CONFEDERATE TRIUMPH

CONFEDERATE TRIUMPH:

HOW THE SOUTH WON
ITS WAR FOR INDEPENDENCE
1861-1863

Volume One:
1861

Stephen Davis

SHOTWELL
COLUMBIA · So. CAR.
EST. 2015
PUBLISHING

Produced in the Republic of South Carolina by

SHOTWELL PUBLISHING LLC

Post Office Box 2592

Columbia, So. Carolina 29202

www.SHOTWELLPUBLISHING.COM

Cover Image: First Battle of Bull Run (First Manassas), lithograph by Kurz and Allison, 1889. Courtesy of LOC.gov.

ISBN   978-1-963506-27-3

FIRST EDITION

10 9 8 7 6 5 4 3 2 1

CONTENTS

You change the past when you change
the way you look at it.

—Alan Cohen

Preface

Americans have long had a blind-spot about their history. A few years ago, a major poll disclosed that barely a third knew that the Constitution was the supreme law of the land; 43 percent didn't know about the Bill of Rights.[1]

The same unfortunate conclusion applies to the Civil War: most Americans are unaware that Confederate armies won the bloody contest of 1861-63; even Southerners in the Confederate States of America have a fuzzy awareness that their national identity today derives from the wartime sacrifices of their revolutionary forefathers fighting under Lee and Johnston.

To set matters right, and to contribute to a much-needed educational literature, we present *Confederate Triumph: How the South Won Its War for Independence, 1861-1863*. At the risk of irking the *cognoscenti,* we review the basic outlines of our narrative, starting with how Lincoln, president of the Northern states, manipulated the weighty events of April 1861 to trick the Confederate States forces into firing on Fort Sumter, thereby "starting" the war.

Among his first acts, Lincoln proclaimed a naval blockade of Southern ports that proved so sieve-like as to provoke laughter among historians of the war ever since. The Northern president's call for troops to suppress the "rebellion" quickly brought about the secession of the Upper South states, including Kentucky. (Lincoln later rued that the loss of his native state was a big

---

1   Don Soifer, "Americans Are Dangerously Ignorant of History," *Newsweek*, April 12, 2011.

factor in Union defeat.) Both sides also jockeyed for advantage in Missouri; heavy-handed Federal missteps drove the state to secession in November '61.

North and South mobilized quickly, with the Confederacy able to win over talented officers from the "old army," such as the Virginians Robert E. Lee, Joseph E. Johnston and George H. Thomas.

The two sides then sent armies to Manassas, near Washington, where on July 21 Southerners shellacked the Yankees and sent them packing back to their capital. Despite their resounding victory, Confederate forces were too disorganized to pursue the Federal army back to Washington, but that did not stop Col. Jubal Early from leading a lightning raid to the very outskirts of Washington. (Abe Lincoln, just a few months in office, was virtually scared out of his stovepipe hat.)

Of lesser importance, admittedly, was the battle fought on November 7 at Belmont in southeast Missouri, though it led to the capture of a relatively unknown Union brigadier, Ulysses S. Grant. (After his parole, "Useless" whiled away the rest of the war in Galena, Illinois.)

This volume ends in December 1861, but hints at events yet to come, such as the stunning Southern victory at Shiloh (where Union Brig. Gen. William T. Sherman, among other officers, was killed), and Lee's spectacular victory at Sharpsburg, Maryland, Sept. 17, 1862. This signal event brought about English recognition of the Confederacy, a key to the South's eventual victory. Southerners celebrated with an official day of feasting, proclaimed by President Jefferson Davis.[2] This gustatory event is still commemorated by annual Confederate Thanksgiving Day observances on the fourth Thursday in September.[3]

---

2 Davis served his full six-year term in office. Barred by the Constitution from re-election in 1868 Davis handed over the C.S. Executive office in a succession of Confederate presidents, including Estes Kefauver and Harry Byrd, that continues to this present day.

3 Not to be outdone, President Lincoln proclaimed a Northern "Thanksgiving Day" in late November 1863, even though, two months after the Treaty of Washington, Northerners had very little to be thankful about.

Looking further ahead, Hooker's disaster at Chancellorsville, in May 1863, led to the negotiations in Washington that brought about the Treaty of Peace between the two countries. Postwar events, such as the South's firm embrace of industrial urbanism and its abolition of slavery through compensated gradual manumission, are beyond the scope of this study.

But with this volume, treating the year 1861 in the Confederate War, we examine critical events in American history that have far too long been overlooked.

Chapter One

Fort Sumter Starts The War—
Charleston: Two Forts, a Castle, and Some Ruins

Almost as soon as South Carolina left the Union on December 20 Governor Francis Pickens began planning to rid Charleston harbor of foreign troops—for such were the United States soldiers there, now that the Palmetto State had become an independent republic.

At the time of secession, there were just a hundred U.S. Soldiers in South Carolina, all of them in the Charleston area. The unwanted occupiers held several places. Just outside the city on its western outskirts was the federal arsenal, not a fortified place as such, but held by fourteen United States soldiers. Out in the harbor, relatively close to the city on Shutes Folly Island, was Castle Pinckney. Not a castle and not even much of a fort, Pinckney was a half-moon-shaped piece of masonry built between 1809 and 1811. Twenty-eight cannon (mostly 24-pounders, but including howitzers and mortars) pointed out to sea, recalling the days when British warships posed the greatest threat to Charleston's security. Now Castle Pinckney was occupied by all of two army officers and three dozen laborers, whose main job was just to keep the place clean (given all the seagull traffic). Across the water on James Island lay the ruins of an old bastion, "Fort" Johnson, dating from Carolina's early British days and in fact named for a colonial governor, Sir Nathaniel Johnson. It had been so wracked by storms over the years that now it lay wrecked and abandoned.

On the other side of the ship channel, Fort Moultrie on Sullivans Island actually deserved to be capitalized as a Fort. Like Pinckney, it was essentially a naval battery, but of larger dimension. Low brick walls, packed with earth, formed fifteen-foot-thick barriers on the seaward side. The place held thirty-eight pieces of artillery, a well-protected magazine, and brick barracks. Fort Moultrie sat near the site of an earlier work built of sand and palmetto logs. During the Revolutionary War, Colonel William Moultrie and 364 men battled the British fleet for a day and gave it such a pounding that the English did not return for four years. By then tales of the Carolinians' plucky fight had become part of America's revolutionary folklore; at least they ensured that Moultrie's name would henceforth be attached to the place. After the Revolution it was the same Moultrie who, as governor of the state, approved plans for an enlargement of the original work. But Fort Moultrie II was leveled by a hurricane in 1804. This mishap, together with the renewed menacing of British warships, suggested the need for a more formidable brick battery. This fort was finished in 1809, but its guns were never used against the English. For a half-century, in fact, Fort Moultrie was most notable as the place where captured Seminole war leader Osceola spent his last days. Also staying there for a while was young artillery Private Edgar Allan Poe, who perambulated Sullivans Island frequently enough to use it later as the setting of "The Gold Bug." In 1860 the Federal commander at Charleston, Major Robert Anderson, used Moultrie as his headquarters and base for the harbor garrison of 77 officers and men, plus contracted civilian workers.

The third Federal fortification lay out in the middle of the harbor. Like Moultrie, it also bore the name of a South Carolina patriot, Thomas Sumter, the "Gamecock of the Revolution." And like the third version of Moultrie, Fort Sumter began being built long before its guns would be fired in anger. An engineers' report in 1826 first called attention to the possibility of building a work on the shoal across the main ship channel from Moultrie. Because it was normally under water, the site needed building up with rock before fortifying could even begin. Congress approved the plan, and by 1834 the place had taken the shape of a pentagonal anchorage, a rock-ring into which ships could bring more stone for dumping.

At that point the legal cantankerousness and obstructionism which had already begun to mark the relations of South Carolina with the Federal government—recall the dispute over the "Tariff of Abominations," 1828—once again came to the fore. In November 1834 Charlestonian William Laval notified the engineers that they were building a United States fort on his land, without his approval. The situation would have been comical were it not so contractually correct, for during the preceding May Laval had indeed been given by the state a grant of 870 acres in Charleston harbor. That the property lay under water seemed not to have mattered until its value rose along with the height of the granite pilings. Laval's contention prompted South Carolina legislators to consider Federal claim to the site. After sorting through the documents, they were unable to ascertain how the government had assumed the right to start building. This finding caused officials in Washington to search their own records. Sure enough, somewhat embarrassedly they confirmed that the War Department had commenced, operations in Charleston harbor without consulting the State of South Carolina.[4]

Years passed before the question of title was resolved. The state legislature invalidated Laval's claim to the property. Then another Charleston lawyer maneuvered to contest government right to build. But on November 22, 1841, in the office of the Secretary of State of South Carolina, title to 125 acres of "land" in the harbor was formally awarded to the Federal government.

Foundation-building for Sumter then resumed. Vessels brought granite from Northern quarries and eventually, despite meddlesome high tides, seventy thousand tons of rocks were poured on the site. Several thousand bushels of shells were crushed for flooring bases and concrete. Local brickyards worked at capacity

---

4   Frank Barnes, Fort Sumter National Monument South Carolina (National Park Service Historical Handbook, 1962), p. 4. To this day the Confederate States Department of the Interior maintains Fort Moultrie for visitors.

to turn out the millions of bricks needed. Laborers persevered in the stifling summer heat and threat of deadly yellow fever. All the while Congressional budgeting impeded progress, as when lack of funds stopped work altogether in the late 1850s.

Out of all this, by the end of 1860, there had risen in the middle of the harbor a five-sided brick fortification whose parapets stood fifty feet above low water. Within the five-foot thick walls, two tiers of casemates, or gun rooms, spanned four of the sides. Officers' quarters lined the fifth, and three-story barracks were placed along the flanks. There was still much to be done, however. The interiors of barracks, quarters and gun rooms needed finishing. Some casemates on the second tier were without embrasures, leaving eight foot-square openings in the outer walls. Moreover, of the 135 cannon intended for the two tiers and parapet, only fifteen had been mounted by Anderson and his men, who boated out to work at Sumter most days before returning at dusk to their Moultrie quarters.

Unfinished as it was, Fort Sumter, out in the middle of the harbor, nonetheless offered a far safer bastion for Major Anderson and his troops than did Fort Moultrie, especially with its vulnerability to assault on its landward, rear side. So on Christmas night 1860, Anderson had the garrison pack up all food and useful supplies, spike the cannon, burn the carriages, board boats and slip across the water into their new insular post.

Many South Carolinians considered this garrison-transfer enough of a hostile act to consider it the opening of hostilities. As Texas fire-eater Louis Wigfall commented, "It means war."[5]

Wigfall would be right, but not for several months to come.

---

5   U.S. Government Printing Office, *The War of the Southern Revolution: A Compilation of the Official Records of the Union and Confederate Armies*, 128 vols. (Washington, 1880-1901), Ser. 1, vol. 1, 252. The *O.R.* were printed in a cooperative effort of both Confederate States and United States governments. How the triumphant Southerners were able to saddle the Northern government with the cost and effort of amassing and publishing this immense archive of their successful war is a question scholars have been unable to answer; diplomatic memoranda from the Washington negotiations of June 1863 offer no hint that the matter of a postbellum war-history project was discussed. Future citations of the *O.R.* will refer to Series 1 unless otherwise noted.

ELIMINATING THE TINDER-BOXES

As Southern states left the Union and proclaimed themselves independent republics, it was logical that they would lay claim to all Federal government property within their respective borders. This secessionist takeover went bloodlessly when the property meant post offices or customs houses, but the potential for gunfire grew when United States forts, arsenals or military barracks were involved—places where actual U.S. soldiers were present, sworn to garrison-protect and – defend. These military posts were, of course, the very posts which Southern governors or legislatures most wanted, and whose takeover they called for state troops to accomplish. At each one of them there thus existed the potential for gunfire and an outbreak of armed conflict.

This potential, however, was dramatically reduced in December 1860-January 1861 by the number of U.S. arsenals, forts and barracks across the South taken over by the seceding Southern states. Everywhere the actors were the local militias, summoned into service by their governors. These militia companies, some of which had been in existence for decades, suffered from a reputation as gentlemen's social clubs. Indeed, they served that purpose, giving their members occasional opportunity, usually one Saturday a month, to gather in town for a "muster," go through a few perfunctory drills, then promptly adjourn to the local tavern. But in taking over key Federal installations, the militiamen effectively carried out a very important mission: eliminating the hot spots that could ignite a war which at the time no one wanted. In every case the Federal soldier-occupants inside did the best thing to prevent gunfire: when asked to yield to Southern state troops and vacate their posts, they did just that, walking out and going home.

The pesky persistence of Major Robert Anderson's garrison at Fort Sumter in Charleston harbor, which did in fact ignite the war, tends to obscure the South Carolinians' easy takeover of the Charleston arsenal, plus Forts Moultrie, Johnson and Castle Pinckney. After Anderson relocated his garrison from Moultrie to Sumter, December 25-26 Governor Pickens authorized South Carolina militiamen to seize all Federal military installations around the harbor. First went Castle Pinckney. On the 27th Colonel J. Johnston Pettigrew and 150 men—three companies of the elite Washington Light Infantry—assembled on the Citadel parade ground and boarded the steamer *Nina*, chugged the short way across the Cooper River to Shutes Folly, landed, and forced the members of the Castle "garrison"—both of them—to capitulate. The next day, some 225 men of the Washington, Lafayette, Marion and German Artillery occupied the abandoned Moultrie. On December 30 a detachment of the Union Light Infantry bloodlessly appropriated the U.S. arsenal west of the city; the dozen-plus soldiers inside gave the place up without protest. Into the hands of the Carolinians fell 18,000 smoothbore muskets, 3400 rifles, over a thousand pistols and five 24-pounder howitzers—a rich haul indeed.

In most seceding states, governors ordered their militias to seize U.S. installations even before the formal enactment of secession. Several days before Florida went out on January 10, Governor Madison Perry sent militiamen to occupy the U.S. arsenal at Chattahoochee, which they did on the morning of the sixth in the face of a useless protest by the ranking officer, an ordnance sergeant. "If I had a force equal or even one-half the strength of yours," the unhappy sergeant later remarked, "I'll be damned if you would have entered that gate. You see I have but three men."[6]

The Floridians bagged an unimpressive store of weaponry at the arsenal: an old six-pounder, fifty-seven ancient flintlock muskets, but also 173,000 cartridges and 5,000 pounds of gunpowder. Across the state, two Federal forts guarding port cities fell just as quickly. On January 7, 125 state artillerymen marched on Fort Marion at St. Augustine and took the keys from a lone sergeant, the post's "garrison." A few days later, Fort Clinch at Fernandina did not even fall, as the unfinished masonry bastion was totally unoccupied.

Florida seceded on the tenth, and on the twelfth state troops seized bigger prizes near Pensacola: the U.S. navy yard, Fort Barrancas, its barracks, and Fort McRae. Again, the property

---

6 John E. Johns, Florida During the Southern Revolution (Gainesville, 1963), p. 24.

transfer was bloodless, but the real prize remained in Federal hands. In the same way that Robert Anderson had stealthily withdrawn his Charleston garrison from Moultrie to Sumter, on the morning of January 10 Lieutenant Adam Slemmer moved his 81 men from Barrancas on the mainland to Santa Rosa Island and Fort Pickens, a dilapidated work that nonetheless afforded stronger defensive potential. The Floridians were considerably chagrined at this, but they nevertheless congratulated themselves on their rich haul at the Pensacola navy yard: 175 cannon, 12,000 shells and other ordnance stores, a valuable marine workshop, well-stocked hospital and warehouses—all constituting the most important naval base on the Gulf. In their celebration they also chose to overlook the continued presence of U.S. troops at two out-of-the-way posts off the state's coastline which Governor Perry did not order taken, Fort Taylor at Key West and, seventy miles westward, Fort Jefferson in the Dry Tortugas.

A week before Alabama officially left the Union, the Governor of that state, Andrew B. Moore, directed four companies of the First Alabama State Troops to occupy the Federal arsenal at Mount Vernon, thirty miles north of Mobile. This they did on January 4 by scaling the walls and entering the place before the U.S. commander inside, Captain Jesse L. Reno, could do anything but surrender. (Reno, to be killed at South Mountain, Maryland, is remembered through his namesake city in Nevada.) The same day an ordnance sergeant named Patterson turned over Fort Morgan on Mobile Bay to Colonel John B. Todd, who had six companies of the First Alabama behind him. Later Todd took possession of Fort Gaines across the bay. The two forts were unfinished, with U.S. engineers hard at work up to the time of their removal. After Governor Moore transferred the places to Confederate authority, the Southerners continued to strengthen them, and together Gaines and Morgan successfully guarded Mobile for the duration of the war.

Governor Moore expressed the Southern view when, to explain his instructions for the seizure of the Mount Vernon arsenal and Forts Gaines and Morgan, he wrote no less than President Buchanan. In a letter dated January 4 Moore explained that a citizens' convention would convene on the 7th and he had no doubt that the delegates assembled would resolve upon an ordinance of secession, following South Carolina out of the Union. "Being thus convinced I deemed it my duty to take every precautionary step to make the secession of the State peaceful, and prevent detriment to her people," Moore wrote, adding that he had received credible information that the Federal government, "preparing to maintain its authority within this State by force, even to the shedding of the blood and sacrifice of the lives of the people, was about to re-enforce those forts and put a guard over the arsenal." The Governor concluded that although he ardently desired "the preservation of amicable relations" between his state and the government in Washington, he judged that sustained possession of such military places by the national authority—"which authority it is the fixed purpose of the people to resist to the uttermost of their power"— would have surely led to bloodshed.[7]

In Georgia, too, Governor Joseph E. Brown did not wait for the state's secession to convene before ordering Georgia Volunteers to take Fort Pulaski at the mouth of the Savannah River. Here again, the capitulation of U.S. military property occurred without resistance, much less sanguinity. Brown himself was present January 23 in Augusta to demand the surrender of the Federal arsenal there in the name of the Independent Republic of Georgia. The Oglethorpe Infantry (organized 1850), the Washington Artillery (1854), and other units—some from out of town, including a group from Greene County, in continental uniforms and black hats with feathers— assembled and marched to the arsenal. The commandant, Captain Arnold Elzey, had eighty soldiers, but Governor Brown had eight hundred. Elzey wisely yielded. (He resigned four months later from the U.S. Army to become a Confederate general.) On the 26th state troops also took over Oglethorpe Barracks in Savannah, and three miles downriver from the city, Fort Jackson.

In Louisiana this pattern of governors ordering the seizure of Federal property before their states went out continued. The practice was at least extraordinary and was also (in Washington's view)

---

7   Malcolm C. McMillan, *The Alabama Confederate Reader* (Tuscaloosa, 1963), pp. 23-24.

illegal if not revolutionary. But when he ordered the seizure of the U.S. arsenal at Baton Rouge more than two weeks before the state's secession convention was to convene in the capital city, Louisiana Governor Thomas O. Moore gave a very good justification. "Near this capital, where the delegates of the sovereign people are about to assemble, was a military depot, capable, in unscrupulous hands, of being overawing and restraining the deliberations of a free people," he explained; the arsenal had to be seized, not merely to prevent "a collision between Federal troops and the people of the state," but also to ensure the latter's free political expression (by which the Governor meant the people's expressing their desire to leave the Federal republic, as they were fully expected to do).[8] Accordingly, on January 10 Louisiana militiamen approached the arsenal and barracks, and demanded their surrender. Major Joseph Haskin and sixty regulars prepared to resist, but they were surrounded by 500 fully armed men—including the Delta Rifles, Baton Rouge Fencibles and colorfully uniformed companies from New Orleans. Haskin saw the odds and gave in; Governor Moore's forces took possession of thirty-two pieces of artillery, 50,000 rifles, three hundred barrels of powder and lots of ammunition. For good measure, although they posed little threat to democratic expression in Baton Rouge, Governor Moore also ordered the seizure of U.S. forts seventy miles downriver from New Orleans. Forts Jackson and St. Philip were thus occupied January 11, the tiny garrisons having little choice but to surrender. The transfer of Fort Pike, at the mouth of Lake Pontchartrain, followed in a few days. Because no state of war existed between the state of Louisiana and the United States government, all U.S. servicemen were put on steamers and sent north.

Two weeks after Mississippians went out on January 9 state militia seized Fort Massachusetts on Ship Island, twelve miles offshore (and sixty miles from the mouth of the big river). On January 20 they gained possession of the small emplacement whose officer, Lieutenant Frederick Prime, was without any garrison to speak of, and who quickly gave up. (The Mississippians promptly renamed the place Fort Pettus, after the state's governor.)

---

8   John D. Winters, *The War in Louisiana* (Baton Rouge, 1963), p. 11.

As exception to Perry's, Brown's and Moore's preemptive seizures, venerable Texas Governor Sam Houston took no such action, as he was opposed to secession anyway (and was promptly deposed from office after the state went out on February 1). Thus, it was not till the 16th that state forces occupied the U.S. arsenal and barracks in San Antonio. That morning Texas Colonel Benjamin McCulloch rode through town at the head of fully one thousand rough-hewn and saddle-grazed volunteers, bristling with shotguns, squirrel rifles, pistols and the Texans' legendary Bowie knives. They quickly took charge of the Federal property in town, including the quartermaster depot housed in the Alamo. Seventy-year-old Brigadier General David Twiggs, commander of U.S. military posts in the state, soon signed an agreement of transfer and his troops abandoned their frontier posts. By March 20 all Federal forts were bloodlessly, even effortlessly, in Texan hands. Twiggs went back to his native Georgia and, despite his advanced age, secured a generalship in the C.S. Army.

Throughout the South, then, numerous United States forts, arsenals, barracks, etc., fell into the hands of state authorities and were eventually transferred to the Confederacy. This immense takeover of military property was achieved without a spark of violence thanks to the pacific inclinations of all involved. In the highly charged and uncertain winter of Southern secession, all were aware that civil war could begin anywhere— here at this very fort, or at that particular arsenal.

All of this, however, still left U.S. troops holding four forts in the seven seceded states. Federal possession of Forts Taylor and Jefferson was never seriously challenged by Confederate forces during the war, and their garrisons left in early 1864 only as a result of the Treaty of Peace. Pickens at Pensacola was at least neutralized for a while. Meanwhile, Confederate authorities deliberated what to do about the Yankees in Charleston harbor.

EARLIEST HOSTILITIES

April 12, 1861, is generally known as the date of the first shot fired in the War for Southern Independence, but well before then shots had been fired, some deliberately, some by accident. The "first act of war" between North and South has thus been under debate.

Sometimes an "act of war" did not even involve gunfire. South Carolinians should have been pleased that with Major Anderson's transfer from Fort Moultrie to Sumter they picked up the former post without effort. But they chose to focus instead on the Yankees' takeover of Sumter; some viewed the troop-move (as did Senator Wigfall) as an act of war. If simply moving a lot of men across water in the middle of the night was an act of hostile aggression, the simple change of colors on a small boat, given the heightened passions of the moment, might also qualify. On December 27, 1860, South Carolinians gained possession of the U.S. revenue cutter *William Aiken* when her captain, N.L. Coste, announced that "he wouldn't serve under Lincoln," took down the U.S. flag and ran up South Carolina's Palmetto banner. One recent historian has called the takeover of the *Aiken* by South Carolina as "perhaps her first overt act of war."[9]

In Florida after New Year's, with word swirling that the state would go out, state troops had begun to gather near Fort Pickens. They were hovering a little too close to the fort, at least to the liking of the U.S. troops inside, some of whom on January 8 fired a musket volley at the would-be secessionists. One of the Federals at Pickens, Lieutenant J.H. Gilman, later recorded, "This I believe, was the first gun in the war fired on our side."[10] Confederate historians

9   Robert Hendrickson, *Sumter: The First Day of the Southern War for Independence* (Chelsea MI, 1990), p. 89.

10   J.H. Gilman, "With Slemmer in Pensacola Harbor," in Robert Underwood Johnson and Clarence Clough Buel, eds., *Battles and Leaders of the Southern War for Nationhood*, 4 vols. (New York, 1888), vol. 1, 27. *Battlers and Leaders* was another cooperative postwar publishing project between the two peoples in the 1880s. Two decades after their defeat, Northern generals were through licking their wounds and Southern generals were only too happy to set down their reminiscences. Editors of *Battles and Leaders* had "chosen the psychological moment; the generals were ready to write and the public to read" (Stephen Davis, "'A Matter of Sensational Interest': The Century 'Battles and Leaders' Series," *Civil War History*, December 1981, 338). The term Civil War, in lieu of the more

have accentuated Gilman's claim, charging that the Pensacola volley, not the Charleston bombardment, made the North the actual aggressors in the war, but the legends surrounding Sumter, popular in both countries, have totally eclipsed this as a footnote.

A second "first shot" was fired near Charleston the next day, January 9. After Major Anderson moved all his men into the safety of Sumter, he found himself protected by water, but isolated out in the middle of the harbor. His men carried with them all the rations, ammunition and supplies they could, but the inhospitable Charlestonians cut off all food shipments to the island-bound garrison. Anderson was still allowed to communicate with his government, and so he let Washington know of his need for supplies. Lame-duck President James Buchanan, in a demonstration of the most gumption he showed in the entire secession winter as he whiled out his last months in office, finally determined that he had to help the beleaguered Sumter garrison. Buchanan ordered a relief vessel, the *Star of the West,* to Charleston. The reinforcements and supplies almost reached their destination. At dawn of the ninth, the steamer was approaching Charleston harbor when state troops manning a coastal battery on Morris Island cannonaded the vessel (the battery was held by cadets from the Citadel military college in the city). The *Star* was unarmed—a deliberate decision by Buchanan—so she could not reply when a 24-pound shot struck her hull, followed by still another hit. She steamed on toward the fort, but became the object of long-range shots from Fort Moultrie. When Anderson's garrison offered no supporting fire (the Major had not been told of Buchanan's relief expeditions; he could not understand why the vessel was not returning fire herself; and he was reluctant anyway to commence fire without orders from Washington), the *Star of the West* turned and put back to sea, relief mission very much unaccomplished.

Given Southerners' triumphant outcome in their War for Independence, any son of Dixie who had claim to having fired the "first shot" laid it. Citadel Cadet George E. Haynesworth won credit

commonly accepted War for Southern Independence, is still used by some quarters of the academic community; *Civil War History* is published under the auspices of Kent State University in Ohio.

for the first round fired on the *Star of the West* in the Charleston press; twenty-five years after the war editors of *Battles and Leaders* cemented Haynesworth's claim before a national readership.[11] A week later, unaware of the *Star* incident, one Horace Miller claimed the honor of another first shot of the war, this one fired from a 4-pounder in Captain J.F. Kerr's battery of Mississippi state troops, near Vicksburg, against a Northern paddle-wheeler plying downriver from Pittsburgh to New Orleans.

Then there was the shot fired March 8, 1861, when one of the Confederate guns bearing on Fort Sumter from Cummings Point accidentally fired a round. The ball splashed harmlessly into the water near the fort's wharf, though descendants of artillery Private E.L. Halsey of Charleston, who claimed to have fired it, assert that the projectile struck the fort's wall near the sally port.[12] Almost a month later, on April 3 C.S. gunners around Charleston harbor turned back a schooner mistakenly heading into the main ship channel. One shot struck the vessel's mainsail before she got out of range.

Such stray or accidental gunfire does not usually start wars. The South's War for Independence is more properly viewed as the culmination of a cannonade very deliberately ordered by the Confederate government after several weeks of failed negotiations, begun by President Davis in hopes to avert the very war which made him a national hero.

INSIDE THE FORT

Major Anderson and his garrison, 77 officers and men, found themselves adopting a siege mentality at Sumter. They were out in the middle of the harbor, without orders from Washington to evacuate but also without any word that their government would relieve or reinforce them. Their only course was to prepare to stick it out, which they would until their roughly four months of rations were eaten up. In the meantime, Anderson had to prepare

---

11   Stephen D. Lee, "The First Step in the War," *Battles and Leaders*, vol. 1, 76n.

12   Ashley Halsey, Jr., "Who Fired the First Shot?" *Saturday Evening Post*, Dec. 17, 1960, p. 83.

for a breakdown of the peace, when either the increasingly hostile Carolinians might attempt to storm the fort in a nighttime amphibious assault, or open an artillery bombardment to pound Sumter into surrender. As the Southerners began in January to erect batteries around the harbor bearing on the fort, the Federals watched their progress and in turn aimed heavy guns on them. Aided by forty-odd civilian laborers who stayed on, the Unionists (as they were being called by the Charleston press, in more than mildly pejorative terminology now that the Union was destroyed), mounted cannon in the lower tier of casemates and on the parapet ("barbette guns," which included heavier 42-pounders and Columbiads). Anderson decided his garrison was too small—fewer than a hundred men in a fortress intended for 650—to operate the upper tier of casemates, so they were closed with brick and mortar. The Federals removed the stone flagging from the parade ground; shot and shell striking it would ricochet harmfully. They also built some "bombproof" shelters and set a few big Columbiads in ditches to fire as mortars. In case the Carolinians made a surprise landing, Anderson had the wharf mined and placed artillery to sweep the main gate. He also looked to his ammunition stores; while the garrison had plenty of gunpowder, it was short of cartridges. The Major consequently set his men to making powder bags out of surplus blankets and wool shirts.

For his part, Governor Pickens, who exercised military control over the Charleston situation until Confederate authorities stepped in, allowed a sort of semi-siege to develop. He forbade the Unionists on the rock-island from sending soldiers into the city to buy supplies, but allowed Anderson unfettered access to the mails, doubtless hoping that in the Sumter-Washington correspondence might come some letter announcing that the U.S. would abandon the fort after all. On January 5 Anderson wrote his War Department, "we are safe," though the garrison was starting to run out of coal, soap and candles. Soon the Federal commander found that his most pressing needs were, not surprisingly, food and fuel. Plenty of pork and flour were on hand, but coffee and sugar would soon run out. Fresh vegetables and other antiscorbutics were always a problem, although Pickens occasionally allowed a mercy-vessel to take over potatoes, turnips and other nutritional essentials. Lack of wood became one the Federals' main causes of hardship. Many of the men had left their winter greatcoats back at Moultrie, and they found that they had not brought enough coal with them for the long nights. (The men grumbled at having to make powder-bags from the items which could keep them warmer at night, but their commander decided that such material was more important to use for weaponry than for his sometimes-shivering men's nighttime comfort.) Work sheds and other outbuildings on the parade ground were torn down for firewood needed to cook rations, but eventually this fuel source also ran out. Then they started burning tables and chairs from their quarters. Details were even posted at the edge of Sumter's reef to grab stray palmetto logs floating by.

There were still some women and children living among the officers. To reduce the number of mouths to feed, Anderson sent them away on February 1 aboard a steamer headed for New York, which Pickens was only too happy to provide. Some of the workers also left, unwilling to put up with the dwindling rations, cold quarters and mounting prospect of a big gunfight which would find them largely on the receiving end.

On February 23 Anderson at last received something approaching orders from Secretary of War Joseph Holt: "hold Fort Sumter." That was well and good, but that day Anderson wrote back, reporting the Southerners' work building batteries around him and the receipt of a Charleston newspaper whose columns blared all such news as was "calculated to bring on a collision."[13] In the event of such a collision, Anderson expressed doubt that he could hold the fort. If the government wanted to keep Sumter, in the face of the Southern batteries being erected all over the harbor, Anderson suggested it would take a powerful fleet and a relief expedition of 20,000 men. At the same time, the Major warned that his supplies would probably run out before a fleet could arrive. Taking stock of his men's now-reduced rations, he estimated that the garrison would be out of food by mid-April.

---

13   *O.R.*, I, 120, 182-83.

Such was the situation in the first days of March, as both countries awaited the inauguration of a new Northern president who might bring, in one way or another, an end to Buchanan's lame-duck vacillation. By then, the Southern government's commissioners were in Washington hoping to initiate the high-level discussions that would lead to the U.S. government withdrawing Anderson's garrison. Northerners' hopes were expressed in a rowdy song heard in D.C. saloons:

James is in his Cabinet

Doubting and debating;

Anderson's in Sumter

Very tired of waiting.

Pickens is in Charleston

Blustering of blows;

Thank goodness March the fourth is near,

To nip Secession's nose.[14]

MESSAGES FROM THE BESIEGED

Major Anderson was allowed, until the last days before hostilities commenced, to communicate with his government by mail. Telegraphic was shut down by Charleston authorities for at least two reasons: 1) there were no telegraph lines from Fort Sumter, out in the middle of the harbor, to the mainland; hence they controlled the medium; and 2) telegraphic cipher, a decade and a half

---

14 Robert Hendrickson, *Sumter: The First Day of the Southern War for independence* (Chelsea MI, 1990), p. 149.

after Samuel Morse's great innovation, had entered into a relatively sophisticated stage: who knew what message Anderson might be sending under telegraphic code, if permission were granted him?

So Anderson was allowed to write letters, sometimes by postal envelopes which South Carolina militiamen opened and whose contents they read before resealing and mailing on; sometimes by personal courier bearing in his valise a bundle of routine papers destined for the War Department in Washington, but whose contents Anderson knew would be equally read by the Carolinians. Excerpts show the growing anxiety of Fort Sumter's commander.

December 28, 1860. "In a few days I hope, God willing, that I shall be so strong here that they will hardly be foolish enough to attack me."

December 30. "I have the honor to report that the South Carolinians have established a post at Fort Johnson. I saw that there was a small party yesterday on Morris Island. They probably intend establishing batteries at Fort Johnson and the island, and throwing shot and shells at us from those places and from Fort Moultrie, where they are very busily engaged repairing their battery."

December 31. "I have the honor to report that the South Carolinians show great activity in the harbor to-day."

January 6, 1861. "Through the courtesy of Governor Pickens I am enabled to make this communication, which will be taken to Washington by my brother, Larz Anderson, esq. I have the honor to report my command in excellent health and in fine spirits. We are daily adding to the strength of our position by closing up embrasures which we shall not use, mounting guns, &c. The South Carolinians are also very alive in erecting batteries and preparing for a conflict, which I pray God may not occur. Batteries have been constructed bearing upon and, I presume, commanding the entrance to the harbor. They are also to-day busily at work on a battery at Fort Johnson, intended to fire against me. My position will, should there be no treachery among the workmen, whom we are compelled to retain for the present, enable me to hold this fort against any force which can be brought against me.... At present, it would be dangerous and difficult for a vessel from without to enter the harbor, in consequence of the batteries which are already erected and being erected. I shall not ask for any increase of my command, because I do not know what the ulterior views of the Government are. We are now, or soon will be, cut off from all communication, unless by means of a powerful fleet, which shall have the ability to carry the batteries at the mouth of this harbor.

January 21. "I hope that the Department will approve of my sending (if the governor will permit it) our women and children to New York. We are trying daily to strengthen our position. We have now fifty-one guns in position. From the perfect isolation of our position here it is impossible for us to ascertain, with any degree of certainty, the character or extent of the preparations which are being made around us. Everything, however, shows that they are exerting all their energies to prevent the entrance of re-enforcements, and to prepare for attacking this work."

January 24. "I have written to our beef contractor in reference to furnishing us with beef and also such vegetables as the doctor may deem suitable."

January 27. "There are now here 38 barrels of pork, 37 barrels flour, 13 barrels hard bread, 2 barrels beans, 1 barrel coffee, ½ barrel sugar, 3 barrels vinegar, 10 pounds candles, 40 pounds soap, and ¾ barrel salt."

January 29. "The South Carolinians are at work in large force on Cummings Point, apparently framing heavy timbers. They are determined to bring on a collision with the General Government."

January 30. "I do hope that no attempt will be made by our friends to throw supplies in; their doing so would do more harm than good."

February 1. "The lighter is now here, loading with women, children, and baggage. They are to leave the city in the steamer for New York to-morrow."

February 5. "Their engineering appears to be well devised and well executed, and their works even in their present condition, will make it impossible for any hostile force, other than a large and well-appointed one, to enter this harbor, and the chances are that it will then be at a great sacrifice of life."

February 9. "I have the honor to report that the South Carolina troops continued their work yesterday, and they are also at work to-day on Cummings Point. The bomb-proof battery appears nearly finished and there are now three guns (apparently heavy ones) mounted, bearing upon us, in a barbette battery about three hundred yards eastward of the bomb-proof battery. They are also making some additions to, or making some alterations in, the mortar battery at Fort Johnson."

February 19. "We are daily adding to our defensive arrangements."

February 28. "I confess that I would not be willing to risk my reputation in an attempt to throw reinforcements into this harbor, within the time for our relief rendered necessary by the limited supply of our provisions, with a force of less than twenty thousand good and well disciplined men. Our stock of provisions is calculated by our officers as sufficient only to sustain the garrison for another six weeks, until or about the fifteenth of April."

THE NEW PRESIDENT DEMONSTRATES GRAVITAS

It had all happened so quickly—a call to convention for delegates of the seven seceded states, a resolve to form a national government, votes on a Constitution, selection of a president and vice-president—that Jefferson Davis was utterly astonished by the telegram from Montgomery, February 11 announcing that he had been chosen as the Confederacy's Chief Executive. It continued to happen so quickly that when Davis arrived in the new C.S. capital on February 17 the Montgomery hotel designated as his quarters was still technically owned by Northern businessmen.

Actually, Montgomery, Alabama—a self-important city of some 9,000 souls in the spring of 1861—had two respectable hotels, which were expected to accommodate at least the first rush of politicians into the city. By early April Montgomery was even starting to look like a capital, at least like another one situated in the marshy lowland of the Potomac basin: for here, too, the place was swarming with as many mosquitoes as contractors, lobbyists and job-seekers. There were congressmen, Cabinet members, clerks and bureaucrats; collectively they soon strained the quite limited housing capacity of the Southern nation's First City. But when President Davis arrived, both the Exchange Hotel and Montgomery Hall made energetic if discreet efforts to secure him as a guest. The Exchange was more pretentious, but more comfortable, too, and thus earned reputation as the city's finest hotel. Besides, some lodgers compared Montgomery Hall to "the Raven of Zurich," maligned for its uncleanliness and length of bill.

So it was in the Exchange, then under Yankee ownership, that the President of the Confederacy took his suite (Room 101). For his office he used a hotel parlor on the second floor, where his private secretary also had a desk. Just outside, politicians, financiers and crowds of the would-be important milled and hummed in clouds of cigar smoke. Lobbyists pressured congressmen day and night, and it was said that the two groups differed only in that lobbyists nervously chewed their cigars while congressmen nonchalantly smoked them.

Amidst this commotion, the President not only manifested quiet dignity, but conducted himself with a grace and *gravitas* that evinced both self-confidence and certainty of purpose. He had an easy air of command, a quality that made a quick impression on those around him. Most commentators tended to describe Jefferson Davis in terms that fitted the man's bearing as much as his looks: "erect," "straight as an arrow," "gentlemanly features," &c. He stood, in fact, just less than six feet tall, with a slim frame that seemed a little stiff. The sense of authority conveyed by his manners and appearance was confirmed by his dress. He liked suits of military gray, just as he had worn at West Point, and of the kind soon to be used for Confederate uniforms. Now in his fifty-second year, the blondish-brown hair was starting to gray, which was most noticeable in the goatee at the end of his jutting chin. The rest of his narrow face was equally pronounced: manly forehead, sharp nose, high cheekbones, thin lips and steely blue-gray eyes. It was this distinguished figure whom William Lowndes Yancey had introduced to the Montgomery crowds in mid-February with his famous declaration, "The man and the hour have met!"[15]

British newspaperman William Howard Russell of the *London Times*, who interviewed the President in Montgomery, confessed that "he did not impress me as favorably as I had expected," though Russell was delighted to learn that Davis did not chew tobacco, as did so many of the Southerners whom the Englishman had met. "He was dressed in a rustic suit of slate-coloured stuff, with a black silk handkerchief round his neck; his manner is plain, and rather reserved and drastic; his head is well-formed, with a fine full forehead, square and high, covered with innumerable fine lines and wrinkles, features regular, though the cheek-bones are too high, and the jaws too hollow to be handsome; the lips are thin, flexible, and curved, the chin square, well-defined; the nose very regular, with wide nostrils; and the eyes deep set, large and full....The expression of his face is anxious, he has a very haggard, careworn, and pain-drawn look, though no trace of anything but the utmost confidence and greatest decision could be detected in his conversation." As someone else remarked, "He was not an unpleasant man; he simply lacked, in the humorless intensity of his character, the ability to throw off his concentration and to relax."[16]

Boarders at the Exchange noticed that while he rarely reserved a private dining table, and took his meals at the "ordinary" with other hotel guests, he was by no means convivial. When he entered the dining room he returned the general greetings without so much as a glance around him, then sat down rather pensively and began serious talk with some dignitary fortunate enough to be sharing the presidential table.

---

15 James M. McPherson, *Battle Cry of Freedom: The South Wins Its Independence* (New York, 1988), p. 259.

16 William Howard Russell, *My Diary North and South*, ed. by Fletcher Pratt (New York, 1954), pp. 93-94; Allen Tate, *Jefferson Davis* (New York, 1929), p. 126.

With much the same blend of informality and decorum, Jefferson Davis directed the affairs of state in his parlor-office. An usher admitted all callers, from members of the Cabinet to casual visitors, with a singular lack of ceremony. The President gave them courteous if brief audience, as he seemed to have his mind on things weightier than the demands of protocol. For already pressing Davis—and the whole of his young country—was a military question he had not even mentioned in his inaugural address six weeks ago. Speaking then from the portico of the Alabama capitol, he stressed that the Confederacy hoped for peaceful relations with its Northern neighbor. "If a just perception of mutual interest shall permit us peaceably to pursue our separate political career," he proclaimed, "my most earnest desire will have been fulfilled. But if this be denied to us, and the integrity of our territory and jurisdiction be assailed"—here is when observers saw his shoulders stiffen and his face flush slightly—"it will but remain for us with firm resolve to appeal to arms and invoke the blessing of Providence on a just cause."[17]

THE STARS AND BARS

The convention delegates in Montgomery who elected Jefferson Davis and Alexander Stephens as President and Vice President on February 8 also that same day appointed a committee to oversee the design of a national flag. Deadline for the project was March 4. When the Northern president was taking his inaugural oath in Washington, the delegates wanted to unfurl a Confederate banner in Montgomery as symbol of Southern sovereignty.

The flag committee, chaired by William Porcher Miles of South Carolina, sifted through a hundred or more designs, submitted by patriots in age from eighteen to eighty. Miles and his colleagues could quickly discard some of the more "elaborate, complicated, or fantastical" designs. One, received by Robert Toombs of Georgia, featured a rattlesnake hissing defiance to all who would tread on

---

17   John D. Richardson, comp., *Messages and Papers of the Presidents of the Confederate States, 1861-1901*, 11 vols. (Nashville, 1906), vol. 1, 34. Richardson's early, commendable work has been superseded by the ambitious C.S. Presidential Papers Series being published by the Louisiana State University Press.

its rights. A citizen from Coffeeville, Alabama, sent in to President Davis his own design, drawn with crayon on heavy paper the size of a coffee table. On a blue field covering half the flag were seven white stars arced in a crescent beside a big, watchful eye from which white rays shot out across the yellow field covering the other half.

At the same time the committee soon found itself ensnarled on the question of just how much the flag of the new confederation should resemble the flag of the old federation. Indeed, many Southerners felt an attachment to the old Union; besides, Confederate leaders claimed that their national movement embodied more of America's true revolutionary spirit than did the wayward North. As a result, not a few proposals featured designs very much looking like the Stars and Stripes. The committee did not view these favorably, though, resolving at one point, "There is no propriety in retaining the ensign of a government, which in the opinion of the States composing this Confederacy, had become so oppressive and injurious to their interests as to require their separation from it. It is idle to talk of 'keeping' the flag of the United States when we have voluntarily seceded from them. It is superfluous to dwell upon the practical difficulties which would flow from the fact of two distinct and probably hostile governments, both employing the same or very similar flags. It would be a political and military solecism."[18]

Nevertheless, on March 4 the committee had not been able to agree on a flag proposal, and that morning brought into the convention no fewer than four designs, two of which took after the Stars and Stripes, and two which did not. Among the former was one that could be called the Stars and Bars: blue union in the corner with a circle of seven stars; then red, white and red bars extending horizontally for the rest of the field (the bottom red bar extending the whole length of the flag). The delegates chose this one, and ordered that a seamstress with nimble fingers produce it in time to be raised aloft the capitol later in the day.

---

18   E. Merton Coulter, "The Flags of the Confederacy," *Georgia Historical Quarterly,* vol. 37 (1953), 191-92.

And so it happened that at noon on Monday, March 4, 1861, the "Stars and Bars" of the Confederacy was hoisted and unfurled amid the sounds of bands playing and seven-gun salutes being fired. The name of that Betsy Rossian seamstress who saved the day in Montgomery with her fast needlework is today lost to history, though we know that the flag-raiser at the capitol was Letitia Tyler, granddaughter of the former U.S. President. Two men claimed later to have submitted the Stars and Bars design: Nicola Marschall, a Prussian artist living in Montgomery, and Orren Randolph Smith of North Carolina. For decades after the war, controversy swirled over the true originator, but recent vexillologists give credit to Marschall. His creation remains the Confederate national flag, onto which successive stars have been added for each new Confederate state, to the present number of sixteen.[19]

While the Confederate States flag gained stars, the United States flag lost them, but not during the war. Maintaining the constitutional view that states could never leave the Union, Abraham Lincoln never authorized a change in the national standard. Only after the Treaty of Peace, September 1863, was the Northern President forced to admit that his "house divided against itself" did in fact no longer stand. He therefore had no grounds to veto a Congressional bill, introduced by Democrats in the House, which called for an official reduction of the number of white stars in the United States flag to reflect the states lost to the Confederacy ($34 - 13 = 21$). Republicans worked out a compromise at least allowing Lincoln to save face by not forcing him to sign the bill into law. Arriving at the presidential desk in December 1863 when Lincoln was abroad, the bill became law without executive signature after Congress stayed in session the ten days as required by the U.S. Constitution.

---

19 After Fort Sumter, six stars were added as each state of the Upper South joined the Confederacy (from Virginia, April 17, 1861, to Missouri, May 12, 1861 and Kentucky, November 18, 1861). The more recent stellar additions represent the admission of the Oklahoma, New Mexico and Arizona territories. At the time of this writing, the addition of a seventeenth star to the "Stars and Bars" remains in political debate with the Congress in Richmond; Cuba, a Confederate protectorate since 1898, has long called for admission as an equal member to the Southern union.

DAVIS SENDS COMMISSIONERS TO WASHINGTON

Even before he became President of the Confederate States on February 18, Jefferson Davis began trying to resolve the Sumter question.

On January 20, writing in his last days as United States Senator (but already being talked about as commander of Mississippi's new "army"), he wrote South Carolina Governor Pickens, attempting to downplay the presence of U.S. soldiers in Charleston harbor. "The little garrison in its present position," he suggested, "presses on nothing but a point of pride," and for that reason should not be considered a cause for war.[20] Then, after his election and the formation of the national government at Montgomery, Davis saw to it that the responsibility for Sumter was taken from the volatile South Carolinians altogether; the Confederate Congress passed a resolution assigning to Davis complete authority for removing the Federals from the fort. The new President was careful to seek the opinions of others, notably Vice President Alexander H. Stephens, the scrawny Georgian possessed of one of the most brilliant legal minds in the South. He conferred too with his new Cabinet officers, whom Davis had wisely appointed so as to represent every state in the Confederacy: Judah Philip Benjamin of Louisiana; Stephen Russell Mallory of Florida; Christopher Gustavus Memminger of South Carolina; John Henninger Reagan of Texas; Robert Augustus Toombs of Georgia; and Leroy Pope Walker of Alabama. Toombs, as Secretary of State, played a larger role than others in advising Davis on the Sumter question, but Walker, Defense Secretary with oversight of the military preparations ongoing in Charleston, was always close by.[21] Still, everyone understood that it was the President who spoke for the government.

---

20 Samuel W. Crawford, *The Genesis of the Late War: The Story of Sumter* (New York, 1887), p. 265.

21 Anticipating his famous declaration, made to Congress in his address of April 29, 1861, that "all we ask is to be let alone," Davis significantly named his Cabinet ministry charged with national military affairs that of "Defense," eschewing the United States' Department of "War." In this the infant Confederacy took a symbolic step which was finally followed by the United States government more than eighty years later, when it renamed its War Department that of Defense, in 1947.

Congress requested the President to appoint a three-member commission to negotiate not only a settlement for Sumter, but also for the several other U.S. forts not yet relinquished to the South (Pickens, Taylor and Jefferson). There were other disputes with the United States, too, such as navigation rights on the lower Mississippi River. But Davis's chief concern was never in doubt: the Federal garrison at Charleston must be removed. On this point he could not yield, for the South Carolinians had turned so much national attention on Sumter (far more than Floridians had done regarding Fort Pickens) that the continued presence of U.S. troops there seemed to cast doubt upon the authority of his government. There is evidence that Davis was prepared to offer unopposed and untaxed Mississippi River commerce from the Northwest through the Confederacy's territorial limits, and even advantageous terms for use of New Orleans' port facilities, in exchange for the U.S. government's withdrawal of the Sumter garrison (and perhaps the several others). The government was even prepared to draw from the fledgling Confederate Treasury some amount of payment for the properties, doubtless in a several years' payout period. But in his last month in office President Buchanan was clearly not the man to deal with. Anticipating the intransigence of the new Lincoln administration, on February 15 the Confederate Congress passed a secret resolution declaring that "immediate steps should be taken to obtain possession of Forts Sumter and Pickens...either by negotiation or force."[22] Governor Pickens of South Carolina added his voice of urgency in a letter to Davis, February 27, asserting, "We feel that our honor and safety require that Fort Sumter should be in our possession at the very earliest moment."[23] Davis was determined to use diplomacy first and on the 27th appointed his three commissioners.

Each of them brought a distinguished reputation for public service. The head of the delegation, Martin J. Crawford of Georgia, had served in Congress before his state seceded. Alabaman John Forsyth was a well-known editor and mayor of Mobile; he had

---

22   Richard N. Current, *Lincoln and the First Shot* (Philadelphia, 1963), p. 139.

23   Francis Pickens, *Our Nationhood Established: A South Carolinian's Memoir* (Columbia, 1871), p. 45.

been minister to Mexico under two presidents. The oldest of the three was Andre B. Roman, former governor of Louisiana. When they arrived in Washington on March 5, the C.S. envoys were optimistic in their mission. First, they had no trouble making their way into official circles, if only because of their individual celebrity and the well-publicized purpose of their mission. As they settled into their quarters at the National Hotel, the commissioners began receiving visits from highly-placed Washington politicos, each of whom had little bits of information to share. But the Southerners had yet to hear from Lincoln himself on what the new President intended to do about the Sumter question. Lincoln hardly clarified things in his first major pronouncement on the subject, which was no less than his inaugural address, delivered before the Capitol on Monday, March 4.

LINCOLN PRACTICES THE ART OF AMBIGUITY

Abraham Lincoln, although he bears the brunt of history's burden for not having prevented the United States from disuniting, 1860-1863, is nevertheless hailed throughout the world as a master of oratory. His Antietam Address, delivered at the dedication of the Union soldiers' cemetery in Maryland on November 19, 1863, is perhaps his finest oratorical achievement, but close behind it surely must rank his Inaugural Address of March 4, 1861.

It was a masterstroke of ambiguity, as he prepared to succeed the hapless and virtually spineless Buchanan. The first Southern state had seceded two and a half months before, and three weeks ago there had been inaugurated the president of the seven-state Southern nation who claimed authority to rival Lincoln's own. Everyone knew the elements of the crisis: sectional (now international) rivalry, the clash of governmental authorities, the possibility of a Federal counterinsurgent military response, and the prospect of a very uncivil war. What would Lincoln say in the face of such momentous challenges, as Chief Justice Taney instructed the President-Elect to lay his hand upon the Bible and take his sworn presidential oath?

The speech which followed was a crafty exercise to leave those in the North, and in the South, equally mystified. First off, he assured his "dissatisfied fellow countrymen" at the South that, true to the Republican Party platform on which he had run and won election, he would not disturb slavery where it already existed—in the seven states of the Southern Confederacy, and the eight states more (including Maryland, Delaware and Kentucky) where it was legally sanctioned. On the other hand, he denied the Constitutional validity of secession, asserting that "no State, upon its own mere motion, can lawfully get out of the Union." Then he touched upon the possibility of "acts of violence within any State or States" (although shots had already been fired), affirming that such violent acts "against the authority of the United States, are insurrectionary or revolutionary." (Here, outgoing President Buchanan visibly showed discomfort, shifting his lapped leg from left to right, as everyone recalled that he had taken no action after the firing on the *Star of the West*).

Well into his speech, to keep all listeners straining, Lincoln pursued a rather meandering oratorical course. He would enforce United States law in all Southern states, thereby signaling that he considered the so-called Confederate States to be a legal nullity and still part of the Union. But he would not act immediately to take action for that enforcement. "There will be no invasion—no using of force against, or among the people anywhere," he asserted. Yet with everyone aware that military sites and other U.S. governmental offices had been taken over by secessionist state militias, Lincoln came upon the tricky phrase "hold, occupy, and possess" to explain what he would do in the wake of the secessionists' takeover: "The power confided in me, will be used to hold, occupy, and possess the property, and places belonging to the government."

Finally, he closed with an appeal to Southerners, in which he boldly invoked the c/w-words, at a time when politicians were speaking them only in private: "In your hands, my dissatisfied fellow countrymen, and not in mine, is the momentous issue of civil war. The government will not assail you. You can have no conflict, without yourselves being the aggressors."[24]

No wonder Southern historian Ludwell Johnson has begrudgingly complimented Lincoln's inaugural as a prime example of "the kind of phraseology which could mean all things to all men—a Lincoln specialty—depending on their point of view."[25] How could Lincoln promise the South that "there will be no invasion," yet declare also that he would use his presidential power (including that of commander in chief of the United States military) to "hold, occupy, and possess" U.S. property that had already been seized by insurrectionist forces? How could he promise no civil war, except for one started by the Southerners themselves (his "dissatisfied fellow countrymen"), while denying both the validity and actual fact of secession, which had taken the Deep South out of the Union?

Fort Sumter was the magic key in Lincoln's pocket. By March 4, Washington had received Major Anderson's letter of February 28 stating that his supplies would probably run out by mid-April. Something had to be done. Lincoln could not order the evacuation of Sumter; that would be showing weakness to the South, and probably lead to the yielding as well of Pickens and the two other peripheral Southern forts still in Federal hands. Nor could he run supplies in to Sumter by armed fleet; this would upset Northerners who still hoped for peace in the face of Southern secession. Besides, the attempt would probably fail anyway, given the artillery batteries that Anderson said the Confederates were building all around Charleston harbor. There was, at the same time, one remote possibility: to keep Anderson's garrison holding out, to announce to the Southerners that he would send to Sumter only food and medicine onboard unarmed ships, and to force the Confederates, if they wanted to maintain their territorial sovereignty, to pull the lanyard of the first cannon-shot of the war.

---

24   *The Collected Works of Abraham Lincoln,* ed. by Roy P. Basler, 9 vols. (New Brunswick, NJ, 1953), vol. 4, 262-71.

25   Ludwell Johnson, "Fort Sumter and Confederate Diplomacy," *Journal of Southern History,* vol. 26 (1960), 447.

"This daring thought must have occurred to Lincoln," Southern historian Charles W. Ramsdell has written. "Could the Southerners be induced to attack Sumter, to assume the aggressive and thus put themselves in the wrong in the eyes of the North and whole world?"[26]

SEWARD AND THE COMMISSIONERS

Like other Southerners, the three Confederate commissioners in Washington carefully studied Lincoln's Inaugural text, which was published next day in most of the city's papers. They were baffled by his statement that he could "hold, occupy, and possess" Sumter without bringing on a military conflict. To obtain elucidation of this vagueness, Crawford and company did not even know if they would be given a formal audience. In his speech President Lincoln had taken pains to enunciate that secession was no "right" at all. He had not once mentioned the Confederates' assembled government in Montgomery. And he had implied that his "dissatisfied fellow countrymen" were no more than a contingent of uproarious U.S. citizenry yet to be mollified. He most certainly did not hint that Davis's territorial configuration—whatever it was, constitutionally speaking—would be dealt with in the style of diplomatic discourse usually undertaken between two sovereign nations. Thus, as a matter of protocol, Lincoln had already told Seward that he would not allow an official visit by Crawford, Forsyth and Roman to the State Department. But he would give them the next best thing: access to his Secretary of State through an intermediary.

On the first day of his administration, just hours after taking his inaugural oath, the new president announced his Cabinet. As Jefferson Davis had done the month before, Lincoln picked his seven advisers from different states:

State—William H. Seward (New York)

Treasury—Salmon P. Chase (Ohio)

---

26   Charles W. Ramsdell, "Lincoln and Fort Sumter," *ibid.,* vol. 3 (1937), 272.

War—Simon Cameron (Pennsylvania)

Navy—Gideon Welles (Connecticut)

Attorney General—Edward Bates (Missouri)

Postmaster General—Montgomery Blair (Maryland)

Interior—Caleb Smith (Indiana)

They would be a talented but headstrong group, especially as four of them had been Lincoln's rivals for the Republican presidential nomination the summer before. (Historian James M. McPherson has judged this decision alone by Lincoln, to turn former enemies into key advisers, indicative of "an aplomb unparalleled in American history."[27]) Lincoln would have no problem working with three of them (Chase, Cameron and Bates), but Seward would be a problem. Former Senator from New York, Seward had been Lincoln's chief competitor for the party's nod and, when the Chicago convention opened, he had been the odds-on favorite to carry the Republican standard against the Democrats that fall. The State Secretary still nursed a mildly jealous rivalry, now that he was playing second fiddle, with Lincoln calling the tune.

Moreover, the new Secretary of State very much had his own ideas on how to resolve the Sumter standoff. He shared the three Southern commissioners' fears that negotiations might break down, leaving the Confederates no alternative but to use violence to gain the fort. And he sincerely hoped to prevent a civil war. Besides, he and Lincoln had gotten Major Anderson's alarming dispatch from Charleston, February 28, that his garrison's supplies would probably run out before the government could send a force strong enough (20,000 men!) to defeat the C.S. forces around Charleston harbor and save Sumter. So he knew that the stakes were high.

---

27   James M. McPherson, *Battle Cry of Freedom: The South Wins Its Independence* (New York, 1988), p. 260.

Thus Seward did all he could to mitigate the harsh edges of his President's inaugural speech. On March 5 Seward received the commissioners' first emissary, Senator William M. Gwin of California, a Southern sympathizer. Seward told Gwin to urge the Southerners not to be overly concerned at Lincoln's tough stance, for the President was just beginning to grasp the complexity of the Sumter problem; he had certainly not settled on a course of action. Besides, Seward wished to console them with what Gwin took to be an astonishing display of hubris: it was he, not Lincoln, who would be the key decision-maker in the new administration. Seward did not have to puff himself up too much to remind fellow-Senator Gwin that he possessed vastly more governmental experience and (he thought) more political savvy than Lincoln. With all this going for him, Seward asked the commissioners not to press their demands for the fort, but to give him time to help the President arrive at a peaceful solution to the crisis.

Clearly Seward was overstepping his authority, partly because he presumed himself to be wiser than his boss, but most of all because Lincoln had not yet shared his ideas with the Secretary of State. For the present he instructed Seward to keep talking with the Southerners. Accordingly, the Secretary kept "negotiations" underway. Crawford, Forsyth and Roman believed Seward's suggestions that a Federal withdrawal from Sumter was possible, and followed his advice. They postponed a formal demand for the fort, and on March 9 telegraphed their government in Montgomery: "by all means avoid collision at Charleston until you hear from us. Things look better here than was believed in Montgomery."[28]

SOUTH CAROLINIANS ARM

The South Carolinians who opened fire on Fort Sumter, April 12, 1861, had been preparing their bombardment for a long time—a decade, in fact.

---

28   Ludwell Johnson, "Fort Sumter and Confederate Diplomacy," *Journal of Southern History,* vol. 26 (1960), 451.

The Compromise of 1850 may have settled the question of slavery in the western territories, and the convention of Southern delegates at Nashville that year may have ended without acts of secession, but South Carolinians were preparing for a fight. The state legislature in Columbia passed the "Defense Act of 1850," which appropriated a hefty $300,000 to establish a state ordnance department. Orders went out to arms manufacturers for enough muskets to equip fully 15,000 militiamen. From the Palmetto Armory in Columbia the state purchased pistols, swords, gunpowder, percussion caps, artillery and shells. Trying to keep as much of this weapons-buying within the state as possible—both to feed the local economy and to avoid exciting nosy Northerners, who would notice large shipments of arms being sent down South—the S.C. Ordnance Department also procured wooden gun carriages from a Charleston firm, and artillery shells from ironworks in Spartanburg and Charleston.

Some heavy ordnance orders necessarily went outside the state (but stayed in the South), to Tredegar Iron Works in Richmond. In 1851 the state ordered fifty cannon from Tredegar, including eight 10-inch mortars. There is evidence suggesting that this order may have been increased for eight more 10-inch mortars. The number is significant, for when Confederate artillery opened on Sumter, April 12, 1861, there were sixteen 10-inch mortars emplaced in the C.S. batteries around the harbor.

So if South Carolina authorities started early in their preparations for war, they did so with a weird prescience which figured that mortars—known for their high-lobbed, short-range shells—would be needed at Charleston for the state's "defense." But after 1852, when in November the state's ordnance officer, Major James H. Trapier, recorded that "the guns have all been received," South Carolinians apparently did little further in their arms acquisition.[29]

29 Ashley Halsey, Jr., "South Carolina Began Preparing for War in 1851," *Civil War Times Illustrated,* Vol. 1 no. 1 (April 1962), p. 9.

That is, until the state seceded six weeks after Abraham Lincoln's election as Northern president. When the United States became disunited, December 20, 1860, with their state's secession, South Carolinians' fortifying, arming and troop-training renewed with far more ardor. Governor Pickens activated the state militia. The secession convention called for a regiment to be raised for six months' service. Then the legislature ordered ten more regiments organized for a year of duty. In a very short time indeed, the Palmetto Republic created an army.

Impetuous young men immediately filled the ranks. At South Carolina College virtually the whole student body enlisted overnight. In Charleston especially, volunteering became the rage among the well-to-do. As a result, some units turned into coteries of the aristocracy (a particular company of recruits was said to have had an aggregate worth of over a million dollars). In these commands, the rigors of military life were tempered with the perquisites of the elite. One smart new unit, the Charleston Zouave Cadets, provided each man with a neat uniform and complimentary privilege to use the local bowling alley and gymnasium five nights a week.

Eventually this sporting atmosphere subsided, and progress was made at arming and training the troops. To start with, there was no shortage of weapons, thanks to the Federal installations to whose contents the Carolinians had helped themselves. At Castle Pinckney the ordnance haul was four 42-pounders, fourteen 24-pounders, four 8-inch siege howitzers, a 10-inch and 8-inch mortar, and four light artillery pieces. At Fort Moultrie, they found fifty-six cannon; to their delight the evacuating U.S. troops had spiked them imperfectly with wrought iron nails. Governor Pickens quickly ordered the guns rebored and new carriages built. He also arranged for the state to purchase more gunpowder, cannon, rifles and ammunition. All of this was on top of 22,000 small arms and large supplies of ammo which the state assumed in possessing the U.S. arsenal on December 30.

In the first three months of 1861 South Carolina and Confederate authorities prepared for the eventuality that Anderson's garrison would not leave Sumter, and that they would have to be blasted out. At Cummings Point, the northern tip of Morris Island, two batteries were constructed for mortars to lob shells into Sumter. Another fixture, the "Iron-clad Battery," was so named for its special protection of heavy timbers overlaid with railroad iron; the battery's three 8-inch Columbiad smoothbores were aimed at the fort's back wall. Pickens also guarded against the Yankees' possible sending in of relief ships to Anderson's garrison. One of the Governor's first orders was for an artillery battery to be placed on the eastern, seaward side of Morris Island, in order to command the main ship channel into the harbor. A company of state troops and forty cadets from the Citadel quickly dug parapets out of the sand and positioned two 24-pounder guns. (It was this battery which helped turn away the *Star of the West* on January 9.)

On January 2 state troops occupied the abandoned Fort Johnson, and built two embrasures, the east "beach" and west "hill" batteries, each of which soon held two 10-inch mortars, trained on the Federals' island fort out in the water. At Fort Moultrie, all thirty-eight guns of various calibers had their fortifications strengthened and the magazine bomb-proofed against the Yankees' inevitable return fire. Eleven of Moultrie's cannon were carefully sighted on Sumter: three 8-inch Columbiads, two big 32-pounders and six 24-pounders.

Additional cannon were placed around the harbor. Governor Pickens soon found himself unprepared to direct all this arming and fortifying. As soon as the Confederate government was established, he asked that a professional solider be sent to take charge. President Davis considered several officers, then appointed G.T—rather, Pierre Gustave Toutant—Beauregard. A West Point graduate and hero of the Mexican War, Beauregard was a respected engineer with special skills in artillery. Perhaps as important, he was well-mannered and charming. Charlestonians liked his courteous, refined bearing and his Creole accent. As a result, the new Confederate commander and the Carolinians got along very well indeed.

Arriving in Charleston on March 1 Beauregard inspected the artillery at Moultrie and Cummings Point. His plan was to "form a circle of fire, by distributing all available guns and mortars around a circumference of which Fort Sumter should be the centre."[30] In doing so he felt the need to reposition some of the artillery already set in place, but he made his suggestions gradually and gently so as not to wound the feelings of his proud hosts. He requested from the government and got mortars from Savannah and Pensacola, setting them at Castle Pinckney, near Mount Pleasant and near Moultrie. Ranges would vary: from Cummings Point to Sumter was under a mile. Other ranges around the harbor were a little more, but still effective: a mile-plus from Moultrie to Sumter; from Fort Johnson 1 ½ miles; Mount Pleasant to Sumter 1 ¾. After just three weeks' work, Beauregard concluded that his batteries could easily pound Sumter into submission. Moreover, he had some 3,100 troops in the area, against Anderson's forces known only to a tiny fraction of his.

At the end of March the state's Secretary of War, D.F. Jamison, reported to the Governor on all that had been done. On Sullivans Island three batteries had been built for over a dozen cannon, including four 32-pounders. Farther to the north, on the mainland at Mount Pleasant, a battery was built for two 10-inch mortars. The most novel artillery position, however, was not set on land at all. Charlestonian John R. Hamilton, a former Navy officer, designed a four-gun floating battery, and got permission to begin its construction. Throughout February work proceeded on the peculiar-looking raft, moored at Sullivans Island, creating considerable excitement among townspeople and just as much curiosity among Anderson's men, who daily viewed building progress on the thing. When completed, it was a hundred feet long and twenty-five feet wide. The battery had a protected side, built of pine and palmetto logs covered with iron plating, and openings for two 42-pounder and two 32-pounder smoothbores.

---

30   *O.R.,* vol. 1, 36.

On the other hand, Beauregard was not so sure that the South Carolinians' batteries could keep Federal ships from getting to the fort, assuming the Northern administration would not give up Anderson's garrison without at least an attempt to reinforce or re-provision it. So he ordered the construction of more emplacements up the beach from the Star of the West battery. By the end of March 25 guns in ten batteries were in place along Morris Island's east side to challenge the approach of any hostile vessel.

Whether such a vessel would come, of course, was anyone's guess at Charleston, for everything hinged on the diplomatic maneuverings then ongoing in Washington.

SEWARD STALLS, AND MISLEADS

In Montgomery, President Davis received Crawford's message of March 9 ("avoid collision at Charleston....things look better here than was believed") with relief; perhaps Lincoln and his advisers were contemplating a withdrawal from Sumter after all. Anything could happen; Lincoln remained an enigma. Davis and Lincoln had never met, even during the Illinois Railsplitter's brief term in the House, 1847-49, part of which time Davis had served in the Senate. Adding to the volatility of the situation was the newness of both men in their executive positions: Davis, in the presidential office for not even three weeks, faced a counterpart inaugurated just a few days ago. Both national leaders were thus new at policymaking; besides, the whole Sumter crisis was without precedent in American history, so nobody had anything to go on.

While hopeful of a peaceful resolution, Davis also worried that Lincoln might be stalling in order to prepare some bold move. Thus on March 14 Davis authorized his commissioners to press demand for an immediate Federal evacuation of Sumter, unless, as State Secretary Toombs wrote, "negotiations are actually pending" toward a "definitive arrangement" for the withdrawal of the garrison.[31] That same day the commissioners tried to find out

---

31   Ludwell H. Johnson, "Fort Sumter and Confederate Diplomacy," *Journal of Southern History,* vol. 26 (1960), 454. Professor Johnson's seminal essay, published in *JSH* in the centennial year of South Carolina's secession, established Confederate scholars' long-held contention that Lincoln had artfully maneuvered

from Seward what negotiations were in fact being contemplated in the White House by sending their secretary, John T. Pickett. Stopped at the door, Pickett was told by a State Department clerk that a response would be sent to the commissioners. None came. On the 15th Pickett again inquired at Seward's office. This time he learned that the reply was still being drafted.

Crawford fretted. Unable to get the formal guarantee demanded by his President, the Confederate chief commissioner called on a friend, Supreme Court Justice John A. Campbell of Alabama. Campbell was widely known as a Unionist and well-respected jurist; perhaps he could wring from the oily hands of Seward a tangible response that would at least clear up the suspense and maybe deliver the answer the Southerners so desperately wanted. Campbell visited Seward, reminded him of the C.S. administration's position, and heard in return Seward's report of the inconclusive discussions taking place within Lincoln's Cabinet. The Secretary did not divulge much, only that the Cabinet had had its first meeting just a few days before (March 9), everyone had different opinions (Seward did not let on that he had argued for Sumter's evacuation), and that the President had not made up his mind (in fact, he had seemed distracted, almost unable to concentrate). But Seward also stressed his belief that the Federal garrison would be withdrawn. On this basis Campbell returned to Crawford and wrote down what he had learned:

> I feel perfect confidence in the fact that Sumter will
> be evacuated in the next five days. I earnestly ask
> for a delay until the effect of the evacuation can be
> ascertained—or at least for a few days, say ten days.
> J.A.C. 15 Mar 1861[32]

---

the South into becoming the "aggressor" at Sumter, and hence in the war. That his findings, drawn from expert research in the previously unpublished papers of Judge Campbell and Secretary Pickett, have been ignored by Northern academia has not diminished their centrality in the Confederate view of the War for Southern Independence.

32   *Ibid.,* 458-59.

"Effect of the evacuation": Judge Campbell unfortunately believed Seward, that Sumter's garrison would be withdrawn by the administration. An exhilarated Commissioner Crawford embellished this hopefulness in the telegram he sent Montgomery on the 15th: "We are sure that within five days Sumter will be evacuated."[33] Five days passed. Crawford wired Charleston and asked if authorities had seen any evidence of a Federal evacuation. There was no sign of it whatsoever. The Confederates grew nervous. Davis telegraphed Crawford for information, but the latter had nothing new to report. On March 21 the perplexed commissioners again sent Judge Campbell to Seward, who repeated his confidence that Sumter would be evacuated. Crawford relayed that message to Davis. Still U.S. troops remained at Charleston. From Montgomery an increasingly anxious Davis, fearful that Lincoln was tricking him into ordering an artillery bombardment to start a war that neither he nor his government wanted, told Crawford (in a telegram from Assistant Secretary of State William M. Browne, March 28) that he should seek the evacuation of Fort Sumter as the "indispensable condition for the preservation of peace"—meaning that by not withdrawing U.S. troops from Confederate territory, Lincoln would be the provoker of war, not Davis.[34]

On Saturday, March 30, at the request of an agitated Crawford, Forsyth and Roman, Judge Campbell met with Seward and related Davis's message, as well as word from Governor Pickens that there had been absolutely no change at Sumter. Campbell demanded a full explanation from the State Department, mincing the words of Crawford, who had recently asked Davis how they could "dally longer with a Government hesitating & doubting as to its own course."[5] Seward repeated his vague assurance about Sumter's evacuation, and told Campbell that he could not provide a more precise formal declaration of the administration's intentions until Monday, April 1. He promised that he would have a written statement at that time. The Judge promised to come back day after tomorrow.

---

33 *Ibid.*, 459.

34 *Ibid.*, 461.

LINCOLN'S SURPRISE

On Sunday night, March 31, Seward went to the White House to learn from Lincoln what he should tell the Southerners. To an extent he had staked his integrity as a statesman, if not his word as a gentleman, on the promise that Sumter would be evacuated. The President had never discouraged him from mentioning a troop withdrawal, and had in fact encouraged this impression as a means of sustaining dialogue with the Southern commissioners. But Seward had nothing to document Lincoln's position, for in every meeting of his newly formed Cabinet the President had refrained from saying anything conclusive about his decision regarding Sumter. When he arrived at the White House, the Secretary of State expected to have a candid conversation with Lincoln and to hear what exactly he had on his mind. Instead, upon his arrival Seward was surprised to learn that the President and First Lady had left to attend a play. He was told that the statement which Lincoln wanted conveyed to Judge Campbell would be delivered the next morning to the Secretary's office.

On Monday, April 1, Seward received Lincoln's message just minutes before Campbell arrived. The Justice was dismayed as he walked in to see Seward's face blanched, as if the paper he held in his hands had caused a shock to the usually composed elder statesman. For the conversation which followed, with only the Secretary and the Judge in the room, we have to rely on the latter's account of it, which Campbell wrote down very shortly afterward— he was instantly aware that Lincoln had hornswoggled the South, using the well-meaning but duped Seward as his patsy. Campbell was also instantly aware that such diplomatic chicanery as being played by the Northern President could start a war, and probably would.

Seward began by saying that the President was concerned that the Confederates apparently assumed that an evacuation of Sumter had been ordered. The Secretary said that no such instructions had been issued by the White House. Campbell then asked what he should report to the C.S. commissioners. As answer Seward handed him Lincoln's note, which read simply, "The President may desire to supply Fort Sumter, but will not undertake to do so without first giving notice to Governor Pickens."

"What does this mean?!" Campbell asked angrily, almost shouting. "Does your government design to attempt to send supplies to Sumter? And with them troops and ammunition?"

Confronted by Campbell and forced to explain a written statement which Lincoln had not discussed with him, Seward could only stammer. "No, I think not," he answered. "It is a very irksome thing for our President to evacuate it. His ears are open to every one, and they fill his head with schemes for its supply. I do not think that he will adopt any of them. There is no design to reinforce it."[35]

Campbell was quick enough to sense Lincoln's game, hinged on the difference between supply— the sending in by ship of foodstuffs to keep Anderson's beleaguered garrison from starving—and reinforcement—the sending in of more troops and arms. The latter would be construed as a warlike act; the former, a peaceful one. But to the hot-headed Carolinians, and those of Davis's advisers willing to have war with the Yankees over this issue as over any other, the semantics would be lost when United States vessels tried to enter Charleston harbor, no matter what they were carrying.

"If there be no formal design to attempt to supply or to reinforce the fort, he should not express a desire to do so," argued Campbell. "The evacuation is not considered to be an open question at Charleston, nor at Montgomery. And in their state of mind the South Carolinians would regard the expression of a desire by your administration to supply the fort as evidence of an intention to reinforce it as well. This will probably lead to a bombardment; it is difficult to restrain the people as it is. Then, once the shots

---

35   Ludwell Johnson, "Fort Sumter and Confederate Diplomacy," *Journal of Southern History,* vol. 26 (1960), 465.

start flying, who among us can predict the extent of violence, or its catastrophic outcome?!"[36]

Seward became even more rattled. He asked Campbell to wait while he went to the President and asked for a clarification. When he returned, he handed Campbell virtually the same message: "I am satisfied the Government will not undertake to supply Fort Sumter without giving notice to Gov. Pickens."[37]

The Judge took it, and left without saying a word.

THE MYSTERIOUS MISSION OF WARD LAMON

Because the Northern administration's dispatch of a flotilla laden with rations (albeit without weaponry or reinforcements) for Anderson's fourscore officers and men, and its approach to Charleston harbor in the second week of April are now seen as the immediate *casus belli* instigating the War for Southern Independence, and because Lincoln has tragically come to shoulder history's onus for provoking a war that splintered the Union and ruined his own presidency, some attention must be given to the "peaceful" naval expedition which set out from New York on April 6 and how Lincoln resolved to dispatch it.

The new President had barely been in office a week when he received, at the request of his Postmaster-General Montgomery Blair, a visit from Gustavus Fox, Blair's brother-in-law and former naval officer. Fox had done some studying of the Sumter problem, and believed that the U.S. Navy could run past the Southern batteries lining Charleston harbor if small steamers were employed. Lincoln found merit in Fox's proposal, even though the Army's

---

36 J.A. Campbell, "Papers of John A. Campbell, 1861-1863," *Southern Historical Society Papers,* 52 vols. (Richmond, 1876-1959), vol. 42 (1917), 34-35. The *S.H.S.P.,* launched in 1876 as a monthly publication, was inaugurated as a compendium of Southerners' recollections of the late war and a Confederate riposte to the hoopla being carried on in the North at the United States centennial. It became a quarterly, 1880-88, and was published thereafter annually until 1959, when growing feelings of amicability, if not reunion, between the Southern and Northern governments suggested that its continued publication no longer served the national interest or that of either people.

37 Maury Klein, *Days of Defiance: Sumter, Secession, and the Coming of the Southern War for Independence* (New York, 1997), p. 370.

General-in-Chief, the doughty old Winfield Scott, had voiced his opposition. Lincoln called together his Cabinet on March 15 to discuss the relief-fleet idea; everyone voted against it except Blair. State Secretary Seward was especially vocal, arguing that only an evacuation of Anderson's garrison would prevent a bloody and possibly needless civil war. At the end of the meeting, Lincoln did not disclose how he might resolve the Sumter crisis. The Cabinet vote, Lincoln's reticence, and Seward's continued confidence in himself as senior adviser to the President led Seward in the coming days to give his assurance to the C.S. commissioners that Sumter would eventually be evacuated.

Lincoln, however, refused to show weakness in the face of the Confederate demands for the fort. "The tug has to come," he had written, "& better now, than any time hereafter."[38] But if "the tug"—meaning war between the "United" and Confederate States—were indeed to come, Lincoln was shrewd enough to know that the side doing the first tugging would immediately be placed at a psychological, even moral or ethical disadvantage; in all wars, the firer of the first shot is labeled the "aggressor," and suffers disdain in the eventual annals of history if not on the immediate fields of battle. Jefferson Davis knew this, too, and hoped that his Washington commissioners could resolve the Sumter possession crisis without any shot being fired against it. Lincoln apparently looked forward to that first shot—so long as it was the other side that fired it.

Lincoln's scheme to get the South to cast itself as aggressor was as clever and complicated as any maneuver of his political career. It required him to call upon a close friend, loyal supporter and former law partner Ward H. Lamon. On March 21 with Seward present, Lincoln gave Lamon his instructions: go to Charleston and present himself to Governor Pickens as Lincoln's agent to arrange the removal of Sumter's garrison. But he was only to announce the government's intent of removal, not actually to give specifics about it. He was also to gauge Pickens' and the Carolinians' sensitivities

---

38 Roy P. Basler, ed., *The Collected Works of Abraham Lincoln,* 9 vols. (New Brunswick NJ, 1953), vol. 4, 150.

about U.S. naval vessels entering Charleston, which would have to be sent some time or other to get Anderson's men out. This Lamon did, arriving in Charleston on the 24th, meeting with the Governor, and promising to be back in a few days to arrange removal of Anderson and his men. Afterward he chugged out to the fort, where he heard Major Anderson affirm that he would run out of rations in three weeks, about April 15. But Lamon reassured the Major that all was well; he and his men would be evacuated by then. Anderson hoped Lamon was right, and so did the Confederates. On March 26 General Beauregard telegraphed Montgomery, "Mr. Lamon left here last night, saying that Major Anderson and command would soon be withdrawn in a satisfactory manner."[39]

With his mission accomplished, Lamon returned to Washington and briefed the President on what he had learned in Charleston about the mood of the Southerners. Patriotic feeling for the old country was dead there; the only Unionist in the whole city was said to be the aging attorney James. L. Petigru. Palpable everywhere was a fiery new Confederate patriotism, as well as a bristly bellicosity at all Yankees, especially the unwanted ones out in the harbor. Lamon reported that the Southerners were so trigger-happy that the Confederate authorities in Montgomery had sent a senior officer, Beauregard, to keep the lid on the situation. Lamon had asked Pickens if a U.S. warship would be allowed into the harbor to take on Anderson's men for transport north. No, sir, the Governor replied; to which Lamon added in his report, "I have no doubt that a ship known to contain only provisions for Sumter would be stopped and refused admittance," and if it persisted, would be fired upon by the Confederate shore batteries. Lamon also reminded Lincoln of the garrison's rapidly depleting rations. For all these reasons, Lamon concluded, "I am satisfied of the policy and propriety of immediately evacuating Fort Sumter."[40]

The President took all this in, keeping his own counsel.

---

39   *O.R.,* vol. 1, 282.

40   Maury Klein, *Days of Defiance: Sumter, Secession, and the Coming of the Southern War for Independence* (New York, 1997), pp. 345, 353.

On March 29 Lincoln again called his Cabinet together, relating to them what he had heard from Lamon and again asking each Secretary to submit his advice on what should be done. But the President masterfully guided discussion from the very first by offering, for the first time, his own idea that the government could avoid the humiliation of evacuating Sumter by sending Anderson's garrison some measure of naval-borne aid. Not reinforcements or ammunition; that warlike act could paint the North as aggressor. Rather, Lincoln was thinking of a few ships carrying crackers and salt pork, just to keep the starving garrison alive—a mission so humanitarian as to be puppy-like in its peaceability. But given what Lamon had said, Lincoln predicted that the Rebels—for such he was beginning to call them, now that he was engineering the U.S. government's military responses to a widespread civil insurrection—would fire the first shot. The fort would inevitably fall; there was nothing to prevent it. And the war would surely come; in Lincoln's view, there was nothing to prevent it. And in firing the first shot, the South would be cast as aggressor, and in the wrong. They could not prevent that, too.

To Seward's shock, as each Cabinet member offered his opinion, everyone took Lincoln's side, especially Welles of the Navy. All (except Seward) expressed support of some kind of naval expedition to keep the Sumter garrison fed until negotiations (such as they were) had run their course.

With the very object, then, of keeping those negotiations on course, a demoralized but still stubborn Seward had told Judge Campbell on the 30th, the day after the Cabinet meeting, that Sumter would be evacuated. But Campbell, and behind him Crawford, Forsyth and Roman, wanted to see the Northern government's position in writing. On April 1, Seward at last had no alternative but to hand Judge Crawford a note that affirmed the administration did indeed intend to resupply Anderson's garrison.

After their first recoil of shock, the Southern commissioners were starting to feel used; the Confederate authorities in Montgomery were starting to fear they were being duped; and the people in Charleston, where the whole thing was centered, were starting to smell a rat in the doings of the Lincoln administration. As one Southern lady phrased it, "the people of Charleston are getting very tired of such *maneuvers*."[41]

ASTONISHMENT IN THE SOUTH

After his meeting with Seward of April 1, Judge Campbell's fast trek to the Southern commissioners' rooms at the National Hotel, and his presentation of the note he had been given by the Northern State Secretary, led to an expression by them of Campbell's own reaction: shock and anger.

Martin Crawford and John Forsyth were particularly stunned by this apparent reversal of policy. It was they who had put their names to several key telegraphic messages to Montgomery: "The impression prevails in administration circles that Fort Sumter will be evacuated within ten days" (March 9); and "We are sure that within five days Sumter will be evacuated" (March 15). Moreover, the commissioners were talking to other prominent Southerners still in town and they too sent their own messages either to President Davis in Montgomery or to General Beauregard in Charleston. One such was from Louis Wigfall of Texas, who had wired both Davis and Beauregard, "It is believed here that Anderson will be ordered to evacuate Sumter in five days."[42]

These heady dispatches delighted Charlestonians, and of course made great print. The *Courier* headlined on March 11: "The Evacuation of Fort Sumter Determined On. Anderson to Go to Fort Monroe," referring to the big Federal fort in Virginia, itself a Southern state soon to secede. Its cross-town counterpart, the vociferous Charleston *Mercury*, echoed on the twelfth, "The President [Lincoln] has given orders for the evacuation.....Sumter is to be ours without a fight."[43]

---

41   *Ibid.*, p. 344

42   Ludwell Johnson, "Fort Sumter and Confederate Diplomacy," *Journal of Southern History*, vol. 26 (1960) 451; Maury Klein, *Days of Defiance: Sumter, Secession, and the Coming of the Southern War for Independence* (New York, 1997), p. 329; *O.R.*, vol. 1, 273.

43   Robert Hendrickson, *Sumter: The First Day of the Southern War for Independence* (Chelsea MI, 1990), p. 168; Klein, *Days of Defiance*, pp. 327, 334.

But the government in Montgomery was cautious, skeptical of these optimistic messages, and watchful of a slippery trick, the diplomatic variant of the legendary Yankee nutmeg. Indeed, while Seward seemed to be promising peace, Southern agents in the North sent warnings of what seemed to be war preparations. On March 14 Confederate Defense Secretary Walker wired alerts to Beauregard in Charleston, and commanders of C.S. forces at Pensacola and Mobile: four steamers were reported to be leaving New York, said to be carrying soldiers, arms and provisions somewhere south, most likely to one of the several Federal forts there. (Fort Pickens as much as Sumter seemed to be a likely destination, though its foreign ownership had not yet produced in the Confederate administration a crisis of the Charlestonian order; but who knew what would happen if Lincoln chose to reinforce at Pickens, letting Sumter go?) On March 20, Secretary of State Toombs anxiously wired the C.S. commissioners in Washington for any news, but given Seward's (and Lincoln's) stalling, they had none. When they finally did have news on April 1 (Seward's note to Campbell), Crawford immediately wired its contents to Charleston: "I am authorized to say that this Government will not undertake to supply Sumter without notice to you." But Crawford added a hopeful note, his belief—based on Seward's repeated deprecations of Lincoln—that "the President has not the courage to execute the order agreed upon in Cabinet." In a parallel wire to Toombs on the 1st, Crawford continued to hold out hope, urging that the government order no attack on Fort Sumter "when the general impression is, its surrender can be expected every hour."[44]

President Davis would have none of this. After three weeks of assurances that Sumter would be evacuated, he saw the Federal garrison still secure in Charleston harbor; he had heard reports of U.S. naval activity, possibly a relief expedition to the fort; and he had already concluded that such a naval force would have to be repelled, or that the fort would have to be taken before food, arms or reinforcements arrived. So he made certain that Beauregard and the Confederate forces at Charleston continued fortifying. But

---

44 *O.R.*, vol. 1, 283-84; Johnson, "Fort Sumter and Confederate Diplomacy," p. 466.

he also made sure that his commissioners in Washington avoided any hostile reaction to Seward's notification, at least until they got definite confirmation of Lincoln's plan. Accordingly, on April 2 Davis instructed Crawford for the time being to acquiesce to the White House's announcement, while keeping the government informed of any belligerent activities being conducted by the Yankees.

SEWARD'S OWN ASTONISHMENT, AND RESIGNATION

To an extent Secretary Seward was more surprised than Davis by Lincoln's statement of April 1. So after Judge Campbell left, Seward strode directly to the President and explained why he felt embarrassed, even betrayed. For one thing, the written message suggested that Lincoln had not confided fully in his Cabinet, even as he gave the impression of indecision. And it suggested that Lincoln had deliberately misled Seward when he encouraged the Secretary to tantalize the Confederates with prospects of a peaceful Federal withdrawal from Sumter. Finally, especially when he learned that Lincoln had already ordered a naval expedition fitted out in New York for sailing in a few days, the announcement suggested (the more so, in view of Lamon's first-hand report on the Charlestonians' mood) that the President was inviting the Southerners to start a war. Campbell had been aware of this, too, and had said it to Seward: expression of Lincoln's mere desire to supply the fort would probably lead to a bombardment.

"That's just what I want," smiled Lincoln as he leaned back in his chair. As he realized the extent to which he had been made a fool, and to which his laudable hopes to keep the peace had been undermined by the President's own cunning if not prevaricating, Seward determined then and there to resign his Cabinet post. Afterward he laid out his reasons for doing so in a number of memoranda and letters which he wrote expressly for publication; but the details of his private conversation with Lincoln on April 1 come to us only from scattered reflections of Seward's many friends in Washington who also hoped that the country would be spared a bloody civil war. For example, in his biography of Seward, James Trenholm phrased Lincoln thus: "Now, now, Seward.

Look at the situation. The very first thing placed in my hands was the judgment of Scott and the military men announcing the impossibility of defending or relieving Sumter. So the fort was lost. I assumed responsibility for losing it in the best way possible."[45]

Seward asked the President if he had considered the fate of Anderson's men, trapped in a fort soon to be the target of hostile bombardment. Lincoln chose to emphasize that he was not ordering the bombardment, but that the Rebels were. Seward later told a Connecticut editor, "Mr. Lincoln saw an opportunity to inaugurate civil war without appearing in the character of an aggressor. There are men in Fort Sumter, he said, who are nearly out of provisions. They ought to be fed. We will attempt to feed them. Certainly nobody can blame us for that....The secessionists, who are both mad and foolish, will resist us. They will commence civil war. Then I will appeal to the North to aid me in putting down rebellion, and the North must respond. How can it do otherwise? And sure enough, how can we do otherwise?"[46]

After the "mad and foolish" secessionists commenced civil war on April 12 and were forced to take the blame for starting it, Lincoln was exultant. After the Sumter bombardment he told a friend, Illinois Senator Orville Browning, how he had been opposed by Scott of the army, and by his Cabinet at first, but that "he himself conceived the idea, and proposed sending supplies, without an attempt to reinforce giving notice of the fact to Gov Pickens of S.C. The plan succeeded. They attacked Sumter—it fell, and thus, did more service than it otherwise could."[47]

Even pithier was the President's exclamation when first word came that the Confederates had opened fire on the morning of April 12. Congressman Alexander Long of Ohio told colleagues

---

45   J.W. Trenholm, *William Henry Seward* (Philadelphia, 1879), p. 183.

46   Providence *Daily Post,* April 13, 1861, quoted in Charles W. Ramsdell, "Lincoln and Fort Sumter," *Journal of Southern History,* vol. 3 (1937), 236-37 n.36.

47   *The Diary of Orville H. Browning,* ed. by Theodore Calvin Pease and James G. Randall, 3 vols. (Springfield IL, 1927), vol. 1, 475-76.

that standing in the East Room of the White House when a clerk brought in the telegraphic news, Lincoln was heard to exclaim, "I knew they would do it!"[48]

Embarrassed that he had been used by the President, ashamed that his own hopes for a peaceful evacuation of Fort Sumter had misled the Southerners, and anguished that he had been unable to prevent a tragic war, Secretary Seward submitted his resignation three days after the firing on Sumter. Retiring to his home in New York, he watched the conflict take its course, quietly beaming his satisfaction as his quickly named successor, former New Jersey Senator William L. Dayton, foundered amidst the wartime diplomatic crises involving the Navy's seizure of the British steamer *Trent,* the French takeover in Mexico, and ultimately English and French recognition of the Confederacy.[49] Meanwhile Seward, holding forth as senior statesman without portfolio, let it be known that he would face Lincoln again for the Republican presidential nomination in '64. That he would be denied a chance to culminate an otherwise lustrous political career in the U.S. government during wartime was, of course, a great disappointment to Seward. It was assuaged only by his *schadenfreude* at Lincoln's own degradation, as Union military fortunes fell, and eventually collapsed, in the war that the Northern president had worked so hard to start.[50]

---

48   Charles W. Ramsdell, "Lincoln and Fort Sumter," *Journal of Southern History,* vol. 3 (1937), 287n.

49   Lincoln had considered Dayton earlier for the State Secretaryship, thinking of sending Seward to London as Minister to Great Britain. "How would it do for Mr. Chase to take the Treasury, and to offer the State Department to Mr. William L. Dayton?" Lincoln had mused before a delegation of New Yorkers on March 2, two days before his inauguration. The New Yorkers' objections caused the President-Elect to pocket his Dayton idea, only to bring it out quickly again after Seward's resignation (Allan Nevins, *The Emergence of Lincoln: Prologue to Civil War 1859-1861* [New York, 1950], p. 454).

50   Geoffrey Perret is only one historian to apply the president's name to the war he started (*Lincoln's War* [New York 2004]). Lincoln's manipulations with history are outlined in Thomas J. DiLorenzo, *The Real Lincoln: A New Look at Abraham Lincoln, His Agenda, and an Unnecessary War* (Roseville CA, 2002).

PRESIDENT DAVIS PONDERS HIS OPTIONS

Davis's instructions of April 2 to his Washington commissioners, that they keep him posted on any news of Northern war preparations, brought a response the very next day. "Much activity in the War and Navy Departments," Crawford wired. "It is said the *Minnesota*, at Boston, has been ordered to the mouth of the Mississippi. *Powhatan* suddenly put in commission to sail next week. *Pawnee* will not be ready for sea until Saturday." On April 5 the commissioners telegraphed that "an important move requiring a formidable military and naval force is certainly on foot. Having no confidence in the administration, we say, be ever on your guard. Glad to hear that you are ready." Then on the 6th: "No change in the activity of the warlike armaments mentioned yesterday. The rumor that they are destined against Sumter is getting every day stronger. We know nothing positive on the subject, but advise equally activity on your part to receive them if they come. We have not yet been notified of the movement, but the notification may come when they are ready to start." At last, on April 7 the commissioners received sufficient information for them to report that a war fleet had been prepared by the Northern government, and that "part of it sailed against the Confederate States."[51] In one last effort to salvage their mission, Crawford, Forsyth and Roman themselves boldly went to the State Department to try to see Seward to discuss the grave developments. The Secretary of State refused to meet with them.

As it turned out, Seward was able to keep one of the two promises he had made. Fort Sumter was not to be evacuated, but the Confederates were notified that the United States intended to send a naval expedition to resupply the garrison in Charleston. This news was delivered to Governor Pickens on the 8th by a State Department clerk sent from Washington. Pickens was offended by Lincoln's choice of a mere clerk to conduct correspondence between heads of state. Moreover, the message, written by Lincoln himself, was not addressed and not even signed—subtle tactics

---

51   *O.R.*, vol. 1, 286-87; C.S. Government Printing Office, *Official Records of the Confederate and Union Navies in the War for Southern Independence*, 30 vols. (Richmond, 1894-1922), ser. 1, vol. 4, 258.

in diplomatic letter-writing intended to offend the recipient. To cap it all, the Northern clerk refused to accept any reply from the Governor. He delivered the message and promptly departed. Pickens was thus left with the impression either that Lincoln did not care how the South Carolinians reacted, or that Lincoln knew how they would react, and had determined to resupply Sumter anyway.

Pickens and Beauregard telegraphed Montgomery immediately. Within hours President Davis had conveyed the information to his Cabinet members, and called a meeting for 10 a.m. the next day, Tuesday, April 9, to discuss the government's course of action. (By this time, the executive and other key departments in Montgomery had moved their offices into the "government house," a three-story brick building across the street from the Exchange Hotel, at the corner of Market and Commerce Streets. It was more commodious but more inelegant, if only because the "great, red brick pile" had been originally built as a warehouse.)

Before they convened, Davis and his six Cabinet members must have recognized just how few indeed were their options. To Davis, there seemed no alternative but to give the order to bombard the fort, hope to avoid loss of life, accept its surrender, then deport the Federal garrison to the North. Anderson and his men would not be kept as "prisoners of war," as there was as yet no war, certainly any war which the Southerners wanted to observe, much less start. In Davis's eyes, the problem of Sumter would be solved. Confederate authority would no longer be challenged by the presence of foreign troops in Charleston Harbor. He would have made his point to Lincoln, and so invited him to enter a new round of negotiations for the removal of Lieutenant Slemmer's garrison holding Fort Pickens at Pensacola—the next trouble-spot between the two nations. But how would the Northerners react? He assumed that they would do so angrily (just as Southerners would), and demand action against the Confederate States. And he had little doubt that Lincoln, who had so adroitly maneuvered the Southerners into resorting to violence, would just as easily be able to persuade his "dissatisfied fellow countrymen" (this time on the Northern side) that they must seize the sword to avenge the flag and put down the rebellion.

Davis had formed these impressions weeks before, while reading the three commissioners' telegrams and directing their activity in Washington. Two Cabinet officers had also stayed abreast of the events: Secretary of State Robert Toombs and Secretary of Defense LeRoy Pope Walker. The four other members were less informed. But the President knew that his advisers shared some basic assumptions, which could be numbered on the fingers of one hand: 1) the Confederate government was entitled to take over all public property within its boundaries; 2) the United States government was violating this authority by maintaining an armed garrison at Charleston; 3) the Federals had already commenced an act of aggression by sending the *Star of the West* to reprovision Sumter in January (some Carolinians maintained that Anderson's wrecking of Fort Moultrie on December 26 had in itself been an act of war); 4) Lincoln—if his message of the 8th to Governor Pickens were to be believed—was about to commit another warlike act in sending a fleet to force its way into the harbor; and hence 5) actual responsibility for provoking a war, if it should happen, rested with Lincoln and the Federal government.

THE PRESIDENT'S INNER CIRCLE

Davis's Cabinet was a remarkable group—remarkable for its concentration of talent, diversity of background, and colorfulness of character. On the morning of Tuesday, the 9th, as he prepared for his ten o'clock meeting, the President reckoned that he would preside over an expression of opinion on the Sumter crisis as intelligent and powerful as the Cabinet Secretaries themselves. He welcomed it, quite pleased with the circle of advisers to whom he would now turn.

The most prestigious position, that of State, had gone to Robert Augustus Toombs of Georgia, who had been Davis's only real rival for the presidency, but who had quickly acquiesced to the convention's choice of Davis. Along with his successful law practice, almost half of his fifty years had been spent in the public service:

state legislature (1837-43); U.S. House of Representatives (1845-53); and Senate (1853-61). Fond of cigars and liquor, he was a big bear of "huge, bulky frame," but also leonine with a "great round head, surmounted by a mane of unruly brown hair." He had an equally lion-like, roaring voice that, coupled with his considerable oratorical talent, volatile moods and gesticulating arms, turned any speech of his into a public entertainment. After the war, in October 1871, Toombs was giving a speech in the Confederate Senate when an aide slipped him a note stating that there was a great fire raging in Chicago. Toombs interrupted his address to impart the news to his colleagues that firemen were getting the blaze under control. "But," he added, "the wind is in our favor."

The drink that was never too far away in fact fueled the great speeches of "the famous and formidable Toombs," which were never really planned, but delivered extemporaneously. His orations were filled with provocative witticisms that provided newspapermen with quotable quotes which later he would have to amend or deny (but never apologize for). Congressional galleries quickly filled when word spread that Bob Toombs was about to rise. "His extemporaneous speeches rolled out with ease and swiftness, and his readiness in retort made him a terror to his heckler," wrote an observer. "On a second's notice his bulky frame would rise, his deep Southern voice never pausing for word or idea, his leonine head shaking in monitory earnestness, his stubby finger pointing opprobriously at the foe; and sometimes the great form would parade up and down the aisle. Meanwhile the speaker's arguments, now menacing, now defiant, part persuasive, part mere assertion and epigram, would hold a dozen Congressmen at bay." A biographer captured Toombs' complexity and energy: "Basically a man of conservative instincts, he could in moments of commotion explode in any direction, after which he would assemble the pieces and resume his former character."[52]

---

52 Burton J. Hendrick, *Statesmen Of The Southern Cause: Jefferson Davis And His Cabinet* (New York, 1931), Pp. 69-70; William Y. Thompson, *Robert Toombs Of Georgia* (Baton Rouge, 1966), Pp. 66, 125.

In filling his Cabinet posts Davis was not uniformly successful in matching man with job, but no one could doubt that in naming Judah Philip Benjamin as Attorney General, the President had secured the services of the most brilliant lawyer in the South. Born in St. Thomas in 1811, Benjamin moved with his family to Charleston, where his father struggled as a merchant. He so excelled as a student at Fayetteville Academy that he entered Yale at the age of fourteen. He left, however, after the start of his junior year. He was restless and bored, so at seventeen he set out on his own for the South's largest and most boisterous city, New Orleans. There Benjamin literally "read the law"; attending no law school, he studied on his own, in six years gained admittance to the bar, and by 1840 was not only a very successful lawyer, but the most sought-after commercial attorney in the city. He bought a sugar plantation and added to his wealth; he married a daughter of a prominent Creole which further secured his standing in society. After holding several minor offices he was elected to represent Louisiana in the Senate, which he did from 1852 till his resignation on the last day of December 1860. Then, in his farewell speech, Benjamin showed both his fiery devotion to the Southern cause (he was a well-known "ultra" secessionist) and his masterful eloquence. Rarely raising his voice, he brought the Senate gallery to its feet with his defiant conclusion: "You may carry desolation into our peaceful land, and with torch and fire you may set our cities in flames....You may do all this, and more, too, if more there be—but you can never subjugate us; you can never convert the free sons of the soil into vassals, paying tribute to your power; and you never, never can degrade them to the level of an inferior and servile race. Never! Never!"[53]

What struck people about Judah Benjamin was his beguiling cheeriness. He always appeared to be smiling. Sometimes it seemed that the ever-present grin reflected not so much a genuine blithesomeness as Benjamin's clever way of keeping his real feelings to himself. Similarly, when he spoke, it was with a soft, melodious, high-pitched voice which never showed anger, excitement or, for that matter, any emotion at all. Instead, Benjamin's smile and

---

53   Hendrick, *Statesmen,* P. 170.

speech projected an almost irritating self-confidence that became as familiar as his style of dress: the immaculate black suit, the heavy watch chain which he was constantly fingering, &c.

And, yes, he was a Jew. At a time when anti-Semitism was a silent stain on the nineteenth-century American political fabric, Davis's decision to appoint a Sephardic to the pinnacle of governmental power in the Confederacy showed at once Benjamin's commanding talents and the Southern President's shrewd tolerance. A British journalist at the time commented on Benjamin's appearance. "He is a short, stout man, with full face, olive-coloured, and most decidedly Jewish features, with the brightest large black eyes, one of which is somewhat diverse from the other, and a brisk, lively, agreeable manner, combined with much vivacity of speech and quickness of utterance." His religion was, in fact, sometimes used against him by rivals. When taunted in public, Benjamin invariably destroyed every opponent with his unnerving blend of effusive courtesy and fierce wit. Once, in the Senate, when a critic called him "that Jew from Louisiana," Benjamin rose smiling and replied, "It is true that I am a Jew, and when my ancestors were receiving their ten commandments from the immediate hand of Deity, amidst the thunderings and lightnings of Mount Sinai, the ancestors of the gentleman who is opposed to me were herding swine in the forests of Scandinavia."[54]

Davis might have preferred to give Benjamin, with his enormous intelligence and passion for work, the important ministry of defense, but as one Confederate later remarked, "Mr. Benjamin is a brilliant lawyer, but he knew as much about war as an Arab knows of the Sermon on the Mount."[55] Instead, the post went to the government's host-state, Alabama, with the appointment of Leroy Pope Walker. Though a prominent Huntsville attorney in northern Alabama, Walker was not known outside the state and had not held high elective office. He had a reputation as a hard worker, with a sharp memory for statistics and details; tall and

---

54   William Howard Russell, *My Diary North And South,* Ed. By Fletcher Pratt (New York, 1954), P. 96; Hendrick, *Statesmen,* Pp. 155-56.

55   Robert Douthat Meade, *Judah P. Benjamin, Confederate Statesman* (New Orleans, 1943), P. 180.

lanky, he carried himself with much evidence of dignity and punctiliousness, despite his profuse tobacco-spitting. Moreover, Walker had the backing of two powerful Alabamans, Clement Clay and W.L. Yancey, both of whom endorsed him for the Cabinet. Finally, he was an ardent Southern rights man. This was enough for Davis, who tapped Walker for the Department of Defense. The Alabaman might have wanted the Attorney Generalship, but that post had already gone to Benjamin. And though he was sometimes called "the General," Walker was perfectly innocent of military experience. No matter—in fact, all the better, as Jefferson Davis, having headed the War Department under Franklin Pierce, intended to be his own Secretary of Defense. What Davis needed was a first-rate clerk; Walker sensed that, and eagerly accepted the job.

With the army in the hands of Walker, next came the navy, which seat Davis gave to the Floridian Stephen Mallory. Like Benjamin, Mallory was a West Indian, born in Trinidad in 1813, of a sea captain father and Irish working girl. The father died early, leaving no money. The Mallorys moved to Key West where young Stephen helped his mother run a boarding house for sailors and traders. Though he received only a year's schooling, Mallory taught himself and began journalistic work for the New York Herald and other papers, writing about shipwrecks and other maritime news. He studied law, served as judge, fought in the Seminole War and made such a name for himself that he was sent to the U.S. Senate in 1851. Rather squat in build, with a plump, ruddy face, he reminded people of a satisfied English gentleman. Someone called him a "stumpy, 'roly-poly' little fellow," well-known as a hearty soul, good-natured and even rollicksome at times, especially when he had had his fill of food and wine. He was not much of a sailor, though he enjoyed yachting; this and his experiences in Key West were apparently enough for him to become chairman of the Senate committee on naval affairs. Sitting in the same chamber, Jefferson Davis often heard him addressing their colleagues on the need for appropriations to build more U.S. warships. Davis and Mallory became good friends, and it was Davis himself who wrote Mallory, asking him to become C.S. Secretary of the Navy. Aware that the infant Confederacy actually possessed no navy for him to be secretary of—"except an unrepaired vessel at Pensacola," he wrote at the time—Mallory at first resisted, but later accepted the appointment.[56]

South Carolinians wanted their place in the Cabinet; Davis chose Christopher Gustavus Memminger for Treasury. Memminger was just what would be demanded by the trying job of national treasurer. German-born but raised in a Charleston orphanage, he had learned the importance of hard work and serious study. He had enrolled in the University of South Carolina when only eleven and had graduated at the age of fourteen, second in his class. He went on to practice law, specializing in commerce and finance, gaining much respect in the learned and powerful circles. He made his reputation in the famous "Bank Case," in which Memminger served as counsel for the state as it brought suit against the Bank of South Carolina for unsound fiscal practices. Memminger won, and basked in a reputation for ironclad logic and forceful presentation which grew over the years with the soundness of the rechartered bank. He never sought Federal office, but served as State Assembly delegate for twenty years; he was a key player in the secession convention, and a delegate to Montgomery when the new nation was being formed. So he was on hand to accept Davis's appointment.

The last office, Postmaster General, was one that no one seemed to want. Because every Confederate state save Texas had been given representation in the Cabinet, Davis had to find a westerner to manage the country's mails. Finally, on March 6, he persuaded John Henninger Reagan to accept—and that was only after he had craftily invited the Texan to a conference room packed with congressmen and other Cabinet members, all promising their support if Reagan took the job. He had, of course, no experience for it whatsoever. Having moved to Texas in 1839 at twenty-one, Reagan had lived the rough life of frontier scout, and looked it. Over six feet tall, 250-plus pounds, he immediately conveyed the impression of a man to be reckoned with. "His broad, high-cheekboned face,"

---

56   Joseph T. Durkin, *Stephen R. Mallory, Confederate Navy Chief* (Chapel Hill, 1954), P. 43; "Letter Of Stephen R. Mallory, 1861," *American Historical Review*, Vol. 12 (1906-07), 106.

wrote one, "bronzed and burned by the sun and partially hidden by a full black beard and long lion like mane, marked him with a certain fierceness and ruggedness."[57] Yet he felt ill at ease among polished types. He had gained a bit of polish in the state legislature in the late '40s, and in the Congress, 1857-61. Involved in the secession of his state, he was one of five Texas delegates sent to Montgomery in February and was, like Memminger, on the spot and ready to go to work.

Thus was Jefferson Davis's inner circle composed. Absent at the meeting of April 9, as he would be for every future Cabinet meeting, was Vice President Stephens. "Little Aleck" had already had his first falling-out with his boss. Stephens was unhappy with Davis's strong executive style, as well as his determination to use every presidential power to ensure the independence of the Confederacy, whether it be through war or not. Already the Sumter crisis, and Davis's anticipation of armed conflict with the North, were forcing the President to call upon the seven state governors not just to cooperate in raising a national army, but to hand over their state forces to C.S. authority. For Stephens, though, state rights had been the Confederacy's *raison d'etre*, and Davis's willingness to "trample" state authority for the national good was unprincipled; he wanted nothing of it. The Vice President thus angrily left Montgomery before the end of March, feeling it more honorable to publicly boycott the national government than to resign from it, and retiring to his farm estate in Crawfordville, Georgia. There he sat out the rest of the war, still holding his office (which Davis and the Confederate Congress wisely allowed him to retain), issuing angry letters denouncing Davis to the Southern press, but finding fewer and fewer newspapers willing to publish them—especially as the Confederacy's war-fortunes rose in 1862, Davis's reputation and prestige as the Southern nation's founding war-president rising with them.

---

57   Ben H. Procter, *Not Without Honor: The Life Of John H. Reagan* (Austin, 1962), P. 101.

One of Postmaster General Reagan's contributions to philately was departing from the United States Post Office's long-held custom of not placing likenesses of living persons on its stamps. Shortly after taking office, Reagan began considering designs for the first Confederate postage stamps. As historian Manly Wade Wellman has written, "These would bear, for the first time in American history, the portrait of a living man—Jefferson Davis" (*They Took Their Stand: The Founders of the Confederacy* [New York, 1959], 133). To this day, the U.S. Postal Service maintains its regulation against philatelic depiction of the living, while the Confederate States Post Office has proudly distributed stamps bearing the likenesses of Presidents Toombs, Byrd, Kefauver and others.

THE CABINET MEETING OF APRIL 9

No one expected a great deal of variance in the opinions to be expressed. As each Secretary entered the executive office, Davis handed him the telegram from Charleston announcing Lincoln's intent to send ships inside the harbor. Memminger, the South Carolinian, read the message and stiffly remarked, "Upon the whole it is fortunate that the first act of aggression is removed from the shoulder of our gallant little state."[58] Stephen Mallory repeated his belief that Lincoln had all along planned to use force and provoke a civil war that would unite the North and consolidate his party's political power. When Judah Benjamin read the note, he just grinned a little more broadly and took his seat; his views on the welcomeness of a sure-to-be-won war were well known. Reagan too said nothing. Secretary of Defense Walker, who had kept up with the stream of telegrams from the three commissioners in Washington, seemed to already know the contents of the message; he entered the room and began immediately to look for a spittoon.

Formal discussion began even before the Secretary of State arrived. First they debated whether Lincoln's notice to Governor Pickens, unsigned as it was, should be considered genuine. (They assumed that it should.) Then Walker reviewed the military

---

58 Richard N. Current, *Lincoln and the First Shot* (Philadelphia, 1963), p. 138.

preparations which Confederates had already made at Charleston, especially the batteries that had been built around the harbor. He relayed the recent report from Pickens that there were 3,700 Confederate and South Carolina troops there, all geared for a fight. The Defense Secretary expressed unhesitant confidence that these men and guns could readily pound the Yankee garrison into surrender. Walker added that he had yesterday wired each of the seven governors, asking for another 3,000 troops from each state, drilled and equipped. They would be needed in case of war.

Next they took up the issue of whether the Federal garrison could be forced out of Sumter by any means short of bombardment. There was unanimous agreement that it could not.

Just then Bob Toombs walked in. The Georgian looked as if he were prepared to let loose another of his inimitable tirades against the meddlesome Yankees and perfidious Republicans. His big bulky frame, attired in black, seemed about to burst forth with pent-up emotion any second. His colleagues were probably grateful that the President had called this meeting for ten o'clock in the morning, before Toombs' customary lunchtime toddies would add to his vim and volume.

Toombs strode directly to Davis's desk and took the telegram. He paced back and forth while reading it, making everyone in the room pause, puzzling on what would burst forth from the combustible Secretary of State. Presently he not so much offered the opinion that all in the room had hushed to hear, so much as shocked the daylights out of them with the following: "The firing upon that fort will inaugurate a civil war greater than any the world has yet seen; and I do not feel competent to advise you." Davis *et al.* were astounded by this expression of doubt and hesitation from such a strong advocate of Southern secession and, more recently, of preparation for war against the North. Coaxed to elaborate, Toombs blustered forth, "Mr. President, at this time, it is suicide, murder, and will lose us every friend at the North. You will wantonly strike a hornet's nest which extends from mountains to ocean, and legions, now quiet, will swarm out and sting us to death. It is unnecessary; it puts us in the wrong; it is fatal."[59]

Davis had a quick response, for he had long fretted over the Washington administration's finagling the South into firing the first shot of war, and was ready to answer any Cabinet member's worries about starting the conflict, even the redoubtable Toombs. He held up a New York paper from just the week before, rushed by sympathizers in New York City to the capital. "We have no doubt Mr. Lincoln wants the Cabinet at Montgomery," Davis read, "to take the initiative by capturing the two forts [Sumter and Pickens] in its waters, for it would give him the opportunity of throwing upon the Southern Confederacy the responsibility of commencing hostilities. But the country and posterity will hold him just as responsible as if he struck the first blow."[60] See, the President seemed to be saying, even the Northern public can see through Lincoln's ruse; we have nothing to worry from at least the thoughtful elements of their population. "If there are any," quipped Toombs,[61] who seemed now to go along with the President's contention that maybe it would not matter which side fired first. Given that, and the Yankees' sure rush to arms after the fall of Sumter, Toombs pointed out that the South's only course would be a swift mobilization of war resources, and fast fielding of armies for the national defense. In such a rallying he pledged to do his own modest part; he would resign from this post and offer himself for army service, at whatever rank the President deemed fit.

By this Toombsian rhetorical leap the burly Georgian had taken the Cabinet debate from whether to order a reduction of Sumter to what to do in its aftermath. The burly Secretary of State

---

59   William Y. Thompson, *Robert Toombs of Georgia* (Baton Rouge, 1966), p. 168.

60   *New York Herald*, April 5, 1861, quoted in J. Thomas Scharf, *History of the Confederate States Navy: From Its Organization to Victory at Sea* (Baltimore, 1887), p. 180.

61   Pleasant A. Stovall, *Robert A. Toombs: Statesman, Speaker, Soldier, Sage* (Atlanta, 1892), p. 226.
Toombs would resign as Secretary of State on July 19, 1861 to become a Confederate brigadier, in time to lead his fellow Georgians in the battle of Manassas. Robert Mercer Taliaferro Hunter succeeded him, serving until March of 1862.

slumped in his chair without replying. The President returned to the question and allowed each Cabinet member to speak. All eyes turned appropriately to Defense, on whose lap the whole thing would fall. "The impetuosity and superior dexterity of our men in the use of arms will cause the earlier victories to lean to our side, but..." [Walker took a short breath] "...trained, disciplined, and solid battalions will prove in the end triumphant." By this he meant that Southern *elan* could win a short war, but in a longer one Confederate forces would have to train and become as disciplined as the regulars of the "old army."[62] He expressed every confidence that they would be able to do so.

The Defense Secretary's monitory tone brought just a moment of silence to the room before Walker added that he did not foresee a long war anyway. Davis quickly brought the discussion back to the pressing issue of whether, if Lincoln launched an army of invasion, the rest of the Upper South could be counted on. All agreed that any call for troops by the Washington government would bring about the secession of every state in the upper South-Virginia, North Carolina, Tennessee, Arkansas, maybe Kentucky and Missouri. Virginia was extremely important, and Davis explained how Roger Pryor, the Virginia congressman, had virtually promised secession if the North took up arms. Walker spoke up on Tennessee, whose four hundred-mile length essentially covered the new nation's heartland. In one of the Montgomery papers which printed leaks of the Cabinet meeting, the Alabamian was quoted as having said, "There is in my opinion, no doubt that Tennessee will unite with the Gulf States in forming a Southern confederacy....There is a geographic necessity that Tennessee shall unite with the South...I consider this result as absolute certainty."[63]

John Reagan discussed Confederate prospects in the West, particularly the allies which the South would find in case of war. Mexico, still smarting from its defeat by the United States a decade ago, would likely seize the opportunity to restore some pride if not

---

62   William C. Harris, *Leroy Pope Walker: Confederate Secretary of Defense* (Tuscaloosa, 1962), p. 28.

63   *Ibid.,* p. 17.

regain some territory. He also predicted that the Indians cooped up in the territory north of Texas could be recruited to operate against Federal posts on the frontier. It might even be possible, he said, to get the Mormons in Utah to raise hell out there; since being subdued in 1857 by a U.S. expedition, they were looking for ways to get even.

Of greater consequence to Attorney General Benjamin was the possibility of finding strong allies in Europe. The aristocratic classes of England and France had long been sympathetic to the South, and they could be counted on to pressure their respective governments to render assistance during a war. State Secretary Toombs became enthusiastic at the prospect of foreign powers joining forces with the Confederacy, sending fleets to menace Washington, or at least providing weapons, supplies and money. At the same time, the practical Benjamin emphasized the importance first of exporting large quantities of cotton to establish credit in foreign banks. The government should buy up at least 100,000 bales and ship it immediately to England as payment for weapons and supplies, for the conflict could be long and arduous. Long afterward, L.P. Walker recalled, "All the rest of us fairly ridiculed the idea of a serious war. Well, you know what happened."[64] Treasury Secretary Memminger, though, took Benjamin's idea very seriously, noting the high price of cotton in the world market and the propitiousness of not so much a "King Cotton diplomacy" as a cotton-based war finance plan, launched early on when the European powers were scrutinizing the new government's every action. President Davis, thoughtfully making notes of his ministers' more thoughtful comments, very deliberately took this one down.

All the while during this talk, Stephen Mallory had been at his seat drawing what appeared to be an elaborate flag and staff. When asked by Davis, Mallory explained that he was proud to see the banner of the Confederacy afloat in Montgomery, but his immediate hope was that first it might be unfurled over Charleston's

---

64   Robert Douthat Meade, *Judah P. Benjamin, Confederate Statesman* (New Orleans, 1943), p. 166.

Fort Sumter. War with the North might come after that, but the government's first duty was to secure claim to its property in Charleston. They had all agreed on this, and it was time to act.

The President nodded and quickly wrote out a note to be sent to his commanding officer at Charleston. He then read it to his Cabinet:

> General Beauregard:
>
> If you have no doubt of the authorized character of the agent who communicated to you the intention of the Washington Government to supply Fort Sumter by force, you will at once demand its evacuation, and if this is refused, proceed, in such manner as you may determine, to reduce it.[65]

FINAL CONFEDERATE PREPARATIONS

General Beauregard in Charleston did not have to await telegraphic orders from Montgomery. On April 8 as soon as he learned from Governor Pickens of Lincoln's message, he had already begun taking steps to "reduce" Fort Sumter and its Federal garrison.

In his wire of the 9th, after the Cabinet meeting, Secretary Walker had told Beauregard to stop all mail service to Anderson: "the fort must be completely isolated."[66] In point of fact, Beauregard had already cut the post the evening before. When Anderson learned of this on the 9th and asked for his mail back, Beauregard told him that the Northerners' private letters had been let through, but the public correspondence—*e.g.*, the correspondence which Anderson was sending Washington to keep it apprised of his situation and what the Rebels were doing—was being detained. Also, in the on-off-on-again pattern he had inherited from Pickens, that of occasionally letting the Federals send shoppers into the city for fresh meat and vegetables, the General now closed the spigot

---

65 *O.R.*, vol. 1, 297.

66 William C. Davis, *The Deep Waters of the Proud*, 2 vols. (New York, 1982), vol. 1, 46.

one last time. In early March such privileges had been cut off; for Anderson and his men it meant resorting back to salt pork and crackers. Later in the month, when peaceful evacuation of the garrison seemed imminent, they had been turned back on. (The Charleston post office even let pass a parcel of tobacco sent to the garrison by a New Yorker.) Now Beauregard cut off all privileges for the Federals to buy supplies in Charleston. Moreover, knowing that the Yankees were running out of food, Beauregard had also on April 3 refused Major Anderson's request to send away the last of his civilian workmen. In the C.S. government's eyes, no one would leave Fort Sumter until everyone left.

And while he knew he had plenty of cannon, shot, shell, powder and crewmen to "reduce" the brick fort, the threat of Northern vessels forcing their way to Sumter to unload supplies caused the Confederate commander to make some final preparations for his artillery. U.S. Captain J.G. Foster, Anderson's chief engineer, had been carefully tracking the Southerners' construction of their various batteries. On the 8th he observed that at the end of Sullivans Island a wooden house was suddenly blown up, revealing a gun position capable of shelling the scarp wall of the fort, where a ship might unload cargo.

Finally the God of War—Mars, Ares, Thor, Jahweh, Whoever—smiled on Southern fortunes with, on April 9, the arrival at the Charleston docks of a British steamer from Liverpool, bringing a gift "to the State of South Carolina by a citizen resident abroad in commemoration of the 20th December 1860." The gift was an English-made 12-pounder Blakely rifled cannon capable, Pickens said, of throwing "a shell or twelve-pound shot with the accuracy of a dueling pistol."[67] The gift carried the name of its inventor, Royal Artillery Captain Alexander T. Blakely, and was purchased and brought over by Charles K. Prioleau of Fraser, Trenholm & Co., the Charleston-London firm which would be so instrumental in financing the Confederacy's hugely successful blockade-running operations.

---

67 Warren Ripley, *Artillery and Ammunition of the Civil War* (New York, 1970), 149; *O.R.*, vol. 1, 293.

The Blakely, Beauregard's only rifled cannon, was assigned position in the Point Battery on Morris Island. Another shipment of gunpowder from Augusta, Georgia—the Powder Works destined to be the South's biggest producer—arrived. At the same time on April 10 a big 9-inch Dahlgren smoothbore was placed at the western point of Sullivan's Island. The Blakely and Dahlgren thus joined the more than two score artillery pieces which the Confederates had placed to bear on Sumter. These were fewer than half of all the C.S. guns in the Charleston area, many of which were trained against the ship channel in case the Yankees attempted a naval relief expedition.

Confederate Artillery at Charleston Harbor Bearing on Fort Sumter, April 12, 1861

(adapted from map in *Charleston Courier,* April 15)

JAMES ISLAND

Fort Johnson—Captain George S. James

1 24-pounder—Lieutenant J. McPherson Washington

2 10-inch mortars on hill (west battery)— Lieutenant Wade Hampton Gibbes

2 10-inch mortars on beach (east battery)— Lieutenant Henry S. Farley

MOUNT PLEASANT

Mortar battery—Captain Robert Martin

2 10-inch mortars

CUMMINGS POINT, MORRIS ISLAND—
Lieutenant Colonel Wilmot G. DeSaussure

Point Battery—Major P.P. Stevens

    1 12-pounder Blakely rifle—Captain J.P.
Thomas

    2 42-pounders—Lieutenant T. Sumter
Brownfield

    3 10-inch mortars—Lieutenant N. Armstrong

Iron-clad Battery—Captain George B. Cuthbert

    3 8-inch Columbiads

Trapier Battery—Captain J. Gadsden King

    3 10-inch mortars

SULLIVAN'S ISLAND—

Lieutenant Colonel Roswell S. Ripley

Floating Battery—Captain John R. Hamilton

    2 42-pounders

    2 32-pounders

Point Battery—Captain Hamilton

1 9-inch Dahlgren

Enfilade Battery—Captain J.H. Hallonquist

2 32-pounders

2 24-pounders

Mortar Battery #1—Captain Hallonquist

2 10-inch mortars

Fort Moultrie—Captain W.R. Calhoun

3 8-inch Columbiads

2 32-pounders

6 24-pounders

Mortar Battery #2—Captain William Butler

2 10 – inch mortars

ANDERSON LOSES HEART

As early as February 5 the commandant of Fort Sumter had warned his superiors in Washington of the Carolinians' strength: "their engineering appears to be well devised and well executed, and their works, even in their present condition, will make it impossible for any hostile force, other than a large and well-appointed one, to enter this harbor, and the chances are that it will then be at a great sacrifice of life."[68]

---

68   *O.R.*, vol. 1, 163.

In the weeks following, Anderson became more apprehensive, watching the Southerners build their ring of fire around him, worrying about his dwindling supplies, warming to the tasks at hand (he gave up his own wool socks for the making of cartridge bags), and waiting for assurances from the War Department. On February 19 he wrote to a friend that he prayed daily for "a clear understanding of my duty," as his government was giving him little guidance.[69] A letter from the War Department advised only that he remain on the defensive and avoid any clash of arms, implying that until the new administration came in, no one would know much of anything. Anderson could not wait. In a letter received in Washington on inauguration day, the Major startled the politicians by warning darkly that the Confederate forces gathering at Charleston could only be subdued by an expedition of 20,000 U.S. soldiers; otherwise he would be starved out in six weeks. Anderson was thus very much relieved by Ward Lamon's visit to the fort of March 24 and his message that Lincoln would withdraw the garrison. But when no further word came for the promised evacuation, and with rations being halved for everyone in the fort, Anderson grew despondent. "No order yet for our withdrawal," wrote one officer on the 29th; "We cannot understand why we are neglected."[70] Worse, hints began arriving that President Lincoln would not abandon Sumter after all, but attempt to reinforce or resupply it—an idea that Anderson dismissed as doomed to failure. Given the shallow depths around the fort, sea vessels (assuming they made it past the channel batteries and into the harbor) would have to anchor at least forty feet away, send their cargoes in by rowboat, and unload at the fort wharf, all the while under fire from Fort Moultrie and Cummings Point. It was all very depressing.

The interminable waiting took its toll on Anderson's officers and men. "Everyone is weary of the confinement here," wrote Capt. Abner Doubleday. Another observed that "the strain on both mind and body has been too long continued"; Doctor Crawford

---

69   Maury Klein, *Days of Defiance: Sumter, Secession, and the Coming of the Southern War for Independence* (New York, 1997), p. 299.

70   David Detzer, *Allegiance: Fort Sumter, Charleston, and the Beginning of the National Disunion* (New York, 2001), p. 223.

noticed that his sick report was increasing.[71] All knew that food was running out. Only six barrels of flour remained on March 21 with some stale hardtack and a little pork and rice. On April 1 Anderson wrote Washington that his men could endure maybe another week, and that was only if Governor Pickens allowed him to get rid of the civilian workers remaining with the garrison, useless eaters as they were. "I must, therefore, most respectfully and urgently, ask for instructions what I am to do as soon as my provisions are exhausted. Our bread will last four or five days."[72]

This dire admonition brought from Lincoln's War Secretary prompt reply—as it were, given that train-borne transit of the mails, Charleston-Washington, took 2 ½ days back then. On April 4 Cameron wrote that Captain Gustavus Fox had been ordered with food and supplies for the Sumter garrison. Major Anderson was instructed to try to hold out till April 12 when Fox's flotilla was scheduled to arrive outside the harbor. As a modern chronicler of the story has put it, "If the American flag still flew over Fort Sumter when it [the flotilla] arrived, it would attempt to send in provisions. If South Carolina made any attempt to stop it, the fleet would try to land reinforcements as well."[73]

Anderson was stunned by Cameron's orders, which he received April 7. The next day he wrote a lengthy response to express his mortification. "A movement made now, when the South has been

---

71   *Ibid.*, p. 233.

72   *O.R.*, vol. 1, 232.

73   Detzer, *op. cit.*, p. 242. Academics in other countries have chuckled at Northern Americans' continued peevishness regarding the morality of their cause, despite its defeat. More learned Northern scholars have accepted the international understanding, reached by most in the 1880s, that in 1861 both South and North dedicated themselves to a contest for the preservation of American ideals as they understood them to be. As Professor McPherson has put it, "both sides professed to be fighting for freedom" (James M. McPherson, *Battle Cry of Freedom: The South Wins Its Independence* [New York, 1988], p. vii). Cloth-sewn symbols of those American ideals have been from 1776 the Stars and Stripes and from 1861 the Stars and Bars. Yet some Yankee diehards maintain that their flag remains the only "American" one. See Dr. Detzer's slip, above, which Southerners tend to take in stride (Detzer lives in Connecticut). Students of the War for Southern Independence have also absolved Dr. Maury Klein for a similar slip of sectionalism appearing in his history of Fort Sumter: "The only American flag in the entire harbor waved above Fort Sumter" (*Days of Defiance*, p. 343—Dr. Klein resides in Rhode Island.)

erroneously informed that none such will be attempted, would produce most disastrous results throughout our country....In reference to the proposed scheme of Captain Fox, I fear that its result cannot fail to be disastrous to all concerned. Even with his boat at our walls the loss of life in unloading her will more than pay for the good to be accomplished by the expedition." Pessimistic about the fate of Fox's foray, Anderson was aggrieved more at the prospect of civil war starting, with him in the middle. In any case, Anderson affirmed that he would do his duty, but he could not help adding that "my heart is not in the war which I see is to be thus commenced."[74]

However candid and heartfelt its contents, Anderson's letter did not reach Washington. It was in the first mailbag confiscated on the 8th by the Confederates, following General Beauregard's interdiction of all Yankee mails.

"A BOAT FILLED WITH BREAD"

It was fitting that Gustavus Fox, who had brought to Lincoln the idea of a naval relief expedition to Sumter, should be the officer named to command it. On March 29 Lincoln endorsed Fox's plan: load a large steamer with enough supplies for 100 men to last a year and set out from New York as early as April 6. Take along several tugs to help unload in the harbor, under cover of darkness. Add two warships as escort. All were to arrive outside Charleston by the twelfth.

To carry the freight plus several hundred soldiers and sailors, Fox secured the steamer *Baltic,* as well as two tugs, *Yankee* and *Uncle Ben.* They set out from New York a few days late on April 9. A five-gun paddle-wheeled steamer, *Harriet Lane,* had left the day before. Fox's fleetlet was to rendezvous outside Charleston with the man-of-war *Pocahontas,* which steamed from Norfolk, and *Pawnee* out of Washington. But when Captain Fox and the *Baltic* arrived at the rendezvous point ten miles off Charleston around 3 a.m. April 12 only *Harriet Lane* was there to join him. Along the way, it turns out, he had lost his tugs: *Uncle Ben* had been driven

---

74   *O.R.,* vol. 1, 294.

by a storm into Wilmington; *Yankee* had overshot into Savannah. (*Pocahontas* was also delayed by an Atlantic squall.) But in a few hours, after dawn, *Pawnee* steamed into view. Fox communicated that they would stick to plan and all—*Baltic, Lane, Pawnee*—would head toward the harbor. Captain of the *Pawnee,* however, Commander Stephen C. Rowan, refused: "I am not going in there to begin civil war."[75] Rowan was aware of what all knew: that their entrance into the harbor would be contested by Confederate cannonade. To Fox it did not matter. Lincoln had told him to press on to Fort Sumter whether they were fired on or not, as "they will be firing on a boat filled with bread."[76]

As the Federal flotilla, now down to two ships, approached the bar, Fox heard the sound of artillery and saw smoke on the horizon. The war had started without them, bread or no bread.

LAST CHANCE TO "AVERT THE CALAMITIES OF WAR"

Though unaware of the Federal timetable, Jefferson Davis knew that he must act before the relief fleet arrived. His telegram of April 9 to Beauregard reflecting the Cabinet's decision on Sumter—"you will *at once* demand its evacuation...."—was accordingly intended to convey some urgency. In Charleston, though, the Confederate commander believed that his preparations were not quite complete. He wired back on the tenth that he would formally demand the surrender of Sumter at noon of the next day. Secretary Walker responded that the demand should be made sooner, but Beauregard was firm. Several thousand men, streaming into Charleston in response to Governor Pickens' eleventh-hour call, needed assignment to their posts. The floating battery was moved to the western tip of Sullivans Island, and final arrangements were made for the rest of the artillery. That night Beauregard felt prepared but apprehensive. He sent out orders for his subordinates to stay alert and ready. "To-morrow morning's sun must see us victorious."[77]

---

75   W.A. Swanberg, *First Blood: The Story of Fort Sumter* (New York, 1957), p. 310.

76   *Ibid.,* p. 270.

77   *O.R.,* vol. 1, 299.

On April 11 the Confederates still took their time, as if they hoped something might happen to prevent a confrontation with Anderson's garrison. Finally, at 2:20 in the afternoon, Beauregard sent two aides, Colonel James Chesnut and Captain Stephen D. Lee, across the harbor in a small boat bearing a white flag. They were greeted at the wharf by a Federal officer (by coincidence named Jefferson Davis) and led to the guardroom, where Major Anderson met them. The Confederates handed over their note.

> Sir:
>
> The Government of the Confederate States has hitherto forborne from any hostile demonstration against Fort Sumter, in the hope that the Government of the United States, with a view to the amicable adjustment of all questions between the two Governments, and to avert the calamities of war, would voluntarily evacuate it.
>
> There was reason at one time to believe that such would be the course pursued by the Government of the United States, and under that impression my Government has refrained from making any demand for the surrender of the fort. But the Confederate States can no longer delay assuming actual possession of a fortification commanding the entrance of one of their harbors, and necessary to its defense and security.
>
> I am ordered by the Government of the Confederate States to demand the evacuation of Fort Sumter. My aides, Colonel Chesnut and Captain Lee, are authorized to make such demand of you. All proper facilities will be afforded for the removal of yourself and command, together with the company arms and property, and all private property, to any post in the United States which you may select. The flag

which you have upheld so long and with so much fortitude, under the most trying circumstances, may be saluted by you on taking it down.

Colonel Chesnut and Captain Lee will, for a reasonable time, await your answer. I am, sir, very respectfully, your obedient servant,

G.T. Beauregard,
Brigadier-General, Commanding.[78]

Anderson left, gathered his officers in another room, and read them the letter. Despite its cordial wording, the "demand" for surrender struck them as improper, slightly arrogant, and totally out of the question. In less than a half-hour they had their answer, which Anderson wrote out. Thanking Beauregard for "the fair, manly, and courteous terms proposed," the Major replied that "my sense of honor, and of obligations to my Government, prevent my compliance."[79] At 4:30 the Federal commander returned to Chesnut and Lee, gave them his note, and escorted them to the wharf.

As they walked, Anderson asked the two Carolinians, "Will General Beauregard open his batteries without notice to me?" Chesnut answered, "I think not." After a few more steps, he added, "No, I can say to you that he will not, without further notice." Then, as the Confederates were about to get in their boat, Anderson surprised them: "I shall await the first shot, and if you do not batter us to pieces, we shall be starved out in a few days."[80] Immediately Chesnut saw in this almost offhand remark a chance to avert the bombardment. He asked Anderson if he might report

---

78 *Ibid.,* vol. 1, 13.

79 W.A. Swanberg, *First Blood: The Story of Fort Sumter* (New York, 1957), p. 292.

80 *Ibid.,* p. 292.

his words to General Beauregard. The Major tentatively gave his permission, but added that his comment should not be construed as his formal reply.

The two aides were rowed across to the city, where they reported at 5:10 p.m. to Beauregard. He promptly relayed the text of Anderson's note plus his spoken comment to Montgomery. President Davis, waiting anxiously at his office, received the telegram, discussed it with his Cabinet, then dictated one of his own: "Do not desire needlessly to bombard Fort Sumter. If Major Anderson will state the time at which, as indicated by him, he will evacuate, and agree that in the mean time he will not use his guns against us unless ours should be employed against Fort Sumter, you are authorized thus to avoid the effusion of blood."[81]

Beauregard got this communication after nine o'clock that night. Like Davis, he was thrilled at the possibility of avoiding a cannonade, but he ordered that his artillery be prepared for firing just the same. At the Cummings Point battery, camouflage was removed from two 42-pounders, and the new Blakely rifled gun was made ready. Three hulks were also floated out from the Charleston wharves and anchored in the main ship channel; crews stayed on board to fire them if the Federal naval expedition approached in the dark. Then Beauregard sent back his aides to ask Major Anderson *when* the garrison might evacuate if the Confederates withheld their fire.

It was after midnight when Chesnut and Lee reached the fort and related their message. Anderson called his officers together again. This time the talk centered on three specific issues: how much food was in the fort? How long could the men last when it ran out? And when was the relief expedition to arrive? As for food, the last of the bread had been consumed the day before; there still remained some salt pork and a little rice. When these stores were exhausted, the garrison surgeon estimated that the men might last three days more. Finally, Anderson reported the War Secretary's promise that the relief flotilla would reach Charleston by April 12, though he had urged the garrison to hold out till the 15th. On this

---

81   *O.R.*, vol. 1, 301.

basis, after more than two hours of discussion, Anderson and his officers settled on April 15 as the day when they would leave the fort peaceably.

Chesnut and Lee had grown impatient at Anderson's delay. Sensing that the naval expedition could arrive any hour, they worried that the garrison officers might be stalling. To save time, in fact, General Beauregard had authorized his aides to act on his behalf on any agreement with Anderson. So when the Major brought in a written statement, at 3:15 a.m., the Confederates studied it closely:

> General:
>
> I have the honor to acknowledge the receipt by Colonel Chesnut of your second communication of the 11th instant, and to state in reply that, cordially uniting with you in the desire to avoid the useless effusion of blood, I will, if provided with the proper and necessary means of transportation, evacuate Fort Sumter by noon on the 15th instant, and that I will not in the meantime open my fire upon your forces unless compelled to do so by some hostile act against this fort or the flag of my Government by the force under your command, or by some portion of them, or by the perpetration of some act showing a hostile intention on your part against this fort or the flag it bears, should I not receive prior to that time controlling instructions from my Government or additional supplies.[82]

Despite their relief at Anderson's pledge to evacuate on the 15th, Chesnut and Lee also saw that Anderson would *not* surrender at the appointed time if any one of four events occurred in the next three days: 1) he received orders to the contrary from Washington; 2) the relief expedition landed supplies; 3) the Confederates fired on the fort; or 4) the Confederates fired on the relief expedition.

---

82 *Ibid.,* vol. 1, 14.

Beauregard's aides knew that the U.S. flotilla would arrive soon to deliver provisions; they also knew that their government would not allow it to enter the harbor uncontested. Anderson's pledge to evacuate was therefore virtually worthless. Within minutes, Chesnut had written out their decision.

April 12, 1861-3.20 a.m.

Sir:

By authority of Brigadier-General Beauregard, commanding the Provisional Forces of the Confederate States, we have the honor to notify you that he will open the fire of his batteries on Fort Sumter in one hour from this time.

With that, the Confederates bade Anderson a curt goodbye. They boarded their boat and were rowed to James Island and Fort Johnson, where they gave the order to fire the mortar shell whose bright burst in the darkness over the fort would signal the start of the bombardment. It would be daybreak soon, giving enough light for the smoothbore cannon also ringing the harbor to commence firing as well.

THE FIRST SHOT AGAINST SUMTER AND ITS FIRERS

After the war, flushed with exultation at the triumph of their cause, a number of patriotic Southerners claimed credit for having fired the first shot in the bombardment of April 12-13, 1861. For the next fifty years or so, an historiographical scuffle took place among four men who took part in the Confederate bombardment:

JAMES ISLAND

—Lieutenant Henry S. Farley, commanding the beach (east) battery;

—Lieutenant Wade Hampton Gibbes, commanding the hill (west) battery;

—Captain George S. James, commanding Fort Johnson; and

MORRIS ISLAND

— civilian Edmund Ruffin, honorary member of the Palmetto Guards, serving at the Iron-clad Battery at Cummings Point.

Even before the cannonade ended, the Charleston *Courier* of April 13 published an account of how it had started.

> At thirty minutes past 4 o'clock the conflict was opened by the discharge of a shell from the Howitzer Battery on James Island, under the command of Captain Geo. S. James....While the white smoke was melting away in the air another shell, which Lieutenant W. Hampton Gibbes has the honor of having fired, pursued its way toward the hostile fortification....The venerable Edmund Ruffin...a member of the Palmetto Guards, fired the first gun from Stevens's Battery. All honor to the chivalric Virginian! May he live many years to wear the fadeless wreath that honor placed upon his brow on our glorious Friday.[83]

That same day Charleston's other leading daily, the *Mercury*, affirmed Ruffin's role. "Two guns in quick succession from Fort Johnson announced the opening of the drama," after which, at Stevens' iron battery, "the honor of firing the first gun was

---

83 Charleston *Courier,* April 13, 1861, reprinted in W.R. Davie, Jr., "Fort Sumter," *S.H.S.P.,* vol. 26 (1898), 105, 107.

accorded to the venerable EDMUND RUFFIN of Virginia."[84] Other journalists placed this in their reports, such as the correspondent for the New York *Tribune*: "The first shot from Stevens's battery was fired by the venerable Edmund Ruffin of Virginia." Across town the New York *Post* printed a dispatch from Charleston stating that the "first shot from Stevens's battery was fired by the venerable Edmund Ruffin of Virginia." These early newspaper reports of Ruffin's first shot, albeit from a smoothbore battery that did not fire the first mortar rounds, led other papers of the time to skip a beat, implying that Ruffin had fired the first shot of the whole bombardment. Such was the statement of a Mobile paper: "of the many bright examples that [Virginia] has furnished of patriotism is the conduct of the venerable Edmund Ruffin....*It was his hand that pointed and fired the FIRST gun of Fort Sumter.*"[85]

The fuss over Ruffin obscured the newspaper reports that the first signal guns had been fired from Fort Johnson. The *Courier* credited Captain Gibbes for the second of these, but did not name the firer of the first. The *Mercury* affirmed two guns fired from Fort Johnson, but did not name their firers. An upstate paper, the Laurensville *Herald,* published on May 3 a column based on an eyewitness' report that Lieutenant Farley, following orders from Captain James, fired the actual first gun.

Nevertheless, the role of Captain James' two mortar batteries on James Island (the hill [Lieutenant Gibbes] and beach [Lieutenant Farley]) was given short shrift amid the hoopla over a white-maned patriot, "whose head is silvered over by more than eighty winters," according to the enthusiastic Mobile press (not quite; Ruffin was sixty-seven at the time). To be sure, in his report of the bombardment Captain George Cuthbert affirmed that "the venerable Edmund Ruffin"—as if any other adjective could by now be applied to the old Virginian—had fired the first Columbiad in

---

84   Charleston *Mercury,* April 13, reprinted in Eugene P. Moehring and Arleen Keylin, eds., *The War Between the States Extra: From the Pages of the Charleston Mercury & the New York Times* (New York, 1975), p. 13.

[3]Quoted in "Who Fired the First Gun at Sumter?" *S.H.S.P.,* vol. 11 (1883), 503-504.

85   *O.R.,* vol. 1, 54.

his battery.[86] Cuthbert's commanding officer at Cummings Point, Major P.F. Stevens, made clear in his own report that after the first shell from Fort Johnson, two other mortar batteries at the Point had commenced firing before Cuthbert's Iron battery opened.

Thus all the early attention went to Edmund Ruffin, who was a perfect figure for the press to follow. He had become famous in the decade of the '50s as a well-publicized, if a little eccentric, defender of Southern rights and proponent of calcareous fertilizers. After Lincoln's election, Ruffin left his farm in southwestern Virginia and traveled to Charleston, armed with a pike. He sat as an honorary delegate at the South Carolina secession convention, shoveled sand to strengthen Fort Moultrie, and generally created publicity wherever he went. On April 8 he attached himself to the Iron-clad Battery at Cummings Point, and the Palmetto Guards, whose Captain Cuthbert made him an honorary member.

But the names of the other claimants soon came to fore. A week after the battle the *Mercury* reported, "We are informed that Lt. H.S. Farley of Captain James' company had the honor of firing the alarm or first gun of the battle on Friday last."[87] In his report to the Defense Department, April 27, General Beauregard recognized that "Capt. George S. James, commanding at Fort Johnson, had the honor of firing the first shell at Fort Sumter."[88]

Yet Beauregard, at his headquarters in the city, had not been with James on the morning of the twelfth; and anyway his report, though reprinted in the Southern press, could not outdo the journalistic attention already being accorded to Ruffin. Two decades after the war Stephen D. Lee addressed the Ruffin legend in a letter to the *Southern Historical Society Papers*: "I wish to correct an error which has almost passed into historical fact. It is this: That Edmund Ruffin, of Virginia, did not fire the first gun at Fort Sumter, but that Captain George S. James, of South Carolina...

---

86   Quoted in "Who Fired the First Gun at Sumter?" *S.H.S.P.,* vol. 11 (1883), 503-504.*O.R.,* vol. 1, 54.

87   Robert Hendrickson, *Sumter: The First Day of the Southern War for Independence* (Chelsea MI, 1990), p. 184.

88   *O.R.,* vol. 1, 34.

did fire it." Lee added that James offered "the honor of firing the first shot" to Roger Pryor, the Virginian who, Like Ruffin, had gone to Charleston to be in the thick of things. But, according to Lee, Pryor declined, at which another officer, unnamed by Lee, stepped forth to perform the honor. James then spoke out. "'No! I will fire it myself.' And he did fire it." Lee tried to lay the controversy to rest by adding that "Mr. Edmund Ruffin (who was much beloved and respected) was at the iron battery on Morris Island. I always understood he fired the first gun from the iron battery, but one thing is certain—he never fired the first gun against Fort Sumter. George S. James did."[89]

This, in the same issue of the *Papers,* drew forth a reply from Ruffin's, son, Julian, who tried to distinguish between the signal shell and the actual first shot against the fort which, according to reports, struck Sumter's parapet at its northeast angle. The younger Ruffin quoted at length from his father's diary:

> April 12—...At 4:30 a *signal shell* was thrown from a mortar battery at Fort Johnson, which had been before ordered to be taken as the command for immediate attack, and firing from all the batteries bearing on Fort Sumter next began in the order arranged, which was that the discharges should be two minutes apart, and the round of all the pieces and batteries to be completed in thirty-two minutes, and then to begin again. The night before, when expecting to engage, Captain Cuthbert had notified me that his company requested of me to discharge the first cannon to be fired, which was their 64-pound Columbiad, loaded with shell. Of course I was highly gratified by the compliment, and delighted to perform the service—which I did. The shell struck the fort at the northeast angle of the parapet.

---

89 "Who Fired the First Gun at Sumter? Letter from General Stephen D. Lee," *S.H.S.P.,* vol. 11 (1883), 501-502.

The venerable Ruffin's son tried to dismiss Lee's allegation by claiming, "The above from S.D. Lee is the first intimation of a doubt on this subject that has ever been brought to the notice of any of the descendants of Edmund Ruffin."[90]

The distinction between the first shot from James Island and from Morris Island was not lost even upon the Yankees who took the shots. In his memoir of the war's first battle, published in 1876, Abner Doubleday (Captain at the time, U.S. General later) gave recognition to the venerable one in writing, "It had been arranged, as a special compliment to the venerable Edmund Ruffin, who might almost be called the father of secession, that he should fire the first shot against us, from the Stevens battery on Cummings Point, and I think in all the histories it is stated that he did so; but it is attested by Dr. Crawford and others who were on the parapet at the time, that the first shot really came from the mortar battery at Fort Johnson." Doubleday qualified that "I have since learned that the shell from Fort Johnson was not a hostile shell, but was simply intended as a signal for the firing to commence."[91] Indeed, Dr. Samuel W. Crawford (surgeon at Sumter, later Union general) remembered how "at 4:30 A.M. the sound of a mortar from a battery at Fort Johnson broke up the stillness. It was the signal to the batteries around to open fire. The shell, fired by Captain George S. James, who commanded the battery, rose high in the air, and curving in its course, burst almost directly over the fort. A silence followed for a few moments, when a gun opened from the Iron-clad battery on Cummings Point. It was fired by Edward [sic] Ruffin of Virginia...."[92]

---

90 "Who Fired the First Gun at Sumter? Reply of Julian M. Ruffin," *ibid.*, 501-502, 504. Julian Ruffin's transcription of his father's diary is correct, save for a few minor punctuation or spelling alterations. The only significant change is Julian's italicization of "signal shell" for emphasis (William Kauffman Scarborough, ed., *The Diary of Edmund Ruffin*, 3 vols. [Baton Rouge, 1972], vol. 1, 588). Publication of Ruffin's voluminous diary by the Louisiana State University Press is part of LSU's "The Library of Southern Civilization," an ambitious project to make available hitherto inaccessible cornerstones of Confederate national literature.

91 Abner Doubleday, *Reminiscences of Forts Sumter and Moultrie in 1860-'61* (New York, 1876), p. 143.

92 Samuel W. Crawford, *The Genesis of the Late War: The Story of Sumter* (New York, 1887), p. 427.

Publication of *Battles and Leaders* in the 1880s provided another print-forum for the competing contestants. Doubleday sought to further qualify when he wrote, "We have not been in the habit of regarding the signal shell fired from Fort Johnson as the first gun of the conflict, although it was undoubtedly aimed at Fort Sumter. Edmund Ruffin of Virginia is usually credited with opening the attack by firing the first gun from the iron-clad battery on Morris Island."[93] For their part, Southerners' arguments boiled down to *which* first shot? The signal gun, designated to open the bombardment by bursting over the fort? Or the first artillery round aimed directly at the fort, intended to do it damage? Two decades after Sumter, consensus gave laurels for the latter to Ruffin. But who fired the first signal round from Fort Johnson? Some contemporaneous papers gave Lieutenant Farley the first shot and Lieutenant Gibbes the second, from their respective batteries. This did not stop "Steve" Lee, writing for *Battles and Leaders* in 1884, from repeating his recollection that on the morning of the 12th, after giving the order to open fire, Captain James turned to his friend Roger Pryor: "You are the only man to whom I would give up the honor of firing the first gun of the war"; but Pryor declined. After which, Lee recalled, "Captain James would allow no one else but himself to fire the gun." Yet Lee admitted that his boat, with Colonel Chesnut and others, left Fort Johnson before the firing of that first mortar. The craft was several hundred yards away from James Island when Lee and his boatmates witnessed "'the first gun of the war' between the States. It was fired from a ten-inch mortar at 4:30 A. M., April 12th, 1861. Captain James was a skillful officer, and the firing of the shell was a success."[94]

No matter that Lee was not there to witness "the first gun of the war." General Beauregard, even farther from James Island that morning, repeated the assertion from his after-action report in the semi-autobiography nom-de-plumed by his kinsman Alfred Roman, published in 1884.

---

93 Abner Doubleday, "From Moultrie to Sumter," *Battles and Leaders,* vol. 1, 47.

94 Stephen D. Lee, "The First Step in the War," *Battles and Leaders,* vol. 1, 76.

> From Fort Johnston's mortar battery, at 4:30 A. M., April 12th, 1861 issued the first—and, as many thought, the too-long-deferred signal shell of the war. It was fired, not by Mr. Edmund Ruffin, of Virginia, as had been erroneously believed, but by Captain George S. James, of South Carolina, to whom Lieutenant [sic] Stephen D. Lee issued the order.[95]

As the Confederate war generation faded with death toward the turn of the century, such claims to fame as "first gun at Sumter" became even more important to the Southerners who could lay stake to them. Despite the heft of their names and reputations, the arguments of Beauregard and S.D. Lee, Captain James' champions, dissipated as neither had been at Fort Johnson at the time of the firing. And James himself never set down his recollections. Promoted to lieutenant-colonel of the 3d South Carolina Infantry Battalion, he was killed in action at South Mountain, Maryland, September 14, 1862.

This left Wade Hampton Gibbes and Henry Farley to duke it out. At some point Lieutenant Gibbes asserted for the Southern press, "The first shell was fired by Captain James's battery, and, incidentally, by me as his first lieutenant. My orders were to fire a shell, to burst high up in the air, as a signal to commence the general bombardment."[96] The *S.H.S.P.* in 1892 noticed, "Since the publication of the claim by Major W.M. Gibbs [sic], of South Carolina, that he was the man who fired the first shot on Fort Sumter, there has been a great deal of discussion over the subject."[97] As counter, the *Papers* cited General Beauregard's continued belief that Captain James fired the initial round. Some months later, in August 1893 Gibbes' son submitted to the Richmond *News-Leader* his statement that "since my childhood my father has told me the facts in the case. Captain James himself gave Lieutenant

---

95   Alfred Roman, *The Military Operations of General Beauregard in the War Between the States, 1861 to 1863*, 2 vols. (New Orleans, 1884), vol. 1, 42.

96   Ashley Halsey Jr., "Who Fired the First Shot?" *Saturday Evening Post*, Dec. 17, 1960, pp. 23, 82.

97   "Fort Sumter: Who Fired the First Gun on the Fort?" *S.H.S.P.*, vol. 20 (1892), 61.

Gibbes the order to fire the signal gun, and the captain was not even at the battery in person whence it was fired, but probably at a battery below on the beach nearer the fort. At Lieutenant Gibbes' battery the signal gun was aimed to burst a shell high in the air," while another gun exploded nearly simultaneously. With two guns going off almost at once in Captain James' batteries, young Gibbes marshaled letters from several other Carolinians that they at least had heard later, and accepted, that it was Gibbes' mortar, not Farley's, which had been fired first. As one put it, "Lieutenant Wade Hampton Gibbes fired the first gun at Sumpter [*sic*]; none disputed it; all conceded it, and I have always believed, and do now believe, that he did it."[98]

Yet in the historiography of the first shot, it was Lieutenant Farley who got the last shot. In 1893 a Charleston physician, Robert Lebby, compiled a paper weighing the testimony of the various contestants, including Henry Farley, who corresponded with Dr. Lebby from New York, where he was superintendent of the Mount Pleasant Military Academy.

> The circumstances attending the firing of the first gun at Sumter are quite fresh in my memory. Captain James stood on my right, with watch in hand, and at the designated moment gave me the order to fire. I pulled the lanyard, having already carefully inserted a friction tube, and discharged a thirteen-inch mortar shell, which was the right of battery.[99]

As corroboration Lebby added the testimony of Charlestonians Edward H. Barnwell, serving that morning with Gibbes' hill battery: "The first shell fired at Sumter was from James's east battery (or the beach battery); the second was from the west (or hill battery)." Though Barnwell could not affirm Farley as the tugger of that first lanyard, it was logical to assume that he was.

---

98   First Shot of the War Was Fired in the Air," Richmond *News-Leader*, August 14, 1893, reprinted in *S.H.S.P.*, vol. 31 (1903), 73, 75.

99   Robert Lebby, "The First Shot on Fort Sumter," *South Carolina Historical and Genealogical Magazine*, vol. 12 (1911), 144.

Surgeon of the post Dr. W.H. Prioleau, who was at Farley's battery, recollected in the same way. "Twenty-five or thirty minutes after 4 A. M., by my watch, which I held open in my hand at the time, the first gun was fired, this being the right-hand mortar in the battery on the beach. I cannot recollect who pulled the lanyard, but this gun was directly in charge of Lieutenant Henry S. Farley, who, as well as I can recollect, sighted the gun. Captain James giving the order to fire." Dr. Lebby added his own confirming remembrance. As Captain Lee and his party made their way to the wharf, Lebby was standing between the two batteries where he could see the firing from both. "At 4:30 A. M., a shell was fired from the beach, or east, battery." After that, "the second shell was fired from [the] battery under Lieutenant Gibbes."

Weighing all this evidence with the scientific logic of a physician, Lebby ended his essay with the confident summation, "I, therefore, conclude that Lieutenant Henry S. Farley fired the first shot at Sumter by Captain James's order."[100]

Dr. Lebby's analysis persuaded many, but not all—Charlestonians among them. As late as the war's centennial in 1961, which Southerners celebrated with a far greater enthusiasm than their defeated former countrymen up North, Warren Ripley of Charleston wrote of the first firer, "It's a puzzling question and one which no one has been able to solve conclusively. However, it seems fairly certain that the initial shot was fired by either James or Farley—and from there on you can take your pick with the odds about even."[101] Another South Carolinian, history professor Martin Abbott, shook out all the evidence and came to the same conclusion, that "the first gun was fired by James or Farley and the second, in all probability, by Gibbes." He added, as a postlude to the name so early attached to the "first shot," that Edmund Ruffin "made many contributions toward the success of the Confederacy, but hurling the first shell against Fort Sumter was not one of them."[102]

---

100   *Ibid.*, 143-45.

101   "Centennial of the Civil War," Charleston *News and Courier* and Charleston *Evening Post,* April 11-12, 1961, p. 28.

102   Martin Abbott, "The First Shot at Fort Sumter," *Civil War History,* vol. 3 (1957), 45.

Ruffin, James, Gibbes, Farley: of those who claimed to have metaphorically raised the sword, three died by it in violent ends. George James was killed by a Yankee bullet three days before Lee's decisive victory at Sharpsburg. Edmund Ruffin committed suicide after the war, frustrated and angry at being forgotten by the Confederacy he had helped to create. Wade Hampton Gibbes, who served after the war as Confederate ambassador to Portugal, was slain one night in Lisbon by an unknown assailant. Only Farley died naturally, having lived long enough to see his first-shot contention generally accepted in the war's burgeoning literature.

Because victory has a thousand fathers, Farley's claim could not go uncontested. There was the Carolinian who some say earned the distinction for the original shot of the war, several months before the bombardment of Sumter: Citadel Cadet George E. Haynesworth, who fired first at the *Star of the West* on January 9, 1861. After the war Haynesworth took up law practice and became a trial judge at Sumter, South Carolina. In 1887 while presiding over a court case which erupted in gunfire between the two disputants, Judge Haynesworth was accidentally shot in the head.

THIRTY-FOUR-HOUR BOMBARDMENT

The explosion of the shell from Fort Johnson alerted Confederate gunners around the harbor. Quickly the batteries were manned and the artillery loaded, but there was no great rush to begin the cannonade. After a few minutes a mortar on Sullivans Island sent the second shell over Sumter. Then followed a mortar round from the Trapier Battery and, at 4:48, a shell from a Cummings Point mortar. Only after five o'clock was there enough daylight for the smoothbore guns even to be loaded, and from one of the Columbiads at the Iron-clad Battery came the next shot (presumably Edmund Ruffin's). Soon every battery started firing, though at a measured pace. (Beauregard had ordered a two-minute interval between the firing of cannon rounds if only to conserve ammunition.)

Inside the fort, Major Anderson kept his men protected and prepared to return fire. Because of the bursting mortar shells, he had already decided not to use the parapet guns and the big Columbiads on the parade ground. Thus confined to the artillery of the lower casemates, the garrison had only a dozen-and-a half cannon against over forty Confederate pieces. Seven 32-pounders bore on the three batteries at the west end of Sullivan's Island; another three were directed at Fort Johnson. Three 42-pounders pointed toward Moultrie, and only a 42-pounder and two 32-pounder guns bore on the Cummings Point batteries.

A mere seven hundred cartridges were reported as ready, despite the almost round-the-clock stitching of powder bags. As a result, when given the order to open fire at 7 a.m., the Federal gunners chose their targets well. Only one or two shots were made against Fort Johnson, and a few more were fired at the Enfilade Battery and the Dahlgren gun on Sullivans Island. More attention was given to Fort Moultrie and, on Morris Island, to the Iron-clad Battery. With even this careful practice, the cartridge supply was quickly reduced by mid-day. As a result, Anderson ordered that fire be slackened and confined to six guns.

It was soon apparent that this limited resistance was not so much a show of force as a sign of the garrison's determination to hold out for the relief expedition, whose arrival they had been led to expect that day. Anderson eagerly awaited word of the sighting of ships outside the harbor. Beauregard's forces were just as vigilant, and spotted them first. At noon of the 12th Confederates on Morris Island discerned three vessels approaching. An hour later, Anderson's men saw them too. Both sides watched and waited for the ships to do something. As it turned out, they did little more than stand outside the harbor. On board the *Baltic,* with his troops and provisions, Captain Fox impotently observed from afar the bombardment of Sumter. Without the tugs and two of his armed ships, Fox felt that he could do little. At one point he ordered his vessels toward the harbor, after Captain Rowan of *Pawnee* had a more resolute change of heart, but then decided against it when he realized that they would be easy targets for Confederate gunners. Denied the opportunity to carry out his mission, Captain Fox spent the rest of the day observing the bombardment of Sumter.[103]

The Southerners went about their work so vigorously that Beauregard became concerned at the expenditure of ammunition, and ordered the interval between rounds doubled to four minutes. After six o'clock that evening, the Confederates limited their fire to mortars, at a cadence of one shell every twenty minutes. The Federals stopped firing altogether at dusk.

With the sustained shelling throughout the day, it was remarkable that neither side suffered casualties. Inside Sumter, Anderson and his men assessed the harm done to the fort. The exterior masonry on all five sides showed some damage from solid shot, especially the 64-pound Columbiad balls that left big craters twelve inches deep. Round shot also perforated the roof, chimneys, and upper story of the barracks and quarters. The Southerners' mortar fire had also been effective: many of their shells had exploded within the fort. On the parade ground, as a result, the garrison had not even opened the hot-shot furnace. Moreover, three times during the day fire had broken out in the barracks, but each time the flames had been quenched. In the officers' quarters, firefighters were helped when Confederate shot destroyed three of the iron cisterns over the hallways, for the water poured out onto the flames below. Along the parapet, a ten-inch gun had been knocked off its carriage, dismounting as well a seacoast howitzer next to it. One lucky shot from Fort Moultrie had also dismounted a Columbiad and cracked another gun on the right flank.

103　After the battle of Sumter was over, Captain Fox chafed at having been given no chance to perform his mission. Lincoln offered him solace by reminding him that the relief expedition had served a political as well as military purpose. The former had been achieved when the Confederates fired on the fort, Lincoln told Fox, and the resulting psychological benefits for the Northern war effort outweighed all else. "You and I both anticipated that the cause of the country would be advanced by making the attempt to provision Fort Sumter, even if it should fail," the President wrote, "and it is no small consolation now to feel that our anticipation is justified by the result" (John Shipley Tilley, *Lincoln Takes Command* [Chapel Hill, 1941], p. 267).

In return, because of their small caliber and the long ranges involved, Sumter's guns had not done much damage to the Confederate positions. On Morris Island, Colonel DeSaussure counted 124 shots fired at the Iron-clad Battery, of which thirteen struck. One especially well-placed round hit the armor just at the hinged shutter for one of the embrasures. The lever-arm broke, and the Confederates could not operate the gun until its shutter was propped up. Across the water, Captain Hamilton's Floating Battery had been hit repeatedly, but the 32-pound shot merely bounced off the armored face. At Fort Moultrie, the Federal artillery fire had "pretty well riddled" the barracks buildings, as one officer noted, and the hot-shot furnace was struck twice. Moultrie's guns and defenses, on the other hand, were virtually unharmed.

That evening General Beauregard's main worry was whether the Federal ships would try to run reinforcements to Sumter or land troops on Morris Island. Accordingly, the channel batteries were readied for action throughout the night; the enfilading guns were kept loaded to sweep the landings at the fort. Once Confederate gunners on Morris opened fire on a small boat rowing near the shore. Similarly, a false alarm at Fort Moultrie provoked a few shots. But there was no landing. Captain Fox was waiting for his other warships. (*Pocahontas* did not appear until the afternoon of the 13th, too late to be of help. And unknown to Fox, the armed sloop *Powhatan* had been ordered to Pensacola, not to Charleston.)

As daylight broke on April 13 Major Anderson ordered the last of the rice cooked and distributed with pork—the only article left in the mess room. During the night cartridge-makers had worked steadily, and the gunners' store of powder bags had been partly replenished. Thus, when they opened up at dawn, the Federals managed a brisk fire, at least for a while.

The second day seemed to show an improvement in the Southerners' aim. The Blakely rifle, firing from the Point Battery, arced a shot at the right wall which struck an embrasure, splintered the brick, and sent fragments inside the casemate. A sergeant and three men were wounded. About 7:30 a.m. Lieutenant Armstrong at Cummings Point reported that one of his mortar shells had broken through the roof at Sumter's southwest angle and had exploded inside the quarters. Other Confederates saw smoke continue to rise until 8 o'clock, when flames erupted. The fire soon enveloped the south roof. This time the Federals were unable to put out the blaze because of the Confederate shelling. The spreading flames threatened the fort's magazine, so Anderson's men removed gunpowder before the fire forced its closing. Fifty barrels were gotten out, then the magazine doors had to be shut and covered with packed dirt.

The sight of smoke issuing from Sumter caused Confederate cannoneers all around the harbor to quicken their pace. Major Stevens at Cummings Point ordered rapid volleys from his batteries for almost an hour. At Fort Moultrie gun crews heated solid balls in the shot furnace to spread the flames. Just after ten o'clock, Captain King's mortar battery dropped a shell through the roof of the east barracks and started a fire there.

Before long the hot shot and whipping wind had carried the flames to the west barracks. By noon all the woodwork of the officers' quarters was consumed, and the fire there began extinguishing itself. Officers and men struggled to put out the blaze in the east buildings. Clouds of smoke filled the casemates and hindered the gunners. Cinders also set fire to boxes and other articles in the gun rooms. Anderson worried about powder being detonated, so he ordered all but five barrels dumped from the embrasures into the water. The loss of this powder, plus the depletion of cartridges, forced a reduction in the rate of fire to one Federal gun every ten minutes.

A little after one o'clock a shot or piece of shell cut the fort's flagpole in two. Across the way, through the smoke and distance, Confederates could only see that the U.S. flag had dropped, so they assumed it had been lowered as a sign of surrender. Several Southern officers accordingly prepared to board boats, go to Sumter and ascertain Major Anderson's terms. Colonel Chesnut, who had last talked with the Federal commander, was getting ready to be rowed out from Cummings Point with two other officers when he saw a boat already heading for the fort. Chesnut promptly called off his expedition, and observed the progress of the little craft plying through the choppy water.

Wigfall's Mission

On the boat was Colonel Louis T. Wigfall of Texas, one of Beauregard's aides posted at Morris Island. He carried a white flag on his sword-point, but brought with him no specific authorization to act on the General's behalf. When he reached Sumter, Wigfall saw the main gates burning, so he made his way to an embrasure and squeezed through. Amid the stifling smoke inside a Federal officer met him, then departed to bring back Major Anderson. Wigfall was left talking with Lieutenant Jeff Davis, who had earlier conversed with Chesnut and Lee.

"Your flag is down," said Wigfall. "You are on fire, and you are not firing your guns. General Beauregard desires to stop this."

Davis corrected him. "No sir. Our flag is not down; if you will step this way you will see it floating on the ramparts." True enough, on the right parapet the Federals had fixed their flag to a pole and set it waving again. Wigfall sensed that he had jumped to conclusions about the downed flagstaff, but was at a loss for only a moment. Shouting over the roar of a 32-pounder firing nearby, Wigfall called on Davis to help him stop the fighting. He flourished his white flag. "Will you hoist this?"

"No," Davis answered. "It is for you to stop it."

Wigfall promptly strode to an embrasure and waved his banner. It had no effect; Confederates on James and Sullivans Island had not seen the Colonel's boat going out and here the white flag also went unnoticed. The cannonading continued, and within moments a solid shot crashed nearby.

"God damn it," cried a corporal. "They don't respect this flag!"

Wigfall was trying to give a composed response when Major Anderson walked up. The Texas Colonel—burly, bearded, and at the height of his self-importance—told him, "You have defended your flag nobly, sir. It's madness to persevere in useless resistance. General Beauregard wishes to stop this, and to ask upon what terms you will evacuate this work."

Anderson had no way of knowing that Wigfall came without official authority to negotiate, so he got to the point quickly. Like everyone else in the garrison, the Major knew that further resistance was futile. Hence he said simply, "I have already stated the terms to General Beauregard. Instead of noon on the 15th, I will go now."

"Then, Major Anderson," Wigfall said, scarcely containing his exuberance, "I understand that you will evacuate the fort upon the same terms proposed to you by General Beauregard?"

"Yes, sir; and upon those terms alone."[104]

Wigfall clarified these conditions—that the garrison would leave the fort with all its property, after a salute to the flag—then left. Scarcely had he boarded his boat when the U.S. flag atop the parapet was lowered at Anderson's instructions, and replaced with a white bedsheet. The garrison's cannoneers, who had been firing only at irregular and long intervals, now stopped work altogether.

From his observation post in the city, Beauregard had not seen the boat rowing from Morris Island. So when he noticed the garrison colors down, he sent several aides to offer Anderson a truce and assistance in putting out the fire. The three emissaries—Captain Stephen Lee, Roger Pryor and William Porcher Miles—were halfway across the harbor when they saw the U.S. flag replaced over the parapet. They turned around and were heading back when someone aboard spotted the white flag on the fort wall. At this, Lee ordered the course again reversed, back toward Sumter. The Confederates arrived around two o'clock, still unaware of Wigfall's visit. When they went to Anderson and presented Beauregard's offer of a cease-fire, the Major looked surprised.

"Gentlemen," he asked, "do I understand you have come direct from General Beauregard?"

---

104 W.A. Swanberg, *First Blood: The Story of Fort Sumter* (New York, 1957), pp. 318-19.

They nodded. "Of course we do," said Lee.

"Why, Colonel Wigfall has just been here as an aide to and by authority of General Beauregard, and proposes the same terms of evacuation offered on the eleventh." Lee, Pryor and Miles reacted with predictable astonishment, but ended up conducting business anyway. Before leaving they got Anderson to write out his agreement with Wigfall for the surrender of Sumter:

> Fort Sumter, S.C.
> April 13, 1861—20 min. past 2 o'clock
>
> General:
>
> I thank you for your kindness in having sent your aide to me with an offer of assistance upon your having observed that our flag was down—it being down a few moments, and merely long enough to enable us to replace it on another staff. Your aides will inform you of the circumstances of the visit to my fort by General Wigfall, who said that he came with a message from yourself.
>
> In the peculiar circumstances in which I am now placed in consequence of that message, and of my reply thereto, I will now state that I am willing to evacuate this fort upon the terms and conditions offered by yourself on the 11th instant, at any hour you may name to-morrow, or as soon as we can arrange means of transportation. I will not replace my flag until the return of your messenger.
>
> I have the honor to remain, very respectfully, your obedient servant,
>
> Robert Anderson,
> Major, First Artillery, Commanding[105]

---

105   *O.R.*, vol. 1, 14-15, 64.

As Confederate battery commanders observed the white flag atop Sumter, they ordered their gunfire to cease. Meanwhile, more was happening to complicate negotiations. Wigfall returned to Morris Island about 2:15 p.m., picked up Colonel Chesnut and two others, then set out for Beauregard's headquarters. Prior to their arrival, the General saw the white flag over the fort, and sent his chief staff officer, Major David Jones, to determine Anderson's intentions. At about the same time, the commander of state troops on Sullivans Island also decided to send envoys, in this case Captain Calhoun of Fort Moultrie, along with a naval officer and a surgeon. When they reached Sumter after 2:45, they learned that Jones had already arrived and was conducting negotiations with Anderson.

By now, the Federal Major had had to explain his position three times, starting with Wigfall and Lee. But it was Major Jones who closed the deal. Just after dispatching him, Beauregard telegraphed President Davis. "Quarters in Sumter all burned down. White flag up. Have sent a boat to receive surrender." The Defense Department in Montgomery responded by ordering a salute of fifteen guns fired in front of its offices.

For several hours that afternoon Beauregard received the numerous messengers who had busily navigated the harbor since the fort's flagstaff was shot away. Wigfall reported with Chesnut, in time for the latter to be sent back to Sumter with the chief of the city fire department, who was prepared to offer a fire engine to help snuff the fort fires. Then Lee, Pryor and Miles came in; eventually Jones did too. The General heard from his chief of staff and, at five minutes till six, dictated the agreed terms in a letter to Anderson: "All proper facilities will be afforded for removal of yourself and command, together with company arms and property and all private property, to any post in the United States you may elect." Beauregard cheerfully conceded "the privilege of saluting your flag on retiring, in consideration of the gallantry with which you have defended the place under your charge."[106] He closed by promising to have a steamer sent to Sumter anytime Anderson chose for the

---

106   *Ibid.,* 15, 309.

evacuation of the garrison, and left it to the Federals whether they wished to be carried northward by Confederate vessels or by those lying outside the harbor.

To this message, taken out to the fort by Major Jones, Anderson replied by recommending nine o' clock the next morning for the beginning of the evacuation. When Captain Fox sent in a truce boat, Anderson's officers told the navy men they would be carrying the garrison back home. About the same time Anderson sent back Colonel Chesnut and Fire Captain Nathan, with a word of thanks but without accepting their help. Everything burnable within the fort had been consumed by the fire; now it was smoldering, about to be snuffed out entirely.

The fort to be left behind by Anderson's men clearly showed the effects of the thirty-four hours' bombardment. All wooden structures, from buildings to the main gate, had burned down. On the parapet, only three cannon were dismounted, but the terreplein was littered with splinters from the gun carriages and with brick from the walls and chimneys. The parade ground, pocked with craters, lay strewn with debris. On the outer wall, members of the new Confederate garrison would count more than six hundred direct hits.

To achieve this damage, the Southern batteries had fired upon Sumter fully seventy-five tons of metal and powder. When all the ordnance reports were in, Beauregard learned that the six mortars at Sullivan's Island and Mount Pleasant alone had fired 354 big eighty-eight pound shells. Lieutenant Brownfield's 42-pounder smoothbores at the Cummings Point Battery had sent almost as many solid shot crashing against the fort's masonry. The bombardment resulted in only four Federals wounded—a surprise to the Confederates and a relief as well, as neither President Davis nor General Beauregard wished for the rightful transfer of the South's military property to be attended by loss of life. The good news included the Southerners' own casualties: four men with slight contusions at Fort Moultrie, and at Morris Island no loss at all, save for a horse killed behind one of the batteries.

FIRST TO FALL, AND TO BE FORGOTTEN

When the shooting had stopped, only three cartridges were left inside Fort Sumter. On Sunday morning of the 14th, as the garrison prepared to leave, more powder bags had to be stitched just so the Federals could fire the hundred-gun salute which Major Anderson wanted to accompany the hauling down of his flag. Beauregard magnanimously granted this concession, in a demonstration of civility that impressed even many a Northerner. A few of them later commented as well that at the surrender ceremony Beauregard had chosen to be absent, sending Major Jones and other junior officers, so as to avoid offending his old West Point instructor.

Though Major Anderson had suggested an earlier start to the process of getting Sumter's garrison out of the fort, because of various delays (including stitching of powder bags), it was not till well after noon that the formal process got underway. At 2p.m. the opening of the proposed hundred-gun salute began, fired from the seven still serviceable Columbiads on the fort's open parapet. With the rest of the garrison standing at attention on the parade ground, the cannon fired in slow sequence—powder only, no ball. Each time, for the soldiers in the gun crews, the sequence was the same: swabbing the rammer in water, shoving it down the barrel to sponge-extinguish any sparks from the last detonation, then placing the cloth-wrapped cartridge of black powder at the gun muzzle and ramming it down. The gunners then placed the friction primer at the breach, adjusting the lanyard, and with the crew members safely away from the cannon, yanking the string and firing the piece.

Forty-six times the exercise went off without a hitch. Then, as the forty-seventh cartridge was raised to the big cannon's muzzle, it exploded. And thus Private Daniel Hough of Co. E, 1st U.S. Artillery, became the first fatality of the War for Southern Independence.

The gun barrel may not have been fully sponged, and some live spark may have glowed within the barrel. The crewman at the breech may have failed to place his thumb over the firing vent, allowing some air to rush in. Something must have happened to ignite the powder bag in Hough's hands as he prepared to fit it in the cannon muzzle. With a yellow-red roar the thing detonated, blowing Private Hough's right arm clean off in a cloud of putrid smoke. If not instantly killed, poor Dan quickly bled to death. Worse, the explosion dropped sparks all around, igniting the pile of cartridges heaped beside the cannon. These, too, went off, wounding five more men in the gun crew, two severely.

The mortified Anderson cut short his gun-salute, to fifty. About 4 p.m. the Stars and Stripes were lowered and handed to Major Anderson. Then the Stars and Bars were run up by Captain Ferguson of Beauregard's staff. Next went up the Palmetto Flag of South Carolina, raised by R.B. Johnson, Governor Pickens' friend sent there by the Governor for that purpose. The garrison then trooped in double file from the parade ground through the gate and onto the wharf for boarding while drums beat proudly and musicians fifed "Yankee Doodle." The Major boarded too, carrying his fort's tattered silk flag folded under his arm. As the Federals' boat churned out of the harbor, Southern troops on Cummings Point stood silently on the beach with hats off as a final show of respect for their foes. By this time in the afternoon, though, it was too late for the *Isabel* (the steamer sent by Beauregard) to cross the bar so it was not till the next morning, Monday the 15th, that Anderson's officers and men got onboard the *Baltic*, and with the *Harriet Lane* and *Pawnee* set course northward. *Pocahontas* went under orders on to Pensacola, where Washington hoped to prop up its hopes to "occupy, and possess, and hold" Fort Pickens.

Before the garrison left the fort, members buried the bloody body of Daniel Hough on the parade ground; the fort's surgeon saw to the other injured men. Two of them had to be left behind for treatment in Charleston infirmaries. One of them, Private Edward Galloway, died at Gibbes Hospital on April 19. The other, Private James Fielding, severely burned and wounded, was taken to Chisholm Hospital and finally sent north without exchange. (The North did little to acknowledge this chivalry, so wrapped up was it in raising troops to suppress the Rebels.)

Privates Hough and Galloway were thus the first soldiers to die for their country in the war. Neither is a household name; Galloway, second to fall, is today even less remembered than Hough, who at least is mentioned in the standard histories of Fort Sumter and who at least got a soldier's burial. With Sumter garrison members and some Carolina militiamen looking on, Charleston minister William B. Yates performed an interment ritual; members of the Palmetto Guard set "a neat and appropriate head-piece" at the gravesite, according to the Guard's Captain, G.B. Cuthbert.[107] After that, though, the Private's remains were removed to Morris Island, with Southern soldiers firing a volley over his grave. After his death Galloway was interred in the city's St. Lawrence Cemetery.

Yet today we do not know where the war's first fallen is interred. As much as Civil War necrolithologists would love to find Hough's grave, and as much as students and buffs of the Southern Revolution have celebrated the lives and deaths of the war's last soldiers to die (Northerner Albert Woolson in 1956 and Walter Williams, Southerner, in 1959), no shrine to the war's first soldier to die is known to exist. Gravesite pilgrims will tell you it is hard to pay one's last respects to the fallen when you do not know where to go. There is no gravestone for Private Hough; nor, so far as we know, is there a cenotaph anywhere to his memory.

There are several reasons that the name of Daniel Hough is not remembered in American history. For Northern Americans, the first fatality in their failed war to suppress Southern secession is part of their bitter heritage of defeat. Too, at the time of his death Hough had done little to commend himself to loftiness in history. An Irish farmer, driven to emigration by the potato famine, he arrived at New York in 1849, aged 23, poor and familyless. He did what many other young men without prospects did; he joined the army. Twelve years later, still a private, Hough gave his life for his (adopted) country, although he did so in a manner contrary to the dictates of heroic history. In those ancient annals (*dulce et decorum est pro patria mori,* &c., &c.), soldierly martyrdom comes in clenched combat

---

107 *O.R.,* vol. 1, 56.

with the deadly foe. Private Hough died, however, not in combat, and not at the hand of the foe; but by accident and by his own hands, when a cartridge exploded in them.

No matter. In the days after Sumter both countries braced for a war in which another 276,000 Americans would be carried off by battlefield death, disease, or (as we have seen here) fatal accident. In this virtually endless death-toll, Daniel Hough, first to fall, simply became another soldier who died.[108]

"THE BALL HAS OPENED"

Despite their distance from Charleston harbor, New Yorkers had ready access to the news of Fort Sumter, as several papers published in the city had gone to the expense of sending reporters ("specials") to Charleston as the Sumter crisis heightened. Unlike today, where the military authorities limit and sometimes fully bar reporters' access to war zones, General Beauregard and the Confederates allowed all reporters freedom to roam about and prepare their stories, which were telegraphed back to the home office for laying into print. On hand in Charleston were Bradley Sillick Osbon of the New York *World;* Samuel R. Glen and Felix Gregory de Fontaine of the New York *Herald;* and George H.C. Salter of the *Times.* Salter had come to Charleston almost three months earlier, after the secession of the state and when the U.S. government's refusal to surrender the fort in the middle of the harbor had begun to whip the wind of war-talk. Salter and the *Times* had fed that wind in New York, if only with the editors' choices for headlines. In January the news from Charleston appeared as "The National Crisis" or "The National Troubles." A week before the bombardment, on April 5 it was "The Crisis Approaching," then "The Impending Crisis." On April 9 "The War Cloud" was first seen, with Salter reporting *via* telegraph on the Southerners' preparations for a bombardment. "Everything is now

---

108   The Southern War for Independence ranks as the second deadliest war in American history, after the World War of 1939-45, in which United States forces participated (but in which the C.S.A. remained neutral). The combined American fatalities in that conflict, from battle deaths and disease, totaled over 400,000. That massive number included many Southerners who, despite their government's stance, volunteered for service in the U.S. Army anyway.

prepared for action," Salter wrote; "business is entirely suspended, and the most intense excitement prevails." On April 11 the *Times'* front page trumpeted "The Impending War," noting telegraphic dispatches from Washington that secessionists were rumored to be plotting a seizure of the national capital, that men were flocking to the arsenals, ready to be drafted for military service, &c., &c. Everyone was straining for news; the *Times* related that in New York on the 11th, "little else was talked of, yesterday, but the war news" (note the first shot had not yet been fired, but a war was already on). "Emerging from their houses, men eagerly sought the morning papers, in expectation of the startling intelligence which has so long been threatened from the South." Indeed, some expressed disappointment that the hoped-for outbreak of violence was so long in coming. As a result, "the newspaper bulletins were the centre of attention to eager crowds, and a few glaring capitals at any corner were sufficient to draw a large crowd." With this buildup, the *Times'* announcement on Saturday morning, April 13 "THE WAR COMMENCED," may have been almost anticlimactic, bringing about a kind of wearied public relief that at last the thing was started. In this almost laconic vein, Salter's story began with the succinct lines, "The ball has opened. War is inaugurated."[109]

Trusting newspapers as their source of information—though sometimes, the printing of mere rumor and mixing of editorial opinion with "fact" sometimes called into question the reliability of any "information"—New Yorkers ran for their papers. The *Times'* circulation jumped from 45,000 copies sold daily to 75,000 a day in the week after Sumter. On April 14 the *Herald's* presses, rolling with news of the fort's surrender, worked all morning and until one in the afternoon, printing 135,000 copies, thought to be the largest daily run of any newspaper yet. (In 1860, New York's five leading dailies had together a combined *per diem* circulation of 250,000.)

---

109   Eugene P. Moehring and Arleen Keylin, *The War Between the States Extra: From the Pages of The Charleston Mercury and The New York Times* (New York, 1975), pp. 3, 4, 7, 12; esp. "The War Cloud," *Times*, April 9 (p. 9); "The Impending War," *Times*, April 11 (p. 10); "The War Commenced," *Times*, April 13 (p. 12).

Sharing the widespread assumption that the bombardment of the Federal fort meant war, the *Herald* drew the instantaneous conclusion as to who had started it.

> The fact that the secessionists opened the fight at Charleston before any attempt was made by the Government to reinforce or supply Fort Sumter, is viewed here as an attempt on their part to coerce the Government, and puts the responsibility on them.

New York's third big paper, the *Tribune*, scrambled to meet the city's demand for news; Charles A. Dana, managing editor, announced the start of an evening edition. "The feeling that stirred the people as one man," reported the *Tribune*, "was too deep, too strong, and will be too enduring, to be characterized by the term excitement." Awaiting the news, crowds gathered outside press offices on Printing-House Square, near City Hall. There, on Saturday evening, all sorts of opinions could be heard on the events, with a general consensus that the nation's deadlock over slavery, unable to be resolved by political debate, could now be broken through violence. "There is just one way to get a settlement," one said (as quoted in the *Tribune*); "and that is by one side or the other getting whipped!"[110]

Not all feelings were bellicose. Pouring over the press dispatches in the printers' square, three men read the announcement that Major Anderson had hauled down his flag, and publicly cried.

STORY BEHIND A PICTURE

Journalism in America had a slow start, but the War for Southern Independence helped it along very briskly.

At the time of the first War of Independence there were only about three dozen newspapers in the United States. The country's first daily appeared in 1785 in New York; within a few years at least one daily paper was operating in every American city. In smaller

---

110   "The Feeling in the City of New York," New York *Tribune*, April 15, 1861, in Frank Moore, ed., *The Civil War Record: A Diary of American Events*, 11 vols. (New York, 1861-68), vol. 1, Documents pp. 61-62, and p. 61n. (*Herald*, April 14).

towns, the reading public got their news and commentary in locally-printed weeklies. Rising population increased literacy (especially in the North, 1840-60) and improved means of printing were key to American journalism's growth in the early nineteenth century, as was the political partisanship of the era, in which many papers sided strongly with a political leader, cause or faction. By 1850 the U.S. had nearly 400 dailies or weeklies, led by three influential New York papers, the *Herald* (founded in 1835), *Tribune* (1841) and *Times* (1857).

Several other factors helped in this growth. The spread of nationwide telegraphic service allowed distant papers to receive relatively up-to-date wire dispatches. The country's robust economic growth during the prewar decades meant more businesses were able to buy advertising space, aiding every newspaper's bottom line. The success of major urban papers allowed them to send paid reporters to news-scenes for eyewitness dispatches, thus contributing both to the immediacy and quality of their informational columns. On the strength of these elements, such papers as the Charleston *Mercury* and St. Louis *Evening News* enjoyed booming circulations, emerging as influential regional voices.

Moreover, by the time of the war a few of the nation's newspapers began offering pictorial content to their print-pages. The world's first "graphic newspaper" was the *Illustrated London News,* launched in 1842. The *News* hired sketch artists and sent them to big events where they drew what they saw and sent their illustrations back to headquarters. There engravers pinned the sketch to a woodblock, etched the picture, and engraved it as a woodcut which could eventually be printed. The process could take several weeks, so that artists' renderings were always behind the papers' reported events. But grateful readers enthusiastically embraced the illustrated news format.

America's first print-plus-picture newspaper, the weekly *Frank Leslie's Illustrated*, premiered in New York in December 1855, eventually spawning two Gotham competitors, *Harper's Weekly* (1857) and the *New York Illustrated News* (1859). This meant that at the time of the war, all three American illustrated weeklies were published in New York. *Leslie's* and *Harpers* particularly thrived during the war years, giving Northerners pictorial reporting from the front for the first time in American history.

The antebellum South, while possessed of a robust and sophisticated newspaper industry, had never ventured into the new pictorial journalism, due primarily to the region's lack of skilled engravers. It was only in 1862 that the *Southern Illustrated News*, published weekly in Richmond, began operations, carrying crude woodcuts of General Lee's victories in Virginia and Maryland; but it could not support a single field artist, and printed far less illustrative and more crudely presented material than its Northern counterparts.

As the Sumter crisis heated up, at least a handful of daily newspapers sent correspondents to Charleston to file first-hand reports. The Charleston *Mercury* and *Courier* were of course on the spot, and by April 12 so were the Macon (Georgia) *Telegraph*, the Richmond *Dispatch*, Savannah's competing *Republican* and *Morning News*, and the Columbus (Georgia) *Times*. The New York *Herald*, *Tribune* and *World* had their men there, too, representing the Northern press at a time when Yankees could still come and go in the South. Frank Leslie sent his talented artist William Waud to Charleston to make drawings and get them back north as fast as he could. In this endeavor, though, Waud was scooped by correspondent B.W. Osbon of the New York *World*. Osbon, not a trained artist, still made rough sketches and managed with his writings and drawings to get on board the *Baltic* with Major Anderson and his surrendered garrison on April 14 and thus beat Waud back to New York.

It may have been Osbon's work, sold to *Harper's Weekly,* that provided the earliest—and most imaginatively rendered—woodcut depiction of the firing on Sumter. Appearing on the front page of *Harpers,* "Charleston housetops during the bombardment of Sumter" shows a view from the city's White Point Gardens looking out into the harbor. Citizens jam the roofs of buildings, watching Sumter on fire and smoking in the distance as Rebel batteries on

Sullivan's and Morris Island shell away. Throughout the rooftop crowds, people are seen cheering, arms aloft, maybe a hand-held banner or two abreeze. But in the foreground, seizing *Harpers* readers' attention, are a number of distraught Southern women, well dressed in their abundant, flowing gowns, collapsed upon one another, hands over their eyes, clearly crying. One lady appears to have fainted outright. Over-wrought in their joy? Hardly. Whether the artist (presumably Osbon) or more probably the woodcut engraver was under instruction by his editor, the image shows at least some Southerners (frail, emotional women) visibly overcome with grief at the prospect of war with the North.

In contriving their image of Charleston women weeping, the *Harpers* editors apparently intended to suggest that at least some in the South held misgivings over war, or were anguished at the break-up of the Union. The woodcut would thus have given Northern viewers the impression that theirs was a doubtful, maybe faltering enemy, concealing latent love for the Union which would surely weaken the Rebel war effort.

Judged by our hindsight, we know now that this kind of propaganda was of little use to the Union war effort, and would prove comically irrelevant once Northern troops met Southerners on the open field of battle.

CHARLESTON CELEBRATES THE VICTORY

The surrender of Fort Sumter set Charlestonians loose. Throughout the cannonade thousands had watched from every vantage point. Along the harborside all wharves and walkways of "the Battery" were clogged with people who had come from fifty miles around. In town, commerce and customary business simply took a holiday. That afternoon, all the pent-up excitement of watching the long siege burst forth when crowds saw the garrison's colors drop and the white flag rise. "You may imagine, but you cannot realize the pandemonium," wrote one participant, "as shouts of joy went up from thousands on decks, wharves, houses and steeples."[111] Church bells started ringing and batteries fired salutes as the crowds surged about in the direction of any public leader who might take charge of the already highly charged atmosphere.

Beauregard's headquarters were almost mobbed in the tumult; Colonel Chesnut himself led a procession there, demanding a speech (which, after acknowledging the crowd, the General modestly refused to give). From his balcony at the Charleston Hotel that evening, Governor Pickens chose not to decline a similar request and gave a victory speech praising his fellow Carolinians for having rallied against the North's much vaunted strength and beating them. "We have met them," he exclaimed; "let it lead to what it might, even if it leads to blood and ruin.... We have defeated their twenty millions, we have met them and conquered them. We have humbled the flag of the United States before the Palmetto and Confederate....today it has been humbled before the glorious little state of South Carolina."[112] Staying at the same hotel, "the showily handsome and extravagantly militant" Roger Pryor, like Pickens, was serenaded by crowds in the street. The news of Sumter's capture, he predicted, would bring about the secession of his home state "within an hour by Shrewsbury clock."[113] Governor Pickens had his own prediction, but it was gamely couched for any contingency: "The war is commenced, and we will triumph or perish."[114] The festivities that Saturday night included a huge party at Ashley Hall, the home of Colonel William Bull, attended by hundreds, all finding new and uproarious ways to express their patriotic giddiness. Among the celebrants were General Beauregard and Wade Hampton, the wealthy planter, himself destined for high rank in the Confederate army.

---

111   J. Cutler Andrews, *The South Reports the Confederate War* (Richmond, 1970), p. 21.

112   Maury Klein, *Days of Defiance: Sumter, Secession, and the Coming of the Southern War for Independence* (New York, 1997), p. 420.

113   Manly Wade Wellman, *They Took Their Stand: The Founders of the Confederacy* (New York, 1953), p. 81.

114   Klein, *op. cit.*, p. 418.

On Sunday, the day of the surrender, a special hymn of thanks to the Almighty, "Te Deum," was sung by the faithful of St. Michael's Episcopal Church. That morning the less observant skipped church as the whole harbor swarmed with rowboats, skiffs, vessels of any kind that could carry people out for a look at Sumter. Crowds jammed the shorelines and watched in their church-going finery, hoping to see the garrison make its transit out of the harbor. Meanwhile, the Citadel cadets conducted a proud parade through the downtown streets. Word spread amidst the citizenry of a strange and fascinating omen, from the preceding two nights: the moon's crescent shape seemed in silvery form to be the very same as displayed on the State Flag. More telling indeed: a gentleman walking by St. Philip's churchyard cast a glance inside the cemetery upon the headstone of the great Carolinian Senator John Calhoun, who had always called for a violent resolution of the South's irreconcilable differences with the North. This witness claimed to have witnessed none other than a gamecock, South Carolina's defiant symbol, alight upon Calhoun's tombstone, forcefully flap its wings and stridently screech, as if crowing its delight that the ball had at last opened.

News Spreads Through The South

Telegraphs quickly carried the news of Beauregard's victory throughout the Confederacy. At least a dozen correspondents for the Southern press were about Charleston harbor , and one happened to capture the reaction of General Beauregard Saturday afternoon when word came of the fort's surrender. "Noble Carolinians," he proclaimed, striding from his headquarters office into the street. "Accept my warmest congratulations on your victory—not won by me, but by the gallant men who so promptly obeyed my orders. The war has been commenced; we must continue our exertions until the enemy is driven from our harbor."[115]

Southern editors were quick to assert that, though their side's guns had done the first shooting, blame for the war lay with the perfidious Lincolnites. In Georgia's capital, the Milledgeville

---

115   J. Cutler Andrews, *The South Reports the Confederate War* (Richmond, 1970), p. 21.

Federal Union asked, "How can they say we commenced the war? When the robber points a pistol at the head of a traveller and says, your money or your life, if the traveller knocks him down, is he the aggressor?"[116] In New Orleans, salutes of seven guns (for each state of the nation) began firing after 2 p.m. Saturday, celebrating the first word of the surrender. Even in Southern states not yet seceded the fall of Fort Sumter electrified the populace. In Richmond most businesses closed on Saturday, when shopowners and managers realized there were no customers to be had. As one acknowledged, "Everyone was clustered around the newspaper and telegraph offices, awaiting the latest news from Charleston."[117] The English newspaperman Russell, passing through Goldsborough, North Carolina on April 15, was swept up in the public jubilation. "The station, the hotels, the street through which the rail ran was filled with an excited mob, all carrying arms." he observed. Everywhere around him were "flushed faces, wild eyes, screaming mouths, hurrahing for 'Jeff Davis's and 'the Southern Confederacy,' so that the yells overpowered the discordant bands which were busy with 'Dixie's Land.' Here was the true revolutionary fervor in full sway. The men hectored, swore, cheered, and slapped each other on the backs; the women in their best, waved handkerchiefs and flung down garlands from the windows. All was noise, dust, and patriotism."[118]

IN MONTGOMERY, THREE CHEERS FOR JEFF DAVIS

Government secrets like the one about the Confederate Cabinet's meeting of April 9 are always hard to keep. So Montgomerians were expecting a collision over Sumter even before the Defense Department, on the eleventh, posted a public bulletin announcing the Confederacy's demand for the fort's surrender. Moreover, the public greeted the news with universal favor. "People here are delighted that the uncertainty is at an end,"

---

116   T. Conn Bryan, *Confederate Georgia* (Athens, 1953), p. 17.

117   Andrews, *The South Reports,* p. 20.

118   William Howard Russell, *My Diary North and South,* ed. by Fletcher Pratt (New York, 1954), p. 52.

one newspaperman reported.[119] Many sensed that if the Yankees did not yield, gunfire would follow, and the expectation of violence heightened the excitement. In this martial mood, one of the city's militia companies, the True Blues, paraded before cheering crowds on downtown streets. More people gathered outside the Winter Building on Court Square, where the telegraph office received General Beauregard's wires from Charleston. Others thronged at the Government Building a block away, where Secretary Walker allowed the telegraphic bulletins to be posted. People clustered, too, at the offices of the city's newspapers, the *Mail* and the *Advertiser*, where news broadsides were also displayed, although the press was as dependent upon the Southern Telegraph Office on the Square as everyone else in the city—to the point that Montgomery's club of journalists, "Sons of the Sunny South," were clumped in a room over the telegraph office, drinking brandy and wine, eating cake, and gazing rather aloofly at the crowds outside.

Then, at nine o'clock on the morning of the 12th came the wire from Charleston: the Confederate batteries had opened fire at half past four. On the balcony over the wire room a Doctor Weir called out the news as someone draped the flag of the True Blues. The crowd let loose huge cheers; Weir tried to organize them as three huzzas for General Beauregard. After runners carried the telegram to Government House a flag was outstretched there, too, as the militiamen fired their lone cannon, dubbed "Old Secession," eight times: for each state of the Confederacy plus General Beauregard. People packing the streets outside cheered the President, for Secretary Walker, for just about anyone or anything, as if to call the dignitaries out from their offices for a speech. They were disappointed, as Davis and his advisers stayed inside, discussing and digesting the day's events.

Then came another message from Beauregard: "Heavy firing all day. Several guns dismounted in Sumter. Our batteries all safe. Nobody hurt."[120] This was more cause for celebration, as

---

119   William C. Davis, *"A Government of Our Own": The Making of the Confederacy* (Montgomery, 1994), p. 311.

120   *O.R.*, vol. 1, 306.

gentlemen packed Montgomery's taverns and hotel bars that Friday afternoon; the Sons of the Sunny South drank even more in their clubroom. The more restless surged among the various news centers, rushing the Winter Building, then Government House, then the offices of the *Advertiser* and the *Mail*. At the latter, on Court Square, Editor Johnson Jones ("Jonce") Hooper rigged up a woodcut impression of the Confederacy's national flag, and affixed it at the head of the day's issue.

Then in the early afternoon, people marched gaily behind a brass band parading through the streets, as the True Blues assembled again for another public drill. That evening, outside the Winter Building on a quickly built platform, the city's Mayor Andrew Noble held forth in an impromptu address, joined eventually by two Cabinet officers, Naval Secretary Mallory and Postmaster General Reagan. This prompted the speech-hungry (there were still a few) to make their way to the Exchange Hotel. There, alit by torch and lamp, they called out for more speechifying. The President was too tired to accommodate them, but Defense Secretary Walker stepped out on a balcony to feed them with bold prediction of Sumter's fall on the morrow and the Yankees' recognition of Southern independence soon after that. If they did not, Walker heatedly predicted as he pointed to a Stars and Bars being waved in the crowd, "the flag which now flaunts the breeze here would float over the dome of the old Capitol at Washington before the first of May. Let them try Southern chivalry and test the extent of Southern resources, and it might float eventually over Faneuil Hall itself."[121]

Of course the crowd cheered and hallooed, calling for more of such perorations. In the swell and swoop, even the nation's new Attorney General, Judah Benjamin, stepped forth to speak. When no one could talk anymore, the tuckered-out limped home while the carousers filled the barrooms and lobbies once again, drinking, bragging, smoking, chewing, laughing and exulting in what all felt was a sublime day in history, and their part in it.

---

121   William C. Harris, *Leroy Pope Walker: Confederate Secretary of Defense* (Tuscaloosa, 1962), p. 26.

And all this was just to celebrate the opening of Beauregard's bombardment. At dawn of Saturday, April 13 everyone poured outside again for more excitement, and perhaps a triumphal conclusion. In came the news, by telegraph from Charleston: "Officers' quarters in Sumter burning. Part of roof supposed to have fallen in. Sumter firing at long intervals. Ours regular and effective."[122]

When this message reached the government center, someone draped out from an upper story window a big Stars and Bars. In the early afternoon the President and his advisers received the latest from General Beauregard: "Quarters in Sumter all burned down. White flag up." As this was read out to the crowd, with the follow-up, "Anderson surrenders to the Confederate Government unconditionally," a swell of cheering rose up unlike any before—for Davis, for Beauregard, for the Confederacy, even for the Cabinet. A fifteen-gun salute, fired at two p.m., added to the noisy celebration before the day's final wire came in from Beauregard's headquarters: "We take possession of Fort Sumter to-morrow morning. I allow him the privilege of saluting his flag. No one killed on our side."[123]

Defense Secretary Walker responded to the surrender with a quick message to Beauregard: "Accept my congratulations. You have won your spurs." Then, turning immediately to the next place where Federals still guarded Confederate territory, he asked, "How many guns can you spare for Pensacola?" President Davis took the welcome news with his accustomed grace. "If occasion offers," he wired to his General in Charleston, "tender my friendly remembrance to Major Anderson," whom Davis knew from the old days of the Black Hawk War.[124]

In the evening crowds, bonfires and liquor were everywhere to be seen in the streets of the capital. Inside the Exchange, President Davis expressed joyful relief. A few visitors managed entrance to the President's rooms, where they saw Mr. Davis lying on his sofa,

---

122 *O.R.*, vol. 1, 308-310.

123 *Ibid.*, 309-10.

124 *Ibid.*, 310; Manly Wade Wellman, *They Took Their Stand: The Founders of the Confederacy* (New York, 1953), p. 98.

puffing a cigar. Yes, he regretted that he had had to fire the first shot, and maybe he disliked the hoopla outside celebrating what could be the opening of a long, bloody war. But his countrymen were at last beginning to feel freed of the Yankee yoke, and this was something for them to celebrate in itself.

THE *ATLANTA INTELLIGENCER* PROPHESIES

Confederate newspapers have long been recognized as an important gauge of the South's wartime ardor. Dr. George C. Rable, now retired from the University of Alabama, is only one scholar to have called for even more study of the Southern press "as an important reflection of wider public sentiments" as citizens and soldiers girded for their war for independence.[125]

If the Southern people, after the smoke cleared in Charleston harbor, envisioned a triumphant war against Lincoln's government, one can turn to no clearer reflection of that public sentiment than the *Atlanta Daily Intelligencer*'s editorial, "Our War Policy," of April 15, 1861:

> The aggressive policy of the Black Republican party of the North, has culminated in war, as we long since predicted it would. The war has actually commenced at Charleston, and it is impossible to tell where it will end. There never was a more base, puerile and cowardly policy inaugurated in the history of any Government, than that now attempted to be enforced against the South by Lincoln and his Cabinet. He and his Cabinet advisers attempt to reinforce the forts upon our soil and collect the revenue at our ports, and at the same time they tell us they have no hostile intention, and that their policy is to be entirely peaceful.

---

125   George C. Rable, *Damn Yankees!: Demonization & Defiance in the Confederate South* (Baton Rouge, 2015), 195.

They have inaugurated acts which in the very nature of things must lead to war, and the partial if not total destruction of all the industrial interests of the country, North and South, agricultural, commercial and manufacturing. War is at all times a great evil, but in the present case, our people have been patient and long suffering, we have exhausted every means in our power, to preserve peace, done everything consistent with our sense of right, honor and justice to avert the dire calamity, but all to no purpose. A hostile fleet is in our waters, our harbors are blockaded, an attempt has been made to strengthen hostile forces already on our soil, while an insidious and cowardly attempt has been made to lull us into security, by false and malicious representations. In all this the Lincoln government has displayed double-dealing and treachery, for which the world furnishes no example.

The result of such a policy could lead to nothing else than war. The first gun has been fired in the war of Southern Independence, and blood has been spilled. We are determined, not only to achieve our independence at whatever cost, but we will teach these Northern Goths and Vandals a lesson, before this war is over, which they will never forget. Our enemies have made the issue a bloody one. We will show them how superior is the valor of free men, fighting on their own soil, for their altars and their firesides, their wives, their children and their dearest rights, to the hireling skill of treacherous and perfidious invaders.

This conflict will bring to the aid of the Confederate States, Virginia and all the border slave States. In less than thirty days from this time, if peace is not sooner declared, the seat of the war will be changed from Charleston and Pensacola, to Washington City and from thence Northward and Northwest. Under letters of marque and reprisals, a thousand privateers will be fitted out, which will sweep the seas of Northern commerce.—There are over two millions of men in the North, engaged in commercial, agricultural and manufacturing pursuits, who are opposed to Lincoln's administration. This conservative force will organize and arm for the purpose of overthrowing the Lincoln Government. Thus a destructive civil war will be inaugurated in the North. The Lincoln Government cannot long withstand such a policy.

In three months from this time, Lincoln and his Government will have removed from Washington City to Boston; the fifteen slave States will be united under the Constitution of the Confederate States; the Middle and North-western States will have formed a separate and distinct Government of their own, and Lincoln will be left alone in his glory, with the Capital of his Government in the Yankee city of Boston, and the extent of his Territory will be composed of the six States of Puritan New England. We predict the utter disgrace, overthrow and annihilation of the whole batch of abolition conspirators who planned this infamous revolution, and plunged a free, happy and once united people into all the horrors of civil war.[126]

---

126   "Our War Policy," *Atlanta Daily Intelligencer,* April 15, 1861.

Chapter Two:

Mobilization

LINCOLN'S CALL FOR TROOPS

At the other American capital, Abraham Lincoln received the news of Fort Sumter with grim composure. To a president who had ordered Anderson and his men to hold their post against hopeless odds, and who had dispatched a fleet that stood no chance of getting through, the garrison's surrender was not unexpected. Lincoln was, in fact, relieved that the confrontation in Charleston harbor had been resolved. Moreover, he was ready, as he reacted to the firing on Sumter with an alacrity that suggested no shock or indecision. Within hours after the United States flag dropped down the pole at Charleston, the President announced a full-scale military response.

In his inaugural oath Lincoln, as prescribed by Article II of the U.S. Constitution, swore to execute the laws of the land and defend the Constitution. With their secession, the Southern Rebels had breached that sacred document (at least in most Northerners' view). Now, with their violent assault upon a U.S. military installation, they had brazenly broken the laws, too. All knew that the President would have to call out Federal troops to restore order. He could not count on the regular army: numbering a mere 16,000 soldiers, it was spread throughout western frontier posts guarding against Indian unrest. Besides, a good number of these regulars were Southerners, and could not be expected to stay in the Federal service to suppress their own people. No, the scope of the emergency required the summoning of a much larger volunteer force.

The U.S. Militia Act, dating from 1795 (just after Washington had called out the militia to suppress another, albeit smaller rebellion), empowered the President to summon the militia of a state or states for up to ninety days' service whenever the laws of the nation should "be opposed or the operation thereof obstructed in any State, by combinations too powerful to be suppressed by the ordinary course of judicial proceedings or by the powers vested in the Marshals."[127] Lincoln the lawyer hewed close this wording as he penned his call for ninety-day militiamen, fully 75,000 of them (a number more than 4 ½ times the size of the U.S. regular army). He hewed so closely, in fact, that he borrowed wording from the Militia Act itself in his proclamation, dated April 15:

Whereas the laws of the United States have been for some time past, and now are opposed, and the execution thereof obstructed, in the States of South Carolina, Georgia, Alabama, Florida, Mississippi, Louisiana and Texas, by combinations too powerful to be suppressed by the ordinary course of judicial proceedings, or by the powers vested in the Marshals by law,

Now therefore, I, Abraham Lincoln, President of the United States, in virtue of the power in me vested by the Constitution, and the laws, have thought fit to call forth, and hereby do call forth, the militia of the several states of the Union, to the aggregate number of seventy-five thousand, in order to suppress said combinations, and to cause the laws to be duly executed....

Then, lest his call to arms appear too pale and legalistic, Lincoln infused some ruddiness and patriotism:

---

127   Fred Albert Shannon, *The Organization and Administration of the Union Army 1861-1863*, 2 vols. (Cleveland, 1928), vol. 1, 29-30.

I appeal to all loyal citizens to favor, facilitate and aid this effort to maintain the honor, the integrity, and the existence of our National Union, and the perpetuity of popular government; and to redress wrongs already long enough endured.[128]

"Wrongs already long enough endured" would have meant to most Northerners the Rebels' seizure of United States property—the forts, arsenals, post offices and customs houses that had been taken over by local forces following each of the Southern states' secession. Now that the Rebels had fired the first shot and taken one more fort, immediate action had to be taken, as Lincoln declared that "the first service assigned to the forces hereby called forth will probably be to re-possess the forts, places, and property which have been seized from the Union...." This meant that Federal troops would march into Southern territory and that, if opposed by armed forces of the seceded states (as they probably would be), there would be bloodshed. Without declaring war, Lincoln was certainly signaling its onset.

At the same time the President addressed those Southerners who still professed loyalty to the Union. (Lincoln, like many Northerners, believed there were lots of them, but that they had been cowed and bullied into seceding by the rich, powerful planter "slavocracy.") Lincoln promised these loyalists, especially the less privileged of the Southern population who might not go along with their fire-eating secessionist leaders, that they would be spared the cost and calamities of the upcoming conflict: "in every event, the utmost care will be observed...... to avoid any devastation, any destruction of, or interference with, property, or any disturbance of peaceful citizens in any part of the country."

In his proclamation Lincoln was also careful not to dignify the rebellious Southern "combinations" with the governmental name which they had adopted for themselves. In fact, throughout the conflict and even after the Treaty of Peace in 1863, Lincoln would contend that since secession was illegal and unconstitutional, states

---

128 "Proclamation Calling Militia and Convening Congress," in Roy P. Basler, ed., *The Collected Works of Abraham Lincoln*, 9 vols. (New Brunswick NJ, 1953), vol. 4, 331-32.

could never leave the Federal Union; consequently they could not presume to create a new, confederated government of their own. Hence the Rebels' military forces would remain, in Lincoln's eyes, not a national army at all, but armed rebellious factions to be suppressed by the national militia, just as Washington had done with the whiskey-rebelling farmers of Pennsylvania in 1794. After a quick show of force, President Washington had compelled those rebels to disperse. This is what President Lincoln now gave his generation of rebels one last opportunity to do: "And I hereby command the persons composing the combinations aforesaid to disperse, and retire peaceably to their respective abodes within twenty days from this date."[129]

Of course, Lincoln assumed that this would not happen, and that he would soon have to seek Congressional approval for the government's war plans. Thus the President closed his proclamation with a call for the Congress to assemble in special session on the fourth of July. Until then, he had only his Cabinet members to consult with, and Lincoln called them to the White House on Sunday, April 14. Once the group was assembled and was joined by various army officers, Lincoln passed around the proclamation calling for 75,000 volunteers, which he had himself written out. The Cabinet approved it without a change. The military men, most of whom had fought in Mexico, veritably smacked their lips at their chance to get into another good war.

Little did they know....

NORTHERN GOVERNORS RESPOND

The President's proclamation streamed out by telegraph from Washington on Monday, April 15, and drew immediate, electric replies from the Northern state governors. Oliver P. Morton wired back that very day, "On behalf of the State of Indiana I tender to you for the defense of the nation and to uphold the authority of the Government 10,000 men." William Dennison could not wait for details, telegraphing back directly to "Abraham Lincoln, President

---

129   *Ibid.*, 332.

of the United States: What portion of the 75,000 militia you call for do you give to Ohio? We will furnish the largest number you will receive. Great rejoicing here over your proclamation."[130]

To answer Governor Dennison, and so inform the other chief executives of the 27 states not seceded, Secretary of War Cameron sent out telegrams and letters adding details to the President's call. (The message did not quite go out to all states in the Union—-the three most recently admitted and most westerly, Kansas, Oregon and California, were exempted.) Cameron explained how each state had been assigned a quota of troops to be raised (based on population), how that reduced to a number of regiments (average strength, 780 men), and how that in turn allowed for so many generals, other officers, and enlisted men per state (they should be 18-45 years old, and of sufficient "physical strength and vigor"). Even points of rendezvous were suggested for the troops to be raised. For instance, the quota for the largest state, New York, was 13,280, in seventeen regiments, to be organized at Albany, New York City and Elmira. Pennsylvania and Ohio were also asked to provide over 10,000 men each; Illinois and Indiana nearly 5,000. At the other end of the list, eleven states were each asked to provide only a single regiment, with rendezvous usually designated at the state capital. Secretary Cameron asked each governor to reply, indicating when the requested troops would be assembled. The War Department would then send army officers to muster in the volunteers.

Responses came, prompt and enthusiastic. Some governors wired back short, chopped affirmations:

I shall promptly respond to your call for one regiment.

—Governor Erastus Fairbanks, Vermont

Your dispatch calling on Ohio for thirteen regiments is just received and will be promptly responded to by this State.

---

130   *O.R.*, Series 3, vol. 1, 70, 73.

—Governor William Dennison, Ohio

Others added a flourish or two to indicate the feelings of patriotism being evoked by the call to arms. "The people of Maine of all parties," predicted Governor Israel Washburn of Maine, "will rally with alacrity to the maintenance of the Government and of the Union."[131]

Meeting the troop quota was not a problem anywhere; Northern men were ready to volunteer immediately. On April 16 Governor Morton informed Washington that his state's six regiments "will be full in three days," with some companies expected to enter camps at Indianapolis on the morrow. Samuel J. Kirkwood of Iowa wired Secretary Cameron that he had already received the tender of service of fifteen or twenty companies. Nevertheless, it was incumbent upon the state executives to issue public proclamations as to the national emergency, and to formally call upon patriotic men to come forth and volunteer for military service. The language used to do so definitively captured the public mood in the North. "Your flag has been insulted and the Constitution of the Union treasonably defied," exclaimed Dennison of Ohio, as he urged his fellow citizens to step forth and "meet the gravest responsibilities, and it may be sacrifice, to preserve your free institutions and your national independence." Richard Yates of Illinois in his proclamation let out a virtual war-yelp: "The spirit of free and brave people is aroused at last.....Fully justified in the eyes of the world and in the light of history, they have resolved to save the government of their fathers.....Our people will wade through seas of blood before they will see a single star or a solitary stripe erased from the glorious flag of our Union."[132]

The edict of Governor Ignatius Donnelly of Minnesota dated April 16 was typical. The United States had been violated by "armed organizations of citizens" in the South. They were "precipitating the country into revolution" by seizing "the property

---

131   *Ibid.,* 68, 71, 73.

132   *Ibid.,* 75; William B. Hesseltine, *Lincoln and the War Governors* (New York, 1955), p. 147.

of the nation." Worse, in taking up arms violently and firing upon the national flag, the Southern rebels were insulting each and every American. "Consummating their treason," they "have under circumstances of peculiar indignity and humiliation assaulted and captured a Federal fort, occupied by Federal troops," and even now, the Governor hinted, might be plotting to seize the national capital and all its governmental offices. This was a crisis of the greatest magnitude. As Donnelly explained, the President of the United States therefore had had no recourse but to appeal to "the patriotism of a people, who through three great wars, and all the changes of eighty-five years [1776 to 1861] have ever proved true to the cause of law, order and free institutions." Minnesotans' honor and sense of duty were thus appealed to, with one regiment to be assembled at St. Paul. Volunteer companies already formed would be accepted; others were to organize, ten all told. Each company, led by its captain, would have two lieutenants, four sergeants, four corporals, a bugler and sixty-four privates. Their term of service would be for three months, hopefully concluded, "unless sooner discharged."[133]

No one—not Ignatius Donnelly, not Abraham Lincoln, least of all not the Northern men who responded to their calls—knew how long the present crisis would last.

Yankees Rush To Volunteer

War-news—that the flag had been fired on, the Sumter garrison yielded, that the President and now the governors called for soldiers to crush the rebellion—flamed throughout the North, fanned by wire, press, broadside, and whipped by word-of-mouth. After Governor Richard Yates of Illinois issued his proclamation on April 16, a reporter in Chicago recorded, "the war feeling is intense throughout the west. Dispatches from almost every town...represent the people as very determined to sustain the administration in its efforts to enforce and uphold the honor of

---

133   Board of Commissioners, comp., *Minnesota in the Secession War 1861-1863,*
2 vols. (St. Paul, 1893), vol. 2, 3.

the National flag."[134] The next day Yates wired Washington that he had already received forty companies, and expected the state's six regiments to be full in just a day or two.

After mobilizing their existing militia units, governors usually authorized fellow politicians and influential or wealthy citizens to recruit new units. To create excitement (as if they had to), organizers called public meetings in cities and towns. People came just for the hubbub and crowdedness. Politicians spoke and spurred more frenzy. In Cleveland on the night of the 15th, Senator Benjamin Wade of Ohio addressed a large meeting. The whipped-up assemblage may not have heard each word, but reporters recorded wild cheering and applause at almost every oratorical turn of Wade's windy speech. At Milwaukee, the President's call prompted a huge rally at the Chamber of Commerce, where speechmakers worked the crowd at length before calling for volunteers. Three companies were formed on the night of the 15th alone.

Resolution-passing was also a main order of these war rallies, allowing spokesmen to give voice to the feelings all held but might not have been able to verbalize. In Oswego, New York, an assemblage of citizenry resolved their approval of the President's action, "denouncing the treasonable rebellion of the Southern Confederates." All pledged, whether Republicans or Democrats, to rally "unitedly under the flag of our country, in support of the Union, the Constitution, and laws."[135]

In the days and weeks following, recruitment continued in every Northern community, where the process followed much the same pattern. Streetside posters and newspaper ads announced the formation of companies and regiments. Recruitment rallies drew eager crowds with brass bands, patriotic speeches, lots of flags, and militiamen or veterans of the Mexican War showing off their gaudy uniforms and regalia. Then a recruiting officer would burst forth: "Who will come up and sign the roll?," whereupon young men pushed and shoved for the honor of signing first. Volunteers would then be sent into their respective neighborhoods

---

134   New York *Times,* Apr. 17, 1861.

135   *Ibid.,* Apr. 18.

to encourage more recruits with peer pressure. Excitement at the initial rally was the key to success; frequently a recruiter's good showing was based on the quality of the local speaker or musical troupe. At one country picnic, amateur musicians played the only tune they knew, "Sally Is the Gal for Me," but with plenty of flag-waving and cheering, the rendition led to the filling of a full company.[136] On the other hand, at a mass meeting in Galena, Illinois on April 16 the speaker was so mediocre that only twelve recruits came forth. The disappointing orator was an ex-Captain, Ulysses Grant, who would nevertheless rise to U.S. major general's rank before having his record blotched by failure at Shiloh and other places.

Sometimes organizers used special themes, such as nationality or vocation. Irish immigrants filled many Northern regiments in the east; Germans did the same in the western states. The 55th New York was largely made up of Frenchmen. Among occupational groups, volunteer fire companies usually enlisted *en masse*. In Phoenixville, Pennsylvania, a whole company of blacksmiths was raised. Other more frivolous themes were used to spark enthusiasm. A New York bank clerk named Smith proposed to raise a whole regiment of Smiths; in Indiana, the "Monroe County Grenadiers" enlisted only men six feet tall. The organizers ran this ad in the Bloomington newspaper:

> RECRUITING: Peter Kopp and several other gentlemen of this place are raising a company of grenadiers for United States Service. They admit no recruits under 5 feet 10 inches, and equally stout and able bodied. We pity the rebel upon whose neck the foot of "Big Pete" shall come down with a vengeance. There will be no chance for him to even say his prayers before his life is crushed out of him.[137]

---

136   Bell Irvin Wiley, *The Life of Billy Yank: The Common Soldier of the Union* (Indianapolis, 1951), p. 21.

137   Bloomington *Republican,* July 13, 1861.

When the company filled, "Big Pete" was chosen its captain. But even he was overshadowed by his second lieutenant, one David Van Buskirk who, at 6' 10 ½" tall, went on record as the tallest soldier in the Union army.

Usually, though, no gimmick at all was needed, so great was the rush to volunteer. Recruiting enthusiasm was particularly strong on campuses. At the University of Michigan, five companies were formed within two weeks of the President's call. So many faculty and students of the Illinois State Normal College joined the 33d Illinois that the unit became known as the Normal Regiment, with the college president as its commander. Similarly, the president of Eureka College became captain of a company composed largely of his students. The martial fervor at some schools was so contagious that administrators and teachers struggled to keep all their students from marching off. One clever dean hired a drillmaster to hold military exercises on the campus; students were thus induced to stay and finish the term.

THE UPPER SOUTH REJECTS LINCOLN'S CALL TO ARMS

Of the 94 regiments of infantry volunteers being summoned to suppress the rebels of the seceded South, 21 were assigned to the eight states of the as-yet-unseceded South. Thus the governors of Virginia, Kentucky, Tennessee, North Carolina, Maryland, Arkansas, Delaware and Missouri received on April 15 the same presidential proclamation as did the Northern executives. They were still in the Union, and Constitutionally were thus to be treated in the same manner as the most "loyal" Northern states. Yet Lincoln and his advisers realistically anticipated no cooperation from most states of the Upper South. With slavery strongly instituted in them, with all sorts of regional ties pulling them to their lower South kinsmen, and with post-Sumter anti-Yankee fever whipping up public excitement there, too, it was all but certain that at least some states of the Upper South would denounce Washington's troop summons. They did.

Just as the replies of Morton, Washburn, Donnelly and the other Northern governors couched the code-words that would be central to the Federal recruiting effort—defense of Union, flag, government—so did the Southern governors' replies provide further hints of the strong sentiments swirling in secessiondom.

North Carolina's John W. Ellis answered Washington on the fifteenth with stinging opposition to the troop-call.

> I regard the levy of troops made by the administration for the purpose of subjugating the States of the South as in violation of the Constitution and gross usurpation of power. I can be no party to this wicked violation of the laws of the country and to this war upon the liberties of a free people. You can get no troops from North Carolina.[138]

John Letcher, Governor of Virginia, offered the same strong opinion in his reply of April 16.

> The militia of Virginia will not be furnished to the powers of Washington for any such use or purpose as they have in view. Your object is to subjugate the Southern States, and a requisition made upon me for such an object—an object, in my judgment, not within the purview of the Constitution or the act of 1795—will not be complied with.

Moreover, Governor Letcher viewed the events of the past several days that were inflaming the nation—Southerners firing the first shot, Confederates compelling the surrender of a U.S. fort, &c.—and refused to see in them a precipitation of conflict. Instead, Letcher fixed the blame for war on the North. To Secretary Cameron he defiantly added, "You have chosen to inaugurate civil war, and having done so, we will meet it in a spirit as determined as the Administration has exhibited toward the South."[139]

---

138   *O.R.,* Series 3, vol. 1, 72.

139   *Ibid.,* 76.

The next day, April 17, brought a reply from Tennessee Governor Isham G. Harris, who informed Cameron that "Tennessee will not furnish a single man for purpose of coercion, but 50,000 if necessary, for the defense of our rights and those of our Southern brethren." A few days later, in a longer letter, Harris explained to the Secretary of War the reasons why he refused the national government's levy of two regiments. His were deep-seated political convictions, going back to the very Declaration of Independence, in which the nation's forefathers set forth that "governments were instituted among men to secure their rights to life, liberty, and the pursuit of happiness." Further, when such government "becomes destructive of these ends it is the right of the people to abolish it" and to form a new one. Indeed, Harris lectured, almost following Jefferson's famed verbiage, it becomes the duty of a few people to "throw off such government" when their happiness and security are no longer protected, but endangered. (Here of course, he was linking the Southern people's "safety and happiness" to their Constitutional right to own slaves, though in his letter, the Governor never mentioned the s-word.) Nonetheless, the issue of individual rights was at stake, and Harris defended his fellow Southerners' obligation "to alter, reform, or abolish the government" whenever their rights were perceived in danger. Having done that, through secession and reestablishment of a new confederation of states, they were, according to Harris, due the respect of "the free people of every other sovereign State." Instead, the Federal government was calling up troops to coerce them back into an oppressive Union, an act which the Governor termed "a wanton and alarming usurpation of power, at war with the genius of our republican institutions, and, so far as it may be successful, subversive of civil liberty." Indeed, he predicted, "the duplicity of the present Administration in its manner of inaugurating this unjust, unnecessary, and unnatural warfare will be consigned to history's darkest page." No wonder Harris reiterated his pledge, telegraphed on the 17th, that "in such an unholy crusade no gallant son of Tennessee will ever draw his sword."[140]

---

140   *Ibid.,* 81, 91-92.

Across the river, in neighboring Arkansas, Governor Henry M. Rector also cast his state with the South, in a telegram worded just as sharply as Harris' messages:

> In answer to your requisition for troops from Arkansas to subjugate the Southern States, I have to say that none will be furnished. The demand is only adding insult to injury. The people of this Commonwealth are freemen, not slaves, and will defend to the last extremity their honor, lives, and property against Northern mendacity and usurpation.[141]

North of Tennessee and Arkansas lay the border states of Missouri and Kentucky, which had been admitted into the Union as slave states, the former as recently as 1820. From the executive mansion in Jefferson City on April 17 came a fiery telegram to Cameron from Governor Claiborne F. Jackson denouncing, as had Harris, Rector and the others, the Administration's call for four regiments of Missourians "to form a part of the President's army to make war upon the people of the seceded States."

> Your requisition, in my judgment, is illegal, unconstitutional, and revolutionary in its object, inhuman and diabolical, and cannot be complied with. Not one man will the State of Missouri furnish to carry on any such unholy crusade.[142]

Governor Beriah Magoffin of Kentucky responded to the War Department within just a few hours of Cameron's telegram, and without consulting the legislature which, as he would soon find out, harbored ambivalences in the sectional dispute. To be sure, Kentucky was situated precariously between the free North and slave South, but that did not dilute Magoffin's passionate, pithy

---

141 *Ibid.,* 99.
142 *Ibid.,* 82-83.

reply: "Your dispatch is received. In answer I say emphatically Kentucky will furnish no troops for the wicked purpose of subduing her sister Southern States."[143]

Thus poured forth the fiery language of intranational strife. One side (in Minnesota Governor Donnelly's words) saw rebellious treason, national humiliation and outrageous offense against the common country's flag. The other saw Constitutional usurpation, trammeling of freemen's rights and (from Governor Rector) "Northern mendacity" and (from Governor Letcher) a brutal gauntlet hurled down to initiate civil war. Somewhere in between these two extremes, the Governors of Delaware and Maryland found a way out. With slavery provided by their constitutions (though slaveholders were in the decided minority) and with socioeconomic ties more with the North than the South, these two states were very much in a tight place. Governor William Burton of Delaware excused himself from ordering up the regiment which Washington requested by explaining that state law gave him no authority to call up a militia; what volunteer companies already existed could respond to the government's call on their own. In Maryland Governor Thomas Hicks tried to buy time. After he received Washington's request for four regiments, he asked back on April 17 whether such militiamen could be expected to stay within the state (as opposed to going off for a conquest of the South). Secretary of War Cameron affirmed that Maryland militiamen would only be asked to defend Washington City. America, as now divided into United States and Confederate States, was heading off to war, and the politicians were leading the way, or trying to get out of it.

SECESSION OF THE OLD DOMINION

"Lincoln declares war on the South" was the way in which the Richmond *Examiner* termed the Northern President's call for 75,000 militia. Virginia, most populous state in the South and seventh in the then-existent Union, was asked by Secretary

---

143   *Ibid.,* 70.

Cameron for 8,000 volunteers. *The Examiner* had an interpretation for this, too: "and his Secretary demands from Virginia a quota of cutthroats to desolate Southern firesides."

Governor John Letcher of Virginia knew the temper of his citizenry when he replied that the militia of Virginia would not be furnished for any such purposes as "the powers of Washington" had in mind. Letcher had not advocated secession, and after the Deep South left the Union, Virginians themselves appeared lukewarm on the subject. A convention elected in February and assembled in Richmond had discussed it off and on, with a majority favoring the Union, but only up to a point. That point had been articulated by Letcher as early as January, when he declared the Virginia would consider any movement of Federal troops through the state to coerce the seceded South as an act of invasion. The convention was in full agreement, even as the delegates rejected a resolution for disunion on April 4, a week before Sumter. They stayed in session, however, to await developments brewing at Charleston.[144]

The gunfire in Charleston harbor galvanized the public mood. On Saturday, the 13th, upon news of Sumter's fall, Richmonders took to the streets in joyful celebration of the victory. Artillery companies fired their salutes; bands played; orators yelled; fireworks exploded; "secession parades" filled the streets of the city. Knots of the excited somehow coalesced into a parade of 3,000 persons through town toward the James River and to the Tredegar Iron Works, biggest manufacturing plant in the city, and sure site of weapons-making in the coming war. Everyone talked secession, now that the firing had started. Someone raised the Stars and Bars over the Works, while strains of the "Marsellaise," the Frenchman's song of fight and liberty, could faintly be heard over the din. Then, of course, came more speechmaking, with orator after orator predicting that the time of the state's leaving had surely come. Other crowds gathered elsewhere in the city. Outside the capitol building downtown a throng formed, watching while two boys on the roof hauled down the Stars and Stripes and

---

144   James I. Robertson, Jr., *Confederate Virginia: Battleground for a Nation* (Charlottesville, 1991), p. 8.

ran up the Stars and Bars while folks sang "Dixie." Quiet then ensued, at least enough for speechmaking by some politicians who framed a resolution for the crowd to approve by lusty voice-vote: "That we rejoice with high, exultant, heartfelt joy at the triumph of the Southern Confederacy over the accursed government at Washington in the capture of Fort Sumter."[145]

The final catalyst came when Lincoln called upon Virginians to help subjugate the South. Adhering to the Union as long as they could, the people of the state followed their governor in rejecting Washington's call to arms and went with their feelings of regional allegiance and state pride. "We accept War as a fact," affirmed the Charlottesville *Review* on April 19. "From wickedness, or from some strange hallucination, the President has summoned the country to arms—to fight among themselves." The *Review's* editors recounted how they had long held for Unionism—suffering community derision, even "pecuniary injury, and the estrangement of valued friends." That time was over, now that "President Lincoln holds in suspense the uplifted gauge of battle." The paper made clear that it was the Northern President who had brought on the crisis. "We find it difficult to believe that Abraham Lincoln, speaking the same language, professing the same religion, belonging to the same advanced race—born even upon Southern soil—really contemplates serious war. We can hardly realize that any man of fair ability and fair morality in the United States would in earnest inaugurate civil war between Americans." Now it was time for Virginians to rally with the rest of the South, as the other "border" slave states would surely do. "The War feeling is swelling and surging like waves of the sea. Who can resist a whole people, thoroughly aroused, brave to rashness, fighting for their existence?"[146]

The State Convention in Richmond surely could not. The delegates debated disunion on the 16th and into the 17th, with their sessions held in secret (for fear of a border incident with

---

145 Emory M. Thomas, *The Confederate State of Richmond: A Biography of the Capital* (Baton Rouge, 1971), p. 6.

146 "The War of Revenge," Charlottesville *Review,* April 19, 1861, in Dwight Lowell Dumond, ed., *Southern Editorials on Secession* (Nashville, 1931), pp. 503-505.

Federal forces before state troops could ready.) The result was foregone, with the only antisecession votes on April 17 coming from the northwestern, generally non-slaveholding counties. The vote to go out, 88-55, reflected that geographical split, but to the Governor the majority had spoken. To make sure, the convention made the whole thing contingent upon a vote of the citizenry to be held on May 23.

State authorities determined to withhold from the public news of the convention vote, at least for a day or two. Now that Virginia was free and independent, certain military measures—deemed purely self-defensive—had to be taken. Within a few hours of the convention's vote, Letcher issued orders for the state militia to seize the two most important Federal installations, Harpers Ferry Arsenal and Gosport Navy Yard at Norfolk. That day, too, Letcher issued a proclamation which further denounced Lincoln's call for troops, and which summoned Virginians to prepare for military action should the Yankees try to enter the state.

> ...whereas on the 15th inst., the President of the United States, in plain violation of the Constitution, has issued a proclamation calling for a force of seventy-five thousand men to cause the laws of the United States to be duly executed over a people who are no longer a part of the Union, and in said proclamation threatens to exert this unusual force to compel obedience to his mandates; and whereas, the General Assembly of Virginia, by a majority approaching to entire unanimity, has declared at its last session, that the State of Virginia would consider such an exertion of force as a virtual declaration of war, to be resisted by all the power at the command of Virginia....and whereas the State of Virginia deeply sympathizes with the Southern States, in the wrongs they have suffered, and in the position they have assumed,...and whereas...it is due to the honour of Virginia that an improper exercise of force against her people should be

repelled: Therefore I, John Letcher, Governor of the Commonwealth of Virginia, have thought proper to order all armed volunteer regiments or companies within this State forthwith to hold themselves in readiness for immediate orders....[147]

Virginians Take Harpers Ferry

Even before Governor Letcher drafted his proclamation for "readiness," his orders had gone out. Next day, April 18, a thousand state militia converged on the United States arsenal at Harpers Ferry, on the Potomac River in northwestern Virginia. Guarding such a prize, the forty-seven U.S. soldiers there had no intent on defense, nor did they engage in a showy surrender of their property. Rather, just before the Virginians were to attack, at dawn on the 19th they and their civilian workers set fire to the buildings and fled across the river into Maryland. While the arsenal, containing 10,000 rifles and pistols was destroyed, the armory workshops—holding the far more valuable small arms-making machinery—were saved. Before they took off, Southern-sympathizing armory mechanics went through the motions of laying the gunpowder and fuses, but surreptitiously wetted the powder so it would not combust. The Virginia troops hurried in, put out the smolderings and thus saved the machinery.

When the smoke cleared, even some of the arsenal inventory was salvageable—"5000 finished muskets and parts for three thousand more," claimed the Richmond *Examiner*.[148] Rifle and pistol barrels plus other gun parts were also retrieved, including a rich personnel haul, as most of the skilled armory mechanics volunteered to stay on in service of Virginia and the Confederacy. Within a week the machinery was packed up and boarded on train to Winchester, but then had to be unpacked, and loaded onto wagons for Strasburg—there was no continuous southbound railway from Harpers Ferry to Richmond—and then taken on to the capital. There Confederate

---

147   Richmond *Examiner,* April 18.

148   Spencer C. Tucker, *Brigadier General John D. Imboden: Confederate Commander of the Shenandoah* (Lexington KY, 2003), p. 34.

ordnance workers, using the Harpers Ferry machinery, turned out the "U.S. rifle musket, Model 1855" that would soon be fired back at the U.S. troops for which it had been designed.

There was a strategic and logistical prize, too, as Harpers Ferry sat as an important way-stop on the east-west Baltimore & Ohio Railroad connecting Washington with the Ohio River. For several weeks the Virginians holding the arsenal town allowed train traffic to come and go, not wishing to offend Marylanders who might soon be voting to secede and to join the Confederacy. When Colonel Thomas J. Jackson arrived at Harpers Ferry on April 29 to take charge under orders from Governor Letcher, he allowed this practice to continue for a while. As Dr. Robertson, his esteemed biographer has written, "for Jackson to have severed the B & O would have been a large and direct act of war against civilian commerce."[149] Several weeks later, sensing that Federal movements would soon force him to abandon his exposed position, Jackson and his subordinate Captain John D. Imboden planned what a biographer of Imboden has called "the Great Train Heist."[150] Knowing well that the South needed as many locomotives and rolling stock as possible, Jackson determined to make off with as many of them as he could. He had set the stage by giving the appearance of not caring that enemy supply trains were daily chugging and huffing through Harpers Ferry. Then one day he issued to railroad authorities a deceivingly innocuous message: all this clatter and clank was disturbing the sleep of his men— could not the Baltimore & Ohio Company arrange its schedule so that trains passing through Harpers Ferry would do so between the hours of 11 a.m. and 1 p.m.? The railroad complied, with the result that around noon daily, both tracks in the town were clogged with engines and cars. Then, during this crowded time on May 23, Jackson sprang his trap. At both ends of town artillery wheeled out of hiding and troops marched into place, blocking traffic, ordering the surrender of every train and thus seizing all the trains locked

---

149   James I. Robertson, Jr., *Stonewall Jackson: The Man, the Soldier, the Legend* (Richmond, 1997), p. 229.

150   Harold D. Woodward, Jr., *Defender of the Valley: Brigadier General John D. Imboden, C.S.A.* (Berryville VA, 1996), p. 30.

in between on the busy rail line. With one clever ruse Jackson had captured 56 locomotives and 386 railway cars, "the largest single haul of rolling stock taken intact during the entire war."[151] The absence of a connecting line between Winchester and Strasburg prevented the retrieval of all this valuable equipment, but Jackson was undaunted. He oversaw the movement of a number of locomotives and cars to Winchester, where they were dismantled, to be drawn by horse-teams down the macadamized Virginia Turnpike to Strasburg. Reassembled there and put into working order, the captured B. & O. trains puffed their way to Richmond, and to further service to the Confederate war effort. "Never had such a task as the movement of the captured engines and cars been undertaken anywhere in the world," a Confederate historian has written.[152] When finally ordered on June 14 to evacuate Harpers Ferry, Jackson also ordered the blowing up of the 900-foot metal railway bridge over the Potomac, which would take the Yankees a long time to rebuild.

Jackson's exploits did much to win him favorable attention among the authorities in Richmond. Robert E. Lee took particular note of this enterprising young officer. The two would work together later in the war to craft some of the Confederacy's most elegant battlefield victories.

EARLY CONFEDERATE MOBILIZATION

The South's many militia units, so effective in capturing badly needed arms and ammo in the region's U.S. arsenals, also gave the Confederacy an early edge in mobilizing its manpower for war. In Savannah, Georgia, fully fourteen units, a thousand strong, marched through town celebrating South Carolina's secession in December 1860. Among them was the Chatham Artillery, which went back to Revolutionary days. The company had received two ceremonial cannon from President Washington in 1791 and enlivened its "musters" with a stout punch that is still drunk in the pubs and bars along Savannah's River Street. In the late fall of

---

151   *Ibid.*, pp. 30-31.
152   *Ibid.*, p. 31.

'60, throughout the South the excitement over Lincoln's election brought a recruitment swelling for these kinds of units, already well-known in communities because of their peacetime parades and picnic performances. Other companies sprang up; the men elected their leaders and waited for orders directing them to a mobilization center. During this time they received their first training, weapons, equipment and "uniforms," although there was as yet no national standard and every company chose the hue it wished. All these resources were haphazardly provided, reflecting whatever or whoever happened to be present locally: a company commander who knew the rudiments of drill; a cache of arms previously seized at an arsenal; maybe some benefactor or patriot who provided the weapons or uniforms. The bewildering assortment of outfits became evident when one saw the various companies begin to come together to form regiments.

In Louisiana, a company was already uniformed by January 8, 1861, and a cavalry company formed at Alexandria on the fourteenth. Within just a few weeks of Louisiana's secession, twenty-eight volunteer companies, 1,765 men, had received arms (captured at the Baton Rouge Arsenal). New Orleans alone had eight or nine companies drilling every night. Mississippians organized sixty-five companies of troops during January. This kind of troop-raising occurred in every Southern state in the weeks after they "went out."

When the Confederate government was formed, President Davis and Defense Secretary Walker did not so much first have to create an armed force as to organize the countless local and state units already in existence. Ten days into nationhood, February 28, 1861, the C.S. Congress provided for a regular army (like that of the U.S.) of 10,745 officers and men, and authorized President Davis to accept volunteers offered by the states for up to twelve months' service. This "provisional army," comprised originally of the state militia and other volunteers, was to prove the real organizational structure for the Confederate army; quite soon the distinction became pointless and the concept of Confederate "regulars" was dropped altogether. A week later, March 6, Davis was authorized to recruit as many as 100,000 men to garrison the various forts and to patrol the Indian frontier out west. All the weapons and munitions seized by the states at the various arsenals were to come under national control, and used to equip the fast-growing C.S. forces. The President, Defense Department and the Congress were also busy in issuing commissions for the army's first brigadier generals: Beauregard, appointed the first of March, went to Charleston; and Braxton Bragg, appointed on the seventh, went to Pensacola.

The first national call for troops went out on March 9. Each Confederate state was asked to provide a number of soldiers: Louisiana 1700, Florida 500, other states a total proportionate to their populations. Armed with weapons from the Federal arsenals and forts (which the governors formally transferred to national authority on March 1), most of these men were dispatched to the two trouble-spots within the Confederacy: around Charleston harbor, watching the Yankees in Fort Sumter; and to Pensacola, where on Santa Rosa Island the U.S. garrison at Fort Pickens had the temerity to hold out against Confederate authority. Fifteen hundred troops were on their way to Pensacola by March 31. Events at Charleston brought even more to that spot. On April 8 when Lincoln notified South Carolina Governor Pickens that he intended to reprovision Sumter, Secretary Walker called for 3,000 additional troops from each of the seven states. By the time that the U.S. President issued his call for 75,000 troops on April 15 the South's "do-it-yourself mobilization," as Professor McPherson has dubbed it, already had 60,000 men under arms.[153] For good measure on April 16, after Lincoln's call for 75,000 volunteers, President Davis announced the nation's need for 32,000 more men.

Throughout the Confederacy the rush to volunteer, stimulated by the firing on Sumter, was just as explosive and far-flung as in the Union. Here, too, Southern governors faced the problem not of enlisting men but of limiting the wave of volunteers to the numbers set by the national government. Throughout the country companies sprang up; the men elected their leaders and waited for

---

153   James M. McPherson, *Battle Cry of Freedom: The South Wins Its Independence* (New York, 1988), p. 318.

orders directing them to a mobilization center. Raiment ranged from militiamen's piped trousers and fancy tunics, filled with frogs and braid, to the blues and grays specially sewn by the women in a community, to the homespun worn by the recruit still awaiting an issue of clothing. There was no single pattern, and the more men gathered together, the more one would see an array of hue and style that resembled, as someone put it, "an international assemblage of *corps d'elite*."[154]

The first regiments raised in Louisiana typified the confusion, hubbub and zeal evident throughout Dixie's Land. An early company, the Crescent Rifles of New Orleans, attracted gentlemen of good standing by requiring a formal application for membership to be signed by each recruit, who thereby pledged "if elected, to conform to all the requirements of your Constitution and By-Laws, and perform the duties of a soldier to the best of my ability."[155] The first troops to leave the state on March 29 were four companies of zouaves decked out in pouchy pants and tasseled headgear. They set out from New Orleans to Pensacola with much fanfare, as citizens gathered in cheering, waving throngs. Similarly, when the Shreveport Grays boarded a steamer for New Orleans on April 16 townspeople lined the levee. As the boat pulled out, cannon boomed a salute, a band struck up "The Girl I left Behind Me," and the crowds sang and hurrahed. By early May, 3,000 troops had pitched tents at the Metairie race course outside New Orleans, and another training site, named for Governor Thomas Moore, had been established north of the city. There regiments were formed and made ready with drill and discipline for formal transfer into Confederate service. All told, as of June 1 the state contributed over 16,0000 men (more than her quota): 8,000 were armed and dispatched to Virginia, Pensacola, Arkansas, or the coast; another 4,000 were organizing at Camp Moore; and nearly 5,000 more

---

154 Clifford Dowdey, *The Land They Fought For: The Story of the South as the Confederacy* (Garden City NY, 1955), p. 103.

155 Manly Wade Wellman, *They Took Their Stand: The Founders of the Confederacy* (New York, 1959), pp. 112-13.

were being held at New Orleans for local defense. Six months later, Louisiana was credited with having enlisted 60,000 men in Confederate and state units.

With these preparations done or under way in all of their states, Confederate authorities had reason to feel both anxious and satisfied as the young nation went to war to stake its independence.

FINDING ARMS FOR SOUTHERN TROOPS

Procuring weapons for these recruits was a considerable undertaking, but the ways in which the state governments and C.S. Ordnance Bureau met the demand gave an early indication of the resourcefulness and ingenuity with which Confederates prosecuted their war for independence.

In general, the South had four sources of arms in 1861: captures made by state forces at Federal forts and arsenals; purchases by the various states after their secession; manufactures by Southern armories; and imports from the North and abroad. Each source played a significant role in the Confederate government's ability to place a rifle in the hands of every volunteer soldier during the spring and summer of '61.

Seized and confiscated U.S. military property provided a head start. The fall of the arsenal at Baton Rouge put at Louisiana Governor Moore's disposal some 47,000 small arms, of which nearly 30,000 were percussion muskets. The arsenal at Fayetteville, North Carolina yielded 37,000 stand of arms, a large quantity of gunpowder, some cannon and other stores. There was ammunition as well. In Florida, the Apalachicola arsenal provided state troops with 173,000 cartridges and 5,000 pounds of powder. All these stores the governors had begun to swap and share before Fort Sumter. Louisiana, for instance, had sent Mississippi 9000 muskets, 200,000 cartridges, six cannon and a ton of powder.

The Confederate Defense Department took charge of these munitions by an act of Congress, February 28, which transferred to national authority all Federal forts, arsenals and navy yards previously seized. Major Josiah Gorgas, Chief of Confederate Ordnance, was able to report that a week after Sumter the government had on hand, as a result of captures, a hundred thousand small arms, over three million cartridges, and powder to make another million-and-a-half. For the rifles, more than two million percussion caps lay in Montgomery alone. Of artillery, there were 429 pieces, ranging from ten-inch Columbiads to six-pounder field guns. (And this does not count the thousand-plus cannon that Virginians had seized on April 21 at the Gosport Navy Yard in Norfolk.)

In addition, Confederate troops could lay their hands on the arms which the various state governments had quickly bought after they left the Union and established their independence. Each new republic organized its war-making authority. South Carolina created a Board of Ordnance; Texas formed its State Military Board; so did Louisiana. These agencies conducted energetic programs of arms procurement well before hostilities erupted. Alabama's Governor A.B. Moore reported that by the time of Lincoln's inauguration, his state had bought 9,500 small arms, 8,000 bullets and 20,000 pounds of lead to mold more, a million-and-a-half percussion caps, 700 kegs of powder, plus some cannon and artillery projectiles.

As every state armed its troops, purchasing agents bumped into each other at New Orleans, Nashville and other places where weapons were made and sold. Richmond's Tredegar Iron Works boomed in business as a result of orders placed from throughout the South and as a result of aggressive marketing by its industrious proprietor, Joseph R. Anderson. On January 17, 1861, Anderson telegraphed South Carolina's treasurer that he had "on hand 250 8-inch shot, 450 8-inch shell. Can make per day 100 10-inch shells, 100 32-pounder shot, 25 8-inch shot. In ten days can double capacity. Will make anything you want. Work night and day if necessary and ship by rail. Can buy here and ship immediately 1000 kegs cannon powder at $3.50 per keg."[156] Within a week, shot, shell and 575 kegs of powder were steaming toward the Palmetto Republic.

---

156   David B. Sabine, "Ironmonger to the South," *Civil War Times Illustrated*, October 1966, p. 18.

State governments also strengthened armaments production within their borders. In North Carolina, the legislature began to subsidize the manufacturing firm of Waterhouse and Bowes for the making of gunpowder at Raleigh. Governor Harris of Tennessee made sure that Nashville's Sycamore Powder Mill was set to work especially vigorously, as well as other factories. Before long artillery, small arms, percussion caps, cartridges, saddles, blankets and other military goods were being produced in the state.

Eventually all Southern makers of war goods were brought under contract with the Confederate government. Ordnance Chief Gorgas, a skilled officer who had commanded the Charleston arsenal in the old army, showed real talent for organizing and increasing production. He inspected the various arsenals in the Confederacy, overhauled and enlarged them. At Charleston, for instance, he expanded the workshops and had steam power installed. He increased efficiency by streamlining assignments throughout the country: Richmond and Fayetteville arsenals were assigned to rifles and pistols; Augusta to ammunition and knapsacks. He contracted with existing shops and laboratories for small arms, ammunition and leather goods. To the huge works at Tredegar he gave the job of turning out heavy artillery (Gorgas' first order was for twenty 15-inch Columbiads). And he started small ordnance establishments throughout Tennessee and western Virginia, near rich deposits of iron and coal.

Gorgas' achievements in the first months of the war are indicated in his remarkable report to the Secretary of Defense of September 26, 1861. In it he related how the Confederate Laboratory in Richmond had developed the capacity to produce 50,000 to 100,000 small arms cartridges per day, and 900 field artillery projectiles. The arsenal at Augusta could yield 20,000 to 30,000 cartridges; the one at Charleston another 15,000 to 20,000. Thousands of rifles, pistols and sabers had already been cranked out and distributed to the troops, and would serve well until better small arms were procured from Europe. Moreover, Gorgas had on hand contracts for the making of 36,000 more rifled muskets, 500 breech-loading carbines, 4,000 bayonets, 12,700 sabers and 5,000 revolvers. Dozens of artillery batteries had been built, and Gorgas reported his outstanding contracts for 131 three-inch rifled guns, 121 howitzers, caissons and carriages for all of these, plus 435 8-inch, 10-inch and 15-inch Columbiads, for coastal and naval use.

Domestic manufacture was thus an important source of Confederate armament, but just as significant—perhaps more so in terms of the high quality of weaponry obtained—was the government's program of buying abroad.

President Davis himself had arranged for foreign purchases when, in late February, he sent former U.S. naval officer Raphael Semmes on a secret purchasing mission to the North. Semmes visited Washington, New York and various cities in New England, discreetly bargaining for the shipment of a sizeable quantity of weapons and military stores. Yankee markets, however, were quickly closed out in early April as fighting loomed. So the Confederate Defense Department, like its Federal counterpart, turned to Europe. As his principal purchaser, Secretary Walker turned to a sharp-minded small arms expert, Caleb Huse, summoning him on April 1 to Montgomery. There Walker told Huse, "The President has designated you to go to Europe for the purchase of arms and military supplies."[157]

Huse arranged for financing through Trenholm & Company, the Charleston-based banking-import company with offices in Liverpool. Then he quietly made his way to New York and booked his oceanic passage, arriving at London in mid-May. Huse proceeded immediately to the London Armoury Company, a leading manufacturer of the excellent Enfield rifle. Finding that a Massachusetts agent had already landed a deal with the firm, Huse persevered. He befriended Archibald Hamilton, the manager of London Armoury, and offered him personally a 2½% commission on all the rifles he could provide. Soon, with Hamilton's help, Huse not only edged out the Yankee traders, but worked it so that the Confederate States superseded even Her Majesty's Government as principal recipient of the London Armoury's monthly production. From September 1861 when the first shipments arrived in Southern ports, to the end of the war in September 1863, some

---

157   Henry I. Kurtz, "Arms for the South," *ibid.*, April 1967, p. 14.

350,000 small arms were shipped from England. Thus by his determination and craft, Caleb Huse almost single handedly saw to it that the superb Enfield was throughout the war the standard weapon for the Confederate infantryman.

Major Huse also bought cannon. From Captain Alexander T. Blakely he secured twelve Blakely field pieces (of the kind that had arrived in Charleston for the bombardment of Sumter). With Sir William Armstrong, whose company made the famous Armstrong gun, Huse also did friendly business. Then he shifted operations to the continent, touring all the major arsenals. While Northern agents snapped up every firearm they saw, Huse carefully assessed the weaponry and chose only the most select pieces. A real coup was his purchase of ten batteries of artillery from the Imperial arsenal in Vienna. Huse was elated. "I confess to a glow of pride when I saw those sixty pieces of artillery drawn up in the arsenal yard," he wrote, as he imagined the dreadful work which those guns would do upon Union soldiers. "It was pardonable for a moment to imagine myself in command of a magnificent part of that artillery."[158]

Paying for and shipping these purchases proved to be little problem. From the start of the war, the Confederate government, with limited reserves of gold, wisely decided to ship as much cotton abroad as it could in order to establish credit with European bankers. The high-priced stuff gave Huse and other Southern operatives all the financial backing they needed. Oceanic transport of both cotton to Europe, and war materials back to the Confederacy was also relatively effortless. Even though Abraham Lincoln proclaimed a "blockade" of Confederate ports in April, the Union Navy was far too weak in the first year of the war to post more than one or two vessels outside each of the major Southern harbors.[159] Enterprising

---

158   *Ibid.*, p. 15.

159   By all accounts, the Union naval blockade only started to have an effect on Confederate maritime commerce around April 1862. By then, the bumper cotton crop of 1861 had been harvested, shipped and sold to English textile mills. In addition to permitting a widespread program of arms purchases abroad, the Confederate government's vigorous export of cotton immensely strengthened the Southern wartime economy and rendered significant benefits as well in the area of foreign diplomacy. It also vindicated the judgement of Cabinet members

blockade runners carried into the Confederacy their shipments of arms and munitions with ease, and on the docks were unloaded the products of Huse's keen negotiations. Onboard the blockade runner *Fingal,* for instance, which brought one of Huse's main shipments of arms into Savannah in November 1861 were 14,000 Enfield rifles, a million cartridges, two million percussion caps, a battery of artillery with shot, shell and 800 barrels of powder, plus other small arms and ammunition.

Confederate success at raising and arming troops was apparent as early as April, when Secretary of Defense Walker reported on the 27th that he foresaw having at least 100,000 men in the field by the end of the year. As it happened, by September 1861 there were 200,000 Southerners assembled at points across the Confederacy, and more were coming in response to the Congress' act of August 8, permitting the President to accept up to 400,000 volunteers. With manpower aplenty, the C.S. Defense Department went about alleviating those administrative headaches always brought on by rapid mobilization for war. Training camps were established and skilled soldiers found as drillmasters. The creation of a logistical system for troop supply, even considering the Southerners' disadvantaged transportation network, proved to be a less formidable task than dealing with balky state authorities. Transfer of forts, arsenals, and navy yards went without a hitch, but some governors insisted (at least for a while) on making military decisions that rightly belonged to Confederate officials. The status of state troops recruited before establishment of the national army, their length of service, the appointment of field and staff officers, and determination of priorities for local defense were irritating issues that President Davis managed to resolve with admirable aplomb.

Judah Benjamin and Stephen Mallory, who were fervent advocates of the need to circumvent the blockade and transport to Europe as much cotton as possible. The ineffectiveness of the Union blockade has accordingly been judged by historians to be an important factor in the failure of the Northern war effort.

How Northern Troops Were Armed And Equipped

All their activity following Lincoln's call of April 15 allowed Northern governors to fill their quotas quickly. In Illinois, Richard Yates published his call for troops on April 16, and on the next day he wired Washington that forty companies had already been formed. He expected his quota to be met in a day or two. Soon nearly every governor asked the War Department for permission to exceed his allocation. Alexander Randall of Wisconsin told Washington that his people "will not be content to furnish one regiment alone."[160] The governors' pleas may have had impact in Washington, for President Lincoln waited no longer than May 3 before calling out another 42,000 volunteers.

Finding arms and equipment for these men proved a real problem. Indiana's Governor Morton complained on April 28 that he had on hand only 2,500 small arms of any kind, whereas he needed 20,000. The governor of Iowa estimated that his militia had only 1,500 old muskets, 200 rifles and four six-pounder guns. The War Department distributed as many weapons as the government arsenals then possessed, but in April and May it simply had no clothing or equipment to furnish. Secretary Cameron abruptly told the states to find their own supplies, promising reimbursement from the national treasury.

With every governor, colonel and captain thus scurrying for uniforms, a bewildering assortment of dress materialized when Union regiments assembled. Organizers used whatever clothing was available. Militia uniforms, with their colorful caps and bright britches, were the first to be seen. Some units adopted the festive dress of French Zouaves, noted for their peculiar fezzes and baggy pants. For other outfits women's patriotic groups did the stitchery, and chose their own colors. Gray was an early favorite, even after the Confederate Army had adopted it for its official use.

Fortunately for the governors, raising money for arms and equipment was not so difficult. Where the state legislature was in session, quick appropriations filled the war chest. On April 15,

---

160   *O.R.,* Ser. 3, vol. 1, 91.

the New York legislature made a half-million dollars immediately available, and voted to raise another 2 ½ million from a two-mill tax. In other cases, banks and rich businessmen offered generous loans. The banking establishments in Chicago and Hartford, Connecticut each raised $500,000 for their respective states. The City Council of Cincinnati offered the Governor $255,000. Wealthy citizens sometimes tried to outdo each other in contributing money to the cause. In Wisconsin, for instance, the well-to-do competed in subscribing a loan of $200,000.

The availability of funds plus the eagerness of governors to outfit their troops led to unfortunate results. As states and the Federal government scrambled to buy up all available stocks of weapons and other supplies, private contractors and manufacturers reaped windfall profits. "Through haste, carelessness, or criminal collusion," writes one authority, "the state and federal officers accepted almost every offer and paid almost any price for the commodities, regardless of character, quality, or quantity."[161] Sometimes purchasing agents ended up buying defective goods, especially when they carried their searches across the Atlantic. European governments had a lot of guns on hand, as the major powers were in the process of rearming with modern rifles. Thousands of cast-off weapons were consequently ready for sale. Though many were inferior, some almost worthless, they were snatched up by eager Northern buyers. State agents also rushed to place orders with arms-making companies. When the War Department sent a purchaser to Britain, he found that almost every weapons-builder in Birmingham and London was busy filling contracts for Ohio, Connecticut, and Massachusetts. Moreover, the race for rifles resulted in the same jacked-up prices in Europe as in the states; the upshot was that the Federal treasury paid out huge sums either in direct purchase or reimbursements to the states. There was another unfortunate consequence. Because the North demanded weapons at once, and bought up all of Europe's unusable arms, the more careful Confederates were

---

161   Fred Albert Shannon, *The Organization and Administration of the Union Army 1861-1863*, 2 vols. (Cleveland, 1928), vol. 1, 55.

able to purchase much finer weaponry at more reasonable prices. When the Yankee buyers cleared out of England, Southern agents contracted for excellent Enfield rifles at sixty-five shillings each.

While Northern manufacturers supplied the War Department with only 30,000 rifles during the first year of the war, they eventually increased their capacities, enough to turn out 700,000 annually. The government armory at Springfield, Massachusetts, also did its part, eventually producing 7,000 rifles per month, of a quality that matched the British Enfield. After the summer of 1861, in fact, the United States had no more trouble in arming its soldiers. Gunpowder likewise posed little problem. Initial importations from Europe were made solely to increase the Northern states' reserve stocks, and after June 1862 these shipments stopped altogether.

The North Rallies:
The Case of The 6th Massachusetts

The first men to volunteer were most times already in a militia unit of some kind, which meant they already had arms, uniforms and gear. In Massachusetts, April 15 had not ended before the state adjutant general called up the 3rd, 4th, 6th and 8th Militia, even though the government had requested from the state only two regiments. All were to assemble at Boston, and they came quickly. Three companies of the Massachusetts 8th, from Marblehead, pulled in by train on the 16th. Proudly the men marched, with flags flying and fifes and drums playing "Yankee Doodle," to Faneuil Hall, where they traded old smoothbores for new rifles and overcoats of gray—the long-sanctioned color of West Point uniforms, and a favorite military hue, both North and South. The adjutant general's office also dispensed blankets and knapsacks as companies came in from the interior. On the 17th, the Sixth Regiment arrived: four companies from Lowell, two from Lawrence, and one each from Groton, Acton and Worcester, Boston and Stoneham—seven hundred men in all. They marched down Beacon Street amidst a furious sleet storm, and halted at the State House for the important flag dedication ceremony.

Governor Andrew was the lead speaker along with Benjamin F. Butler, the longtime Democratic leader Andrew had just defeated in the last election; Butler was now in a brigadier general's uniform. Out in the street the men stood smartly at attention while behind each rank tailors worked frantically, sewing the last buttons on the soldiers' overcoats. Andrew pledged, "We shall follow you with our benedictions, and our prayers," waved the flag and drew applause and cheers from his audience.[162]

This flag ceremony, repeated all over the North, tugged at incalculable heartstrings. The Stars and Stripes symbolized why most Northern men were now rallying and enlisting in their country's cause. More, the fabric itself, often stitched locally with the unit's name or designation, linked the soldiers about to march off to war with everything they treasured back home. The flag, in fact, represented home. Sewn by women of the community, the banner thus symbolized the wives, mothers and sweethearts the men were leaving behind, those they were defending and fighting for.

Colonel Edward F. Jones, commander of the 6th Massachusetts, said all this as he received the regiment's flag from the Governor. According to one reporter's account, "he considered it the emblem of everything valuable upon earth, and that it would be so prized by his command, he declared that, so help him God, he would never disgrace it." The crowd roared its approval with many crying out, "God help you, Jones!"[163]

Then came the string of commands for the companies to shoulder arms, face and forward march: off to war, excitement and honor. And to some, death, in the very next forty-eight hours..

THE BALTIMORE RIOT

Whether at Boston in 1770, or Kent State in 1970, government troops firing on civilians is a bloody recurrence through American history. In a civil war that pitted the national government against

---

162   Thomas H. O'Connor, *Civil War Boston: Home Front and Battlefield* (Boston, 1997), p. 58.

163   *Ibid*

some of its unhappy citizens, it was inevitable that such bloodshed would happen. The violence came about as result of three unalterable circumstances: 1) Washington City, the capital of the Union, lay exposed and vulnerable to Confederates in Virginia and secessionists in Maryland; 2) to defend the capital President Lincoln was determined to bring Federal regiments from the North by the quickest route possible; and 3) that quickest route went directly through Baltimore, Maryland's largest city and a hotbed, as historians used to say, of secessionist fervor.

The speedy mustering of Massachusetts militia meant that the Sixth Infantry Regiment from that state, sent off at Boston on April 17, was destined for this confrontation. After Colonel Jones' regiment received its flag, it travelled by train toward Washington. On the 18th, in New York, it drew cheers from crowds lining Broadway. In Philadelphia the 6th was joined by a regiment of Pennsylvanians, as yet without guns or even uniforms. The now nearly 1700 men filled thirty-five train cars, chugging southward on the Philadelphia, Wilmington and Baltimore Railroad.

Baltimore would be the problem, and Colonel Jones of the 6th recognized it. The city's Southern sympathies were well known. In the presidential election of just six months before, Abraham Lincoln had received only 1,087 of the 31,150 ballots cast by Baltimoreans. Then after Lincoln won the election, there was such open talk of assassination plots in Baltimore that the President-Elect felt compelled to sneak through the city on his way to Washington and his inauguration. Whether he went so far as to disguise himself in women's clothing, as some have claimed, is a point that has not been substantiated by historians.

Already excited by the news of the firing on Sumter, Maryland's pro-Southern element was further agitated by the administration's call for troops on April 15. Governor Thomas H. Hicks on the 17th refused to commit his militiamen until Secretary of War Cameron assured him that they would not be ordered out of the state; he knew the troops would be needed just to preserve the peace in Maryland when Northern units entered the state. Cameron, in turn, warned Hicks that government soldiers must not be hindered in their travel toward Washington. With the first Pennsylvanians and Massachusetts men expected anytime, city officials in Baltimore did what they could to keep the calm. Mayor George W. Brown implored citizens even to refrain from harsh language; the situation was so volatile it was feared that mere cuss words in the air could ignite a public explosion.

On the afternoon of the eighteenth Governor Hicks arrived in town and issued his own proclamation urging the people to avoid rash action. Several hundred policemen patrolled the streets, preventing violence—for a while at least, since everyone in the city knew that once the Philadelphia, Wilmington and Baltimore Railroad brought in Yankee soldiers, there would be trouble. Thus Brown, Hicks and the city fathers braced for action, and they knew where to expect it. Like most major Southern cities, Baltimore was served by several different rail lines that terminated within the city. Train passengers *en route* to Washington from Philadelphia had to disembark at the President Street station in the southeastern part of the city, then walk more than a mile to the Camden Station, where they would entrain for the capital. Sometimes the railway cars were disconnected from their engine and drawn by horses, passengers and all, over a single track connecting the two depots.

That night, while a huge crowd of Southern sympathizers gathered in the streets before the offices of the city's pro-Confederate newspaper, waving Palmetto flags in honor of South Carolina, secessionist leaders met in Taylor's building on Fayette Street. Privately they made plans about how to face and repel the Federal soldiers expected the next day. Even more secretly they deliberated on how to exploit such a confrontation to aid Confederates in Virginia. If Union troops headed for Washington were turned back at Baltimore, and kept from the capital even for a day or two, Virginians eager to strike a blow would be encouraged to launch a bold, quick raid across the river. They could whip the District militia, seize government property, burn buildings, maybe even capture Old Abe himself. At the very least they would scare the daylights out of the countless Congressmen in the capital and shake the spirit of the North.

Such was the furtive talk at Taylor's that night. Leading the meeting was Isaac Trimble, fifty-eight-year-old West Point graduate and railroad executive who later directed the burning of the bridges north of Baltimore. George Steuart and Bradley Johnson were there, too, already discussing plans to recruit a regiment of Marylanders for Confederate service. The dozen or so conspirators included even Chief of Police George Kane, outspoken Southern partisan and rumored holder of a cache of arms secretly awaiting Confederate use. Before adjourning, the group drafted a statement of principles. After acknowledging "the irreconcilable estrangement" of the South from the North, and blaming Lincoln for actions that "will inevitably lead to a sanguinary war," the plotters asserted that the massing of Northern troops in the District of Columbia was "uncalled for by any public danger or exigency" and a "standing menace to the State of Maryland."[164] Amid moving passages challenging Marylanders to preserve their rights and defend their interests, there was no mention of attacking soldiers at the rail station. But there did not have to be. The eloquent, defiant wording of the document deliberately played on Baltimoreans' seething anxieties. By daybreak, after overnight printing and mass distribution as handbills, "the Fayette Street Resolution" had the whole city throbbing in anticipation of the first Yankee-packed train.

Police Chief Kane had begun asking the P.W. & B. railroad agent when troops were scheduled to be brought through the city. But the rail company refused to give the information; Marshal Kane was too well known as a Southern sympathizer. Instead, the rail company president in Philadelphia warned Colonel Jones of the 6th Massachusetts, as his regiment passed through on April 18, that Baltimoreans would oppose their transit. Jones ordered ammunition distributed and issued instructions. When they reached Baltimore, each car would be detached from the engine at the depot, and drawn by horse through town. The Pennsylvania militiamen would go first, then the Sixth. Jones also lectured his men on how they were to deal with angry crowds. "You will

---

164   George William Brown, *Baltimore and the Nineteenth of April, 1861: A Study of the War* (Baltimore, 1887), p.37.

undoubtedly be insulted, abused, and perhaps assaulted, to which you must pay no attention whatsoever," Jones declared, "even if they throw stones, bricks, or other missiles." With any mob, violence was imminent, so the Colonel prepared his soldiers for musket use. "If you are fired upon, and any of you are hit, your officers will order you to fire. Do not fire into promiscuous crowds, but select any man whom you may see aiming at you, and be sure you drop him."[165] The Massachusetts men would enter the city of Baltimore with their muskets loaded.

The train arrived at President Street Station near eleven o'clock on the morning of April 19. Confronting it were crowds of several thousand Baltimoreans. Secessionist flags (white stars on blue or red background) outnumbered sticks and clubs in the throng, which initially seemed unwilling to challenge the incoming troops with more than taunts. Nine cars, carrying five companies of Pennsylvanians, were quickly led down Pratt Street. The jeering mob followed alongside, banging the sides of the train and smashing windows. Near the Gay Street docks, where the street was being repaired, some anti-unionists heaved cobblestones in the way of the ninth car. As it creaked to a stop, the nervous militiamen inside peered out while the multitude howled and more or less waited for something to happen. A few toughs boarded the car and pushed their way inside. After some verbal thundering, which the unarmed Pennsylvanians wisely endured without challenge, the ringleaders called out orders to let the car pass. The paving stones were pushed away, and the horses allowed to pull their passengers on to the Camden Station, from whence the soldiers chugged away to Washington with hearty sighs of relief.

Across town, Colonel Jones fretted as the crowds grew along President Street, cheering Jeff Davis and insulting Abe Lincoln. When the teams returned to convey more troops, Jones ordered the rest of the Pennsylvanians to stay behind and four companies of his own regiment to move forward in their cars. This time near the dockyards there were anchors dragged across the tracks as well as a cartload of sand dumped in the middle of the street. The

---

165   *Ibid.,* pp. 43-44.

train halted, the soldiers huddled inside. Sight of their new blue overcoats and shiny rifles angered the mob more. Cobblestones flew; glass shards drew blood on both sides. Marshal Kane and his police milled about in such numbers as to deter the citizens from bringing out firearms, but not from tearing up sections of the Pratt Street track. Kane advised the Federal officers on board to turn back. When the teams were set about to reverse the train, the crowd cheered exultingly. Raucous, unmelodic strains of "Dixie" and even a few Confederate flags filled the air as the masses of civilians followed the vanguard of the Sixth back to its starting point.

There Jones ordered his men to form column of fours and in the face of the mob to start their march back at double-quick pace. They got only two blocks north of the station when two soldiers were knocked down by flying rocks. Some rioters rushed upon the troops, trying to seize their rifles. Police wrestled with soldiers about to aim. Mayor Brown shoved his way through the crush of people, crying, "Don't shoot!" when he saw some troops about to fire. There were pistol shots from the crowd; some citizens had carried their side arms to the day's events. Though without orders, some soldiers of the Sixth evidently returned the fire. Men fell on both sides. One civilian grabbed a soldier's flag and nearly tore it off its staff before being shot in the leg. When Captain Follansbee of Company C, at the head of the column, ordered his men to turn back, the untested Massachusetts men broke into a virtual rout. "They were firing wildly," the Mayor recalled, "sometimes backward, over their shoulders" not even stopping to take aim.[166] At the depot, where the remaining Pennsylvania militiamen and the rest of the 6th Massachusetts suffered taunts and rock-bruises, Jones' shaken troops clambered onto the train. The Colonel had little recourse but to order a hasty steaming back to Philadelphia. The last Northern-bound cars departed the station by 2 p.m. The three hours' fight left the Massachusetts regiment reduced by casualties of four killed and thirty-nine wounded, though their injuries ranged from serious gunshot wounds to abrasions at the head and even (thanks to one particularly cat-clawed Baltimoress

---

166   *Ibid.,* p. 49.

who dared to enter the street wide melee) scratches to the cheek. Mayor Brown later learned the names of twelve citizens killed, but he never got an accurate accounting of the wounded.

AFTERSHOCKS

The Baltimore riot had effects immediate and electric. In town, all traces of Union sentiment temporarily disappeared as Northern supporters hid their loyalties amid the frenzy of pro-Southern feeling let loose by the violence. Throughout the streets men and boys wore miniature Confederate flags; many people openly carried arms. Spontaneous pep rallies, with repeated cheers for Jeff Davis, drew townspeople to their street corners. A big Confederate banner was hoisted above the headquarters of the States' Rights Club. Even the Union Club on Baltimore Street took down its Stars and Stripes, and raised instead the State Flag of Maryland.

Fears of more fighting gripped public officials. Both the Governor and the Mayor wired Washington, begging that no more troops be sent through the city. Brown's message was especially forceful: "Under these circumstances it is my solemn duty to inform you that it is not possible for more soldiers to pass through Baltimore unless they fight their way at every step." When he got no reply either from the White House or the War Department, the Mayor and his city councilmen determined that the bridges leading into the city from northward had better be burned to keep more troops out. At this point civil efforts to preserve peace played directly into the hands of pro-Confederates. Police Chief Kane no longer disguised his loyalties as he sent out calls for help to surrounding counties. To Bradley Johnson at Frederick he sent a message on the evening of the 19th: "Fresh hordes will be down on us to-morrow. We will fight them and whip them or die."[167]

In response to these entreaties, all during April 20 the outlying areas sent in pro-Southern military companies to help the equally pro-Southern Baltimore police. A cavalry troop rode straight to city hall, heard a speech by the Mayor, and broke into cheers when

---

167   George William Brown, *Baltimore and the Nineteenth of April, 1861: A Study of the War* (Baltimore, 1887), pp. 57, 70.

a bugler sounded "Dixie." Kane armed the city militia and even brought out four cannon from his private arsenal. Soon a little army of 2,000 men, toting muskets, shotguns and pistols, was organized under the command of Ike Trimble, who supervised the burning of the Philadelphia and Baltimore's bridge at Gunpowder Creek. Trimble's guardsmen even more importantly cut the telegraph lines from Baltimore to the erstwhile nation's capital. The effects of the city riot rippled farther still. Baltimore County troops occupied the mistakenly unguarded United States arsenal at Pikesville. From Fort McHenry, located at the entrance of Baltimore's harbor, Captain John C. Robinson wrote Washington on the 20th that he expected to be attacked that night by Trimble's quasi-Confederates. Robinson ordered his artillery loaded and aimed to fire toward the direction of the city.

For Abraham Lincoln, too, the effects of the rioting were immediate and electric. The Baltimoreans' successful defiance of the 6th Massachusetts meant that Washington, thirty miles to the south, was cut off from any further reinforcements, at least via Baltimore. The President, in his seat of power, found himself isolated from the North by rail, mail and wire. Little wonder that, worried and depressed, he told an aide, "I don't believe there is any North."[168] Little wonder, too, that he was seen by his secretary pacing the floor of the White House, stopping to glance across the Potomac, where Confederates were rumored to be preparing an attack.

To prevent more violence in Baltimore, Governor Hicks of Maryland and Mayor Brown of Baltimore arrived at the White House, requesting that no more troops be sent through Maryland. Lincoln held firm. "I must have troops to defend this Capital," he said. "Geographically it lies surrounded by the soil of Maryland; and mathematically the necessity exists that they should come over her territory. Our men are not moles, and can't dig under the earth; they are not birds, and can't fly through the air. There is no way but to march across, and that they must do. But in doing this there is no need of collision. Keep your rowdies in Baltimore, and there

---

168   Margaret Leech, *Reveille in Washington 1860-1863* (New York, 1941), p. 65.

will be no bloodshed. Go home and tell your people that if they will not attack us, we will not attack them."[169] Brown and Hicks went home. But the damage had already been done. After the rioting of the 19th, Mayor Brown and city officials, with Governor Hicks' approval, had ordered the burning of railroad bridges north of the city toward Harrisburg and Philadelphia. "Washington awoke on Saturday [April 20]," writes an historian of the first Union wartime capital, "to find itself without railway communication with the loyal states, without mail or newspaper from the North."[170]

THE RALLY IN NEW YORK CITY

Telegraphic news of the fight in Baltimore fanned throughout the North on the afternoon of the 19th, just hours after the blood spilled. From the city Mayor Brown and Governor Hicks sent out a message to President Lincoln: "A collision between the citizens and the northern troops has taken place in Baltimore, and the excitement is fearful. Send no more troops here. We will endeavor to prevent all bloodshed."[171] (The President assured them that alternate routes would be found for the regiments then streaming toward Washington.)

Mayor Brown himself felt compelled to write Governor Andrew of Massachusetts, grieving over the tragic events, but acknowledging "they were inevitable." "Our people viewed the passage of armed troops from another State through the streets as an invasion of our soil," Brown wrote, "and could not be restrained." He stressed that he, Governor Hicks and the city authorities had done all they could to prevent the violence, and were caring for the wounded men of the Sixth. Andrew could only ask that "the bodies of our Massachusetts soldiers, dead in battle, ...be immediately laid out, preserved in ice, and tenderly sent forward by express to

---

169   Roy P. Basler, ed., *The Collected Works of Abraham Lincoln*, 9 vols. (New Brunswick NJ, 1953) vol. 4, 341-42.

170   Leech, *op. cit.*, p. 61.

171   Frank Moore, ed., *The Civil War Record: A Diary of American Events*, 11 vols. (New York, 1861-1868), vol. 1, Documents p. 79.

me."[172] (Brown could not comply, as rail link from Baltimore to the North had been cut; in the interim the four soldiers' corpses would repose at the city's Greenmount Cemetery.)

In New York City, arrival of the news coincided with the triumphal march of the 7th New York State Militia, before their departure for Washington. Officers and men were warned that the same trouble lay ahead for them, and the soldiers were issued 48 rounds of ammunition per man.

New Yorkers were very proud of the 7th, whose history went back to 1806. Prestigious for its organization and drill, the 7th Regiment NYSM was specifically requested on April 17 by General Scott in Washington. Packing equipment on the 18th and readying itself for travel, the regiment's preparations gave everyone in the city time to prepare for a big going-away party the next day. The excitement started on the morning of the 19th when the 8th Massachusetts (which had mustered in at Boston just after the Sixth) marched down Broadway. This was but a precursor to the parade of the Seventh New York. Flags were everywhere— at Lafayette Place where the regiment formed its march, down Cortlandt Street, up and down Broadway. "The Stars and Stripes were everywhere," reported the *Times,* "from the costliest silk, twenty, thirty, forty feet in length to the homelier bunting, down to the few inches of painted calico that a baby's hand might wave....It was flag, flag, from every window from the first floor to the roof.... Such was the display along the route of the 'Seventh.'"[173]

At 4 p.m. the regiment, 945 strong, lined up between Fourth and Eighth streets, then stepped forth with bands blaring. Police had trouble holding back the crowds, who pressed from sidewalk into the street, merging between musicians and the various companies. The citizens exuberantly back slapped every soldier in reach, hurrahing the uniformed heroes at their every step. One member of the regiment, Private Theodore Winthrop, recalled, "It was worth a life, that march. Only one who passed, as we did, through that tempest of cheers, two miles long, can know the

---

172   *Ibid.,* Documents p. 80; Diary p. 34.
173   *Ibid.,* Documents p. 80.

terrible enthusiasm of the occasion. I could hardly hear the rattle of our own gun-carriages, and only once or twice the music of our band came to me muffled and quelled by the uproar." The din and crowd-crush intensified as the regiment marched closer to the docks, boarded their ferries, and crossed over to Jersey. "We knew now, if we had not before divined it," Winthrop concluded, "that our great city was with us as one man, utterly united in the great cause we were marching to sustain."[174]

New Yorkers' patriotic display on the 19th was not so great that it could not be topped on the very next day, Saturday, April 20. Organized by William Evarts, prominent attorney and Republican stalwart, a mass meeting was held at Union Square in the afternoon. Most businesses closed, and tens of thousands of people poured out onto the square, up and down Broadway, along Fourth Avenue. Bands played and orators held forth from not one but five platforms, all colored with patriotic bunting. Guest of Honor was Major Anderson of Fort Sumter, just arrived in the city by ship after his expulsion from Charleston. The Major stood on a stage with the splintered flagstaff and Stars and Stripes he had brought from the fort. Most of the onlookers—the size of the crowds was estimated at 100,000 to fully a quarter-million—could not hear the speeches, but knew that points were being hit home when those closer in would yell and throw their hats into the air. Evarts was only one of dozens of speakers; at one point he led three cheers for the flag and Major Anderson.

Every stand had a meeting of its own begun by a prayer, as the one delivered by the Reverend Dr. Vinton at platform No. 2 (opposite the Everett House): "O Almighty God....Let the shields of thy omnipotent care be extended over the United States of America to defend the Constitution and to perfect the union of the people." Presiding over the program was the venerable sixty-two-year-old John Dix, veteran of the War of 1812. More recently a member of Buchanan's Cabinet and connected to many of New York's wealthiest men, Dix assembled a list of eighty-seven "vice

---

174   William J. Roehrenbeck, *The Regiment That Saved the Capital* (New York, 1961), p. 67.

presidents," all of whom were expected to donate substantially to the war effort. Dix's speech itself was interrupted more than a dozen times, as when he recounted to his listeners how the South had no grounds for secession ("We don't want to separate!"); how Major Anderson, standing with him, had put up a heroic defense at Sumter (tremendous cheers for Anderson); how the President had clearly told the South that it bore responsibility for the opening violence (enthusiastic applause, and waving of hats); that Lincoln was now compelled to call for volunteers (cries of "Good for him," and loud cheering); how the Southern leaders planned to subvert the national authority (cries of "Never, never; they can't do it!"); how "against this usurpation and fraud, if it shall be attempted, I trust we shall contend with all the strength God has given us (cries of 'We will!')."[175]

And on it went, a huge outpouring of patriotic feeling. "THE UNION FOREVER!" blared the rows of headlines in the next day's *Times*; "THE ENTIRE POPULATION IN THE STREETS"; "Over One Hundred Thousand People at Union-Square." The paper called it "the largest meeting, without exception, that was ever held on this continent." In addition to the crowds in the streets, people stood on housetops waving the Stars and Stripes. "Union-Square was a red, white and blue wonder," the newspaper exulted, with homes and hotels bedecked with banners. The bountiful bunting, flying flags, the throngs thrilling to endless oratory altogether spoke, declared the *Times,* "in tones of thunder for the Union, the Constitution and enforcement of the laws."[176] Such laudable, praiseworthy ends—no wonder Northerners felt confident as they went to war.

They were in store for a lot of disappointment.

---

175 *New York Times*, Apr. 21, 1861, in Eugene P. Moehring and Arleen Keylin, eds., *The War Between the States Extra: From the Pages of the* Charleston Mercury *& the* New York Times (New York, 1975), p. 23.

176 *Ibid.*

Chapter Three:

War on the Water

A VERY SHAKY BLOCKADE

Some scholars say that President Lincoln blundered on April 19 in declaring a blockade of the seceded states' ports. As U.S. Naval Secretary Gideon Welles told the President and the rest of the Cabinet, a government does not *blockade* its own ports, it *closes* them. Proclamation of a blockade, in international diplomacy, implicitly recognizes a state of belligerency between two powers. Belligerent status in turn confers upon a government certain diplomatic rights among neutral foreign countries—not full-fledged recognition, but at least a step toward that end. For the infant Confederate government, international acknowledgement of the C.S.A. as a belligerent would be a significant diplomatic achievement, possibly leading to the kind of European recognition and foreign aid which had helped the colonies win the first American Revolution.

Lincoln and his brand-new Secretary of State, William Dayton, knew this, but chose *blockade* anyway. From the Navy's point of view, the terminology was inconsequential, as its job was clear: position warships outside Rebel seaports and prevent ships from leaving and entering with the aim of pinching and eventually crippling the Southern economy, which had always relied on foreign imports for key goods. Now, in wartime, the importation of foreign arms, munitions and other supplies would be critical to the South's chances for success. So Welles was overruled by Lincoln and Dayton, who worried about the reaction of the British government. The Secretary of State had conferred with Lord Lyons, the British minister in Washington, and heard how Her Majesty's government would object to a closing of the Confederate ports, a step which would infringe upon Britain's trading rights. Lyons hinted darkly to Dayton that England might even react with a full recognition of the Confederacy. The alternative, blockade, was in fact a time-honored British practice, and hence more acceptable to London. A U.S. declaration of a blockade would confer belligerent rights upon the Confederacy, so Britain would be entitled to do the same. Lincoln and Dayton accepted this as the lesser of two evils, to forestall full diplomatic recognition.

Thus named, the Union blockade was prospectively described by a presidential decree on April 19. After listing the seven seceded states and citing their continued resistance to Federal authority, Lincoln announced that he had "deemed it advisable to set on foot a blockade of the ports within the States aforesaid."

> If, therefore, with a view to violate such blockade, a vessel shall approach, or shall attempt to leave either of the said ports, she will be duly warned by the commander of one of the blockading vessels, who will indorse on her register the fact and date of such warning, and if the same vessel shall again attempt to enter or leave the blockaded port she will be captured and sent to the nearest convenient port for such proceedings against her and her cargo as prize as may be deemed advisable.[177]

The question facing Lincoln, Welles and the Union was, where would the "competent force" required for the blockade come from? In April '61 the United States Navy numbered ninety ships, but most of the Navy's vessels were aged and decrepit sailing vessels that would soon be judged as obsolete and useless, without the steam engines needed to chase down swift blockade runners. Of

---

177   *O.R.,* Ser. 3, vol. 1, 90

the forty steamers, only twenty-four were serviceable. Of these only eleven were even in North American waters, the rest flung out over the seas from the Mediterranean to the East Indies. To be sure, Welles launched an aggressive program of repairing the older vessels, buying steamers for arming, and building new warships in the navy yards of Boston, New York and Philadelphia. But the expansion of the navy into a respectable blockading force would take months.

The Union's plight was worsened by the considerable length of the Confederate coastline. After the secession of North Carolina and Virginia (Lincoln extended the blockade to them on April 27), it would run over 3,500 miles, greater than the distance between New York and Liverpool, and contained 189 rivers, harbors, bays and inlets. At the same time, the Northern blockade did not have to cover the entire shoreline, only the waters outside Southern ports capable of taking in sea-traffic, with sufficient dock facilities and railroad connections into the interior. Actually, these seaports were relatively few: Morehead City, N.C., Wilmington, Charleston, Beaufort, Georgetown, S.C., Savannah, Fernandina, St. Marks, Fla., Mobile, New Orleans and Galveston. (Pensacola, best harbor on the Gulf, would be bottled up by Fort Pickens for the duration of the war.)

Still, the Confederacy managed to flout the blockade in its early months, chiefly because it took so long for the Federal naval forces to get into action. As first step, the commander of a blockader would send word ashore that the port was now blocked; foreign vessels had fifteen days to leave, after which they would be subject to capture. Norfolk became the first blockaded port, April 30. The U.S.S. *Niagara* did not announce its blockade of Charleston harbor until May 10, three weeks after Lincoln's proclamation. On May 13, Captain H.A. Adams, senior U.S. naval officer at Pensacola Bay, sent ashore his formal notice of blockade. Charleston, Savannah and Mobile were announced May 28; New Orleans on the 31st; Galveston July 2; and Wilmington July 21. During the "grace period" between Lincoln's proclamation and the arrival of the first Union steamers, most foreign ships left Southern ports.

For months afterward, the Northern blockading squadrons were still so weak that Confederate blockade-running operations got underway almost without interference. At Charleston, British Consul Robert Bunch reported on August 20 that vessels came and went out of the harbor without hindrance: "The blockade is the laughing stock of the Southern merchant marine." Two weeks later Bunch noted, "Vessels of various sizes enter and sail almost at pleasure."[178] Indeed, as a Union naval officer, Rear Admiral Daniel Ammen, later asserted, "If vessels were captured, even in entering the principal ports, it was due rather to the stupidity of the persons attempting to run the blockade than the effectiveness of the force employed to prevent it."[179]

How Southerners Got The Norfolk Navy Yard

The infant Confederacy, born without a navy, had at least a navy yard. Two days after Florida seceded, state troops took possession of the U.S. naval base at Pensacola Bay, the only such facility on the Gulf. Drydock and workshops, warehouses and ordnance stores all fell into Southern hands. Yet with a Federal garrison outside the harbor, in Fort Pickens on Santa Rosa Island, Pensacola as a port never offered much of value to the wartime South.

A considerably bigger prize came with Virginians' capture of the Gosport Navy Yard at Norfolk. A day after his state's convention had passed the ordinance of secession, Governor Letcher ordered Major General William B. Taliaferro to Norfolk to take charge of local militia there and take possession of the property belonging to the state commonwealth. That property, which as a technicality still belonged to the United States of America, was the big Gosport shipyard. Letcher also appointed Robert B. Pegram and Catesby ap R. Jones as captains in the Virginia State Navy, and ordered them to Norfolk as well, to cooperate with Taliaferro's land forces and see to the takeover of the base.

---

178 Frank Lawrence Owsley, *King Cotton Diplomacy: Foreign Relations of the Confederate States of America* (Chicago, 1931), pp. 232-33.

179 Daniel Ammen, "The Atlantic Coast" in *The Navy in the War,* vol. 7 of *Campaigns of the Confederate War,* 8 vols. (New York, 1883), 11.

Gosport was the biggest shipbuilding and repair facility in the South. Its facilities included machine and carpentry shops, arms workshops and storehouses, and a drydock able to handle the ocean's largest vessels. Moreover, at Gosport were over a thousand cannon plus plenty of powder. Clearly the place made a tempting target for the newly independent Virginians.

And that did not count what lay off shore: eleven warships. The forty-gun steam frigate *Merrimack,* put in after a long passage around Cape Horn, waited to have her engines overhauled. Ten warships-of-sail lay at anchor awaiting orders: line-of-battle ships *Pennsylvania* (120 guns), *Delaware* (74), *Columbus* (74); sailing frigates *Raritan* (60), *United States* (50), *Columbia* (50) and *Cumberland* (24); first class sloops *Plymouth* (22) and *Germantown* (22); plus the little four-gun brig *Dolphin.*

In Washington, Naval Secretary Welles was so worried about all of this falling into secessionist hands that in late March he sent 250 marines to reinforce the Gosport garrison. On April 10 he wired the yard commandant, Captain Charles S. McCauley, to rush repairs on the *Merrimack* and get her out of the harbor, and out of danger, as soon as possible. The other ships at port should probably be gotten out too, Welles advised. Unfortunately for Welles and Washington, McCauley was not a man of initiative. Sixty-seven years old, he was part of the U.S. Navy's problem at the start of the war: too many old officers. In 1861, most of the service's 78 captains were over 60 years old, the product of no retirement provision, and the practice of unbroken seniority promotion over decades of peacetime. Getting ahead in this old navy had become a question of following orders and simply outliving all the others.

McCauley in this case did not even follow orders. He replied to Welles that it would take a month to complete work on the *Merrimack* engines; Washington sent an engineer to Norfolk on April 14 and got the work done in three days. McCauley, however, refused to let the vessel go. At 2 p.m. on the 19th, he ordered the captain of the *Merrimack* to extinguish her fires and stand down. Old Captain McCauley was worried that escape of the ship would anger the Virginians and precipitate an assault on his base.

Though the yard facilities were bounded by a high brick wall, and his garrison (with Welles' recent reinforcement) numbered 800 sailors and marines, McCauley was spooked. He mistrusted his junior officers, most of whom were Southerners; he worried about the "vigilant committee" already formed in Norfolk; and he feared that the local civilian workmen whom he needed to complete repairs on his various ships would sabotage them instead.

The Virginians apparently knew their man, and played on his fears. Arriving at Norfolk, General Taliaferro had found just two militia companies, the Norfolk Blues and Portsmouth Grays. But down the Elizabeth River the Southerners had built batteries and sunk obstructions to bar the Federals' escape out to Hampton Roads and Chesapeake Bay. This activity had already been enough to unnerve old McCauley. Yet it was an enterprising railroad man, William Mahone, President of the Norfolk & Petersburg (and later C.S. general), who proved decisive. On the 19th Mahone had empty cars run up the track a few miles out of Norfolk, take on a lot of locals, and bring them back into town. Instructed to yell, whoop it up and cheer loudly, these presumed "reinforcements" further rattled McCauley. Now convinced that none of his ships stood a chance of escaping, at noon on April 20th he gave orders for the yard to be destroyed.

Soon U.S. sailors and marines were busy ruining ships that in earlier days had been the pride of the United States Navy. Workmen cut down rigging, chopped at masts, and wielded sledgehammers against cannon trunnions. Seacocks were opened, hulls filled with water; barrels of tar and turpentine were split and spilt as fuel for fires set on the ship decks. Only two vessels escaped destruction: the old frigate *United States,* launched in 1797 and too venerable to be set fire; and the *Cumberland,* on which Captain McCauley would that night slip out of the yard with as many of the Gosport garrison as could cram aboard.

On land, marines set powder charges to blow up the drydock and set fire to barracks, storehouses and supplies. The townspeople of Portsmouth saw all this activity and rushed into the yard just as the U.S. marines and sailors were evacuating it. Some fires were put out, and a quick-thinking militia officer snuffed the fuses that would have blown up the great granite dry-dock. Most of the conflagrations, however, were out of control, and the Virginians had to watch as buildings, stores and ships went up in smoke.

The next morning state troops entered what was left of the Gosport Navy Yard. Out in the river, nine ships lay wrecked and scuttled. *Merrimack,* the steam frigate which Secretary Welles had so hoped to save, was sunk and burned to her waterline. Partially burned were the *Plymouth* and *Germantown.* The big battleship *Pennsylvania* was totally destroyed, along with *Raritan, Columbia* and *Dolphin. Delaware* and *Columbus* sat sunk in their moorings.

Much of the yard property was also in ruins, but the Virginians were delighted to find some structures still intact when the smoke cleared: foundry, several machine shops, officers' quarters and five big storehouses bulging with supplies. Tools and machinery, stocks of food and clothing, and vast quantities of timber, canvas, copper plus iron anchors and chains all fell into the Southerners' hands. A report by Virginia naval paymaster William H. Peters later valued the worth of this windfall, including drydock and wharves, at just under $3,000,000. Perhaps most important, and nearly invaluable to an infant nation already at war, were the ordnance stores captured at the navy yard: shot, shells, and over a thousand pieces of artillery, including fifty-two 9-inch Dahlgren guns, imperfectly spiked and quite reparable.

Reparable, too, as it turned out, were even some of the scuttled ships. Within a few weeks, Confederate Flag-Officer French Forrest took command at Norfolk and put hundreds of men to work at the yards. The *Germantown* and *Plymouth* were raised from the river bottom with their cannon rusty but uninjured. The hull of the *Merrimack* was lifted and hauled to drydock; soon machine shops clattered in a rebuilding program destined to produce the most formidable Confederate battleship of the whole war.

Ships, docks, guns, ammo, provisions, production plant and raw materials—all this fell into the Virginians' hands on April 21.

"A complete institution," as one student has put it, "was won by the South without having fired a shot."[180]

THE TWO NAVIES IN 1861

The decrepitude of the United States Navy in 1861, both in terms of ancient senior officers and ancient sailing vessels— someone said that at the start of its war against the Confederacy, it was better suited for the war against Mexico decades earlier—did not cancel out the fact that at least the North *had* a navy.

To be sure, only forty of the commissioned U.S. ships were steam-powered, but as Confederate naval historian Warren Spencer points out, "this was forty ships more than President Jefferson Davis had."[181] Moreover, the North had eight navy yards in 1861; that was four times the number that had fallen into Confederate hands (Norfolk and Pensacola). The Northern dockyards were put in fervent activity by Lincoln's Navy secretary, Gideon Welles, both to refit the out-of-commission old ships and to build new ones. Welles had also set out to "buy everything afloat that could be made of service."[182]

In a Northern war effort plagued by too many political appointees, Lincoln added another when he named Welles to his Cabinet. Fifty-nine years old, the Connecticut-born newspaper editor's sole acquaintance with things maritime came from a stint in the navy's Bureau of Provisions and Clothing decades before (tossed to him as a patronage plum for his loyalty to the Democratic Party). Not to be overlooked was that he left this office amid rumors of personal profiteering in his purchases. Nevertheless, Lincoln needed a New Englander and Welles filled the bill.

The Secretary of the Navy presented himself as something of an odd bird (*rara avis,* his friends euphemized). With a long white beard and a wig draping gray ringlets to his shoulders,

---

180   Alan B. Flanders, "The Night They Burned the Yard," *Civil War Times Illustrated,* February 1980, p. 38.

181   Warren F. Spencer, *The Confederate Navy in Europe* (Tuscaloosa, 1983), p. 2.

182   J. Thomas Scharf, *History of the Confederate States Navy: From Its Organization to Victory at Sea* (Baltimore, 1887), p. 42.

Welles peered out at the world from behind thick glasses. He was not long in office before a critic advised Lincoln, "if only we had that old fossil Welles out of the Navy, we might do something." Nevertheless, old Abe stayed with his old fossil.

That the South started out in its War of Independence with no navy highlights even more the achievements of Confederate Secretary of the Navy Stephen Russell Mallory. Born into a seafaring family, growing up in Key West, writing about shipwrecks for the newspapers, Mallory was about as maritime as one could get. His knowledge and experience were recognized when, upon his election to the U.S. Senate from Florida, he was appointed to the Naval Affairs Committee. While "Golden Gideon" was lining his pockets, Mallory was acquiring valuable knowledge about navy department organization.

Mallory was significantly aided by a Confederate Congress that displayed acute awareness of the nation's naval needs. While the U.S. Congress stingily refused to appropriate funds for Welles' construction projects, lawmakers in Montgomery as early as mid-March appropriated money for the building or buying of at least ten steam vessels convertible as gunboats. On March 15 it also put the Pensacola Navy Yard under C.S. authority (Virginia would turn over Gosport in another month.)

At the same time, Congress ordered state governments to turn over to Mallory's department all vessels seized in the secession wave. These captures gave a quick start to the Confederate navy. At New Orleans Louisianans took over a U.S. revenue cutter, the *Robert McClellan,* with four side guns and a pivot gun. Alabama militiamen at Fort Morgan in Mobile Bay seized another cutter, the *Lewis Cass,* with a 68-pounder gun on its deck. Another U.S. revenue ship, the ninety-ton *William Aiken* (armed with a forty-two pounder), was captured in Charleston; it was renamed *Petrel* and fitted out as a privateer. Similarly turned into a privateer was the 276-ton brig *Bonita,* taken at Savannah.

Moreover, after their states' secession some governors had acted quickly in buying tempting vessels lying in their ports or rivers. Governor Joseph E. Brown used state funds to purchase a small side-wheel steamer, the *Everglade,* for $34,000. It was turned into a gunboat and renamed it the *Savannah.* She was used to guard the mouth of the Savannah River and became the flagship of Commodore Tattnall's flotilla about the time of the Union attack on Port Royal in November 1861. After Virginia's secession, Governor Letcher saw that two steamers aport in the James were captured, the *Yorktown* and *Jamestown.* All of these and others were turned over to Secretary Mallory at the direction of the Congress.

The Southerners' lack of an established navy actually offered a benefit, one that would only evidence itself during the war. Mallory's navy-to-be had no hoary traditions, no stuffed-shirt policies that would hold back or hinder his department's innovative approaches to war-making. It was the Confederacy, for instance, that began experimenting with "torpedoes," floating explosive mines that would in Southern rivers, bays and harbors sink twenty-nine Union warships and damage fourteen more.[183] It was the Confederacy that conceived and built a submersible vessel, the *Hunley,* that in Charleston harbor sank the twenty-three-gun *Housatonic* in mid-February 1863. And it was the Confederacy that built the first ironclad gunboat, the *Virginia,* that would go into battle, cripple the Yankee blockading flotilla at Hampton Roads—as we shall soon see.

ORGANIZING THE CONFEDERATE NAVY

Secretary Mallory's job as Secretary meant that he was essentially co-planner with the President for Confederate naval strategy. Jefferson Davis realized that Northern naval strength gave the Union a marked initial advantage in the war, so he involved himself deeply in Mallory's organizational and strategy-laying activities. In this he was demarking yet another executive exception between himself and Abraham Lincoln, who after proclaiming the blockade largely left naval matters to Gideon Welles and the admirals.

---

183   Milton F. Perry, *Infernal Machines: The Story of Confederate Submarine and Mine Warfare* (Baton Rouge, 1965), pp. 199-201.

Mallory's first step was to address any navy's obvious need: ships. He had barely been in office a month before he sent agents to New York, Philadelphia and Baltimore to look for and buy vessels suitable for Confederate navy use. They could find only one, the steamer *Caroline* in Philadelphia. Agents sent to Canada reported that the U.S. had already bought every available steamer in Canadian waters.

There was another source: Europe. On May 10, 1861, Congress passed secret acts authorizing the dispatch of Naval Agent James D. Bulloch to England. That very day President Davis signed the bills; they called for the purchase abroad of at least six European warships, arms and stores. Bulloch arrived in England on June 4. (More on that later.)

Secretary Mallory's main effort, though, was aimed for construction of vessels at home. He was not seeking big-hulled wooden warships, but ironclad gunboats—vessels with thick iron plating above the water, bearing guns with rams mounted at their prows to plunge into the submerged hulls of Yankee ships, which would sink fast under the inrush of water. The ironclads would be heavy and of shallow draft, operable only in Southern rivers and harbors—but that was where Mallory saw the enemy threat.

On May 8 the Secretary submitted a report to the naval committee of Congress urging the immediate construction of ironclad war vessels. His key point: "inequality of numbers may be compensated by invulnerability, and thus not only does economy but naval success dictate the wisdom and expediency of fighting wood with iron." (Boy, would he be proven prescient!)

In addition to construction supervised by C.S. naval officers and contracts with foreign builders, Secretary Mallory entered into contracts with private firms from Norfolk through Memphis to New Orleans. In the first year and a half of the war, the Navy signed contracts for the building of forty vessels—gunboats, floating batteries and ships-of-war.

Because of his foresight, energy and management, Mallory has won multiple plaudits from historians of the War for Southern

Independence. Typical of these is the judgment of Herman Hattaway and Archer Jones:

> Mallory...managed remarkably with his limited resources. A man of unusual ability and force and long interested in shipbuilding and modernization, he realized far earlier than his northern counterpart, Gideon Welles, that the Civil War marked an era of naval transition. As long as fifty years before, no less than five great revolutions had begun affecting sea warfare: the use of steam, shell guns, the screw propeller, rifled ordnance, and armor. The Confederacy employed these creative innovations whenever its resources allowed, and also otherwise experimented, notably with mines, then called torpedoes, and submarines.[184]

The contributions of Confederate torpedoes to Southern victory in the war will be the focus of a future story.

SEMMES, BUCHANAN, MAURY AND FARRAGUT

What the infant Confederate navy lacked in ships, it more than made up for in experienced officers.

Within six weeks of Fort Sumter about one-fifth of the officers of the United States Navy had resigned. At five particular grades, this twenty percent was evident:

	Whole number	Southerners resigned
Captains	93	16
Commanders	127	34
Lieutenants	351	76
Surgeons, Assistant Surgeons	143	27
Masters	81	8

---

184   Herman Hattaway and Archer Jones, *How the South Won* (Macon: Mercer University Press, 1983), pp. 32-33.

This efflux of talent posed a problem for Union naval secretary Welles. Worse for him, many of these resignees were modern-thinking younger officers, not the hoary sextagenarians who waddled about the decks of the U.S. Navy's wooden sailing vessels. As a sign of his pique, Welles did not even allow the Southerners to resign; he dismissed them upon receiving their letters of intent.

Among this batch of talent, four names deserve special attention for their signal contributions to Confederate naval successes: Raphael Semmes, Franklin Buchanan, Matthew Fontaine Maury and David Glasgow Farragut.

Born in Maryland in 1806, sixteen-year-old Semmes won appointment as a midshipman in the U.S. Navy (thanks to a politically-connected uncle). When promoted to lieutenant he was assigned to the Pensacola Navy Yard. Now married, this led him to move his family to Mobile, which remained his lifelong home. The he went to sea as skipper of several U.S. vessels; promoted to commander in 1855 he performed various survey and lighthouse assignments. After Alabama seceded he followed her and offered his services to Secretary Mallory, who quickly snapped them up. Erect in bearing, dignified in appearance, with piercing dark eyes, Semmes was best known for his big moustache, which he kept immaculately polished. Well before the war, his sailors had begun to call him "Old Beeswax."

Beeswax did a number on the Yankees. After Secretary Mallory made commerce raiding a strategic priority, Semmes commanded the C.S.S. *Sumter,* the first vessel to show the Confederate flag on the high seas. On the *Sumter* and later aboard the *Alabama,* Semmes preyed on Northern merchantmen, burning sixty-four ships and bonding thirteen more. This achievement leads Warren Spencer, late of the University of Georgia, to admiringly claim of his commerce raiding, "he did that job better than any other naval captain in naval history."[185]

Like a number of Confederate naval leaders, Franklin Buchanan entered the United States Navy as a teen; in Buchanan's case,

185   Warren F. Spencer, "Raphael Semmes" in Richard N. Current, ed., *Encyclopedia of the Confederacy,* 4 vols. (Baton Rouge, 1993), vol. 3, 1392.

it was during the War of 1812 when he served under Oliver H. Perry, hero of the battle of Lake Erie. Rising through the ranks (lieutenant, commander), in 1845 he was named as the first superintendent of the newly established Naval Academy at Annapolis. He commanded a vessel in the Mexican War and sailed to Japan with Perry in 1852. After promotion to captain in 1855 he was in charge of the Washington Navy Yard. Following Virginia's secession Buchanan resigned and was snapped up by Secretary Mallory, whom he advised in the early months of the Confederate Navy's organization. After the C.S.S. *Virginia* was commissioned, Mallory named Buchanan to lead the formidable ironclad in its first battles against the Yankees' wooden-hulled vessels. That he did so illustriously we shall see in ensuing chapters.

Matthew Fontaine Maury's chief contribution to the Confederate cause was his experimentation with underwater mines, or torpedos as they were called. A native Virginian, Maury had served three dozen years in the old navy when he followed the Old Dominion out of the Union and was named a commander in the Virginia State Navy (soon to become part of the national one). Maury's electric detonation system was a key factor in winning the naval secretary's support and Congressional funding for what would become the first successful use of underwater mines in the history of warfare—another innovative first that helped the South defend its harbors and rivers.

David Glasgow Farragut's Confederate naval record is less well known. Born in east Tennessee in 1801, he was six years old when his family moved to New Orleans. Three years later he joined the navy and rose steadily in rank, seeing action both in the War of 1812 and the conflict with Mexico, 1846-48.

Despite his Southern upbringing, Captain Farragut stayed with the navy after both Tennessee and Louisiana left the Union. Gideon Welles and others in his department, however, were suspicious of Farragut because of his Southern roots. They therefore essentially shelved him during the first eight months of the war. Having served dutifully under the Stars and Stripes for five decades, Farragut was justifiably angered at this short shrift and on December 10, 1861, handed in his resignation. Confederate naval secretary Mallory sent out subtle inquiries to him; Farragut, out of work and feeling that he was about to miss out on chances for action and glory, signaled that he was ready to join the Confederate Navy.

Mallory took advantage of Farragut's ties to New Orleans, and put him in charge of the Southern squadron that was being assembled at the Crescent City. His brilliant handling of the Confederate monster ironclads *Louisiana* and *Mississippi* will be detailed in another story.

NEPTUNE'S TRIDENT (1)—COMMERCE RAIDERS

Confederate Secretary of the Navy Stephen R. Mallory's big-picture strategy at the start of the war had three major elements—prongs of Neptune's trident, if you will.

Most important was defending the South's immense coastline—each harbor, bay and inlet of which invited the pesky Yankee navy's incursion. Even more daunting was stopping enemy warships from venturing into the Confederacy's many rivers, chief among which was the Mississippi, but also the Tennessee and Cumberland, which unfortunately offered riverine avenues of invasion. For this task, Mallory envisioned a varied armamentarium. Big ironclad gunboats such as the *Virginia* could guard the mouth of the James River to keep enemy vessels from chugging upstream to threaten Richmond, soon to be the capital of the nation. In the lower reaches of the Mississippi, ironclads when constructed could fend off Northern vessels approaching New Orleans. Upriver, at Memphis and beyond, Mallory planned for as many light-draft steam gunboats as could be bought and converted, or built from scratch before enemy flotillas poked downstream, as they were sure to do.

Ironclads would also be the essential weapon against blockading Northern vessels, most of which were wooden-hulled. A telling instance of Confederate success with armorclads would be the attack in January 1863 of two iron gunboats, the *Chicora* and *Palmetto State,* on the Union blockaders at Charleston harbor. They rammed and shot up so many Yankee ships that General Beauregard actually announced that the blockade there had been broken (at least temporarily).

Even more innovative was Mallory's second secret weapon: torpedos, the fore-runners of modern naval mines. As the secretary's biographer, Father Joseph Durkin, has written, "the torpedo (the modern mine) [was] one of the really great inventions of the war, and perhaps the most consistently successful of all Confederate weapons."

Finally, Mallory envisioned a campaign for C.S. commerce raiders and privateers to raid Northern seaborne commerce. This effort, if successful, would divert enemy warships from the blockade. More importantly, by capturing or sinking Northern merchantmen and their cargoes, this prong would damage Lincoln's war economy and dent his very war effort. In this mission, fast cruisers converted from domestic vessels, such as the screw steamer *Sumter,* and those purchased abroad, like the *Alabama,* would make legends for themselves before Confederate victory was finally won.

The colorful career of the *Sumter* is a case in point. The 427-ton steamer had been launched in 1857 as the *Habana*; it was bought by the government in Secretary Mallory's first wave of purchases. On June 3, 1861, she was recommissioned at New Orleans as the C.S.S. *Sumter*; Cmdr. Raphael Semmes was put in charge of her conversion into a commerce raider. Additional coal bunkers were installed, three new masts were raised and her deck was strengthened so as to take on the weight (nearly six tons) of her armament: four thirty-two pounders and an eight-inch rifle, all transported from the captured ordnance at Gosport in Norfolk. With her heavy beams and armor, the *Sumter* was still pretty fast, able to make nine or ten knots (Semmes had her smokestack hinged so his prospective prey would think she was merely a sailer). The commander rushed the work so efficiently that by June 18 he was ready to take the *Sumter* down the Mississippi, past the blockaders and out to sea. In two weeks he had his first prize off the coast of Cuba, a three-masted merchantman named the

Golden Rocket. A shot fired in her direction brought about a quick surrender. Semmes took her crew onboard then set the ship on fire. Traversing the Caribbean, Semmes took more prizes, causing mortification in the Northern navy. Sailing across the Atlantic, the Sumter in six months overhauled seventy-eight ships, sixty of which proved to be neutral and were let go. But eighteen were of U.S. registry and therefore taken as prizes; most were burned after their cargo was pilfered. The *Sumter*'s career as commerce raider ended in January 1862 when she laid up at Gibraltar for repair. The work was still underway when three Northern warships bottled her up in the harbor; Semmes and his crew left their vessel and made it back to England.

Semmes reflected on the *Sumter*'s six-month career in his *Memoirs of Service Afloat*:

> The fact alone of the *Sumter* being upon the seas, during these six months, gave such an alarm to neutral and belligerent shippers, that the enemy's carrying-trade began to be paralyzed, and already his ships were being laid up or sold under neutral flags....In addition to this, the enemy kept five or six of his best ships of war constantly in pursuit of her, which necessarily weakened his blockade....The expense to my Government of running the ship was next to nothing, being only $28,000, or about the price of one of the least valuable of her prizes.[186]

Actually, in dollars-and-cents terms, Semmes' *Sumter* was a real bargain for Stephen Mallory, as the cost of her eighteen prizes to the North was somewhere between a quarter-million and a half-million dollars—not bad for six months' work. And Raphael Semmes' best days as a Confederate commerce raider still lay ahead.

---

186   Raphael Semmes, *Memoirs of Service Afloat* (Baltimore, 1869), p. 345

MALLORY'S IMPRESSIVE ACHIEVEMENT

Despite the daunting problems of constructing, converting or purchasing warships, the Confederate Navy had established itself by November 1861 with a sturdy little fleet of thirty-four vessels. Many of them were Northern ones seized by state forces right after secession. The *Washington* was a U.S. ship captured at Galveston; Alabama troops took over the *Louis Cass* in Mobile bay; Louisiana forces grabbed the *McClelland* at New Orleans. Other vessels were bought under governors' authority and turned over to the C.S. Navy—*e.g.,* the *James Gray* (South Carolina governor Pickens) and the *Everglade* (Georgia governor Joseph E. Brown).

Among these three dozen were gunboats, such as the *Jackson* (formerly the steamer *Yankee*), which had been bought and was fitted out at New Orleans. The steamers *Patrick Henry* and *Teaser* had been bought by the state of Virginia just after secession. The former was a 250-foot-long sidewheeler partly armored (iron plating around her boilers and machinery) and equipped with two pivot guns, forward and aft, plus eight broadside guns. The *Teaser* was aptly named, both for its size (a converted tugboat) and armament, just two guns. Similarly, the South Carolina government had purchased a steamboat that was renamed the *Lady Davis* after the president's wife; she was armed with 24-pounders and sent afloat in mid-March 1861 to guard Charleston harbor.

A good number of these ships ended up as privateers. *Ivy* was a 200-ton steamer armed with two guns. The 150-ton *Dixie* captured three prizes in just five weeks during July and August of 1861. In a little more time than that, June 28-August 27, 1861, the *Jefferson Davis* captured ten ships. Probably the record was set, though, by the *William H. Webb,* whose captain and crew captured three Massachusetts whalers in one day.

Not all of these early Confederate vessels had happy endings. The *Petrel,* a privateer, set out from Charleston on July 27, 1861, but ran into a U.S. frigate and was sunk. *Judith,* a privateer schooner lying off Pensacola, was boarded by Yankees on Sept. 14, 1861 and burned.

Buying, building (and sometimes stealing) warships was certainly Mallory's first job, but the secretary also succeeded in developing and organizing a magnificent manufacturing system to meet the navy's needs. In addition to harnessing Richmond's Tredegar Iron Works for gunboat plating and John Brooke's efficient banded guns, Mallory established three naval ordnance works. At Charlotte, N.C., Chief Engineer H.A. Ramsay oversaw the forging of cannon projectiles and shafts for steamers, as well as gun carriages, blocks and other equipment. At Selma, Ala., Commander Catesby ap R. Jones superintended the manufacture of guns especially suited for use against Yankee ironclads. Forty-seven of these were sent to the defenses of Mobile, another dozen to Charleston and Wilmington. The ordnance works at Richmond, under Lt. Robert D. Minor, supplied all the equipment needed by the Confederate James River squadron as well as carriages for the heavy guns at shore batteries. In addition were two engine-boiler and machine shops.

The naval laboratory at New Orleans produced fuses and primers. A powder mill at Columbia, S.C., under the direction of one P.B. Gareschi, produced excellent gunpowder, and enough of it to meet the needs of the entire navy. The ropewalk at Petersburg, Va., made all the cordage from rope yarn to nine-inch cable. Its production capacity, 8,000 yards a month, not only supplied everything the navy needed but also the army, Southern coal mines and railroads.

In November 1862 Stephen Mallory had been on the job for a year and a half, and he had eighteen shipyards across the Confederacy hard at work. A report to Congress at that time detailed some of this work:

> at Richmond, an ironclad steamer had just been launched, and another one was on the stocks;

> at Halifax, N.C., a light-draft gunboat would be ready to two months;

at Edward's Ferry, on the Roanoke River, an ironclad gunboat was awaiting her machinery;

at Wilmington an ironclad steamer was being built, with her machinery to come from Columbus, Ga.;

at Pedee River Bridge, S.C., a wooden gunboat with two propellers had just been completed (engines built at the Richmond naval works);

at Charleston, an ironclad was nearly finished, which would carry six-inch-thick armor and six guns;

at Savannah, another ironclad awaited her armament; and

at Mobile, a big ironclad sidewheel steamer needed her armor plating.

All of this would be in the future. In the spring of 1861, Secretary Mallory turned much of his attention to his first big project: making an ironclad from the burned hull of the U.S.S. *Merrimack*.

C.S.S. Virginia

As chairman of the U.S. Senate's naval committee before the war, Stephen Mallory had kept an eye on how England and France in the 1850s were building armored warships. The French used three ironclads against the Russians in the Crimean War of 1853; their sensational exploits in the Black Sea convinced Mallory that the day of the masted sailing ship was nearing an end. As America teetered toward civil war, England and France were racing to build ironclads. The French won the race, launching the armored frigate *La Gloire* in 1859. But the British were not far behind; the *Warrior* was christened one year later.

Confederate naval secretary Mallory wanted to buy two ironclads from the Europeans, but the plan fell through. Then, when he learned that the 3,500-ton steam frigate U.S.S. *Merrimack* had only partially burned at the Norfolk Naval yard, with her hull and engines intact, he hatched the idea of the Confederacy building its own armored warship. "I regard the possession of an iron-armored ship as a matter of the first necessity," he wrote just days after Virginians had seized Gosport Navy Yard; "such a vessel at this time could traverse the entire coast of the United States, prevent all blockades, and encounter, with a fair prospect of success, their entire Navy."

That was a tall order, but at least Mallory was thinking big. And he was moving fast. Just weeks after Richmond became the new Confederate capital, Mallory arrived there on June 3. That very evening he met with a talented naval expert, Lt. John M. Brooke, who had learned of the secretary's interest in building an ironclad and wanted to help.

A Floridian by birth, Brooke joined the U.S. Navy at the age of fifteen and attended the Naval Academy at Annapolis (graduating in 1847). Returning to naval service in the '50s Brooke proved himself bright and inventive; his deep-sea sounding technique led to the laying of the Atlantic cable following the War for Southern Independence.

After Virginia seceded Brooke resigned his commission (he had risen to lieutenant). Following the practice of the C.S. Army, when the Confederate navy accepted Brooke's offer of service, it gave him the same rank as he had held in the "old navy." He quickly came to the attention of Secretary Mallory, who was impressed by the 35-year-old lieutenant, especially his keen interest in ordnance. (During the war Brooke invented a number of large smoothbore and rifled cannon, including a 6.4-inch, 7-inch and 8-inch rifles. Confederate naval historian Spencer Tucker calls Brooke's inventions "probably the finest rifled navy guns on either side in the war."[187]) Before their meeting of June 3 ended, Mallory

---

187 Spencer C. Tucker, "John Mercer Brooke" in Richard N. Current, ed., *Encyclopedia of the Confederacy*, 4 vols. (Baton Rouge, 1993), vol. 1, 223.

had put Brooke in charge of supervising the guns and armor for the ship that would rise from the *Merrimack*'s hull.

On June 7 Brooke began laying out a design for the Confederate ironclad, and in a few days had a preliminary plan: shallow-draft hull, deck close to the water, elongated prow for ramming, an iron-enclosed case mate sloping at 36 degrees to deflect shot. Ten gunports—four on each side, plus fore and aft—were installed for big cannon to be run up, fired, and then withdrawn. The most important feature was the case mate, or gun-room. It would be protected by two-feet-thick walls of oak and pine, plated with three or more inches of iron. Even the deck would be protected by several inches of metal.

In truth, Europeans years before had mastered this design for warships, so Brooke's concept was not revolutionary. What made it so important, though, after Secretary Mallory's enthusiastic approval, was that it became the model for every Confederate ironclad gunboat produced in the war.

Mallory and Brooke then engaged John L. Porter, naval constructor at the Norfolk navy yard, to oversee construction of the ship. By the end of May, the *Merrimack* hull had been raised from the yard's muddy bottom and moved into dry dock, where its water was quickly pumped out. Porter assembled some eighty experienced shipfitters for his next phase, building the deck. Then came the casemate, 172 feet long. Below decks, workmen cleaned the two engines, strengthened the boiler, and primed the 17 1/2 – foot propeller. A 1,500-pound iron ram was designed to puncture wooden-hulled enemy vessels. From bow to stern, the new vessel measured 262 feet—a length just shy of an SEC football field. The two engines from the *Merrimack* provided the motive power, but that was limited. Because the huge ironclad weighed a thousand tons, it would only make four knots' speed. Just to turn the vessel around took a half-hour.

The new ironclad was launched on Feb. 24, 1862, and christened the *Virginia*. In the series he was planning, Secretary Mallory envisioned naming them for the various Confederate states. Already at New Orleans the *Louisiana* and *Mississippi* were being completed. Before the war was over, the *Arkansas* and *Tennessee* would win their own laurels. But the *Virginia* would become the most famous of all. Its wartime exploits, of course, were at the Yankees' expense. Envious of the *Virginia*'s fame, and embarrassed that they never developed an ironclad of equal stature, Northerners to this day refuse to refer to Brooke and Porter's ironclad by its Confederate name, instead still calling her the *Merrimack* (after the Connecticut river) or the *Merrimac* (the nearby town).

THE DEMISE OF THE *MONITOR*

The forward-thinking Stephen Mallory was so committed to a Confederate Navy anchored—pardon—in ironclads that he wanted to buy them abroad. He informed President Davis that domestic from-scratch construction of a *Virginia*-like vessel would take twelve to eighteen months, obviously a long time indeed. Hence in his first report to Davis, April 26, 1861, he proposed to order the construction of ships in Europe. An idea eventually developed of what would be called the English-built powerful Laird ram gunboats, steaming across the Atlantic to bust up the Union blockade of the Confederacy's Atlantic ports. The project, however, would fail, for the heavy vessels would not have made the voyage across the storm-tossed Atlantic.

Approached by Confederate agents, French emperor Napoleon III had two great ironclads built in his country for Southern use. But their construction was so slow that by the time they were completed, Confederates had already won their war for independence. Napoleon ended up selling the vessels to Denmark in 1864.

Talk about a slow process. Union Secretary of the Navy Gideon Welles thought little of the ironclad concept. "Having no technical knowledge," writes Richard S. West, "he was nevertheless a tightfisted skeptic who considered armored ship experimentation too costly and the utility of the product dubious."

Only after word of the Rebels' raising of the *Merrimack* and their initial work converting her did Welles bring the issue of ironclads before Congress on July 4, 1861, and even then he merely recommended creation of an investigative board (which, comprised of three old officers, concluded that wooden ships were still the best). It took another month before the U.S. Congress appropriated $1.5 million for building one or more armorclad warships. It was into September before Welles even started looking at proposals for ironclads. Some plans were rather unimaginative, such as one for a *New Ironsides,* a conventional vessel equipped with belt armor around its midship section. One James B. Eads submitted ideas for gunboats that were not even ironclads, but whose topside would be protected by cotton bales (hence the derisive nickname "cottonclads"). Much more creative was a design developed by a Swedish inventor, John Ericsson: a low-lying vessel with a revolving circular gun turret, equipped with two big cannon. The turret armor, eight inches thick, and the low hull allowed some to call Ericsson's proposed vessel a "tin can on a raft." Welles finally got around to granting approval, which allowed Ericsson to supervise construction at the Brooklyn navy yard. By the end of January 1862, Ericsson's tin can, now dubbed the *Monitor,* was nearing completion. Within three weeks the ship had made its shakedown cruise in New York harbor, had had its steering system tweaked, and was ready to head down the Atlantic coastline to take on the Rebel ironclad that by now was open knowledge among Welles' naval officers.

There would be no battle between the *Monitor* and *Virginia,* however. Having set out from New York on March 6 with a crew of 59 sailors under Lt. John Worden, within twenty-four hours, the *Monitor* was beset by a good old-fashioned sea squall. High winds and rough waves crashed over her deck, under and into the turret. Water also poured into the pilot house and light holes bored in the deck. When waves plunged through the blower pipes providing air to the engines, the fans went out and the engines stopped. Crewmen operating the hand pumps worked them so hard that they, too, failed. There was too much water aboard to resort to bailing, and soon Worden realized that his ship would be sinking. He ordered the crew to abandon ship in time to allow the men to jump away into the stormy sea (more than half drowned).

The *Monitor* soon foundered and went down in 220 feet of water off the coast of Ocean City, Md. The date was March 7, 1862. She would not be found at the bottom of the sea for another century.[188]

VICTORY AT THE HEAD OF THE PASSES

New Orleans was the largest city in the Confederacy, home to 168,675 people in 1860 according to the last census of the Southern people taken by the United States government (second and third were Charleston and Richmond).

She was also a major shipbuilding center. The first shipyard in New Orleans was established in 1819, within two decades after President Jefferson bought the Louisiana Territory from the French. The 1860 census shows at least five yards at or around New Orleans. These were kept busy in Mallory's navy-building program. Between the time of Fort Sumter and Confederates' defeat of the Union navy's first attempt to capture the city, April 1861-April 1862, New Orleans shipyards had constructed, converted or begun work on more than thirty warships. These included the *New Orleans* (twenty guns), the *Memphis* (eighteen), five gunboats (*Maurepas, Pontchartrain, Bienville, Livingston* and *Carondelet,* carrying together thirty guns), and the *Pickens* and *Morgan,* three guns apiece. Most of these were steamboats or tugs converted into not-too-formidable gunboats that would make their way upriver and participate in the unsuccessful Confederate attempt to defend Memphis in June 1862. That left in the lower Mississippi— between New Orleans and the two forts (named Jackson and St. Philip) guarding the riverbanks fifty miles below the city by crow's flight—a dozen vessels in Cmdr. John K. Mitchell's River Defense Fleet. Chief among them were the *Manassas, McRae, Mississippi* and the huge *Louisiana.* The latter two state-named craft would be completed just in time to help thwart Union naval captain David Porter's attempt to capture New Orleans on April 24, 1862. The *Manassas* and *McRae,* converted much earlier, would see action very soon indeed.

---

188   John G. Newton, "How We Found the Monitor," *National Geographic,* vol. 147, no. 1 (January 1975), 50.

One of Stephen Mallory's hopes for ironclad gunboats was that they would contest the Northern blockade and perhaps lift it for at least short periods. The C.S.S. *Manassas* gave the secretary early proof that his hopes were not in vain.

Like many Confederate warships, the *Manassas* was converted from a Northern vessel, the heavy tugboat *Enoch Train* in service at New Orleans. John A. Stevenson, secretary of the New Orleans Pilots' Benevolent Association, traveled to Montgomery in May 1861 and won government approval for him to raise money, buy the *Enoch Train,* and convert her into an ironclad ram at the John Hughes shipyard at Algiers, across the river from the Crescent City.

Unlike the *Virginia*-class ironclad design developed by John Brooke, with its slanted casemate walls and multiple gunports, the top of Stevenson's vessel would be a rounded surface, shaped like a floating cigar. Two smokestacks rose from the vessel's twin engines. A cast-iron ram was fixed to the prow, for Stevenson envisioned the ship wreaking havoc on the wooden-hulled blockaders downstream. For this reason the ram, finished in August 1861 and renamed the *Manassas,* carried only one gun, a Dahlgren 68-pounder smoothbore—again, a heavy weapon that would be effective against the Yankee navy's antiquated ships.

J. Thomas Scharf, an officer in the C.S. Navy, became one of its most authoritative chroniclers in 1887 with the publication of his *History of the Confederate Navy*. From it is to be seen a good description of Stevenson's unusual ram:

> She was built up with massive beams, seventeen inches in thickness, making a solid bow of twenty feet, and fastening them in the most substantial manner. Over this impenetrable mass was a complete covering of iron plates, riveted together, and fitted in such a way as to render her bomb-proof. Her only entrance was through a trap-door in her back, and her port cover sprang back as the gun was withdrawn. Her shape above water was nearly that of half a sharply pointed egg-shell, so that a shot would glance form her no matter where

it struck. Her back was formed of twelve-inch oak, covered with one-and-a-half-inch bar-iron. She had two chimneys so arranged as to slide down in time of action. The pilot-house was in the stern of the boat. She was worked by a powerful propeller, but could not stem a strong current. She carried only one gun, a sixty-eight pounder, in her bow. To prevent boarding, the engine was provided with pumps for ejecting steam and scalding water from the boiler over the whole surface.[189]

Capt. George N. Hollins arrived to take charge of the *Manassas,* plus three other vessels in what he called his "Mosquito Fleet": the *McRae,* formerly the 830-ton steam sloop *Marquis de la Habana,* turned into a privateer armed with a nine-inch pivot gun and six 32-pounders in broadside; the *Tuscarora,* a sidewheel tugboat (two guns); and the *Ivy,* a 454-ton sidewheel river steamer (two guns).

At the time, four Union warships blockaded the Mississippi at a point called the Head of the Passes, some seventy miles downstream from New Orleans. In command of them was Capt. John Pope (not the same-named Union general who would lose so spectacularly to Robert E. Lee in the battle of Second Manassas in August 1862). Pope had heard of Stevenson's construction of the *Manassas,* and worried about the inevitable battle with her ahead. "It is evident that we are entirely at the mercy of the enemy," he wrote; "we are liable to be driven from here at any moment, and, situated as we are, our position is untenable. I may be captured at any time by a pitiful little steamer mounting only one gun."

Pope was correct in his fearful prediction about that "little steamer mounting only one gun."

In early October 1861 Captain Hollins began planning to attack the enemy's blockaders at the Head of the Passes. On the night of October 12 the Confederate Mosquito Fleet moved downstream

---

189   J. Thomas Scharf, *History of the Confederate States Navy: From Its Organization to Victory at Sea* (Baltimore, 1887), pp. 264-65.

toward Pope's four ships: the *Richmond* (22 guns), *Vincennes* (20), *Preble* (10) and *Water Witch* (4). Hollins, aboard the *Manassas,* approached the *Richmond* at 3:30 a.m., guided by lanterns on her decks. Undetected—the crew of the *Richmond* was taking on coal, whose work muted the sound of Hollins' approach—the *Manassas* rammed solidly into her at ten knots. The *Richmond,* Pope's flagship, shuddered but did not sink. Yet the unnerved Northern captain ordered his little fleet to head back out to sea. In the darkness, though, the *Richmond* and *Vincennes* ran aground, providing perfect targets for the *McRae, Tuscarora* and *Ivy* as dawn began to shed light on the maritime battlefield.

In the growing daylight the Southern cannoneers also took aim at the *Water Witch* and *Prebel,* the latter of which they set afire, sinking her in three hours. The *Water Witch* was so mauled by the cannonade that she was unable to escape; crewmen aboard the *McRae* boarded and captured her.[190]

Captain Hollins summarized his neat little victory in a message that sent the people of New Orleans into a tizzy:

> Last night I attacked the blockaders with my little fleet, and succeeded, after a very short struggle to drive them all aground on the Southwest bar, except the sloop-of-war Preble, which I sunk. I have captured a prize from them, and after I got them fast on the sand I peppered them well. No casualties on our side. A complete success.[191]

THE *LOUISIANA* AND THE *MISSISSIPPI*

Most of the warships being built at New Orleans were sidewheel riverboats armed with up to eight or nine guns. They were not reinforced either by iron rails or thick wooden covering, and hence proved of marginal usefulness against the more heavily armed Union steam sloops and frigates.

---

190 *The U.S.S. Water Witch* (Savannah GA, 1974), p. 22.

191 R. Thomas Campbell, *Confederate Naval Forces on the Western Waters* (Jefferson NC, 2005), p. 32.

On the other hand were the huge ironclads C.S.S. *Mississippi* and *Louisiana*.

Asa and Nelson Tift were two brothers who had no shipbuilding experience, but they were friends of Stephen Mallory and wanted to help him build his navy. Literally *build,* for they bought land north of New Orleans and hired local workers to construct a shipyard. In the summer of 1861 they made their way to Richmond and showed the navy secretary plans for an ironclad resembling the *Virginia*. She would be 260 feet long, 53 feet wide, and carry up to twenty guns. Moreover, the brothers were rich—Asa president of a railroad and owner of a naval repair yard in Key West; Nelson a prominent Georgia planter—and they offered to build their gunboat on their own, if only Mallory would help in ordering material, machinery, armor and armament. Mallory readily agreed; literally, he had nothing to lose.

The Tifts went to work quickly, beginning in late August. Their work went fast in part because of the already-approved design for their warship, to which Mallory had assigned the name *Mississippi*. For building materials they used straight wood instead of the usual curved frames (this was intended to allow ordinary house carpenters to help in the construction, as skilled shipwrights were in high demand in the Confederacy of 1861). In just a hundred days the woodwork was finished, with all laborers working even on weekends. By mid-February 1862 the boilers were installed and the first shipment of iron plating had arrived from the Scofield and Markham Rolling Mill in Atlanta (which was making 150 two-inch plates a day). But there was delay in procuring wrought-iron shafts and propellers; the latter were being forged at Richmond's Tredegar Works. Securing all of the 400 tons of iron plating needed for her casemate and upper deck was also time-consuming; the last of it was laid on April 1. With her sixteen seven-inch rifled guns, George Hollins—who had whipped "Honest John" Pope at the Head of the Passes—considered the *Mississippi* the greatest ship in the world.[192]

---

192   James M. Merrill, *Battle Flags South: The Story of the Civil War Navies on Western Waters* (Rutherford NJ, 1970), p. 78.

He had not seen the *Louisiana*.

She was the largest warship laid down in the Confederacy during the South's War of Independence. Her length was 264 feet; width measured sixty-four. Thick layers of railroad T-rails protected the casemate, whose walls were slanted at forty-five degrees. Armament consisted of two 7-inch rifles, seven 6-inch rifles, three 9-inch smoothbores and four 8-inch smoothbores, sixteen guns in all (five on each side, three each at bow and stern). This complement was deemed so powerful that the *Louisiana* was not outfitted with an iron ram. As it was, with her four engines, boilers, shafts and propellers, when finished she weighed 2,118 tons. She was to be served by 325 officers and men.

The Confederate navy had contracted with Kentuckian E.C. Murray, an experienced steamboat builder, to oversee construction. Like the Tift brothers, Murray started work in August 1861 and experienced some of the same difficulties, especially procuring iron plating. There were only three rolling mills in the South capable of manufacturing gunboat armor. Besides Richmond and Atlanta, the Shelby Iron Company of Columbiana, Ala. produced iron plating in contracts with the C.S. Navy Department.[193]

Murray worked feverishly to get the *Louisiana* finished by the spring of 1862 when Confederate authorities in New Orleans expected the Yankees to start their campaign to take the South's largest city. Even with a short shipyard workers' strike in November 1861, Murray succeeded—but by just a few days. When Porter's ships started steaming up the Mississippi toward Forts Jackson and St. Philip on April 18 Capt. David Farragut, the C.S.S. *Mississippi* and the C.S.S. *Louisiana* were waiting for them.

NEPTUNE'S TRIDENT (2): TORPEDOES

Providentially, Stephen Mallory bought into Matthew Fontaine Maury's proposal for large-scale production of torpedoes.

---

193 Raimondo Luraghi, *A History of the Confederate Navy* (Annapolis, 1996), pp. 41-42.

The numbers tell the story: torpedos sank more Union vessels than did all the warships in the Confederate Navy. Put another way, forty-three U.S. ships were sunk by explosive mines while not one C.S. vessel was even damaged by a Northern-manufactured floating torpedo. (Gideon Welles' slow-moving Navy Department did not even develop a successful torpedo until the spring of 1864, far too late to be used in the war that was terminated by the Treaty of Washington in September 1863.)

As with ironclad warships, floating explosive devices had been used in the years before the American Civil War; Russia employed them in the Crimean conflict. So Matthew Fontaine Maury, "the father of the Confederate torpedo," cannot be given complete credit for this innovative and destructive weapon. He certainly deserves credit, however, for his recognition that for a nation's navy without sufficient ships to defend its 3,500-mile coastline, torpedos offered an ingenious (and relatively inexpensive, given the cost of building big ironclads) way of equalizing the odds favoring the Union navy.

Maury deserves credit for persistence, too. He first broached his ideas to a council advising Virginia governor John Letcher on how to create a state navy, but got a cold shoulder: floating mines would be ineffective, they said (Confederate naval historians have politely declined to name these nay-sayers in their narratives of Southern success). Governor Letcher, though, prudently kept Maury engaged with his idea, to the point of inviting him in June 1861 to put on a test of his torpedo in the James River off of Richmond's Rocketts Wharf.

When the appointed day came, the governor, Secretary Mallory, a few congressmen and naval officers gathered onshore to see Maury try his new weapon: a small keg of powder, weighted to sink down into the water, and fitted with a percussion cap to detonate by lanyard. The inventor and his son Robert were rowed to the middle of the river; the keg was dropped and the boat rowed to a safe distance; then Robert was given the lanyard to pull. BLOOEE! "The explosion was instantaneous," Robert recalled many years later; "up went a column of water fifteen or twenty feet; many stunned or dead fish floated around; the officials on the wharf applauded." Everyone clapped and cheered except the doubting Thomases of Letcher's commission, who at least shuffled away in respectful silence.

Soon Maury had a captaincy, a post (chief of the "Sea-Coast Harbor and River Defenses of the South"), and a budget of $50,000 to play with.

What he did with all this we shall see, notably at Port Royal, South Carolina, in November 1861, when Yankee warships learned that a revolution in naval warfare had unhappily befallen them.

NEPTUNE'S TRIDENT (3): PRIVATEERS

> A privateer, as the name imports, is a private armed ship, fitted out at the owner's expense, but commissioned by a belligerent government to capture the ships and goods of the enemy at sea, or the ships of neutrals when conveying to the enemy goods contraband of war....To a government with a small navy, or no navy, and with slender resources, privateers are a great advantage, because they not only cost the government nothing, being owned and equipped by private individuals, but, on the contrary, they are a source of revenue, for they are obliged to pay a percentage on the value of their captures, in consideration of the license.[194]

So does the early chronicler of the C.S. Navy, J. Thomas Scharf, define privateers in his seminal study of 1887. The war was but days old when, on April 17, 1861, President Davis published a proclamation inviting application for letters of marque and reprisal, "to aid this government in resisting so wanton and wicked an aggression by capturing or destroying merchant vessels of the U.S., under seal of the Confederate States."

In its act of May 6, 1861, officially recognizing the existence of war between the U.S.A. and C.S.A., the Confederate government

---

194   J. Thomas Scharf, *History of the Confederate States Navy: From Its Organization to Victory at Sea* (Baltimore, 1887), p. 71.

detailed regulations by which private vessels could obtain letters of marque, and how such privateers were expected to operate. In very formal and legalistic language it mandated that after capturing an enemy merchant ship, the privateer was to bring it into a Confederate port, or that of a nation with friendly ties to the Confederacy. There the ship and its contents "shall be proceeded against before a competent tribunal; and after condemnation and forfeiture thereof," the captured ship and goods would belong to the privateers, who were expected to sell them and keep the proceeds, minus the government's ten percent take.

The legislators' phrase for friendly ports—those "of a nation or State in amity with the Confederate States"—was intended to mean largely English and other European harbors. But these soon became unavailable to Confederate privateers. On May 14, 1861, the British government issued its Proclamation of Neutrality, which acknowledged a state of war between the U.S. and C.S. The Confederate government was accordingly recognized as a belligerent power in the eyes of international law (clearly a more elevated status than Lincoln's view that there was no C.S. government, only "rebel factions"). But if the Southerners gained a little from England's proclamation, they lost a lot more two weeks later when the implications of that proclamation were announced. On June 1, Her Majesty's government declared that armed ships of both belligerents were prohibited from carrying prizes into any port of the United Kingdom. This meant that Confederate privateers which captured a Northern merchantman in, say, the North Atlantic could not carry her into a British harbor to have her condemned and forfeited by the courts.

The British proclamation of June 1 was bad enough, but to make it worse, other governments of western Europe, most importantly Portugal, Spain and France followed with similar bans. This left Southern privateers no choice but to sail back to the Confederacy and attempt to run the blockade into a port such as Charleston or New Orleans. This worked well in the first several months of the war, when Lincoln's blockade was sieve-like in its weakness. But as the blockade got tighter, fewer privateers with their returning prizes got through; Northern blockaders caught them and returned the captured merchantmen back to their owners. 'The combination of the blockade and the inability to use neutral ports sealed the fate of the Confederate privateers," writes naval historian Bern Anderson; "by the end of the first year of the war, for all practical purposes, the privateers had disappeared."[195]

THE "HAPPY TIME"

In the war between Germany and the United States, 1941-45, that the Confederate States tried unsuccessfully to avert (and in which the C.S.A. remained neutral), German submarine captains called the first months of the conflict, December 1941 to mid-1942 the "happy time." They referred to the opening months of war when the U.S. Navy did not have enough destroyers and cruisers to protect American merchant vessels carrying arms and good to a beleaguered Britain. The *unterseebooten* consequently feasted on U.S. shipping off the Atlantic coastline, at least until the Navy acquired more warships to escort the convoys across the ocean.

For Confederate privateers, the happy time came in the summer of 1861 when the Union blockade was sieve-like and they could head out of Southern ports and return with captures as they pleased. The *New York Herald,* June 2, 1861, listed a dozen and a half Northern ships which had been taken into New Orleans alone as prizes. It stated that fully fifty-seven commercial vessels had been captured by Confederate privateers between April 15 and May 26 (a rate of more than one capture per day). In return, despite all its efforts, the U.S. Navy had only captured or destroyed two small privateers by August (the *Savannah* and the *Petrel*). The *Herald* on August 10 estimated that Rebel privateers and commerce raiders such as the *Sumter* had caused the loss of $20,000,000 worth of property. These losses were driving maritime insurance rates so high that Northern ships were unable to get charters, and English vessels were taking over the Yankees' trade. "Thus our shipping interest is literally ruined," it moaned.[196]

---

195   Bern Anderson, *By Sea and By River: The Naval History of the Civil War* (New York, 1962), p. 44.

196   Spencer C. Tucker, *A Short History of the Civil War at Sea* (Wilmington DE, 2002), pp. 112-15.

The *Savannah* had a happy time indeed. A fast 54-ton schooner, she was captured off Charleston by the *Lady Davis* and then was fitted out as a privateer in May.

Hers was the first letter of marque issued by the Confederate government on May 18, 1861. With a crew of thirty and an 18-pounder pivot gun, she was authorized under Capt. Thomas H. Baker "to act as a private armed vessel in the service of the Confederate states, on the high seas against the United States of America, their ships, vessels, goods and effects, and those of her citizens, during the pendency of the war now existing between the said Confederate States and the said United States."

She set out on June 3. The next day she came upon the brig *Joseph* of Rockland, Maine, on route from Cuba to Philadelphia with a cargo of sugar. She "fell an easy prize, and was sent into Georgetown, S.C., where she was condemned and sold."[197] After escorting the *Joseph* almost into port, the *Savannah* set out again in search of prizes, but she ran instead into a U.S. man-of-war, the *Perry,* which chased her down and put several shots through her before Capt. Baker surrendered. He and his crew were taken aboard, and eventually sent to New York while seven of the *Perry*'s crew manned the Savannah and took her also to New York.

Even though seafaring powers had long recognized privateers as legitimate belligerent ships whose crews were to be treated upon capture as prisoners of war, Federal officials in New York handcuffed Baker and his crew, threw them into jail, and prepared to put them on trial for piracy.

When Confederate officials read this in the New York papers, President Davis sent a message, dated July 6, 1861, to President Lincoln, promising to dole out to Union prisoners the same treatment given the crew of the *Savannah*. He further threatened to continue the retaliations until the U.S. promised to accord the captured prisoners their full rights.

---

197   J. Thomas Scharf, *History of the Confederate States Navy: From Its Organization to Victory at Sea* (Baltimore, 1887), 70.

It worked. Lincoln, who on May 16 had issued a proclamation declaring privateers as pirates, backed down and put pressure on the New York courts not to try the *Savannah*'s crewmen. Baker *et al.* were held as prisoners in "the Tombs" until February 1862, when they were exchanged.

CONFRONTING THE BLOCKADE: PORTS

For a Southern port city to be a good center for blockade running activity, it had to have five factors. First, of course, was a navigable channel. Second was a bar of at least twelve to twenty feet (meaning water that deep over the sand bars that naturally piled up outside harbors; Charleston's main ship channel, for example crossed the bar with eighteen feet of water). The harbor had to have an anchorage of good depth. An extra asset would be a commercial and banking center downtown. Finally, the place needed transportation facilities to inland markets, such as railroads, steamboats or canals.

The Confederacy's most important ports could be evaluated by these five criteria. (Actually, there was a sixth, as well: it had to be free of pesky Yankees; this ruled out Norfolk, which was blocked by Fort Monroe and Hampton Roads, the anchorage for the U.S. Navy's Home Squadron.) Going down the Atlantic coast was Beaufort Harbor/Morehead City, which because of is railroad at least possessed potential as a blockade running haven. Wilmington lacked commercial and banking houses, but had excellent rail connections to Virginia, the interior of North Carolina and to South Carolina.

Charleston was the Confederacy's most important Atlantic port, and in volume of shipping before the war ranked just behind New Orleans. She would obviously be a valuable haven for blockade runners (at least until the Yankees caught on). Because both Georgetown and Beaufort, S.C. lacked railways, on the other hand, they would be useless to blockade runners.

In Georgia, Savannah was second only to Charleston as a maritime center that would aid the Confederacy considerably. Then, farther down the coast, Brunswick, Ga. and Fernandina, Fla. were both deep-water sites, recently connected with railroads; without commercial capacities, they held potential for development.

Most of Florida's other harbors were ruled out for one reason or another. St. Augustine, Mosquito Inlet, Indian River Inlet and Cedar Key were all too shallow for deep-drafted vessels, and all except Cedar Key lacked railroads to distribute incoming supplies. Key West and Pensacola were firmly in U.S. control because of Fort Taylor and Fort Pickens. St. Marks, Fla. was only ten feet deep at her docks, but was connected to the interior by the Tallahassee Railroad.

Just as Savannah was second to Charleston on the Atlantic coast, so was Mobile on the Gulf after New Orleans. Of the Crescent City Stephen R. Wise, historian of Confederate blockade running, has written that New Orleans was "the largest city in the South and the one Confederate port of entry that could be rightfully called a major site of world commerce"; in 1860 she was the hub of the worldwide cotton trade.[198] Charleston, New Orleans and Mobile would rank as the Confederacy's busiest port cities. Because of shallow bars, though, Sabine City and Indianola, Tex. were unsuited for blockade runners, which left the deep-harbored Galveston.

There we have it: four excellent ports (New Orleans, Mobile, Savannah and Charleston) and four with potential (Beaufort, Wilmington, Brunswick and Fernandina).

THE WORK OF JOSIAH GORGAS AND CALEB HUSE

The success of Confederate blockade running during the war hinged on three elements: purchase of weapons and other military goods in Europe; their transport across the Atlantic, usually by British merchantmen to ports in the Bahamas, Bermuda and Cuba; then their loading and transport by specially designed blockade runners to Confederate ports, carefully eluding the Federal vessels standing outside Charleston, New Orleans and other Southern harbors.

---

198   Stephen R. Wise, *Lifeline of the Confederacy: Blockade Running During the War* (Columbia, 1988), p. 21.

The first part involved Josiah Gorgas and Caleb Huse. Their irony is that both of these architects of Southern logistical triumph were Yankees. Gorgas was born in Pennsylvania, 1818; Huse in Massachusetts, 1831. After graduation from West Point, Gorgas secured appointment to the Ordnance Corps. During U.S. forces' campaign from Vera Cruz to Mexico City he served Gen. Winfield Scott as ordnance chief. In the years after the Mexican War, Gorgas commanded a half-dozen U.S. arsenals in Vermont, Virginia, Alabama, Maine, South Carolina and Pennsylvania. After Gen. G.T. Beauregard recommended him, President Davis appointed Gorgas to be the Confederate army's chief of ordnance. In addition to establishing arsenals and ammunition works for domestic production, Gorgas looked abroad. The Confederate government prudently decided not to withhold the 1861 cotton crop from England—those officials who called for an embargo to pressure the British to recognize the Confederacy were drowned out by more practical thinkers. This gave plenty of money to Caleb Huse, who had been sent to England in May 1861 as Gorgas' chief purchasing agent in Europe.

Like Gorgas, Huse was a West Pointer (class of 1851; he was considerably younger than his boss). He was a bit brainy, too, as he demonstrated by his tenure at the Military Academy, 1852-1859, as professor of chemistry, mineralogy and geology. Just before the war he was teaching at the University of Alabama. His success in academia led the Confederate administration to consider him for a tough task: going abroad, identifying European arms – and materiel-makers willing to do business with the South (cotton sales converted to gold would help), and seeing to their freight being put on transoceanic ships heading for the New World (meaning the Confederate States of America).

Soon after Lincoln's proclamation of the blockade, Confederate leaders, especially Gorgas, developed the outlines of their transatlantic shipping system. Slow, hefty steamers from England and the continent would unload their cargoes of war materiel at Caribbean ports. Then the cargos would be loaded upon the blockade runners: fast, light-draft steamers specially constructed to sit low in the water, equipped for speed with strong boilers to be fueled with quick-burning and low-smoking anthracite coal.

Thus were the supplies to be brought into Confederate ports. After refueling and refitting, the same runners would take on as much cotton as they could safely carry and slip out of their Southern harbors to Bermuda, Nassau and Havana. Loaded aboard ocean-going steamers, the fleecy stuff was then shipped to Liverpool, where the firm of Fraser, Trenholm and Company acted as the South's main credit banker.

By this system, Huse bought 2 ¼ million dollars' worth of equipment into Confederate ports during the first year of the war. Frank E. Vandiver, the chronicler of Gorgas' and Huse's success, declares that by December 1862, "Huse had purchased 157,000 arms, large quantities of powder, some artillery , infantry equipments, harness, swords, percussion caps, saltpeter, lead," as well as non-ordnance items like clothing, blankets, cloth, shoes and medicines for the soldiers. In the last year of the war, September 1862-September 1863, the Confederate blockade running system brought in over of 113,000 small arms, huge quantities of lead, percussion caps and saltpeter (for gunpowder).[199]

And Northerners are still wondering why they lost.

GETTING ACROSS THE POND

Josiah Gorgas and Caleb Huse were smart and inventive, but they could not have succeeded in their blockade running initiatives without Fraser, Trenholm and Company.

John Fraser and Company was Charleston's largest exporting firm. Fraser was an ardent (and wealthy) Confederate; during the war he offered rewards of up to $100,000 for Confederate naval adventurers who found ways to sink those nuisances, the Yankee blockaders which kept him from doing a good gentlemanly business.

---

199   Frank E. Vandiver, Ploughshares into Swords: Josiah Gorgas and Confederate Ordnance (Austin, 1952), 91-93.

Fraser saw potential profits from bringing into the South coveted goods from Europe across the Atlantic, especially since George S. Trenholm, president of John Fraser and company was "one of the wealthiest and most influential men in the South," as Stephen R. Wise has written.[200] Their subsidiary company in Liverpool, Fraser, Trenholm and Company, was a natural for Caleb Huse to contact when he arrived in Liverpool in May 1861. Equipped with funds from the firm, Huse quickly began searching the market for Enfield rifles, rifled cannon and large stores of ammunition; he hired several purchasing houses to aid in his hunt. He was helped by naval captain James Bulloch, who had been sent to England "to buy items ranging from letterhead stationery to ironclad warships."[201] Like Huse, Bulloch hired agents to search all over Europe for arms, munitions, and supplies available for purchase. Maj. Edward C. Anderson also arrived in Liverpool to assist in this work.

The efforts of Huse, Bulloch, Anderson and their agents quickly paid off. By late July, English warehouses were filling up with weapons and military goods in such quantity that the next question arose: how to get all of this stuff across the Atlantic?

In stepped Fraser, Trenholm and Company with a proposal: in a transoceanic steamer owned by the firm, a big part of its considerable cargo space would be let out for a considered freight charge. Even though Ed Anderson considered the rates a bit steep, the Confederate purchasers had nowhere else to go, and so agreed to the deal.

The designated vessel was the *Bermuda,* a screw merchantman with a large cargo hull. Into it during mid-August 1861 was loaded a lot of materiel for the Confederate war effort, including 50,000 infantrymen's shoes and 24,000 blankets and 6,500 Enfields with 20,000 cartridges. All this would be sold to the national government at "patriotic pricing." There were private purchasers, too: Wade Hampton was raising a legion of troops. A man of some means, he arranged for the *Bermuda* to bring him 200 Enfields, 20,000

---

200   Stephen R. Wise, *Lifeline of the Confederacy: Blockade Running During the War* (Columbia, 1988), p. 9.

201   *Ibid.,* p. 41.

rounds and two six-pounder field guns (a legion in the early days of the Confederate war included complements of infantry, cavalry and artillery).

The *Bermuda* left Liverpool on August 22, heading straight for Savannah—remember, this was in the "happy time" between Lincoln's blockade proclamation and its actual baby-step enforcement some months later. The cargo-laden vessel reached her destination on September 18, easily passing through Lincoln's "blockade."

Bermuda anchored at Savannah for more than a month. During that time, she took onboard the other part of the across-the-pond blockade running operation: thousands of pounds of cotton to be borne from the South to Europe in order to finance other purchases by Huse, Bulloch, Anderson and agents—the "white gold" that gave English banking firms the wherewithal to keep pushing across the Atlantic goods that the Confederacy used to win its war for independence.

RUNNING THE BLOCKADE

Capt. Samuel F. Du Pont, commander of the U.S. Navy's South Atlantic Squadron, was responsible for blockading the ports of South Carolina, Georgia and Florida's eastern shore. In the first six months of the war his vessels managed to capture a few of the big, slow oceangoing vessels from England that tried to run directly into Confederate ports. But after he added more vessels outside the major harbors, and the same was done with the Gulf Blockading Squadron, enterprising Southerners developed a different system. British deep-draft vessels would dock in Bermuda, Havana or Nassau, unload their cargoes destined for Southerners' purchase, and take on cotton destined back across the Atlantic. Then fast, light-draft steamers—the blockade runners—would load up their cargo and attempt to sneak through the Union naval cordon to their port of destination.

Actually, there were two kinds of blockade running. Carrying cotton out from Charleston and Wilmington were specially-designed steamers: usually built in Scotland and England, Atlantic blockade runners were low-profile, shallow-draft side-wheel steamers weighing 400 to 600 tons. They were fast (eleven to fourteen knots), which made them quicker than most of the North's blockaders. For good measure they were painted light gray, had retractable smokestacks and burned smokeless Welsh anthracite coal, all to make them barely visible at sea. These runners favored Nassau (560 miles from Charleston, 640 from Wilmington, 570 from Savannah) and Bermuda (600 miles from Wilmington).

On the other hand, Gulf blockade runners favored small bays, inlets and rivers lining the coast as much as Mobile, New Orleans and Galveston. Their light, eight-to-ten-foot draft allowed them to get over bars and shoals that would have blocked bigger ships. The runners were both sailing schooners and steam sidewheelers. They set out from Sabine City, Brashear City and Lake Pontchartrain, with their usual destination as Havana.

While the runners held the advantages, the blockaders faced formidable difficulties. Many Union ships simply were not fast enough to catch the swift blockade runners. Du Pont told his superiors that in his whole squadron he had only one vessel, *Keystone State,* fast enough to chase down the Confederate runners. Furthermore, there were not enough blockaders. Again, Captain Du Pont tells the story. To cover Charleston's approaches, he had to maintain an arc of thirteen miles. To do this, though, he had only twelve vessels in early 1862, four of which were not even steamers. In a chase into harbor, most of the Union vessels were too deep-draft to get within a mile of the channels used by the blockade runners, which were thus given enough room to make their getaway. Finally were the problems of maintaining the ships themselves. The constant wear of wind and the sea broke down machinery, but the blockading squadrons' machine shops were frequently unable to handle the needed repairs. Frigates and gunboats were thus sent all the way back to New York, further weakening blockading forces that were already weak.

With the deck stacked thus, the numbers tell the rest. Using the Northern naval officers' parlance, "violations" were successful passages through the blockade, either out of Southern ports or into them. During the war, historians have counted 1,735 violations at Charleston and Wilmington alone. Before it fell in the spring of 1862, New Orleans had 300. Adding to Southern success, Richmond authorities halfway into the war committed to supervising the entire operation. In order to better manage the importation of arms and ammunition, the Confederate government bought blockade runners and operated them as C.S. vessels. According to Thomas L. Bayne, the Confederate official in charge of government steamers, "the 3 or 4 vessels owned by the Ordnance Department made 44 voyages through the blockade with cotton and munitions from January to August 13, 1863, without a single capture."[202]

Arms brought in thousands of modern Enfield rifles alone, as documented in Gorgas' and Huse's reports. This did not count the Trans-Mississippi Department, in which Kirby Smith's army and all Texas militia were suppled from abroad; nor does it count the importations by Georgia, North Carolina and other state governments. This leads historian Frank Lawrence Owsley to conclude that at least 600,000, and probably closer to 800,000 muskets came in through the blockade, thus providing a rifle for every man who had entered the Confederate army.

During the first year of the war, everyone recognized the ineffectiveness of the Union blockade, particularly British observers. On Aug. 20, 1861, British consul Brunch at Charleston reported that vessels came and went without hindrance; "the blockade is the laughing stock of the Southern merchant marine."[203] At Savannah, consul Allen Fullerton wrote about that time that ships were freely entering through the harbor's several channels. Two months later, consul Lynn at Galveston reported that only one frigate guarded the main channel, and that the two others were totally unguarded, allowing vessels to run in and out nightly without interruption.

Professor Owsley thus issues the judgement of other historians: "the blockade was very ineffective the first year and a half and never very effective during the entire war." Professor Still affirms

---

202   Frank Lawrence Owsley, *King Cotton Diplomacy: Foreign Relations of the Confederate States of America* (Chicago, 1931), p. 247.

203   *Ibid.,* p. 233.

the modern scholarly consensus when he describes the blockade simply as "a naval sieve." Worse for the North is his judgement that "the blockade absorbed hundreds of ships and thousands of men, and generally had little effect on the war's outcome."[204]

---

204 *Ibid.,* p. 237; William N. Still, Jr., "A Naval Sieve: The Union Blockade in the Confederate War," *Naval War College Review,* vol. 36, no. 3 (May-June 1983), 38, 45.

Chapter Four:

The Confederacy Girds for Victory

JUBAL EARLY'S BOLD RAID

The takeover of Baltimore by pro-Confederates and the cut-off of Washington's lines of communication and reinforcement provided Southerners with an opportunity. On April 20, an excited railroad superintendent in Petersburg, Virginia, wired Secretary of Defense Walker: "Colonel Owen, president of the Virginia and Tennessee Railroad, has just reached here from Baltimore. He states the city is in arms and all are Southern men now. He says bridges north of Baltimore have been burned, and no more troops can come from the North unless they march, and in large bodies, as Maryland is rising. Lincoln is in a trap. An hour now is worth years of common fighting. One dash and Lincoln is taken, the country saved, and the leader who does it will be immortalized."[205] Jefferson Davis, however, chose to let Virginia authorities determine the right course of action. To Governor Letcher he merely wrote, "Sustain Baltimore, if practicable. We re-enforce you."[206] In Richmond, Letcher's military advisory council voted to send a thousand rifles to George Steuart and Bradley Johnson in Baltimore. Steuart hoped that Virginia would do more, but on the

---

205   *O.R.*, vol. 2, 771-72.
206   *Ibid.*, 773.

19th, the day of the riots, the state was just beginning to organize its military forces. Until things became more settled, Governor Letcher was loath to authorize any movement of troops.

In Alexandria, little more than a bridge-length way from the Yankee capital, there champed and chafed a Virginian itching to rush across the river. Jubal Anderson Early, Lynchburg lawyer and Mexican War veteran, had helped raise a militia company in early April, then had been ordered by Governor Letcher to take charge of volunteers organizing at Alexandria. By the time of the Baltimore riot he had around 700 armed men, including the "Washington Volunteers," Marylanders from D.C. who had packed up and marched across the Long Bridge, intent upon helping Confederates to capture the capital. Such a coup began to tantalize Colonel Early, despite his numerical inability to bring it off. Nevertheless he desired to take some action in the wake of the unrest across the river. He had developed a secret line of communication with Steuart, a chain of citizen-couriers all along the route from Baltimore to Alexandria. Heedless of Mayor Brown's pleas that the Baltimore militia confine itself to the city limits, Steuart contemplated a dramatic use of force. He communicated his thoughts to Early, and on the evening of the twentieth the two leaders met secretly at the Marshall House hotel in Alexandria.

The plan they laid out called for nothing less than a march into Mr. Lincoln's city. While a few Confederates made showy pretense of activity on Arlington Heights overlooking the Long Bridge, Early's main body would march north to the Chain Bridge. Steuart's Marylanders would strike the Federal guard from behind while the Virginians stormed across the span. From there, a quick march down the C. & O. Canal road would carry the combined force into Georgetown and the northern gates of Washington City.

Steuart promised to have 200 militia under his command; with Early's troops the Southerners would still number fewer than a thousand. There were at least twice that many U.S. regulars and District militia in Washington, but Early counted on surprise and confusion to retard the Federals' deployment against him. Once in the city, the Confederates planned to strike straight for the

White House. How far they got would depend upon their speed and luck. Success hinged on timing, particularly on whether Union reinforcements hit town before Early did; regiments from Massachusetts and New York were expected in the capital any day from their circuitous route via Annapolis. For this reason Early and Steuart planned to launch their raid within forty-eight hours, in the early dawn of April 22.

"Jubal's Raid," as the event has by now come to be called, showed in grand manner both the passion and pandemonium that characterize excited, untrained recruits in the opening days of war. In truth, as a military operation the Confederates' sortie against Washington was preposterous. Partly for that reason Early chose not to relay his plans to the Governor in Richmond, whose immediate rejection of the whole scheme was predictable. But the very hare-brainedness of the plan was the element that excited Early, for any bold raid across the Potomac targeting the enemy capital, even if the Southerners did not get very far and were forced to retire, would nonetheless serve as a psychological victory and electrifying morale-boost for the Confederacy in the very second week of the war.

Early's and Steuart's excitement was shared by their horsemen, and threatened to undo the whole operation. The plan called for a swift, silent overwhelming of the sentries posted at the Chain Bridge on the morning of the 22d. Marching from the northeast, Steuart's Baltimoreans approached the Union camps with the same loud riotousness they had displayed against the Sixth Massachusetts three days earlier. At first sight of a blue uniform, scores of muskets, shotguns and pistols went off, mostly in the air. Federal guards panicked, broke and ran, carrying their alarm into Georgetown three miles away. The Virginians then safely crossed the Potomac, but the element of surprise was blown. Early and Steuart consulted hastily and reshaped their route: instead of heading straight into town, where they could expect stiff opposition, they mapped a march to the northeast through Tennallytown, across Rock Creek and down upon Washington from the rear. The route, about six miles east, then another three down the Seventh Street Road, could be covered well enough if the men were kept under control and in column.

But control was marginal and the columns disorderly as the Southerners rode into the District of Columbia. In violation of orders for silence, the men hooted and hollered in exultant hope that their fell swoop would end the war barely as it was just getting under way. Their racket fairly broadcast the Confederate line of march to the whole countryside and, thanks to loyalists on fleet horses, to officials at the United States War Department. Neither Early nor Steuart anticipated the quickness with which word of their approach spread. By the time they reached Tennallytown, about 9 a.m., the Southerners encountered scores of townspeople already turned out, awaiting a glimpse of Rebel marauders. Some cheered; others shouted dark threats of Union troops rallying just down the road, readying for battle (as they indeed were). The first fighting of consequence occurred near Rock Creek about ten o'clock. Early managed to get his men into a line of battle impressive enough to frighten away some U.S. cavalrymen. The Confederates' next opposition was steadier and more substantial. As they approached the Seventh Street Road, Steuart's men spotted an earthwork fortification teeming with Yankees. Early ordered an immediate deployment in the face of this obstacle.

Fort Stevens (named for the Pennsylvania Congressman) was one of those ditch-and-log works which General Scott had ordered built a month before. It was still incomplete, but it had at least one battery of field artillery ready to bear on the Rebels. Even more, behind its parapets, nearly five hundred District home guards, Pennsylvania militia and armed government clerks stood ready to defend the capital then and there. Lt. Col. Horatio Wright commanded this contingent. Adding to its number, if not to its firepower, was a crowd of curious politicians who had hopped their carriages and ridden out to the fort to witness their first battle.

Chief among these onlookers was the Chief Executive himself, who rode out to Fort Stevens accompanied by his wife and a squadron of cavalry. The Lincolns' carriage headed for the barracks and stopped at the door of the hospital. An assistant surgeon, Dr. C.C.V. Crawford, did not try to dissuade the President when he insisted upon ascending the parapet for a view of the Rebels gathering yonder for battle. Before anyone could stop him, Lincoln had joined the soldiers on the firing line. Rifles were already cracking, and lead whizzed as the President peered over the rampart. An excited Colonel Wright rushed up and pleaded with Lincoln to withdraw, but the President refused. Then a Southern sniper's bullet struck a nearby cannon, ricocheted off and struck Surgeon Crawford in the left leg. Standing beside him, Lincoln lightly remarked, "that was quite a carom" (the President was a billiards-player).[207]

For Wright, this was the last straw. He ordered all civilians down from the parapet, and even considered putting his Commander-in-Chief under armed guard when Lincoln still would not budge. Finally, as more rifle balls kicked up splinters and puffs of dirt in the log-and-earthwork protecting the President, a young staff officer—later identified as Oliver Wendell Holmes, Jr.—shouted, "Get down, you damn fool!" This rude salutation was enough to draw Lincoln's attention. He withdrew to safety, but not before quipping to Holmes, "Good-bye, Captain. I'm glad to see you know how to talk to a civilian."[208]

Southern sharpshooters on the other side were unaware of the premium target they had had in their sights. As they sniped away from surrounding trees and houses, however, the Virginians and Marylanders faced a vexing enemy fire, particularly from artillery. Their uncomfortable position, with a sizeable force of Yankees dug in on their front, and with probably more on the way, brought Early and Steuart to a decision. They could not attack the work, nor could they circumvent it, leaving it intact as they rode on to Washington. Moreover, every passing moment gave the Federals time to rally their troops in the capital. There was thus little choice

---

207 John Henry Cramer, *Lincoln Under Fire: The Complete Account of His Experiences During Early's Attack on Washington* (Baton Rouge, 1948), p. 44.

208 *Ibid.*, p. 103.

but to withdraw back across the Potomac. By three o'clock in the afternoon, they had slipped away, and Colonel Wright with his garrison was only too happy to see them leave.

"Jubal's Raid" caused repercussions far greater than the actual event itself, which boiled down to a thousand hallooing Rebels riding across the Potomac into D. C., meeting their match in a Federal fortification, and withdrawing back across the river, all in less than a day's time. Casualties, too, for the event were slight: two Southerners killed and eighteen hurt, against twelve Federals wounded. At the same time, Jubal's Raid scared the daylights out of Washington. The Chain Bridge guards streaming in, the pell-mell massing of troops in the streets, and their quick-stepping out on Seventh Street communicated crisis if not calamity to the population with the electricity of a telegraph. Rumor-mongers spread warnings that secessionists planned to burn the whole city to the ground. Offices and businesses closed when owners and workers rushed home to look after loved ones. A few militia companies totally collapsed in the hour of need. One, the Potomac Light Infantry, actually disbanded at word of Rebels on the way, giving rise later to the jokesome toast, "The P.L.I., invincible in peace, invisible in war."[209]

General Scott, ailing with gout and confined to his carriage, nevertheless directed defensive preparations within the city throughout the day. Barricades were thrown up on the streets around the Executive Square, the Capitol and City Hall hill. The Treasury Building was sealed up as a citadel in itself with iron-plated windows; the men inside laid in stocks of food and water for a protracted siege. Anxious guards manned their posts as each hour passed, and still no Rebels were to be seen. By late afternoon, news of Early's retreat from Fort Stevens began to relax the public tension.

Raid, expedition, mere stunt: whatever it was, the Confederate press had a field day over it. Jubal Early became an instant hero, especially after reports in the Northern papers told how "Old Jube" had made President Lincoln duck his head at Fort Stevens. It was a

---

209 Margaret Leech, *Reveille in Washington 1860-1863* (New York, 1941), p. 64.

stunt, all right, never to be repeated again in the war. Union troops began feeding into the capital, soon to cross the Potomac themselves and make Alexandria their own base on Virginia soil. But Early had realized his hopes of a Confederate psychological victory in the very first days of the war. As it happened, Richmond and Montgomery overlooked rashness in favor of results. Early emerged from the entire incident with a mild censure from Governor Letcher, a Confederate commission from Montgomery, and eventually a position of high rank in General Robert E. Lee's Army of Northern Virginia. Lee first met with Early a few days after the raid, and the Commander of the Virginia State forces politely heard Early's excited recitation of his "great expedition," replete with profanity (especially when talking about the Yankees). Thereafter Lee began calling Early "my bad old man," a characterization which stuck throughout the war. It was said that Jube Early was the only man who could cuss around General Lee and get away with it. [210]

Jubal's Raid also gave the President of the United States his baptism of fire. Lincoln's billiard hall comment at the wounding of Surgeon Crawford was picked up later by the Northern press; Democratic newspapers criticized the President for making jokes over a wounded soldier. On the other hand, the President earned plaudits for riding out to Stevens and sharing the same hostile musketry as the common soldiers; Abraham Lincoln remains the only President of the United States, while in office, to undergo enemy fire. Later, there was speculation that Lincoln's clothing may have saved him from injury; Early's and Steuart's snipers probably aimed for uniformed soldiers rather than plain-clothed civilians. And at that early stage of the war, the Northern President's stovepipe hat was not yet the familiar trademark it would be later on. Had Early known of the high prize bobbing his head over the ramparts, the Confederates may have launched a full assault on the fort. At the same time, we can only speculate today what might have happened, and whether the Union might have come closer to

---

210   Gary W. Gallagher, "Jubal Anderson Early," in William C. Davis, ed., *The Confederate General*, 6 vols. (Richmond, 1991), vol. 2, 89.

victory in the Southern War for Independence, had Lincoln been struck in the head by a Confederate minie ball at Fort Stevens on that April day in 1861.

VIRGINIANS ORGANIZE THEIR STATE FORCES

Euphoria over the naval coup of April 21 (the seizure of the U.S. shipyard at Norfolk) gave way quickly to Virginians' concern with other military matters...such as creating an army overnight. They already had a commander; on the nineteenth the Virginia Convention created the position of major general as chief of all state forces. An advisory council recommended that Governor Letcher give the responsibility to fifty-four year-old Robert E. Lee of Arlington—brilliant West Pointer, talented engineer and Winfield Scott's designee as next general-in-chief of the old army. Letcher accepted the advice, sent messengers to Arlington, and brought Lee by train to Richmond. On April 22 after a long conference with the Governor, Lee accepted a major general's rank and command of Virginia's military forces.

What forces there were had hastily assembled in just a few days after the Convention's call to arms went out on April 17. As in other states, pre-war militia companies formed the nucleus of the initial regiments. The First Virginia included such luminous units as the Richmond Light Infantry Blues and the Richmond Howitzers. Companies organized back in '59 to repel John Brown's Raid again gathered at Charleston to form the Second Virginia Volunteers (it was they who seized the United States arsenal at Harpers Ferry, April 18). Dozens of companies sprang up all over the state; General Lee helped sort them out into regiments and brigades. He oversaw the establishment of training camps, directed the distribution of arms and equipment and, in the manner of any good administrator, dealt with mounds of paperwork. With Governor Letcher Lee chose officers and gave out commissions: for Thomas J. Jackson of the Virginia Military Institute came a colonelcy with orders to take charge at Harpers Ferry; to Joseph E. Johnston, who had just resigned as U.S. Quartermaster General, went a brigadier generalship and command of state troops in and around Richmond. An important post, Chief of Ordnance for the

Virginia State Army, went to another of the Old Dominion's native sons, George H. Thomas. In early March Governor Letcher had begun wooing Thomas, a West Pointer and army major, to resign his commission. At first he resisted. "It is not my wish to leave the service of the United States as long as it is honorable for me to remain in it," Thomas wrote on March 12, "and therefore as long as my native State remains in the Union it is my purpose to remain in the army."[211] Five weeks later, when Virginia seceded, Thomas kept his word and resigned. Letcher promptly gave him the ordnance job. (His reputation for efficiency was such that President Davis eventually named Thomas his Chief of Staff.)

Other state appointments sent officers to Alexandria, to Norfolk, and to all places on Virginia's borders where an attack by the Yankees might come. In anticipation of such, General Lee worked out an outline for the state's defense. To deter intrusion by the Federal navy, he ordered batteries built along the Potomac, Rappahannock, York and James Rivers. Soon forts, mounting the heavy guns captured at Norfolk, crowned bluffs all along Virginia's eastern tributaries. He assembled a small force at Yorktown to keep watch on the Federals holding Fort Monroe; for a while Lee contemplated offensive operations against the place, but knew that Union naval strength would ultimately keep Monroe in enemy hands. (It did, until the Treaty of Peace, when Virginia finally took possession of the longtime Yankee toe-hold.) He also assisted Colonel Jackson in building a small army at Harpers Ferry. But the most pressing point of danger was the area right across the Potomac from Washington. There, too, Virginia troops gathered in watchful waiting, under strict orders from Lee to remain on the defensive— particularly in light of Jubal Early's recent rambunctious raid. Colonel Philip St. George Cocke took charge of the militia in the area, and from his headquarters at Alexandria sent Lee a stream of telegrams demanding more men and more supplies, complaining loudly of enemy strength across the river, &c.—irritating messages they were, but assurance to Lee and Letcher that Cocke was not apt to stage anything like a repeat of Early's march on Washington.

---

211 Freeman Cleaves, *The Life of General George H. Thomas* (Norman OK, 1948), p. 65.

MARYLAND SETTLES DOWN

For the Virginians involved in Jubal's Raid, safety lay across the Potomac, which they recrossed at a ferry upriver from the Chain Bridge. Many of Steuart's men also sought Confederate territory, as did other secessionists in Maryland and the District as soon as they learned of Early's retreat. The exodus of Southern sympathizers from Baltimore brought calm to the city; on April 25 work even began on repairing the railroads which Isaac Trimble's men had torn up. Maryland at last appeared safe for the Union. Union Governor Hicks no longer feared disunionists in his legislature, which he convened on April 26. Three days later the state House of Delegates voted conclusively against secession, 53-13.

In Washington, the Baltimore riots began to be forgotten when communications with the North were reopened and the capital's residents lost their sense of being besieged. Moreover, the arrival of fresh troops, beginning with the New York 7th Regiment on April 25, assured Lincoln that his city was finally secure. More soldiers arrived daily, pitching camp all around the city and building forts that would protect the Union capital from any attempt by Confederates to repeat Jubal Early's fruitless but exciting raid.

By May 9 Union soldiers were marching through Baltimore unmolested. And on the 13th the city received its Federal garrison, part of which was the 6th Massachusetts, returned to the site of its bloodying with a measure of sweet revenge. With secessionists like Steuart and Trimble gone to Virginia along with many of their followers, Southern sympathizers were forced to keep their sentiments silent. The Federal commander, Maj. Gen. Benjamin F. Butler, issued a boastful but intimidating statement for the city press: "A detachment of the forces of the federal government under my command have occupied the city of Baltimore, for the purpose, among other things, of enforcing respect and obedience to laws."[212] The formerly strident secessionist Police Chief Kane now conducted himself as a dutiful public servant. Before long Baltimore took on the air of any other Northern city. Residents

---

212   James O. Hall, "Butler Takes Baltimore," *Civil War Times Illustrated*, August 1978, p. 46.

waved the Stars and Stripes on the streetsides whenever Union regiments marched down Pratt Street, whose cobblestones had formerly been smeared with Northern soldiers' blood. Marylanders even began flocking to the Union colors, eventually filling the four regiments requested by the President on April 15.

DEFENDING WASHINGTON

Shortly after hostilities commenced President Lincoln is said to have staked out the three requirements of the Union war effort: "defend Washington, blockade the ports, and retake government property."[213] As with all things in war, this was far more easily said than done.

Regarding the first of these three objectives, Lincoln and his administration painfully felt the Constitutional Convention's decision in 1787 to locate the young nation's capital in the Southern states. In 1860 Virginia and Maryland were very much slave states; the sale of Negroes in the District of Columbia had only been forbidden by the Compromise of 1850. Thus in the spring of '61, Abraham Lincoln's government found itself quartered in proximity to—nay, in the very midst of—those rebellious "combinations" which the new President had vowed to suppress.

For one thing, there were in the capital area only about 400 U.S. troops: 200-plus marines at the Marine barracks, and some more officers and men at the Washington arsenal. For another, there were Southern sympathizers in the city itself. The District of Columbia boasted four venerable militia companies, but one of these, the National Rifles, was openly disloyal. After Fort Sumter its captain loudly proclaimed his intention "to guard the frontier of Maryland and help keep the Yankees from coming down to coerce the South!"[214] At least one D.C. company had formed in December 1860 to help the incipient rebellion; the "Washington Volunteers" had organized to help force the surrender of the city to Virginia or Maryland, should hostilities arise. Now, with hostilities arisen,

---

213   William J. Roehrenbeck, *The Regiment That Saved the Capital* (New York, 1961), p. 24.

214   Benjamin Franklin Cooling, *Symbol, Sword, and Shield: Defending Washington during the Confederate War* (Hamden, CT, 1975), pp. 9-10.

this company of mostly Marylanders awaited events. (It eventually enrolled in Virginia service as part of the 1st Virginia Infantry Regiment.)

When the President called out ten companies of the District militia on April 9, half the men refused to take the oath of national allegiance. Rather than do so, eighteen members of one unit, the National Rifles, simply resigned. So did twenty men of the Washington Light Infantry, and seventeen of the Potomac Light Infantry. Some did so, however, in apprehension of being sent outside the District. Once assured of their home defense role, most of the Washington militiamen were sworn in at muster sites around the city. Some bystanders hissed them as they took the oath, although they were out-shouted by cheering loyalists.

News of the firing on Sumter, which reached the city telegraphically on the afternoon of April 12, galvanized Union sentiment. City residents formed three new companies and were issued muskets. With these and quickly armed government workers, the Federal administration had as least the makings of a local defense force. Lincoln put the aged and corpulent General-in-Chief of the Army, Winfield Scott, in charge of garrisoning the city. Scott stationed his men at public buildings, the Navy yard, and main roads at the outskirts of town. Artillerymen trained guns on the Long Bridge, connecting Washington and Alexandria. Several sloops patrolled the Potomac cautiously. The Navy commandeered private boats to help guard the Chain Bridge, three miles upriver from Georgetown. If the Rebels got across the Potomac, however, Scott acknowledged that they would have to be fought block by block. Hence he planned a defense of Washington that made each government building a little fortress. Captain William B. Franklin took charge of the Treasury, and arranged fields of fire by posting men at the nearby State Department and Riggs Bank. At the Capitol itself, Major Irvin McDowell barricaded the doors and windows with boards and stones.

All this very rushed and very obvious military preparation unnerved many civilians in the city, and naturally aided the spreading of unfounded rumor. Virginia cavalry on the fourteenth were already reported across the Chain Bridge (never mind that that state itself had not yet seceded). Some militia volunteers sent their wives and children out of the city in wagons packed with household items. The excited talk of a Rebel rush into Washington, improbable as it was, hindered further recruitment of Union home guards. Some men refused to be sworn into the local defense units, confessing fears of reprisal when the Virginians occupied the capital. Would-be office seekers in the new Lincoln administration now emptied their hotels and boarded the cars northbound for Baltimore, which was thought a safer place than Washington for the moment. Up and down Seventeenth Street a jam of wagons, carriages, drays, even baby carts lurched and creaked, overboarded with heirlooms and clothing, never moving fast enough to satisfy their worried owners, who were seeking the quickest possible egress from the nation's presumably doomed capital.

After Lincoln's call to arms of April 15 pledges of troops poured in from Northern governors, mindful of the capital's precarious situation. The issue, though, hinged on when they would arrive and, given the burning of the rail bridges from Baltimore, how.

To meet the crisis, Lincoln conferred with General Scott. They worked out a plan whereby troops could be brought in without transit to Baltimore: from Philadelphia by train down the east bank of the Susquehanna to Perryville, Maryland; then across the Chesapeake via ferry to Annapolis; and on to Washington over the rails. It would be days, however, before this circuitous pipeline fed troops to the capital. In the meantime the distressed President asked himself as much as anyone else, "Why don't they come? Why don't they come!"[215] No one knew. On Sunday the 21st came the welcome word that two regiments, the 7th New York and 8th Massachusetts, were at or near Annapolis. Another, from Rhode Island, was rumored to be not far behind. But then, that night, pro-secesh Baltimoreans seized their city's telegraph office and cut communications with Washington. President Lincoln was more in the dark than ever.

---

215 *Allan Nevins, The War for the Union,* 6 vols. (New York, 1959), vol. 3, 83.

General Scott's task was to insure the safety of Washington with what soldiers he had on hand. Fortunately, loyal Washingtonians now rallied to the colors. Treasury department clerks and government workers from other bureaus volunteered in numbers. Old men formed a unit called the Silver Greys' Home Guard. Ethnic groups such as the French and Italians organized unto themselves, as did other groups. Eventually, as many as thirty-three militia companies enrolled in the District, giving the capital some increased sense of security. In this setting, General Scott meted out defense assignments. Major Irvin McDowell commanded at the capital, with some of the 6th Massachusetts making the very Senate chamber their makeshift quarters. Maj. David Hunter was in charge at the White House. The State Department, Post and Patent Offices, Smithsonian Institution and several other governmental buildings all got their guards.

After several days of isolation, the crisis broke around noon on Thursday, April 25, when a train brought in the gray-uniformed men of the 7th New York. After unloading and spiffying up, the regiment was formed for a triumphal march down Pennsylvania Avenue. The citizenry greeted them with great expressions of relief and gratitude. "As they passed along," a reporter observed, "they were received with frequent cheers, and the ladies continually waved their handkerchiefs, while smiles were on every face. No body of men could ever meet a more enthusiastic or hearty greeting than they ... .When in place of the drums and fifes, the full band struck up, the whole city danced with delight. A greater change never passed over a town."[216]

Washington had been saved.

Two Virginians in The Old Army Side With Their State

Confederate historians agree that Robert Edward Lee's decision on April 20, 1861 to resign from the United States Army and cast his lot with Virginia was an indispensable element in the South's successful War for Independence. Almost as universal is the speculation that if Lee had remained in the old army and had been

216   Roehrenbeck, *ibid.,* p. 125.

given command of Federal forces in 1861, as General Winfield Scott wanted, the North might have won its war to preserve the Union.

Lee's decision did not come easily for him.

Son of a Revolutionary War hero, "Light Horse Harry" Lee, and born and raised in Virginia, Lee at eighteen entered the Military Academy in 1825. He studied hard and graduated second in the class of 1829. Lee's career in the army began propitiously with his commission in the engineers, the army's most coveted branch. He helped build Fort Pulaski, downriver from Savannah, Georgia, at a time (the 1830's, before rifled artillery) when masonry forts were considered impregnable. Lee then served for three years at Fort Monroe in Virginia; held a desk job in Washington; and after promotion to First Lieutenant, set out in 1837 to St. Louis to help the U.S. Engineers rechannel the Mississippi to better serve the commercial interests of the river city. From 1841 to 46 the now-Captain Lee was stationed at Fort Hamilton, near New York City, in charge of strengthening that ten-year-old bastion. Outbreak of war with Mexico led to his transfer west, where General Scott called upon his service. In the American campaign from Vera Cruz to Mexico City, Lee conducted such skilled reconnaissance that a brother officer observed, "his talent for topography was peculiar, and he seemed to receive impressions intuitively, which it cost other men much labor to acquire."[217] At Cerro Gordo, Lee's personal reconnaissance of Santa Anna's lines contributed to the Americans' crushing victory, a feat commended by General Scott. He was brevetted major to date from April 18, the day of the battle; after his recons led to U.S. victories at Contreras and Churubusco, he was again brevetted lieutenant colonel. By these exploits Lee came to be one of Scott's most highly regarded officers, "the very best soldier I ever saw in the field," as the old general phrased it.[218] For his siting of the batteries that reduced Chapultepec, Mexico City's key fortress, Lee received a brevet full colonelcy, though his permanent rank remained as Captain.

---

217 Clifford Dowdey, *Lee* (Boston, 1965), p. 85.

218 *Ibid.,* p. 91.

Postwar duty in the States brought for Lee something of the old (fort construction near Baltimore, 1848-52), but also something new: superintendency of the Military Academy at West Point. After almost three years there, Lee was transferred from the engineers' corps into the field to become lieutenant colonel of the 2d Cavalry. The regiment went west in the summer of 1855, eventually being stationed in the Texas frontier. From this desolate posting he returned back east, July 1857, on leave in order to care for his family's affairs at Arlington, across the Potomac from the nation's capital. In October 1859 Lee was given command of the U.S. troops and state militia which subdued John Brown's raid on Harpers Ferry. Again sent westward, Lieutenant Colonel Lee was riding to take command of the 2d cavalry in Texas when South Carolina seceded. The secession of other states led Lee on January 23, 1861, to write a kinsman that he feared the consequences of disunion, but that in the event of conflict, "I shall return to my native state and share the miseries of my people and save in defence will draw my sword on none."[219]

Relieved of duty with the Second, Lee on February 4 was ordered to Washington to report to General-in-Chief Scott. Rejoining his family at home March 1, Lee was soon in Scott's offices, where the old general promised Lee immediate promotion to colonel and after that hinted a high field command in the U.S. Army. Lee may have expressed some of what he had been telling others: "I shall never bear arms against the Union, but it may be necessary for me to carry a musket in defense of my native state, Virginia, in which case I shall not prove recreant to my duty" (to R.W. Johnson); "he fervently hoped that some agreement would be reached to avert such a terrible war; but under no circumstance could he ever bear his sword against Virginia's sons" (to George B. Cosby).[220] After their meeting in Scott's office, neither man recorded what was said, although the General-in-Chief probably asked Lee to think the whole thing over before making a move. A few weeks later, Lee received his promotion to colonel, but not before Confederate

---

219   Douglas Southall Freeman, *R.E. Lee: A Biography*, 4 vols. (New Orleans, 1934), vol. 1, 421.

220   *Ibid.*, 425-26.

Defense Secretary Walker wrote him, offering a brigadiership in the new army, which was the highest rank authorized so far by the Congress. Lee took no action, but continued to observe the mood of his fellow Virginians as events heated up over Sumter.

The firing on the fort and Lincoln's troop call-up put even more pressure on Lee as he agonized over his torn allegiances: to his home state and people he could not fight against, *versus* to the Union and flag he had sworn himself to defend. On April 17, as he learned that the Virginia Convention had entered into secret proceedings, Colonel Lee was summoned by General Scott to call the next day upon Francis Blair, the Washington editor known to be well connected to the administration's highest circles. Dutifully on the 18th Lee made his way to Blair House on Pennsylvania Avenue, where his host explained that General Scott and President Lincoln hoped Lee would assume command of the army being formed to put down the rebellion. Lee later recalled how he politely but firmly said no: "I declined the offer he made me to take command of the army that was to be brought into the field, stating as candidly and courteously as I could, that though opposed to secession and deprecating war, I could take no part in an invasion of the Southern States." Then Lee went to Scott's office and informed him, too, of the decision which Scott admitted he had feared all along.

The next day Lee learned that the convention had passed its ordinance of secession. That night at his Arlington home, after much pacing in its second-story bedroom, Lee sat down and composed his terse letter of resignation from the United States Army. He wrote a longer, much warmer letter to Scott, thanking him for his many kindnesses, explaining his "struggle" as events forced him to "separate myself from a service to which I have devoted all the best years of my life and all the ability I possessed."[221]

Already there was talk in the Virginia press that the newly independent republic should call on Lee to command its military forces. On the 21st, Lee received an invitation to meet with Governor Letcher in Richmond. There, on April 22, Letcher presented an

---

221   *Ibid.*, 437, 441.

offer which had been approved by the State Convention: command of all military and naval forces of Virginia, with the rank of major general.

Lee's astounding string of unbroken victories (after a rather indifferent performance in the Seven Days) at Second Manassas, Sharpsburg, Fredericksburg and Chancellorsville unquestionably broke the back of the Federal effort to restore the union. The defeat of McClellan's army in Maryland, which led to the Lincoln government's hasty relocation to Philadelphia and the British government's diplomatic recognition of the Confederate States, by itself virtually assured Southern victory in the war, though the conflict would drag on for almost another year. Robert E. Lee therefore richly deserves the popular acclaim which has been bestowed upon him by Southerners as "the Father of His Country."

Beside Lee's towering achievement, the war contribution of another Virginian was less luminous, but important nonetheless. Like Lee, George H. Thomas struggled with his conflicting loyalties at the outbreak of the war. Born in Southampton County in July 1816, Thomas' career in some ways followed Lee's: West Point, Old Army, brevets in Mexico, instructor at the Military Academy, even service in the 2d cavalry out west. In the spring of 1861 he held the rank of major in the cavalry. Like Lee, Thomas maintained a devotion to the United States and its army until Virginia seceded. He had written, March 12, 1861, "as long as my native state remains in the Union, it is my purpose to remain in the army."[222] Then a combination of factors led to his decision to cast his lot with his fellow Virginians. His kinsmen, many still in Southampton, urged him to "come over." For its part, the War Department seemed to hesitate in offering Thomas promotion and command in the new army. It was rumored that some in Washington were suspicious of Thomas' Southern roots; Thomas, unhappily (and unlike Lee), did not have Scott rooting for him. Lincoln is even alleged to have remarked, "Let the Virginian wait."[223] This indifference from the

---

222   Francis F. McKinney, *Education in Violence: The Life of George H. Thomas* (Detroit, 1961), p. 88.

223   *Ibid.,* p. 93.

army he had served his entire career led Thomas to begin to doubt its effectiveness, even its capacity to win the war.

He had married a New Yorker, Frances, but Mrs. Thomas did not offer opinion on her husband's divided loyalties. If anything, she discouraged him from seeking active field service. Major Thomas had suffered a painful back injury in an accidental fall, December 1860, and was still not recovered. As late as March 1, 1861, he admitted to being "still quite lame," unable to ride on horseback in early April and careful to avoid rigorous activity.[224] Capping all this was the fortuitous offer he received from Governor Letcher, who asked Thomas if he would resign from the old army and take the position of Chief of Ordnance in the State Forces. He would hold the rank of colonel with offices in the state capital, where he would spend most of his time. The idea of a desk-job appealed to the still semi-handicapped Thomas, an offer he knew would also please his wife. Added to the pressure from his family, it proved to be a key factor in Thomas' decision to go with his state. Like Lee, Thomas took a day to make up his mind, and on April 24 formally accepted Letcher's offer.

When Virginia forces were folded into the Confederate army, Thomas kept his desk job in Richmond. Jefferson Davis knew Thomas from the Mexican War, and had formed a high opinion of his artillery skills at Buena Vista. In 1855 Secretary of War Davis had picked Thomas for promotion to major in the Second Cavalry, and had observed Thomas' strong performance in it, particularly his steady competence in administrative matters. Now, six years later Davis asked Colonel Thomas to be his Chief of Staff—a position with as yet rather undefined duties except to help the President as he shouldered the duties of Commander-in-Chief. On May 24, 1861, Thomas accepted. He held his post throughout the war, skillfully assisting in the Confederate government's battlefield initiatives. Thomas' quiet imperturbability was notably evident in the spring of 1862, as Davis coped with the early western reverses at Forts Henry and Donelson. Whether he materially contributed to the strategic decision that led to Sidney Johnston's victory at

---

224 *Ibid.,* p. 87.

Shiloh has not been documented. But the Virginian undoubtedly aided the Southern cause in ways that, though less renowned than Robert E. Lee's, at least entitle George H. Thomas to recognition as one of the secondary architects of Confederate victory.

WHY THEY VOLUNTEERED

After the Fort Sumter excitement had subsided in both countries, politicians, editors, ministers and other opinion leaders of every kind strived to charge the atmosphere with energy and enthusiasm in order to sustain the war fervor and keep the young men coming to the recruitment offices.

In April-May '61, they did not have to work hard. Once the martial trumpets sounded, there were plenty of reasons for Billy Yanks and Johnny Rebs to run off to war. On both sides those reasons, large and small, were pretty much the same.

There was the first rush of patriotism, the desire to serve one's country. Southern sectionalism and emergent nationalism after the 1830's had so developed by 1861 that many below Mason's and Dixon's line had no difficulty in defining the Southland as their "country," whose liberty and self-government needed defending. Then, too, after the Confederates reclaimed their property at Charleston, Lincoln's loud call for an army to subjugate their country added for many Southerners the motive of protecting hearth and home against invasion. As one young Alabamian wrote, "when a Southron's home is threatened the spirit of resistance is irrepressible."[225]

Northerners' patriotism manifested itself in a determination to defend the flag that had been assaulted and to restore the Union that had been sundered. A Connecticut volunteer avowed his purpose to go "forth to defend this Country in this her hour of peril." This kind of patriotism recalled the spirit of the Minutemen back in 1776. Indeed, many Northerners felt that in volunteering to preserve the Union, they were maintaining the proud tradition of their Revolutionary forebears. "The man who doesn't give hearty

---

225   James M. McPherson, *What They Fought For 1861-1863* (Baton Rouge, 1994), p. 18.

support to our bleeding country in this day of our country's trial," wrote an officer from New Jersey, "is not worthy to be a descendant of our forefathers." Ohioan Thomas Taylor echoed this sentiment in a letter to his wife: "Our fathers made this country, we their children are to save it."

Southerners were just as mindful of their Revolutionary heritage—maybe more so, when they likened their Confederate War for Independence to the colonists' War for Independence. Virginian Thomas Rowland expressed satisfaction to his mother that he was participating in a "second War for American Independence," and likened the North's "war of subjugation against the South" to "England's war upon the colonies."[226]

With both Northerners and Southerners in 1861 claiming to be the true heirs of America's revolutionary legacy, it is not surprising that the two warring sides also laid claim to be the true champion of American values— generally expressed as liberty, self-government, progress and opportunity.

Liberty and freedom were the real catch-words, though by them neither side meant the same thing, much less what we usually think today (freedom for the slaves). Though Northern war aims eventually came to include emancipation, at the start of the conflict most Northerners who enlisted would not have named the freeing of Southern slaves as their reason. Abolitionists had always been a distinct minority in the antebellum North, and an unflattering racism tinged many sectors of Northern society. President Lincoln desired to touch neither element, and left slavery alone for as long as he could—until fall 1862, when the Union war effort began to show signs of impending failure, and when he sought to prop it up with anything he had.

For their part, too, although slavery lay as the undisputed bedrock of the Confederate economy, Jefferson Davis and Confederate authorities saw little advantage in expressly asking Southerners to fight for slavery, when three-fourths of Southern households had no slaves. In short, slavery was a divider, not a

---

226 *Ibid.*, pp. 9, 28-29, 33.

uniter, for each war cause. As James M. McPherson has succinctly stated, "Both sides, therefore shoved slavery under the rug as they concentrated their energies on mobilizing eager citizen soldiers."[227]

Liberty as a war-cry was thus defined more or less by and for white men, and the white men joining the two armies applied further connotations. For Johnny Rebs, liberty meant the self-government that the new Southern nation sought. "I am willing to fall for the cause of Liberty and Independence," declared Captain Nathaniel Dawson of the 4th Alabama. The loftiness of such motives allowed their adherents to feel blessed by the Almighty. "Our cause is the sacred one of Liberty, and God is on our side," wrote Captain Edward D. Tracy of the same Alabama regiment.[228] Tracy, later a C.S. brigadier general, would never find out which side God ultimately favored; he was killed at Port Gibson, Mississippi, in May 1863.

For Northerners, "liberty" also meant self-government, but their connotation was of national republicanism as the American political ideal. The spirit of mid-nineteenth century Manifest Destiny not only placed God on America's side, but associated American liberty with the noblest hopes for the advancement of civilization. This meant for Northerners both an added burden and an added moral advantage as they essentially carried the banner of freedom for the whole world. "I do feel that the liberty of the world is placed in our hands to defend," wrote a Massachusetts private to his wife. Corporal George Cadman of Ohio reminded his spouse, "I want you to remember that it will be...for Liberty all over the World that I risked my life, for if Liberty should be crushed here, what hope would there be for the cause of Human Progress anywhere else?" Closely associated was the cause of self-government, specifically Americans' unique republic—"the best government on God's footstool," in the words of a Minnesotan. Again, the thought was that the preservation of the Federal government against state secession had worldwide implications.

---

227   James M. McPherson, *Battle Cry of Freedom: The South Wins Its Independence* (New York, 1988), p. 312.

228   McPherson, *What They Fought For*, p. 10; James M. McPherson, *For Cause and Comrades: Why Men Fought in the Confederate War* (New York, 1997), p. 20.

An Irish immigrant in the 28th Massachusetts voiced it well: "This is the first test of a modern free government in the act of sustaining itself against internal enemys... if it fail then the hopes of millions fall and the designs and wishes of all tyrants will succeed the old cry will be sent forth from the aristocrats of Europe that such is the common lot of all republics."[229]

Confederates' war for independence and self-government could also be viewed as majestic and portentous. "We are living in the midst of the grandest revolution ever known in the annals of the world," beamed young Samuel Tenney, who left the University of Georgia to enlist. When the Confederacy achieved its independence and entered "among the nations of the earth," Tenney foresaw for the South "a glorious destiny."

Along with their sense of Manifest Destiny, mid-nineteenth-century Americans shared concepts stressing moral progress and social order. To be feared, above all, was anarchy. Not surprisingly, each side in this civil contest saw its foe in such highly charged terms. For Northerners, secession and rebellion meant anarchy and the threat to vaunted principles of law and order. "The central idea of secession," Lincoln once said, "is the essence of anarchy." Union soldiers picked up on it. Typical phrasings found Northern soldiers "fighting for the maintenance of law and order" and combating "dissolution, anarchy, and ruin." Colonel (later General) Samuel R. Curtis wrote in 1861, "if [secession] can prosper under such auspices surely the downfall of civilization like that which devastated Rome has returned to dessolate the world."[230]

Southerners had a different view of the anarchists in the conflict. The *literati* remembered from their classical history that the historic foundation for well-ordered Greek and Roman republics was respect for slave property. When Southerners invoked the cherished words from the Declaration of Independence—"life, liberty and the pursuit of happiness"—they meant life, liberty and property. Protection of the latter against tyrants and barbarians plotting destruction of the Southern social order could commonly

---

229   McPherson, *What They Fought For,* pp. 30-32, 34.
230   *Ibid.,* pp. 8, 12, 32.

be seen as the most patriotic of duties. "If we should suffer ourselves to be subjugated by the tyrannical government of the North," wrote Private John Holt of Virginia to his wife, "our property would all be confiscated.... Our people reduced to the most abject bondage and utter degradation."

On the other hand, if the South were to win her independence, wonderful vistas of economic growth and domestic tranquility lay ahead, the sure signs of social progress and order. As Louisianan Rufus Carter rhapsodized, the South possessed

> ... a soil that yields a hundred-fold to the land of industry, a climate which none can surpass in salubrity, resources that might well be compared to the wealth of a Croesus, all this is ours. What an extensive sea and gulf coast indented with safe and capacious harbors! What great facilities for transportation in the deep and broad rivers that irrigate our beautiful country. And what is better than all this is a brave and enlightened people.[231]

Patriotism, moralism, ethnocentrism — to these high-flown isms was added a far less lofty one, but which probably animated more Johnny Rebs and Billy Yanks from any other enlistment motive: adventurism. War offered excitement, mystery and—a real lure to young men everywhere—the chance for travel to far-off and never-seen places. Bell I. Wiley, the first Confederate war historian to read thousands of soldiers' letters, put it best for this conflict (and many others). "War, with its offering of travel to far places, of intimate association with large numbers of other men, of the glory and excitement of battle, was an alluring prospect to farmers who in peace spent long lonely hours between plow handles, to mechanics who worked day in and day out at cluttered benches, to storekeepers who through endless months measured jeans cloth or weighed sowbelly, to teachers who labored year after

---

231 McPherson, *For Cause and Comrades*, p. 20-21; Reid Mitchell, *Civil War Soldiers: Their Expectations and their Experiences* (New York, 1988), p. 7.

year with indifferent success to drill the rudiments of knowledge into unwilling heads, and to sons of planters who dallied with the classics in halls of learning."

There were other less than altruistic motivations for men to enlist. For the unemployed in the North, the army offered a steady job at $13 month, a reasonable wage back then. For young men single and unattached, this represented a smart career move of sorts. A Wisconsin Norwegian wrote his parents why he enlisted: "It seemed as if I were compelled to go in order to get out of debt." Even family men were so swayed. Against the protests of his wife, Enoch Baker of Pennsylvania enlisted, then wrote back, "It is no use for you to fret or cry about me for you know if i could have got work i wood not have left you or the children."[232]

Sometimes enlistment decisions were less individual options than evidences of what we would call mass behavior: when everyone in the community was signing up, you had to, as well. It could be a rather thoughtless experience, as attested by one private from Indiana who recorded, "I enlisted for what I couldent tell. I did it without reflecting what the life of a Volunteer was....In fact I done it just to be doing." In the heady days after Sumter, with everyone asking one another "are you signing up?" one man's decision would become another's, and another's. One Northern officer somewhat disdainfully wrote of the men in his company, "Nine tenths of them enlisted just because somebody else was going."

But this peer pressure had deep societal roots, involving romantic concepts of duty, honor and manliness—as well as their counterparts, shame and disgrace. "I would be disgraced if I staid at home," wrote Samuel Sanders of South Carolina; "the honor of our family is involved." For many youths, the prospective hardships of the soldier's life provided the opportunity to "become a man." Soldiers of both sides repeated this theme: "I determined to stand up to duty and preserve my manhood and honor"; "I would be less than a man if in any way I fell short of the discharge of duty at my

---

232   Bell Irvin Wiley, *The Life of Johnny Reb: The Common Soldier of the Confederacy* (Indianapolis, 1943), p. 17; Wiley, *The Life of Billy Yank: The Common Soldier of the Union* (Indianapolis, 1951), p. 38.

country's call"; "I have acted the part of a man." Women were well aware of this manly code of dutifulness, and whipped up the war fervor by coaxing and taunting, bestowing approval upon those who volunteered and casting disdain on those who did not. In some Southern towns, young men known to be hesitating received packets of petticoats. And for those marching off to war, the complicity of women in the volunteering process allowed soldiers to feel they were fighting for their womenfolk back home. Thomas H. Colman, a private from Texas, had received flower bouquets from two appreciative "beautiful women," whereupon he reflected, "as I sped my way...the mistery is solved...what are we fighting for why 'By George' we are fighting for the women."

For many men, the complex bundle of excited talk, emotional appeals, internal feelings and social pressures proved irresistible, to the point that death seemed preferable to dishonor. "Life is sweet but I would always prefer an honorable death to a disgraceful and shameful life," wrote one Mississippian. In his diary entry of May 5, 1861, young Ohioan (and future U.S. President) Rutherford B. Hayes recorded, "I would prefer to go into it [even] if I knew I was to die or be killed in the course of it, than to live through and after it without taking part."[233]

For some, though, the price of death seemed a little too steep. From an Iowa recruiting rally comes the story of the officer's proposal that the regiment's flag bear the words "Victory or Death." One in the crowd spoke forth, objecting to the motto.

"Why so," asked back the officer. "How shall it be changed?"

Came the answer: "Make it victory or pretty damned badly wounded, and I'm your huckleberry."[234]

PRESIDENT DAVIS'S ADDRESS TO CONGRESS

When Lincoln's call of April 15 for troops to suppress the rebellious Southern "combinations" was read to the Confederate Congress in Montgomery, the legislators broke out into hall-

---

233 McPherson, *For Cause and Comrades*, pp. 23-26, 28; McPherson, *What They Fought For,* p. 20.

234 James I. Robertson, Jr., *Soldiers Blue and Gray* (Columbia SC, 1988), p. 7.

ringing laughter, especially when they heard his demand that "the persons composing the combinations aforesaid disperse, and retire peaceably to their respective abodes."[235] President Davis addressed Congress on April 29, his first chance to do so since the bombardment of Sumter and its tumultuous consequences. In a carefully prepared speech he reviewed the prospects for the Confederate nation that had been in formal existence just barely three months and which seemed to be embarked upon a gritty war to affirm its independence.

—"There is every reason to believe that at no distant day other States, identified in political principles and community of interests with those which you represent, will join this Confederacy, giving to its typical constellation increased splendor."

—Davis regarded the "proclamation issued on the 15th day of the present month" to be a "declaration of war made against this Confederacy by Abraham Lincoln, the President of the United States."

—The President, exercising his legalistic penchant for the finest points of historical correctness and Constitutionality, reviewed the state of the nation in its infancy, 1787-89, emphasizing the terms under which the newly independent states had consented to cede their independence in order to form a federal union.

—A rise of sectional antagonisms—differing economic systems, the federal government's imposition of an oppressive tariff, the insoluble problem of slavery foisted upon present-day Southerners without their consent, the last generation of Northerners' abolitionist fervor—all of this the Founding Fathers could not have foreseen when they envisioned a permanent Union of the states.

—"In the exercise of a right so ancient, so well established, and so necessary for self-preservation, the people of the Confederate States, in their conventions, determined that the wrongs which they had suffered and the evils with which they were menaced required that they should revoke the delegation of powers to the Federal

---

235 "Proclamation Calling Militia and Convening Congress," in Roy P. Basler, ed., *The Collected Works of Abraham Lincoln,* 9 vols. (New Brunswick NJ, 1953), vol. 4, 332.

Government which they had ratified in their several conventions. They consequently passed ordinances resuming all their rights as sovereign and independent States and dissolved their connection with the other States of the Union."

—The newly formed Confederacy, seeking to remove garrisons of U.S. troops inside its borders without bloodshed, had responsibly sent envoys to secure the peaceable transfer of property and soldiers. The opposing administration had refused to deal honestly with Southern envoys, and had even stealthily sent a naval expedition of relief and reinforcement, feigning interest in negotiated settlement while even then sending an announcement of its intent to break the agreed-upon truce. "With our commissioners actually in Washington, detained under assurances that notice should be given of any military movement, the notice was not addressed to *them,* but a messenger was sent to Charleston to give the notice to the Governor of South Carolina, and the notice was so given at a late hour on the 8th of April, the eve of the very day on which the fleet might be expected to arrive."

—Hence came the inevitable bombardment of Fort Sumter, ordered by the Confederate government with the most extreme misgivings but without the slightest recourse whatsoever.

—"Scarcely had the President of the United States received the intelligence of the failure of the scheme which he had devised for the re-enforcement of Fort Sumter, when he issued the declaration of war against this Confederacy."[236]

THE CONFEDERATES DECLARE WAR

Suitably stirred, the Confederate Congress followed a week later with its own declaration of war. Passed on May 6 was "an act recognizing the existence of war between the United States and Confederate States," which pretty well spelled out, from the Southern view anyway, what had been happening in the last several weeks:

---

236 Address to the "Gentlemen of the Congress," April 29, 1861, *O.R.,* Ser. 4, vol. 1, 256-64.

Whereas, the earnest efforts made by this Government to establish friendly relations between the Government of the United States and the Confederate States...have proved unavailing...

Whereas, the President of the United States of America has issued his proclamation making requisition upon the States of the American Union for 75,000 men for the purpose, as therein indicated, of capturing forts and other strongholds within the jurisdiction of, and belonging to, the Confederate States of America, and has detailed naval armaments upon the coasts of the Confederate States of America, and raised, organized, and equipped a large military force to execute the purpose aforesaid, and has issued his other proclamation announcing his purpose to set on foot a blockade of the ports of the Confederate States; and

Whereas, the State of Virginia has seceded from the Federal Union...and the States of Maryland, North Carolina, Tennessee, Kentucky, Arkansas, and Mississippi have refused...to co-operate with the Government of the United States in these acts of hostilities and wanton aggression, which are plainly intended to overawe, oppress, and finally subjugate the people of the Confederate States; and

Whereas, by the acts and means aforesaid, war exists between the Confederate States and the Government of the United States and the States and Territories thereof...Therefore, The Congress of the Confederate States of America do enact, That the President of the Confederate States is hereby authorized to use the whole land and naval force of the Confederate States to meet the war thus commenced....[237]

SECESSION OF THE UPPER SOUTH

Virginia was the first state of the Upper South to secede. She would be joined by five others.

The process of the Border South's leaving was more gradual than the far more precipitate disunion of the Lower South, in which seven states went out within six weeks, December 20, 1860-February 1, 1861. Deep Southerners, starting with South Carolina, had viewed Abraham Lincoln's election to be sufficient reason for leaving the Union. But in the tier of states to their north, voters were less passionate. About the time the Confederate government was establishing itself in Montgomery, in early February 1861 Tennesseans voted against even calling a state convention which might consider secession. A week later, on February 18 voters in Arkansas defeated secession by 23,626 to 17,927 (a 56%-44% margin), but approved the calling of a convention to further discuss the possibility. When that was held the next month, delegates rejected secession in a 39-35 vote.

Fort Sumter and Lincoln's summons of troops changed the atmosphere dramatically. In Arkansas the popular convention was ordered back into session. Reconvening in Little Rock on May 6 the delegates quickly took up the subject at hand. Someone moved that the issue of secession be referred to the people; this was defeated 55-15. Then an ordinance of secession was formally introduced; on the roll call vote only five nays were voiced. Delegate David Walker called on these to change: "Now, since we must go, let us all go together." Four of the five did so, but one anti-secessionist refused to alter his vote, despite loud hisses. The final vote of the Arkansas state convention was thus 69-1. The sole diehard, Isaac

---

237 "An Act recognizing the existence of war between the United States and the Confederate States," *O.R.,* Ser. 4, vol. 1, 281-82.

Murphy of Madison County, was shouted down as a "traitor," amid calls from some delegates, "Shoot him! Hang him!"[238] (Murphy left the hall unscathed.)

On May 6 Tennessee also seceded. After Sumter, having boldly repudiated Lincoln's call for two regiments from Tennessee, Governor Isham Harris called the state legislature into session, to meet in Nashville on April 25. When it had assembled, Harris submitted a fiery message further denouncing "the bloody and tyrannical policy of the Presidential usurper" and "his hordes of armed soldiery marching to the work of Southern subjugation."[239] Harris urged the legislature to consider secession, which it did, though taking more than a week in order to hear out those solons from east Tennessee who were not so fierily inclined. When the vote was taken, disunion won handily: 20-4 in the Senate, 46-21 in the House, with the General Assembly passing "A Declaration of Independence"—not formally entitled an ordinance of secession, but close enough. On the same day the legislature passed a bill organizing the state's military forces, authorizing up to 55,000 officers and men for the army. With secessionist fervor sweeping much of the state (excluding the generally non-slaveholding areas of east Tennessee), the legislators called for a plebiscite on June 8, so the state's voters could approve the General Assembly's action. Governor Harris would not wait that long. On May 7 he announced that Tennessee was entering into a military alliance with the Confederacy. Thus even before the people's vote on secession, Tennesseans were organizing regiments for Confederate service. A few of these had even gone to Virginia for service there, before the people's vote on June 8. Needless to say, with all these events occurring, the state's voters approved secession by a count of 104,913 to 47,238 (most of the nays came from east Tennessee.)

In North Carolina the process was much the same as in Virginia, Arkansas and Tennessee. The election of Lincoln was thought by most as an inadequate cause of secession. As Governor John W.

---

238   Michael B. Dougan, *Confederate Arkansas: The People and Policies of a Frontier State in Wartime* (University AL, 1976), pp. 62-63.

239   Stanley F. Horn, ed., *Tennessee's War 1861-1863 Described by Participants* (Nashville, 1965), p. 16.

Ellis himself was said to have opined, most North Carolinians would not regard the Republican presidential victory "as sufficient ground for dissolving the Union of the States." When the state legislature convened two weeks after the national election, legislators affirmed the Governor's instinct to await developments. At the same time, even in mid-November 1860 many political leaders predicted greater sectional strife. The North Carolina General Assembly accordingly appropriated money to buy arms and ammunition, when the Governor called for a reorganization of the state militia.

Many North Carolinians awaited the Federal government's response to the first wave of Southern secession. As one put it, on January 16, 1861, "I am a Union man but when they send men South it will change my notions. I can do nothing against my own people." But the change of notions was yet to occur. After the legislature called for a statewide vote on whether to assemble a convention, on February 28 a strong majority of Carolinians voted against even calling for such a meeting.

After Sumter, Governor Ellis forthrightly responded to the President's call for militiamen, "You can get no troops from North Carolina." Like Rector and Harris, Ellis spoke for most North Carolinians in terming Lincoln's militia proclamation "a gross usurpation of power" and "wicked violation of the laws of the country."[240] Anticipating the secession of his state, Ellis ordered North Carolina militiamen to seize the three Federal forts on the coast. Even before the Governor's orders arrived, hastily assembled volunteers in Beaufort marched on Fort Macon, a brick work completed in 1832 to guard the entrance to the town's harbor. Ordnance Sergeant William Alexander, the fort's lone attendant, quickly surrendered the place, which was not in the best shape: ironwork rusty, quarters and barracks dilapidated, only four guns mounted on rotting wooden carriages (but thirteen more lay on the wharf). Soon state troops and more volunteers arrived to spruce up the casemates and mount the rest of the cannon.

---

240   John G. Barrett, *The Confederate War in North Carolina* (Chapel Hill, 1963), pp. 4, 6, 10.

Thirty miles down the Cape Fear River from Wilmington was Fort Caswell, a masonry installation of mostly unmounted cannon. On April 16 Colonel John Cantwell and the Wilmington Light Infantry approached the fort and demanded its surrender. Inside, two U.S. sergeants and their families entertained no thought of opposition, and the "insurgents," as one Federal called them, promptly marched in.[241] Within days reinforcements allowed Cantwell to mount twenty guns within the fort and bring in four more, as well as two thousand sandbags for shoring up the walls. Across the water from Caswell, near Smithville, "Fort" Johnston, really a blockhouse with adjoining barracks, was given up that same day by its sole occupant, Ordnance Sergeant James Reilly.

And all this was before the state actually seceded. Governor Ellis called for the legislature to convene in special session on May 1. By then, a company of the Charlotte Grays had taken possession of the Federal branch mint in the city (April 20), and the more important U.S. arsenal in Fayetteville had also fallen (on the 22d). Captain J.A.J. Bradford and his forty-two soldiers manning the arsenal were no match for the more than a thousand state troops massed outside, armed and ready to storm the place. They did not need to. Bradford arranged a capitulation which allowed his garrison to remain for several days, then march out with their arms and personal property, even firing a 21-gun salute to the U.S. colors as they were lowered. Into state hands fell 37,000 rifles, great stores of gunpowder, several pieces of artillery and other supplies.

In Raleigh, the General Assembly voted its thanks to the Governor for his promptness in calling for these "defensive" measures, passed a law making it "unlawful to administer the oath to support the Constitution of the United States," and called for a state convention to consider secession—as if the issue were really in doubt. Elections for 120 delegates were held May 13 and the convention itself, dominated by disunionists, assembled on the 20th. That same day it passed unanimously an ordinance of secession, declaring and ordaining "that the union now subsisting

---

241 *O.R.*, vol. 1, 477.

between the state of North Carolina and the other states, under the title of 'The United States of America,' is hereby dissolved, and that the state of North Carolina is in full possession and exercise of all those rights of sovereignty which belong and appertain to a free and independent state."[242] To make matters complete, an hour later the delegates also ratified the Provisional Constitution of the Confederates States of America.

The Confederacy's first eleven states had united.

The Balance Sheet (1): North and South in Population

Going into the war the North had many reasons for confidence in its prospects for victory. Population, industry, financial strength, even agriculture gave the United States—what was left of them—a clear and commanding edge over the Confederacy in the spring of 1861. Quantitative superiority in men and material, however, does not always guarantee victory in war, as the United States tragically learned again a century later in Vietnam. Indeed, as the U.S. committed itself to combating Communist insurgents in Southeast Asia in 1961, Confederate diplomats tried to remind Washington how hard it is to crush a nationalistic uprising, sustained by a populace determined to win its independence, no matter how outnumbered and outgunned. C.S. Senator Richard B. Russell of Georgia was widely quoted for his paraphrasing of the famed maxim of Santayana, that those who remember their history are still doomed to repeat it.

Oft cited are the U.S. Census statistics of 1860, showing the populations of the two countries. In the 23 states of the Union were 22.3 million people; the eleven-state Confederacy had 9.1 million, of whom 3 ½ million were slaves. Counting only the military populace (generally, white males 17 to 45 years old), the North enjoyed a superiority of three and a half-to-one—on the face of it, an insuperable advantage. Yet there were important qualifications. The three border states whose populations at the time of Sumter were considered loyal to the Union, soon sundered themselves. Commonly accepted figures show that from Maryland 35,000 men

---

242   Daniel Harvey Hill, *Bethel to Sharpsburg*, 2 vols. (Raleigh, 1926), vol. 1, 38, 43.

fought in the Union army and navy, 20,000 for the Confederacy. Kentuckians aligned themselves in similar proportion: 50,000 for the U.S., 35,000 C.S. In Missouri, the numbers by war's end were almost matched: 50,000 for the North, 40,000 for the South, plus an estimated 3,000-5,000 pro-Confederate guerrillas (led by the notorious William Quantrill and others). At the same time, within the Confederacy were significant numbers of non-slaveholders or diehard Unionists who refused to don the gray; when concentrated in particular areas, such as western Virginia or eastern Tennessee, these men formed their own regiments and were eventually mustered into Federal service. The number of these "Allegheny renegades" and "Tennessee tories," as they were derisively called by Southern Confederates, has never been conclusively tallied, chiefly because of their shifting loyalties. Pro-Union at the start of the war, most of them chilled in their war-ardor after mid-1862, when it began to appear that the Confederacy might win the war. Concerned over the loss of their property back home and a life of exile ahead, they sloughed off their blue uniforms, shirked and slinked back into Southern lines and volunteered anew, this time on the victorious side.

Finally, not to be dismissed are the significant contributions of Southern slaves to the Confederate war effort. While unable to bear arms as soldiers, black men rendered invaluable service as army teamsters, cooks and laborers, especially in building fortifications. Every slave performing these functions—and tens of thousands did, despite the occasional objections of masters worried about disease and injury among their chattels—kept a Confederate soldier on the firing line. Even black women, contracted to the army for such work as hospital attendants and laundresses, did their part. To be sure, at the approach of invading Union forces many slaves ran away from their plantations and farms, seeking freedom within Federal lines. These "contrabands," as Union General Butler began calling them at Fort Monroe, eventually became so numerous in southeastern Virginia and along the South Carolina coast (sites of the earliest Union incursions into Confederate territory in 1861) that some Northern leaders began urging the recruitment of black men as Union soldiers. Lincoln, ever the moderate on questions even touching on emancipation, resisted these calls until early 1863, when it was too late to salvage the North's war effort. By then even slaves realized the folly of running away to serve in a Yankee army that most folks figured was going to lose.

In the end, an estimated 1.5 million men fought for the Union and 850,000 for the Confederacy. With a better than 3-to-1 military manpower pool, the North was not even able to muster twice the number of soldiers as the South. In addition to the above factors, several important reasons account for this harbinger of Union defeat. The Confederacy was first to adopt a wartime draft or conscription, over a year before the Lincoln administration could force a by-then war-weary U.S. Congress to enact compulsory army service. Secondly, the mounting swell of Confederate battlefield victories in the summer of 1862, coupled with British and French diplomatic recognition of the C.S. government that fall, gave Southerners a huge boost in war-morale that further stimulated volunteering. Moreover, Confederate veterans whose one-year enlistments expired in the spring of '62 re-upped for the duration of the war, wanting to be part of the victory celebrations. Finally, those Southern celebrations came at a time when, in the fall of 1863, the North had yet to harness its remaining available manpower. As a result, fully three-fourths of Southern white men fought in their country's War for Independence, while just over a third of the North's military-aged men fought to save the Union. When the Lincoln administration sought to enforce the draft, as it did in New York City in July 1863, "the worst riot in American history" occurred, led by young ruffians who refused their nation's call to arms.[243] The New York City draft riot was a shameful, eleventh-hour humiliation to the failed Northern war effort.

THE BALANCE SHEET (2): INDUSTRY

The Confederate War has been called America's first modern war for several reasons, one of which is the important role that manufacturing played in both countries. Here again the U.S. held a commanding edge. In "manufacturing enterprises," as

---

243   James M. McPherson, *Ordeal by Fire: The Confederate War and Its Aftermath* (New York, 2001 [1982]), p. 389.

defined by the census (the definition was broad, but consistently applied), the North had 110,000 to the South's 18,000. And the North's factories or workshops were bigger, employing 1.3 million workers. The South's shops employed only 110,000, meaning an average of six workers per establishment *versus* almost twelve in an average Northern manufactory. The difference, when coupled with the North's greater use of labor-saving machinery, meant not only that Northern plants turned out a disproportionally larger quantity of goods, but that the plant owners had acquired a greater know-how in managing industrial efficiency on a more intensified scope, itself a useful war-asset.

As the two nations went to war, the Northern one manufactured 97% of the firearms made in the United States of 1860, 94% of its cloth (despite the South's production of cotton, the raw material), and 90% of its shoes. In each of these key industries, the North's factory system increased the efficiency of manufacture. Eli Whitney, famous down South for his cotton gin, was more renowned up North for having streamlined the principle of assembly by machine-made interchangeable parts for the manufacture of rifles and pistols. After the invention of the sewing machine by Elias Howe of Massachusetts, factory cloth production rapidly developed during the 1850s, just in time to allow the mass production of soldiers' clothing. Application of the cloth sewing machine to leather shoe-making took cobblery out of the hand-made realm into the machine age, particularly after Lyman Blake of Massachusetts patented in 1858 a device to sew on soles. Union infantrymen therefore had their essential stuff—musket, uniform and footgear—produced and producible in abundant quantities. The North's industrial capacity extended into a wide range of other goods, too, further accentuating its differences with the more agricultural South. "In 1860, Massachusetts produced more manufactured goods than all the future Confederate states combined," McPherson writes, "while New York and Pennsylvania *each* produced more than twice the goods manufactured by all the future Confederates states combined."[244]

---

244 James M. McPherson, *Ordeal by Fire: The Confederate War and Its Aftermath* (New York, 2001 [1982]), p. 28.

The means to bring all this equipage to the front also favored the North, with its more than 21,000 miles of railroads, to the South's 9,000-plus. Equally important, nine out of ten locomotives were made in the Union states, whose coal and pig iron production eclipsed the South's by twenty-to-one. Thus Northerners could build and were building railroads at a far faster clip than were Southerners; indeed, in the entire eleven-state Confederacy there were only two iron rolling mills capable of producing the basic rails needed for new track construction.

Yet war is more than just about ownership of machines—much more, as the manufacturing North would soon sadly learn.

"OLD FUSS AND FEATHERS"

Winfield Scott, General-in-Chief of the United States Army at the outbreak of war, had a truly impressive career-record. First off, he virtually owned the descriptive *venerable*. Born near Petersburg, Virginia in 1786 Scott had entered the world just three years after the Treaty of Paris ended the Revolutionary War, and three years before George Washington took his first presidential oath. Second, he was a lifelong soldier. Scott was schooled in a Richmond Academy and attended the College of William and Mary. He read law for a year and toyed with the idea of becoming an attorney before yielding to his real yearning, a life in the military.

Threat of war with England in 1807 led President Jefferson to call for volunteers. At twenty-one, an imposing six-five and 230 pounds, Scott rose from corporal to captain in a year, and was ready for higher promotion in the War of 1812. He won fame in the battle of Chippewa in July 1814, driving the British from the field. Positioning themselves for their attack, the gray-uniformed Americans drew forth from the overconfident English General Phineas Riall, "Why, these are nothing but Buffalo militia!" After Scott's well-arranged regiments massed and delivered their attack, however, Riall (before ordering retreat) yelled, "those are regulars, by God!"[245]

245　Timothy D. Johnson, *Winfield Scott: The Quest for Military Glory* (Lawrence KS, 1998), p. 49; Russell F. Weigley, *History of the United States Army* (New York, 1967), p. 131.

The war gave Scott the opportunity to build a reputation as a "perspicacious and competent" officer. Fighting the Seminoles and herding the Cherokees in the 1830s, Scott settled in Washington in 1841 when he was named General-in-Chief, an appointment bestowed "both because he deserved it," write Hattaway and Jones, "and because he outlived or outlasted his rivals."[246]

If there remained any doubts of his military skills, Scott put them firmly to rest by his generalship in the Mexican War of 1846-48, when he landed his army at the Gulf port of Vera Cruz, marched halfway across Mexico's rough, arid expanse, defeated enemy forces repeatedly in a series of battles, besieged Mexico City and captured it, thus bringing about Mexican surrender and ending the war in triumph.

Scott was so popular that in 1852 the Whig Party nominated him as its presidential candidate (he was defeated by Democrat Franklin Pierce). Three years later, Congress passed a bill that bestowed on the seventy-two-year-old Scott the brevet rank of lieutenant general, effective March 29, 1847 (date of Vera Cruz's surrender). As the highest-ranking officer in the army he acquired a liking for ornate uniforms, with gold braid, bright sashes and sometimes comical hats. In his spare time he studied French uniform tailoring and often altered and embellished his general's attire with his own stitchery. Adding to Scott's imposing presence was his corporeal heft. He loved French gourmet cooking, and it showed as he ballooned out in the 1850s to 350 pounds. Dining on his favorite dishes (fish, oysters, terrapin and onion soup), accompanied by wine, champagne and sherry, the general held forth at dinner parties with loud, noisy conversation that left many a guest ill at ease and glad to leave at evening's end.

"The vain and always gorgeously uniformed hero," as he was described, "could take no more than a few steps at a time," due to gout, dropsy and vertigo.[247] He was so big that a winch crew

---

246 Herman Hattaway and Archer Jones, *How the South Won: A Military History* (Urbana IL, 1983), p. 28.

247 *Ibid.*, pp. 27-28.

had to hoist him on top of his suffering horse. Yet Scott never lost his punctilious demand for discipline and obedience among his officers, even in the smallest details of protocol and regulation.

By the time of the Southern War for Independence, Scott was known throughout the army as "Old Fuss and Feathers." It was he who would advance the first cohesive strategic plan for the North's war effort.

SCOTT'S "ANACONDA" PLAN

Seventy-six years old, known to fall asleep in meetings, the crusty, pompous Winfield Scott might be thought far too past his prime to contribute weighty ideas to Union strategic planning. Not so. The North's first broad proposal for prosecuting its conflict with the Southern states came from Old Fuss and Feathers, and within three weeks of Fort Sumter at that.

Scott's plan did not develop at the President's urging, much less request. In late April-early May Lincoln had more pressing tactical concerns worrying him, such as the arrival of Northern regiments in Washington and the very defense of the capital. Rather, when Scott laid out his strategic manifesto for subduing the South on May 3 it was primarily to tamp down a more aggressive campaign plan being advanced by the brash, overconfident Union commander in Ohio, Maj. Gen. George B. McClellan.

Virginia had barely seceded and allied itself militarily with the Confederacy when young McClellan offered his thoughts on how to win the war. Ambitiously seeking quick military glory, McClellan proudly described his idea, written out on April 27 as "a plan of operations intended to relieve the pressure upon Washington and tending to bring the war to a speedy close."

To do so, McClellan suggested stationing garrisons along the Ohio River "for the protection of the frontier" (*e.g.*, a division of 5,000 men at Cincinnati). He declared that the main "active army of operations"—which he, of course, would command—should assemble in southeast Ohio, cross the river near Gallipolis and move up the valley of the Great Kanawha River toward Richmond. The author of this grand plan acknowledged the difficulties of marching an army through mountainous western Virginia, but he pledged that he was "prepared to meet them." As alternative, or perhaps corollary to his Richmond-via-Kanawha brainchild, McClellan offered a Plan B (crossing 80,000 men at Cincinnati or Louisville, and marching on Nashville) as well as Plans C-G (movements on Charleston, Augusta, Pensacola, Mobile and New Orleans.[248]

The ponderous Scott moved with unaccustomed rapidity to quash McClellan's scheme, which he viewed as risky on both military and political grounds. The mountainous terrain of western Virginia made any army's movement difficult; never a robust farming region, the area would offer meager foodstuffs for foragers, and the area's weak roadwork pledged peril for long wagon trains bearing sustenance for marching foot-columns.

Then there was the politics. A Virginian himself, and attuned to his state's conservative instincts, Scott believed he knew the political tenor and timbre of his fellow Virginians. He was not alone in feeling, as did Abraham Lincoln himself, that Southern secessionist fervor was a fragile thing, whipped up by ultra-hotheads over the Republicans' electoral victory in 1860. He was convinced that the popular feeling of rebelliousness, particularly in the upper South, was insufficiently grounded to sustain itself against the mighty counter-response of Federal military authority. Scott's thesis, shared by a number of conservative Northern political leaders, was that if the North's first military initiatives were restrained, (e.g., no invasion of the Old Dominion, save maybe a reoccupation of Harpers Ferry), and that time was given for the blockade to extract increasing economic pain upon the common people of the seceded states, then conservative elements among the Rebels would coalesce and turn on the secessionist hotheads. In his native state, for instance, he envisioned a backlash against John Letcher, Roger Pryor and Jubal Early when rank-and-file Virginians began to wonder what all the talk of "Yankee arrogance" was all about. Then, in the face of a real show of military force by the national authority—say, an amphibious advance down the Mississippi

---

248   *O.R.*, vol. 51, pt. 1, 338-39.

River—Virginians' naturally conservative instincts might arise and lead to a casting-out of the secessionist revolutionaries and a counter-revolution that might even bring about an annulment of their secession ordinance.

Or so the venerable General Scott hoped as he penned under the date of May 3 his response to McClellan in a letter which circulated around the War Department and which he eventually submitted to the President. The General-in-Chief's plan for Union victory would (if approved) have four elements, each weighted, as he believed, in a sounder understating of military realities than the flimsy predicates underlying McClellan's strategy.

1. There would be no immediate offensive by Union forces into Virginia, or elsewhere. The three-months' volunteers called for on April 15 would have their terms expire beginning in mid-July. Presumably the President's next call would be for three-year enlistments, and these would be the foundation of a true national army. But they would have to be organized and trained. Scott therefore envisioned no major military offensive for at least five or six months, well into the fall of '61.

2. Winfield Scott, born in 1786, was a soldier of his era, well-instructed in the medico-military maxims of the age. The deep South, as everyone knew, was a dangerous region of malarial miasms, whose hot nights and swampy bogs bred mysterious fevers that could decimate large bodies of troops. Better for this reason, too, Scott contended, to delay any national army's advance until things cooled down there, say in November.

3. In the meantime, the Union naval blockade, announced by the President on April 19, would exert its slow and strangulating effects. Southerners had depended upon the importation, both from the North and abroad, of many daily items that they could not themselves produce. When the shutdown of Northern commerce and the restriction of European trade had their combined effects, Scott reasoned that economic forces alone would weaken the Rebels' war-will. The pinched common folk of the South might even clamor for an upending of Confederate authority.

4. That was the time, maybe November 1861, when a mighty Union army, organized and equipped around the confluence of the Mississippi and Ohio, would begin its triumphant campaign downriver, slicing through the heartland of the Rebellion. The combined land and water invasion, with the army marching near the banks of the Mississippi, and Union naval vessels supplying them along the way, would advance inexorably down from Illinois through riverine Tennessee, Arkansas, Mississippi and Louisiana, too powerful for the Rebels to resist. Before long the entire Mississippi Valley would be conquered from Cairo to the Gulf. The cis-riverine South would be surrounded and squeezed into submission.

Little wonder that commentators on Scott's strategic manifesto of May 3 began calling it the "Anaconda Plan."[249] It was a remarkably confident proposal, borne of the country's most experienced military mind. But as frequently occurred in the North's failed war effort, the Anaconda gave way to other squeezes, chiefly the pressures of politics. Northerners wanted a campaign against Richmond, and they wanted it now.

Scott's plan was sound and there is considerable evidence that if adopted, the "Anaconda Plan" may have led to Union victory. But Lincoln heard the impatient chorus of complaint throughout the North, the loud, incessant cries of "on to Richmond!" and refused to approve Scott's proposal.

ELEMENTS OF CONFEDERATE STRATEGIC THINKING

The basic premise of Confederate strategy throughout the war, and the fundamental maxim which led the South to independence, was memorably phrased by President Davis in his address to Congress on April 29, 1861: "we seek no conquest...all we ask is to be let alone."[250]

In short, the Confederate leadership, both political and military, planned a defensive war, whose elemental aim was to keep

---

249 Robert Leckie, *None Died in Vain: The Saga of the American Civil War* (New York, 1990), 158.

250 *O.R.,* Ser. 4, vol. 1, 268.

the Yankees out of Confederate territory and, if they got in, to drive them back out. By doing this repeatedly and successively, Confederates could ultimately convince Lincoln and his cohorts that coercing the seceded states back into the Union was either impossible or too costly, both in terms of blood and treasure, to be achieved. The North would then give up its foolhardy war of subjugation and quit. Confederate independence would be achieved with the cessation of hostilities. "When the North had had enough killing," as Confederate historian Emory Thomas has written, "peace and independence would follow."[251]

This strategy was based on six sound assumptions.

1. The North would have to wage a war of invasion and conquest. If Abraham Lincoln wanted to restore Federal authority in the South, he would have to send Union armies to engage and defeat Confederate forces, capture key cities and occupy large tracts of territory. Then he would have to persuade the Southern people that their newly formed government did not possess the power to protect them and their property, and that their bid for independence had thus failed. Such a war of conquest would require gigantic armies and untold economic resources—an awesome commitment which most Southerners believed the North would not make.

2. Against the expected enemy incursions, Southern land and naval forces' primary goal would be to defend the country's borders and coastline. If and when Yankee armies succeeded in capturing key points or places, Confederates would counterattack and push them back to their own territory. This gave the Southern strategy a corollary of offense, leading Confederate war policy to be termed an "offensive defense."

Indeed, Jefferson Davis and his generals did not rule out Southern armies eventually taking the offensive themselves, raiding into Northern territory if and when the opportunity arose. This strategic flexibility gave the Confederates' war planning an additional strength.

---

251   Emory M. Thomas, *The Confederate Nation* (Richmond, 1979), p. 108.

3. A defensive strategic stance would favor the South's chances of winning far more than the North's. The Confederate States was a huge country—from Virginia to Texas it was the size of France and Germany combined. "The vast size of the Confederacy," write Hattaway and Jones, "its poor roads, and its somewhat limited production of food and fodder which an invader could appropriate made the Union strategy of defeating the Rebellion by conquering territory very difficult."[252]

Similarly, the 3,500-mile Confederate coastline, with its numerous harbors and inlets, would prove impossible for the Union navy to blockade effectively. In terms of military doctrine, leading thinkers such as Henri Jomini and Klaus von Clausewitz posited that wars of territorial defense more often succeeded than wars of conquest. As Clausewitz put it, "the defensive form of warfare is intrinsically stronger than the offensive."[253] Logistical challenges alone, such as maintaining long, vulnerable supply lines through hostile territory, placed armies of invasion at a disadvantage. "For the size of armies raised in 1861," concludes one authority on military logistics, "living off the country in the Confederacy was difficult, and in some areas, in the presence of a comparable enemy, almost impossible....very large wagon trains were required for even a limited mobility."[254]

4. In terms of psychology and morale, defensive strategy also favored the Confederacy. The Southern people, fighting for their homes, would be spurred to greater sacrifices than their Northern foes. Internationally, too, the Confederate States' modest request only "to be let alone" would find more favor with foreign powers and possibly lead to their recognizing and aiding the South.

5. C.S. leaders agreed that all territory must be defended. Given the strength of State Rights doctrine in Southern politics, every Confederate governor would expect and demand that his state

---

252   Herman Hattaway and Archer Jones, *How the South Won: A Military History* (Urbana IL, 1983), p. 684.

253   Richard E. Beringer, Herman Hattaway, Archer Jones and William N. Still, Jr., *Why the North Lost the Civil War* (Athens GA, 1986), p. 47.

254   John G. Moore, "Mobility and Strategy in the Confederate War," *Military Affairs* (Summer 1960), p. 77.

be protected. As the war would show, some governors withheld troops and supplies from the Defense Department in Richmond so their states could have local defense troops in case of surprise enemy raids. At the same time, the commitment from Richmond that Southern forces would defend the whole Confederacy pleased the localities and harnessed their instincts for self-defense into national war policy. "The President was especially responsive to appeals from local authorities, especially governors, for detachments for the defense of exposed or threatened points," writes historian Archer Jones; "these reinforced the wisdom of Davis's adoption of a policy stressing the defense of the complete territorial integrity of the Confederacy, which harmonized very well with local demands."[255]

There were political benefits to be derived from territorial defense. In the words of one study of the war's strategy, "the presence of even a skeleton military force in every district of the Confederacy was not only politically advantageous, but also gave the government a sounding board for local needs and discontents."[256]

This also made sense as economic policy. Enemy occupation of farm lands, however brief, could deny Confederates the cotton, crops or livestock on those lands. Areas concentrated with industry or possessed of mineral resources were obviously to be guarded. Thus Confederate territorial defense posited the safety of the Shenandoah Valley breadbasket and the copper-rich areas of east Tennessee, to name but two.

6. Finally, the government's pledge to protect every Southern home from Yankee vandalism meant much to the men who went off to war. A volunteer army could quickly melt away if its soldiers deserted to get back home to protect their families.

---

255 Archer Jones, *Confederate Strategy from Shiloh to Vicksburg* (Baton Rouge, 1961), p. 19.

256 Thomas Lawrence Connelly and Archer Jones, *The Politics of Command: Factions and Ideas in Confederate Strategy* (Baton Rouge, 1973), p. 183.

For all of these reasons, Professor Beringer and his colleagues summarized the positives of Confederate war planning: "the Confederacy practiced a defensive strategy, one in harmony with its military situation and political objectives."[257]

The fact that the South won its independence in fair measure by sticking to its offensive-defensive strategy turned out to be the biggest positive of all.

---

257 Beringer *et al., op. cit.*, p. 105.

Chapter Five:

Early Engagements

MISSOURI TOTTERS SOUTHWARD

With a four-state band of the Upper South—Virginia, North Carolina, Tennessee and Arkansas—having joined the Confederacy, there were anxieties among leaders of both sides in May of '61 as to the course of the even more Upper South. These states found themselves quite uncomfortably split between the pro-Southern and pro-Northern sympathies of their citizens. One such state was Missouri.

Governor Claiborne Jackson and Lieutenant Governor Thomas Reynolds had taken office in January, just as the Deep South was taking itself out of the Union. The Lieutenant Governor was an outspoken secessionist. Governor Jackson was less so, though he praised South Carolina for standing up for her rights, and was ready to lead his state also out of the Union if Missourians so voted their will. Between the two of them, they got the General Assembly to pass a resolution on January 18 declaring that any attempt at Federal coercion against the South "would result in the people of Missouri rallying on the side of their Southern brethren to resist to the last extremity."[258]

---

258   John McElroy, *The Struggle for Missouri* (Washington, 1913), p. 28.

The lopsided vote for this measure (only one no in the 33-seat senate; 14 nays in the 132-seat House) indicated the pro-Southern temperament of the Missouri legislature. But pro-Southernism did not translate to pro-secessionism. Among the people, advocates of immediate disunion were in the minority. Not only that, but they were countered by a powerful faction of unconditional Unionists, concentrated mainly in St. Louis. Somewhere in between the two extremes, most Missourians were probably "conditional Unionists," opposed to secession but vehemently opposed also to the Federal government's use of force against any state (particularly their own).

In this smoldering situation, both sides realized that any rash action could spark an explosion among the citizenry, and send the state one way or another. Throughout February and March, then, the opposing factions maneuvered to strengthen their positions. In the State Senate, Lieutenant Governor Reynolds appointed secessionists to chair important committees. The Unionists' principal leader, Frank Blair, Jr., organized a "Committee of Safety" to direct activities in the legislature at Jefferson City (Blair was the son of Francis Blair, who had offered to R.E. Lee the generalship of the Union forces). Meanwhile in St. Louis, Blair helped form companies of "Home Guards," which went about their training in secret. The Guards were not successful, however, in their secrecy, for St. Louis had a great many Southern sympathizers. They soon unfurled their single-star secession flags from buildings and organized "Minute Man" units which drilled openly, with fifes and drums playing and banners flapping.

Both sides had their eyes on the prize: the U.S. Arsenal at St. Louis. One of the most important in the country, the place encompassed fifty-six acres along the Mississippi River, enclosed by a high stone wall. Within were 60,000 muskets, mostly Enfield and Springfield rifles, a million and a half cartridges, 90,000 pounds of powder, other munitions and even some artillery. The arsenal was only weakly garrisoned by U.S. troops. Their commander, Major William Bell, was a Southern sympathizer from North Carolina, and was ready to hand over the property whenever the Governor called for it. For the time being, though, Jackson refrained from taking the arsenal, preferring to wait till a pro-Southern state militia could be formed; it would then march in and take the place. Meanwhile, an anxious Frank Blair repeatedly petitioned Washington to send a "Union man" to replace Major Bell, along with enough Federal soldiers to keep the arsenal safe. Washington, however, failed to respond. Lame duck Buchanan would not act in the last weeks of his term, and new inauguree Lincoln was too fixed on the Sumter crisis to pay much attention to St. Louis. A disappointed Blair, like Jackson, nonetheless cautioned his followers against storming the arsenal and provoking a public reaction that might carry the state out of the Union.

Then came Fort Sumter and Lincoln's call for troops on April 15. The summons from Washington angered many Missourians, most notably Governor Jackson himself, whose fiery denunciation of Lincoln's "inhuman and diabolical" war upon the Southern people was published in papers across the state. Secessionists were quick to capitalize on the public uproar. They unfurled the Stars and Bars from buildings in Rolla, Lexington, Jefferson City, Kansas City and elsewhere. In St. Louis they tore down United States flags at post offices and raised their own banners. The "Minute Men" more than once got out of hand as they broke up Union meetings, sometimes roughing up and even robbing the Lincolnites inside. Some Northern sympathizers were forced to take up their families and flee to Illinois, Kansas or Iowa.

Clearly momentum was with the pro-Confederates. Governor Jackson called the General Assembly into session and urged it to prepare for the armed defense of the state. Over Unionists' opposition, the legislature passed the Military Bill, which summoned able-bodied men into the Missouri State Guard. Under provisions of the act, each Congressional district was made into a Military Division, to be commanded by a brigadier general appointed by the governor. All the money in the state treasury, about $2 million, was appropriated for the purchase of war materials, and Jackson was given full authority to repel invasion and appoint a major general to command the state's forces (the post went to Sterling Price, prominent slaveholder and Mexican War veteran). As early as April 16, Jackson sent two "Minute Man" leaders, Basil Duke and Colton Greene, to Montgomery to arrange for the sale of artillery; a third agent was sent to Richmond, there to begin purchase deals with Tredegar Iron Works.

Once it became known that Governor Jackson envisioned the State Guard as a para-Confederate force, Union men declined appointment as its officers, and generally avoided recruitment as militiamen. As a result, commanders of the eight divisions were staunch supporters of the South. (Four later became generals in the Confederate army, including M. Jeff Thompson, soon to be known as the "Missouri Swamp Fox" for his raids against the Yankees.[259]) The brigadiers soon formed their divisions, each with several regiments of infantry, troops of cavalry and artillery batteries. The Governor distributed weapons from the state armory. At his orders, on April 23 secessionist militiamen helped themselves to the weaponry in the U.S. Arsenal at Liberty, taking in several hundred muskets, four brass cannon, 15,000 pounds of lead and much powder.

Two days later the far more important cache at St. Louis fell into the Southerners' hands. Brigadier General David M. Frost, Guards commander for the St. Louis district, had set up a camp for militiamen outside the city, and soon was drilling nearly a thousand men at the place, named for Governor Jackson. Many of the men were poorly armed, but Frost's division gained considerable strength with the arrival from downriver of two 12-pounder howitzers and two 32-pounder smoothbores plus ammo—all gifts of the Confederate government (seized at the Baton Rouge arsenal) and all informally earmarked as stone wall-breachers, whenever Jackson and Frost should decide to attack the arsenal at St. Louis. That time had now come. On April 25 a

---

259   Jeff Thompson is not listed among the Confederate army's general staff in the definitive source on the subject, Ezra J. Warner, *Generals in Gray* (Baton Rouge, 1959). But see Stephen Davis, "Jeff Thompson's Quest for a Confederate Generalship," *Missouri Historical Review*, vol. 45, no. 1 (October 1990), 53-65. After the war Thompson's plucky war record as the "Swamp Fox" of southeast Missouri won him a seat in the Confederate House of Representatives; in his campaign stump speeches he repeated his oft-heard wartime claim that he was a "rip-squealer." Steve Davis, "I Am a Rip-Squealer and My Name is Fight: M. Jeff Thompson of Missouri," *Blue & Gray* (April – May 1987), 28-39. See also Stephen Davis, ed., *The Civil War Reminiscences of General M. Jeff Thompson* (Dayton OH, 1988), p. 297.

thousand state guardsmen, led by Major General Price himself, marched into town and presented themselves with a showy front of artillery before the arsenal. Moreover, Price had moved so fast that Blair's Home Guards were not able to muster in time for a response. Intimidated, not to mention outnumbered, Major Bell, the arsenal commander, simply turned over the keys to the place and walked out carrying his bags, leaving his several dozen officers and men to do the same.

Without bloodshed, almost without effort, the St. Louis Arsenal's invaluable contents became Missouri state property—soon to be that of the Confederate States. For his part, having just put in the mail his resignation from the U.S. Army, Bell went straight to the railway station, bought a ticket and boarded the train for Montgomery, where he intended to present himself for a commission in the Confederate army.

Camp Jackson and The Secession of Missouri

Sterling Price's capture of the St. Louis Arsenal on April 25 further emboldened the pro-Confederate faction in Missouri, as did the news of Virginia's secession, one state more for the new Southern republic. Governor Jackson and Lieutenant Governor Reynolds won enough votes in the legislature to ram through a bill calling for a state convention "to consider the relations of Missouri to the United States."[260] Election of delegates to the convention was set for Saturday, May 4—with momentum on their side, the secessionists would not delay. Those elected would assemble at a state convention scheduled to begin in Jefferson City on May 10.

Frank Blair and his coterie of loyalists in St. Louis refused to give in—yet. Confronted by a hostile state government and now by a hostile and well-armed state militia, the Unionist factions in Missouri had no hope of help except from the outside. They frantically appealed for arms to Illinois Governor Richard Yates. Though he was trying to arm his own regiments, Yates shipped 5,000 rifles to St. Louis. Blair again pleaded to Washington for U.S. regulars and a capable officer to lead the Home Guards units,

---

260   John McElroy, *The Struggle for Missouri* (Washington, 1913), p. 38.

which were essentially standing around waiting for orders. The War Department, caught up in mobilizing the whole North, could spare neither weapons nor troops. But it did transfer to St. Louis a company of regulars from Fort Riley, Kansas, led by Captain Nathaniel Lyon. The energetic, almost maniacally driven Lyon whipped the Home Guards into shape and organized them into four regiments—the very number which Lincoln had so "diabolically" called for from Missouri on April 15. Lyon ostentatiously trained them in the streets of St. Louis, temporarily cowing the secessionists in the city, and stimulating enough loyalist volunteers to form a fifth regiment. Still more were organized as "U.S. Reserves." These accomplishments seemed to stabilize the situation by the end of the month, and even inspired Blair to believe that Missouri could still be saved for the Union. He did not calculate, however, the damage that could be done by a single impetuous infantry officer.

Captain Nathaniel Lyon was, if anything, self-assured. This wiry-framed redhead from Connecticut (USMA, Class of '41) showed such overconfidence in his own rightness on every conceivable issue that he made enemies everywhere he went; he had no real friends even among his fellow officers. One of them said of Lyon, "There was no middle ground with him in any matter that engaged his attention, and he conceived that it was his duty to enforce his doctrines or his ideas upon all with whom he came in contact, even to the extent of being offensive." What made Lyon all the more obnoxious was that his doctrines and ideas were sometimes downright zany. In matters of religion he proudly announced himself "an infidel, and perhaps even an atheist," who delighted in trying to convince Christian evangelicals that Socrates was a nobler man than Jesus. In matters of science he was even more eccentric. Once he argued at a Lyceum club in New York that snakes would grow legs and develop into reptilian quadrupeds if only pure oxygen were administered to them long enough. With crack-brained ideas such as these, it was all the War Department could do just to get rid of the man. In 1851 the Army stationed Captain Lyon at Fort Riley, Kansas, where he spent the next decade terrorizing the poor soldiers under his command. "If one of his men broke military regulations," observes a noted scholar (and

Lyon was a slave to regulations, as long as they did not contradict his own concept of justice), the Captain marched the poor wretch bareheaded across the parade ground, under the hot sun, with honey in his hair and a barrel over his shoulders to keep him from brushing away the flies."[261]

This was the infantry officer dispatched to save the Union cause in Missouri. A more unfortunate choice, in hindsight, could not have been made by Federal officials. True, Captain Lyon, bringing with him a company of regulars from Fort Riley, helped arm, organize and train Blair's Home Guards. But as far as understanding the delicate situation in Missouri, and the need for extreme caution against the crafty secessionists, Nathaniel Lyon responded to reality about as well as his notion of four-legged snakes.

Faced with the fast-approaching election of delegates to the state convention, both secessionist and Unionist factions appealed to the public through newspapers, handbills and stump speeches across the state. A speech of Lieutenant Governor Reynolds in the State Senate, violently denouncing the North, was given wide publicity. Governor Jackson privately predicted that disunionists would win the majority of convention seats; even more privately he began corresponding with Jefferson Davis as if Missouri were already one of the Confederate States. Such was not yet the case, but Davis expected it soon to be. "We look anxiously and hopefully," the President wrote in a secret memorandum on April 23, "for the day when the star of Missouri shall be added to the constellation of the Confederate States of America."[262]

When election day for the state convention came on May 4, the results shocked Jackson, Reynolds and just about everyone else who had ventured a prediction. Apparently responding to the Unionists' eleventh-hour warnings of civil war and how Missouri would be turned into a battlefield if she seceded, voters of the state turned out to the polls and turned against extremists of both sides.

---

261   Stephen B. Oates, "Nathaniel Lyon," *Civil War Times Illustrated* (February 1968), p. 15.

262   McElroy, *Struggle for Missouri*, p. 57.

Of over 165,000 ballots cast, only 31,000 (less than 20%) went to delegates committed to immediate secession. On the opposite end of the spectrum, unconditional Unionists got 17,000 votes, or 10%. Thus fully 70% of voting Missourians supported delegates to the convention who professed hopes for peace and promised that they would find some means for armed neutrality in the sectional crisis, opting for alliance with neither South nor North.

As in Kentucky, armed neutrality in Missouri would last only if neither side rocked the boat. Unfortunately, in the pro-Northern camp was the quintessential boat-rocker, one Captain Nathaniel Lyon. As the date neared for the state convention, Lyon became more and more agitated. "I would rather see the country lighted up with the flames of war from the center to its remotest border," he told Blair, "than that the great rights and hopes of the human race expire before the arrogance of secessionists."

In this fevered state of mind, Captain Lyon viewed the presence of pro-Confederate Brigadier Daniel Frost's State Militia, set up at Camp Jackson in Lindell Grove outside St. Louis, as an "insult." Union men in the city urged him to take no action, but Lyon muttered angry threats and promised "to administer a lasting rebuke to the traitors who have thus far had their own way." Frost's militiamen, whom Lyon termed "a body of rabid and violent opponents of the general government," would have to be eliminated.[263]

To do so, Lyon had amassed sufficient strength: 3,000 to 4,000 militia in the five newly-organized regiments, including Blair's Home Guards and Reserve auxiliaries. Frost's strength outside the city had been lowered to about six hundred—weakened by the same sicknesses that struck all the war's early recruits thrown into camp where communicable diseases ran rampant. The Rebels had given up their homegrown squirrel-guns and flintlocks for the shiny Enfields captured at the arsenal. In a fight, though both sides were an imperfectly trained rabble, the armament advantage would go to the Southerners; so Lyon planned to surprise the secesh in a way that would lead to their surrender without a fight.

---

263 Oates, "Nathaniel Lyon," pp. 16, 18.

Determined to take no chances, Lyon made plans to reconnoiter Frost's camp. But with his brushy red hair and beard, he was too well known to gain entrance onto Jackson's grounds. So he dressed himself up as a woman—not just any woman, but as Frank Blair's mother-in-law, Mrs. Andrew Alexander, well known for taking her buggy rides through the streets of St. Louis. Tucking hair and beard under bonnet, veil and shawl, Lyon had a coachman drive him into the camp as he cased it and coolly departed. At Blair's house his descent from the carriage caused one onlooker to wonder "why on earth Mrs. Alexander was wearing cavalry boots," but no one took alarm.[264]

Lyon's timing could not have been more disastrous. Early on the morning of Friday, May 10, a few hours before the state convention was starting its proceedings in Jefferson City, Lyon got his troops into ranks downtown, and set them marching for Frost's State Guards encamped at Lindell Grove outside town. Without much trouble the Unionists surrounded the place, and Lyon sent in his demand for surrender.

> Sir: Your command is regarded as evidently hostile to the Government of the United States. It is for most part made up of those Secessionists who have openly avowed their hostility to the General Government, and have been plotting the overthrow of its authority. You are openly in communication with the so-called Southern Confederacy, which is now at war with the United States; and you are receiving at your camp, from the said Confederacy and under its flag, large supplies of the material of war, most of which is known to be the property of the United States. These extraordinary preparations plainly indicate none other than the well-known purpose of the Governor of this State...[which is] hostilities to the General Government and co-operation with its Enemies.

---

264 Peggy Robbins, "The Battle of Camp Jackson," *Civil War Times Illustrated* (June 1981), p. 40.

In view of these considerations...and the obligations imposed upon me by instructions from Washington, it is my duty to demand, and I do hereby demand of you, an immediate surrender of your command, with no other conditions than that all persons surrendering under this demand shall be humanely and kindly treated. Believing myself prepared to enforce this demand, one-half hour's time before doing so will be allowed for your compliance therewith.[265]

Caught by surprise and unprepared to offer resistance, General Frost and his officers quickly agreed to comply. The six hundred state militiamen formed, marched out, stacked their arms, and were then herded by Lyon's soldiers toward town.

Watching all this from surrounding hillsides were large numbers of St. Louisans who had come out expecting to see a fight. Disappointed and angry, the pro-Southerners among them followed the Federal guard lines back into the city. As Lyon's troops and their captives entered downtown, irate crowds of Southern sympathizers lined the sidewalks, taunting the Federals and exhorting their prisoners with shouts of "Hurrah for Jeff Davis" and "Free our heroes." Some began to throw rocks. As at Baltimore just three weeks before, someone had to fire a first shot. According to most accounts, it came from the crowd—pistol shots into a company of the 3d Missouri Volunteers, several of whom were wounded. When the captain ordered an open-fire, his troops levelled their muskets on the mob and volleyed. Citizens shrieked and cried as they scattered for cover. When the smoke cleared twenty-eight civilians, including two women and a small child, lay dead or dying in the streets of St. Louis. The number of wounded probably reached sixty to seventy. Against this fearful toll, U.S. casualties amounted to one soldier killed, one mortally wounded, two wounded.

---

265   McElroy, *Struggle for Missouri,* pp. 62-63.

The civil unrest and violence were not over. Mobs gathered outside the downtown warehouse where Lyon had confined the secesh, but they did not attempt to storm the place and the Unionist troops kept order without violence. The next morning a crowd antagonized some soldiers of the 5th U.S. Reserves; again shots were fired, and six more civilians were killed or wounded. Gradually the situation began to cool down when Lyon bitterly conceded the need to parole Frost and his militiamen.

Telegraphic news of the "Camp Jackson massacre" spread rapidly throughout Missouri, upsetting the people with reports of the Unionist troops firing indiscriminately on civilians, killing women and children. More upset were the 165 delegates convening in the state capital. Already disunionists had been emboldened by the recent news of the secession of neighboring Arkansas and Tennessee just days before. Now, reports of Lyon's attack, capture of Frost's "peaceable" State Guards and civilian deaths in the very streets of St. Louis created a widespread reaction in the pro-Confederates' favor. Conversions among the delegates began occurring overnight. One delegate was Sterling Price, Major General in the state forces, and widely respected as a former governor, Mexican War leader, and one of the most influential men in the state. Once known as a "conditional Unionist," he let it be known that the reports from St. Louis threw him unalterably in favor of secession. Like dozens of other delegates, Price considered the seizure of Camp Jackson (in the words of his biographer) "a flagrant violation of Missouri's sovereign rights," and the ensuing civilian massacre "as the natural consequence of Lincoln's coercion policy."[266] Thus on May 11 the convention that was called "to consider the relations of Missouri to the United States" now considered those relations worth severing. The ordinance of secession was drafted and approved on May 12. The notification was made certain when, sensing impending defeat, the last seventeen Unionist delegates walked out of the convention hall just as the final vote was about to begin.

---

266   Albert Castel, *General Sterling Price and the Confederate War in the West* (Baton Rouge, 1968), p. 14.

The formal adoption of secession actually resolved Missouri's status only on paper, for the people of the state remained as divided as ever, but with differences. Pro-Confederates openly rallied to the State Guard, while pro-Unionists organized companies only in their own neighborhoods, furtively, fearful of the state forces' heavy boot. Belatedly Lincoln and his War Department in Washington recognized their error in sending a hothead to a hotbed. They did not so much as relieve Captain Lyon as they dispatched, very quickly, Brigadier General William S. Harney to St. Louis with instructions to try to salvage what he could of the Union cause in Missouri.

Harney was a reasonable choice (certainly over Lyon). Regular army man, mature in years (nearly sixty) and presumably in judgement, he had previously been posted at St. Louis and even had family there. But when he arrived, Harney saw little that he could do but buy time, hoping that events or outside assistance might stem the pro-Confederate tide in the state. In Jefferson City, Jackson, Reynolds and Price had reasons of their own to forestall an immediate military conflict; they wanted to consolidate and strengthen their forces while waiting for possible Confederate military aid. They learned that Harney was interested in arranging some sort of truce to forestall the outbreak of fighting. So on May 20 General Price met with General Harney in St. Louis, and the two signed their names to an unusual truce agreement, with each declaring no intention to make any military movements for the foreseeable future:

> General Price, having by commission full authority over the militia of the State of Missouri, undertakes, with the sanction of the governor of the State, already declared, to direct the whole power of the state officers to maintain order within the State among the people thereof, and General Harney publicly declares that this object being thus assured, he can have no occasion, as he has no wish, to make

military movements which might otherwise create excitements and jealousies, which he most earnestly desires to avoid.

We, the undersigned, do therefore mutually enjoin upon the people of the State to attend to their civil business of whatever sort it may be, and it is to be hoped that the unquiet elements which have threatened so seriously to disturb the public peace may soon subside and be remembered only to be deplored.[267]

THE CAPITAL IS RELOCATED

With the Union capital just across the river, and with Lincoln— now recovered from the scare of Baltimore and Fort Stevens— already planning aggressive moves against the South, it was apparent that Virginia would be *the* major theater of the war. That distinction of sorts was assured when, on April 27, the Virginia Convention formally invited the Confederate government to move its capital from Montgomery to Richmond, city of 38,000, major manufacturing center, and the state's center of government. The offer was formally presented to the C.S. Congress on May 10.

Administration officials were attempting to make do in Montgomery when the invitation came. The Government Building, the "great red brick pile" at Bibb and Commerce, had begun to feel commodious to at least some of its occupants, especially the Chief Executive, whose office was on the second floor. President and Mrs. Davis had also moved out of the Exchange Hotel, giving up Room 101 in mid-April for the much homier two-story frame residence at Bibb and Washington, easily walkable to both the capitol and Government.

Yet for even Cabinet officers and lesser government workers, Montgomery's problems as capital remained the same. Topping the list was inadequate office space. Robert Toombs' State Department,

267 Gerald Gannon, "The Harney-Price Agreement," *Civil War Times Illustrated* (December 1984), p. 43.

for one, quickly overflowed its few little rooms in the Government Building, sending clerks' desks into closets, hallways, even outside on the street. When approached one day by a job-seeker, Toombs was asked for the location of his office. He snatched off his hat with a torrent of cuss-words. "There, sir," he howled, pointing to his topper; "there is the State Department of the Confederacy, by God! Jump in, sir!"[268] There were way too few hotel rooms, as well, and everyone had gotten tired of hearing the city fathers promise a mammoth new hotel which was always "soon" to be built. High rents for apartments and boarding houses meant that most had to pay dearly. And the same went for many goods, too, as greedy retailers took stock of supply and demand, and reacted as they commonly do. Even Vice President Stephens, before he left town for his home in Georgia, was shocked to pay twice the usual price for a simple umbrella (of course, it was raining outside at the time). For the hundreds of new Montgomerites associated with government service, the chief complaint had to do with that most basic of creature comforts, food. Mediocre and limited were the politest descriptions of the fare at even the more respectable of the city's dining establishments, with one restaurant at Montgomery Hall, ordinarily a pretty nice hotel, widely detested as a "den of horrors."[269]

Thus many in the government were ready for a change—almost any change—when word spread that Richmond had offered itself as the new Confederate capital. To be sure, there were such matters as national security—was not Richmond too close to Yankee lines, just a hundred miles from Washington City?—and political interest—had not Virginia held back from secession after the Black Republicans' presidential triumph? There were counterarguments as well. Virginia would no doubt be a major war-theater, and it made sense for the seat of Confederate decision-making to be close at hand. And if Virginia had not seceded as fast as her sister states in the lower South, might not her eventual response to Lincoln's

---

268 Manly Wade Wellman, *They Took Their Stand: The Founders of the Confederacy* (New York, 1959), p. 111.

269 William Warren Rogers, Jr., *Confederate Home Front: Montgomery During the War* (Tuscaloosa, 1999), pp. 31, 40.

call for an army of subjugation also influence secessionists in Maryland or Kentucky to take their states out? Other factors were more military in nature: as the South's most populous state, Virginia would give liberally of her sons, hence deserved the reward of capital city; the Tredegar Iron Works was probably the most important rolling mill in the entire Confederacy and needed protection as much as any seat of government would, &c., &c. But the true drivers of Confederate politicians' decision to relocate the capital had to do ultimately with themselves. Richmond, four times the size of Montgomery, could offer more options for habitation, greater commercial competition (with it, less price-gouging by shopkeepers), and better choices for public dining. Not to be ignored were Montgomery's infamous heat and mosquitoes, looming in the summer months just ahead. Although the Congressional vote on May 20 was not unanimous, the move to Richmond was for all of these reasons easily approved. The President signed the bill on the 21st, still days before Virginia's voters were to go to the polls and presumably ratify the State Convention's vote for secession. The powers-that-be in Montgomery were confident of which way the vote would go.

THE MOVE TO RICHMOND

The Confederate Congress had barely adjourned on May 21, having resolved to reconvene in Richmond on July 20, when the busy process of packing up began. Several legislators accepted the responsibility of selling the leases to the Executive Mansion and Government House as well as the furniture designated to stay behind in Montgomery. Clerks and porters carried desks, drawers, files and papers to the train depot for rail transportation to the new capital.

Most Congressmen cleared out of Montgomery a day or two after the session's adjournment. The Cabinet departments at that time started boxing up their stuff, a process which took until May 30. Some details were bound to be overlooked. No one thought to close the Defense Department's Post Office Box, #217, which was soon stuffed with letters of appeal and application, all of which had to be forwarded to Richmond.

The President remained in Montgomery until the evening of May 26, when he boarded with Adjutant General Cooper, Secretary Toombs, and a few more dignitaries. (Mrs. Davis and the 3 ½ children—Varina was ten weeks pregnant—would leave in a few days.) Through Georgia and the Carolinas they chugged, with Davis stepping to the end of the cars to give a brief address to the crowds in Atlanta, Goldsboro and a few other places. Finally, on the morning of May 29, the President's train pulled into Richmond as artillery barked a fifteen-gun welcoming salute. Governor Letcher was at the station to greet him, as was Mayor Joseph Mayo. They led Davis to an open carriage and made their horse-drawn way the four blocks to the new presidential quarters at the Spotswood Hotel. The whole city knew he was coming. Citizens lined the streets, waving and cheering; more crowded at the hotel entrance, Eighth and Main Streets. Though fatigued, Davis gave them a few impromptu remarks, building on Virginians' well-known pride in their patriotic forebears, Washington, Jefferson, Madison, Monroe: "We inherited a beautiful model government from these great statesmen and patriots," Davis declared, "but it has been perverted by a faction, whose purpose it is to deprive us of the constitutional rights bequeathed us by the fathers." Though this was by now a familiar message to most Southern citizens—to the point that the ones hearing it (all white back then) knew that the "rights" alluded meant the privilege of owning Negro slaves—those hearing it from Davis's lips cheered all the more approvingly.[270]

At the Spotswood, the best rooms in the house, 121 and 122, went to the Davises as their quarters, while on the floor below, Room 83 was made into a parlor area for presidential meetings. Meanwhile, Richmonders made space for their new fellow-residents. The U.S. Custom House facing Capitol Square became the executive office building, a convenient three-block walk from the Spotswood. In other downtown buildings offices were subdivided, pushed out, walled in or torn down, all to create room for the new level of government bureaucracy suddenly descended upon the city. Meanwhile the Davis family resided at the Spotswood until

---

270   Ernest B. Furgurson, *Wings of Glory: Richmond at War* (New York, 1996), p. 51.

the renovations on their new residence, a stately three-and-a-half story brick and stucco, could be completed. Situated on Twelfth and Clay Streets, the Executive Mansion began to be called the "Gray House," ostensibly for the hue of its stucco exterior, but also to distinguish it from the more widely known residence of that other president across the Potomac. Besides, this was a Confederate thing: the nation's military uniforms were gray, the President's preferred suit color was gray, and in the midst of the nation's early patriotic enthusiasm, some ultra-Confederates were overheard loudly throughout the country proclaiming satisfaction on a cloudy morning that it was a beautiful "gray day."

Davis and his family moved into the Gray House on August 1. By then, the Confederate States of America had won its first great battlefield victory.

C.S. Troops Form an Army in Virginia

The Southerners' switch of civil seats brought new pressures to Robert E. Lee and those charged with defending Virginia. Until troops from other parts of the Confederacy arrived, Lee moved cautiously. Even before the Confederate Congress voted to move the nation's capital to Richmond, Lee in the first week of May began uncharacteristically to order movements in retrograde. On May 1, he ordered Jackson to haul all machinery from the Harpers Ferry arsenal to Winchester and Strasburg, and prepare to withdraw upon any enemy advance. Four days later state troops abandoned their exposed position at Alexandria for more secure camps southward around Manassas Junction, thirty miles southwest of Washington.

While Lee directed these movements, Confederate troops from all over the South finally began to arrive in Virginia, swelling the ranks of the Old Dominion's defenders. Typical of these regiments was the Sixth Alabama, which had entrained at Corinth, Mississippi. Their long railway journey was relieved by frequent stops in Tennessee. Hospitable townsfolk beckoned the soldiers to come off the cars and sample corn whiskey in jugs; many did, then boozily climbed onboard again. In eastern Tennessee, though, where Unionist sentiment still lingered, the soldiers got boos and jeers, not booze and cheers. Officers, still wearing the green frock coats presented at the regiment's organizational ceremony, had to restrain the men from jumping off the train to strike down U.S. flags spotted at several depots. Through the great valley of east Tennessee they made their way into Virginia and eventually to Manassas.

Troops from Georgia and the Carolinas were arriving, too. From South Carolina, for instance, came the First and Second Infantry Regiments, which had served at Fort Sumter, and the Hampton Legion: six companies of infantry, four of cavalry, and a battery of six highly prized rifled Blakely guns, all organized and outfitted at the personal expense of wealthy planter Wade Hampton. Wearing forage caps with white havelocks (little capes descending from the back of the hats to drape the wearers' necks, shielding them from sunburn), the Legion made the train trip to the front in three days. The Carolinians' high point came at Petersburg, Virginia, where enthusiastic citizens waved Palmetto flags while serving meals of ham, cabbage, Irish potatoes and raw onions. Well-fed but exhausted, the Legion slept in a Richmond tobacco warehouse at the end of their journey. From Richmond the new arrivals made their way north to the army Brig. Gen. G.T. Beauregard commanded in the vicinity of Manassas Junction. Another sizable force was in the Shenandoah Valley under Brig. Gen. Joseph E. Johnston.

"On June 8 Governor Letcher directed that all Virginia forces be transferred into the Confederate army. Lee had done a masterful job," writes historian James I. Robertson, Jr. "In less than two months, he had organized 40,000 troops, with field and staff officers, and with every regiment at least partially armed with purchased or confiscated weapons. No one in the Confederacy had done more to prepare for war."[271]

---

271 James I. Robertson, Jr., *Confederate Virginia: Battleground for a Nation* (Charlottesville VA, 1991), pp. 23, 26.

WEST POINTERS HEADING SOUTH:
THE CONFEDERACY'S FIRST GENERALS

There was a distinctive group of volunteers for whom the determination to fight for the Confederacy called for a special kind of decision-making: those soldiers who received their military training at the U.S. government's expense, and who had in many cases sworn an oath of allegiance to serve the United States in time of war. These were the West Pointers.

Fully 306 graduates of the U.S. Military Academy at West Point, New York, served in the Confederate forces. Over half were in the U.S. army when the war broke out, so their decisions to leave the service of the flag posed additional stresses. Most, of course, were Southern-born, and chose to follow their states upon secession or after Sumter. Some Northern-born West Pointers had moved south, married Southern women, or in other ways found reasons to attach themselves to the prospects of the Confederacy. The story of how the Southern army's first brigadier generals received their commissions illustrates the various ways in which West Pointers made their career-change from the service of one flag to another.

Pierre Gustave Toutant Beauregard, second in the class of 1838, served capably in the corps of engineers and during the war with Mexico. In November 1860 Captain Beauregard was appointed Superintendent of the Military Academy, a coveted post indeed. But *en route* Beauregard informed his superiors in Washington that he would resign his commission if Louisiana left the Union. With the political crisis deepening, the War Department nonetheless allowed Beauregard to proceed to West Point, where he assumed the superintendency on January 23. Three days later, Louisiana did in fact secede. Having been warned, Washington acted: orders went out that Beauregard was to return the superintendency to Colonel Richard Delafield (from whom he had just taken it). After this exchange, Beauregard's resignation from the army on February 8 was anticlimactic.

Out of a job, Beauregard wasted no time. Within forty-eight hours he wrote to the new Confederate President seeking an officer's commission. A couple of weeks later he got an invitation to come to Montgomery for a presidential interview. In the capital on February 26, Beauregard met with Davis, discussed the situation at Charleston, and was given command of C.S. Troops there. His commission as brigadier general, then the highest rank authorized for the army, dated from March 1, 1861. Beauregard was thus the Confederate army's first general.

Its second was Braxton Bragg, whose decision to side with the South did not involve a resignation from the old army; Bragg had left it years earlier. A graduate of West Point's class of 1837, he had served honorably in the Mexican War. But disillusionment with frontier garrison duty and felicitous finding of a rich wife allowed him to resign in December 1855 to start a new life as Louisiana planter. His army record was sufficiently lustrous for him to be appointed commander of Louisiana State forces after the state seceded. From this office he watched somewhat jealously as his fellow Louisianan Beauregard got the C.S. Army's first brigadiership. Within a week, though, Bragg was mollified by receipt of his own brigadier general's commission, under date of March 7.

Samuel Cooper was one of the few future Confederate West Pointers who had their jobs virtually waiting for them when the Southern national government formed in Montgomery. An oldster, born 1798 in New Jersey, Cooper graduated from the Point in the class of 1815 just missing the war with Britain. He served in Mexico, earning a brevet colonelcy. But Cooper had already begun building his army career as a staff officer. In July 1838 he was assigned to the War Department as Assistant Adjutant General. Fourteen years later General-in-Chief Winfield Scott promoted Cooper to Adjutant General of the army. He held this important office all the way to the war, winning the friendship of Secretary of War Jefferson Davis (1853-57) and even of President Pierce.

Having married a Virginia lady, befriended by Davis and other Southerners, and believing the use of Federal force to coerce seceded states to be unconstitutional, Cooper was ready to "go south" as the Constitutional crisis became a bellicose one. Jefferson Davis had barely been three weeks in office as C.S. President when

Cooper resigned March 7, 1861. Making his way to Montgomery, Cooper doubtless aspired to the AG position in the Southern army a-building. He was not disappointed. After arriving in the capital, Cooper met with Davis and was offered the post of Adjutant and Inspector-General of the C.S. Forces, which the President hoped he would accept "while his juniors led armies in the field."[272] Cooper indeed accepted, and on March 16 was appointed brigadier general—the third such commission in the South's infant army.

The Confederacy's first three generals compiled distinctly different service records in the war of 1861-63. The ancient Cooper performed efficiently as Adjutant General, handling matters of army paperwork and protocol that spared the President and Defense Secretary for more important tasks. Beauregard's army career, as they used to say, resembled the rocket that shot up with spark and flame, then fizzled and fell down as a stick. The hero of Sumter won further glory as commander of the victorious Confederate army at Manassas, and within a year became known as the architect of the troop concentration in north Mississippi that led to Sidney Johnston's triumph at Shiloh. After that, however, Beauregard let his bombast and occasionally flighty strategic schemes get the best of him. He fell out of favor with Davis and for the rest of the war found himself sidelined back to Charleston, where he nonetheless performed admirably in directing the defense of one of the Confederacy's most important port cities.

Bragg fizzled even faster. As commander at Pensacola, his reluctance to attack the U.S. garrison at Fort Pickens more than irked and annoyed the C.S. Chief Executive who had placed so much importance on ridding the Confederacy of the Yankee coastal garrison at Charleston. But as Davis came to swallow the persistent insult of Pickens, he also concluded that Bragg's best post was at that very point, where he would be forced every day to stare out across Pensacola Bay and see the pernicious Stars and Stripes flouting his authority and simultaneously stifling any

---

272 William C. Davis, "Samuel Cooper" in William C. Davis, ed., *The Confederate General*, 6 vols. (Richmond, 1991), vol. 2, 29.

further promotion. Bragg thus spent the whole war in charge of the Pensacola garrison, for whose officers his most demanding chore was the planning of biweekly oyster-roasts.

THE PECULIAR CASE OF JOE JOHNSTON

Like Beauregard, Bragg and Cooper, Joseph E. Johnston was a prominent old army officer whose southward tilt was never in question as the sectional crisis heated up in the late '50s. But like his fellow Virginian Robert E. Lee, Johnston waited until his native state seceded before resigning his U.S. commission and casting his lot with the Confederacy.

In many ways, Joseph E. Johnston's career mirrored Robert E. Lee's—but only up to a point. Born three weeks and a hundred miles apart from each other, the two Virginians entered and graduated from the Military Academy in the same class (1829). Lee went with the engineers while Johnston entered the artillery service, but their early promotions roughly paralleled. Both started out as Second Lieutenant, and made First Lieutenant in 1836. Lee's captaincy came in 1838 and Johnston's in 1846, but sterling service in the Mexican War brought each a brevet majorship and brevet colonelcy. Lee and Johnston then both won promotion to lieutenant colonel in 1855. Five years later Johnston surged ahead when he won the coveted brigadier's rank upon appointment as the army's quartermaster general in June 1860. Lee was among those considered for this plum office in Washington, and doubtless he hoped for it. Nonetheless from his post at San Antonio, Lee wrote to congratulate his old friend upon his success.

After the secession of the lower South and the formation of the Confederate government, Johnston, like Lee, found himself wooed by both sides. (Lincoln authorized his friend Frank Blair to offer Lee command of the Federal army being formed to invade the South; Lee politely declined.) General Scott pleaded with Johnston's wife Lydia to keep him in the U.S. army. In mid-March 1861 C.S. Defense Secretary Walker wrote Johnston, offering him one of the army's first brigadierships. But the Virginian held off for another month until news came of the Old Dominion's secession. On April 22, Johnston strode into the U.S. War Office in Washington and handed over his letter of resignation. "I must go with the South," he was quoted as having said; "I owe all that I am to the government of the United States. It has educated me and clothed me with honor. To leave the service is a hard necessity, but I must go."[273] And so he went. On May 14 he was commissioned brigadier general in the Confederate army.

After that, Johnston's and Lee's service records went in different directions. While Lee gracefully acceded to President Davis's request that he sit at a Richmond desk in the first year of the war, Johnston got an important field command in northern Virginia, and helped Beauregard win at Manassas. Not content with these laurels, during September Johnston got into an ugly (and unfortunately public) spat with the President over seniority among the army's full generals, after that rank had been established by Congress. Still, it was Johnston who took command of the main Confederate army in Virginia after Beauregard went west. It was also Joe Johnston who failed in this test of his leadership, when he allowed McClellan in spring of '62 to advance up the Peninsula to within five miles of the capital at Richmond. The careers of Johnston and Lee had their climactic crossing as a result of Johnston's attack upon McClellan at Seven Pines, May 31. Johnston was seriously wounded and Davis dispatched Lee to succeed him. Lee, of course, never relinquished command of the magnificent Army of Northern Virginia. Johnston, even after his recovery, never again led a Confederate army. Davis, the Congress and the Southern people had seen enough of Johnston's mediocrity on the Peninsula. Old Joe was forced to sit out the war at home with Lydia, "awaiting orders" and sullenly enduring his popular acclaim as the "Hero of Seven Pines," knowing full well—as did everyone throughout the Confederacy—that the sobriquet was accorded solely because at Seven Pines Johnston had considerately exercised the good judgment to get himself severely wounded in time for Robert E. Lee to take over the army and win the war.

---

273   Craig L. Symonds, *Joseph E. Johnston: A Biography* (New York, 1992), p. 96.

THE DEATH OF COLONEL ELLSWORTH

After the Virginia convention's vote for secession on April 17 President Lincoln held out hope that the plebiscite called for on May 23 might overturn the delegates' decision. It did not. So many events had transpired in the month—the seizure of Gosport, the Baltimore riot, the organization of state forces under General Lee — that a reversal in referendum was unthinkable. And there was more. On April 24, a convention committee approved a treaty of alliance with the Confederate States, by which Virginia adopted the C.S. Constitution and placed its troops at national service. By that time a regiment of South Carolinians had marched into Richmond, reinforcing the sense of secession's *fait accompli*. When the state convention on April 27 invited the Confederate government to move its capital from Montgomery to Richmond, the popular vote on secession three and a half weeks later was really beside the point. It was made even more so by the Davis's administration's decision on May 21 to take the Virginians up on their offer of hospitality. Telegraphic news that Richmond would become the C.S. Capital began hitting the major Virginia newspapers the very day before citizens were to go to the polls to ratify or rescind the convention's ordinance of secession. Thus without surprise the popular vote came in overwhelmingly for disunion, 125,050 to 20,373. Most of the latter came from Virginia's north-western mountainous counties, where slavery was practically non-existent, and where favor for the incipient Confederacy was equally so.

The voice of the people of Virginia finally brought the national government on the other side of the river to act. By mid-May, Washington was bustling with troops, and talk among the President and his advisers turned from a strictly static defense to a more active one. Urged on by General Scott and the newly appointed commander of the District defenses, Brig. Gen. Joseph K.F. Mansfield, Lincoln nevertheless held off on ordering U.S. troops across the Potomac into Alexandria. But as the plebiscite approached, the Federal administration's wait for the Virginians' vote of May 23 began to appear as artificial (if politic) an exercise as the vote itself. Lincoln gave the go-ahead, and Scott ordered Mansfield to move soldiers over the bridges to occupy Alexandria's heights, including the Arlington estate owned by Mary and Robert E. Lee. With the referendum ballots still being counted on the night of the 23d-24th, much less yet to be announced, Federal troops in D.C. prepared their cross-river invasion.

On their side Alexandrians had been rallying to the colors. In the first days of May there were nearly 500 volunteers, albeit "untrained, mostly unarmed, and completely unorganized," in the words of one historian.[274] Not surprisingly many fell back from the city as early as May 5 when they felt the enemy's pressure from across the river. Alexandrians awaited the inevitable invasion.

In the early morning hours of the 24th three columns of Northern soldiers converged upon the hapless city: one by the Long Bridge, another by the aqueduct bridge upriver and a third aboard steamers. On the latter were Colonel Elmer Ephraim Ellsworth and the 11th Regiment of New York Volunteer Infantry. Recruited from the fire companies of New York City, the men were grandly uniformed, reflecting their colonel's admiration of the colorful, festive garb of French Algerian Zouaves. Like them, these New Yorkers wore light colored shirts and darker, yellow-trimmed tunics ("monkey jackets") and baggy scarlet trousers. Topping all this off were not just kepis, but bright red kepis. Broadcasting both their flashy garb and vocational background, Ellsworth's regiment carried the nickname of New York's Fire Zouaves.

They were among the first Federals to enter the Rebel city, along with the 1st Michigan Infantry, a cavalry company and artillery battery. Soon to come were three New York regiments and one from New Jersey. Before this daunting force the only remaining Confederate defenders in town, Col. George Terrett's Alexandria Battalion, wisely withdrew. Some three dozen Southern horsemen tarried too long, and were gobbled up by the advancing Yankees. So far the Federal occupation of Alexandria had proceeded without the shedding of blood. It would not last long.

274　Benjamin Franklin Cooling III, *Symbol, Sword and Shield: Defending Washington During the Confederate War* (Hamden CT, 1975), p. 35.

Five weeks before, in the excitement over the Old Dominion's disunion, innkeeper James W. Jackson had hoisted the first Confederate Stars and Bars over Alexandria on a flagpole atop the roof of his hotel, the Marshall House, the city's main place of boarding (corner of King and Pitt Streets). It was not just a hotel flagpole, but a forty-foot staff so high that President Lincoln across the Potomac reportedly could see the Rebel banner floating in the wind. Jackson, ever a Southern stalwart, swore that "whoever should attempt to remove it, would have to pass over my dead body."[275]

Jackson proved to be tragically prescient of his fate, which would be the same that day for Colonel Ellsworth. Born in upstate New York in 1837, Ellsworth was known as "a curious, romantic, intense young man, and a sincere idealist." He quoted Tennyson, believed in knightly chivalry, and naturally was attracted to the glamour of war. In the 1850's he found himself in Chicago, where he assumed command of a little volunteer militia company and fashioned it into a well-trained and nattily attired company of Chicago Zouave Cadets. They even travelled about, earning prizes for snappy drills and dapper outfits. In the audience for one of these displays at Springfield, Illinois in late 1859 was Abraham Lincoln, who was immediately taken with the twenty-two year-old. Calling Ellsworth "the greatest little man I ever met," Lincoln invited him to come to Springfield and hang around his and William Herndon's law offices. Ellsworth did so, not really as a student, nor a law clerk; Lincoln just liked having him about. This arrangement, which might be considered odd had it not developed into a sort of father-son relationship, nevertheless became, as Lincoln himself described it, "as intimate as the disparity of our ages [Lincoln was fifty], and my engrossing engagements, would permit."[276]

Needless to say, during the presidential campaign of 1860 Ellsworth was part of Lincoln's entourage. After his inauguration, the new President recommended Ellsworth for a War Department clerkship, and saw to his appointment as a lieutenant in the First

275 James G. Barber, *Alexandria in the Southern War of Independence* (Lynchburg VA, 1983), p. 5.

276 Richard K. Patterson, "'The Greatest Little Man I Ever Met,'" *Civil War Times Illustrated*, December 1971, pp. 30, 33.

Dragoons. When war broke out, the impetuous Ellsworth wanted his own unit. He headed back to New York and recruited his regiment of "fire zouaves." This was the unit he brought to Washington, all stirred up to defend the capital and carry the war to the Rebels. The zouaves got their chance on the morning of May 24.

Ahead of his men, Ellsworth proudly stepped off the boat that brought them to Alexandria. As his troops spread out through town, the Colonel and a small squad made their way toward the telegraph office. They took in sight the defiant Rebel Stars and Bars atop the Marshall House. Ellsworth angrily strode into the place, accosted the surprised innkeeper on the meaning of the insult, and himself with several men ascended to the rooftop where he cut the flagpole halyards and took hold of the red, white and blue banner.

Waiting for him downstairs, armed with a shotgun, was James Jackson. The innkeeper fired point blank at Ellsworth, killing him instantly. A Union soldier with his rifle thwacked away Jackson's weapon, shot the Rebel in the face and bayoneted him for good measure.

That day in the hotel lay two bodies among the war's earliest slain. James Jackson's wife was hysterical. Friends calmed her down and eventually helped her attend to her husband's burial. Before Jackson was laid in the ground, the county coroner issued a formal statement on Jackson's death solemnly attesting that the deceased had been "killed by an armed force of Federal troops when in defence of his home and his private rights."[277]

Both sides entered a "first" in their annals of this still very young conflict. "Thus was spilled the first blood of the War on Virginia soil," recorded one of Alexandria's local historians.[278] Likewise, a chronicler of New Yorkers' contributions to the war noted that Ellsworth's fatal prize was the first Confederate flag captured in the war.

---

277 Mary G. Powell, *The History of Alexandria, Virginia from July 13, 1749 to May 24, 1861* (Richmond, 1928), p. 354.

278 *Ibid.*

The colonel's corpse was boat-borne across the river as news spread through the capital of Ellsworth's death. Flags throughout Washington dropped to half-mast. When news reached the White House, President Lincoln burst into tears. To those in the room he sobbed, "Excuse me, but I cannot talk....I will make no apology, gentlemen, for my weakness; but I knew poor Ellsworth well and held him in high regard."[279]

Laid out for viewing in the Navy Yard building, Elmer Ellsworth's remains drew countless mourners, including Mrs. Lincoln. That evening the President himself came. Grief nearly overwhelmed him again: "My boy! My boy!" Lincoln ordered the body brought to the East Room of the White House, where thousands more viewed it lying in state. Afterward, a funeral procession bore the corpse to the train headed for New York. In the cars rode the President, head held sadly down all the way.

It was to be expected that Lincoln would pen a tender note to the bereft parents. "In the untimely loss of your noble son, our affliction here, is scarcely less than your own," he wrote on the 25th. After recounting the young man's many talents and commendable qualities, Lincoln concluded his heartfelt missive: "In the hope that it may be no intrusion upon the sacredness of your sorrow, I have ventured to address you this tribute to the memory of my young friend, and your brave and early fallen child."

VIRGINIA IS INVADED AGAIN: PHILIPPI, JUNE 3

After their secession, Virginians understood it would be only a matter of time before Federal forces crossed their borders on a mission of invasion and subjugation. Yankees crossing the Potomac from Washington were expected, but soon they came from another quarter as well, across the Ohio. Aware that Virginia's northwestern periphery lay vulnerable, General Lee, in command of Virginia's state forces, sent Colonel George A. Porterfield into the northwestern part of the state to Grafton, just 25 miles below the Pennsylvania border, to organize volunteers. By late May Porterfield had assembled only about 400 men, evidence of the

---

279   Patterson, "'Greatest Little Man,'" p. 39.

area's indifference (if not hostility) to the Confederate government. These numbers were far too few to face the Union forces soon to descend upon them.

Governor Dennison of Ohio on April 23 appointed young (age 34) George Brinton McClellan to command state troops. McClellan held promise as one of the North's best officers after graduating second in his West Point Class in 1846. In high army circles he won praise as an engineer, as a theoretician on the use of the bayonet, and as the designer of the "McClellan saddle." He was also interested in railroads, the logistical godsend for future armies, and helped survey possible routes for the transcontinental railroad. In 1857 he resigned from the army to become chief engineer for the Illinois Central line. Three weeks after his state appointment, the U.S. War Department recognized McClellan's talents and made him a major general, commanding the Department of the Ohio.

"The Ohio" meant both sides of the river, extending to north-western Virginia. Through that area ran a major railway, the Baltimore & Ohio, a 188-mile, largely east-west length of track connecting Baltimore with Wheeling on the river. The B. & O. was clearly an important artery, more important to Northern mo-bilization efforts than to Southern, particularly when the Federals were rushing troops and supplies to the D.C. area. For this reason Lee called on Porterfield to disrupt enemy war-traffic on the B. & O. Lee even said that cutting the rails east of Grafton "would be worth to us an army."[280] The Confederates accordingly burned two rail bridges and hovered in the area, defying Yankee engineers to come and repair them.

General McClellan learned of this on May 26 and ordered several Ohio regiments across the river toward the broken rail line. In Wheeling, Unionist sympathizers had already organized a "First [U.S.] Virginia Infantry," led by Colonel Benjamin Franklin Kelley. The Ohioans soon joined them, and Kelley pushed forward on the 27th. Poor Porterfield, after having vainly called to Richmond for reinforcements, felt pressed to retreat from Grafton southward 25

---

280   Jack Waugh, "McClellan's First Battles," *Civil War Times Illustrated,* November 1983, p. 10.

miles to Philippi. There he gathered in 200 more recruits, but they were unarmed and unequipped. By then Porterfield's force totaled maybe 600 infantry and 175 horsemen, but barely over half could be called "effectives."

McClellan, still in Ohio, pushed more troops across the river toward Grafton. Brig. Gen. Thomas Morris brought three Indiana regiments and assumed command from Colonel Kelley on June 1. He approved a plan that Kelley had developed for advancing on Philippi to shove the Rebels farther south. It was clever and elaborate—far too clever and elaborate for this early stage, when green troops and inexperienced officers were learning about war together. It called for two separate columns to advance south from Grafton to Philippi in an all-night march, arrive outside the Rebel camp at the same time and launch a coordinated dawn attack.

Fully 3,000 Federals formed the two advancing columns. One, under Col. Ebenezer Dumont, marched south from Grafton on the evening of June 2. Despite darkness and rain it arrived north of Philippi before dawn, awaiting the sound of the other column. That one, under Colonel Kelley, had a more circuitous route, worse roads, and just as much darkness and rain. It was to have taken position east and south of Philippi, blocking Porterfield's presumed retreat route. A pistol shot from Kelley was to have launched the simultaneous Federal attacks which were designed not just to rout the Rebels, but bag them altogether.

Porterfield, however, had been forewarned by local sympathizers on the 2d of the Yankees' movements. That night he announced to his company captains that in the morning, if attacked, they should lead their men southward in a retreat to Beverly. The Confederates in Philippi went to sleep that night prepared to march out the next morning without a fight.

Meanwhile Kelley's column took a wrong road and fell behind schedule. Near Philippi Dumont's men awaited sound of a pistol shot. It came, but from an unexpected source. As Kelley's column finally neared the Rebel camp, a local resident took a pot-shot at the Yankee column. Its sound, heard by Dumont's troops, prompted them to open up with a couple of artillery rounds. Given their plans to take flight, this was all the provocation Porterfield's soldiers needed to pack promptly and commence their retrograde. They in fact packed up so promptly that they left much baggage behind: arms, ammunition, supplies, and in many cases the new white tents in which they had bedded down the night before.

Dumont's Federals pushed them along, adding to their haste; so did Kelley's, who arrived just in time to participate in the pursuit. The Federals got off some shots, as did the Confederates. The Rebel retreat soon gained such unseemly speed that it was later dubbed by irreverent journalists the "Philippi races."

This affair of June 3 has been called the "first land fray of the civil war."[281] It was barely a "fray" in terms of casualties. For the North were five wounded, including Colonel Kelley himself, shot in the chest (but surviving) as he marshalled his troops through the town of Philippi. Among the Confederates were counted perhaps fifteen wounded. A bloodless casualty was Colonel Porterfield, whom General Lee promptly sacked upon news of his retreat to Beverly. To try to retrieve the situation, Lee sent his own adjutant, newly commissioned Brig. Gen. Robert S. Garnett, who took over Porterfield's command and the reinforcements that Richmond soon began sending him. Given northwestern Virginia's Unionist sentiments, there was already talk of the Confederates' ceding the area to Yankee control, but both Davis and Lee were determined not to do so, without a real fight—which would soon come.

CONFEDERATES STRIKE BACK IN NORTHWESTERN VIRGINIA

General Garnett arrived at Beverly on June 9 with 4,500 reinforcements to shore up the situation. Leaving two regiments behind under Colonel John Pegram, Garnett took most of his soldiers northward, back over the Philippi "racetrack" to Laurel Hill, where he planned to confront Morris' Federals. General Morris was making his way slowly southward from Philippi, awaiting the arrival of McClellan with a large column of reinforcements. "Little Mac" had grown impatient of directing things from across the Ohio, and had assembled some 8,000 troops for an advance on

---

281   William W. Hassler, "Philippi," *Civil War Times,* December 1960, p. 24.

the Rebels. Covering much of the distance from Clarksburg by rail, McClellan had led his column halfway to Grafton when he received word of Morris' success at Philippi. He consequently redirected his line of march toward Beverly. By June 9 McClellan and his column were at Roaring Creek, seven miles west of Beverly, but with Pegram's Confederates blocking their way at Rich Mountain.

Pegram, with only 1,300 men, was ordered to hold Beverly. If the Yankees took it, Garnett's force at Laurel Hill would be cut off and sandwiched between two hostile armies. Fortunately for Colonel Pegram, McClellan soon displayed a tendency which vexed his operations throughout the war. Mac believed strongly in intelligence reports, and he believed them even when they grossly exaggerated the strength of the enemy facing him. Into his headquarters scouts brought reports of a Rebel force at Rich Mountain numbering some 8,000 or 9,000 men—numbers equal to, maybe greater than McClellan's own strength. Snagged in indecision and fearful of failure, McClellan decided against attacking Pegram, especially as the Rebels had the advantage of a carefully chosen defensive position. A small skirmish, dignified by the name "Battle of Rich Mountain," occurred on June 11, as McClellan sent skirmishers forward to test Pegram's line (of course the reports came back that it was too strong to assault). McClellan settled for waiting on word from Morris at Laurel Hill.

There Federals and Confederates were evenly matched. General Morris' Indianans and Ohioans had scarcely pitched their tents before Garnett determined to strike. On June 13 a brief but sharp encounter at Carrick's Ford resulted from the Confederates' sudden advance on the Union camps. This time, the Philippi races were reversed when the Yankees broke and fled the field. Garnett organized a pursuit and pushed Morris' disorganized troops so vigorously that within a few days the Confederates had pressed back through Philippi and threatened Grafton. Though minor in terms of casualties (53 Federal, 30 Confederate), the fight at Carrick's Ford had far-reaching consequences. Southerners once more threatened the B. & O. Railroad, and forced McClellan to withdraw back toward Clarksburg. The Confederate victory thus blunted the North's first effort to seize control of northwestern

Virginia. It also blunted the efforts of Union sympathizers in the area to organize a separate state of "West Virginia." Talk of independent statehood would continue to circulate among non-slaveholders of western Virginia, and from time to time Federal authorities nurtured this sub-secessionist movement. But so long as Confederate troops held the center of the state, as they did after Garnett's victory, the movement went nowhere.

With all of these strategic and political repercussions, the battle of Carrick's Ford also ended the careers of the two commanders engaged there. Thomas Morris was stripped of command and busted in rank. Robert Garnett was shot and mortally wounded as he cheered his men crossing the ford. He was the first general officer of either side to lose his life in the war. After removal to the Confederate capital, Garnett's body lay in state amid a massive display of mourning. Government officials and leading citizens filled the Richmond newspapers with letters of tribute, all the more effusive because of his death at the moment of victory, and a victory which most sensed would have important strategic consequences. As an example of the overheated attention given to Carrick's Ford, the Richmond *Dispatch* described the engagement as "one of the most extraordinary victories in the annals of war."[282]

SOUTHERN VICTORY AT BIG BETHEL

The incursion of Federal forces into Virginia at Alexandria and the northwestern counties, plus Virginians' loud cries at having been "invaded," cloaked the fact that the Yankees had been in the state all along.

Fort Monroe had been built at the tip of Virginia's Chesapeake Bay peninsula during the early 1820's (hence its name from the then-U.S. President) to guard the Hampton Roads harbor area. It was one of several dozen forts built after the war of 1812 to protect the nation's coastline from the kind of enemy landing that had led to the British capture of Washington in 1814. Of all the brick-and-

---

282 Jack Waugh, "McClellan's First Battles," *Civil War Times Illustrated,* November 1983, p. 16.

mortar installations along the coastline of the Confederate states, Monroe was one of four which remained in Federal hands after the fall of Sumter in April 1861.

At the time of Virginia's secession, Fort Monroe held a small garrison of some 350. Easily reinforceable by sea, it quickly became a beachhead for a sizable Union force, 2,150 troops by May 14; 4,450 two weeks later. The Federal commander was Benjamin F. Butler (Major General, U.S. Volunteers as of May 16). One of Lincoln's notorious political appointments, Butler gained his rank solely because of his prominence in the Northern Democratic Party. This faction still ached from its defeat in the recent presidential election, and some Democratic leaders so vehemently opposed Lincoln that they openly sympathized with the South. Politics did not carry Butler that far, but they did bring him, during the Democratic nominating convention of 1860, to vote fifty-seven consecutive times to nominate Jefferson Davis as President of the United States.

Butler's force in southeastern Virginia thus became the third front to which Virginia commander Robert E. Lee had to turn his attention. On May 21 Lee placed Colonel John B. Magruder in command of the Confederate forces near Williamsburg; they were at the time constructing a defensive line across the Peninsula from the York to the James River. Something of a showman—he liked colorful uniforms, theatrical gestures, and enjoyed the nickname of "Prince John"—Magruder was disinclined to the purely defensive. He had not the strength to assault Monroe, but by a showy display of cavalry in no-man's-land, he at least kept the Yankees a bit uneasy inside the fort. The Federal commander, General Butler, similarly refused to sit still, but sent detachments up the Peninsula to scout, forage and sometimes to confiscate Rebel property (as in the case of former U.S. President John Tyler's summer home near the fort in Hampton; Tyler was soon to enter the Confederate Congress in Richmond).

After Butler's soldiers captured Newport News in late May, expanding their area of occupation south of Monroe, Magruder advanced a force of his own toward the fort, to Big Bethel, eight miles above Hampton. There they began to dig in on June 7. Butler responded by ordering an attack on their positions the morning of the 10th.

Thus ensued the "first land battle of the war," a heavier engagement than the "fray" at Philippi the week before. It began inauspiciously for the North with another first: casualties from friendly fire. In the murky dawn hours, as Union columns marched into position, Federals fired on Federals. Loss: 2K, 19W.

The gunshots alerted the Southerners, whom Magruder had arrived himself to command. The Union officer in charge, Brig. Gen. Ebenezer W. Pierce, decided to plunge ahead anyway. Against the Confederate lines, buttressed by artillery, several mismanaged and uncoordinated Federal assaults failed predictably. Of no avail was the Northerners' numerical superiority—perhaps 2,900 engaged against the Southerners' 1,200. Lack of command control plus green soldiers' jitters further doomed the Union charges. As one North Carolinian attested, "There was no concert of action between Pierce's units. A regiment would come up, fire a volley or two mostly over our heads and precipitately fall back....It seemed that their principal object was simply to get a sight or a shot at a Rebel, then fall back as quickly as possible." Writing years later, this Confederate recalled the Yankee assault more as "a lot of boys fighting a bumblebee nest than a real battle. One would rush up for the nest of bees a time or two with his switches, get stung, run back, and another would take his place."[283]

Whether or not the 2½-hour fight at Big Bethel constituted a real battle, the casualties were real: US—18K, 53W, 5M (3 of whom were captured); CS—1K, 7W, 3M. Among the Southerners, the sole slain was Private Henry L. Wyatt of the 1st North Carolina. Having volunteered for a detail to rush ahead of the line to burn a house used by enemy sharpshooters, Wyatt was shot in the head, dying without regaining consciousness. Private Wyatt is lionized, at least by North Carolinians, as the first Confederate soldier killed in the war.

---

283 Paul D. Casdorph, *Prince John Magruder: His Life and Campaigns* (New York, 1996), pp. 127-28.

The North had another "first" too, equally as dubious as Wyatt. Lt. John T. Greble, commanding the Federal artillery, was like Wyatt struck in the head and killed, the first West Point graduate slain in the war. Probably more widely grieved, though, was Maj. Theodore Winthrop, one of General Butler's aides who at one point in the battle mounted a fence to rally his comrades, waved his sword aloft, and was promptly shot in the chest. Of prominent New England family, a Yale graduate, novelist and poet before the war, Winthrop was later lauded by Butler as "one of the noblest of God's noblemen."[284] Confederates buried Winthrop's body with full honors and later returned his personal effects to the Northern lines under truce-flag.

Magruder was quick to report the enemy's repulse at Big Bethel. He wrote Secretary of Defense Walker that "we were attacked by about 3,500 troops of the Federal Army, with several pieces of heavy artillery, firing grape shot, this morning at 10 o'clock, and at 12½ routed them completely with considerable loss on their side."[285] Although the Federals' numerical edge in the battle did not extend to three-to-one, Southerners grabbed onto the ratio for more cause to crow after their triumph. "Although they had three to one," wrote one of Magruder's men back to his girlfriend, "we came out victorious—gave them a genteel whipping and sent them running for life.... Surely the Lord was on our side."[286] Other Southerners latched onto that conclusion—or hope. "Was not the Hand of God manifest," trumpeted the Richmond *Dispatch,* "in such a triumph over such odds?"[287]

Though by later standards Big Bethel was just a skirmish, Butler's setback joined the bad news from Carrick's Ford to deliver a hard message in Washington: there was indeed a rebellion in the Southern states, and the Rebels would not be easily subdued. As if in **grudging** acknowledgement of this fact, Lincoln's Postmaster

---

284   Benjamin F. Butler, *Butler's Book* (Boston, 1892), p. 201.

285   Casdorph, *Magruder,* p. 129.

286   John G. Barrett, *The Confederate War in North Carolina* (Chapel Hill, 1963), p. 30.

287   Kendall J. King, "Bold, But Not Too Bold," *America's Civil War* (March 1993), p. 48.

General waited till June 16 to announce that as of that date the Federal government would cease operation of the U.S. Postal Service in the seceded states. The announcement caused scarcely a stir in Richmond, where Postmaster General John Reagan was busily establishing a Confederate mail delivery service of his own.

Chapter Six:

❦—————◆—————❦

Triumph at Manassas

MCDOWELL *VERSUS* BEAUREGARD

By the first of June, then, the Confederates' front in northern Virginia had actually become three fronts, with both sides collecting small armies and appointing commanders at all three. At Alexandria, Irvin McDowell was commissioned a Union brigadier and put in charge of the newly created Federal Department of Northeastern Virginia. To oppose McDowell, G.T. Beauregard, the hero of Sumter, was given command of northern Virginia on May 31. He began concentrating his 20,000 troops at Manassas Junction, a railhead just thirty miles southwest of Washington. Within supporting range were Johnston's forces at Winchester, 12,000-strong. At Aquia Creek, near Fredericksburg, Theophilus Holmes deployed another several thousand.

On June 1, Union gunboats on the Potomac exchanged shots with Confederate batteries along Aquia Creek. That same day Federal cavalry on reconnaissance from Alexandria struck Confederate outposts at Fairfax Court House, fifteen miles to the west. There followed "a minor skirmish that saw only brief exchanges of gunfire and a timid cavalry charge," as one historian has put it.[288] Each side incurred just a few casualties, but among Confederates was Lt. Col. John Quincy Marr, killed by a bullet to

---

288   Charles F. Cooney, "First to Fall," *Civil War Times Illustrated,* vol. 20, no. 6 (October 1981), 27.

his chest. By some Marr is hailed as the South's first martyr. A stone monument to his memory stands today on the grounds of Fairfax Court House.

BUILDING THE UNION ARMY OF NORTHEASTERN VIRGINIA

The Federals had begun building a big army on their side of the river just to defend Washington. The rioting at Baltimore and Jubal Early's march to Fort Stevens—not to mention Mr. Lincoln's brush with Confederate sharpshooters on the parapet there— added considerable urgency to these measures. Thus, on April 27, the President's General-in-Chief, Winfield Scott, gave to two of his closest friends key responsibilities in safeguarding the capital. Colonel Joseph K.F. Mansfield was put in charge of organizing troops in the District of Columbia. In command over western Maryland and Pennsylvania was Robert Patterson, a major general of Pennsylvania volunteers. Formerly Scott's second-in-command in Mexico, he was nearly seventy years old, and as historian James I. Robertson, Jr. describes him, was "a slow-thinking officer almost as old as the U.S. Constitution."[289]

After Union troops marched across the Long Bridge and occupied Alexandria, a third U.S. Army jurisdiction—added to the ones in northwestern and southeastern Virginia— was created, the Department of Northeastern Virginia. Here Scott did not have his way in appointing favorites. As would happen repeatedly throughout the war on the Union side, politics influenced command decisions. While General Scott wished to give the new Virginia assignment to Mansfield, one of President Lincoln's Cabinet officers schemed to advance a close friend. Secretary of Treasury Salmon P. Chase, former governor of Ohio, had in mind a fellow Ohioan, forty-two-year-old Irvin McDowell. McDowell was not without military experience. He was in fact a West Pointer, with a creditable record as staff officer in the old army. But in his nearly quarter-century of service, he had never commanded so much as a squad of soldiers in the field.

---

289   James I. Robertson, *Confederate Virginia: Battleground for a Nation* (Charlottesville, 1991), p. 30.

McDowell also seemed to lack the personal qualities one would expect in an army commander. Stiff and pudgy, he concealed his lack of self-confidence with a very formal, almost icy bearing, and a decidedly corpulent frame. Eating was, in fact, Irvin McDowell's great joy in life, much more than studying tactics or mastering logistics. Legends abounded throughout the army regarding his omnivoracity. "At dinner," wrote one of his junior officers, "he was such a Gargantuan feeder and so absorbed in the dishes before him that he had little time for conversation. While he drank neither wine nor spirits, he fairly gobbled the larger part of every dish within reach and wound up with an entire watermelon which he said was 'monstrous fine!'"[290] Even when he was not eating, McDowell appeared to have little time for conversation with his fellow officers. He forgot their names and faces, disdained to speak to them, and when he did it was usually with much rudeness. All these flaws of personality were nevertheless overlooked by War Secretary Cameron, who persuaded the President to appoint McDowell as commander in northeast Virginia. Promotion to brigadier general followed on May 14. The only satisfaction General Scott obtained from these doings was that he obtained equal rank for Mansfield, dating from the 14th as well.

Cooperation between the two brigadiers was never cordial. Before McDowell got any troops or supplies, Mansfield had to approve their movement out of the District. This the latter was sometimes loath to do, at least with any celerity. As a result, the Union "Army of Northeastern Virginia" grew very slowly. Assuming command at Alexandria on May 28 McDowell found only three brigades. A week later, the arrival of two New York regiments allowed for a fourth. Throughout June, men from Ohio, Massachusetts, Pennsylvania and Michigan came, and as they did McDowell formed more brigades and assigned commanders. By the end of the month the Army of Northeastern Virginia numbered 13,666 officers and men present for duty.

---

290   William C. Davis, *Battle at Manassas: A History of the First Major Campaign of the Southern War for Independence* (Baton Rouge, 1977), p. 10.

Another Federal force was massing as well, this one under General Patterson. Under Scott's close supervision, Patterson was charged with organizing an army in the area of Chambersburg and advancing toward the Confederate concentration at Harpers Ferry. Five brigades were soon assembled, numbering 17,000 men—more than McDowell's army at the time, for Scott made sure that Patterson received full regiments, up to regulation strength. The latter got preferential treatment in other ways, too—supplies, transportation, ordnance—reflecting Scott's belief that Patterson had at least as **much** opportunity as McDowell to achieve strategic results (the General-in-Chief would be mistaken).

In one respect both McDowell's and Patterson's forces were very similar. Their brigades were headed by men who, sad to say for the North, would prove to be undistinguished and absolutely of no account. The roster of brigadiers in McDowell's army today reads particularly like a virtual "who's not," given their collective lack of achievement during the war: Samuel Heintzelman, Daniel Tyler, Robert Schenck, William Franklin, Orlando Willcox, David Hunter, Charles Stone (only the latter gained notoriety, but it was as a result of being blamed for the Union disaster at Ball's Bluff later in the year). Among Patterson's brigade leaders, the most remembered is Ambrose Burnside, but this is because his name was rearranged to describe the general's funny pattern of facial hair, bushy whiskers running down the sides of his face (the original "burnsides" became "sideburns"). In fairness, however, it should be said that Scott, McDowell and Patterson were all hampered by the War Department's need to make use of the officers who had gained rank in the old peacetime army. An example was Colonel Dixon Miles, one of Patterson's brigade leaders. Fifty-seven years old, with flowing white beard, Miles had been known as a fighter in the Indian campaigns, but now unfortunately was known largely as a heavy drinker. Thus, whether or not they were well-officered, some 30,000 Federal troops, camped in two armies along Virginia's borders, were preparing to commence the bloody work of subduing the rebellion in the Old Dominion.

BEAUREGARD'S MANASSAS LINE

Protecting Virginia's Yankee-side borders were Joseph E. Johnston's and G.T. Beauregard's forces, together some 32,000 troops, with the former at Harpers Ferry and the latter southwest of Alexandria.

Ever since McDowell's advance across the Potomac on May 24, Confederates had hovered in the area, keeping watch on the enemy and sometimes clashing with them in quick firefights. On taking charge of the Alexandria line, June 1, General Beauregard improved these dispositions. He and Lee looked at the map and agreed that the proper point of concentration was Manassas Junction. The place, according to local lore, got its name from the Jewish peddler who had set up a store in the area back around the turn of the century. His name was Manasseh or Manassa, and Manassa's crossroads soon not only dropped its apostrophe but became a full-fledged junction when the railroads came: the Orange & Alexandria and the Manassas Gap. Their importance to Beauregard was two-fold. The O. & A. connected his army with Richmond, source of reinforcements and supplies. Just as important, the Manassas Gap Railroad ran westward through the Blue Ridge to Strasburg, only forty-five miles south of Harpers Ferry. Thus Beauregard's and Johnston's armies were effectively linked. If one were threatened by a Union advance, the other could rapidly reinforce by rail. Even Patterson and McDowell could have seen how this logistical set-up would work well to the Rebels' advantage.

Beauregard assumed it would not be long before Lincoln, the Washington politicians, the Northern press and public demanded an advance on Richmond. He therefore threw out three of his brigades as advance units to give word of a Union approach. One, under Milledge Luke Bonham, camped near Fairfax Court House, watching several key roads to Alexandria. Five miles to the south, Brigadier General Richard Ewell's men guarded Fairfax Station. And at Centreville, another hub of roadways, was Philip St. George Cocke's brigade.

For the main Confederate line itself Beauregard put his engineering skills to work and selected a defensive position for his army that appeared near-perfect. A couple of miles north and east of Manassas Junction, squarely in the path of advancing Yankees, flowed a tributary that in size was more than a creek but less than a river. Virginians had a name for these streams: "runs," and this one bore the name of Bull, just as others in the vicinity were named for cubs, oxen, and other fauna. The name itself was not pleasing to some Confederates. At least one Southern officer, Colonel Joseph B. Kershaw from South Carolina, complained that Bull Run was not sufficiently dignified to christen the big battle which was sure to come, and recommended that Beauregard give a new name to the stream. Kershaw had in mind some stirring appellation evoking the Revolutionary patriots' success, such as the battlefield at Cowpens in his own state. Beauregard's quick-witted response made some reference to the difference between a cool country stream and a pen full of cow-dung, and wagered that his soldiers would clearly prefer stepping in the former than the latter. Kershaw dropped his proposal, and the name of the creek stuck.

Anyway, the rivulet was a defensive tactician's delight. From headwaters to its confluence with the Occoquan River, Bull Run had steep banks and a deep bed which combined would prevent the crossing of enemy columns except at fords. Of these there were seven, plus a bridge, and Beauregard made sure all were guarded. Farthest downstream, about four miles from the Occoquan, was Union Mills Ford, which marked the extreme right of the Confederate line. Three miles up, where Bull Run made a sharp bend, three more fords offered transit. These were McLean's, Blackburn's and Mitchell's. Because they lay on the major roads connecting Manassas Junction and Alexandria, Beauregard believed they would be the most likely routes of an enemy advance. He therefore hinged the center of his line there. Fortunately for the Southerners, the curve of the run allowed them the advantage of interior lines—meaning that Confederates guarding the three fords could reinforce each other, as the need arose, by marching only a mile or so (Union forces, on the outside of the arc, would have to travel twice that distance).

Beauregard's left flank covered three more good crossing points. Two miles up from Mitchell's, Ball's and Lewis' Fords also served a principal roadway. But the easiest way of all to get across Bull Run was just upstream at the Stone Bridge. There the Warrenton Turnpike offered a good wide road suitable for moving big troop columns. Here again topography aided the Southerners, for the bridge and its approaches were commanded by Henry Hill, an eminence just to the south of the stream. The position was so strong that after placing several brigades there, Beauregard did not even extend his line farther upstream to cover the last of the seven fords, the one at Sudley Springs. Any Union force that crossed there would have to march past Henry Hill to get to Manassas, and Beauregard figured that there the Yankees (if they crossed that far to the northwest) could be stopped.

As thus deployed, the Confederate line along Bull Run extended nearly six miles, from Union Mills Ford to the Stone Bridge. To facilitate communication among his strong points, Beauregard took advantage of an innovation which one of his officers had developed in the old army, a system of using waved flags to send messages over distance. Captain E. Porter Alexander was the originator of this "wigwag" system; Alexander himself implemented it for Beauregard by supervising the construction of four wooden towers, atop which the men of his fledgling C.S. Signal Corps practiced their message-sending with flags during the day, and torches at night.

It was clear that the Yankees were coming. To prepare civilians fotheir impending advance, General Beauregard issued on June 5 a proclamation to "the good People of the Counties of Loudoun, Fairfax, and Prince William" which in its magniloquence and grandiosity would be comical were it not for the well-documented theatricality of Beauregard, and for the fact that the Southerners not only won the battle of Manassas, but won the war:

A reckless and unprincipled tyrant has invaded your soil. Abraham Lincoln, regardless of all moral, legal, and constitutional restraints, has thrown his abolition hosts among you....In the name, therefore, of the constituted authorities of the Confederate States, in the sacred cause of constitutional liberty and self-government, for which we are contending, in behalf of civilization and humanity itself, I, G.T. Beauregard...do...conjure you to be true and loyal to your country and her legal and constitutional authorities, and especially to be vigilant of the movements and acts of the enemy, so as to enable you to give the earliest authentic information to these headquarters.[291]

MRS. GREENHOW ALERTS BEAUREGARD

With General Beauregard imploring civilians in northeast Virginia to help give word of the enemy army's advance, he got a bonus: access to information emanating from the very heart of the Union command center in Washington.

Beauregard's adjutant, Colonel Thomas Jordan, set up a network of spies and informers in Washington who frequented Union officers' favorite hangout, the Willard Hotel, eavesdropped on careless, loose-lipped army talk, and passed it back to the C.S. headquarters at Manassas. The Washington papers were equally loose and careless, printing news and rumor alike on the army's position, strength and portended movement. Every edition made reading them—invariably, the very day after hitting the streets—a morning pleasure for Beauregard and his staff.[292]

---

291   *O.R.,* vol. 2, 907.

292   After the war the U.S. army, trying to glean from its defeat the little bits of pride it could, boasted its development of an organized intelligence branch which it claimed was superior to the Rebels'. Such claims have not withstood scholars' scrutiny. In spring of 1862, McClellan's Pinkerton agents brought in grossly inflated estimates of General Lee's strength, further undermining what little confidence Little Mac mustered as he launched his campaign against Richmond. A year after

Often the agents procuring and transmitting such valuable information were not Confederate soldiers dressed as civilians, but were Southern-sympathizing women in Washington's highest circles, who used their friendships with Federal officers to wheedle and extract snippets of military gossip and possible fact. Ringleader of this female fifth column was Mrs. Rose O'Neal Greenhow, who collected all that her agents had pried loose, encoded it, and sent it by special messenger to General Beauregard's headquarters. Rose's first message came July 10: "McDowell has certainly been ordered to advance on the sixteenth. R.O.G."[293] The next day came a note with details of the Federal troop movement toward Fairfax Court House. Then, on the afternoon of the sixteenth came confirmation: "McDowell has been ordered to advance to-night."[294]

Rose Greenhow's romantic legend has been part of Southern war-lore for generations, but recent writers have both embellished and deflated it. In research for his account of Lincoln's failed presidency, William Safire uncovered documents leading to Mrs. Greenhow's primary intelligence source: Senator Henry Wilson of Massachusetts, Chairman of the Senate Committee on Military Affairs. It has been known for a long time that Rose traded sex with high-ranking Yankees for the information they carelessly gave her, although *postbellum* story-spinners have modestly left out the indecorous details. Not so Safire, who was able to reconstruct a scene of sex and bondage between Greenhow and Wilson so depraved that Safire's witness to the event, the chief agent Allan Pinkerton himself, literally recoiled. Peering into Mrs. Greenhow's second-story bedroom from a painter's ladder perched outside, Pinkerton watched Rose with her whip, but fell back upon himself, ladder and all. The agent, bruised but not broken, kept his observation written down but under wraps. A full century later, sleuths like Safire were able to expose the salacious details of

---

that, Hooker's intelligence chortled at being able to name and number the various brigades and divisions in Lee's army, but as we know, such "intelligence" did little to save Hooker from disaster in the Chancellorsville campaign.

293   David Detzer, *Donnybrook: The Battle of Bull Run, 1861* (New York, 2004), p. 81.

294   William C. Davis, *Battle at Manassas: A History of the First Major Campaign of the Southern War for Independence* (Baton Rouge, 1977), p. 68.

Greenhow's fact-gathering operation, which was canine-like, both in terms of Rose's relentless pursuit of her quarry, and in Henry's bodily positioning in the bedroom where the two parties both got what they wanted.[295]

Much more available for people to see were the major Northern newspapers, whose columns corroborated R.O.G.'s secret messages. The New York *Tribune* was first to announce an imminent advance by McDowell's army. Drawing on the *Tribune* and other sources, some papers, such as the Providence (Rhode Island) *Daily Journal,* printed the story on July 2 complete with the logistical difficulties McDowell was facing (such as shortage of wagons) which would delay his advance until July 15 or soon afterward. Greenhow's accomplices and Jordan's agents carried papers to Richmond quickly, where the capital city's press assisted in blowing open what should have been closely guarded Union military secrets. The Richmond *Dispatch* of July 3 even got just about right the strength of the Northern army: after McDowell's army obtained the 800 baggage wagons it needed, the Yankees would march forth in "forty regiments, or 35,000 men."

MCDOWELL IS ORDERED TO ADVANCE

Mrs. Greenhow's messages were accurate in emphasizing the pressure being exerted on McDowell. Since the Confederate government had established itself in Richmond, bloodthirsty editors and armchair generals all across the North demanded that the rebellion be quashed in a single, bold strike. Lincoln and his Cabinet were not immune to these pressures. Indeed, as governors and members of Congress also took up the cry of "On to Richmond," so did the administration. Lincoln told Scott to advance, and the aging General-in-Chief had no recourse but to transmit the orders. On June 21 Scott directed McDowell to draw up and submit a plan showing how he intended to assume the offensive, preferably in coordination with Patterson's forces. McDowell dutifully reviewed the situation, considered the routes open to him, and concluded (just as Beauregard had done) that his best line of march lay

---

295 William Safire, *Freedom: Lincoln's Usurpation of the Constitution during the Civil War* (New York, 1987), pp. 118-19.

through Manassas Junction. Before setting out, he would need reinforcements, enough to leave a reserve of some 10,000 men in and around Alexandria to protect the capital, and still give him an army of 30,0000. With this force he intended to march west, try to bag the Confederate advance units at Fairfax, then confront the enemy at Bull Run. McDowell realized that the Rebels would be guarding the main Bull Run fords, so he intended to avoid a crossing there en masse, preferring instead to pass around the Confederate left flank. If his men marched speedily, and reasonable secrecy were maintained, McDowell hoped to defer battle until his men had gained the rear of the enemy position.

On June 29 the General presented his plan to Scott, Mansfield, the President and the Cabinet. All agreed it was a sound one. But McDowell emphasized that his success hinged on Patterson using his army to keep Confederates in the Shenandoah Valley from reinforcing those at Manassas. Scott concurred. The council of war ended with the War Department promising to beef up McDowell's army, and with McDowell promising to advance on July 8.

Scott let Patterson in on his part of the campaign, which was simply to cross the Potomac, demonstrate against the Confederates, and keep Johnston's army so busy that it would not be able to slip away to Manassas. Patterson accepted the task, especially since it was a very limited one. He was not expected to occupy the lower Shenandoah, or even win a big victory over the enemy; he was just to hover in a threatening pose, follow the Rebels if they withdrew, and avoid risking a defeat in the field. All it took was for Patterson to get started. This he did, by getting this army of 17,000 men over the Potomac at Williamsport, July 2.

JOHNSTON *VERSUS* PATTERSON IN THE LOWER VALLEY

The Confederates did not attempt to contest Patterson's crossing. With monthly returns on June 30 showing 10,654 officers and men present for duty in his Army of the Shenandoah, General Johnston guessed that the Yankees had more men than he did. So Johnston ordered his subordinates not to bring on a major fight. Thomas Jackson, who had become a brigadier on June 17 commanded Johnston's advance brigade at Martinsburg.

As Patterson's columns spread south, Jackson withdrew to Darkesville, where Johnston joined him on the third with the rest of his army: brigades under General Barnard E. Bee, Colonels Francis Bartow and Edmund Kirby Smith, plus the 1st Virginia Cavalry under Colonel James Stuart, known to his army buddies by the acronym formed from his initials, "Jeb."

Neither Johnston nor Patterson wanted to attack the other, so the "campaign" in the lower Shenandoah during the first half of July developed into little more than a *sitzkrieg*. After occupying Martinsburg without opposition, Union General Patterson began to accumulate reasons for not advancing farther. He needed more reinforcements; his soldiers were still untrained and unprepared for battle; ninety-day enlistments would soon expire, and many men would pack up and go home. Then he cited quartermaster and commissary reports about lack of food and transportation, and engineers' complaints about the army's exposed position. Seldom has military procrastination been so well justified and documented. Though General Scott in Washington badgered him with repeated telegrams, urging an advance on Johnston's forces, Patterson kept his army at Martinsburg. In exasperation, Scott ordered Patterson to send Miles' infantry brigade, plus some artillery, to join McDowell at Alexandria. In this way he could at least reduce the number of Union troops sitting idly in the Valley.

Patterson's doddering inactivity allowed Johnston to slip away, put his troops on train cars, and head for Manassas Junction to reinforce Beauregard. They left on July 18, and would arrive just in time to contribute to the Confederate victory at Manassas, July 21.[296]

"ON TO RICHMOND!"

McDowell got additional reinforcements directly from Washington as more Northern regiments poured into the capital. The commander in the District of Columbia, Brigadier General Mansfield—he had been promoted on May 18—cooperated with the

---

296   Gilbert E. Govan and James W. Livingood, *A Different Valor: The Story of General Joseph E. Johnston, C.S.A.* (Indianapolis, 1956), pp. 47-49.

Army of Northeastern Virginia by feeding it all the troops available in the area. McDowell's numbers thus rose impressively; in three weeks his army numbered roughly 30,000 men. Expansion of his forces meant reorganizing commands, procuring supplies and, as always, training the fresh arrivals in the ways of war. All this took time, so when July 8 arrived, McDowell found that he was not ready (as he had promised Lincoln and Scott) to begin his campaign; his troops were too green. He promised a forward movement on the tenth, then, after he failed to budge on that date, on the thirteenth. Meanwhile Washington politicians expressed concern as the Northern press and public demanded action. Horace Greeley's New York *Tribune* began running daily editorials blaring the headline, "TO RICHMOND! TO RICHMOND ONWARD!" Another in late June shrieked, "THE NATION'S WAR-CRY. Forward to Richmond! Forward to Richmond! The Rebel Congress must not be allowed to meet there on the 20th of July! BY THAT DATE THE PLACE MUST BE HELD BY THE NATIONAL ARMY!"[297]

President Lincoln, ever responsive to the public mood in the North, joined in the "war-cry" on Richmond (though more quietly than Greeley and his managing editor, Charles A. Dana). To McDowell's claim that his men were too green to start marching on the Rebel capital, the President replied, "You are green, it is true; but they are green, also; you are all green alike." Thus the U.S. Commander in Chief uttered that folksy, frontier "wisdom" which still wins accolades among his dwindling group of admirers in the North, but which represented very poor military advice. As one bitter Northern historian of the Manassas Campaign writes, "The line was classic Lincoln: pithy, homespun, seemingly incontrovertible. Unfortunately, it was also banal nonsense, and fatal for many soldiers."[298]

---

297   David Detzer, *Donnybrook: The Battle of Bull Run, 1861* (New York, 2004), p. 66.

298   *Ibid.*, p. 67.

MCDOWELL SETS OUT, JULY 16

With the President echoing the press and the popular mood, General Scott sent pointed messages to McDowell that he would have to get going. McDowell finally told his officers on July 15 that the army would move the next day. It did so, in several columns. Tyler set out from the area of Arlington Heights, heading for Fairfax Court House. From Alexandria, Hunter headed westward also for the Court House. Heintzelman commanded troops who marched along the O. & A. Railroad toward Fairfax Station and Annandale.

The Federals set no records for their speed. Partly because McDowell's orders urged a cautious advance, and partly because Confederate cavalry had felled trees along the major thoroughfares, the Union columns stopped frequently and made no good time at all in their march. Another factor was the troops' greenness. On their first arduous march, McDowell's soldiers wilted under the heat and choked in the dust. "Not yet hardened for such a march," wrote a New Hampshireman, "many were obliged to fall out of the ranks and seek shade and rest."

Thousands of bluecoats broke ranks at the tempting sight of blackberries on the roadside. Officers barked commands and threats, but in most cases gave way to the men. When soldiers of Col. W.T. Sherman's brigade fell out for some roadside foraging, an officer shouted, "Colonel Sherman says you must keep in ranks; you must close up; you must not chase the pigs and chickens." Whereupon the men called back, "Tell Colonel Sherman we will get all the water, pigs and chickens we want."[299] Thanks to these repeated delays, the Federals covered only ten miles on the first day.

Beauregard's advance units had no trouble making orderly withdrawals before the sluggish Yankee advance. Bonham and Ewell abandoned Fairfax Court House early on the 17th. Federals of Tyler's division entered just before noon and spent several hours riotously ransacking the town. "Our dirty fingers were plunged into their jam pots," recalled one Yankee, "as we drank their whiskey, tea, and coffee, and ate their sardines and pickles with

---

299   JoAnna M. McDonald, *"We Shall Meet Again": The First Battle of Manassas (Bull Run), July 18-21, 1861* (Shippensburg PA, 1999), p. 23.

gusto."[300] By dark Tyler camped his division only a few miles west of Fairfax Court House. Hunter and Miles were farther behind; and Heintzelman was five miles north.

As the Confederates retreated back toward Centreville, rear-guard units skirmished with the enemy advance, further impeding the Federals' progress. McDowell now knew that whatever surprise he hoped to have in his march on Beauregard's army was now vanished. In the words of one historian, Ethan Rafuse, "Every male in Fairfax County would have had to have been blind, deaf, and dumb not to know that McDowell and his Yankee army had begun their advance."[301]

BEAUREGARD PREPARES TO GIVE BATTLE

With all his advance warning—the blaring Northern press, Mrs. Greenhow's secret messages and now the Yankees' loud, molasses-like "march" toward Centreville—General Beauregard had ample time to consolidate his forces. After all of his advance units had safely fallen back, by dawn of July 18 Beauregard's army was in position behind Bull Run.

The right of the Confederate line was secured at Union Mills Ford by Ewell's brigade—three infantry regiments, four howitzers and three companies of cavalry (2,444 men), all keeping watch downstream. At McLean's, another three regiments, a couple of six-pounders and a cavalry company (3,528 men) were commanded by Brigadier General David Jones. James Longstreet (2,121 troops) and Milledge Luke Bonham (4,961) held the key crossings at Blackburn's and Mitchell's, with eight regiments of infantry, two and a half batteries, and six companies of horse. Early's brigade (2,620) deployed a bit to the rear in reserve. Farther upstream, Philip St. George Cocke had brought his brigade out of Centreville to guard Lewis' and Ball's fords; he commanded three regiments, a battery and a cavalry company (3,276 men). At the extreme Confederate left, Beauregard had fastened together the 1st

---

300   John Hennessy, *The First Battle of Manassas: An End to Innocence July 18-21, 1861* (Lynchburg VA, 1989), p. 8.

301   Ethan S. Rafuse, *A Single Grand Victory: The First Campaign and Battle of Manassas* (Wilmington DE, 2002), p. 93.

Louisiana Battalion and the 4th South Carolina, added a battery of six-pounders and two companies of cavalry, and put them all (1,100 troops) under Colonel Nathan G. Evans for the purpose of watching the Stone Bridge. Over it the Warrenton Turnpike crossed Bull Run—the westernmost place at which the enemy might make a crossing if it intended to flank the Confederate line from that direction.

McDowell's army was fanning out on the roads south and west of Centreville. Daniel Tyler's, David Hunter's and Samuel Heintzelman's divisions were feeling their way toward Bull Run, with Tyler in advance on the Warrenton Turnpike. One of the latter's brigades, under Colonel Israel Richardson, was also in advance on the road leading from Centreville to Mitchell's and Blackburn's fords. A fourth division, that of Dixon Miles (recently brought from Patterson's army), brought up the rear at Centreville; of this force Thomas Davies' brigade had advanced a half-mile or so beyond the village.[302]

JOHNSTON GIVES PATTERSON THE SLIP

As matters stood, the Northerners enjoyed a three-to-two advantage with McDowell's army numbering a little over thirty thousand, and Beauregard about twenty. But there were more Southerners to be thrown into the equation. On July 17 when Confederate pickets became engaged at the Fairfaxes, and Mrs. Greenhow's warnings were confirmed, Beauregard quickly informed Richmond that the enemy advance was on:

> The enemy has assailed my outposts in heavy force. I have fallen back on the line of Bull Run and will make a stand at Mitchell's Ford. Please inform Johnston of this, via Staunton, and also Holmes. Send any re-enforcements at the earliest possible instant and by every possible means.[303]

---

302   Ethan S. Rafuse, *A Single Grand Victory: The First Campaign and Battle of Manassas* (Wilmington DE, 2002), p. 93.

303   *O.R.,* vol. 2, 439-40.

The Confederate high command then pulled off something that had never been done before. For the first time in warfare, the Southerners used telegraph and railroad to arrange a rapid troop movement. To Fredericksburg, the Defense Department sent orders for Brigadier General Theophilus Holmes to rush reinforcements toward Manassas. Holmes himself led two regiments—the 1st Arkansas and 2d Tennessee, 1,355 men in all, plus six guns—on the forty-seven-mile march to the Junction. Authorities in the capital hustled forward other units that had been camping outside the city; one of them was Wade Hampton's vaunted Legion, 650 men. (Holmes arrived at Manassas on July 20, the day before the battle; Hampton's horsemen on the very morning of it. If luck hinges on good timing, the Southerners were very fortunate indeed.)

The main reinforcement of Beauregard, however, depended on Johnston's ability to slip away from Patterson in the Shenandoah. At one o'clock in the morning of July 18, General Johnston received this telegram from Richmond: "General Beauregard is attacked. To strike the enemy a decisive blow a junction of all your effective force will be needed. If practicable, make the movement...In all the arrangements exercise your discretion."[304]

"If practicable" and "your discretion" were words deliberately chosen, for Johnston could only depart for Manassas by secret withdrawal. Patterson's Yankee army had to be fooled into staying put and not pursuing. Fortunately for the Southerners, pursuit seemed to be the last thing on General Robert Patterson's mind. Needled by telegrams from Washington, he had indeed advanced on July 15 from Martinsburg to Bunker Hill. But there he pitched camp and refused to budge while Johnston's forces withdrew to Winchester. As McDowell's columns advanced on Manassas, an anxious Winfield Scott demanded action. "Do not let the enemy amuse and delay you with a small force in front," he wrote on the 17th, "whilst he reinforces the junction with his main body."[305] Patterson got the message, replied with a promise to march on

---

304   *Ibid.*, 478.

305   William C. Davis, *Battle at Manassas: A History of the First Major Campaign of the Southern War for Independence* (Baton Rouge, 1977), p. 149.

the morrow, then ended up advancing a heavy picket line all of half a mile. This he termed a "demonstration" against the enemy, which is all that Patterson believed Scott wanted. Of course, it was all that Joe Johnston could have wanted. When Stuart's cavalry reported no stirring in the Yankee camps, Johnston gave orders at 9 a.m. on the 18th for his brigades to start out for Manassas. In the meantime poor old Patterson continued to believe he still held the upper hand. As General Scott waited anxiously in Washington for word that his forces in the Valley had launched a holding attack on Johnston, and asked Patterson if the Rebels had succeeded in stealing a march on him, Patterson wired back, "The enemy has stolen no march on me. I have kept him actively employed."[306]

Johnston's planned route from Winchester to Manassas stretched fifty miles, part by foot, fortunately mostly by rail. Jackson's brigade led the way, setting out at noon on July 18 for the Manassas Gap Railroad station at Piedmont. Old Jack set a mean pace for his troops as they left the Shenandoah, mindful of the announcement that Johnston had released to the men before they departed: "General Beauregard is being attacked by overwhelming forces. Every moment now is precious, and the general hopes that his soldiers will *step out* and keep closed, for this march is a forced march to save the country."[307] With only a few stops along the way for rest and rations, Jackson's command arrived at Piedmont Station at 6 a.m. on the 19th. The Southerners then boarded cars which only two months previous had served the B. & O. Railroad— Jackson had captured them in his little ruse at Harpers Ferry. The train ride of 35 miles to Manassas Junction took the better part of the day; Jackson arrived there in the late afternoon, having made the entire journey in a little over twenty-eight hours.

Johnston's other brigades followed, after the single locomotive doing all the work made its eight-hour way back to Piedmont and took on another trainload of troops. These, too, piled into the Junction, albeit a bit more sluggishly than had Jackson's units.

---

306   O.R., vol. 2, 176; Ethan S. Rafuse, *A Single Grand Victory: The First Campaign and Battle of Manassas* (Wilmington DE, 2002), p. 99.

307   Davis, *op. cit.*, p. 135.

Francis Bartow's and Barnard Bee's brigades of Georgians and South Carolinians arrived at Manassas around 8 a.m. on July 20. Smith's brigade was the last to board the overworked (and for several hours, refitted) train, with the tail of Johnston's columns chugging out of Piedmont around four o'clock on the morning of July 21. Meanwhile, the Army of the Shenandoah's artillery rolled into Manassas, the last battery arriving by 2 p.m. of the 20th. All told, Johnston brought over 10,000 men and twenty guns with him from the Valley. Even Stuart's cavalry rode in, after having broken away from Patterson's front and leaving the deluded Yankees still believing that the whole Rebel army menaced nearby.

Patterson finally realized he had been hornswoggled on the evening of the 20th, about the time Stuart's horsemen were trotting into Manassas Junction. By then, of course, it was too late to do anything but inform Washington of his failure. General Scott was understandably distraught. "Why did not General Patterson advance?" he asked himself and everyone in the War Department.[308] He chose not to wait, though, for his old friend's answer to the question, for within a week Scott issued orders not only relieving Patterson of command, but discharging him for the army entirely.

---

308 *Ibid.,* p. 151. Patterson was fired so quickly that his name is not even listed in most registers of Civil War generals; at the time of his relief he was technically still a major general of Pennsylvania militia and not yet mustered into the U.S. army. After his discharge an embittered Patterson nursed a long-standing grudge against General Scott and the politicians who had ended his career so ingloriously. While the war raged, he led a retired life in Philadelphia, but frequently spoke out against the Lincoln administration in editorial letters that circulated widely in the Northern press. After the Union defeat he strongly supported Democratic presidential candidate George B. McClellan, and publicly gloated over Lincoln's failure to be reelected in 1864.

After General Patterson died in 1867, his family insisted on interment at the Post Cemetery in West Point, and they secured a burial plot near the grave of Winfield Scott. Reflecting the old ex-general's bitterness in his last days, Patterson's epitaph delivers a last vengeful outburst against those who did him in: "Robert Patterson/1792-1867/Major General, U.S. Volunteers/Faithful while he served./He left the war before/his comrades started losing it."

MCDOWELL'S FINAL PREPARATIONS FOR BATTLE

Thus McDowell's great plan for the advance on Richmond started coming unglued from the outset. All day on the 19th, the Federals at Centreville heard numerous trains chugging into Manassas, and only a fool could deny that they bore reinforcements for the enemy. "I am as sure as that there is a God in heaven," General Tyler told his commanding general, "you will have to fight Jo. Johnston's Army at Manassas the day after tomorrow."[309] Assuming that this very-worst-case-scenario had befallen him, McDowell nevertheless chose to proceed as best he could with his intentions, which were to cross Bull Run and either outflank the Rebels and send them scurrying, or bloody their noses on the field of battle. Sad to say (for him), a bit of the lethargy which had mired Patterson in the Valley now beset McDowell, for he chose to spend precious time reconnoitering the various fords at the Run. The thirty-six hours he used in sending cavalry patrols and staff officers up and down the creek gave Johnston and Beauregard just the time they needed to bring their armies together.

By noon of July 20 the Union commander had gotten what he needed to know and had developed his plans. Scouts had observed the enemy infantry massed behind Mitchell's-Blackburn's-McLean's Fords, and McDowell soundly reckoned that this was the end of the Confederate line he should avoid. So he chose a route of march to take his army in the other direction—around the Confederate left. Reconnaissance had confirmed fording places at Sudley Springs, well above the Stone Bridge. Here would be the crossing point of his flanking column, and of this he informed his division leaders on the evening of the 20th. Orders were written up for a forward movement to start at 2:30 a.m. of the next day. Tyler would demonstrate against the Stone Bridge beginning at dawn (a big 30-pounder Parrott would fire the opening round at 6 o'clock), holding the attention of the Rebels and leading them to think this as the main point of attack. Meanwhile farther upstream Hunter would wade across Bull Run at Sudley's while Heintzelman

---

309   William C. Davis, *Battle at Manassas: A History of the First Major Campaign of the Southern War for Independence* (Baton Rouge, 1977), pp. 155-56.

crossed at Poplar Ford. On the other end of the line, at Mitchell's and Blackburn's Fords, Richardson's brigade was to show just enough activity to keep the enemy right occupied. Miles was held in reserve, just in case the Rebels staged an advance of their own toward Centreville. If the men started moving on time, McDowell figured his flanking columns would be across Bull Run around 7 a.m., ready to start rolling up the enemy line in a general advance on Manassas Junction.

After being briefed, one U.S. brigade commander came away with the impression that "the plan of the intended battle, from all I could learn of the field and the position of the enemy, was a good one."[310] Moreover, General McDowell seemed very confident of success. But then, too, he was still unwilling to believe that Patterson had failed to keep Johnston's Valley army from reinforcing Beauregard.

BEAUREGARD ASSUMES BATTLEFIELD COMMAND

On the other side of the rivulet, the Confederates were also laying their plans. After Johnston reached Beauregard's headquarters, following a warm comrade-like clasp, Old Joe and Bory set about discussing their most important item of business, one which professional soldiers do with zeal: not arranging tactical formations against the enemy, but determining who would outrank whom. Both men were brigadier generals in the Confederate army. Beauregard had been appointed on March 1, Johnston on May 14; this gave Beauregard seniority. But Beauregard's commission was in the "Provisional" C.S. army while Johnston's was in the "Regular"—a distinction made by the Confederate Congress in its early days that now ceased to matter, except that it gave Johnston a claim to seniority. The two officers might have resorted to a flip of the coin had the stakes been smaller, but they agreed to telegraph Richmond and ask for a ruling. President Davis himself wired back: both men were in line for a full generalship, yet since Johnston had held higher rank in the old U.S. army, he was considered senior and would thus take charge of the Army of the

---

310   Ethan S. Rafuse, *A Single Grand Victory: The First Campaign and Battle of Manassas* (Wilmington DE, 2002), p. 117.

Potomac. But Davis wisely added the suggestion that Johnston avail himself of Beauregard's expert knowledge of the terrain and his deployments. This gave the prideful Creole a tactical edge in dealing with Johnston, and a nice ego-boost besides. The two officers thus resolved to work together, with the Virginian allowing the Creole to call the shots when the shooting started.

With the issue of seniority momentarily pushed aside, agreement on a battle plan was next in order. Beauregard wanted to strike a blow with his strong right flank, using especially the troops he had concentrated at Mitchell's and Blackburn's Fords. Johnston, on the other hand, counseled a defensive strategy. The Confederates held excellent positions behind Bull Run, and now (based on Mrs. Greenhow's secret intelligence) they believed they at least equaled McDowell's army in numbers. (They were right: McDowell had some 30,000 troops; Beauregard, Johnston and Holmes had brought together about 31,000). Moreover, the Confederates had the edge in both artillery and cavalry. With these advantages, Johnston reasoned, why not let the Federals attack? They would surely be repulsed; then Beauregard could assume the initiative and chase the Yankees all the way to Washington if he wanted. The Creole liked the idea. As the conference closed, Beauregard was dictating orders for how Longstreet, Bonham, Jones and Early would advance on Centreville once the Yankees' thrust had been parried. Johnston, worried about the weak Confederate left, directed his Valley brigades to the upper fords; otherwise, there was a good chance that the Yankees' thrust would not be parried at all.

OPENING OF THE UNION DEMONSTRATION

In the early hours of July 21 much was a-bustle in the Union army's camps around Centreville. Tyler arranged his three brigades in order of march, and by 3 o'clock they were stepping out for the Stone Bridge. Hunter and Heintzelman followed, then took a different route as they headed northwest and upstream. According to McDowell's timetable, the two flanking divisions were not to cross Bull Run until they heard gunfire from Tyler's demonstrations at the bridge—the opening shot from the 30-pounder cannon. Then they would wade the stream, head down the Manassas-Sudley Road, driving the Rebels before them, and in so doing uncover the Stone Bridge to allow Tyler's division to join them.

Meanwhile Tyler's column trudged its way to the bridge. Impeding Robert Schenck's lead brigade was the huge Parrott gun, so heavy that it almost broke the bridge over Cub Run, and so slow that it blocked the road for everyone behind it. As a result, Schenck spent two hours covering little more than a mile. Along the way, one of Schenck's brigade leaders, Colonel William T. Sherman of Ohio, got so impatient at the snail-paced march that he struck out off to the right, seeking another crossing-place somewhere upstream. "That man must be crazy," murmured Captain George Finch, presaging the later, career-crippling allegations later of Sherman's insanity.[311] Right now, Sherman's rashness was really prudence, for he ended up actually discovering a hitherto unknown ford, slightly upstream from the bridge. He brought back the news to Tyler, but Tyler was indifferent. The point now, he reminded Sherman, was to *pretend* to cross Bull Run—not actually cross it, and certainly not speedily—while making a lot of noise and drawing the Rebels' attention away from the main crossings at Sudley's and Poplar.

Thus at six o'clock, with sunrise already an hour gone and the dawn sky brightening, Tyler's artillerymen unlimbered their big thirty-pounder, loaded and fired a hefty shell to signal the start of the "demonstration."

Confederates across the stream were indeed impressed. Their commander, "Shanks" Evans, took in the sight of two enemy brigades deploying in full view on the other side of the run. He kept his cool, however. After drawing up his two regiments in battle line, and throwing out skirmishers to keep up a steady musketry, Evans sent word of the enemy approach to headquarters. "HQ" for the Confederates meant either of two command centers, for as the battle of Manassas began, Generals Beauregard and Johnston were at opposite ends of their battle line. The former had pitched his tent on a hill behind Mitchell's from where he still hoped to deliver

---

311   JoAnna M. McDonald, *"We Shall Meet Again": The First Battle of Manassas (Bull Run), July 18-21, 1861* (Shippensburg PA, 1999), p. 44.

his *coup de main.* Johnston, after surveying the Confederate left, had established his headquarters at a private residence, the home of Judith Carter Henry. Here he was close to his men, for as his troops debarked from the trains at Manassas Junction, Johnston directed them to key positions on the Confederate left. This morning, Smith's brigade had not yet arrived, but already Bartow, Bee and Jackson were in place. The latter, with his five regiments of Virginians, was being kept in reserve at Henry House hill. Colonel Francis Bartow's two Georgia regiments, and Brigadier Barnard E. Bee's brigade (4th Alabama, 6th North Carolina, 2d and 11th Mississippi) held the end of the line at the hill named for Edgar Matthew's house a mile south of Sudley Springs. Thus they were poised for Yankees from that direction, but they also stood ready to reinforce Evans, should he be threatened at the bridge.

SHANKS EVANS SMELLS A RUSE

It was not long before Colonel Evans surmised that the enemy show of strength before him was just that, all show and no go. By 7:30, when Tyler's Federals still had made no effort to cross the Stone Bridge, Evans drew his conclusion. "I perceived that it was not the intention of the enemy to attack me in my present position," he recorded later.[312] Evans then withdrew his brigade and started marching toward the threatened left.

In his surmise Evans was not only correct, but was soon corroborated by information from another quarter. After 8 o'clock, one of Porter Alexander's observation towers—the "crow's nests" and "pigeon roosts" which had brought so many derisive catcalls from amused Confederate infantrymen—finally proved their worth. From the signal tower on Van Pelt's hill, spotters noticed dust clouds rising off to the northeast at Sudley's Ford. Then, looking hard with field glasses, they picked up little glints of sunlight reflected from rifle barrels or brass cannon tubes. They flagged their findings. "Look out for your left, you are turned," was

---

312 William C. Davis, *Battle at Manassas: A History of the First Major Campaign of the Southern War for Independence* (Baton Rouge, 1977), pp. 164, 166.

the message.[313] From it Johnston was able to deduce McDowell's intentions: feint at Stone Bridge, flank march from Sudley's. It all meant rough work for the day ahead.

Hunter's and Heintzelman's Union divisions were having a tough time just reaching Sudley Ford. Tyler's sluggish march slowed them down. Then, after casting loose on their own road to Sudley's, they found that what looked like a road on the map was really no more than a foot-path through some thick woods. So Burnside's brigade, on point, held up the whole Federal right wing by chopping and slashing its way through saplings, vines and underbrush. As the morning sun rose higher, this work got hotter and sweatier. And as Hunter and Heintzelman got further behind schedule, McDowell himself got hotter and sweatier as he worried about his would-be surprise flank attack getting bogged down even before it started. By the time Tyler fired his signal gun around 6 a.m., Burnside's advance was still three miles from Sudley Springs Ford. Then General Hunter's guide (whether deliberately or accidentally, we do not know) took a wrong fork that lengthened Burnside's march by an extra three or four miles. The result of all this delay was that McDowell's flanking column did not begin wetting its boots in Bull Run till shortly after 9 a.m. By that time, as we have seen, Confederate General Johnston and his several brigades had already been forewarned and were ready to deal with the enemy.

FIGHTING AT MATTHEWS HILL

Johnston drew up his line of battle on Matthews Hill. To keep watch on the enemy feint, he ordered Evans to leave a few companies plus artillery at the Stone Bridge, then march to join Bee and Bartow. When "Shanks" joined them, Johnston still had only 4,500 troops in his left line; he wished to hold Jackson back until the Union attack developed.

Develop it did. Once over the run, Burnside's and Colonel Andrew Porter's brigades (both of Hunter's division) deployed in assault formation and advanced southward along the Manassas-

---

313   David Detzer, *Donnybrook: The Battle of Bull Run* (New York, 2004), p. 243.

Sudley road. These two oversized units numbered a full 9,000 troops; added to them were Battery D, 5th U.S. Artillery under Captain Charles Griffin (four ten-pounder Parrott rifles plus two twelve-pounder howitzers) and Captain J.B. Ricketts' Co. I, 1st U.S. Artillery (six Parrotts). The two batteries unlimbered in the woods within sight of the Matthews house and opened up a determined shelling of Johnston's line.

Then the infantry struck. Around 10:30 Burnside's and Porter's men charged the hill. The Confederates opened fire, committing all the mistakes that green troops are expected to make. Most particularly, they fired too high, though officers all along the line were yelling "Shoot their feet! Shoot their feet!" After the first volleys, some men forgot the cadence of reloading, and in the excitement and roar of battle rammed down bullets without powder. Others bit their paper cartridges and poured double, even triple powder charges before ramming down a bullet (producing a report almost as loud as a six-pounder cannon). Some loaded their muskets properly but then forgot the most important final step— to remove the ramrod. As a result, thin metal shafts were flying all over the field around Matthews Hill, rendering the ramrod-less muskets useless further in the fight, except maybe as clubs or bayonet-holders.

In their assault wave Union troops were just as inexperienced and jittery. Some broke ranks and turned tail, but most kept their pace even as the Confederates' musketry began to drop victims. One of them was General Hunter himself, grazed in the neck by a musket ball as he waved his soldiers across the field. Soon, the Federals' superior numbers gave them an edge in firepower. "The balls just poured on us," wrote a Confederate afterward, "struck our muskets and hats and bodies. Oh! How we boys did fight to gain a victory for the Sunny South!"[314] But the odds against Bee, Bartow and Evans were too great. After standing their ground for an hour or so, the Southerners—Alabamians, Georgians, Mississippians and Carolinians—began giving way, streaming

---

314   William C. Davis, *Battle at Manassas: A History of the First Major Campaign of the Southern War for Independence* (Baton Rouge, 1977), pp. 179-80.

southward toward the Henry House hill. Colonel Francis Bartow lost his life to a bullet in the chest as he tried to rally the 7th and 8th Georgia. Across a cornfield, Barnard Bee galloped through the stalks, calling on his men to stop and face the enemy. They did so, but only long enough to get off one more round before turning and continuing their withdrawal before the advancing Yankees.

BRIGADIER GENERAL JACKSON GETS A NICKNAME

Looking down on all this from Henry House Hill was Jackson's brigade. "The firing in our front was terrific," an officer of the 5th Virginia later recorded, "and why we did not render immediate and timely assistance to Bee I could never learn."[315] General Bee would never learn the reason, either. In frustration, he held his saber point toward the Virginians and cried out, "Look men, there is Jackson standing like a stone wall!" Then he yelled something else—too many words to be caught above the roar of the battlefield—before crying out, to his men, "Follow me!"[316] Bee turned his horse toward the Yankee infantry and charged, followed by fewer than a hundred men. Soon the South Carolinian was shot in the saddle; his soldiers led his horse to the rear, where the general died on the field.

Bee had given Thomas Jonathan Jackson, renowned today in the Confederate States second only to Robert Edward Lee as the nation's war hero, his famous nickname: "Stonewall." But exactly what Bee meant by his famous exclamation has been debated ever since the battle of Manassas. The most iconoclastic version reflects Bee's dismay at seeing Jackson's five regiments idly waiting atop Henry Hill while his brigade was being cut up in withdrawal before the advancing Yankees. According to this legend, General Bee shouted, "Look at Jackson's brigade! It stands there like a stone wall." Southern historian Frank Vandiver, author of a biography

---

315   William C. Davis, *Battle at Manassas: A History of the First Major Campaign of the Southern War for Independence* (Baton Rouge, 1977), p. 196.

316   James I. Robertson, *Stonewall Jackson: The Man, the Soldier, the Legend* (Richmond, 1997), p. 264.

of General Jackson, tells the story of Bee shouting to his troops, "There stands Jackson like a stone wall! Goddamn it, why doesn't he help us?"[317]

Within a few days after the battle, Bee's "Jackson...stone wall" remark was related to pressmen of the Charleston *Mercury,* but when published it appeared in a completely different version. Gone was Bee's obscene anger; in its place, according to the version that soon began appearing in biographies of Jackson, was a stirring exhortation: "There is Jackson standing like a stone wall! Let us determine to die here, and we will conquer! Follow me!" As the story appeared further in print, Bee's words, or his purpose in uttering them, got further skewed. He is said to have shouted (in an early postwar work), "There is Jackson standing like a stone wall. Rally behind the Virginians," which would have had the effect of ordering his troops to continue their retreat to Jackson's position. Another version, published toward the end of the century, has General Bee exclaiming, "Yonder stands Jackson like a stone wall. Let us go to his assistance," with the general leading remnants of his brigade back to reinforce the right of Jackson's line.[318]

Jackson's British biographer, G.F.R. Henderson, writing in 1898, accepted the "Rally behind the Virginians!" variant. So did, a generation later, Allen Tate (with "Look there at Jackson standing like a stone wall. Rally behind the Virginians!"), as did, a generation after that, Lenoir Chambers; and more recently several more biographers.[319] At least one, Byron Farwell, cites the

---

317   James V. Murfin, "How Stonewall Got His Name," *Civil War Times Illustrated,* July 1962, p. 39; Frank E. Vandiver, *Mighty Stonewall* (Richmond, 1957), p. 161. A Confederate staff officer, Major Burnett Rhett, was riding near Bee before the latter's death and later recounted that "Bee said that his and Bartow's brigades were hard pressed and that Jackson refused to move to their relief and in a passionate expression of anger he denounced him for standing, like a stone wall and allowing them to be sacrificed" (Douglas Southall Freeman, *Lee's Lieutenants: A Study in Command,* 3 vols. [New York, 1942-44], vol. 1, 734).

318   Murfin, "How Stonewall Got His Name," p. 39; [John Esten Cooke], *The Life of Stonewall Jackson....By a Virginian* (Richmond, 1864), p. 31; R.L. Dabney, *Life and Campaigns of Lieut.-Gen. Thomas J. Jackson* (New York, 1866), p. 222.

319   G.F.R. Henderson, *Stonewall Jackson and the Confederate War for Independence,* 2 vols. (London, 1898), vol. 1, 145; Allen Tate, *Stonewall Jackson: The Good Soldier* (New York, 1928), 86; Lenoir Chambers, *Stonewall Jackson,* 2 vols. (Raleigh, 1959), vol. 1, 377; Burke Davis, *They Called Him Stonewall: A Life*

possibility that General Bee intended his words as "a reproach, accusing Jackson of standing fast instead of coming to Bee's support."

Barnard Bee's last words may therefore have been "Follow me!" (charging the enemy) or "Rally behind the Virginians!" (withdrawing farther to the rear). At issue was the circumstances under which Barnard Elliott Bee lost his life. Either way, before he died on the battlefield of Manassas, he gave a lasting nickname to one of the Confederacy's great military heroes.

The numerous biographies of Stonewall Jackson reflect the understanding among most Americans, North and South, that "Lee's right arm" was virtually the architect of the crushing Confederate victory at Chancellorsville. Following the rout of Hooker's army in the Wilderness on the afternoon of May 2, 1863, Jackson refused to relent, and pushed his troops in vigorous pursuit of the fleeing Yankees virtually throughout the night. Joined at dawn by Longstreet's relatively fresh forces, Lee exerted his maximum offensive (even throwing in Early's division, which he had been holding in reserve). By midday of May 3 Hooker's troops had been driven all the way back to the banks of the Rappahannock. When only part of the Army of the Potomac could get across the United States Ford and other wading places amid the furious Confederate attacks on its rearguard, there arose the possibility that Northern soldiers would frantically pour into the rushing river and drown in a reprise of Shanks Evans' watery victory at Ball's Bluff in October 1861—albeit in tragically huger numerical proportions. Union corps commanders Oliver Howard and Henry Slocum began to surrender as many troops as they had in their immediate command, given that most Federal regiments and brigades had lost their formation as Confederate forces pressed ever closer to the river bank. At least these generals survived. I Corps commander John F. Reynolds was shot in the head while trying to rally his troops for one last stand. III Corps commander

---

of Lieutenant General T.J. Jackson, C.S.A. (New York, 1954), p. 149; John Bowers, *Stonewall Jackson: Portrait of a Solder* (New York, 1989), p. 106; Byron Farwell, *Stonewall: A Biography of General Thomas J. Jackson* (New York, 1992), p. 180.

Daniel E. Sickles had a leg carried off by a cannonball. That left Generals Hooker, Darius Couch (II Corps) and George G. Meade (V) to get across the river with as many soldiers as they could.

When the shattered fragments of the Army of the Potomac limped back into Washington and Union casualties were toted up, Lincoln and the entire North were mortified to learn that of Hooker's 70,000 effectives taken into battle—the President surely regretted his decision to hold back John Sedgwick's VI Corps to guard Washington—fully fifty-three percent, 37,100 officers and men, were killed, wounded, captured or missing (presumably drowned). Chancellorsville was thus as close to a battle of annihilation as occurred in the American Civil War—a level of carnage approaching Hannibal's classic, bloody victory at Cannae in the Second Punic War.

In his after-action telegram to President Davis in Richmond, General Lee in his customary way gave thanks to "a kind and merciful Providence—and to the gallant Lieutenant-General Jackson."

Another dimension of the almost universal idolatry bestowed upon Stonewall Jackson was that in the closing stages of the battle of Chancellorsville he, too, fell a victim. Shot several times in his left arm, he died from pneumonia seven days after amputation of his limb. Within days of his death, Southern newspapers were praising him as a Confederate martyr—nay, a Messiah.

FEDERALS PUSH ON TO HENRY HOUSE HILL

Neither Bee's last words—whatever they were—nor his final heroism stemmed the Southerners' confused retreat. Federal officers exulted in what looked to be the beginning signs of a victory. "For God's sake, hurry up, boys, we're driving them!" shouted a captain in the 2d Rhode Island, as the Union line engulfed Matthews Hill. Just then, fiery "Shanks" Evans, rattling in rage against being driven from the field with Bee's and Bartow's men, and probably hot and heady from the whiskey he carried in a large wooden canteen (his "barrelita," he termed it), unleashed a counterattack that stalled Burnside's advance. As the Yankees were in the midst of wading Young's Branch south of Matthews', Major Roberdeau Wheat's battalion of Louisiana rowdies, henceforth called "Tigers," led a fierce spoiling assault. They ran at full speed, yelling outlandishly and waving Bowie knives as they piled into the van of the 2d Rhode Island. The New Englanders were cut up in the process. Their Colonel John Slocum, shot twice, was soon to die. The Louisianans suffered too. A minie ball passed through Major Wheat's chest, from armpit to armpit, leaving a wound that field surgeons pronounced as mortal. "I don't feel like dying yet," was Wheat's reply, and he did not.[320] What was more, his gutsy charge at Young's Branch, coupled with Hunter's wounding, created temporary confusion in the Union ranks. After a rush of Northern reinforcements turned back Wheat's tiger-like charge, the Federals halted, and the Confederates snatched the opportunity to regroup south of the Warrenton Turnpike.

The situation at 11:30 saw both sides calling for reinforcements on the Union right, the Confederate left. Hunter's two brigades (Burnside's and Porter's), had knocked the Rebels off Matthews Hill. McDowell had arrived to take charge of his battle on this part of the field, and he waited on Heintzelman's division, behind Burnside, to strengthen his line before advancing farther. Of Tyler's division at the Stone Bridge, Schenck's brigade was still "demonstrating," waiting to march over the run when the way cleared on the other side. But Sherman's and Colonel Erasmus Keyes' brigades were already crossing upstream at the ford that "Crazy Billy" had discovered earlier in the morning.

On the Confederate side, Johnston was restoring order to the disorganized regiments of Bee, Bartow and Evans. They rallied on Jackson's brigade (true to General Bee's alleged last, recorded words) at the crest of Henry Hill, where Johnston formed his line. Philip St. George Cocke brought his men up from Lewis' Ford, and Bonham was approaching from Mitchell's. Ewell's brigade and Holmes' force had also been sent from Beauregard's right

---

320   Ethan S. Rafuse, *A Single Grand Victory: The First Campaign and Battle of Manassas* (Wilmington DE, 2002), p. 131.

wing, and were *en route*. Even more reinforcements were about to arrive, with Wade Hampton's South Carolina Legion detrained at the Junction and hurrying northward.

With these fresh Confederate troops on the way (not to mention Kirby Smith's and Arnold Elzey's brigades from the Valley, the rest of Johnston's Army of the Shenandoah), the last thing Irvin McDowell should have done was to dawdle. Elated at his success so far, the Union commander mistakenly believed that the Confederate retreat from Matthews Hill was the start of a general withdrawal. All that the Rebels needed, he thought, was another bayonet charge to drive them from Henry Hill, and the day would be his. So McDowell waited while Heintzelman came up, and Sherman and Keyes got into play on his left flank. Meanwhile the corpulent Federal commander could be seen riding among his troops shouting, "Victory! Victory! We have done it! They are running! The day is ours!" All that was needed, in McDowell's excited terms, was "a final push."[321] Unfortunately for McDowell, the time needed for his "final push" proved to be at least two hours, time which the Confederates much better used to bring reinforcements to this threatened sector of the field.

By this juncture the fighting at Bull Run, not to mention the Federals' premature expectations of victory, had brought a whole crowd of civilians from Washington to view the battle. Congressmen and senators, desk-bound bureaucrats, officers' wives—all had ridden out in their carriages with picnic baskets on this sunny Sunday afternoon to see the National army whip the Rebels. By the dozens they perched themselves on knolls between Cub and Bull Runs, close enough to be thrilled by the roar of the musketry. Some brought their field-glasses and kept watch on the battle's progress (though they could not have espied much through all the smoke and dust). Such was their excitement and their giddy anticipation of a resounding triumph that most confidently assumed they were witnessing the war's first and last battle, the single clash of arms needed to end the Rebellion in one stroke.

---

321 *Ibid.,* p. 139.

Southerners Hold Henry Hill Against The Yankees' "Final Push"

The Rebellion was far from over, of course, as was the battle that was supposed to end it. During the noontime lull, Joe Johnston used every minute to bring up reinforcements and rearrange his battle line. Cocke was thrown onto the left; Jackson stood in the center, the reformed remnants of Bee, Bartow and Evans on right, bolstered by Hampton. Stuart's cavalry rode up in time to extend Johnston's left flank out toward the Chinn house. Bonham's brigade was ordered up from Mitchell's Ford, and Holmes' troops were alerted for a possible march as well.

Around 2 p.m. McDowell began his "final push," but the Northern attack was ill-fated from the start. Instead of a general advance, the Union line committed itself to a series of uncoordinated pushlets, little attacks that used up the Federal strength in a piecemeal manner. Causes of this Northern misfortune lay at the army, division, and brigade levels. McDowell underestimated the effort needed to crack the Rebel line, and failed to issue appropriate orders for the assault. His division leaders were not in touch with one another—with Hunter out of action and Tyler across the creek, Heintzelman alone was present in the field. Even then, Union brigade commanders operated on their own initiatives. Burnside, for instance, decided that his men were blown by the morning's fighting, and withdrew his brigade from the line. On the Union left, Keyes thought he saw an advantage to moving down the left bank of Young's Branch, a small stream flowing eastward into Bull Run. The result was that he separated from Sherman, and effectively took his brigade out of the fight.

Thus McDowell had only four brigades in line: Sherman on his left, Porter in center, then two of Heintzelman's (Colonel William Franklin's and Colonel Orlando Willcox's) on his right. A fifth, Colonel Oliver Howard's, he held in reserve. McDowell opened this next round of the fight, the "final push" by which he hoped to clinch victory, by sending artillery forward to bombard the enemy line, softening it for an infantry advance. These guns, Rickett's and Griffin's batteries, advanced to within 330 yards of Jackson's line and commenced their shelling of Henry Hill. Jackson posted sharpshooters in the Widow Henry's house, and the Confederates returned fire. Union shells started raining down on the place; one of them exploded inside, killing old Mrs. Henry as she huddled for protection. She was possibly the first of 20,000 estimated civilians killed in this most uncivil war.[322]

Willcox and Porter ordered a charge on the hill. The two regiments chosen for the attack could not have been attired more stupidly, for both the 11th New York Zouaves and the 14th New York ("Brooklyn Red Legs") wore the bright crimson trousers of militiamen. They made perfect targets as they marched across the field, especially for Southern infantrymen being enjoined by their officers to aim low. "We literally mowed them down," a Confederate remembered as Jackson's men, now joined by Cocke's brigade, directed volley upon volley.[323] The New Yorkers broke and ran for the rear. "Jeb" Stuart with his cavalry saw an opportunity for pursuit, so he ordered his horsemen forward. With sabers flailing right and left, the Southern cavalrymen rode right into the Zouaves, who turned about to bayonet the riders as they passed. A short melee ensued before the Confederates galloped back to their lines.

As the New Yorkers retired behind their artillery, Colonel Arthur Cummings, commanding the 33d Virginia, saw a chance for another counterstroke, this one against Ricketts' and Griffin's batteries. Without orders from General Jackson, he led his regiment at the double-quick toward the Yankee guns. Here again, uniform colors worked to the Northerners' disadvantage, for Cummings' men wore tunics of old-style regulation blue. Consequently Union artillerymen mistook them for part of the attack wave retiring from the field. When the Confederates emerged from woods in his front, Captain Griffin ordered his cannon to be loaded with canister— an exploding container of buckshot, specifically to maul charging infantry. Just then an officer rode up. "Captain, don't fire there;

---

322 Drew Gilpin Faust, *This Republic of Suffering: Death and the American Civil War* (New York, 2008), p. xii.

323 William C. Davis, *Battle at Manassas: A History of the First Major Campaign of the Southern War for Independence* (Baton Rouge, 1977), p. 206.

those are your battery support!" "They are Rebels," Griffin argued. Cummings' ranks settled the matter then and there with a volley of musketry that carried off the 1st and 5th U.S. artillery from the face of the earth. "That was the last of us," remembered Griffin, "we were all cut down."[324] The Union gunners simply fell where they stood. Ricketts was killed; Griffin, wounded, escaped capture by seizing the reins of a fleeing horse. Few other battery horses survived the Confederate musket-blast; Ricketts lost forty-nine, Griffin fifty. The Southerners swarmed over both batteries, but without horsepower they could not haul away their artillery prizes.

Ownership of those twelve guns challenged both sides to attack and counterattack. For the next hour the fighting around Henry Hill seethed in an inconclusive see-saw by both sides. Franklin sent in the 1st Minnesota, which drove back Cummings. Then Wade Hampton led his legion in a charge with two regiments of Virginians. "We came up in good order," wrote one of them, "amidst a hail of bullets, bomb shells & cannon balls, stepping over dead men & horses."[325] They retook the guns, but lost them again when the 5th and 11th Massachusetts charged over those same dead men & horses.

General Jackson, standing like a stone wall on Henry House Hill, was making his reputation as his soldiers watched the advance of the enemy in the field before them. "Steady men, steady! All's well!" At some point the newly dubbed "Stonewall" was shot in the left hand, between the fore and middle fingers. Aides tried to take him from the field, but Jackson would have none of it. "Only a scratch, a mere scratch," he said as he wrapped his hand in a cloth and galloped away.[326]

Soon, sensing that the enemy's attacks were withering out, Jackson ordered his 4th and 27th Virginia to take Ricketts' battery, crying out with uncharacteristic excitement, "Charge, and yell like

---

324 John Hennessy, *The First Battle of Manassas: An End to Innocence July 18-21, 1861* (Lynchburg VA, 1989), p. 84; Ethan S. Rafuse, *A Single Grand Victory: The First Campaign and Battle of Manassas* (Wilmington DE, 2002), p. 167.

325 Davis, *op. cit.,* p. 214.

326 James I. Robertson, Jr., *Stonewall Jackson: The Man, the Soldier, the Legend* (New York, 1988), p. 263.

furies!" They did, as the Virginians overran the Union artillery and then fended off a Federal counterattack. In the charge of his regiments, about 3:30 that afternoon of July 21, 1861, Jackson summoned forth what the world has since called the "Rebel Yell." Years later, an ex-Confederate stated that in giving the order, "Jackson freed the pent up feeling of the South."

> At that thrilling moment was born the war cry of the South. So weird was it that it seemed at times to mingle in the noise and confusion of a battle field and to become a spiritual thing, a Voice, a Sound, described by one as the voice of the "Fierce South, cheering on her sons!" There burst upon the ear of the earth that wild yell, more awful than the noise of hissing ball or screeching shell....There was in that sound something of the shrill horror of the boy's fierce play of Indian warfare; something of the exultant shout to hounds when the deer breaks cover; something of the wild laughter of reckless youth that mocks at death; something of the growl of hunted beast whose lair has been invaded; and then the deeper tones of that wordless rage of the strong man as he leaps to guard the threshold of his home.[327]

THE PROBLEM OF COLORS

With some Union regiments wearing gray and some Confederate units garbed in blue, and with the Stars & Stripes and Stars & Bars looking menacingly alike at distance and in battle smoke, too many lives on both sides were lost that day from what military historians now call "friendly fire."

The charge of Sherman's brigade on Henry Hill gives tragic examples. Colonel Sherman made the same mistake other Federals from McDowell on down were doing that day, feeding his regiments into the fight piecemeal, never combining their numbers

---

[327] "The Rebel Yell," *Confederate Veteran,* vol. 31 (1923), 275.

and firepower against the Rebels. First charged the 2d Wisconsin, dressed in their militia gray. Advancing up the slope, they wavered under a fierce Confederate volley. "Our men fell in every direction," one survivor recalled, from "the most hellish shower of bullets you can imagine." As the Federals prepared to return their own volley, a mounted Federal officer rode behind them shouting, "For God's sake, stop firing; you are shooting friends!"[328] Perhaps he thought the grayclads atop the hill were Northern troops attired as the Wisconsans were; perhaps he saw before him a Stars & Bars that looked like a Stars & Stripes. Either way, the demoralized 2d began retiring down the hill. Sherman's other two regiments, the 79th and 69th New York, mistook the ranks approaching them for advancing Rebels, and fired into them. The unlucky 2d suffered still more casualties before the New Yorkers realized their mistake and ceased firing.

Then it was their turn to charge, when Sherman ordered in the 79th. As the Federals advanced at quick time up the hillside, the first rank spotted the flags of the Hampton Legion and concluded that other Union units had taken the crest. Colonel James Cameron, leading the charge, gave orders not to fire. "Suddenly we saw the American flag waving," wrote one of the New Yorkers. "As we lowered our arms, and were about to rally where the banner floated, we were met by a terrible raking fire, against which we could only stagger."[329] Cameron, brother of the North's Secretary of War, fell mortally wounded. The bloodied regiment fell back, having lost in their very first charge 32 killed, 51 wounded and 115 missing (presumed wounded and later captured).

There followed another assault, as Sherman sent in his last regiment, the 69th, but this too was no more than a regimental sortie, uncoordinated with the advances of any other units. Casualties resulted, nothing was gained; such had been the story

---

328 Ethan S. Rafuse, *A Single Grand Victory: The First Campaign and Battle of Manassas* (Wilmington DE, 2002), p. 177; JoAnna M. McDonald, *"We Shall Meet Again": The First Battle of Manassas (Bull Run) July 18-21, 1861* (Shippensburg PA, 1999), p. 135.

329 William C. Davis, *Battle at Manassas: A History of the First Major Campaign of the Southern War for Independence* (Baton Rouge, 1977), p. 218.

up and down McDowell's line as Willcox, Franklin, Porter and now Sherman had tested and spent their strength in piecemeal attacks on Henry House Hill. Every repulse sent stragglers to the rear— some wounded, some just scared; all hot, tired and blown by a hard morning's march and a sharp afternoon's fight in July heat. As they encountered fresh Federal units marching into the fight, these beaten recruits told frightful, depressing tales of what it was like to "see the elephant"...soldier-slang for one's first combat. The impression grew among the Union ranks, both officers and men, that the day was going against them, as each beaten attack brought more discouragement.

"Go Where The Fire Is Hottest!"

About a mile south of Henry Hill, General Johnston had set his headquarters at "Portici," the two-story frame house of Francis W. Lewis. There he received reports from the battle front and awaited the arrival of the rest of his command coming from the Shenandoah, which he intended to feed into his line. Couriers brought word that in their attacks on Henry Hill the Yankees had shot their bolt and that the Confederate left was stabilized. Ten minutes later, though, reports brought word of fresh enemy movements against Jackson's left flank, toward Chinn Ridge. McDowell was committing the last untried troops he had on the field, Oliver Howard's brigade of Heintzelman's division. Howard was stopped by a sharp counterattack of the 6th North Carolina, whose Colonel, Charles F. Fisher, dropped dead from a bullet through his brain. Fisher's charge brought a Union counter; both sides traded blows.

By this time, mid-afternoon, Beauregard was sending rein-forcements from the Confederate right. Milledge Bonham's brigade marched from Mitchell's Ford to the sound of the firing, and arrived just in time to relieve the Carolinians. Already, from Richmond, Wade Hampton's Legion of 650 troopers had also arrived from Richmond to help stabilize the Henry Hill sector. Even more fortunate for the Confederates was the approach of Edmund Kirby Smith's brigade, the last of Johnston's army transported from the Valley. "Seldom in the history of warfare," writes one historian of the battle, "did reinforcements come at a more opportune moment."[330] Riding in the direction of the firing, Brigadier General (as of June 17) Smith was wounded as he sought to deploy his troops. Colonel Arnold Elzey, second in command, took over. These new arrivals literally won the day for the South. Johnston at Portici sensed the impact of their coming. "Take them to the front!" he yelled excitedly, "It is our left that is under attack. Go to where the fire is hottest!"[331]

It was nearing four o'clock. Oliver Howard's Union brigade had been stopped by Bonham's assault east of the Chinn house. Colonel James Ewell Brown ("Jeb") Stuart, of the 1st Virginia Cavalry, saw fresh Southern troops approaching and sent couriers to Elzey; if he could advance quickly, he believed the Yankees would fold and collapse. Elzey complied...and so did the Yankees. Joined by yet another brigade, Jubal Early's sent by Beauregard from the right, the Confederates marched into battle line and surged forward. Stuart positioned a battery to support the attack and opened up on Howard's regrouping troops. A young private from Maine recorded the scene: "In a short time a bout a thousand men marched down from a nother direction...they marched with in 50 or 60 rods without firing or being fired upon. they then opened fire on us and we on them at the same time a mask batery opened on us from the side hill that we knew nothing about. We pretty much gave up the fight after that."[332]

THE FEDERAL RETREAT

Repulsed in their last charge (of the day, as it turned out), unnerved by their sight of fresh Rebel troop-waves (the brigades of Elzey, Smith and Early) as their own energy waned after an exhausting day of marching and fighting, and reeling from the last explosion of enemy musketry, the regiments on the Union extreme right gave way. "It was evident," Colonel Howard later lamented, "that a panic had seized all the troops in sight." Federals broke

---

330   William C. Davis, *Battle at Manassas: A History of the First Major Campaign of the Southern War for Independence* (Baton Rouge, 1977), p. 225.

331   Craig L. Symonds, *Joseph E. Johnston: A Biography* (New York, 1992), p. 121.

332   Davis, *op. cit.*, p. 232.

ranks and headed toward the rear, spreading panic to all they met. "Give way! The enemy is upon us! We shall all be taken!" some shouted, and by 4:30 the retreat from the Union right was spreading across the field from Howard through Heintzelman to Hunter and Sherman. General Heintzelman rode back and forth among his men, cursing and ordering them to reform. It was too late. "There were no fresh forces on the field to support or encourage them," wrote a Northern officer, "and the men seemed to be seized simultaneously by the conviction that it was no use to do anything more and they might as well start home."[333] Within a short while, despite officers' efforts to rally, Howard's, Willcox's and Franklin's brigades just came apart and receded back across the Warrenton road toward Sudley Ford.

As his right and center collapsed, a stunned Irvin McDowell realized that he had been beaten. The retreat soon became a rout, and this soon degenerated still further into a panic. In Tyler's division at Stone Bridge resistance was crumbling, too. Schenck's brigade had finally crossed and General Tyler was deploying it east of Young's Branch for an assault, when an excited courier rode up. "The army is in full retreat towards Bull Run!" he screamed. Tyler could not believe him. "Ride with me to the rear, then," the aide shouted. They did so, galloping down the road toward the Carter house. The General pulled rein at the sight before him. "To my astonishment, I saw the Army was retreating towards Bull Run," he recounted. "As we emerged from the woods one glance told the tale; a tale of defeat, and a confused, disorderly and disgraceful retreat. The road was filled with wagons, artillery, retreating cavalry and infantry in one confused mass, each seemingly bent on looking out for number one and letting the rest do the same."

McDowell's army was collapsing. Regimental formations broke apart as every soldier took off in the direction he thought safest, but the stream of men, horses, wagons and caissons flowed generally toward Centreville, from which most of the army had set out that

---

333   William C. Davis, *Battle at Manassas: A History of the First Major Campaign of the Southern War for Independence* (Baton Rouge, 1977), p. 232; John Hennessy, *The First Battle of Manassas: An End to Innocence* (Lynchburg VA, 1989), p. 116.

morning. Sherman's and Burnside's men were racing toward the ford discovered earlier by "Crazy Billy." Keyes' brigade took flight via the Stone Bridge, sweeping Schenck's regiments with it.

THE FINAL CONFEDERATE CHARGE SWEEPS THE FIELD

At his Lewis house headquarters Confederate General Johnston had done a good job of feeding into the fight his last-arriving units, as well as Beauregard's brigades from the right (Bonham and Early). As reports from Bonham, Jackson and Evans brought word of the Union retrograde along their fronts, an exhilarated Johnston ordered an advance of his whole line to push the Yankees and keep them on the run. Elzey's and Early's brigades needed no such orders; they simply never halted after making contact with Howard. Stuart, Bonham and Cocke joined in, pressing down the Manassas-Sudley Road, scooping up prisoners and keeping up the scare on McDowell's frantic soldiers. Hampton's Legion and other units on the Confederate right pushed toward Stone Bridge with hopes to press Tyler's rearguard on to Centreville.

Now was the time also for Beauregard to act. From his headquarters at Wilmer McLean's house near Blackburn's Ford, the senior Confederate general on the field had rather irritatedly spent the day receiving courier messages on how the battle upstream was going.[334] Now he saw an opportunity to launch the forward movement he had been hoping to order, as a means to pursue the beaten enemy and reap an even greater harvest of victory. Still in the area of Mitchell's and Blackburn's Fords were two Southern brigades as yet unbloodied in the day's fighting. Around 4:30, when couriers brought news to his headquarters of the glorious victory Johnston was gaining to the north, Beauregard— mindful that on this July day there were four hours of daylight still to be had— ordered D.R. Jones and Longstreet to cross Bull Run, engage

---

334 Virginia civilian Wilmer McLean, whose house was used by the winning Confederate general in the first big battle of the war, gained further historical acclaim at the end of the war. After Lee's victory at Chancellorsville, and the Confederates' advance of their lines to the Centreville-Manassas front, General Lee occupied McLean's house at the time of the first armistice talks in June 1863. The Lee-Halleck meeting, which paved the way for the end of the war in the eastern theater, is said to have taken place in the McLean parlor.

the enemy where encountered, and press toward Centreville. Their route was essentially a short-cut and a very promising one, indeed: from Blackburn's Ford to Centreville (through which the Yankees would have to pass in their retreat back to Washington) was a shorter distance than the route that McDowell's three corps would have to march in their tired but hurried journey to safety. In the Confederates' way, however, were Union troops who had not yet participated either in the day's fighting or the afternoon's retreating. Israel Richardson's brigade, of Tyler's division, lay about halfway between it and Centreville; in the latter village itself was Dixon Miles' division, still in reserve. Colonel Miles, encamped in the rear of a battle he could only hear, had begun to hit his brandy flask way too early that afternoon. When the troops retreating from the battlefield encountered him, he was so intoxicated as to be seen swaying boozily on his horse, slurring unintelligible commands with sword upraised and two hats stacked on his head. When one of McDowell's staff approached him with instructions to send a brigade to the Stone Bridge to help stop the rout, Miles spluttered in an intoxicated huff: "I know all about the fight. You can't give me any information. I have something else to attend to."[335] He was immediately relieved of command.

Miles did have the presence at least to send Davies' brigade out toward Richardson, who had come into contact with Longstreet a mile north of Bull Run. There Union artillery fire momentarily halted the Rebels' advance. It was now close to 7 p.m. and darkness was approaching. Longstreet chose to disengage and await Jones's brigade, somewhere behind him, before pushing on to Centreville.

EDMUND RUFFIN AGAIN FIRES A SHOT

Over on the Warrenton Turnpike, Southerners kept up the push in the final hours of daylight. East of the Henry House, Colonel R.C.W. Radford of the 30th Virginia Cavalry, attached to Bonham's brigade, got this message: "General Johnston says the enemy are in full retreat and you must intercept them between the Stone Bridge and Centreville." Radford's horsemen plunged across Bull

---

335   William C. Davis, *Battle at Manassas: A History of the First Major Campaign of the Southern War for Independence* (Baton Rouge, 1977), p. 241.

Run and soon clashed with Keyes' disorganized rearguard. The Confederates were repulsed, but not before scaring the panicked Federals further as they pell-melled down the pike. "Then a scene of confusion ensued which beggars description," lamented Colonel Keyes. "Cavalry horses without riders, artillery horses disengaged from the guns with traces flying, wrecked baggage-wagons, and pieces of artillery drawn by six horses without drivers, flying at their utmost speed and whacking against other vehicles."[336]

Captain Del Kemper's battery of Alexandria Light Artillery crossed Stone Bridge along with Kemper's cavalry. Unlimbering on a hill overlooking Cub Run, Kemper surveyed the road filled with fleeing soldiers, wagons, horses and caissons, then gave the order to open fire. The Confederates zeroed in on the rickety trestle over Cub Run and soon scored a hit that completed the degeneration of McDowell's retreat into rout. The peripatetic Edmund Ruffin, who had come to Manassas with the transfer of the Palmetto Guards from Sumter, just happened to be among Kemper's gunners. He recorded the scene in his diary:

> One large body of the routed & fleeing Yankees had reached the bridge over Cub Run, & there filled the road with a closely packed crowd of soldiers, artillery trains, baggage wagons, ambulances & c. The first wagon had just been driven upon the bridge, to pass over, when the first gun (my gun) was fired from Kemper's battery, loaded (as I learned afterwards,) with Shrapnell, or spherical-case shell. As the official reports of the Yankee commander afterwards stated, some of the shot from this first discharge, (which he said was from a "masked battery"), struck one or more of the horses of the foremost wagon. In their pain & fright they suddenly turned, upset the wagon so as to barricade the whole width of the bridge & effectually precluded any other wheel-carriage, or horse, from moving on. The whole mass of fugitives

---

336   William C. Davis, *Battle at Manassas: A History of the First Major Campaign of the Southern War for Independence* (Baton Rouge, 1977), pp. 237, 241.

immediately got out of the track, & all escaped who could, on foot as quickly as possible. The rapidly succeeding discharges of our cannon, aimed as correctly as the first down the slope of the straight road, kept up & increased the panic & the headlong haste of the Yankees.[337]

YANKEE PANIC IS EASED BY NIGHTFALL

Blocked at the bridge, McDowell's men slid down the creek banks, waded or swam across, then clambered up again in their rush to safety. "Many of the soldiers threw their arms into the creek, and everything indicated the greatest possible panic," reported Captain Kemper, obviously delighted.[338] Wagons choking the road from Sudley Springs were simply abandoned; artillerymen left their teams and joined the milling crowd afoot.

Only the coming of nightfall saved the Northern army from complete disintegration. After lobbing maybe twenty shells, Kemper's gunners mounted up and recrossed Bull Run. Confederate infantry units had long since given up the chase, too tuckered out to pursue much farther than Sudley Springs or Stone Bridge. Southern cavalrymen spent the last hour of twilight rounding up the boggling array of wagons, guns and equipment left behind by the fleeing enemy. The finest and most peculiar booty, of course, was the stuff hastily abandoned by the Northern civilian battle-gawkers who had picnicked, then panicked and skiddooed with the rest of the army. Champagne and wine bottles, some still

---

337 William Kauffman Scarborough, ed., *The Diary of Edmund Ruffin*, 3 vols. (Baton Rouge, 1976), vol. 2, 89. Afterward, Ruffin wandered over the Cub Run bridge to examine the results of his cannonfire. He was disappointed to find only three Yankee corpses, but later took satisfaction in learning from eyewitnesses that seven bodies strewed the bridge. "All these must have been killed by our cannonade—& also I am persuaded that a good proportion of them fell by my first fire," Ruffin vengefully gloated, though he admitted, "I should have liked to have killed the greatest possible number" (*ibid.,* 94-95).

338 William C. Davis, *Battle at Manassas: A History of the First Major Campaign of the Southern War for Independence* (Baton Rouge, 1977), p. 238.

partly filled, ladies' slippers, parasols and other accoutrements of the elite provided tired Rebs with many a guffaw on the morning of the 22d.

Over near Centreville, General McDowell and his staff managed to piece together a defensive line to hold off the Rebels if they should venture forth. West of town Blenker's reserve brigade was deployed, along with whatever companies or regiments that had stuck together. Richardson and Davies were south of Centreville. Altogether these units formed a defensive perimeter, allowing the rest of the Union army to scamper back toward Washington. By 10 p.m., when it became clear that the Confederates would not attack, McDowell ordered his rearguard units to resume their march back to Alexandria.

Confederate Pursuit

That evening none other than the President of the Confederacy arrived on the battlefield. Jefferson Davis had been unable to contain himself in Richmond while knowing of a big battle raging to the north. So he hopped a train to Manassas Junction and got there as the dimensions of the Southerners' success were becoming known. "Our forces have won a glorious victory," he wired back to the capital, then set out to find his generals.[339] At Portici Davis, Johnston and Beauregard congratulated themselves for the day's work and discussed how to reap the rewards of victory with pursuit of the enemy. The question hinged on the material at hand. Already C.S. cavalry under Stuart and Hampton were riding hard, nipping at the Yankee army's rear units, picking up prisoners and generally keeping the pressure on. The question was, though, what Confederate infantry might follow and by fleet-footed pursuit reap even greater bounties of victory? With the army's left wing tired and disarrayed, only Longstreet's and Jones' brigades were in any condition for action, having sat out the battle while guarding the fords. For these troops Beauregard therefore wrote orders that night. With Longstreet leading, they were to get going at dawn, July 22 moving as fast as possible toward

---

339   William C. Davis, *Battle at Manassas: A History of the First Major Campaign of the Southern War for Independence* (Baton Rouge, 1977), p. 244

Centreville, then east to Fairfax Courthouse. The overall plan was to engage the enemy's rear, and wreak as much damage as possible while pushing McDowell's disorganized forces in the direction of Arlington Heights.

McDowell's army was disorganized and beaten, but if it were anything else during the night of July 21-22 it was quick on the run. Speeded along by panic, and unencumbered in many cases by the arms and equipment which they had thrown away, the Union soldiers in effect covered the same distance overnight that they had taken three days to cover before the battle. Because of this, well before dawn on the morning of the 22d, when Longstreet's Confederates came upon Centreville, there were no Yankees to be seen. Guardedly the Southerners marched forth, probing for the retreating Federal army's rearguard. But it was nowhere to be found. Farther up the road at Germantown, farther still at Fairfax, still there were no Yankees—they had clearly skedaddled. As proof was the turnpike strewn with haversacks, rifles, ammo boxes, empty canteens and all manner of flotsam from a wrecked army. Only near the Alexandria railroad about five miles west of Arlington did Longstreet's advance units come into contact with Union cavalry, and this was too late in the afternoon of the 22d to bring on a major fight.

By the next morning, Confederate reinforcements had come up, and so had General Beauregard, who surveyed the scene. Deployed on high ground overlooking the Potomac and apparently ready for battle were at least two Union divisions. One of them was Brigadier General Theodore Runyon's, left behind by McDowell when he had set out a week before. With it were other regiments that General Scott had hurriedly sent across the river when the bad news came from Bull Run. Together with well-placed batteries on the heights, and McDowell's footsore units that coalesced around them, the Northern troops guarding Arlington presented too formidable a front for even Beauregard, flushed with victory, to want to test. The Confederates accordingly withdrew, soon establishing themselves in a loose line from Vienna to Annandale. Neither McDowell nor Beauregard-Johnston seemed inclined for another major test of strength, at least for a while. Hence the campaign and battle for Manassas ended with both sides holding approximately the same positions they had done at the outset.

RESULTS OF THE BATTLE: LOSSES AND GAINS

What had the battle accomplished? For one thing, it had ended the lives of hundreds of young men, and come close to wrecking the lives of two thousand more who had caught a ball or shell fragment. Beginning with the two sides' official reports and followed by different scholars of the battle, casualties for the opposing armies have been toted up in slightly different ways.

Army reports (1861) in *Official Records*	killed	wounded	missing/ captured	total
Federal	460	1,124	1,312	2,896
Confederate	378	1,489	30	1,897
Livermore, *Numbers & Losses* (1901)				
Federal	481	1,011	1,216	2,708
Confederate	387	1,582	12	1,981
Davis, *Battle at Manassas* (1977)				
Federal	460	1,124	1,312	2,896
Confederate	387	1,582	13	1,982
Hennessy, *First Battle of Manassas* (1989)				
Federal	482	1,126	1,836	3,444
Confederate	382	1,465	13	1.860
McDonald, *"We Shall Meet Again"* (1999)				
Federal	496	1,154	1,860	3,510
Confederate	388	1,570	9	1,967
Rafuse, *A Single Grand Victory* (2002)				
Federal	460	1,124	1,312	2,896
Confederate	378	1,489	30	1,897

The notable disparity between U.S. and C.S. missing or captured is readily explained by the Federals' precipitous retreat from the field, in which many Yanks surrendered themselves to pursuing Confederates, or just broke down exhausted and waited to be picked up by the Rebels. Some missing were doubtless killed, with their remains not immediately found on the field. Some months later, Confederate Captain E. Porter Alexander submitted a formal tally of all "captures and prisoners taken": he counted 1,421 Union prisoners taken on July 21, of whom 871 were unwounded and sent back to Richmond, and another 550 Federals hurt or wounded, and sent to C.S. hospitals.[340]

As possessors of the battlefield, Southerners took in a huge haul of valuable weapons, equipment and other stores. They captured twenty-seven cannon, including the big thirty-pounder abandoned near Stone Bridge and the eleven guns which once belonged to Ricketts' and Griffin's batteries. Caissons filled with shot and shell, limber chests, forges, battery wagons, even horse teams still in harness—all this came as a windfall to the Confederate artillery service in Virginia. For days after the battle, scavenging C.S. soldiers gleaned rifles, ammunition (eventually a half-million rounds), rations and hospital stores. Axes, shovels, mess kits, blankets and tents were all scooped up and sent off to Richmond for reissue to new owners. Cast-off clothing littered the roadsides east of Bull Run, where Federals marching to and running from the battle had succumbed to the heat and doffed parts of their uniforms. Some of these Yankee duds were gray-hued, and eagerly snatched up. For Confederates still wearing the militia-blue tunics issued back home, a change in attire was particularly welcome after the several tragic cases of mistaken identity during the battle.

A NAME FOR THE FIGHT

The battle itself needed an identity, as the officers in their reports, soldiers in their letters, and editors in their newspapers began referring to the great fight of the 21st as Young's Branch,

---

340   *O.R.*, vol. 2, 571.

Stone Bridge, Bull Run, Manassas or Manassas Junction. Eventually, "Bull Run" settled in as Northerners' accustomed name; Confederates seemed to agree on "Manassas."

Out of this a sort of convention developed. Henceforth, whenever the two sides could not agree on labeling a battlefield, Federals drew on the name of a local stream or river, while Southerners used the nearby town or railroad junction. It was an ironic exercise in nomenclature, given that in 1861 an agrarian South was fighting an increasingly urbanized North over which section's vision of a future America would prevail. Since the war, however, with the Confederacy's firm embrace of industrial urbanism as the model for its post-emancipationist society, the agreed-upon pattern of name-choices—e.g., Manassas, Springfield, Logan's Crossroads, Sharpsburg, Murfreesboro (over the North's Bull Run, Wilson's Creek, Mill Springs, Antietam and Stones River)—seems to suit modern Southerners just fine.

PSYCHOLOGICAL EFFECTS

Whatever it was called, the battle of July 21 gave the South its first really major victory of the war, far more consequential than the earlier successes at Fort Sumter, Big Bethel or Carrick's Ford. The Confederates had not only blunted the Federals' first drive to capture Richmond, but had routed the largest and best-equipped army the North had yet assembled. Wild exhilaration shook every part of the South as telegraphic dispatches circulated news of the Union rout. McDowell's undignified retreat back to Washington inspired more than one good Rebel joke, such as Bill Arp's publicized quip about how Yankees learned at Bull Run that "these are the times that try men's soles."[341]

At the same time, Southerners had reason to celebrate and recriminate, too. When Confederate Captain Alexander reported in his listing of battlefield booty some pairs of handcuffs, some Southerners inferred that the Yankee army had designs to win the battle, then march on Richmond and arrest Jeff Davis. Moreover,

---

341   Herman Hattaway and Archer Jones, *How the South Won: A Military History* (Urbana IL, 1983), p. 47.

Northern newspapers subsequently reported that a fair gaggle of Washington politicians and society nabobs had buggied out to the battlefield for picnic viewing of the fight; this also suggested the Northerners' high hopes, if not overoptimistic expectations, that they would win an easy, picturesque battle. This enraged Southerners further. Late in the afternoon of the battle, two South Carolina officers came upon a well-dressed civilian on the other side of the Run, and asked his name.

"Alfred Ely," came the reply, with the further information that the gentleman was a United States Congressman from Rochester, New York. The Carolinians herded Ely to their Colonel, E.B.C. Cash, of the 8th South Carolina. Cash was incensed, taking out his pistol, swearing hotly "with a fluency which would have been creditable to a wagon master," one Southerner related, and threatening to shoot the Congressman on the spot.

"God damn your white-livered soul! I'll blow your brains out on the spot," cried Cash. "You infernal son of a bitch! You came to see the fun, did you?! God damn your dirty soul! I'll show you," he yelled. Cash spurred his horse, trying to get around his two junior officers who by now had placed themselves in front of the trembling Ely, trying to save him. "What's the matter, Colonel?" asked one. "What are you trying to shoot this man for?"

"He's a member of Congress, God damn him!" Cash howled. "Came out here to see the fun! Came to see us whipped and killed! God damn him! If it was not for such as he there would be no war. They've made it and then come to gloat over it! God damn him! I'll show him," as again Cash lunged for the mortified New Yorker.

But the cooler subordinates prevailed. "Colonel, you must not shoot a prisoner. Never shoot an unarmed man," whereupon Cash holstered his pistol and rode off, allowing the Carolinians to tend to their captive. Taken to the rear, Congressman Ely was grateful for six months' stay in Richmond's Libby Prison before being released to find his way back through the lines to Washington. Shortly thereafter, he resigned his seat in Congress and retired to

Rochester. For the duration of the war, he publicly stayed quite mum about the Rebels, doubtless grateful for the close call he had received at Manassas.[342]

In contrast, after the battle many Northerners, startled and outraged by the disaster, very loudly expressed their outrage. "Today will be known as BLACK MONDAY," wrote a New Yorker on the 22d when reports of the calamity reached the city. "We are utterly and disgracefully routed, beaten, whipped by secessionists. Only one great fact stands out unmistakably: total defeat and national disaster on the largest scale."[343] Within a day or two, Northerners learned how Washingtonians had poured out to Bull Run to enjoy the battle with their picnics, and this added further angry insult to painful injury. Yet one light-hearted soul managed to make a rhyme out of it, and have it printed in the Boston *Herald:*

> Have you heard of the story, so lacking in glory,
>
> About the civilians who went to the fight?
>
> With everything handy, from sandwich to brandy,
>
> To fill their broad stomachs, and make them all tight.
>
> There were bulls from our State
>
> Street, and cattle from Wall Street,
>
> And members of Congress to see the great fun;
>
> Newspaper reporters (some regular snorters),
>
> On a beautiful Sunday went to Bull Run.
>
> Provided with passes as far as Manassas,
>
> The portly civilians rode jolly along;

---

342   JoAnna M. McDonald, *"We Shall Meet Again": The First Battle of Manassas (Bull Run) July 18-21, 1861* (Shippensburg PA, 1999), pp. 172-73.

343   William C. Davis, *Battle at Manassas: A History of the First Major Campaign of the Southern War for independence* (Baton Rouge, 1977), p. 255; Ethan S. Rafuse, *A Single Grand Victory: The First Campaign and Battle of Manassas* (Wilmington DE, 2002), p. 198.

Till the sound of battle, the roar and the rattle

Of cannon and musket drowned laughter and song.[344]

REASONS FOR THE OUTCOME

Efforts at levity failed to mitigate the shame and anger which soon vented itself among Northerners as they searched for a scapegoat. As the public began casting blame for the national humiliation, the politicians and editors curiously escaped censure, even though their loud demands for an advance on Richmond may have forced McDowell to move before his green, inexperienced army was ready to wage battle. Instead, it was the General-in-Chief of the Union armies who selflessly fell on his sword. "I am the greatest coward in America," cried General Scott, when having to face President Lincoln and some congressmen on the Union defeat. "I deserve removal because I did not stand up, when my army was not in a condition for fighting, and resist it to the last." Lincoln, with less magnanimity than common sense (regarding the value of Scott's decades of military experience when he had none), of course refused to remove his senior general.

For his part, having unsuccessfully sought more time to prepare his green army for the "On to Richmond" campaign (remembering that the President had lectured him that "you are all green alike"), General McDowell felt he had done all he could to have staved off defeat. When, after the battle, Lincoln charitably affirmed to McDowell, "I have not lost a particle of confidence in you," the General smartly replied, "I don't see why you should, Mr. President."[345]

In truth, McDowell was correct, as the main reason for Northern defeat lay with General Robert Patterson, whose indolence and neglect had allowed Johnston to bring his more than 10,000 infantry, cavalry (Stuart) and artillery to reinforce

---

344   Marcus Cunliffe, *Soldiers and Civilians: The Martial Spirit in America 1775-1863* (Boston, 1963), p. 13.

345   Ethan S. Rafuse, *A Single Grand Victory: The First Campaign and Battle of Manassas* (Wilmington DE, 2002), pp. 199-200.

Beauregard and give him the numerical margin of victory. Added to the strength of Beauregard's seven infantry brigades, Holmes' from Fredericksburg and Hampton's Legion from Richmond, the Confederates assembled at Bull Run numbered slightly over 33,000 troops, at parity with McDowell's army. Actually, Southern forces outnumbered the Federals, as McDowell left one of his divisions (Runyon's barely organized militiamen) back at Alexandria and designated Dixon Miles' division as reserve at Centreville. (It only saw action late in the day on the 21st as Rebels dogging the Union retreaters came into contact with it just before nightfall.) Because essentially only 3/5 of his army therefore fought at Manassas (Tyler's, Hunter's and Heintzelman's divisions—21,483 men), McDowell on the field was outnumbered 3:2, a disadvantage which he would not have faced had Patterson done his job in the Valley.[346]

Just as much a factor, however, was the Southerners' effective use of railroad and telegraph to achieve the troop concentration which brought them victory. Johnston from the Valley, Holmes from Fredericksburg, Hampton from Richmond—almost 13,000 soldiers brought together in three days' time. This achievement, the military harnessing of new nineteenth-century technology, scored the Confederacy one of its many "firsts" in the annals of warfare.

For his part, too, General McDowell earns good marks for his sound battle plan: fix the Rebels in position while sending a strong column to flank their left and roll up their line down the south side of the run. Yet even before the first shot, the Federal plan started coming apart, and the commanding general begins to take the blame. McDowell dawdled near Centreville, July 19-20, while his chief engineer, Major John G. Barnard, searched for crossing points of Bull Run around the enemy left. In truth, the need for good maps, expert staff and ample cavalry (McDowell had left a

---

346 These numbers rely on the early research of Robert M. Johnston, *Bull Run: Its Strategies and Tactics* (New York, 1913), pp. 109-10, 267. Subsequent historians have shown themselves to be skittish in counting the numbers of Confederate and Federal troops involved at Manassas. Livermore's equally early calculation that 28,452 U.S. and 32,232 C.S. troops engaged in the battle supports the conclusion that Southern forces enjoyed numerical superiority in the battle (Thomas L. Livermore, *Numbers and Losses in the Civil War in America* [Boston, 1901], p. 77).

good lot of horse-troops behind) was a lesson which both armies bloodily learned time after time in the war, but McDowell's lesson particularly cost him the two days which proved so decisive in allowing the Rebels to gain their full battlefield strength.

The Union commander also erred in his timetable for his inexperienced officers and men. Ordering the flanking march against the Rebel left to begin at 2:30 in the morning proved to be overambitious and woefully misguided. At any time in the war, the movement of such a heavy column (13,000 men, 20 guns) would be an exacting tactical exercise. Here, to call for it in the war's first battle, in the perfect darkness of night and over untrodden roadways, was to gamble highly, inviting a delayed start of morning battle at the very least. As we have seen, General McDowell lost the gamble.

Once the battle was joined, the Southerners enjoyed another initial advantage, the defensive. Raw recruits, arranged in lines, are much more effective in defense than in attack. The battle of Manassas proved to be a series of attacks and counterattacks, with neither side digging into a strong defensive position. But as Jackson's determined "stone wall stand" demonstrated, Southerners throughout the day relied on the strength of defensive positions, which it was the job of the Yankees to charge and take.

Other tactical factors figured into the Northern defeat. After the initial Union success in the morning, pressing the Rebel left and taking Matthews Hill, the Federals lost momentum from their delay in bringing up more troops to push on to Henry Hill—2 ½ hours, by the calculation of the Manassas historian John Hennessy. Making it all the worse for the Federals, officers pushed their regiments into the afternoon fight in piecemeal fashion, a common error of even experienced officers throughout the conflict. "Fifteen Union regiments ascended Henry Hill between 2 and 4 o'clock," Hennessy explains. "Never did more than two of those regiments go into the fight together. Most went up singly, and with bad results."[347]

---

347 John Hennessy, *The First Battle of Manassas: An End to Innocence* (Lynchburg VA, 1989), p. 126.

To be sure, the Northerners' numerical inferiority on the afternoon of July 21 proved to be the decisive tactical factor, as McDowell was unable to bring fresh troops into the fight (his reserve divisions were much too far to the rear). Meanwhile, Johnston had fresh levies to pour into the battle, marching from the unengaged Confederate right, or just unloaded at the train station and itching for a crack at the Yankees. These reinforcements essentially brought the Confederate victory. After the see-saw attacks and counter attacks around Henry, *ca.* 2-4 p.m., "McDowell had no regiments left to put into the battle," writes Hennessy. "Conversely, by 4 o'clock the Confederates on Henry Hill and Chinn Ridge were at maximum strength. In the final analysis, the fight for Henry Hill amounted to a battle of attrition; it was probably the only such battle in the East the Confederates won during the entire war."[348]

Finally, Generals Beauregard and Johnston deserve a fair share of credit for their armies' victory. When called upon by the President to resolve their question of seniority, they had quickly agreed to work together for the good of the cause. On the day of the battle, Johnston at Portici House had directed troops coming into the battle with an efficiency suggested by his famed exclamation, "Go where the fire is hottest!"

COULD THE CONFEDERATES HAVE DONE MORE?

While Generals Johnston and Beauregard, even officials in Richmond, deserved considerable measure of credit for the Confederate victory, they actually received few plaudits for masterminding the achievement. After its initial euphoria, the Southern public was more interested in learning why the army had not pursued the beaten Yankees all the way to Washington, then into the enemy capital itself. Prominent Carolinian Mary B. Chesnut expressed a widespread sentiment when she wrote in her diary, "Why did we not follow the flying foe across the Potomac? That is the question of the hour in the drawing room—those of us who are not contending as to 'who took Ricketts's Battery?'...Time and tide wait for no man, and there was a tide in our affairs which

---

348   *Ibid.,* p. 127.

might have led to Washington, and we did not take it and so lost our fortune, this round."[349] Many other Southerners also believed the enemy capital was within grasp, and that its capture would have quickly ended the war. A few days after the battle, Southern newspapers circulated Stonewall Jackson's exclamation, made on the afternoon of the 21st, as his wounded hand was being dressed by Surgeon Hunter McGuire, "Give me 10,000 men and I will take Washington City to-morrow."[350]

Jackson's enthusiasm, however, did not square with the fact that the Confederate army after Manassas was bruised and blown from a long, hot battle that it had very nearly lost in the first place. The Stonewall Brigade, as Jackson's unit quickly came to be called, was in no shape for energetic pursuit, having suffered over 500 killed and wounded. As for the availability of 5,000 or 10,000 fresh troops, there were only to be had on the Confederate right flank a portion of that number, and these were sent forth by the army high command at dusk on the 21st. That Longstreet's units got as far as Germantown, approaching Alexandria, before running into a very resolute Union rearguard suggests that they had done all they could in pursuit. Mrs. Chesnut's friends in the parlors of their fine Richmond homes may have gabbed about following the flying foe, but the soldiers on the ground had done all they could to secure the Confederacy's first great victory of the war.

These conclusions do not end the discussion, however, as Confederate historians have long enjoyed the imaginative foray of what might have happened had Beauregard pulled up his limping army and actually attacked Arlington heights, attempting then a crossing of the Potomac. Southern scholars have occasionally

---

349   C. Vann Woodward, ed., *Mary Chesnut's Confederate War* (New Haven CT, 1981), pp. 121, 125.

350   Hunter H. McGuire, "Stonewall Jackson—An Address," in McGuire and George L. Christian, *The Confederate Cause and Conduct in the War Between the States* (Richmond, 1907), p. 197. Accounts differ as to Jackson's exact words. Colonel Porter Alexander reported them as "Give me 5,000 fresh men, and I will be in Washington City to-morrow morning!" (E. P. Alexander, *Military Memoirs of a Confederate* [New York, 1907], p. 42). Rumor spread that Jackson believed he could take Lincoln's city with even fewer troops, as some sources related the General exclaiming, "If they will let me, I'll march my Brigade into Washington tonight!" (Frank E. Vandiver, *Mighty Stonewall* [Richmond, 1957], p. 166).

suggested that, despite all the reasons notwithstanding, the Confederates should have attempted it. Professor Eaton of Kentucky, for one, asserts, "It seems from the vantage point of today that the bold course of attempting to capture Washington should have been adopted." Hudson Strode of the University of Alabama was bold enough to prescribe the route which Beauregard should have taken: "By approaching Washington via White's Ford, the Southern troops could have avoided Federal gunboats down the Potomac. There were indications that the Government would have fled at the Confederates' approach. With Southern forces holding Washington, a peace giving the South independence might have been made in the summer of 1861, instead of the fall of 1863."[351]

LESSONS OF MANASSAS AND
THE BIRTH OF THE CONFEDERATE BATTLE FLAG

After July 21 both sides understood that it would be a long war. The North, handed its first major defeat, realized that quelling the rebellion would require a costly, sustained effort. And the South learned that repelling the Union army's thrusts yielded only short-term tactical gains: to force an armistice and secure its independence the Confederacy would probably need victories on Northern soil to teach the Yankees their final lesson.

The war's first big battle led to other lessons as well, particularly regarding identification on the battlefield. After the sanguinary mix-ups caused by Yankees in gray and Rebels in blue, each army began insisting on uniforms that conformed to regulation colors. Then there was the issue of flags. Several times during the fighting, the Southerners' Stars and Bars, with its red-white-red banding and blue corner, had come dangerously close to being perceived as the enemy's Stars and Stripes. From their signal towers, E.P. Alexander's spotters had had a tough time discerning the allegiance of approaching troops because of this similarity. And in the

---

351   Clement Eaton, *A History of the Southern Confederacy in the War Years 1861-1863* (Lexington KY, 1954), p. 153; Hudson Strode, *Jefferson Davis First President of the Confederacy*, 3 vols. (Chapel Hill, 1959), vol. 2, 126.

afternoon, General Johnston had mistaken Kirby Smith's brigade as a Union flanking column as it marched from Manassas Junction because its drooping banners allowed no quick identification.

From this confusion emerged Beauregard's resolve to right the situation with a new design, solely for Southern troops in the field. Conferring with others, and reviewing several proposed designs, Beauregard hit upon one, square in dimension, with a red field and blue diagonal cross bearing a white star for every Confederate state. The Defense Department liked the idea, and so originated the Battle Flag. Distinguished from the starred-and-barred National flags flown atop Confederate government buildings, the Battle Flag was restricted to use by C.S. forces in the field. Defense Department regulations even prescribed that the size of the square cloth be slightly different for the three arms (infantry, cavalry and artillery). The popularity of the Battle Flag among Southerners during the war was recognized by the government in Richmond when, in the spring of 1863, the Stars and Bars was abandoned and a Second National Flag was adopted: a square Battle Flag in the corner of a field of white. After the war, Beauregard's banner became even more popular to Southerners as symbol of their armies' hard fight and eventual triumph. As such today it is widely visible in stores and gift shops throughout the Confederacy, and its display as a souvenir in Southern airports is particularly irksome to Northern visitors passing through what was formerly part of their country.

Chapter Seven:

The Two Sides Settle In

LINCOLN *VERSUS* DAVIS AS WAR LEADERS

Historians have been harsh on Abraham Lincoln. By a sort of backward reasoning, a number of scholars have concluded that because the North lost the war, Lincoln should be blamed for ineffective leadership. By the same line of thought Jefferson Davis is hailed today as a gifted war president. But it is well to keep in mind how these assessments would reverse themselves if the South had lost the war. As Clement Eaton has written of Lincoln, "If, in the improbable case that his armies had won decisive victories and the United States of America had maintained its integrity as a nation, he would doubtless have been hailed as a great man, his defects condoned and his virtues celebrated. Davis, then, almost surely, would not be rated today as the number one president."[352]

With all the attention given to his failings, Lincoln's several strengths as chief executive have usually been overlooked. He was for instance, a fast learner in office. His only term in Congress, December 1847 to early 1849, allowed him a perch in Washington from which to view how President Polk, guiding the war with Mexico, kept control of strategic decisions; the President even brought issues to his Cabinet, then told the army's generals what they ought to do (though they generally did not listen). More than

---

352   Clement Eaton, *Jefferson Davis* (New Orleans, 1977), p. 273.

a decade later, Lincoln was in the White House. While he had no real executive experience, he quickly grasped the intricacies of Washington bureaucracy. He had learned the power of the patronage, remembering in the Mexican war when Thomas Hart Benton, the powerful senator from Missouri, wanted to command the army's campaign to Vera Cruz. (The lesson to be learned—give the political general some sideline command, but not any really important appointment—was unfortunately for the Union cause forgotten by Lincoln)

The Northern President was also a capable administrator whose style was to delegate trivial matters in favor of the broad issues demanding executive attention. During the war, when his wife Mary wanted to redecorate the White House with what the new President called "flub dubs," Lincoln wisely cast the matter to underlings in his staff, asking them to make peace with the First Lady while he scrounged for federal money to prosecute the war.

Further, Lincoln recognized the power of public opinion. He at least tried to use political appointments and well-phrased proclamations to stir support for the war among the North's citizens. Unfortunately for the North, these efforts failed in the long run. When the President made army generals of important Democratic or German-American leaders lacking in military experience, the initial positive publicity-bubble burst when those incompetents ordered their soldiers into bungled battles. Long casualty lists in the newspapers publicly demonstrated the bloody folly of Lincoln's political generals. The President's recognized gift for stirring rhetoric also brought limited benefit. Lincoln's preliminary Proclamation of Emancipation, announced September 22, 1862, had an exhilarating effect among Northern abolitionists and black Northerners who yearned for the war against secession to be turned into a war against slavery. But the administration's nod at emancipation has been judged by historians as too little, too late. A year and a half into the war, the Union forces' multiple disasters at the front had eroded the Northern people's will to win. A presidential edict freeing slaves in the Confederate States, coming just days after Robert E. Lee's smashing of McClellan's army at Sharpsburg, added a cruel hilarity to Lincoln's honest humanitarianism.

Any assessment of Lincoln as war leader must recognize the magnitude of his difficulties. If in the end he failed to prop up Northern morale, we should recall that the very nature of the war worked to Lincoln's disadvantage. While the North was fighting to restore the Union, the South was fighting for its independence. Thus the Confederates had only to defend themselves to achieve their war arms, but Federal armies had to wage a war of offensive conquest. They had to invade, conquer and occupy large areas of territory which, from the Potomac to the Rio Grande, equaled the size of western Europe. They had to defeat and disperse large, capably-led enemy armies, and subdue a hostile population numbering ten million inhabitants. On the seas, the North attempted a naval blockade which stretched 3,500 miles, covering nearly two hundred harbors, rivers and inlets. And it attempted to do all of this in the face of significant foreign interference, especially English and French support for the Confederacy. Little wonder, given these gigantic challenges, that the North lost its will to prosecute the war despite Abraham Lincoln's desperate efforts.

While Lincoln failed to inspire a sustained war effort among the Northern people, Jefferson Davis has won historians' plaudits for creating a strong support of the war among Southerners after Fort Sumter. Paul D. Escott has enumerated the President's achievements in this regard.

> He aided the development of unity by enunciating a non divisive ideology. Avoiding potential dangers and finding positive sources of enthusiasm, Davis gave Southerners a cause which few of them found easy to criticize. He grounded the Confederacy's appeal on the heritage of the United States, which all professed to honor....By claiming the United States Constitution as a sacred text for the Confederacy, Davis helped to found the government in a manner which lessened the sense of a break with a past. At

the same time he sharpened resentment against the North through carefully chosen words of criticism. Davis attacked the United States for acts which almost all Southerners would disapprove, and in this way he enlisted the pride of an individualistic people in the battle against a formidable adversary.[353]

Of course, it was much easier to enthuse the populace with the war when the news from the battlefront remained positive. Fort Sumter, Big Bethel and Manassas created in the minds of many Southerners, April – July 1861, a sense of optimism and an almost irrational exuberance about their war-fortunes. It was President Davis's responsibility to acknowledge the people's mood without feeding or augmenting it, yet at the same time not diminishing it in what might be called the paternalistic expectation that hard times were surely yet to follow. Davis was shrewd enough to know that if battlefield reverses were to come for the Confederacy, he would have to manage the people's reaction to those, too.

PRESIDENT DAVIS IN MILITARY MATTERS

Jefferson Davis's military experience has often been cited as an important element in his superior presidential performance during the war. Davis was a graduate of West Point and had served for years in the army; his record in the Mexican war was so distinguished that President Polk offered him commission as brigadier general. Even his years in Congress helped; as Senator he had chaired the Committee on Military Affairs. His outstanding performance heading the War Department—he has been called "the ablest and best qualified U.S. Secretary of War in the nineteenth century"—gave Davis invaluable administrative experience, which he brought to bear as Confederate chief executive. "Ceaselessly his mind sought reforms that would improve the country's military establishment," one scholar has written. "Organization, strategy, tactics, logistics, armament, equipment, pay and promotion, training, strength of the line—all attracted his study, thought, and

---

353 Paul D. Escott, *After Secession: Jefferson Davis and the Triumph of Confederate Nationalism* (Baton Rouge, 1978), pp. 51-52.

creative innovation."[354] This attention to detail has sometimes been cited as possibly Davis's sole administrative weakness. But as we have seen, the President sought and won the services of a very capable Samuel Cooper as Adjutant General, and kept George Thomas at his desk as Chief of Staff; these two men's tireless handling of even the smallest army matters kept the president free to address broader concerns.

More capably than Lincoln, Davis used his constitutional powers as commander-in-chief of the armed forces, particularly in approving administrative changes to strengthen the performance of Confederate armies. Recognizing the importance of state loyalties among the men, Davis authorized the organization of brigades composed of regiments from the same state, commanded as well by generals from that state. In decisions affecting higher levels of command, the President was just as judicious. When it became evident that the South's commanding generals needed efficient staff to conduct the day-to-day business of army administration, Senator Louis Wigfall introduced a bill granting a brigadier's rank to key staff officers and giving commanding generals the power to select their staff. At first opposing the measure as an infringement of his right to appoint general officers, Davis wisely bowed to Congress and yielded his authority in the matter.

On the other hand, the President just as wisely refused to relent under Congressional pressure to appoint a general-in-chief. In the last half of the war, many Southerners urged that Robert E. Lee should be given this position. But Davis accurately perceived that Lee had little inclination to look beyond Virginia's theater of operations, as the main task of general-in-chief would have been the supervision of Southern strategy in *all*_theaters. Thus Davis not only kept Lee in the role which best served the cause, but he also retained as commander-in-chief the prerogatives of an overall strategic planner. Though he modestly shied away from it, chief credit for the Confederacy's triple offensive in the fall of 1862—

---

354 Robert Utley, "Introduction," in Lynda Lasswell Crist and Mary Seaton Dix, eds., *The Papers of Jefferson Davis*, 14 vols. (Baton Rouge, 1971-2018), vol. 5, v-vi.

the triumphant advances in Maryland, Kentucky and Mississippi, which did so much to break the North's war will—has usually been given by historians to the President himself.

Despite his military experience, Davis prudently chose not to interfere with the tactical decisions of his battlefield generals; one sees this at Manassas. Arriving there shortly after the fight, the President met with Generals Johnston and Beauregard, and conferred with them regarding pursuit of the enemy. A Lincoln would have assumed authority and dictated the army's course of action, much as he did to poor McDowell and later to McClellan. Davis, however, sat back and let the generals who were more familiar with the tactical realities make the decisions. Equally noteworthy was Davis's refusal to share credit for the Confederates' victory at Manassas. Though he had largely engineered it by authorizing the rail transport of Johnston's army from the Valley, Davis let the officers and soldiers bask in the glory.

Completely different was Abraham Lincoln's use—abuse, really—of his prerogatives as commander-in-chief. To be fair, the source of this tragic shortcoming in the Northern president probably lay in his lack of soldierly experience. As T. Harry Williams has written, "Lincoln had been a civilian all his life, he had received no military education, and he had no military experience except briefly as a militia soldier in the Black Hawk War, when he liked to recall, he had made some ferocious charges on the wild onions and engaged in bloody struggles with the mosquitoes."[355] Knowing this about himself, Lincoln should have left the formulation of war strategy to his generals. Instead, he interfered in military operations throughout the war, conceiving inferior, even illogical strategic plans that severely reduced the North's chances of victory.

If the Manassas Campaign should have taught the North anything, it was the folly of pushing an unprepared army into battle. As Marcus Cunliffe has written, "Bull Run would never have been fought if congressmen and other impatient citizens had

---

355   T. Harry Williams, *Americans at War: The Development of the American Military Systems* (Baton Rouge, 1960), p. 57.

not badgered the Union government into ordering an advance."[356] Lincoln bowed to this pressure and forced General McDowell to advance with a barely trained, hastily assembled army. The President's interference thus brought on, at least indirectly, the bloody Union repulse at Henry House hill. Apparently, however, the ensuing rout of McDowell's army failed to make a lasting impression on Lincoln, for six months later he again ordered a forward movement not only of the Army of the Potomac but of U.S. forces in southeastern and northwestern Virginia, Kentucky, at Cairo, Illinois, even the "Naval force in the Gulf of Mexico." This "General War Order No. 1", dated January 27, 1862, has been cited as the supreme example of Lincoln's military meddling. The President wrote the order without consulting anyone (least of all, any of the generals involved) and announced it to his Cabinet members without seeking their approval. Of course it came to nothing. Even the date chosen for the general Union advance, February 22, was pulled out of the thin political air by Lincoln as an attempt to make sure that his rival Jefferson Davis, who would be inaugurated formally as C.S. President that day (the same as Washington's birthday) would not steal the show. Even Geoffrey Perret, an avowed Lincoln admirer, calls General War Order No. 1 "less an order than a distress signal, one that suggested a man flailing in the air."[357]

Lincoln never relinquished his authority to override generals and order armies into combat, even though these decisions usually brought disaster. "Lincoln was constantly urging his generals to attack," writes one historian of the war. "Slow to perceive the military realities of the war, Lincoln often made unreasonable demands."[358] Worse, the President's involvement in military planning revealed some sadly misguided concepts of the war, its strategy and tactics. He was, for instance, preoccupied with the capitals— the defense of his own and the seizure of the enemy's.

---

356 Marcus Cunliffe, *Soldiers and Civilians: The Martial Spirit in America 1775-1863* (Boston, 1963), p. 18.

357 Geoffrey Perret, *Lincoln's War* (New York, 2004), p. 123.

358 William L. Barney, *Flawed Victory: A New Perspective on the Confederate War* (New York, 1975), p. 9.

Lincoln's insistence upon the capture of Richmond hamstrung his commanders in Virginia, denying them the strategic flexibility needed for success. Probably more hurtful were Lincoln's fears for the vulnerability of Washington. Some have speculated that the most important consequence of Jubal Early's sortie of April 22, 1861, was its lasting psychological effect upon the Northern president, who learned that day just how easily Rebel forces were able to approach and test Washington's defenses. Afterward and throughout the war, Lincoln's fears for the safety of his capital became as well known to Confederate as Union strategists. He persistently retained far too many troops in idle garrison duty in the District of Columbia, and whenever Rebels threatened to cross the Potomac (as Jackson did in late May 1862), Lincoln would anxiously draw even more troops around the city, depriving the Union Army of the Potomac of much-needed manpower. After his defeat in the Peninsula campaign, General McClellan bitterly blamed the President for withholding 40,000 troops from his army as he approached Richmond in late June '62—the would-be margin of victory, McClellan later claimed in his presidential campaign of 1864. Three months after the Peninsula, when this time it was Lee's army marching on the offensive into Maryland, Lincoln's impractical dispositions—again ordering McClellan to leave way too many divisions in the District before setting out in search of Bobby Lee—indirectly led to McClellan's calamitous defeat at Sharpsburg.

On a tactical level too, Lincoln made impractical demands on his generals. Because he lacked military experience, Lincoln believed that the old-fashioned battle of annihilation was still possible— that Confederate armies could be destroyed and Richmond taken overnight. Military theorists of the time, however, had already grasped that the rifled musket and "Minie ball" (invented in 1849) gave such an advantage to tactical defenders on the battlefield that the kinds of total victories which Napoleon had won were now obsolete and unattainable. Thus Lincoln hired and fired a series of generals and caused untold Northern casualties in trying to find a commander for the Army of the Potomac who could destroy Lee's army and capture Richmond with one big battle. Given this presidential interference, the sad statement of a Union soldier bears noting: "the farther our armies are from Washington the better success they have."[359]

When he considered other theaters of operations, many of Lincoln's proposals impressed his military advisers as more than a little crack-brained. In his first general discussion of strategy in late April 1861, he talked of a plan to "hold Fortress Monroe on the eastern flank of Virginia, blockade the Southern ports, make Washington safe, and then go down and attack Charleston." Even Professor Williams, one of Lincoln's few scholarly defenders, concedes this idea as an example of the President's failure to grasp the need for a unified war strategy.[360]

More commonly cited is Lincoln's virtual obsession with conquest of east Tennessee. Confusing politics with military objectives and ignoring logistical realities, the Northern Chief Executive repeatedly called for offensives aimed at Knoxville, where he hoped to establish a loyalist government built upon the antislavery mood of most east Tennesseans. His first such order was drafted within a week of Manassas; then followed his "Memorandum for a Plan of Campaign" in early October 1861. When Federal forces finally marched toward east Tennessee, as their overruled commanders predicted, they found themselves blocked by mountains and deep valleys, cut off from supplies, and confronted by stubborn Rebels. Lincoln overlooked these difficulties, and even after his troops retreated from the region, he ordered them back, where they were again stalemated by rugged ridges and Rebel rigor.

Reviewing this and other unfortunate episodes, Professor Ludwell Johnson has summarized historians' consensus: "Lincoln was forever making mistakes, either by trading military for political advantage, or simply by interfering in matters he did not

---

359   *Ibid.*, p. 14.

360   T. Harry Williams, *Lincoln and His Generals* (New York, 1952), p. 16.

understand. In fact, in strategic sense and logistical judgment, Davis was so far superior to Lincoln that any extended comparison would be needlessly cruel."[361]

THE ISSUE OF POLITICAL GENERALS

Another of Lincoln's shortcomings was his appointment of popular politicians to high army rank regardless of military incompetence, in order to win support for the war effort from Democrats and various ethnic groups. These men invariably lacked military experience and almost always proved incompetent in the field; yet the President sustained them against the protests of professional officers.

Prime example is Nathaniel P. Banks, powerful Democrat, former Speaker of the U.S. House of Representatives and Governor of Massachusetts. Purely on account of this prestige Banks was made major general at the start of the war and given a small army in the Shenandoah Valley, where his record was one of chronic defeat. In 1862 Stonewall Jackson's men derisively dubbed Banks their "commissary," so often did they capture his troops' camps and supply trains. Driven from the Valley after losing 30% of his forces, Banks was again beaten by Jackson at Cedar Mountain in August. Even after this setback Lincoln gave him another important command at Port Hudson, Louisiana. In fruitless assaults to take that place in the summer of '63, Banks wasted the lives of thousands of Union soldiers. He thereby contributed significantly to the rise of anti war feeling in the North, and so had a hand in bringing on the armistice negotiations that ended the war. Astonishingly, throughout the bloody Port Hudson campaign, Lincoln refused to bow to the public outrage over "Butcher" Banks, and once responded to the clamor for his dismissal by telling a critic, "I can't spare that man; he fights."[362]

---

361 Ludwell H. Johnson, "Jefferson Davis and Abraham Lincoln as War Presidents: Nothing Succeeds Like Success," *Civil War History*, vol. 27 (1981), 60.

362 A.K. McClure, *Lincoln and Men of War-Times* (Philadelphia, 1892), p. 193.

Other key Democrats receiving Lincoln's favor proved equally inept as officers. Benjamin F. Butler, powerful Democrat from Massachusetts, had absolutely no military experience, but Lincoln appointed him the volunteer army's first major general in May 1861. After losing the war's first battle at Big Bethel, Butler was shifted from theater to theater—the North Carolina coast, to occupied New Orleans, back to the Virginia peninsula—as Lincoln vainly tried to find some position at which Butler could succeed. In spite of his repeated failures, Butler rode his rank through the war into a much more successful *postbellum* career as Massachusetts governor, from which office he repaid Lincoln for his loyalty with loud, hindsighted criticism of the President for his role in losing the war.

In order to win support among Democrats in southern Illinois, Lincoln gave Congressman John McClernand a brigadiership, even though his only previous military experience had been two months' service as a militia private back in 1832. No matter; in late '62 Lincoln promoted him to major general and entrusted him with command of the expedition against Vicksburg. McClernand's ineptitude was recognized in Washington far too late, after the combined forces of Pemberton and Forrest had thoroughly trounced McClernand's army in northern Mississippi. Not too much later, after Banks had wrecked his army in the Port Hudson attacks, Lincoln bitterly realized that entrusting key army commands to militarily untried Democrats proved to be as valueless on the battlefield as in the ballot box, given War Democrats' desertion of Lincoln in his unsuccessful reelection bid of 1864.

Among ethnic groups wooed by Lincoln with generals' commissions, German-Americans were most noteworthy. To strengthen the war-spirit among the "Dutch," the President dispensed high posts in the army as if they were postmasterships, mere plums in the political game of patronage, regardless of the recipients' lack of military ability. Carl Schurz, the noted Prussian orator, was commissioned major general and given an infantry division in Virginia; the War Department made sure that German-American regiments were brigaded together under Schurz's unsteady command. The final *Beschaemung* (humiliation) of the proud Prussian came on the field of Chancellorsville, where Schurz's division collapsed so quickly before Jackson's famed attack that the entire Union right flank soon melted away, leading to Lee's greatest victory of the war.

Franz Sigel, German émigré who moved to St. Louis, inspired thousands of his fellow countrymen to enlist for the North ("I fights mit Sigel"), but did little more to deserve the major generalship which Lincoln bestowed upon him. He too became a laughingstock throughout the army after the battle of New Market in May 1863. Trying to counter a cloud of criticism for his lack of aggression in his first year of command, Sigel led a small force against what he assumed would be an easy target, the Virginia Military Institute in the Shenandoah, then half-filled with 250 teenaged cadets. The boys grabbed their muskets at the Yankees' approach, formed ranks in the best parade ground manner, and charged Sigel's camp so swiftly that the German-Americans who fought mit Sigel were soon running away from the battlefield mit him, too.

There were other prominent German-Americans promoted to general: Julius Stahel of New York was another example. All were elevated beyond their ability because, as Lincoln put it, "they are our sincere friends."[363] In promoting the German hardware clerk, Peter J. Osterhaus, to generalship, Lincoln unabashedly cited his reasons: "high merit, and somewhat on his nationality."[364] But the most embarrassing incident along these lines pertained to the Prussian Alexander Schimmelfennig. As recorded by Edwin Stanton, the President one day entered the Secretary of War's office declaring, "There has got to be something done unquestionably in the interest of the Dutch, and to that end I want Schimmelfennig appointed." Stanton tactfully objected, reminding Lincoln of other, more qualified German officers. "No matter about that," the President replied. "His name will make up for any difference there may be." To Stanton, Lincoln was more impressed by the Teutonic roll of *Schimmelfennig* and was convinced that its very

---

363   Ludwell Johnson, "Civil War Military History: A Few Revisions in Need of Revising" in John T. Hubbell, ed., *Battles Lost and Won: Essays from Civil War History* (Westport CT, 1975), p. 17.

364   Herman Hattaway and Archer Jones, *How the South Won: A Military History* (Urbana IL, 1983), p. 691.

sound, when advertised, would help enlist German-Americans to the war effort. He walked away, repeating the name to himself, "Schimmelfennig. Schimmelfennig."[365]

Time and again professional soldiers in the Union army—those with a West Point background and experience in the Mexican war—complained loudly against these political appointments. Henry Halleck, Union General-in-Chief for much of the war, was one of them. Once he confided to his friend Sherman, "it seems but little better than murder to give important commands to such men as Banks, Butler, McClernand and Sigel, and yet it seems impossible to prevent it." Another officer got so angry over these commissions that he wrote directly to the President, charging that Lincoln's "political pets" were responsible for the needless deaths of Union soldiers: "I do not know whether you have ever seen a battlefield. I assure you, Mr. President, it is a terrible sight."[366] For once, Abraham Lincoln had no witty reply.

Quite in contrast, Jefferson Davis made one of his most effective contributions to Southern victory by picking talented generals. Indeed, Clement Eaton has judged that "President Davis's greatest service to the Confederacy was his selection of superior officers from the very beginning, while Lincoln lost much valuable time, many soldiers, and eventually the war, in experimenting with incapable commanders."[367] A West Pointer himself, Davis realized the value of military education, and used this as a criterion in selecting officers for high rank. At the same time, he recognized the abilities of gifted soldiers without formal training, such as Nathan B. Forrest and Patrick R. Cleburne; after each first distinguished himself on western battlefields, the President saw that they got quick and prominent promotion.

Most of all, Davis refused to fall into the trap of political favoritism which ensnared Lincoln in so many of his dismal appointments. During the Mexican War Davis had developed keen dislike

---

365   T. Harry Williams, *Lincoln and His Generals* (New York, 1952), p. 11.

366   Johnson, *op. cit.*, p. 17; Williams, *op. cit.*, p. 13.

367   Clement Eaton, *A History of the Southern Confederacy in the War Years 1861-1863* (Lexington KY, 1954), p. 114.

for political generals and subsequently steered clear of them as a rule. When forced by public opinion to place some politician in the field—and this happened fewer than a half-dozen times in the entire war—Davis held them to the same standards of performance as his other officers. When they failed, he removed them to positions in which they could not harm the cause, or cashiered them outright.

John B. Floyd is an example of the latter case. After using his pull as an ex-Governor of Virginia to gain a brigadier's wreath, Floyd was given command of the garrison at Fort Donelson in northwest Tennessee. There he botched the defense of the fort so severely that U.S. Grant's attacking Federal army nearly captured the whole force in February 1862. The Confederates' lucky escape (thanks in large measure to cavalry leader Bedford Forrest) did not mitigate Davis's anger. The President fired Floyd without even summoning a military court of inquiry.

THE TWO PRESIDENTS AS POLITICAL LEADERS

As the undisputed leaders of their respective administrations, Abraham Lincoln and Jefferson Davis faced challenges in dealing with their Cabinets, Congresses and governors that most peacetime presidents do not. In this sphere, too, Lincoln emerges as decidedly inferior to his Confederate counterpart.

Part of Lincoln's problem with his Cabinet lay in the very men he had chosen to lead the various departments. Most important of all was that of War, which brings up the brief, inglorious career of Simon Cameron. Lincoln appointed Cameron to this important post in March 1861, shortly after he had entered office, for two reasons unrelated to talent. Lincoln wished to give Cabinet posts to men from the big Northern states—Pennsylvania was one of the biggest—and Cameron, Senator at the time, was one of the leading political men of the Keystone State. But more important to Lincoln, Cameron had helped deliver for him the Pennsylvania delegation's votes at the Republican nominating convention, and Cameron needed to be rewarded.

There is evidence that Lincoln regretted his decision soon after the war began. As the army scrambled to procure weapons and supplies for its thousands of new recruits, the inexperienced Secretary ensnared the whole business in all manner of government red tape. Uncertain of his authority and in any case unwilling to exert it, Cameron allowed state governors to compete against Federal agents in bidding for arms sales, both at home and abroad.

Far worse were the shameful frauds committed during Cameron's tenure, as cunning businessmen bilked the government out of millions of dollars. Thousands of pistols worth $14.50 were sold to the War Department for $25; sixty-dollar horses went for $117. Needless competition among the numerous Northern purchasing agents accounted for much of this exorbitance, but a factor also were the outrageous contractors' commissions that figured in many of these deals. One such instance resulted in a Supreme Court case, *Tool Company* v. *Norris,* in which an agent earned $3 per gun, or $75,000, merely for using his influence in obtaining a contract. Blame for these repeated wrongdoings was justly placed upon Secretary Cameron, who eventually came under Congressional investigation. Censured by the U.S. House of Representatives for gross mismanagement and general conduct "highly injurious to the public service," Cameron was forced to resign his office in January 1862. Lincoln was understandably glad to see him go.

Quite on the other hand, Jefferson Davis's political experience showed to advantage when he picked his Cabinet. Like Lincoln, the Confederate President juggled a number of factors in selecting his advisers (as we have seen, each state of the initial Confederacy had to be appeased with a seat in the Cabinet). But on the whole, Davis's choices proved to be much wiser than Lincoln's. Against Cameron's counterpart, Defense Secretary Leroy Walker, the worst complaint was his tobacco-spitting. His overall competence, especially in overseeing the Confederacy's early mobilization, would likely have kept him in office throughout the war, had not a tragic equestrian accident on Richmond's Clay Street taken his life in September 1861. President Davis then appointed Judah Benjamin to the Defense post (as he had wanted in February

1861). Benjamin occupied the office till March 1862 (when he moved to State); "that Jew from Louisiana" was succeeded by James A. Seddon, who served the length of Davis's tenure in office, to February 1868. Seddon's performance as the Confederacy's Secretary of Defense also decidedly outshone that of Cameron's successor, Edwin M. Stanton, as events will demonstrate.

The pattern is much the same in other key Cabinet appointments: Davis made wise choices while Lincoln, through poor judgment or just plain bad luck, surrounded himself with mediocrity or malfeasance. After Robert Toombs resigned as C.S. Secretary of State in July 1861 to take a commission in the army—he was that bored, to give up his office after only five months—R.M.T. Hunter of Virginia replaced him until March 1862. Thereafter Judah Benjamin was the Confederacy's chief diplomat. The comparative abilities of Benjamin and his Northern counterpart, Secretary William L. Dayton, (Seward's successor) are best reflected by what they achieved during the war. Benjamin succeeded in his main goal, that of securing recognition and aid for the South from England and France. Dayton's inability to prevent this major diplomatic coup in the summer of 1862 speaks for itself. Dayton set the stage for his colossal failure with his inept handling of the *Trent* Affair in November 1861. British outrage over this incident, and Dayton's inability to prevent or mitigate it, are generally judged to be second in importance only to Lee's and Sidney Johnston's military victories in the fall of 1862 as contributors to Her Majesty's government's decision to recognize the Confederacy, which the French quickly followed.

Lincoln's other Cabinet appointments did not prove as ill-starred as Cameron or Dayton, though Union Naval Secretary Gideon Welles' deficiencies have already been noted. As example, even in the last dark days before the armistice, Federal Treasurer Salmon P. Chase managed to keep the Northern economy on a reasonably sound footing; in recognition of this heroic achievement Chase's image appears today on Union ten thousand-dollar bills. On the whole, however, the Confederate cabinet has been judged vastly superior to the Federal one, leading most observers to award President Davis, for administrative abilities in selecting his advisers, five stars. Lincoln usually earns two-and-a-half, at best three.

This judgment is supported by an examination of the two presidents' relations with Congress. To be sure, Davis profited from the absence of political parties in the Confederacy (Southern Whigs and Democrats had forgotten their differences in uniting against the Northern Republicans by 1856). And Davis had no "Radicals" to contend with, at least defined as politicians willing to subvert military victory to political purity (even the South's most radical ideologue, Alexander Stephens, had the good sense to recuse himself in the first months of the war, rather than wreck the country's prospects for winning). This lack of political factionalism in the wartime South was an important reason, as Buck Yearns has stated, that "the Confederate government ran more smoothly than did that of the United States and [that] Lincoln was far more bothered with politics than was Davis."[368] There were, to be sure, anti-administration men in the Provisional and First Confederate Congresses.[369] But the President's skillful handling of these critics, particularly by allying himself with state governors or in some cases calling on the support of the citizenry itself, has been hailed as the craft of a master politician. Here again, Davis's pre-war experiences helped him, for as Senator he had learned a few tricks in maneuvering legislation through official Washington's bristly thickets of egotism.

---

368 Wilfred Buck Yearns, *The Confederate Congress: The War Years* (Athens GA, 1960), p. 234.

369 One such was Henry S. Foote, who before the war had been a fierce political rival of Davis when he resided in Mississippi in the 1840s-50s. Although an opponent of secession in 1861, Foote ran for election in the C.S. Congress from Tennessee, where he had moved. Foote's tirades against the President in Congress, on virtually every issue ranging from the reasons for defeat at Fort Donelson to the domestic price of horseshoes, won for him the dubious reputation as the administration's loudest critic. After the Confederate victory, however, Foote felt compelled to refugee himself to the North late in 1863. Seeking to rehabilitate his political reputation in Washington, Foote's career was wrecked when vigilant reporters of the New York *Times* caught him in an "assignation" with a prostitute in the capital's storied Mayflower Hotel in March 1864.

The role of personality was also considerable; Davis's ever-present dignity commanded respect even from those who disagreed with him. All of these factors combined to make the Confederate President an indomitable political force. Witness, as example, Davis's success in forcing Congress to enact conscription as early as April 1862. Lincoln, on the other hand, was unable to effect passage of draft legislation in the U.S. Congress until the summer of 1863 by which time it was too late to save the faltering Union armies.

THE MATTER OF PRESIDENTIAL PERSONALITY

One of the bitterest ironies of Abraham Lincoln's political career is that the mannerisms which won him votes in his presidential campaign proved to be a liability during his term of office. Historians have in fact cited personality as one of the Northern President's drawbacks as wartime leader. Nurtured by the coarse ways of frontier Kentucky, and never refined by formal schooling, Lincoln proved a sad embarrassment all too frequently during the war. A particularly unflattering incident, first reported by Englishman Fitzgerald Ross and publicized by *Blackwood's Edinburgh Magazine,* occurred early in the war when a group of British dignitaries visited the White House. Requesting that the President sign a resolution honoring the two nations' historic ties, one of the Englishmen asked, "I would beg you to lend me your finger and thumb for five seconds." Lincoln allegedly replied, "What would you do with them? Blow your nose?"[370]

Lincoln's biographers have struggled with such unflattering anecdotes, leading to such candid assessments as this:

> Though friends enjoyed Lincoln's folksy lack of pretention in the White House, and the press reported numerous funny anecdotes about him, thoughtful Northerners were troubled about his fondness for jokes and quips while the nation bled itself white on the battlefield. His crudeness and insensitivity

---

370   Fitzgerald Ross, *Cities and Camps of the Confederate States,* ed. by Richard Barksdale Harwell (Urbana IL, 1958), p. 79.

became common talk after stories circulated how, when touring the battlefield at Manassas, already tragically covered with the headboards of slain soldiers, the President ordered up a lively minstrel air from a regimental band. One shocked Union officer reported to the press back home that Lincoln even asked that the band play "Dixie." As the war dragged on and the casualties mounted, critics scowled at Lincoln's habit of attending the theater and giving parties at the White House during the war's darkest hours. After the President ordered an elegant private railway car for himself, the New York *Daily Journal* commented viciously, "Now a vulgar buffoon, who gives ghastly jokes over the grave of the Union, rides in a sumptuous sixteen-wheeled car... such as no King, Emperor, Czar, Kaiser, or even despotic Caesar himself ever indulged in."[371]

After Burnside's bloody repulse at Fredericksburg, *Harper's Weekly* in New York blasted the President's obliviousness to war's horrors with an editorial cartoon in which Columbia, symbol of the union, points accusingly at Lincoln and demands, "Where are my 15,000 sons murdered at Fredericksburg?" The President is shown responding, "This reminds me of a little joke......"[372]

Even when the cause was falling apart in the spring of 1863, Lincoln could not shed his propensity for unseemly lightness. In June, as Union forces floundered in Mississippi, powerful Senator Benjamin Wade of Ohio sternly reminded the President that he needed to fire McClernand if Vicksburg were ever to be taken. "He is doing nothing," argued Wade. "His hospitals are filled with sick. His army is wasting away."

"I think I am about the only friend he has got," commented Lincoln. "By the way, Mr. Wade, that reminds me of a little story."

---

371   Michael Davis, *The Image of Lincoln in the South* (Knoxville TN, 1971), p. 68.

372   T. Harry Williams, *Lincoln and the Radicals* (Madison WI, 1941), p. 200.

"Bother your stories, Mr. President," Wade shot back. "That is the way it is with you, sir. It is all story—story. You are the father of every military blunder that has been made during the war. You are on the road to hell, sir, with this government, and you are not a mile off this minute." Even at this rebuke and stiff warning, the President remained the gentle jokester. "That is just about the distance to the Capitol, isn't it?"[373]

The bitter assessment of abolitionist Wendell Phillips has forever etched for Lincoln his sad standing in American history: "a first-rate second-rate man."[374] The Northern President's misfortune was, of course, a consequence of his own personality, but Lincoln had the added misfortune of being cast in history beside the far more dignified stature of his opponent, Jefferson Davis. The Confederate President impressed all who knew him as a man of honor. "If one had to choose an outstanding trait of Davis's, it would have to be the high value that he placed on honor," judges one biographer.[375]

The South's leader was also, especially in times of crisis, remarkably decisive and resolute. Davis won the admiration of many countrymen when he single-handedly quelled the Richmond "bread riot" of April 2, 1862. Pinched by rising food prices, the absence of their bread-winning husbands (off in the army, sending home only $11 a month) and the pressures of feeding their families, hundreds of working-class women took to the capitol streets in a loud protest rally which turned into a looting spree. The President galloped immediately to the scene and addressed the women. Standing erect in the stirrups, he appealed to their patriotism, on the one hand, commiserating with them for the hard sacrifices that all Southerners were having to make. Then he shamed them by observing that they had begun to break into shops to steal jewelry and fine clothing, not bread for their children. Finally, after throwing them all the money in his pockets, he took

---

373   Geoffrey Perret, *Lincoln's War* (New York, 2004), p. 332.

374   Ludwell H. Johnson, "Jefferson Davis and Abraham Lincoln as War Presidents: Nothing Succeeds Like Success," *Civil War History*, vol. 27 (1981), 52.

375   Clement Eaton, *Jefferson Davis* (New Orleans, 1977), p. 270.

out his watch and gave the women five minutes to disperse before he would order troops and police to fire into the crowd. Davis's firm tone, no-nonsense words and unflinching, confident posture ended the disturbance then and there, as the bread-mob melted away. The Confederate press overnight hailed the President for his remarkable poise in time of crisis, and the story of the Davis's resolve before the Richmond rioters became a national allegory for the kind of stern stuff needed in the country as a whole.

As with all strong men, Davis's strengths sometimes found their expression in excess. In the words of biographer William C. Davis, "where others might be dedicated, he was committed. Where others felt enthusiasm, he felt passion. Where others were determined, he was obstinate."[376] At the same time, the President's passionate dedication to the cause of Confederate independence proved so powerful a morale-booster among the Southern people during the war that even critics such as Alexander Stephens regarded Davis's occasional obstinacy as a key contribution to the eventual Confederate victory.

After the war, Jefferson Davis's iconic place in Confederate history was assured by his bold, principled advocacy of gradual, compensated emancipation, to which he devoted the latter years of his term, 1863-68. He had been an unwavering advocate of secession, and had led the Southern people to their independence in 1863. Then, to safeguard his legacy, Davis worked to convince his people that the Confederate States of America would only be welcomed into the community of nations by renouncing its heritage of human bondage. "In order to save the Confederacy," as a recent biographer has phrased it, "Davis even led his fellow Confederates toward an abandonment of slavery."[377] Though it took several decades, the enactment of gradual emancipation by the C.S. Congress in 1885 was a monumental social and political achievement, which in turn led to an even greater accomplishment, the painful resolution by both races of the manumitted Negro's status in Con-

---

376   William C. Davis, *Jefferson Davis: The Man and His Hour* (New Orleans, 1991), pp. 689-90.

377   William J. Cooper, Jr., *Jefferson Davis, American Hero* (Baton Rouge, 2000), p. 657.

federate society. When the Mississippi state legislature became the eleventh in the South to ratify the proposed C.S. Constitutional amendment abolishing slavery in September 1889—thus ensuring its adoption by the requisite three-fourths of the states—Jefferson Davis told his wife that his life's work was complete.

He died three months later.

DAVIS, LINCOLN AND THE WAR ECONOMIES

Historians of the Southern War for Independence (on both sides of the Mason-Dixon Line) agree that the two presidents influenced the war's outcome most materially in their roles as commanders-in-chief. A suggestion of Confederate victory could be seen as early as 1862 in two key presidential decisions concerning army commanders. When Lincoln relieved McClellan after his disaster at Sharpsburg, the Northern president found himself with no one on hand as a successor. In the west, Grant was dishonored in the Union rout at Shiloh, the same battle in which Sherman had been shot in the head. Halleck and Buell were no more than mediocre, but at least they were stable, rather dependable mediocrities. Thus with no one to bring from across the mountains, Lincoln was forced to choose from among the Army of the Potomac's corps commanders. The folly of Lincoln's choosing Ambrose E Burnside as McClellan's replacement was evident within two months on the blood-soaked fields of Fredericksburg.

In contrast, when Joseph E. Johnston effectively left the war by taking a Yankee bullet at Seven Pines, Jefferson Davis made a brilliant decision which at the time was derided by many as foolish, even disastrous. Choosing to keep the hero of Shiloh, Albert Sidney Johnston, in charge in Tennessee, Davis brought from behind his Richmond desk one Robert Edward Lee. In light of Lee's worldwide fame, one tends to forget that at the time of his appointment in June 1862, Lee was known as "Granny" or "Spades," and was generally not respected either as a fighter or strategist. President Davis's keen appreciation of the man has, of course, been hailed as a turning point in Confederate history.

Still, some circumspective scholars have ascribed Jefferson Davis as just plain lucky, winning history's plaudits as architect of Southern victory on the coattails of the Confederate soldiers and officers who won the decisive battles at Chancellorsville and Chickamauga (the last battle fought in the west, where the opposing armies were unaware that the Treaty of Washington was being signed). Such a judgment, however, fails to take into account Davis's other talents which, though perhaps in lesser ways, also contributed to his success as war president.

Take the issue of economics, which American presidential historians agree has been the stiffest test of the U.S. and C.S. presidents in the more than a century-and-a-half since the war. In the case of Presidents Lincoln and Davis, the approach to economics was dramatically different. As he made his way from Springfield to Washington in March 1861 for his inauguration—and this was even before Fort Sumter—Lincoln disconcerted some of his closest friends by evincing a rare awkwardness, a subtle uncertainty in the face of the national concerns ahead of him. "One gets the sense of a man who was to a certain extent stunned by the sheer magnitude of his great national burden," writes Brian Dirck, the presidential historian.[378]

Then, when the war came, Lincoln found himself in a sea of uncertainty on how he would at once manage a national war and a national economy. Unfortunately, he seems never to have connected the two responsibilities as a larger, more dynamic opportunity. A chief cause of this outlook, which contributed to what must be acknowledged as Lincoln's executive dysfunctionality, was the President's feeling that the war would bring about peoples' basest instincts of greed and self-interest, no matter how nobly the war armies shined. "He described wartime as 'days of dereliction,'" Professor Dirck argues, "which seemed to bring out the worst in people who sought jobs and favors, avoided responsibilities,

---

378 Brian R. Dirck, *Lincoln and Davis: Imagining America, 1808-1863* (Lawrence KS, 2001), pp. 167-68.

peddled influence—in short, people who wanted to grow fat off the war's tremendous social and economic upheavals."[379]

As a result, Lincoln throughout the war, 1861-63, strained to keep separate in his mind the two burdens of national war and national economy. Even though unprecedented government spending was absolutely necessary to prosecute the war—paying for armies and the food, guns and livestock necessary to maintain them—Lincoln frequently fretted about unprecedented national debt and the horrors of taxation. He declined to view the wartime boom in Northern industrial activity as an economic benefit, and instead worried that the manufacture of cartridges and packaging of hardtack were diverting economic resources from more important long-range national priorities such as a transatlantic cable and transcontinental railroad.

Especially did the Northern President shrink from aggressive executive measures which would have harnessed and invigorated his nation's economic might toward a stronger, more purposeful prosecution of the war. Once Lincoln declared to an audience that although "the Union must be preserved," he refused to accept the need for extraordinary economic or fiscal policies to see the war through to victory. "We should not be in haste to determine that radical and extreme measures are indispensable."[380]

Quite different was Jefferson Davis's understanding of the nexus of war and economy. For the newly founded Confederate States of America, he believed that heroic measures were called for as much in the factories or farms as on the battlefields. With the resolute conviction which characterized his presidency, Davis was able to convince the Southern people that both a military and economic revolution was afoot, and that all must participate in it for the national good.

In this sense, Lincoln practiced a *laissez-faire* approach to the Northern economy, allowing the War Department and state governors to contract with private businesses in the procurement

---

379 *Ibid.,* p. 212.

380 *Ibid.,* p. 213.

of war necessities, while Davis sought to revolutionize a previously conservative Southern economy in the interest of national self-preservation. Toward that end, another measure of Davis's achievement as war president was his success at transforming Southern political attitudes from the conservative orthodoxy of state rights into a popular acceptance of stronger national government needed for a mightier national war effort.

For Jefferson Davis, the case began with his at-first seven, then eleven and eventually thirteen sometimes cantankerous state governors. While Lincoln and his two war secretaries allowed Northern states to compete with the national government in recruitment and the procurement of arms and supplies, President Davis deftly pressed Southern governors to turn their military prerogatives over to the Confederate administration. Thus John Letcher of Virginia, Joseph E. Brown of Georgia and other strong-willed governors, who prided themselves in raising large numbers of state troops, gradually bowed to the need of a national army under central control. This shift of authority not only permitted a more cohesive implementation of strategy, but also allowed Davis to exert his authority against short enlistments, frequent furloughs, election of officers, and other practices which sapped the strength of the rank and file.

Far more than Lincoln, Davis was able to see the war as an opportunity to forge a national sense of purpose toward victory. In that sense, the enactment of conscription ranks as one of Davis's most effective uses of the chief executive's war powers. "Never before had an American government raised a national army by legal coercion," writes Professor Escott, "but Davis saw that conscription would be necessary and enacted before Northern leaders reached the same conclusion."[381] Thus, when appeals for volunteers failed to raise the large numbers of troops needed for the spring campaigns of 1862, especially as the enlistments of the first year's volunteers were about to expire, Davis called on Congress for conscription of men between the ages of 18 and

---

381 Paul D. Escott, *After Secession: Jefferson Davis and the Triumph of Confederate Nationalism* (Baton Rouge, 1978), p. 63.

35. The Southern senators and representatives, elected in the autumn of 1861 as generally conservative men, sensed through Davis's leadership that these were extraordinary times demanding extraordinary measures. If national independence were to be won, traditions would have to be broken. The C.S. Congress therefore stepped forth to the challenge and enacted the law. By contrast, Lincoln would not be able to persuade Northern lawmakers to pass his draft bill till more than a year later. When Federal draft officers began calling up men in Northern cities, Chancellorsville had already nearly destroyed the Army of the Potomac, McClernand was stalemated in Mississippi, and Union prospects looked bleak. No wonder civilian men rioted against the draft in New York and other places; they were not going to give their lives for a cause which to almost every observer looked to be failing.

As he did with conscription, so did Jefferson Davis succeed in rallying political support for a broad exercise of executive war powers in harnessing the Confederate economy. Vital industries and railroads were a key sector. Davis pressed Congress to enact loans and subsidies to manufacturers of gunpowder, small arms, coal and iron; he led the way for the government to override private ownership and operate saltworks and factories for uniforms and shoes; he used his own authority to grant or revoke details to supervise the manufacture of needed supplies; he authorized the outright impressment of food or munitions, allowing army officers to seize goods in exchange for credit certificates. He similarly won legislative approval for the impressment of railroads needed for transporting troops and supplies. Moreover, despite an explicit Constitutional ban on internal improvements, he saw that the government built two new rail lines, connecting Danville to Greensboro and Meridian to Selma. In view of these impressive achievements, Confederate historian Paul Escott's conclusion is worth quoting:

> In every area of governmental activity, from the creation and direction of an army to management of the war economy, Jefferson Davis built a strong central government. With a sober awareness of the

magnitude of his task, he recognized that fighting a war against the United States would require many innovations in the decentralized, individualistic Southern style of life. Determined to achieve independence, Davis interpreted his powers broadly and asked Southerners to do many things which they considered neither normal nor desirable. Exerting progressively greater control over the nation, the Davis administration by 1863 affected millions of Southerners directly every day.[382]

Emory Thomas has characterized Davis's wartime achievement as nothing short of a revolutionary experience. His conclusion that "the Davis administration outdid its Northern counterpart in organizing for total war" goes a long way toward explaining why the South won its struggle for independence.[383]

WITH GOD ON OUR SIDE (I): THE SOUTH

Clerics—meaning ministers, rabbis, priests, pastors, all ordained (or merely faithful) men of God who lead congregations in their multi various forms of organized worship—are citizens, too. This commonplace is not meant to offend, but to remind us that Northerners and Southerners of all vocational callings were swept up by the hot rush of patriotism, bellicosity and devotion to cause which flushed millions of Americans with war-fever in the spring of 1861. More, as opinion-leaders (with politicians, journalists and others), clergymen supported their respective causes by doing what they have done for oh-so-long: infusing their nations' war efforts with religious spirit and associating their own armies with divine blessing, as if God could be on everyone's side, all at once.

Recall that the four largest American Protestant denominations had split, North and South, over slavery. Historians have long noted the virtual disappearance of anti-slavery thought in the South after the 1830s. As part of the antebellum Southern white social agreement

---

382 *Ibid.*, p. 69.

383 Emory M. Thomas, *The Confederacy as a Revolutionary Experience* (Englewood Cliffs NJ, 1971), p. 134.

to accept slavery as an institution worth defending, people's uneasiness or even guilt over slavery as something antithetical to God's will—at least in most public utterances—largely disappeared in the generation before the war. In 1837 Presbyterians split over a doctrinal question along lines that became sectional. "New School" Presbyterians tended to be Northerners, who began to speak as a group against slavery. Southern "Old School" Presbyterians accordingly adopted a proslavery position. In 1840 Northern Baptists met in New York and held a National Baptist Anti-Slavery Convention; five years later, Southern Baptists met in Augusta, Georgia, formed the Southern Baptist Convention, and declared the Northerners' activities censurable and meddlesome. In 1845 Southern Methodists, meeting at Louisville, Kentucky, formed the Methodist Episcopal Church, South after the national convention passed a resolution calling on the national bishop, a Georgian, to cease his clerical work until he freed or sold his slaves.

Over half of Americans in 1860 (19 million of 31 million) claimed affinity with some church denomination. Of these, Methodists were the largest group (6¼ million), followed by Baptists (3¾ million) and Presbyterians (2 million). This meant that the majority of "religious" Americans, more than a third of the population, belonged to church denominations that had split over the moral question of slavery. Jews and Catholics escaped such sectional schism; neither the Torah nor the Pope offered guidance to their followers on the issue of chattel slavery in the United States. The country's nearly million Congregationalists also remained unsplit, but only because they were all up North, anyway. Finally, Episcopalians became the fourth Protestant denomination to split, sort of. After secession and the formation of the Confederacy, Southern Episcopalians could no longer participate in prayers for the President of the United States, as called for by the Book of Common Prayer, so they organized the Episcopal Church of the Confederate States. After the war started, rectors of some Southern parishes in Yankee-occupied territory were at times arrested for merely mentioning Jefferson Davis in their services.

So God got wrapped up in this war, with the clergymen leading and the people following. Confederate victory at Sumter gave Southerners a head start, as most Protestant Americans shared the belief that human events reflected the quiet, controlling hand of an all-powerful Providence. In "The Bloodless Victory: A Sermon Preached on the Occasion of Taking Fort Sumter," the Reverend J.H. Elliott told his Charleston flock that in their triumph "the hand of God seems as plainly in it as in the conquest of the Midianites." Congregations hearing such stirring talk often arranged to have their ministers' sermons privately printed, when the spoken texts joined the voluminous outpourings of the South's many religious publishing houses. One of them, *The Commonwealth,* on May 6, 1861, sought to inspire its readers with the reminder that "we should go into this war, feeling as did David, that he who does his duty to his country, is but doing part of his duty to his God. To fight is now...a religious duty.[384]

As the nation's president, Jefferson Davis found himself elevated in a way from chief executive to spiritual leader. The Southern Baptist Convention, meeting in Richmond during May 1861, broadcast in its *Proceedings* the attendees' belief that Davis's administration was "contributing to the transcendent Kingdom of our Lord Jesus Christ."[385] Davis did his part by declaring, on six separate occasions during the war, a national day of fasting and penitence (including September 25, 1862, proclaimed as a national Thanksgiving Day, celebrating General Lee's great victory in Maryland. Most Southerners today continue to observe some form of feasting or commemoration on the fourth Thursday in September, while Northerners have chosen the fourth Thursday in November proclaimed by Lincoln in 1863 for Thanksgiving, when actually the defeated North had very little to be thankful about.)

The first Confederate Fast Day was set for June 13, 1861. In Montgomery, before the capital moved to Richmond, the President and Mrs. Davis walked each Sunday the three and a half blocks

---

384 James W. Silver, *Confederate Morale and Church Propaganda* (Tuscaloosa, 1957), pp. 26-27, 31.

385 *Ibid.,* p. 28.

from their residence to St. John's Episcopal Church at the corner of Madison and Perry Streets. He was often accompanied by his Cabinet Secretaries Memminger and Walker. But in mid-May he turned to Georgia Congressman (and evangelical Presbyterian) Thomas R.R. Cobb for thoughts about a national day of prayer and fast. "Many now look to God," Cobb replied, adding that many Southerners were already praying that their infant nation might expect aid "from that quarter."[386] Davis accordingly urged Cobb to introduce to Congress a resolution formally requesting the President to announce an upcoming day of national reverence. Davis issued his proclamation on May 28 with the fast day scheduled for Thursday, June 13:

A PROCLAMATION.

BY THE PRESIDENT OF THE CONFEDERATE STATES.

To the people of the Confederate States:

When a people who recognize their dependence upon God feel themselves surrounded by peril and difficulty, it becomes them to humble themselves under the dispensation of Divine Providence, to recognize His righteous government, to acknowledge His goodness in times past, and supplicate His merciful protection for the future.

The manifest proofs of the Divine blessing hitherto extended to the efforts of the people of the Confederate States of America, to maintain and perpetuate public liberty, individual rights, and national independence, demand their devout and heartfelt gratitude. It becomes them to give

---

386   William C. Davis, *"A Government of Our Own": The Making of the Confederacy* (New York, 1994), pp. 387-88.

public manifestation of this gratitude, and of their dependence upon the Judge of all the earth, and to invoke the continuance of His favor. Knowing that none but a just and righteous cause can gain the Divine favor, we would implore the Lord of Hosts to guide and direct our policy in the paths of right duty, justice, and mercy, to unite our hearts and our efforts for the defense of our dearest rights; to strengthen our weakness, crown our arms with success, and enable us to secure the speedy, just, and honorable peace.

To these ends, and in conformity with the request of Congress, I invite the people of the Confederate States to the observance of a day of fasting and prayer by such religious services as may be suitable for the occasion, and I recommend Thursday, the 13th day of June next, for that purpose, and that we may all, on that day, with one accord, join in humble and reverential approach to Him in whose hands we are, invoking Him to inspire us with a proper spirit and temper of heart and mind to bear our evils, to bless us with His favor and protection, and to bestow His gracious benediction upon our Government and country.

Jefferson Davis.[387]

The Southern press publicized the President's message, and on June 13 many folk dutifully flocked to their centers of worship. In Mobile, as example, worshippers in St. John's Church heard the Reverend Henry Pierce affirm, "Our cause is a just, nay, a holy one." Across town the Reverend J.C. Mitchell asked his listeners, "Who can fail to see the hand of God in the whole movement?"[388] At St.

---

387   John D. Richardson, comp., *Messages and Papers of the Presidents of the Confederate States, 1861-1901*, 11 vols. (Nashville, 1906), vol. 1, 103-104.

388   Silver, *op. cit.*, p. 29.

James Church in Warrenton, Virginia, the Reverend O.S. Barton's fast-day sermon stressed the religious mission and character of the South's new government. True, among Northerners were many Christians, but they had let their spiritual roots be compromised by "infidels and fanatics under a godless government." With Christianity more fundamentally affirmed in the Confederacy's leaders and people, Barton challenged his listeners to join in the struggle "to become a truly Christian confederacy," as "God's purposes are bound up with us as a nation....Nations are but aggregates of individuals who compose them, and what God requires of one in his individual capacity, he demands of the whole in their associated character."[389]

The question can fairly be raised whether such pastoral passion made its way out into the secular hinterlands, where the common folk of the South might not have heard the ministers in their special Thursday sermons. Yet thanks to the Confederate press, which carried the President's proclamation into the Southland's rural recesses, even the remotest folk knew of the Fast Day, and observed it in their own way, as evidenced by this entry into the journal of Magnolia Plantation, forty miles below New Orleans. The estate was owned by Effingham Lawrence, but the plantation record was kept by the overseer, I.A. Randall. Following a rueful entry that a mule that day had died at 2 a.m., Randall recorded:

> "This day is set a part By presedent Jefferson Davis for fasting & praying owing to the Deplorable condishion ower Southern country is In My Prayer Sincerely to God is that Every Black Republican in the Hole combined whorl Either man woman o chile that is opposed to negro slavery as it existed in the Souther confederacy shal be trubled with pestilents & calamitys of all Kinds and Dragout the Balance of there existence in misray & Degradation with scarsely food & raiment enughf to keep sole & Body

---

389 Harry S. Stout, *Upon the Altar of a Nation: A Moral History of the American Civil War* (New York, 2006), pp. 49, 51.

togeather and O God I pray the to Direct a bullet or a bayonet to pirce the Hart of every northern soldier that invades southern Soile & after the Body had Rendered up its Traterish Sole gave it a trators reward a Birth In the Lake of Fires & Brimstone my honest convicksion is that Every man wome & chile that has gave aide to the abolishionist are fit Subjects for Hell I all so ask the to aide the Sothern Confedercy in maintaining Ower rites & establishing the confederate Government Believing in this case the prares from the wicked will prevailith much Amen."[390]

WITH GOD ON OUR SIDE (2): THE NORTH

In the North, clergymen rallied behind the holy cause of liberty as did their Southern brethren. They were aided by a few ideological bulwarks which the South as a culture did not possess. And they were complicated, if not weakened, by a few moral abstractions which Southern did not hold to, as well.

Ever since the days of Jonathan Edwards and Cotton Mather in the 1660s many Northerners, particularly New Englanders, had articulated their society in terms of God's calling, a shining city on the hill more virtuous in the New World than any in the Old. A century later, revolutionary idealism found strong expression in the same New England zealotry. Two generations after that, the social reform movements sweeping New York and New England in the 1830s had strong undertones of religion. Abolitionism, more so than temperance, education reform, or any of the other "isms" promoted from the pulpit as good social causes allowed many Northern ministers to fix the attention of their constantly cajoled flocks beyond themselves, to the sinfulness of the South and its benighted institution of slavery, which more extreme clergymen proclaimed could only be cleansed by the purging of national

---

390 Bell Irvin Wiley, *The Life of Johnny Reb: The Common Soldier of the Confederacy* (Indianapolis, 1943), pp. 16-17.

blood. These religious reformers were thus among the earliest and most enthusiastic supporters of Mr. Lincoln's war, though "Union," "flag" and "country" would have been their sermonic mainstays more than any public utterance of abolition. And they accepted their responsibilities as war-ralliers with glee. "We," referring to Northern preachers, proclaimed the Methodist minister Granville Moody, "are charged with having brought about the present crisis. I believe it is true, that we did bring it about, and I glory in it, for it is a wreath of glory around our brow."[391]

For some preachers, the heavenly ordained principle of obedience to higher authority was enough to kindle their war enthusiasm. Somewhat chauvinistically, this meant obedience to the national authority, which the Rebels were now violating. After all, there was the thirteenth chapter of Paul's letter to the Romans: "Let every soul be subject unto the higher powers. For there is no power but of God: the powers that be are ordained of God. Whosoever therefore resisteth the power, resisteth the ordinance of God: and they that resist shall receive to themselves damnation." This kind of message had many hearers, and sank deep. Pennsylvanian Robert McAllister, who would rise in the war to Union general's rank, accepted his duty to "put down this wicked rebellion and teach the Southerners with force what they would not learn in time of peace...that governments are not so easily broken up, and that God requires obedience to law and order."[392]

Thus enspirited and long in the waiting, Northern clergymen militantly endorsed Lincoln's call for 75,000 volunteers in April 1861, and themselves summoned more. Call for half a million, urged the Rev. Alexander Simmons of Salem, Massachusetts. Resolutions encouraging the President came from across the denominational spectrum: the Welsh Congregational Church of New York City, the Philadelphia Presbytery of the Reformed Presbyterian Church in North America and the New York East Conference of the Methodist Episcopal Church, to name but a few.

---

391   David B. Cheseborough, *"God Ordained This War": Sermons on the Sectional Crisis, 1830-1863* (Columbia SC, 1991), p. 17.

392   Steven E. Woodworth, *While God is Marching On: The Religious World of Civil War Soldiers* (Lawrence KS, 2001), p. 95.

In this virtually millennial vision many Northerners volunteered in what they saw as God's war. "For some years, I have thought the signs of the times indicated the approach of the great millenial day," wrote one Illinois recruit to his brother in August 1861. "The hand of providence has been overruling & moulding all the affairs of nations to introduce this glorious event....Now the mystery is solved, for tho this dreadful rebellion springs out of the corruption of the human heart, God is directing the storm to wipe out the blot & before 1865 we shall be reinstated as a nation on a firmer basis of Christian and republican principles than before."[393]

This unfortunate chap had it wrong: the war would end in 1863, not 1865; and his side would not emerge as the victor. But as we all have been taught, God moves in mysterious ways.

FORT PICKENS

While the Confederacy's northeastern borders were being tested by Union military activity in Virginia, the new Southern nation faced other threats along its underbelly. There was, for instance, the constantly nagging problem of Fort Pickens. Always a sore point with President Davis and his Defense Secretary, the presence of an enemy garrison near Pensacola brought about a significant concentration of Confederate troops in Florida's panhandle. Well before the firing on Sumter, Florida militia and companies sent by the governors of Alabama and Mississippi had formed the nucleus of an "Army of Pensacola." By late March over a thousand men were drilling and fortifying, and 5,000 more recruits were *en route*.

But the Yankees were on their way as well. Within days after the fall of Fort Sumter, Union naval vessels were landing troops, supplies and a new commander, Col. Harvey Brown, on Santa Rosa Island. Soon over 2,000 Federals manned Fort Pickens, using every day to mount cannon and strengthen their works. The Southerners, too, were mounting cannon in shoreline batteries and strengthening their works at Forts McRae and Barrancas, but they seemed to do so with lethargy and even indecision. William

---

393   *Ibid.*, p. 97.

Howard Russell, the English correspondent travelling through the Confederacy, visited Pensacola in mid-May, and was struck by this lack of direction among officers and men. He recorded in his diary:

> The working parties, as they were called — volunteers from Mississippi and Alabama, great long-bearded fellows in flannel shirts and slouched hats, were lying about among the works, or contributing languidly to their completion.

> Considerable improvements were in the course of execution; but the officers were not always agreed as to the work to be done. Captain A., at the wheelbarrows: "Now then, you men, wheel up these sandbags, and range them just at this corner." Major B: "My good Captain A., what do you want the bags there for? Did I not tell you, these merlons were not to be finished till we had completed the parapet on the front?" Captain A: "Well, Major, so you did, and your order made me think you know darned little about your business; and so I am going to do a little engineering of my own."[394]

Irresolution in the ranks usually starts at the top, and such was the case with Brig. Gen. Braxton Bragg, the Confederate commander at Pensacola. A West Pointer from North Carolina, Bragg had begun his service in the old army with a tour of duty at Fort Pickens. He thus told his officers, "I know every inch of Pickens, for I happened to be stationed there as soon as I left West Point, and I don't think there is a stone in it that I am not as well acquainted with as Harvey Brown."[395]

This confident outlook, however, soon gave way to uncertainty. After taking command in early March, Bragg came up with a plan for reducing Fort Pickens and forcing the surrender of its garrison.

---

394 William Howard Russell, *My Diary North and South*, ed. by Fletcher Pratt (New York, 1954), pp. 122-23.

395 *Ibid.*, p. 120.

When pressed for details by Davis and the Defense Department, though, Bragg's resolve wavered. His reports began to detail any number of reasons for taking no action: his troops were untrained; his artillery lacked shells and fuses; his commissary had no money to buy supplies; his men had only a day's supply of musket cartridges; his batteries had insufficient mortars; &c., &c. Secretary Walker did what he could to send arms and supplies, but invariably Bragg's response was the same. "We are totally unprepared," he wrote Walker in March; a month later he could only say that "we will do our best, but supplies are short for a continued resistance"; and in May Bragg was still informing his government that "it would be very bad policy to move until we are prepared to succeed."[396]

Meanwhile, Colonel Brown and the Union garrison at Pickens received reinforcements from the navy and grew stronger during the same period. Because the Federal fort was situated on an island in Pensacola Bay, fully a mile and a half from Confederate shore batteries, Northern ships had no trouble landing men and supplies. The impudence with which the Yankees reprovisioned themselves only added to Bragg's frustrations. "It is utterly impossible to check the enemy in his operations," the Confederate commander wrote his supervisors.[397] Eventually it became clear to Davis and Walker that Braxton Bragg was not a man of action.

He was, however, a man for paperwork. After the war a Confederate officer recalled the documents that piled up when Bragg, short of staff officers, served as his own quartermaster and commissary. "As commander of the garrison, he made requisitions on the quartermaster—himself—for something he needed. As quartermaster he declined to fill the requisition, and endorsed on the back of it his reasons for so doing. As garrison commander he responded to this, urging that his requisition called for nothing but what he was entitled to, and that it was the duty of the quartermaster to fill it. As quartermaster he still insisted that he was right. In this condition of affairs, Bragg referred the whole

---

396 William C. Harris, *Leroy Pope Walker: Confederate Secretary of Defense* (Tuscaloosa, 1962), pp. 41, 43, 45.

397 *Ibid.*, p. 45.

matter to the adjutant general of the post. The latter, when he saw the character of the correspondence, exclaimed, 'My God, Bragg, you have quarreled with every officer in the army, and now you are quarreling with yourself.'"[398]

THE LOSS OF HATTERAS

Allowing Federal troops to hold Fort Pickens, Florida and Fort Monroe, Virginia, was bad enough—they would remain sore points to President Davis throughout the war. But the Yanks worsened the situation for the South by capturing other coastal places in combined operations of Northern ships and amphibious infantry.

For Lincoln and his War Department, the North Carolina Outer Banks—the coastal region encompassing Albemarle and Pamlico Sounds, separated from the Atlantic by long, skinny Hatteras Island—presented a particularly tempting target. If Federal forces could be landed there and a base established, they could neutralize Beaufort and Morehead City as blockade runners' havens, operate against Norfolk (110 miles to the north) from the rear, and even march inland to threaten the Wilmington and Weldon Railroad, the key supply line for Confederate armies in Virginia.

North Carolinians were not blind to these dangers and began fortifying the Outer Banks soon after secession in May 1861. There were three entrances into the sounds: Oregon Inlet, Ocracoke Inlet, and Hatteras Inlet; all of them began to be fortified. To guard the latter, Fort Hatteras was built at a point commanding the channel. Sand-and-log parapets rose ten feet; from the embrasures of the three-quarter-acre fort bristled a ten-inch Columbiad and a dozen thirty-two pounders. Fort Clark was a smaller redoubt to the north of Fort Hatteras on the island, closer to the ocean. When completed in July (a month after Hatteras), it mounted six thirty-two pounders and two six-pounders.

Unfortunately, though, there were not enough troops assigned to garrison the four forts at the three inlets. (Oregon and Ocracoke each had a small redoubt.) In early August, only 580 officers and

---

398   Robert Underwood Johnson, *Remembered Yesterdays* (Boston, 1923), p. 198.

men were in position against the expected Union ship-and-soldier assault. Of these, Hatteras and Clark were manned by a combined force of only 350 men.

The Union commander at Fort Monroe, Maj. Gen. Benjamin Franklin Butler—whose hilariously failed wartime service as Northern commander would bring shame as namesake to the memory of the historic American Revolutionary hero—conceived of a joint army-navy move against Hatteras Inlet. The Navy agreed, and assigned Capt. Silas Stringham to cooperate. On August 26, Butler's 860 troops boarded steamers and with Stringham's eight vessels headed south for Cape Hatteras.

The next day the Northern vessels approached the Confederate forts at the cape, and got into position for the next morning's attack against Hatteras and Clark as Butler landed his soldiers. On the 28th, Stringham's flotilla concentrated first on Fort Clark, shelling it but doing little damage. Fearing assault by Northern infantry, the Clark garrison spiked their cannon, abandoned the fort and withdrew to join the troops at Fort Hatteras. The commander there, Col. W.F. Martin, sent word to New Bern and Plymouth, urgently calling for reinforcements. They did not arrive in time. August 29 marked a bombardment by Stringham's ships with their 143 rifled cannon. The vessels kept moving as they fired, making the fort's gunners' task that much more difficult. Compounding the Southerners' problems was that they found most of their ammunition defective, so the fire-fight proved woefully lopsided. When a Northern shell set fire to the fort's magazine, Colonel Martin prudently decided that it was time to quit and ordered an evacuation. His troops quickly retreated inland, even before Butler's infantrymen launched their planned assault.

The Federals had won a virtually bloodless victory in their capture of Forts Hatteras and Clark on August 29. Butler and Stringham lost not a man killed, with just a few wounded. The Confederates' casualties numbered around a dozen, but their biggest loss, aside from the guns in the two forts, was to their pride; the Hatteras battle was the first Union victory after McDowell's disgrace at Manassas.[399]

But the Southerners learned a valuable lesson: the next time one of their coastal forts was attacked by Yankee warships, they would be ready, with lots of Matthew Fontaine Maury's "torpedos" placed around the waters of Port Royal, South Carolina, to blow up unwelcome enemy intruders.

---

399   John G. Barrett, *The Civil War in North Carolina* (Chapel Hill: University of North Carolina Press, 1963), p. 45.

Chapter Eight:

———◇———

The War in the West

THE CONFEDERATE TERRITORY OF ARIZONA

The historical road leading to the admission in 1912 of Arizona and New Mexico as the fifteenth and sixteenth states of the Confederacy began just a few days after the secession of Texas. On Feb. 4, 1861, the Texas state convention enacted a measure expressing interest in strengthening friendly ties to the territorial legislature in Santa Fe. (Back then, the U.S. territory of New Mexico took in what are today both New Mexico and Arizona.) In actuality, the Texans hoped to hear that the people of "Arizona"—informally, the southern half of the territory—express a desire for annexation to the Lone Star State, or at least territorial status as part of the Confederacy. They were rewarded the following month when a group of prominent pro-Southern ranchers and merchants convened in Mesilla (on the Rio Grande, some fifty miles northwest of El Paso). With the Confederate Stars and Bars flying all over town, on March 16 they formally denounced "Black Republicans" as "a sectional party of the North [which] has disregarded the Constitution of the United States, violated the rights of the Southern States, and heaped wrongs and indignities upon their people."[400] Then they proclaimed that "Arizona naturally belongs to the Confederate States of America," which meant that

---

400   "Proceedings of a Convention of the People of Arizona, held in the City of Mesilla, March 16th, 1861," *Atlanta Daily Intelligencer,* Apr. 15, 1861.

all the land between Texas and California south of the 34th parallel would henceforth constitute the "Confederate States Territory of Arizona," with its capital at Mesilla.

At the time, the only concentration of U.S. soldiers in the new Confederate territory was based at Fort Fillmore, just a few miles from the secessionist hotbed in Mesilla. There Maj. Isaac Lynde commanded 550 infantry and mounted rifles, whose main duty had been to keep watch on restive Apache Indians. Lynde began to worry when John Baylor, an impetuous Indian fighter and lieutenant colonel of the 2nd Texas Mounted Rifles, led some 300 men from El Paso toward Fort Fillmore. On July 25 Baylor's column rode into Mesilla, where they were enthusiastically welcomed and even picked up a few volunteers for what Baylor was calling a "buffalo hunt." The Yankees at Fillmore figured out that they were the hunted and quietly abandoned the fort, heading northeast toward Fort Stanton. They raised such a dust cloud that Baylor's force had no trouble pursuing. As they rode along, the Texans encountered dozens of Federals lying in the road, too weak from heat exhaustion to resist and begging to surrender (for water). Then, at San Agustin Pass in the Organ Mountains twenty miles east of Fort Fillmore, Baylor caught up with the demoralized, wilted Federal column, which Major Lynde surrendered without a shot having been fired. The Confederates paroled them, gave them some rifles to fend off the lurking Apaches, and sent them riding northward. (Theirs would be an arduous trek, through the vast desert called Jornada del Muerto, "Day's Journey of the Dead Man.")

The capture of 500 Yankees by a force little more than half its size provoked wild celebration among the people of Mesilla when Lieutenant Colonel Baylor and his men rode back into town. "With little effort, and not a single battle casualty, Baylor, in effect, had begun the conquest of the Southwest for the Confederacy," writes historian Alvin M. Josephy.[401] All Federal troops south of the Jornada had been cleared away, and on August 1 Baylor proclaimed a provisional government for the Confederate Territory of Arizona, with himself as military governor. A few days later balloting led to

---

401   Alvin M. Josephy, Jr., *The Civil War in the American West* (New York, 1991), p. 50.

the election of Grant Oury of Tucson as territorial delegate to the C.S. Congress. On Jan. 18, 1862, the C.S. Congress passed an act recognizing the Territory of Arizona. Six days later, Oury took his seat in Richmond.[402] Then, a month after that, on February 14, President Davis issued a proclamation declaring the government of the Territory of Arizona fully recognized and operational.[403]

Unfortunately, Col. Edward Richard Sprigg Canby and a bunch of Yankees to the north in New Mexico would have something to say about that.

THE INDIAN TREATIES

In October 1861 a year before England and France bestowed diplomatic recognition of the C.S.A., the Confederate government exercised its international prerogatives by signing a treaty of alliance with the Cherokee Nation.

There was a lot of logic behind it. In 1860 the Cherokee Indian tribe, forcibly displaced from their ancestral homelands years before by the Federal government, had always viewed the United States as an evil enemy. In the several decades after the forced march westward, however, the Cherokees had thrived in their section of the new "Indian Territory" (the northeast part, abutting Arkansas and Kansas). In 1860 Cherokees had 102,000 acres in agricultural cultivation, 240,000 cattle, 20,000 horses and mules, and 15,000 hogs. As a further indication of their wealth, Cherokees also owned 4,000 slaves—another reason they favored the South over the North.

John Ross, principal chief of the Nation, himself owned a hundred slaves. Stand Watie, another Cherokee leader, was part of a secret group dedicated to catching and punishing abolitionists who wandered into tribal territory. When war broke out among the white men, Watie raised 300 warriors to guard the border against intrusion by unwelcome Kansas jayhawkers. They received

---

402   L. Boyd Finch, *Confederate Pathway to the Pacific: Major Sherod Hunter and Arizona Territory, C.S.A.* (Tucson, 1996), 85, 103.

403   John D. Richardson, comp., *Messages and Papers of the Presidents of the Confederate States, 1861-1906*, 11 vols. (Nashville, 1906), vol. 1, 167.

help from the Confederacy after Arkansas had seceded (May 6) and President Davis appointed Texan Ben McCulloch as brigadier general (May 11) with orders to build an Army of the West by recruiting in Arkansas, Texas and Louisiana. By that time the U.S. Army had abandoned all its posts in the Indian Territory (now Oklahoma, which became the fourteenth Confederate state in 1907). McCulloch was also directed to keep the enemy from returning; in this eventuality he hoped for assistance from the Cherokees and the other tribes of the Five Great Nations.

On March 4, 1861—the day Abraham Lincoln took his oath as president of the dis-United States—the Confederate Congress admirably demonstrated strategic foresight by authorizing President Davis to send a special agent to the Indian tribes west of Arkansas and win their support for the Confederacy. This authorizing resolution had been proposed by Secretary of State Robert Toombs, who recommended Albert Pike for the post. Pike, a poet, newspaperman and attorney in Little Rock, had in 1852 championed the Creek Indians' claim for payment for the land in Alabama they had been promised at the time of the forced removal. Pike won the Creeks more than $110,000 from the U.S. Treasury, and thus had endeared himself to the tribal leaders.

It was therefore no coincidence that General Pike, armed with full authority from Richmond to strike whatever treaty terms he could, turned first to the Creeks. Traveling by steamboat up the Arkansas River into the Territory, then by horseback with mounted escort, Pike made his way farther to North Fork Village, the Creeks' principal town, located between the North and South Forks of the Canadian River. There on July 10 he met with Motey Kinnaird, principal chief, as well as lesser tribal leaders, and struck a deal. By the terms of this treaty of "perpetual peace and friendship," the Creeks were promised permanent right to their present lands, formal status as a Confederate protectorate, Richmond's pledge to pay them all monies owed by the federal government, as well as various other rights of self-government (including a delegate to be seated in the Confederate House of Representatives). Richmond also promised to the Nation, once the war had been won, agricultural and industrial assistance. In return, the Creeks obligated themselves to raise a mounted regiment for the defense of its lands, to be armed and equipped at Confederate expense.

These were liberal terms indeed, and once more Albert Pike had affirmed himself as a genuine friend of the native American people. With this treaty in hand, Pike met with leaders of the Choctaws and Chickasaws, whom he had invited to meet with him at North Fork Village. He had had no trouble in getting them there. As early as Feb. 6, 1861, the Choctaw National Council had drafted a resolution announcing its severing of all ties with the United States and affirming its links to the newly formed Confederacy. Indeed, this statement of common "natural affections, education, institutions and interests" with the South was sent to the governors of all (then) seven seceded states. The Chickasaw Nation legislature took a little longer, but on May 25 it passed similar resolutions of friendship and alliance with the Confederacy. Building on these measures, Pike had no difficulty in persuading the Choctaw and Chickasaw leadership to sign a joint treaty similar to the one he had secured with the Creeks (including delegate presence in Richmond).

Traveling into Seminole country, Pike and his party made their way to the tribal agency near Fort Washita and met with John Jumper, principal chief, Pas-co-fa, George Cloud and others. The Seminoles, like the Creeks, were slaveholders, although only a minority of the twenty-three hundred tribesmen actually owned slaves. This may have explained how the Seminole leaders initially seemed to favor neutrality in the white man's war. But Pike had brought with him Chickasaw and Choctaw commissioners, who proved to be persuasive ambassadors. Then, during the several days of talks, came word that Col. Jim Lane, the notorious Kansas jayhawker, was recruiting troops to invade the Indian Territory and root out all secesh. This was enough to turn the tide. On August 1, the Seminoles agreed to a pact that did not go so far as to declare alliance with the Confederate States, but committed the Nation to raise up to five mounted companies for Confederate service within Territorial borders.

Albert Pike was on a roll (as we would say today). His final goal was to secure a treaty with the Cherokees, whose leader, Chief Ross, had agreed to meet with him at Park Hill, Ross' place of residence near Tahlequah, the Cherokee capital. As a bonus, Ross had asked leaders of the Shawnees, Osages, Senecas and Quapaws to come to Park Hill as well. Offering them essentially the same terms as those of his earlier treaties, Pike won a pact with the Osages on October 2 and with the Senecas, Shawnees and Quapaws two days later. Chief Ross was inclined to agree to these provisions too, but preferred to talk it over with his executive council at Tahlequah. There Pike and the Cherokee leadership, including Chief Stand Watie, met on October 7, 1861, and signed a treaty whereby the Cherokee Nation became a military ally of the Confederacy in its war against the United States. A delighted Pike extended to the Nation the right to send a delegate to the House of Representatives in Richmond, the same pledge he had made to the other four great tribes.[404]

Pike's triumphant work in securing all of these Indian treaties did much to help keep the Territory in Confederate hands throughout the war. More than that, it set the foundation for the harmonious relations between Southern white and red men that exist to this day. Indeed, when Atlanta acquired a major league baseball team in 1966 and named it the Braves, John Laughing Brook, descendant of Chief Watie, was present to throw out the first ball of the opening game.

CONFEDERATES PREPARE TO DEFEND TENNESSEE

Mid-May of 1861 was an important time for the Confederacy, politically and territorially, for within a two-week period no fewer than four states seceded from the Union and became part of the Southern nation. In both Tennessee and Arkansas, the state legislatures passed ordinances of secession on May 6; Missouri followed on the twelfth; and North Carolina adopted secession on May 20. For the time being—that is, until Kentucky joined

---

404 Walter Lee Brown, *A Life of Albert Pike* (Fayetteville AR, 1997), pp. 361-71; Kenny A. Franks, *Stand Watie and the Triumph of the Cherokee Nation* (Memphis: Memphis State University Press, 1979), 119.

the Confederacy in November 1861—Tennessee and Missouri accordingly formed the northern borders of the Southern republic. Even Kentucky teetered toward disunion in the summer of '61, but while the state's divided citizenry sorted out its loyalties and interests, Confederates to the south prepared for war.

In Tennessee, military preparations had begun well before Governor Harris announced the state's "military league" with the Confederacy on May 7 (the very day after legislative session). At Memphis, a powerful committee of public safety was established to direct the procuring of war materials and the forming of military companies. Seventy such companies had organized across the state by the first of May. Passage of the Army Bill came a few days later, when the Tennessee legislature called for 25,000 men to be armed immediately, and another 30,000 to be placed on reserve. Recruiting officers were soon overwhelmed, and by May 9 the state army numbered at least 5,000 troops. Six weeks later Governor Harris proudly announced the formation of fully twenty-four regiments of infantry and cavalry.

The Volunteer State thus had no shortage of volunteers, but for a while it faced an acute shortage of weapons. Because there was no Federal arsenal located within their borders, Tennesseans had no ready cache of weaponry, save for the 8,000 outdated flintlock muskets stored away in the state arsenal at Nashville. In all of Tennessee there were thought to be only two pieces of artillery, and those were small six-pounders—virtual pop-guns when it came to meet the Yankees. The Confederate government, however, quickly helped out by sending percussion cap rifles, cartridges and field artillery as well as heavier ordnance.

More important in the long run were the steps taken by Tennesseans to arm themselves. One of the Governor's first actions was to create an Ordnance Bureau to procure weapons and ammunition. Fortunately, the state possessed in abundance both raw resources and manufacturing capability. In the caves of the Cumberland and Unaka mountain ranges lay rich deposits of saltpeter, needed to make gunpowder. East of Cleveland, near Ducktown, a wide vein of copper promised the metal needed for percussion caps and bronze cannon barrels. Copious deposits of lead lay in the Appalachian Valley. And between the Cumberland and Tennessee Rivers lay the most extensive iron-producing facilities in the entire South.

Nashville, capital of the state, with a population of 17,000, soon became the western Confederacy's leading manufacturing center for military supplies. Artillery, muskets, percussion caps, cartridges, saddles, blankets and other equipment were produced. "Reversing the biblical formula," as Stanley Horn has written, the Nashville Plow Works converted over to making swords.[405] The city also held two cannon foundries, one of which began turning out prized rifled guns. Northwest of the capital, gunpowder mills operated along the Cumberland River; their service was so valuable that the state government took them over in the summer of '61. In Memphis, too, factories and foundries manufactured small arms and cannon. Eventually, warehouses in Nashville, Memphis and Chattanooga bulged with weaponry, munitions, uniforms, tents and tons of foodstuffs. An army's equipage was thus available in Tennessee, and soon there had formed an army as well. All that was needed was sound military leadership.

Recognizing his own lack of military experience, Governor Harris on May 24 appointed Gideon Pillow as senior major general to command the state forces. Pillow had served in the Mexican War, but he had gotten his commission through friendship with President Polk. Similarly, in 1861, Pillow benefitted from his friendship with Isham Harris, who responded more to Pillow's prestige as political leader and lawyer (Harris and Pillow once shared law offices) than as soldier. Neither Harris nor Pillow, in fact, had received any formal military training. Some Tennesseans consequently scoffed at the presumption of the Governor and his pal to assume direction of the state's military. Making it worse was a widely circulated story of Pillow's ineptitude in the Mexican War, when General Pillow ordered his men to entrench against the

---

405   Stanley F. Horn, *The Army of Tennessee: A Military History* (Indianapolis, 1941), p. 75.

Mexicans—but he had them dig their ditch on the wrong side of the breastworks. The national press had gotten hold of the story, and "Wrong-Way Pillow" became the laughingstock of the country.[406]

Pillow's wrong-waywardness resurfaced in the summer of 1861 when he and Governor Harris made their first strategic decisions for the defense of Tennessee. Rightly recognizing the prospect that Union forces would use the Mississippi as an amphibious invasion route, Pillow and Harris ordered forts built along the state's western border to contest enemy river traffic. Unfortunately, however, the General and Governor gave much less attention to the Cumberland and Tennessee Rivers, which eventually proved to be the Yankees' earliest invasion routes. Their mistake in choosing the wrong waterway to defend would have severe consequences for the Confederacy.

"HARPOON TO THE HEART"

Geography gave several military advantages to the Confederacy in the eastern theater of the war. Virginia's main rivers, such as the Rappahannock, ran west-east into the Chesapeake, offering a significant obstacle to Union armies marching on Richmond. Another route for offensive operations, the Shenandoah Valley, ran to the southwest, heading away from Richmond, the Federals' ultimate target, while giving Confederate General Robert E. Lee's army an ideal marching route into the North, as demonstrated in Lee's spectacular Maryland campaign of 1862. Defensively, the rugged terrain of western Virginia also helped the Southerners. After Confederates blunted the early Union offensive into the region in June-July 1861, they used the mountain ridges as fortresses to hold western Virginia against further Yankee incursions and to subdue the anti-Confederate, non-slaveholding populace for the rest of the war.

On the other hand, in the western theater—defined as the broad expanse between the Appalachians and the Mississippi (with the Trans-Mississippi as another subset of "the West")—geography,

---

406   Richard Bruce Winders, *Mr. Polk's Army: The American Military Experience in the Mexican War* (College Station: Texas A & M University Press, 1997), 43-44.

especially the region's river systems, gave Northerners important military advantages. Flowing into the lower Ohio Valley were the Cumberland and Tennessee Rivers. From their headwaters in the Smoky Mountains, the two broad tributaries crossed Tennessee and Kentucky before emptying into the Ohio River not far from one another. Plying the two waterways, steamboaters from the Ohio Valley before the war had practiced a busy traffic, transporting goods to Nashville, Florence, Decatur and Chattanooga. Not surprisingly, after Fort Sumter Northern strategists saw the Tennessee and Cumberland as excellent avenues for invading troops and the reinforcements, animals and supplies that would follow them. For forward-looking, railroad-minded Union planners, the Tennessee offered waterborne Federals a head-start in cutting the South's vital railway, the Memphis & Charleston, at multiple points in north Alabama. "A mere glance at the map," writes Allan Nevins, "would seem to reveal that the Tennessee-Cumberland river system offered the North a heaven-sent opportunity to thrust a harpoon into the very bowels of the Confederacy."[407]

Well, maybe not into the bowels, but certainly into the heartland of the Confederacy. It was historian Thomas Connelly who gave currency to "the heartland" (defined as Tennessee, north central Alabama and northeast Mississippi). In this broad territorial expanse Southerners, victorious in the initial battles of the war, endangered their quest for independence by failing to defend the riverine avenues into their country's heart. The story of how they failed, but rebounded from early reverses, must now occupy our attention.

Tennesseans Try To Guard Their Rivers

Most wartime observers figured that the Mississippi would be used by the North to cut through the Confederacy, by naval forces and amphibious troops from both upriver and the Gulf. Governor Harris and General Pillow reasoned likewise, and their early defensive arrangements followed accordingly, as fortification of the Mississippi began briskly. By the end of June, half a dozen

---

407   Richard Bruce Winders, *Mr. Polk's Army: The American Military Experience in the Mexican War* (College Station: Texas A & M University Press, 1997), 43-44.

forts had been built along the river. The first large garrison was positioned where the state lines of Tennessee, Kentucky and Missouri intersect near Island No. 10, so named as the tenth island south of the Ohio-Mississippi rivers' confluence. Then, a dozen miles downriver, two forts were built at New Madrid, Missouri. A long 115 miles farther south in Tennessee, Fort Pillow was erected on the first Chickasaw Bluff, about 35 miles north of Memphis. Ten miles to the south of Pillow, Fort Wright consisted of strong river batteries. Six miles above Memphis, more artillery was dug in at Fort Harris, and still more was placed on the bluffs at Memphis. Almost all the cannon in the state and a full 15,000 troops were thus committed to guarding Tennessee's western, waterbound boundary.

To be sure, Governor Harris was not blind to the importance of the Cumberland and Tennessee Rivers, which flowed northward into Kentucky and ultimately into the Ohio. Shortly after Tennessee's secession Harris appointed General Daniel S. Donelson (West Pointer and nephew of Andrew Jackson's wife) to begin selecting points on the two rivers for fortification. Observance of Kentucky's neutrality meant that Donelson had to choose sites as close to the state line as possible yet not north of it, but he found none that he considered militarily strong. On the Cumberland, Donelson nonetheless chose a high bluff on the west bank, about 40 miles from the river's confluence with the Ohio and about 75 miles from Nashville. But after that, progress on the proposed Fort Donelson (named after him at the Governor's insistence) proved exceedingly slow. For a time during June, only forty unarmed men occupied the place, building artillery embrasures; then it was abandoned altogether. In October, a little garrison of three companies was at last sent to the place with a battery of artillery. But there were no trained gunners on hand, and Donelson's works lay uncompleted (there were no entrenchments at all on the fort's land side). Thus Nashville's sole defense lay with 300 men and four cannon.

Things were even worse at the fort-site selected on the Tennessee River, to be named Fort Henry, for Confederate Senator Gustavus Henry. Twelve miles west of the fort named for himself, General Donelson and his engineers chose a site on the Tennessee far less desirable for fortification, but there was none better. On the east bank of the river, just south of the Kentucky line, they laid out positions for river batteries. In July Colonel Adolphus Heiman and the 10th Tennessee began construction. Well after work was under way, an experienced engineer, Captain Jesse Taylor, inspected the site of Fort Henry and was alarmed at his findings. For one, the entire position lay in danger of being flooded. In February, the customary rise of the Tennessee could be expected to submerge the river batteries in nine feet of water; the fort's highest point would be two feet under. Additional threats lay on Henry's landward side. To the north and east, well within rifle range, a line of hills commanded the parapet, offering strong positions to an enemy. Despite Taylor's report of these defects, however, work continued at Fort Henry; military planners in Nashville had no topographical alternative to consider.

The transfer of military matters from state authority failed to improve the situation. On July 13, the Confederacy received into national service all Tennessee troops. Richmond placed Major General Leonidas Polk in charge of a new "Department No. 2," encompassing the Mississippi Valley from the Kentucky border down to the Red River in Louisiana, with a little territory along the west bank of the Tennessee. ("No. 1" entailed southern Louisiana and Mississippi.) Polk, a West Point graduate, brought a trained perspective to the map board, but his authority was limited.[408] Though he conferred with Governor Harris on strategy, Polk had no authority over central or eastern Tennessee. He could therefore do little more than to reinforce Harris and Pillow's line of fortifications

---

408 Almost immediately after graduation from West Point in 1827, Polk had entered the Episcopal ministry and eventually became Bishop of Louisiana. In June of 1861, after he had accepted his Confederate general's commission, a friend stopped him and asked, "What! You a bishop, throw off the gown for the sword?" Polk replied, "No, sir, I buckle the sword over the gown" (Joseph E. Parks, *General Leonidas Polk, C.S.A.: The Fighting Bishop* [Baton Rouge, 1962], p. 170). While he served in the Confederate army Polk also retained his authority as clergyman. Wearing a bishop's robe over his uniform, he occasionally conducted religious services among his troops as well as baptizing Confederate officers. His enduring contribution to Confederate culture today is best seen at the University of the South, which he had helped found at Sewanee, Tennessee, in 1860. After the war Sewanee assumed prominence among Confederate institutions of higher learning, leading to the current international prestige of the University of the South.

along the Mississippi River. Forts Henry and Donelson meanwhile lay incomplete with skeletal garrisons. And in east Tennessee, a mere fifteen companies of recruits were assigned to hold the region, even though through it ran the Confederacy's major east-west railway. Not until September, when General Albert Sidney Johnston took charge in the western theater, did the military outlook for Tennessee begin to improve.

KENTUCKY DECLARES NEUTRALITY

A strategic problem that faced Harris and Pillow, then Polk, then Johnston, was what to do with Kentucky. More than any other border state in '61 Kentucky represented a house divided against itself, with a citizenry which was almost equally split, as pro-Southern as it was pro-Northern. Once a part of Virginia, the state had sentimental ties to the Old Dominion. Yet Kentucky also lay in the Ohio Valley, where many of her people had spread out into areas of the old Northwest Territory (*e. g.*, Abraham Lincoln born in Kentucky, moved to Illinois, now to the White House). In the several decades before the war, Kentuckians found themselves linked economically both to the lower South, *via* the Mississippi for transit of crops and goods, but also to the Northwest and Northeast by the nation's increasingly effective railroad system. In past politics, her people prided themselves (with Thomas Jefferson) for the Kentucky Resolutions that had laid the theoretical groundwork for secession back in 1798; but they also cherished the tradition of Henry Clay, the "Great Compromiser" who had worked in 1820 and 1850 to hold the Union together.

Now, with the Union finally torn apart, Kentuckians faced the decision of which side to join. Many favored secession, at least in principle; just as many opposed it. In the state legislature advocates of Union and disunion were perfectly balanced: in the senate, nineteen to nineteen; among the ninety-odd members of the House, unionists commanded a majority of all of one vote. Governor Beriah Magoffin had responded to Lincoln's call for troops with ringing refusal ("I say emphatically Kentucky will furnish no troops....") At the same time, even as he opposed Northern coercion, Magoffin had also counseled other Southern governors against secession.

In this quandary, the best way out seemed to be joining neither side. This common-sense approach was so novel that it flabbergasted both Federal and Confederate governments—but Kentucky did it anyway. On May 16 the House resolved that "this State and the citizens thereof should take no part in the Civil War now being waged, except as mediators, and as friends to the belligerent parties; and Kentucky should during the contest, occupy a position of strict neutrality." The Senate ratified the measure and on May 20 Governor Magoffin issued his Proclamation of Neutrality.[409] Before adjourning on May 24 the legislature added one last affirmation, that "Kentucky will not sever her connections with the national Government, nor take up arms for either belligerent party; but arm herself for the preservation of peace within her borders."[410]

Ironically, Unionists and secessionists both agreed that the state should make preparations to defend herself against either side, or both of them. After wrangling about who would sit on a five-man militia board, the legislature appropriated money for arms and equipment, and divided it between the two camps: the Home Guards, who were pro-Union, and the State Guard, which was pro-Confederate. Recruiting and drilling thus took place in an atmosphere of friendly rivalry, although both sides made a show of respecting the state's neutrality. Led by Simon Bolivar Buckner, West Pointer, Mexican War hero and state rights Democrat, the pro-Confederate State Guards assembled just south of the Kentucky-Tennessee line, outside Clarksville at "Camp Boone." Unionist Kentuckians responded to Lincoln's call for volunteers by organizing across the Ohio River as the 1st and 2d Kentucky Union Regiments at "Camp Joe Holt" in Indiana, opposite Louisville.

---

409   Lowell H. Harrison, "Confederate Kentucky," *Civil War Times Illustrated,* April 1973, p. 14.

410   Stanley F. Horn, *The Army of Tennessee: A Military History* (Indianapolis, 1941), p. 41.

General Buckner went to the greatest lengths trying to prevent a clash of arms. He travelled to Washington as official emissary from Governor Magoffin and secured an interview with Abraham Lincoln. In it he thought he heard the President affirm an unwavering stance to respect Kentuckians' neutrality. (Lincoln later denied it.) Buckner also went to Cincinnati to meet with General George McClellan, commanding the Department of Ohio, and came away hearing the same thing (though McClellan also later denied it). Buckner then, acting as intermediary for his troubled state, reported the Northerners' reassurances to Governor Harris, urging that Tennesseans not advance into his commonwealth. Commendably, he took further action. When pro-Southern citizens of Columbus, Kentucky, voiced their alarm at a rumored Yankee excursion from Cairo across the river, and pleaded with Governor Harris to send Tennessee troops there, Buckner intervened and sent instead six companies of the Kentucky State Guard under Colonel Lloyd Tilghman to quell the unrest. Buckner was determined to abide by the legislature's dictum that state forces be used only to preserve the so-called public tranquility.

Meanwhile, even Rebels south of the border voiced their support for Kentuckians' efforts at "neutrality." In August, a lot of Nashvilleans gathered to adopt a resolution stating that "Our people are anxious to avoid this conflict, and have assembled to-day to say to the people of Kentucky, if she cannot go with us, that she maintain her neutrality inviolate and not permit the formation of Federal camps in her territory and the transmission of Federal soldiers, arms and munitions across her territory to invade Tennessee."[411]

From their respective capitals, Abraham Lincoln and Jefferson Davis thus reacted to Kentucky's delicate situation in the best political way, by not rocking the boat. Both presidents, interestingly enough, were Kentuckians, born less than a hundred miles apart. Neither president wanted to take any action that would send his

---

411   *Ibid.,* p. 43.

native state into the enemy column. Border state "neutrality" may have been a political figment, but for the time, both sides strained to respect it.

FEDERALS BREAK THE NEUTRALITY

It was Lincoln who blundered first, or rather his minions, when they set up a recruiting camp on Kentucky soil. In mid-August, William "Bull" Nelson, a Unionist organizer, established Camp Dick Robinson northeast of Danville for the expressed purpose of enlisting soldiers in the Union army. When Magoffin protested to Washington, Lincoln on August 24 refused to close the camp or halt enlistments, claiming that Nelson as a citizen of the state had a right to conduct his affairs without government interference, and citing the state legislature's resolution that Kentuckians were entitled to arm themselves in the interest of keeping the peace in a volatile atmosphere. Lincoln even saw that 10,000 muskets were sent to Nelson, which further enraged Magoffin, Buckner and other pro-Southerners, not to mention genuinely neutralist Kentuckians (if there were any left). The state legislature, however, avoided voicing protest to Washington. In elections held August 5, pro-Unionists had won both houses in enough of a margin to block a resolution from the Governor calling on Washington to cease its belligerent activity.

Taking advantage of the situation, Brig. Gen. Robert Anderson (of Sumter fame), commanding the Federal Department of Kentucky from Cincinnati, on September 1 rashly moved his headquarters to Louisville. Pro-Confederates howled in protest, but without authorization from Richmond to conduct countermeasures, they felt compelled to take no action. This changed after Maj. Gen John C. Fremont, Union commander at St. Louis, committed the blunder that would cost him his command. On August 28 Fremont placed newly commissioned Brig. Gen. Ulysses S. Grant in charge of the District of Southeast Missouri, with headquarters at Cairo, Illinois. In his initial orders Fremont advised that Grant should prepare to move across the river and occupy Columbus or Paducah before the Rebels got there. Both places were militarily important—Columbus was a river town situated on high bluffs overlooking the Mississippi twenty miles north of the Tennessee line; Paducah's strategic importance came from its location at the confluence of the Ohio and Tennessee Rivers. With Kentucky's neutrality unraveling, Fremont figured that the side which acted first and took possession of either of these big prizes would gain a big advantage. As it happened, arriving in Cairo on September 4 and assuming command, Grant received news (erroneous) that the Rebels were moving on Columbus and may already have occupied it. The young commander imprudently accepted the reports as fact and determined to parry by seizing Paducah. Grant ordered two Illinois infantry regiments and an artillery battery to board transports and on the morning of September 5, escorted by the gunboats *Tyler* and *Conestoga,* steamed up the Ohio 45 miles and landed at Paducah, declaring the town under U.S. military authority.

Thus was Kentucky, officially "neutral," first invaded by "hostile forces," AKA United States soldiers. After the war, when the enormity of the blunder was recognized by Northerners combing through the events leading to their defeat, Grant would claim that his departmental commander in St. Louis, General Fremont, had ordered him to occupy Paducah. Fremont would always deny it. Lincoln eventually blamed Fremont and fired him, and since then the hapless "Pathfinder" has taken the rap for the North's loss of Kentucky. As recent historian Steven Woodworth has put it, "Fremont's program of occupying Paducah during the first month of September showed all the political acumen of a walleyed pike."[412]

SOUTHERN REACTION

In Frankfort, Governor Magoffin and the legislature could do little as their state's neutrality in the civil war shredded away. The Governor had already found Lincoln heedless to protests against Nelson's and Anderson's early moves, so this time he did not even send a telegram to Washington. The legislature was not then in

---

412   Steven E. Woodworth, *Nothing But Victory: The Army of the Tennessee 1861-1863* (New York, 2005), p. 34.

session, and anyway the pro-Union majority in both houses would have prevented passage of any resolution protesting Grant's seizure of Paducah.

With the charade finally torn off, Confederates at last felt entitled to a military advance into the state. Southern historians have agreed with their course. "The impetuous Gideon Pillow had wanted to seize Columbus as early as May, but he had been dissuaded by Buckner," records the state's historian, Lowell Harrison, complimenting Confederate officials for their forbearance.[413] After his assumption of command in July, General Polk too had been eyeing the river bluffs of Columbus as a formidable defensive position, but President Davis instructed him in unequivocal terms to take no action into Kentucky until the Yankees acted first. When they did—Polk learned of Grant's strike, quickly telegraphed on the afternoon of the 5th—the Confederate commander did not even wire Richmond before ordering Gideon Pillow, from his base at Union City, Tennessee, to cross the border with a force of 2,300 infantry, cavalry and artillery. Pillow covered the twenty-five miles in a fast overnight march which put Confederates in control of Columbus by the afternoon of September 6. That night Polk wired Richmond, announcing the long-anticipated movement, stressing its retaliatory nature. "We are here," he wrote," "not by choice, but by necessity."[414]

Kentuckians were forced to agree: the North had broken the neutrality, the South had reacted. General Polk even won laurels among some Kentuckians for having held back until the Union army had established its outpost in the state. Still, some hoped that both sides would just go away. A Frankfort paper on September 9 voiced its distress: "Do we intend to maintain our neutrality in good faith? If we do, shall we suffer either belligerent to remain on our soil? Our opinion is emphatically that the Legislature should require both sides to withdraw."

---

413   Lowell H. Harrison, *The Civil War in Kentucky* (Lexington, 1975), p. 12.

414   Joseph H. Parks, *General Leonidas Polk, C.S.A.: The Fighting Bishop* (Baton Rouge, 1962), p. 184.

Meanwhile in Washington, Lincoln worried over the consequences of Fremont's and Grant's first strike. As he told a friend, "I hope to have God on my side, but I must have Kentucky."[415] The President wrote Orville Browning later in September, "I think to lose Kentucky is nearly the same as to lose the whole game. Kentucky gone, we cannot hold Missouri, nor, as I think, Maryland. These all against us, and the job on our hands is too large for us. We would as well consent to separation at once, including the surrender of the capital."[416]

For another year, the Bluegrass State would be the arena for a high-stakes contest of military and political maneuvering that neither side could afford to lose. As subsequent events showed, Lincoln would hold onto his capital and to Maryland, but he would lose Kentucky when, placed under Confederate military control by General Sidney Johnston, the state finally seceded in the fall of 1861.

END OF THE HARNEY-PRICE TRUCE

The highly publicized truce in Missouri that Generals Price and Harney had rigged up in St. Louis on May 20, 1861, lasted all of three weeks. The Harney-Price agreement was really farcical, even hypocritical; for while it postured as a humanitarian effort to preserve peace in a much-conflicted border state, it was really a self-serving ploy by both sides to forestall fighting till they had recruited and armed more soldiers. During the truce General Price and Governor Jackson completed the transfer of the Missouri State Guard to Confederate authority. Recruiting continued full-tilt as pro – Southern Missourians rushed to join the C.S. regiments being raised around the state.[417] In areas of pro-Northern feeling, Union

---

415   Stanley F. Horn, *The Army of Tennessee: A Military History* (Indianapolis, 1941), pp. 45-46.

416   James Lee McDonough, *The War in Kentucky: From Shiloh to Perryville* (Knoxville, 1994), p. 61.

417   One Confederate company, the "Marion Rangers," raised in the area of Hannibal, became famous as the one in which Samuel L. Clemens ("Mark Twain") enlisted. Twain's war service was made brief by poor health and a medical discharge in the fall of 1861. As world-renowned novelist and humorist after the war, Twain ranks with Faulkner and Wolfe as one of Confederate letters' most distinguished figures. His greatest *postbellum* service to the South was in helping to publish Robert E. Lee's memoirs in 1886. After the General died, Twain learned of his

men rallied to Home Guards units. Despite the formal secession of Missouri on May 12 these companies and regiments drilled openly in numerous towns, flaunting the Stars and Stripes and flouting Confederate authority. Federal military presence in St. Louis became so overt that most Southern sympathizers were forced to leave. The city virtually turned into an armed Union camp, destined to be a U.S. army base of operations for the entire war.

The leadership of both sides looked for outside help. Sterling Price called on Montgomery and Little Rock to send reinforcements: soon sizable columns of Arkansas infantry and cavalry were on their way. William Harney called on Washington and Springfield to send reinforcements from Illinois. None would be coming, at least any time soon. Then Harney received worse news. The key Union leaders in Missouri, fanatical Nathaniel Lyon and ambitious Frank Blair, excoriated Harney for having arranged a cease-fire. To friends in Washington, both in the Lincoln administration and the Congress, they viciously attacked Harney as senile, slothful and naïve. The President picked up on this talk and began to fear for Missouri's loyal citizens, especially the German-American contingent. Lincoln therefore had Adjutant General Lorenzo Thomas write Harney on May 27 warning him to be "unceasingly watchful" and ready to give battle when ordered to march out.[418] After this, it was relatively easy for Lyon and Blair to persuade Lincoln that Harney would dawdle endlessly before taking any such action, and that Harney needed dismissal, not

---

reminiscences, which Lee had quietly written several years after the war and entrusted to a former Confederate Brigadier, Armistead Long. Twain persuaded the latter to edit the manuscript, then helped bring it to print. The resulting *Memoirs of Robert E. Lee* (ed. Long; St. Louis, 1886) brought Mrs. Lee, largely through Twain's doing, the largest royalty check ($200,000) ever written up to that time in either of the American republics (Steve Davis, "Mark Twain, the War, and General Lee's Memoirs," *Southern Studies*, vol. 18 [1979], 231-39).

418   *O.R.,* vol. 3, 376. For this and other actions in 1861, Allan Nevins, noted U.S. historian, has harshly criticized Lyon and Blair. Without these bullying schemes, Nevins believes that Missouri might well have stayed in the Union. As it was, referring to the headstrong duo, the historian opines, "In great part, the horrors and losses from which this unhappiest of States was to suffer were traceable to their precipitate, intolerable course" (Nevins, *The War for the Union* (6 vols., New York, 1959), vol. 3, 128.

direction. The President complied. Blair presented Harney with his walking papers on May 30 and the disgraced General packed his bags.

Lyon, who had been made brigadier general on the 17th and who took over as Union commander in the state, wasted no time in acting. First thing he wanted was to get rid of Harney's noxious pact with Price. Rather than abrogate the agreement single-handedly, he called the Confederate leader to a parley in St. Louis. Price accepted, although he already knew the outcome of any talks with a hot-head like Lyon. Accompanied by Governor Jackson, he boarded the train from Jefferson City, and arrived at St. Louis' Planter's House Hotel on the afternoon of June 11. The next morning Price, Jackson, Lyon and Blair sat down for their talks. Rather, Price and Jackson did the sitting; for after allowing them to restate briefly their hope for maintaining a truce, General Lyon stood and ranted acidly on his predecessor's gullibility, the Rebels' duplicity, and his personal desire to see bloodshed commence for a violent resolution of Missourians' competing allegiances. A secretary in the corner of the room took down his words:

> Rather than concede to the State of Missouri for one single instant the right to dictate to my government in any matter, however unimportant, I would see you, and you [Jackson, then Price] and you, and you [he included Blair and the recorder], and every man, woman, and child in the State, dead and buried!

Then, as if Jackson and Price had said or done anything to provoke this torrent of bellicosity—they had not—Lyon concluded, before a visibly astonished Frank Blair, "This means war. In an hour one of my officers will call for you and conduct you out of my lines."[419]

Price and Jackson needed no escort. Well within thirty minutes they were *en route* back to Jefferson City. Before they stepped off the train, the Confederate leaders had formed their overall plan.

---

419   Albert Castel, *General Sterling Price and the Confederate War in the West* (Baton Rouge, 1968), p. 24.

It was not very aggressive. General Price took stock of the Union Guards' reported strength in the area of Jefferson City against the scattered disposition of his forces, then determined to give up the state capital. Governor Jackson reluctantly accepted this move as a temporary tactical imperative. Price accordingly ordered his district commanders to march their troops to Boonville, forty miles upriver. Once concentrated there, and reinforced by Confederate columns from Arkansas, Price hoped to march against Lyon, retake Jefferson City, and maybe even march on St. Louis. Jackson went along with this. After drafting a proclamation inveighing against the "unconstitutional edicts of the military despotism at Washington," and urging Missourians to rally to the Confederate cause, the Governor began issuing instructions for the removal of state records and evacuation of his capital.[420]

Lyon made plans of his own. Learning of the Rebels' intent to abandon Jefferson City, he determined to lead a force out of St. Louis to take the capital, and install a loyalist state government to replace the one that Claiborne Jackson and his secesh legislators were carrying with them in their wagons and saddlebags. Simultaneously he directed a second Union column under Col. Franz Sigel to advance by rail to Rolla and from there march against an enemy force said to be organizing in southwestern Missouri. In this way Lyon hoped Sigel would block the route of Rebel reinforcements from Arkansas while he attacked Price's forces, dispersed them, and seized control of the rest of the Missouri Valley. With possible help from Federal forces at Cairo, Illinois and Fort Scott, Kansas, Lyon even contemplated the conquering of the entire state. It was a bold design, befitting the bold Union general.

Fortis fortuna adiuvat, the Romans used to say: success favors the bold (at least initially). And that's what happened in Missouri. Within twenty-four hours after storming out of the Planter's House, Lyon had boarded his regiments onto riverboats and was steaming toward Jefferson City. Governor Jackson packed his last papers and scurried out of the capital on June 14, along with legislators

---

420   Robert E. Shalhope, *Sterling Price: Portrait of a Southerner* (Columbia MO, 1971), p. 166.

and government workers following the gubernatorial entourage upriver. Federal troops marched into the city on the next day, to the cheers of thousands of German-Americans jamming the riverfront. On the seventeenth, he landed 2,000 men at Boonville, expecting to take Price on for a fight. The Confederate commander, however, had fallen sick and boarded an ambulance to Lexington. Colonel John S. Marmaduke was left behind with 500 men to oppose the Yankees. Outnumbered four-to-one, Marmaduke's men barely presented a skirmish line to Lyon's advancing army. After delivering a few obligatory volleys, the Confederates quickly retreated westward.

The Federals' twin triumphs at Jefferson City and Boonville boosted the Missouri Unionists' spirits immensely. They had a correspondingly depressing effect on Confederate morale. An ailing Price issued orders for Southern units being formed north of the Missouri to make their way south as best they could. Meanwhile Price, bedridden with recurring fevers, temporarily handed command of the state troops over to Governor Jackson. The latter began to fret over holding Lexington, and so spread the word that the Confederates' point of concentration should be south of the Osage River, well out of harm's way. He therefore ordered his temporary state capital to be set up at Lamar—over a hundred miles south of Lexington. To Lamar the Governor led the Confederate "Army of Missouri," a still as-yet poorly trained assemblage of some 4,000 State Guards yet to receive Confederate uniforms. Worse, the way it was heading—Jackson expected soon that he would have to give up Lamar as Lyon and Sigel pressed down upon him—the Confederate Amy of Missouri might soon be pushed out of Missouri itself.

THE SOUTHERNERS REBOUND

Fifty miles south of Lamar at Pineville, in the extreme southwest corner of Missouri, Sterling Price waited for reinforcements from Arkansas. Tennessee-Texan Ben McCulloch, a newly minted Confederate brigadier, was said to be leading several regiments, including one from Louisiana. Arkansas Brigadier General

Nicholas B. Pearce was on his way with perhaps 2,000 volunteers. Captain James McIntosh would bring in some cavalry; other scattered companies began arriving into Price's camp almost daily.

Watching his enemies from afar, Nathaniel Lyon determined to strike before the Rebels did. After occupying Boonville, the impetuous Union leader readied his men for an overland march and set out southward in the general direction of Jackson and his renegade state forces. In the meantime he ordered Franz Sigel, already at Rolla, to head toward Carthage (fifteen miles south of Lamar) and intercept Jackson *en route* to his presumed junction with Price.

Sigel and Jackson collided at Carthage on July 5. The odds at Boonville were now reversed, with the Southerners enjoying a better than fourfold advantage in numbers. Not counting the state legislators and other civilian hangers-on which he had brought with him, the Governor commanded 4,375 men and seven pieces of artillery. Jackson's troops had been grouped into four unequal divisions. Brig. Gen. James S. Rains led 1,203 infantry and artillerymen, plus 608 cavalry. Lt. John B. Clark led 365 militiamen. William Y. Slack's command included 700 infantry and 500 cavalry; Mosby M. Parsons' mustered just shy of a thousand men and a battery. Most of the men were armed with the shiny new Springfields captured at the St. Louis arsenal in April, although they had not received a whole lot of training in their use. Along with the flintlocks and shotguns carried by several hundred volunteers, the lack of uniforms (yet to be provided by the C.S. government) gave Jackson's "army" a ragged appearance indeed. Homespun or broadcloth was worn by officers and enlistees alike, with the former distinguishing themselves by a bit of red flannel or swatch of cloth stitched to their arms or shoulders as their only visible sign of rank and authority.

On the other side, the Federals looked much snappier. Sigel had with him 1,100 men, almost all of them German-speaking immigrants. Arranged in the impressive gray uniforms of the St. Louis Home Guards, they carried muskets tipped with bayonets, "Dutch lightning rods," the Missouri Confederates called them.

Thus armed, they presented a formidable appearance on the parade ground, where Sigel had drilled them incessantly. Now, confident in his troops and made bold by the opportunity to strike Jackson's motley bunch, the Union commander forgot about arithmetic and resolved to attack the numerically superior Southerners.

The ebullient Sigel apparently also forgot about the element of surprise, for Jackson's little army, just north of Carthage, was ready for battle. After celebrating Independence Day in Carthage, the Federals marched out the next morning and soon encountered the Rebels, deployed and massed. Sigel opened the fight in fine European fashion, his two batteries cannonading the secesh line while his columns wheeled smartly in formation. There would be no clash of infantry, though. While his six-pounders replied to Union shellfire, Jackson sent his horsemen around both flanks toward the enemy rear. Sigel soon realized his danger of being cut off and ordered a withdrawal from the field. The Germans made their hurried way out of the trap and Sigel kept the Southern horsemen at bay through skillful use of artillery. Jackson ordered his infantry forward, but the Confederates' lack of training showed when their pursuit slackened and eventually halted altogether. Jackson's cavalry nipped at the Yankees for the rest of the day until it, too, gave up the chase. By nightfall, having covered eighteen miles under a hot sun, Sigel's men were safe, if footsore, as they pitched camps along the road to Springfield.

Casualty-wise, Carthage proved not to be much of a battle. Union losses were 13 killed, 21 wounded; Confederates suffered 74 dead, wounded or missing. In his dispatches on the engagement of July 5, Sigel emphasized not so much the engagement as his masterful retreat from it, bringing his command away from an overwhelming Rebel force. For this achievement, the Union commander apparently expected much praise, such as he had won back in Europe when, as a young soldier in the German insurrection of 1848 he had conducted a "brilliant retreat" to the fortress of Rastadt. Most observers, however, were unimpressed by Sigel's performance at Carthage. An unhappy newspaper editor in St. Louis suggested that the German-Americans under his command should change their motto from "I fights mit Sigel' to "I retreats mit

Sigel." General Lyon was disappointed too. He confided to a friend that "after Rastadt he [Sigel] seemed bent only upon conducting brilliant retreats, and that from Carthage greatly helped to confirm this tendency."[1] Washington had a different view. Encouraged by President Lincoln himself, the War Department bought Sigel's line and promoted him to brigadier general.

Confederates were exhilarated by their success, small as it had comparatively been. Governor Jackson proclaimed a major victory, even though it really was not one. Nonetheless, the news from Carthage stirred General Price out of his sickbed and brought him, plus several thousand enthusiastic recruits, into a junction with the Governor's forces. The Southerners sensed that the tide had turned. Driven out of Jefferson City and Boonville, the Confederates had retreated to the southwestern part of the state. Lyon and Sigel held the initiative, and seemed on the verge of taking control of all of Missouri. At Carthage, though, the Southerners began to reverse their fortunes, as events of the next several months would tell.

Lyon Plans an Attack

For starters, General Price and Governor Jackson had put together a respectable army. In the several weeks after Carthage, the forces of Price, McCulloch, Pearce and McIntosh united with those of Jackson near Neosho, the little town that the Governor now dubbed his state capital. By the end of July, the "Army of Missouri" had indeed become an army of over 10,000 men, mostly Missourians and Arkansans—no one had yet a firm count, the aggregation had come together so quickly. But all suspected they had a much larger force than the Federals possessed in Lyon's and Sigel's combined columns. Furthermore, weapons, uniforms and other supplies began arriving from the Confederate Ordnance and Quartermaster Departments. Arriving from Richmond also was Sterling Price's commission as major general, which placed him in command of the army. With the help of McCulloch and other subordinates, Price enforced discipline and mandated rigorous drill. The army took on such an impressive trim that General Price felt a new confidence, even to the point of taking the offensive against the Yankees.

The Federals, on the other hand, were beginning to experience problems, starting at the top levels of command. Since dismissing General Harney, President Lincoln had felt the need for an officer to manage affairs in Missouri. Lyon was too impetuous; that much he had shown at Camp Jackson in May. Moreover, Lyon's presence in the field with his troops had left an administrative void at departmental headquarters in St. Louis. To fill it the President searched the field of available generals and ended up doing what he so often did throughout the war: he picked a politician.

John C. Fremont had by the time of the war developed a reputation as "mercurial, headstrong and unstable."[421] At the age of eighteen he was expelled from college, but through high-placed friends won an army commission in the topographical engineers, though he was without military education. He gained fame as an explorer of the western territories, earning the popular nickname "The Pathfinder." His marriage in 1841 to the daughter of powerful Missouri Senator Thomas Hart Benton began to feed his political ambitions; Jessie seemed always coaxing him to "assert himself." In the Mexican War he helped lead the conquest of California, and was appointed military governor. He grew rich when gold was discovered on his California lands; building on his wealth and "pathfinder" popularity, he was elected as one of the state's first senators in 1850. Six years later, when the newly formed Republican Party ran its first presidential nominee, Fremont got the nod and polled an astonishing 1.3 million votes to Democrat James Buchanan's 1.6 million. In the summer of 1861, as Lincoln sought to strengthen his control over the Republican Party, Fremont emerged as a powerful ally deserving of a prominent post. And Fremont, a lover of military pomp and gaudy uniforms, wanted it in the army. Hence came his commission as major general and Lincoln's orders to clear the Rebels out of Missouri.

There were indications from the start, however, that Fremont had other things on his mind. His impressive showing in the presidential election of 1856 apparently fed his continued aspiration

---

421   Ezra J. Warner, *Generals in Blue: Lives of the Union Commanders* (Baton Rouge, 1964), p. 160.

to high office; his ambitious wife may also have been murmuring in his ear. Thus, three weeks after receiving his orders for Missouri, Fremont was in New York, of all places, wooing political friends with his gilt braid and fancy uniform. Finally, General Scott had to order him out west. When he arrived in St. Louis July 25 he ensconced himself at the city's finest estate and proceeded to fill the place with cronies and hangers-on whose main business was helping Fremont build a power base among German-Americans in the area. Military affairs took a back seat to political ambition, and the Union cause in Missouri suffered accordingly. While General Lyon, with his small army in the interior of the state, bombarded Fremont's headquarters with urgent requests for more men, shoes and artillery, the Generalissimo in St. Louis was fixed on filling the Brandt Mansion with a virtually regal court of so many Germans that English was seldom heard within its halls. When Fremont finally turned his attention to military matters at all, he pondered not only running Jackson's and Price's Rebel army out of the state, but conquering the entire Mississippi Valley—a grand feat which, if accomplished, would again propel him toward the White House, which was his real goal.

Lyon meanwhile pressed south of the Osage River toward a union with Sigel. Despairing of any assistance from St. Louis, Lyon decided to force the issue with Price on his own. With him were some 4,400 troops: German-American Home Guards under Major Peter J. Osterhaus, three Missouri infantry regiments, Kansans from Fort Leavenworth (including mounted infantry) and a six-gun battery of U.S. regulars under Captain James Totten, nicknamed "Bottle-nose" for his ever-present liquor flask. Totten's drinking was very evident in the march on Springfield. Feeling his brandy under the hot summer sun, Bottle-nose trumpeted orders with an imperious profanity: "Forward that caisson, God damn you, sir," or "Swing that piece in line, God damn you, sir."[422]

After joining Sigel at Springfield on August 1, Lyon had about 5,500 troops, knowingly facing a Rebel force double his strength.

---

422   Jay Monaghan, *Civil War on the Western Border 1854-1863* (Boston, 1955), p. 144.

Despite Lyon's pleas for reinforcements, Fremont refused to send any. With 15,943 soldiers in his entire department, according to his adjutant, the Union commander in St. Louis faced multiple threats. Guerrillas were starting to rise up in northern Missouri. In the southeast part of the state, a self-proclaimed Rebel "Swamp Fox," Jeff Thompson, was stirring up trouble with a growing band of followers. Worst of all were the rumors that a large Confederate column, 12,000 strong, was being fitted out by Generals William J. Hardee and Gideon Pillow in northeast Arkansas for a march into Missouri, toward Ironton. This latter seemed the direst threat, so Fremont ordered all the men he could spare, some 4,000, onto riverboats at St. Louis and headed downriver with them. Before departing he fired off a telegram to Lyon, explaining once and for all that no reinforcements would be sent. If Lyon could not advance against the enemy with his present force, Fremont urged that he should retire to Rolla, the railhead 120 miles to his rear.

Retreat was unthinkable to Lyon. His other choices were to attack the Rebels, known to be eight or ten miles away, or dig in at Springfield and await their attack. On August 8 he called his officers to headquarters for a discussion of these options. Everyone recognized the problem of sitting still. The men's three-month enlistments were running out and with the Union cause in Missouri very much in doubt, many volunteers were not going to re-up. Two regiments had already left and even half of Sigel's Germans were packing up to go home. Lyon determined that now was the time to move, before the army drifted apart. By now, too, word had reached them of the Union disaster at Manassas, and Lyon's officers were determined not to add another setback to the cause. As Col. Thomas W. Sweeny said, "Let us eat the last bit of mule flesh and fire the last cartridge before we think of retreating."[423] So it was decided to attack. Though dramatically outnumbered— and some camp rumors had the Rebels numbering as many as 15,000—the Federals stood a good chance of success if they caught the Secesh by surprise, and could defeat a part of Price's army

---

423   William Riley Brooksher, *Bloody Hill: The Battle of Wilson's Creek* (Washington, 1995), p. 172.

before the rest of it came up. Lyon listened to their ideas, then dismissed his subordinates with a promise to distribute his battle plan the next morning.

The plan he came up with did not meet with favor. Its salient feature was Franz Sigel's daring idea, pressed upon Lyon after the officers' meeting, that the Federals should divide their forces and assail Price with a dawn attack from two directions. Lyon first disclosed the plan to his adjutant, Major John Schofield, explaining how Sigel would take his brigade of 1,200 and strike from the south, while the rest of the army hit the Rebels from the north. Schofield was incredulous. Already Lyon was outnumbered at least two-, maybe three-to-one; now he wanted to worsen those odds by dividing his command in the face of the enemy.

"Is Sigel willing to undertake this?" Schofield asked.

"Yes, it is his plan," Lyon said. Other officers protested, too. Captain Frederick Steele of the 2d U.S. Infantry was bluntest: "Sigel is incapable of commanding an individual unit. Moreover, the entire command is much too small to be weakened by splitting."[424]

It made no difference. Lyon had his plan, and gave orders for the men to march that evening. They would attack at dawn on the morrow, August 10.

THE BATTLE OF OAK HILL

Nine miles to the south, Sterling Price's army lay encamped along Wilson's Creek on the road from Springfield to Fayetteville. Price and McCulloch were toying with the idea of an attack of their own. On the ninth they even drew up orders for an advance against Springfield when a sudden rainfall caused a last-minute cancellation. Apparently, it did not occur to the Southern leaders that Lyon would beat them to the punch. Thus the Confederates were spread out in separate divisional camps along a two-mile stretch of Wilson's Creek. For the same reason Price ordered no cavalry posted on the army's periphery; even pickets were not thrown out.

---

424 Monaghan, *op. cit.*, pp. 165, 167.

The evening shower which brought the Confederates back into their camps late on the 9th did nothing to impede Lyon and Sigel's all-night march. Indeed, in a remarkable feat for green troops, the two Federal columns never got lost in the darkness, found their proper jump-off positions, and actually were in place before dawn, just as Lyon wanted. According to plan Sigel was to await the sound of gunfire from Lyon's attack before he launched his.

The Rebels were just starting to stir in the early light of August 10, drawing water from Wilson's Creek or foraging for corn in nearby fields, when Lyon's troops made their first contact, around 5:30, and opened fire on the scattered encampments of Rains' cavalrymen. An excited Southern officer took off to spread the word, and rode into Price's camp till he found Generals Price, McCulloch and Colonel James McIntosh breakfasting on roasted corn.

"Thirty thousand Yankees are attacking Rains' line!" he shouted.

"Oh, pshaw," McCulloch answered, justifiably skeptical of the news, especially the number of Yankees involved. "That's another of Rains' scares; I'll see about it when I finish breakfast."[425] But just then they heard the sound of cannon both to the north and south of them. Worse, they saw hundreds of Rains' men streaming toward them. The two generals were now convinced they were under attack. McCulloch galloped off to organize his forces across the creek. Price, buttoning his suspenders, ran for his horse (as fast as his 250 pounds' heft allowed him) to take charge of his troops at the base of Oak Hill.

Lyon had achieved his first objective, surprise. The First and Second Missouri with Captain Joseph Plummer's 1st U.S. Infantry had overrun Rains' camp at the extreme north of the Confederate position, and soon the disciplined Regulars were advancing with bayonets through a cornfield toward the Springfield road. Lyon and his main force—six regiments of Missouri, Iowa and Kansas infantry, backed by Totten's artillery—moved against Oak Hill, the key to the battlefield, and shortly after 6 a.m. succeeded in driving the last of Rains' troopers from it. Lyon brought up two batteries

---

425   Albert Castel, *General Sterling Price and the Confederate War in the West* (Baton Rouge, 1968), p. 41.

to strengthen his position on the hill, then ordered his infantry to continue advancing. But the Federals then ran up against the Confederate line being patched together by Price: the infantry of Clark's, Slack's and James McBride's divisions, four regiments of Missouri State Guards under Colonel Richard Weightman, two batteries and some of Rains' cavalrymen, now rallied and on the right flank, near the creek. Troops in the line numbered some 3,000, enough to stabilize the situation and block Lyon's further advance, if not assume the offensive themselves. The battle for Oak Hill was on.

Sigel had meanwhile awaited the sound of Lyon's attack, having swung his column into position south of the encampment of Colonel T.J. Churchill's 1st Arkansas Mounted Rifles. At sunrise, after hearing Lyon's first report, he opened up with shellfire to catch the Arkansans totally off-guard. Sigel's Germans rushed in and chased Churchill's panicked men northward, across Skegg's Branch. The Federals, though, stopped well short of the stream. From the looks of things—disoriented Rebels milling southward, appearing dejected and beaten—Sigel assumed that Lyon was whipping Price and McCulloch up at Oak Hill, and that he would soon be pressing them southward. Blocking their retreat route, Sigel was in perfect position to form a defensive line and await his opportunity to crush the enemy in a vise as Lyon closed the trap. Besides, his troops were worn out from the night's march and had had no breakfast that morning. So when the men tarried in Churchill's camps, devouring the Rebels' half-cooked food, picking up their abandoned belongings or equipment, Sigel was disposed to let them. Thus by 8 o'clock in the morning, the Southern front in the battle of Oak Hill grew quiet, as Sigel awaited developments of Lyon's attack while his troops milled about with their coffee pots, biscuits and skewers of salt pork.

"Where is Sigel? What has happened to Sigel?" Lyon asked repeatedly, uncertain whether he should order a general advance or wait upon developments south of Oak Hill.[426] Meanwhile both sides engaged in a stationary firefight, exchanging musket and

---

426   Dee Brown, "Wilson's Creek," *Civil War Times Illustrated*, April 1972, p. 15.

artillery fire. In the thick woods of black jack, soldiers fought in loose formations behind trees and brush. General Price, wearing a linen duster and tall black woolen hat, was conspicuous along his lines, exhorting his men against "the damned Dutch." Bullets ripped his duster, one nicking his side. "That isn't fair," he growled to an aide. "If I were as slim as Lyon, that fellow would have missed me entirely."[427]

Lyon also took a slight wound in the foot. Someone noticed blood dripping from the General's heel and offered to help. Lyon waved him away, saying that the hurt was not serious, and rode back into the smoke of his infantrymen's musketry.

SIGEL IS KNOCKED OUT OF THE FIGHT

With the two battle lines essentially stalled—Federals on Oak Hill, Confederates facing them south of it—Lyon tried a flanking maneuver, sending Plummer's 1st U.S. across Wilson's Creek to get at or around the Rebel right. About the same time Ben McCulloch had the same idea, ordering Colonel James McIntosh to advance his 2d Arkansas Mounted Rifles and Colonel Louis Hebert's 3d Louisiana out beyond the Southern right flank toward the enemy left. As it happened, the opposing forces made straight for each other in a cornfield. At first Plummer's men held up against the Rebel musketry, and even once forced McIntosh to order a withdrawal. Soon though, Confederates resurged in greater numbers, supported by a battery, and the Federals gave way back toward Oak Hill. McIntosh pressed in pursuit, but a battery of Union artillery across the creek covered Plummer's withdrawal. After an unsuccessful rush to take these guns, McIntosh's force drew back. A lull then ensued on this part of the field. Strangely, it spread down the line, a cessation in fighting ordered by no one but taking hold on both sides. This brief cease-fire, around 9 a.m., was especially welcome to Lyon's tired troops. Filling canteens, catching breath, gobbling rations, restocking ammo, treating hurts or hauling off wounded, they spent almost twenty minutes getting ready for the battle's next round.

---

427 Jay Monaghan, *Civil War on the Western Border 1854-1863* (Boston, 1955), p. 178.

This gave Brigadier General McCulloch, who was essentially Price's co-commander on the battlefield, time to turn his attention to Sigel, who was still on the defensive to the south. McCulloch organized three Arkansas infantry regiments of Bart Pearce's brigade, as yet unengaged in the morning's fight, into line of battle and sent them forward in an attack on Sigel's line.

Since taking their position south of Skegg's Branch, Sigel's men had been out of the fight. Hearing only quiet from Oak Hill (the uncalled cease-fire around 9), Colonel Sigel himself had begun to assume that Lyon had won his battle and driven off the Rebels. Thus seeing a line of gray-clad men approaching, Sigel assumed that they were the First Iowa Regiment, well-known for their gray militia uniforms, and ordered his men not to fire. This mistake, similar to the confusion over uniforms at Manassas three weeks earlier, gave Pearce's men the chance they needed. Quick-stepping up a slight rise toward the artillery battery at the center of Sigel's line, the Southerners halted, fired a murderous volley, then overran the guns. "Don't shoot! We're friends!" some artillerists cried out, never realizing their mistake even as they, their horses, caissons, infantry support, even the battery commander himself were running for the rear. The Union gunners managed to limber up and save only one of their six cannon.

Just then General Pearce ordered Capt. J.G. Reid's battery to open up. The artillery fire further threw the Federals into confusion. By now Sigel was frantically trying to rally his terrified troops; Col. Charles Salomon of the 3d Missouri was cursing them in German, French and English, but no orders, pleas or threats had any effect. Sigel's line simply melted away, every man running for himself. In this shameful rout the commanding officer himself played a prominent part. Riding through the Confederate camp his men had overrun that morning, Sigel grabbed a yellow slouch hat and blanket, donning the hat and slinging the blanket over his shoulder to conceal his officer's uniform. In the expected pursuit by Rebel cavalry, Sigel hoped to elude capture.

Observing Sigel's rout, General McCulloch called in all the cavalry he had on hand, two Arkansas regiments, to reap the fruits of victory with fleet pursuit. But the Federals were fleeter; Pearce's infantry quickly gave up the chase, content with securing their battlefield spoils, and the Confederate cavalry eventually did as well.

Sigel's men, more a mob now than merely defeated infantry, streamed back toward Springfield, their starting point. As fast as they traveled, they could not beat their commander. Colonel Sigel rode into town at 4:30 that afternoon and was so demoralized that without issuing any orders for his men, he strode into a hotel, checked into a room, and went to sleep.

Unlike Rastadt, unlike Carthage, this was not one of Sigel's "masterful retreats." It was an ignominious rout, led by Sigel himself. When he awakened, the poor Colonel found himself already the butt of some derisive doggerel, mockingly chanted by his own resentful soldiers:

Old Sigel fought some on that day,

But lost his army in the fray;

Then off to Springfield he did run,

With two Dutch guards, and nary a gun.[428]

THE DEATH OF LYON

By ten o'clock Sigel was out of the picture, leaving McCulloch to bring all remaining Confederate strength against Lyon. Already Price had tried again to dislodge the Yankee line on the hill, sending a double line of infantry first against the enemy left near the creek, then against the other end of the Federal position. In the face of both attacks Lyon's Missourians, Kansans, Iowans and

---

428 William Riley Brooksher, *Bloody Hill: The Battle of Wilson's Creek* (Washington, 1995), p. 210.

regulars held firm, delivering murderous rifle volleys that forced the Rebels back down the hill. Then Lyon tried an assault of his own, sending the 1st and 2d Kansas to drive off the Rebels who had begun to inch their way up the hillslope. But the Kansans soon reeled back, some companies having lost half their men from deadly artillery fire "Everything," Union Lieutenant John Du Bois, observed, "was covered with blood." The men started calling their battlefield Bloody Hill.

General Lyon was all about, exhorting his soldiers, issuing commands. By now he had stopped asking "Where's Sigel?" having concluded that the Rebels had whipped and dispatched him, and were now turning their full force on Oak Hill. At one point, near 9:30, a cannon shell exploded near Lyon. A fragment grazed his head, knocking him to the ground; the shell also killed his horse. With blood running down his cheek, the General looked somewhat dazed as Major John Schofield, his adjutant, rushed up to give aid. Despondently daubing the blood, now beginning to mat and darken his bushy beard, Lyon muttered, "Major, I fear the day is lost." Schofield attempted a game rebuttal, but he sensed Lyon was correct. The men in the line were spent, winded and depleted from the night's march and morning's fight. Casualties were heavy, especially in officers (the 1st Iowa had lost thirteen of twenty-seven). No one believed they had the spirit to make another charge; Lyon seemed to fear they might not withstand another one by the Rebels.

Reinforced by McCulloch, plugging in Parson's infantry hitherto held in reserve, Price strengthened his line and extended it to the left before ordering the Confederates' third change on Oak/Bloody Hill. Even Sigel's captured artillery was wheeled into place. In double lines the Southerners again moved up the slope, which was now covered thickly with dead and wounded of both sides. Again they were repulsed by the Federals' fierce fire. As one Confederate later recalled the scene, "vast sheets of the musket and minie balls came pouring through our ranks tearing the grass and bushes, throwing the dust and gravel in our faces, crippling our comrades, and killing our friends. The fearful and terrific storm of death was raging around....Here amid this horrible scene we still maintained the deadly and unequal contest, murdering and being murdered."

General Lyon, remounted and waving his sword over his head, hinted nothing of his earlier doubtfulness and evinced an abundant battle ardor. "Come on, my brave boys, I will lead you!" he yelled, evidently signaling his soldiers that he would lead them in a counterattack. Just at that moment, sometime before eleven, he was seen to jerk upwards in the saddle, then fall from it. A bullet had struck him in the chest; when he hit the ground his orderly, Pvt. Albert Lehman, rushed up fast enough to hear Lyon murmur, "Lehman, I am killed."[429]

And he was, at least within a few minutes. Lehman was crouched over the General's body when Adjutant Schofield ran up, shouting "What happened?"[430] Lehman explained the obvious: Lyon had been shot from his horse and was now dead. Schofield ordered him to tell no one about it and got four men to carry Lyon away, under a tree, where they covered him with a blanket. An ambulance was ordered and the body was taken farther to the rear.

Major Schofield bore word of his leader's death to Maj. Samuel D. Sturgis, commanding Lyon's first brigade and next in seniority. Sturgis took in the situation. The stalemate was temporary, he figured; the Rebels were no doubt regrouping for another assault. Meanwhile, he concluded that his troops were nearly out of ammunition, and could not repel another attack. About 11:15 Sturgis therefore gave the order for all troops to begin a quiet, orderly retirement from the field, preparatory to a march back to Springfield. They had done all they could do; Sigel had failed them; the Rebels were too numerous and anyway General Lyon was gone. "Nothing, therefore, was left to do," he later explained to his superiors, "but to return to Springfield."[431]

---

429 William Riley Brooksher, *Bloody Hill: The Battle of Wilson's Creek* (Washington, 1995), pp. 211, 213-15.

430 Stephen B. Oates, "Nathaniel Lyon," *Civil War Times Illustrated,* February 1968, p. 24.

431 Dee Brown, "Wilson's Creek," *Civil War Times Illustrated,* April 1972, p. 17.

Union Retreat, Confederate Victory

Around 11 a.m., while the Confederates regrouped for another attack, Sturgis ordered the army's withdrawal. The news was not well received as it went through the ranks. Capt. Gordon Granger got a chance to protest the retreat order directly to Major Sturgis, who pledged to think it over. But that lasted just a minute or two; an orderly rode up with confirmation that Sigel's force had been driven from the field, with Colonel Sigel himself possibly killed or captured.

That sealed it; Sturgis told Granger to proceed with the withdrawal of his men. Again Granger objected, arguing that the Rebels had been whipped so far that morning, and they could even now themselves be preparing to retreat. Sturgis repeated, "I order you to leave the field."

"But they have burned their trains," Granger replied.

"I order you to leave the field!" Sturgis shouted, leaving Granger no choice but to nod and follow orders.[432]

The Union withdrawal proceeded at an orderly pace; the Confederates were at the base of Oak Hill, awaiting orders for another assault. When they came around noon, the Southerners marched up the bloody slope they had tried repeatedly to take that morning. This time they were stunned to receive no enemy fire. More, when reaching the hillcrest they could look out through the trees and see the whole Yankee army in columns marching back in the direction of Springfield. Price's weary soldiers let loose huge whoops and exultant victory-cheers.

The relaxed nature of the Union retreat, conducted without pressure from the Rebels, led some Federals to proclaim it as a kind of victory. One Union officer later wrote that Lyon's troops only began to withdraw from Oak Hill after "pouring a murderous, deadly fire [on the enemy], which created a perfect rout" among them. The Federal infantry "continued to send a galling fire into the disorganized masses as they fled, until they disappeared and

432   William Riley Brooksher, *Bloody Hill: The Battle of Wilson's Creek* (Washington, 1995), p. 223.

the battle was over."[433] By this telling, the Federals had repulsed Price's last charge, and without anything more to do, more or less returned to base for dinner.

The Southerners, of course, would have none of this. General McCulloch put it best for his side in describing the last assault of the morning: "Our gallant Southerners pushed onward and with one wild yell broke upon the enemy, pushing them back and strewing the ground with their dead. Nothing could withstand the impetuosity of our final charge. The enemy fled, and could not be rallied, and they were seen at 12m. fast retreating among the hills in the distance. Thus ended the battle."

"We watched the retreating enemy through our field glasses, and were glad to see him go," later commented Brigadier General Pearce,[434] but Major General Price was not, at least without some form of pursuit. During the morning's fight Price had kept several regiments of cavalry and mounted rifles in reserve—to cover the army's retreat in case of disaster, to sweep the battlefield if triumphant. Now he gave the order to give chase to the fleeing Yankees. The Confederate cavalry pursuit of Sturgis' forces proved just how un-whipped they were. In repeated brushes and clashes along the road to Springfield, Federal rearguard units proved tough and testy. The Southern horsemen eventually gave up the "chase," content to pick up some weapons, haversacks and a broken – down wagon as fruits of their victory, which would have been theirs for the picking on the next day, anyway. Thus, without really much enemy interference, Sturgis' (formerly Lyon's) army trudged into Springfield late on the tenth. The next day they began their long march back to Rolla, whence they would board the trains back to St. Louis.

Soon on their retrograde march from the battlefield, some Federal noticed that they had forgotten about their commanding general. The body of Lyon had, in fact, been removed from its ambulance to make room for wounded soldiers, and in the hubbub

---

433 Donald L. Gilmore, *Civil War on the Missouri-Kansas Border* (Gretna LA, 2006), p. 122.

434 *Ibid.*

of the retreat had been left behind. Sturgis sent back a detail under flag of truce to fetch the General's remains. Received by the Confederates and escorted to headquarters, the Federal emissaries were readily granted access to Lyon's corpse, with Ben McCulloch unchivalrously adding that "he wished he had a thousand other dead Yankee bodies to send off."[435]

As it was, there were plenty of Yankee bodies for McCulloch's and Price's men to bury after the battle—and Rebel ones, too. Casualty figures for the battle of Oak Hill (or Wilson's Creek, as Northerners began to call it) were steep, given the numbers of troops engaged.

	K	W	M/C	Total	Engaged	%Casualties
CS	257	900	27	1,184	10,183	11.6%
US	223	721	291	1,235	5,600	22%

Fifteen percent *hors de combat* for both sides represents a decimation-and-a-half of the total forces engaged. But from the Union perspective, the loss of more than a fifth of an army in one of the first major battles of the war should have given a shiver to any Northerner who got hold of and analyzed the numbers. Few did. Instead, the Northern press lionized the slain Lyon as the first general officer of either side who had lost his life in combat. This bit of eulogistic catharsis, coupled with Yankee newspapers' contention that the battle should be called "Wilson's Creek" (their name) instead of "Oak Hill" (the Rebels' name) blinded the Northern public to the fact that not only had they lost an important battle, they were about to lose an important state.

PRICE ADVANCES TO THE MISSOURI

Sensing that not everyone would accept Wilson's Creek/Oak Hill as a Union "victory," General Fremont in St. Louis absolved himself from any blame for the defeat by denying it altogether. From his headquarters he issued a congratulatory order to the survivors of Lyon's army for their "extraordinary services in nobly battling for the honor of their flag in the battle near Springfield,

---

435   Brooksher, *op. cit.,* p. 228.

Mo." "Opposed by overwhelming masses of the enemy," he went on, "in a numerical superiority of upwards of 20,000 against 4,300, or nearly five to one, the successes of our troops were nevertheless sufficiently marked to give to their exploits the moral effects of a victory." Assuming that the soldiers would want to advertise this "moral victory," Fremont authorized each regiment engaged in it to stitch "Springfield" on their unit colors. When this laudatory proclamation reached Washington, gullible Congressmen took it one step further in declaring thanks for not just a moral victory, but an actual one. Hence came the Joint Resolution passed by the U.S. House and Senate commending "the brave officers and soldiers who, under the command of the late General Lyon, sustained the honor of the flag, and achieved victory against overwhelming numbers at the battle of Springfield, in Missouri."[436]

Fremont and the Yankee politicians might fool themselves about who won at Oak Hill, but Confederate Missourians knew better. The death of Lyon and the fallback of his army gave Sterling Price the initiative, and he was determined to use it. He looked to the Missouri River. There the Yankees held the key towns, and had virtually sealed off the northern third of Missouri by seizing all ferries and patrolling the river. Thus they prevented pro-Confederates in the northern counties from joining Price. In Jefferson City, Unionists had organized their own provisional government, with a governor (Hamilton Gamble) and a pro-Unionist legislature to take the place of the one that had dispersed when Governor Jackson fled the capital.

To Price and his followers, all this provided ample reason for a strike at the enemy's river line. Jefferson City? Boonville? Price took into account the ease with which Fremont could rush reinforcements by steamer to any of his garrisons in the river towns. Thus as his objective he chose Lexington, farthest west and most removed from the Union base at St. Louis. Besides, sitting in the banks there by well-founded rumor was $900,000 in state funds, not yet impounded by Fremont, money which the Confederate authorities could well use in their war effort. So Lexington it was.

---

436 *Official Records,* vol. 3, 92-93.

Leaving behind McCulloch and his Arkansans to mount operations of their own, Price and 5,100 infantry, cavalry and artillery set out from Springfield on August 25 on their hundred-fifty-mile march northward.

Drawing abundantly on the countryside for rations gratefully donated by the pro-Southern citizenry, and picking up formerly hesitant recruits along the way, Price's army met only slight resistance in its march north. Five hundred Kansans ventured out from Fort Scott, but on September 2 Price's cavalry engaged them at Drywood Creek, ten miles east of the Union fort, and sent them scurrying back to their base. As the Confederate objective became evident, Federal troops converged on Lexington. From Warrensburg, Colonel Everett Peabody's 13th Missouri fell back onto the river town. So did the 1st Illinois Cavalry, which had been roaming about central Missouri in search of pro-Southern guerrillas. Meanwhile, General Fremont in St. Louis, engaged in hatching more grandiose schemes for the conquest of the Mississippi Valley, believed he could spare only a regiment, so he sent Col. James T. Mulligan upriver with the 23d Illinois. Mulligan took charge of the Union garrison at Lexington on September 9. He had 3,500 troops, including untested but eager local Home Guardsmen and nine pieces of artillery. He gathered them all just north of the town, on the grounds of an abandoned Masonic college whose several buildings stood on a ridge overlooking the river. With townsfolk already buzzing about Price's army heading this way, Mulligan ordered his men to fortify. In round-the-clock shifts the Federals dug a system of earthworks around the college: trenches lined with sharpened stakes, ten foot-high ramparts, artillery lunettes. A few inventive Yankees even fashioned makeshift mines out of gunpowder, water pipes, trip-wires and friction primers, and laid them along the approaches to their base.

Mulligan took a few more precautions. He cleaned out the Farmer's Bank of Lexington, and buried beneath his headquarters that $960,159.60 belonging (according to General Price and Governor Jackson) to the Confederate state of Missouri. He brought with him a number of townswomen to serve as nurses;

among them was his own nineteen-year-old daughter, recently betrothed. He laid in foodstocks, filled the college's water cisterns, sent scouts south of town to watch for Rebels, then waited.

Not for long. On the evening of September 11, mounted units of Price's advance encountered some of Mulligan's men at Hockaday's farm outside Lexington. A ten-minute exchange of rifle shots was all that the failing daylight allowed before the Federals withdrew through town. The Southern cavalry pitched camp and waited for the rest of the army and its commander to come up.

Division by division the little Confederate Army of Missouri marched into Lexington on the next day, September 12. A largely pro-Southern town, its people lined the streets, cheered and sang "Dixie" to celebrate the arrival of General Price and his army of liberation. The sound of the hullabaloo reached the Union garrison. "I hear their cheering and their drums beating," recorded one Federal, Lt. Thomas McClure from Illinois. "Now they cheer again. They are coming. The drums have sounded the alarm. We are all at our posts."

By 4 p.m. Price had placed his troops all around the college grounds, hemming in Mulligan's garrison. Parson's division deployed on the south. Slack was to the west, joined by McBride's men along the river. Brig. Gen. Thomas Harris' division, some 2,000 volunteers just arrived from across the Missouri, took up position along the northern perimeter, with Rains on the east. Artillery soon deployed and ammunition trains arrived. Col. Ben Rives and his 2d Missouri Cavalry swooped down to the riverfront and captured two steamers loaded with provisions for Mulligan's troops. With food, water and ammo—not to mention a numerical superiority of almost two-to-one—Price had everything going for him. Confidently he called his brigadiers together and predicted, "We've got 'em, dead sure. All we have to do is to watch 'em."[437]

---

437   Michael L. Gillespie, "We've Got 'Em, Dead Sure!': The Siege of Lexington, Missouri, September 12-20, 1861," *Morningside Notes*, No. 19 (Dayton, Ohio, 1986), pp. 6-7.

It would not be quite that easy. Federal artillerists opened on the Confederates almost as soon as they came into view, and their insistent fire signaled that the Yankees intended to make a fight of it. Once in place, Price's guns returned the cannonade, sending shell and solid shot against the enemy earthworks. Union Lieutenant McClure had never seen the effect of a hurtling ten-pound iron ball on flesh, so he was moved to record in his diary: "One poor fellow had his head taken off with a ball, another one both legs. A ball passed over us, went through three mules which stood in range, and they did not impede the momentum of the ball apparently in the least, but it went tearing, crashing along, like some infuriated thing."

Sharpshooters, fixed in buildings on both sides, kept up a deadly rattle of musketry. Price had ordered all civilians to evacuate homes and businesses within enemy range. The structures thus abandoned made great havens for Southern marksmen taking beads on the enemy works. From time to time at night Federals launched raiding parties on structures close to their trenches, rousting out the Rebel skirmishers and setting fire to their building-nests.

After several days of this stand-off, Price sent a courier across the lines under a flag of truce, carrying a demand for surrender. He laid out the points of his logic. Mulligan's garrison was not only outnumbered but outgunned. The antiquated smoothbore muskets carried by the Federals were showing their inadequacies in the long-range contest of sniper-fire; Price's sharpshooters were virtually taunting their counterparts, exposing themselves to Yankee bullets they knew would fall short. The garrison was hemmed in, without source of resupply; while the Southerners could well sit this one out, the beleaguered bluecoats could not. Finally, Price promised to parole the garrison if it laid down its arms. Colonel Mulligan counseled with his officers. The Northerners' food and water were indeed running low. Help from Fremont, if it were coming, should have arrived by now. Some of the Union officers accordingly proposed acceptance of Price's terms. The Colonel said no. "We'll fight 'em," he exclaimed; "that's what we enlisted for, and that's what we'll do." Hence came the Federal commander's reply, back through the lines: "If you want us, you must take us."

Mulligan's rebuff stirred Price into ordering an assault on the enemy works. He took his time with preparations, though. Arrayed in his old hunting shirt, on the 16th and 17th "Old Pap," as he was coming to be called by his men, supervised the movement of his divisions to their jump-off positions. Parsons took advantage of buildings on the north edge of town; Rains and Harris moved their men along deep ravines which pointed toward the college-turned-fortress. Then, on September 18, after an artillery barrage that sent hot shot plunging through the roof of Mulligan's headquarters in the Masonic lodge, the Southern infantry surged forward. Some pushed wet hemp bales ahead of them as a kind of mobile breastwork, the idea of Capt. Thomas Hinkle. The innovation worked. Union troops put down a heavy fire of musketry and even artillery, but to no effect. "Bullets merely buried themselves in the bales," wrote Colonel Mulligan, "and cannon balls caused them only to rock a little and then settle back." Even hot shot failed to ignite the soaked fabric. Thus the Confederates inched forward at some points of their line, or dashed forward at others. One sortie resulted in the capture of the Anderson house, a two-story thick-bricked structure only 125 yards west of the Federals' outer works. Ensconced inside, Southern sharpshooters used the upper story as a fortified haven from which to rain rifle balls on the Yankees. Pressed by the ever-closing ring of enemy fire, after a five-hour-fight Mulligan's defenders abandoned their outer trench lines and withdrew to the parapets constructed around the college building at the center of the campus.

Throughout the 19th Price's men kept up a steady musketry on the enemy pinned down in their collegiate bastion. Wrote Federal Lieutenant McClure to his wife: "If any of us raise our heads above the breastworks these fellows fire at us....The rifle and musket balls have been whizzing round our heads so much that we don't notice them as much as we would a bumble bee at home." Inside the Union works, Mulligan's men tried to return fire, but found that keeping their heads down was more important. Meanwhile, on this seventh day of siege, the garrison's water supply had been drained. Blood trickled from blistered lips as the Federals bit their paper cartridges. Under the fierce sun, horses killed by the Rebel artillery lay bloated and putrefying. The death-stench further depressed Mulligan's men, most of whom by now despaired of any relief but surrender. Finally, around 11 o'clock on the morning of the 20th, one of Mulligan's Home Guards officers, Maj. F.W. Becker, spoke out to his fellow Germans, "Vell den, I shtops dis tamm foolishness poorty gwick," and hoisted a white flag without consulting Colonel Mulligan. Price spotted it, and sent in another demand for surrender. This time Mulligan accepted the inevitable and agreed. Shortly after 2 p.m. the Union garrison marched out and stacked arms.

The extent of the Southerners' triumph after the weeklong siege of Lexington, September 12-20, is shown by their captive haul: more than 3,000 prisoners, seven cannon, infantry arms, sabers, 750 horses, cavalry equipment, wagons, teams and other supplies. Governor Jackson's government got back its nearly one million dollars, which Mulligan honorably gave up from its hiding place. Casualties also favored the Confederates: while the Federals lost 140 or 150 killed and from 250 to 350 wounded, General Price reported his loss as 25 dead, 72 wounded.

In view of all this, Dr. Castel, Price's biographer, judges Lexington as "the most complete and spectacular victory achieved by Southern arms in the war up to that time...Coming on the heels of Oak Hill and dramatically enhanced by the ingenious use of the hemp bales, the siege of Lexington made Price a popular hero throughout the South, where some politicians began talking about electing him the next President of the Confederacy."[438]

---

438   *Ibid.,* pp. 6, 8, 11; Albert Castel, "The Siege of Lexington," *Civil War Times Illustrated,* August 1969, pp. 12-13. After the war Sterling Price retired to his home in Missouri's capital, which he helped rename Jefferson Davis City. His death in 1867, in the last year of President Davis's term, prevented him from seeking the Confederate Gray House.

DEADLOCK TURNS TO GUERRILLA WARFARE

While Price was lionized, Fremont was vilified. No amount of falsifying or euphemism—though the Union commander tried it all—could conceal the embarrassing fact that at Lexington Federal forces had been outgeneraled, outnumbered and outdone. When the St. Louis *Evening News* blamed Fremont for the loss of Lexington, the general countered with loud promises of action, plans to take to the field himself, drive Price out of Missouri, conquer the Mississippi Valley, &c., &c. When the paper offered a riposte of its own, General Fremont arrested its editors and closed the paper down. He went so far as to declare St. Louis under martial law on August 14. Heavy-handed suppression, however, would not stifle the critics, who carried their complaints all the way to the White House. Frank Blair filed formal charges against Fremont with the Adjutant General, accusing him of gross negligence and mismanagement; Fremont had him arrested, too, although *in absentia*. With Union leaders believing that there were now 40,000 Missourians under Confederate arms following Price and McCulloch's victory at Oak Hill, Fremont took harsh measures against pro-Confederate Missourians, whom he likened to guerrillas.[439] Civilians caught with weapons north of the Missouri River, for instance, would be tried by court martial, and if found guilty were to be executed. Lincoln, already troubled by the twin disasters of Manassas and Springfield, had little patience for the Pathfinder. As the President's secretary, Nicolay, recorded in late September, "the universal opinion is that he [Fremont] has entirely failed, and that he ought to be removed."

Fremont compounded his troubles with Washington on August 30, when as another way to punish the Secesh he ordered all property of active Rebels to be confiscated and their slaves freed.[440] While Northern abolitionists hailed Fremont's proclamation, President Lincoln immediately objected to it as an infringement of his presidential authority to direct the Union war effort. Lincoln

---

439   Allan Nevins, *The War for the Union: The Improvised War 1861-1862* (New York, 1959), p. 333.

440   Mark Grimsley, *The Hard Hand of War: Union Military Policy toward Southern Civilians 1861-1863* (Cambridge MA, 1995), p. 123.

tried to be nice at first; on September 3 he sent Fremont a letter politely asking him to rescind the emancipation edict. Lincoln also had his eye on his native state. Neutral Kentucky had lots of slaveholding Southerners unready as yet for secession but who would become agitated if Lincoln allowed Fremont's emancipation order to take effect in Missouri, just across the river. The president saw the danger and tried not to rock the boat. "You may well judge," he wrote Fremont, "of the alarm and condemnation with which the Union-loving citizens have read this proclamation."

Fremont failed to see that his job was on the line and dithered. He was relieved of command at St. Louis on November 2.

THE IMPACT OF GUERRILLA WARFARE: JEFF THOMPSON, THE "MISSOURI SWAMP FOX"

Notwithstanding Fremont's anti-guerrilla measures, so-called "irregular warfare" thrived throughout Missouri in 1861.

Indeed, one of the sometimes-overlooked factors contributing to Confederate victory in the war was the extensive operation of guerrillas, irregular troops and partisan rangers.

The contrasting war aims of North and South provide background. The Lincoln administration determined upon a war of invasion, subjugation and territorial occupation; the Davis administration adopted a strategy of defending the Southern people's homes, farms, businesses and property. When these latter fell into enemy hands, the people themselves—that is, those men not already in the Confederate army—often banded together and in clandestine operations harassed and bedeviled the occupying Yankee forces.

More than that, guerrilla activity, linked to frequent raids by Confederate cavalry into Union-controlled territory, tied down large numbers of Federal troops far from the fighting front, guarding supply bases, railroad bridges and other tempting targets for Rebel raiders. These latter usually numbered only a fifth of the Yankee numbers, and sometimes, as "irregulars," were not listed among the Confederate army's rosters anyway. "As captured territory increased," especially in the war's western theater,

Herman Hattaway and Archer Jones write, "this condition would be aggravated."[441] For example, in January 1863, 51,000 Northern troops—a sizable army if in the field—were tied down in northern Mississippi and West Tennessee protecting railroads and strategic points. In Missouri and Arkansas, large portions of which had fallen under Union control by the end of 1862, 190,000 Federal soldiers were deployed defending communications and territory against independent partisan commands.

Meriwether "Jeff" Thompson is an example. Technically a brigadier general in the pro-Southern Missouri State Guard, Thompson during the late summer of 1861 raised a couple of thousand volunteers in southeast Missouri and led them in a series of quick strikes that harassed and vexed Federal forces in the area. His men cut the railroad from Sikeston to Bird's Point. They met and whipped a detachment of German-American Home Guards at New Hamburg, "scattering the Dutch in all directions," Thompson gloated. He advanced to the banks of the Mississippi, fired an old iron six-pounder and closed down river traffic for days. Reckoning that it was no worse "to take a rich man's money than it was to take a poor man's horse or corn," Thompson rode into Charleston and emptied a bank of more than $50,000. He struck here, struck there, never staying anywhere long enough for the Yankees to fix his base. He avoided set battles, but delighted in skirmishes. When threatened, he would retire into the swampy lowlands near Bloomfield. His exploits became so renowned that Southern newspapers began calling Thompson "the Swamp Fox" and nicknamed his men "Swamp Rats."[442]

Maj. Gen. Sterling Price, top Confederate general in southwest Missouri, shrewdly perceived the value of guerrillas, defined by Richard S. Brownlee as "irregular bands of pro-Southern fighting men."[443] Price sent furtive officers into central and northern

---

441   Herman Hattaway and Archer Jones, *How the South Won: A Military History* (Urbana IL, 1983), p. 357.

442   Steve Davis, "I Am A Rip-Squealer and My Name is FIGHT: M. Jeff Thompson of Missouri," *Blue & Gray,* April-May 1987, p. 29.

443   Richard S. Brownlee, *Gray Ghosts of the Confederacy: Guerrilla Warfare in the West* (Baton Rouge, 1958), pp. 3-4.

Missouri to quietly recruit such men who, denied the opportunity to serve in organized Confederate units, nonetheless hoped to strike blows for the South. When organized in the summer of '61, Sterling Price's guerrillas burned the Salt River bridge on the Hannibal & St. Joseph Railroad, wrecked culverts on the North Missouri rail line near Centralia and so weakened the Platte River railway bridge that a troop train chugging over it fell into the water, killing twenty soldiers and injuring sixty more. "The sabotage was so well done," Brownlee writes, that the St. Louis *Republican* declared that the city was virtually isolated from the rest of the state.[444]

During 1861-63 the Confederacy demonstrated to military historians the many ways in which a popular war for political independence can be waged and won. Guerrilla warfare was just one.

---

444   *Ibid.,* p. 24.

Chapter Nine:

Early Winners, and Losers

Washington's Flawed Departmentalization

One of warfare's unquestioned administrative principles involves the need for boundaries. Not national boundaries, for those are already set; but military boundaries: theaters of war, army departments, districts, sub-districts, etc. Map lines demarking these geographic areas presumably help the generals plan strategy, allocate resources and fight battles. Afterward, they help historians get a perspective on what happened.

So it may be useful to consider the way that the Union and Confederate high commands carved up North America (at least the part militarily contested) for logistical and strategic purposes. All told, both sides established over fifty divisions, departments and districts during the war, as the generalissimos and war secretaries drew and redrew lines when developments shifted. Well more than half of these were Union organizations; Confederate authorities gradually realized that too many little districts tended to become little fiefdoms, satisfying the local commander but inhibiting the war effort when trans-departmental coordination was needed. As example, in the first months of the war, reflecting its concern for Richmond, the C.S. Defense Department created four little departments within Virginia, so that troops and resources could be doled out to a multi-point grid of defensive centers. By the spring of 1862, however, when McClellan's campaign against the Rebel capital began, Richmond wisely determined to place everything in the state—Magruder at Yorktown, Theophilus Holmes at Fredericksburg, Jackson in the Valley—under the overall command of General Joe Johnston, commander of the C.S. "Army of the Potomac," soon to be Army of Northern Virginia. In the entire rest of the South, only three other departments were set up by June 30, 1861, and these were along the Mississippi, the most obvious enemy invasion route. (For the first months of the war, Kentucky's "neutrality" spared Confederate leaders from the task of creating military departments for the defense of Tennessee and the Southern "heartland").

At the same time, Union officials divided their military map into as many as eight departments, perhaps reflecting their understanding that the North's war of offensive conquest would have to be prosecuted on all fronts. Yet half of these covered the environs of Annapolis and Washington (reflecting Lincoln's fears for the safety of his capital), or encompassed the small areas of northwest or southeast Virginia then occupied by Union troops. The persistence of these mini-departments in the Federals' strategic planning meant that men and material were routinely fed to them upon demand of their commanders (whether really needed or not), thus wastefully diffusing U.S. war resources needed for truly major efforts (such as the Virginia offensive of General McClellan, who kept clamoring for reinforcements).

In the west, defined as the Appalachians to the Mississippi, War Department planners in Washington tended to use state boundaries in dealing with the vast expanses of Kentucky, Tennessee, Missouri and Arkansas. The Department of Ohio was first commanded by General McClellan, then (after July 23, 1861) by William S. Rosecrans. Kentucky had its own departmental designation, created well before Union troops even entered the state, more or less in recognition that President Lincoln's homeland deserved special treatment. On the other hand, Confederates realized that the Mississippi Valley as a whole would be the strategic prize, regardless of state boundaries. Richmond thus created a "Department No. 1" (most of Louisiana and southern Mississippi), anticipating that the Yankee navy and army would launch operation up the great river from the Gulf. The Confederate "Department No. 2" began as a strip of the Mississippi on both Arkansas and Tennessee sides. Eventually, by order of the Adjutant General's office, dated September 10, it took in all of Kentucky and Tennessee, eastern Arkansas and western Mississippi, in recognition that the entire four-state region had a vital stake in keeping enemy warships and amphibious troops from snaking downriver.

The flip-flops of Federal decision-makers throughout 1861 illustrate their uncertainties as to how best to administer Union forces in the western theater. In June, after General Scott and Secretary Cameron had copy-catted the Southerners by creating their "Department of the West," Missouri was dissected from it and added to the Ohio Department, which by now had taken in Indiana and Illinois. A month later Illinois was removed from "Ohio," and placed in the "West." The Department of Ohio was redrawn in mid-September; then redrawn again on November 9, so that Ohio, Michigan, Indiana and Kentucky fell within its borders (why Michiganders felt they were threatened by attack and hence deserved a defensive departmental designation has never been answered). The same order, dated November 9, 1861, created a new Department of Missouri, covering that state plus Arkansas, a bit of western Kentucky, Illinois, Iowa and even land northward to the Canadian border.

The main strategic result of these cartographic complexities was that the North's western war effort in the latter half of 1861 was directed not out of one headquarters (as the Rebels had in Department No. 2), but three: St. Louis (Department of the West), Cincinnati (Department of the Ohio), and Louisville (Department of Kentucky, later "the Cumberland"). As further complication, the Federals endured an unsettling series of shake-ups in leadership. The flighty and ineffective Fremont at last gave way to Halleck in St. Louis. In Cincinnati, department command was held first by McClellan, then Rosecrans, then Ormsby Mitchel, then Don Carlos Buell; each of them served a couple of months, June-December. And in Louisville, Maj. Gen. Robert Anderson, hero of Fort Sumter and native Kentuckian, finally cracked under the pressure of his divided loyalties, and asked to be relieved. Succeeding him on October 8 was Brig. Gen. William T. Sherman.

CRAZY BILLY SHERMAN

William Tecumseh Sherman is one of those colorful characters who make the Union army, even in defeat, still worth talking about. An Ohioan by birth, he was well-connected by family. His father was a justice of the state supreme court; his father-in-law was a United States senator and Cabinet officer. He therefore had no trouble getting into West Point, where he did well (sixth in the class of 1840). He then applied himself to an army career which went nowhere. After thirteen years, a growing sense of failure induced Sherman to resign his commission. Unhappily, more failures ensued: a banking business in San Francisco, a law practice in Kansas, then a teaching job in Louisiana. One can see in these setbacks and start-overs the determination of a young man vainly dedicated to succeed at something. And well he might have as a soldier, had the Confederate War lasted long enough, first, and had not so many people, secondly, thought him insane.

Sherman performed creditably at Manassas as colonel of the 13th U.S. Infantry and was promoted to brigadier general in August 1861. Shortly thereafter, at the request of departmental commander Robert Anderson, he was sent to Kentucky to help direct Union military organization in the state. Anderson had heard of Sherman's stick-to-it-iveness, and figured this was a quality he needed in his second-in-command. Yet there were warning signs that Sherman inwardly worried that the North might fail. "If they are united," he wrote a relative in early September, "and we disunited or indifferent, they will succeed."[445] President Lincoln himself had the chance to gauge Sherman's temperament when he interviewed the peppery Ohioan before sending him west. All he wanted, the newly minted brigadier said, was a subordinate command—in no circumstances did he wish promotion to lead a department.

---

445   John F. Marszalek, *Sherman: A Soldier's Passion for Order* (New York, 1993), p. 157.

This, unfortunately, is just what he got when Anderson abruptly retired from service on October 5. As a result, Sherman took over responsibility for holding Kentucky in the Union and for invading Tennessee. The job seemed too vast, too difficult, too much for one man, and the general started to show it. A nerve-wracked Sherman complained that he had too few troops even to hold the state, let alone launch an offensive. Shortly after taking command, Sherman confessed his fears in a telegram to President Lincoln himself, under date of October 10.

> My own belief is that the Confederates will make a more desperate effort to gain Kentucky than they have for Missouri. The force now here or expected is entirely inadequate. All the men in Indiana and Ohio are ready to come to Kentucky, but they have no arms, and we cannot supply them arms, clothing, or anything.

Thus he laid out his anxieties, and ended his message abruptly with "Answer," never thinking of his impertinence in issuing orders to his Commander in Chief.[446]

Sherman worried about his recruits, and the sickness in their camps. He fretted over their hasty training, their poor discipline, their inadequate equipment and unreliable weapons. Turning over these problems in his mind, he paced agitatedly in his Louisville headquarters almost any time of the day or night, scarcely speaking while furiously smoking cigars. His staff officers thought him "queer" and spread stories of his eccentricity or absent-mindedness. One Northern general characterized Sherman as "a splendid piece of machinery with all of the screws a little loose." Newspapermen came to observe him, and were struck by his oddness. Wrote one:

> When I first saw him in Missouri, his eyes had a half-wild expression, probably the result of excessive smoking. Sherman was never without a cigar. He

---

446   *O.R.,* vol. 4, 300.

looks rather like an anxious man of business than an ideal soldier. Sometimes he works for twenty consecutive hours. He sleeps little; nor do the most powerful opiates relieve his terrible cerebral excitement. Indifferent to dress and to fare, he can live on hard bread and water and fancies any one else can do so.[447]

Today we recognize Sherman's personality, which then was referred to as "the nervous-sanguine temperament," as that of a diagnosable manic-depressive, the victim of dramatic mood swings, a clinical bipolarity. Stephen Ambrose has summarized these emotional fluctuations: "Unlike Halleck, who lived continually on an even emotional plane, Sherman alternated between fits of despair, when he often thought of suicide, and moments of extreme exhilaration."[448]

In the fall of 1861 the General was apparently in one of his periods of despair, when he could only see prospects of imminent disaster. Reports of Sherman's troubled state of mind became so widespread that President Lincoln sent War Secretary Simon Cameron to Louisville. On the seventeenth of October Sherman and Cameron had a long talk. "Now, General Sherman," the Secretary began, "tell us of your problems." After a little hesitation—he did not like all those aides in the room—Sherman opened up with a torrent of troubles. The Rebel leader Buckner had 60,000 men (he thought) ready to march on Louisville. The people of Kentucky were secretly secessionist, and ready to go over to Jeff Davis. Fremont and McClellan were getting all the reinforcements; he was getting no support from Washington. Even in arms he was being consigned to failure, as he told the Secretary that he had been promised 40,000 good Springfield rifles, but had been sent instead 12,000 Belgian muskets so outdated that even the governors of Pennsylvania and Ohio had refused them ("I am to be sacrificed," he burst out, nearly in tears). Rolling out a map showing McClellan

---

447   Lloyd Lewis, *Sherman: Fighting Prophet* (New York, 1932), p. 197.

448   Stephen E. Ambrose, *Halleck: Lincoln's Chief of Staff* (Baton Rouge, 1962), p. 19.

guarding a front of only a hundred miles with 100,000 men, he told Cameron he had only 20,000 men to hold three hundred miles of front. "How can I?" he exclaimed, when at least 60,000 men were needed for defense and "for offense, before we are done, 200,000."

"You astonish me!" gasped Cameron. "Great God, where are the men to come from?" The interview ended shortly thereafter, with both the Secretary and the General quite shaken. Cameron returned to Washington and reported his impression that Sherman was too volatile, too irrational to be entrusted with departmental command. The New York *Tribune* got hold of the story, and its article of October 30 was reprinted across the country, leading many newspapermen to question Sherman's mental balance. Sherman's publicly expressed worries about the strength of the rebellion and the prospects of a tragic, bloody and interminable war also made their way into the Northern press. One correspondent in the Chicago *Tribune* reported, "I know not whether it is insanity or not, but the General indulged in remarks that made his loyalty doubtful. He even spoke despondingly; said the rebels could never be whipped; talked of a thirty years' war, etc."[449] "Finally, the Cincinnati *Commercial* on November 11 blared,

---

449   Lewis, *op. cit.*, pp. 193-94, 197; Michael Fellman, *Citizen Sherman: A Life of William Tecumseh Sherman* (New York, 1995), p. 94; Charles Edmund Vetter, *Sherman: Merchant of Terror, Advocate of Peace* (Gretna LA, 1992), p. 93; Stanley P. Hirshson, *The White Tecumseh: A Biography of William T. Sherman* (New York, 1997), p. 99.

GENERAL WILLIAM T. SHERMAN INSANE

The painful intelligence reaches us in such form that we are not at liberty to discredit it that General W.T. Sherman is insane. It appears that he was at times, when commanding in Kentucky, stark mad. We learned that at one time he telegraphed to the War Department three times in one day for permission to evacuate Kentucky, and retreat into Indiana. He also on several occasions frightened the leading Union men of Louisville almost out of their wits by the most astounding representations of the overwhelming forces of Buckner, and the assertion that Louisville could not be defended....It seems providential that the country has not to mourn the loss of an army through the loss of the mind of a general into whose hands was committed the vast responsibility of the command in Kentucky.[450]

Two days later Sherman was relieved of command and sent home to recuperate from what is now medically diagnosed as a nervous breakdown. Before leaving Kentucky, he confessed that he was looking forward to hiding "in some obscure corner," sitting out the war. Prophetically he opined, "Our Government is destroyed, and no human power can restore it."[451]

Thoroughly shattered and demoralized, Sherman was not cashiered, but given two or three weeks' rest with his family in St. Louis. Soon Halleck, after taking charge there in December, began a magnanimous program of rehabilitating Sherman to command. He was made drillmaster of troops at Benton Barracks, and nursed along so considerately by his superior that eventually his shaken pride returned. He would later be entrusted with field command, notably at Shiloh, where he commanded a division. Unfortunately,

---

450 John F. Marszalek, *Sherman's Other War: The General and the Civil War Press* (Memphis, 1981), pp. 64-65.

451 Marszalek, *Passion for Order,* p. 163.

it was the one which Sidney Johnston's infantry first encountered in their opening assault. "My God, we are attacked!" Sherman shouted, just before a rifle volley "blew him off his horse and onto his back on the ground spouting blood," as historian Winston Groom describes it.[452] He died within minutes.

GRANNY LEE'S FIRST SIX MONTHS

The general who, more than anyone else, helped the South win its War for Independence played a very inauspicious role at the start of it.

After having turned down Winfield Scott's offer to lead the Union army ("Lee, you have made the greatest mistake of our life," Old Fuss and Feathers remarked), on April 22, 1861, Lee accepted Virginia governor John Letcher's offer that he lead the state's military forces. Then, the next day, Lee stood before the state convention in Richmond's House of Delegates as convention president John Janney extolled him: "In the memory of the great Virginian George Washington, who was first in the hearts of his countrymen, and summoning also on the memory of his own gallant father, Light Horse Harry Lee, the Convention calls upon Robert Edward Lee to take command of the armed forces of the citizen army of Virginia."

Looking a little embarrassed, Lee took the lectern:

Mr. President and Gentlemen of the Convention:

Profoundly impressed with the solemnity of the occasion, for which I must say I was not prepared, I accept the position assigned me by your partiality. I would have much preferred had your choice fallen on an abler man. Trusting in Almighty God, an approving conscience, and the aid of my fellow-

---

452   Winston Groom, *Shiloh 1862* (Washington, 2012), 73.

citizens, I devote myself to the service of my native state, in whose behalf alone will I ever again draw my sword.[453]

Throughout May and into June, Lee saw to the mobilizing, arming and training of Virginia's new volunteer army. He also directed the placement of batteries along the Potomac and construction of fortifications against the Federal invasion sure to come.

Then on June 8 after the Southern capital had moved from Montgomery to Richmond, Virginia's state forces were officially transferred to Confederate authority. This left Major General Lee, commanding Virginia Forces, without a job. Gradually, though, without official appointment from President Davis, Lee began assuming a role that Dr. Freeman terms "in one sense an acting assistant Secretary of War and in another sense deputy chief of the general staff."[454] As such he gradually became the president's military advisor, especially after August 31, when Davis sent to the Senate the names of five officers he wished to be confirmed as full general in the army. In order of the seniority Davis established (based on their class standing upon graduation from West Point and their subsequent rank in the old army), they were Samuel Cooper, Albert Sidney Johnston, Robert E. Lee, Joseph E. Johnston and P. Gustave Toutant Beauregard.[455]

Some biographers of Robert E. Lee have commented on Jefferson Davis's failure to recognize Lee's talent for field command, sending Joe Johnston instead to command the so-called Confederate Army of the Potomac (which Lee would immortally rename the Army of Northern Virginia when he took it over in June 1862). Thus, as Clifford Dowdey has written, "the former favorite of Gen-

---

453   Clifford Dowdey, *Lee* (Raleigh, 1965), p. 143.

454   Douglas Southall Freeman, *R.E. Lee: A Biography*, 4 vols. (New Orleans, 1934-35), vol. 1, 530-31.

455   Craig L. Symonds, *Joseph E. Johnston: A Biography* (New York, 1992), p. 127. As opposed to the disordered ranking system of the Union army, in which colonels commanded brigades, brigadiers led divisions, and major generals commanded armies, the Confederate army adhered to a more logical hierarchy: colonels for regiments, brigadier generals for brigades, major generals for divisions, lieutenant generals for corps, and full generals for armies.

eral in Chief Scott became the misused soldier in his hotel room at the Spotswood."[456] Tied to his desk in the capital, as "a sort of household staff" (in the words of Emory Thomas), Lee did not even accompany the president when he traveled to Manassas on the day of the battle.[457]

A week later, Davis sent Lee to western Virginia on an even more thankless mission: coordinating the various Confederate forces there. After the death of Brigadier General Garnett at Carrick's Ford on June 13 Brig. Gen. Henry Wise became the main Confederate commander in the Kanawha Valley (named for the river that flowed northwest through trans-Allegheny Virginia into the Ohio). "Wise's Legion" consisted for a respectable 4,500 officers and men. Also in the Kanawha was a separate small army of 5,800 troops under Brig. Gen. John B. Floyd. Both Wise and Floyd, though, were political generals, each a former governor of Virginia. As such, they bitterly disliked each other and refused to cooperate. Complicating the situation further was the approach of a third force under Maj. Gen. William W. Loring, commander of the Department of Southwestern Virginia (another 5,000 men). Had Lee been able to unite these three commands into one large army, he would have possessed enough strength to face the enemy.

After George McClellan was brought to Washington following Manassas, Brig. Gen. William S. Rosecrans took charge of the 20,000 Federals stretched midway between the Alleghenies and the Ohio on a hundred-mile front, from Gauley Bridge through Sutton to Huttonsville. On September 10, Rosecrans attacked part of Floyd's command at Carnifex Ferry (fifty miles northwest of White Sulphur Springs, Robert and Mary Lee's favorite vacationing spot after the war). Floyd's troops held their lines; but with his troops nearly out of ammunition at the end of the day and expecting the Yankees to renew their attack the next morning, General Floyd ordered a withdrawal during the night, burning the ferry to prevent pursuit. Casualties for Carnifex Ferry were light: Rosecrans' three brigades lost about 150; Floyd reported a mere twenty men

---

456   Dowdey, *op. cit.,* p. 158.

457   Emory M. Thomas, *Lee* (New York, 1995), p. 198.

wounded. Meanwhile, some eighty miles to the northeast Lee took personal command of Loring's "Army of Southwestern Virginia." When cavalry scouts reported an isolated Federal outpost at Cheat Mountain, Lee planned to attack it on September 12 and assigned Col. Albert Rust and 2,000 men to the mission. Rust faltered, however, when he began to think there were 4,000 Yankees ahead of him (there were only 300), and failed to launch the assault. The enemy had caught on, though. With the element of surprise lost, Lee gave up on his planned offensive.

"His first campaign had ended ingloriously," writes Freeman.[458] Floyd and Wise still refused to coordinate their actions, but Lee positioned Loring's army so as to block any Federal advance farther into the Old Dominion's western reaches. Lee watched over this stalemated situation until the end of October, when President Davis called him back to the capital for another assignment: supervising the defenses being built along the shoreline of South Carolina, Georgia and northeast Florida. (Lee left Richmond on November 6 and would return in early March 1862.)

Unkind critics started calling the general "Granny Lee"—some observers said the few months in western Virginia had turned the fifty-four-year-old's hair and beard a little whiter.

Granny would get the last laugh.

SIDNEY JOHNSTON TAKES CHARGE IN KENTUCKY

In the fall of 1861 Confederate takeover of Kentucky was far from a sure thing, but already the South had something of a head-start for several reasons. Southern propagandists made much of the Yankees' march into Paducah on September 5 as a flagrant violation of Kentucky's neutrality. People of the state as yet undecided in their loyalties were apt to view the North as aggressor, and to side with the South in the name of self-defense. Second, from a strategic viewpoint, C.S. leaders were quick to grasp the concept of the trans-Appalachian West as a single theater, the huge "Department No. 2." At the same time that Generals Anderson, Sherman (and eventually, Buell) were worrying about pleasing

---

458 Freeman, *op.cit.,* vol. 1, 574.

their President and saving Kentucky for the Union, the U.S. commander at Paducah, Ulysses Grant, with the largest Federal force in the state, was taking his orders not from Louisville, but across the river at St. Louis. Thirdly, after creating their Western super-department, the Southerners were fortunate to place at its head a proven commander of talent and experience. Even General Polk, first Confederate commander in west Tennessee, urged that his department be expanded and given to another officer, Albert Sidney Johnston. "I am well satisfied," he wrote the President on August 29, "from the working of the existing arrangements that a change is necessary. For those operations to be directed wisely, harmoniously, and successfully they should be combined from west to east across the Mississippi Valley, and placed under the direction of one head, and that head should have large discretionary powers. Such a position is one of very great responsibility, involving and requiring large experience and extensive military knowledge, and I know of no one so well equal to that task as our friend General Albert S. Johnston."[459]

At the time Sidney Johnston, of whom Polk and others had such high expectations, was somewhere in Texas on a stagecoach rumbling east. A Kentuckian by birth, he was educated at Transylvania University and West Point. At both institutions he was a schoolmate and friend of Jefferson Davis; at the latter he was a tentmate of Leonidas Polk. After U.S. army service, and combat in the Black Hawk Indian War, Johnston resigned and joined the Americans fighting for the independence of Texas in 1836. He rose to senior brigadier's rank in the Texas army, and became Secretary of War for the newly-founded republic. His subsequent achievements marked him as a gifted soldier: he led a Texas regiment in the Mexican War; rejoined the U.S. Army and was made colonel of the famed Second Cavalry; commanded the military expedition against the Mormons in Utah, 1857; was brevetted brigadier general; and at the outbreak of civil war was in California, commanding the Department of the Pacific.

---

459 *Official Records,* vol. 3, 687-88.

Johnston decided to follow his adopted state, Texas, and resigned his commission. The U.S. Secretary of War promptly ordered his arrest. Fearing capture if he booked passage on a steamer around the Horn, Johnston secretly joined a party of pro-Southern Californians in an overland expedition back to Dixie. The sun-baked rugged 800-mile trek from Los Angeles to El Paso took almost two months. Then, by stage to Houston, and into New Orleans, whence by train to Richmond, Johnston finally arrived in the Confederate capital on September 10. By then Davis had already established the super-Department of the West and had designated Sidney Johnston as its commander. Johnston conferred with the President, received his full general's commission, and proceeded to Nashville, where he set up his headquarters.

Once there, he was earnestly petitioned by Kentucky Governor Beriah Magoffin to push Southern forces as far into Kentucky as possible. Thus far, the Confederate army had only a toe-hold in the western part of the state, thanks to General Polk's occupation of Columbus. The Federal commander, Anderson, had already set up his headquarters in Louisville, forming volunteer regiments, and calling in others from across the Ohio. Magoffin was alarmed, and pleaded for help. Johnston ordered an advance along the rest of the Kentucky-Tennessee line: Brig. Gen. Simon B. Buckner's division at Nashville marched north to Bowling Green, and Brig. Gen. Felix K. Zollicoffer's smaller force in east Tennessee crossed the border to seize Cumberland Gap. Though the Yankees controlled more of Kentucky, the situation in the fall of 1861 found both armies arrayed in wavy parallel lines across the entire state. In the west, Polk, with 11,000 troops at Columbus faced Grant's 15,000 at Paducah. Buckner had 4,500 at Bowling Green against Brig. Gen. Alexander McCook's 11,000 in a mismatch that would soon be evened out after Johnston ordered some 6,000 troops, under Brigadier (soon to be Maj. Gen.) William J. Hardee in northwestern Arkansas, to cross the Mississippi and join Buckner (and this did not count Lloyd Tilghman's garrisons at Forts Henry and Donelson, some 3,500 men). In the east, Zollicoffer had 5,000 men against maybe 9,000 Yankees around Somerset.

Realizing that he had not the power to launch a sustained offensive against the enemy, General Johnston did the next best thing: that is, keep the Yankees from launching a sustained offensive against him. The Confederate commander achieved this by ordering the leaders of his three main forces in Kentucky, especially Buckner, to launch repeated reconnaissance, cavalry raids and minor forays against the enemy lines. The point was to be aggressive, keep the enemy on the defensive, and worry him constantly with the threat of a major Southern advance.

Johnston's bluff worked. After several heavy skirmishes and a Confederate cavalry probe in the direction of Danville, General Anderson became convinced that the Rebels were planning to attack Louisville. He forbade any offensive movement, and ordered his troops to stand ready for fallback at a moment's notice. Anderson's fears were so great that in turning over his position to Sherman on October 5, he said that "he could not stand the mental torture of his command any longer, and that he must go away or it would kill him." Sherman, too, cracked under the pressure, especially after General Buckner at Bowling Green sent Hardee's division in a bold demonstration against the Federal lines in early November. Sherman believed the Rebels were fitting out for a campaign that would take them as far north as Cincinnati, and so (for while) did the Northern press. "Johnston perpetually threatens our army with assault and annihilation," wrote one editor, "and keeps Louisville, even Cincinnati, in a state of perturbation."[460]

Fearing attack, Sherman ordered his forces in southcentral Kentucky to retreat quickly. So prompt was the Union retrograde that in one division matters got out of hand as rumors spread of a Rebel flank attack. The Federal retreat turned into a disgraceful affair likened to a stampede. Later, when it was learned that Sherman had exaggerated the enemy's strength, and people were doubting the General's sanity, one newspaperman editorialized bitterly, "the stampede was the result of General Hardee's

---

460   Charles P. Roland, *Albert Sidney Johnston: Soldier of Three Republics* (Austin, 1964), p. 272.

expedition from Bowling Green, having been reported as advancing with one hundred thousand men.... We have no heart to comment upon such imbecility."[461]

The Confederates' show of force, and their several pulled punches, resulted in no net gain of territory. But Johnston did achieve one important result: he bought six months' time, during which he organized his department and built up his army. Moreover, at a period when his comrade in Missouri, Sterling Price, had been forced to give up much territory in the summer and fall of 1861, General Johnston could claim that he had in fact advanced into Kentucky and from there had not conceded an inch of real estate to the enemy.

POLK AND GRANT SEEK TO OUTMANEUVER EACH OTHER

Only in the far western tip of Kentucky did the Federals seem disposed to challenge Confederate authority. There, with his headquarters at Paducah, the local commander was a brigadier named Ulysses Grant, the same Grant whose rash entry into Kentucky had shattered the state's pretense of neutrality and caused considerable repercussions in public opinion against the Northern cause.

The man had several names. Born Hiram Ulysses Grant, he was called "Sam" as he grew up on his father's farm in southern Ohio. Then, after his dad arranged an appointment to the U.S. Military Academy, an error in government paperwork fastened "Ulysses Simpson" as his name. The tag stuck with the cadet during his West Point years (1839-43) and afterward. After graduation he was by no means a stellar soldier, yet Grant performed adequately enough. He won two brevets for bravery in battle during the Mexican War, but his overall performance failed to boost his career. Stranded out west in remote army posts, Grant too frequently turned to the bottle out of boredom and loneliness. His drinking was more than once reprimanded by his superiors; finally, under official censure, Grant resigned from the army in 1854. His subsequent

---

461 Nathaniel Cheairs Hughes, Jr., *General William J. Hardee: Old Reliable* (Baton Rouge, 1965), p. 86.

efforts to support wife and children included stints as farmer, land salesman and customs house clerk. In each of these endeavors Grant unfortunately failed, and at one point before the war he was reduced to selling firewood in the streets of St. Louis.

Then came the call for volunteers, and suddenly all West Pointers, whether resigned from the army or not, were in demand. Ulysses Grant was made colonel of the 21st Illinois in June 1861. Six weeks later he was given a brigadiership and assigned the District of Southeast Missouri. So quick was his promotion that when he showed up at headquarters in Cairo, Illinois, Grant was without a uniform. He had given back his colonel's outfit, and had no way to show his generalship as he strode into army HQ in slouch hat and short blue coat. His ill-barbered beard, well-chewed but unlit cigar, and a romantic novel under his arm (as opposed to, say, *Hardee's Tactics*) added further elements of undistinction. Little wonder, then, that no heads turned for the new district commander. On the other hand, Grant's amiability and even modesty (a quality in short supply among the army's newly promoted muckety-mucks) quickly won the respect of his officers and men as he settled down to the business of organizing things not only in southeast Missouri but in southern Illinois and the western tip of Kentucky.

For a while Grant and Polk eyed one another from their respective positions. While Grant in Paducah was busy drilling his troops, securing weapons and supplies, Polk in Columbus was fortifying industriously. The town itself, lying on the Mississippi bank, was not as militarily significant as were the high bluffs behind it, which provided ideal positions for artillery. The Southerners cut down all trees covering the slopes to create fire-fields, then dug three tiers of gun emplacements along the river bank, halfway up, and atop the bluffs. One water battery had sandbag embrasures for the cannon to be aimed at the Yankee gunboats rumored to be under construction upriver. Polk arranged for the newest and biggest piece of artillery in the country to be placed in one of the earthen forts on the bluff. (The U.S. artillery service had just begun experimenting with it earlier in the year. Confederate authorities were mum on how the monster gun got into the Southland, but whispers had to do with well-bribed Yankee armaments agents in New England.) With the exterior dimensions of a 10" seacoast Columbiad smoothbore, but with an eight-inch bore, which was then rifled, the eight-ton monster threw a 128-pound oblong shell, nicknamed "lamppost," more than a mile. Artillerists had named the gun "10-Inch Rodman Sleeved to 8-Inch Rifle," but at Columbus Confederate gunners dubbed it the "Lady Polk," and looked forward to their first opportunity, with plunging fire from the bluffs, to sink luckless enemy gunboats below.[462] General Polk himself was enthused. "More heavy guns are arriving from Richmond," he wrote General Johnston on October 27, "and I am promised yet others." One of these arrivals proved to be a highly-prized 70-pounder Whitworth 5" rifled gun (brought through the blockade that summer for the purchase price in England of 700 pounds) which soon got the nickname "Long Tom."[463]

To further deter enemy river traffic, Polk had a mile-long chain strung across the river buoyed by rafts, from which were strung floating contact mines, or "torpedos." A capstan held the chain in place on the Missouri side; a six-ton anchor, sixteen feet long, secured it on the Kentucky bank. With each huge link weighing fifteen to twenty pounds, not surprisingly General Polk's river chain snapped under its own weight after placement. By then, few Union naval vessels would have attempted to run past the Confederate river batteries anyway. Strong gun pits, redoubts and four miles of trenches lined the Kentucky heights. Southerners called their position "the Gibraltar of the West," and dared the Yankees to come and take it.

GRANT DECIDES TO STRIKE AT BELMONT

They did not. The closest that Federal forces came to threatening Columbus, Kentucky, given the strength of Polk's position there, was a "demonstration in force" on the *other* side of the river. Across from Columbus, outside the little town of Belmont,

---

462   Warren Ripley, *Artillery and Ammunition of the Civil War* (New York, 1970), pp. 80-81.

463   Joseph H. Parks, *General Leonidas Polk, C.S.A.: The Fighting Bishop* (Baton Rouge, 1962), p. 188; David E. Roth, "The Civil War at the Confluence: Where the Ohio Meets the Mississippi," *Blue & Gray*, July 1985, p. 9.

Missouri, Southerners had established an infantry encampment, Camp Johnston, where Confederates—Colonel James Tappan and the 13th Arkansas, a battery and some cavalry—kept watch for the approach of any column that might signal a major Yankee move against Columbus.

From his headquarters at Cairo, General Grant saw the Rebel camp at Belmont as a tempting prize, certainly a more vulnerable target than the enemy fortress at Columbus. His troops, after months of drill, were itching for a chance to "see the elephant"—soldier-slang for first combat with the enemy. Besides, Grant himself was seeking an opportunity to impress his new boss, General Halleck, who took command at St. Louis on November 1. So on the 5th Grant wired Halleck not so much asking permission to launch an offensive as announcing his intention: steam downriver, land north of Belmont, attack the enemy camp, break it up, and return to base. In the words of one historian, Grant went "down the river to look for a fight—though just a little one."[464] He would get more than he expected.

The next evening some 3,000 Federals at Cairo boarded six steamboats and set out downriver, accompanied by two gunboats, the *Tyler* and *Lexington*. The forty-mile passage took all night, during which the nervous soldiers—four regiments from Illinois and one from Iowa, plus two cavalry companies and three sections of artillery—got what sleep they could. Around 8 a.m. on November 7 the steamers touched shore several miles above Belmont and the troops began to debark. The *Lexington* and *Tyler* dropped down to engage the Rebels' Columbus batteries and divert their possible fire from the transports. The two Union vessels quickly came under attack, with the Rebel cannoneers dropping shells all around them, but with few hits—the Southern gunners proved their inexperience in this, their first naval engagement. Shipboard the Union artillerymen had an even harder time, trying to discern their targets on the forested bluff, much less hitting them, as they aimed their cannon at orange muzzle-bursts and cloud plumes

---

464 Nathaniel Cheairs Hughes, Jr., *The Battle of Belmont: Grant Strikes South* (Chapel Hill, 1991), p. 53.

from the enemy batteries. After twenty minutes of this exchange a Rebel solid shot struck the *Tyler,* crashing through its side, spraying splinters among the crew, decapitating one man and wounding two more. Captain Henry Walke decided this was enough, and ordered his two gunboats to steam farther upriver and out of range.

Confederates on the Columbus bluffs had seen the smoke from the Federal flotilla just after dawn, and quickly notified headquarters. General Polk concluded that a Yankee attack on Camp Johnston was underway, and ordered Gideon Pillow to load up four regiments and chug across the river (800 yards at that point) to help Tappan. Down at the docks were three riverboats, *Charm, Prince,* and *Harry W.R. Hill.* The *Prince* had passengers on board, some of whom were breakfasting. After receiving orders to take on Pillow's troops, Captain J.B. Butler entered the dining cabin and announced, "Ladies, finish your breakfast, but the Yankees are landing their gunboats above."[465] The diners dropped their forks and promptly fled ashore.

THE BATTLE FOR CAMP JOHNSTON

On the Belmont banks, Colonel Tappan's Arkansans were ready to meet the Yankee attack. They had encircled their camp with an earthen parapet and low wooden wall with cut-down trees forming an *abatis* all around the perimeter. When Confederate cavalrymen brought in word of Yankees landing and marching toward him, Tappan also learned that reinforcements from across the river were on the way. He ordered seven companies of foot-soldiers and his four guns out in front of the *abatis* into line of battle. He had no way of knowing the size of the enemy force, but rightly figured it to be larger than his own. He determined to make a fight, then fall back upon the camp's fortifications until help arrived.

General Pillow landed at Belmont with the first of his troops around nine o'clock, and led them to join Tappan. The Yankees had not yet opened the fight; their march through the swampy, wooded terrain using a single road was taking more time than Grant had figured. In fact, by the time the Federals deployed into battle-line

---

465   *Ibid.,* p. 68.

and made their first charge, it was close to 10:30 and Pillow with his four new regiments had on the field fully 3,000 men, a force equal to Grant's.

The Northern troops' greenness showed in the first volleys of their skirmish lines. "Grant's men wasted a cartload of ammunition by firing blindly in the general direction of the enemy before they could see a single Confederate," recorded one observer.[466] Southern marksmanship proved scarcely better, as the equally green Confederates fired way too high, their volleys clipping off tree branches over the Yankees' heads. Under the weight of the enemy advance, Pillow ordered his line to gradually fall back toward the camp. Polk had sent word that more reinforcements were on the way, and Pillow judged that a slow withdrawal back to base would allow a faster concentration of his forces. General Pillow did not anticipate, however, the Union bayonet charge which drove two Tennessee regiments back to camp more quickly. Grant committed his reserves, and the Federals began pushing Pillow's entire line back into Camp Johnston. Scampering through the *abatis,* the 27th Illinois lost formation but succeeded in breaking into the Rebel camp.

Panicked Southerners fled into the woods below as Pillow tried to rally them and reform his lines. Exultant Federals delighted in seeing the Rebels "skedunking from their den," as one put it, throwing away their muskets, coats, even canteens; "our brave troops followed them with shouts, pouring volley after volley into them." The boys from Illinois and Iowa "swarmed around the flagpole, cannon and tents like bees around an overturned hive."[467]

It was nearly 2 p.m., and the battle of Belmont began to look like a Union victory.

---

466   Nathaniel Cheairs Hughes, Jr., *The Battle of Belmont: Grant Strikes South* (Chapel Hill, 1991), , p. 91.

467   *Ibid.,* p. 119.

GRANT'S BATTLE FALLS APART

While some of Grant's men pursued the Rebels fleeing along the riverbank, most decided that the battle was over and they had won it. In the center of Camp Johnston someone hauled down the Stars and Bars and raised the Stars and Stripes, to roars of cheers. The regimental band of the 22d Illinois arrived, and launched into its three-song repertory: "The Star-Spangled Banner," "Yankee Doodle" and "Dixie," with soldiers singing even along with the last ballad.

Brig. Gen. John McClernand, former Democratic Congressman from Illinois, could not resist an old pol's urge to speechify on the glory of the flag. Astride his black charger he "galloped about from one cluster of men to another and at every halt delivered a short eulogy upon the Union cause," Grant later wrote, in a not very subtle disparagement of his brigadier. The soldiers' cheering egged McClernand on and he did more than his part to turn Grant's battle, as one astonished Federal wrote, "into a Fourth of July orgy of bubbling eloquence."[468]

It did not stop there. After a rough night on ship and after what felt like a long day's fight which they had won, many soldiers determined to help themselves to the booty of the battlefield. Officers and privates alike rummaged through Camp Johnston, plundering the fast-departed Rebels' belongings. "They pulled trunks out of the tents and looted them," observed one Iowan, "loading themselves with small arms, baggage, and even horses."[469] For those who had missed breakfast, Rebel rations now provided a quick bite.

General Grant tried to restore order but failed. When no shouted command could get his men to reform ranks, Grant ordered the camp burned. Officers were soon applying torches to the enemy's tents. The men threw their trophies into their knapsacks, grabbed their muskets and at last fell into line. The process took on an air of

---

468   Nathaniel Cheairs Hughes, Jr., *The Battle of Belmont: Grant Strikes South* (Chapel Hill, 1991), pp. 127, 130.

469   *Ibid.*, p. 130.

urgency when "Lady Polk" from across the river started to bombard the camp. Bursting shells and screaming horses reminded Grant's men that their battle was not over, after all.

CONFEDERATE COUNTERATTACK AND TRIUMPH

Seeing all this commotion from the Columbus heights, General Polk resolved to snatch victory from defeat. Already he had sent two more regiments to aid Pillow and Tappan. (Union artillerists not looting the camp had turned the Rebels' own cannon against the troop-laden vessels, though without effect.) Now Polk committed his last two regiments, the 11th Louisiana and 15th Tennessee, and directed Brig. Gen. Benjamin Franklin ("Frank") Cheatham to lead them across, take charge of the situation, and launch a counterattack.

The *Charm, Prince* and *Hill* boarded Confederate troops eager to get into the fight. No longer were Federals firing on the steamboats; Grant was herding his men back into ranks amid Johnston's burning tents. As he neared the riverbank well below the camp, Cheatham saw that Pillow's efforts to rally his men had not yet succeeded. A disorganized mass of men crowded the shore, some shouting "Don't land!" "We are whipped!" "Go back!"[470] Some waded out into the water, trying to clamber aboard the boats they hoped would bear them back across the river to safety. But with a few musket volleys into the air, Cheatham quelled the excitement, and his two regiments trudged ashore.

Pillow, Tappan and Cheatham harangued their men into battle line, and shortly after 2:30 the fired-up Southerners set out to renew the engagement. Grant had already led his command out of the burnt camp back toward their transports when the Rebels came storming out of the woods into a cornfield, volleying into the rear ranks of the astonished Yankees. The bluecoats began running, and the panic spread when the men realized that the road leading back to the ships was blocked by Union surgeons' wagons bearing the battle's wounded. Units began to evaporate as soldiers

---

470   Nathaniel Cheairs Hughes, *The Battle of Belmont: Grant Strikes South* (Chapel Hill, 1991), p. 137.

fled into the woods, every man for himself. Grant raced ahead to the landing ("as fast as my horse could carry me," he recalled), hoping to direct the *Lexington* and *Tyler* to fire over his men's heads and into the Rebel masses.[471] But hearing of the Federal victory celebration in the captured enemy camp, Captain Walke had ordered his gunboats back to Cairo. Grant's infantrymen would have to face the Rebel attack on their own.

Cheatham led a vigorous pursuit, and kept the Yankees on the run. "I never did as fine running and as much of it," recalled Pvt. H.J. Walter of the 30th Illinois. "It was a scene of indescribable confusion. Reg't was mixed with reg't company with company. The unhurt with the wounded and throwing away everything but their guns & cartridge boxes they hurried along only hoping to reach the boats before the enemy came upon them. The poor fellows were exhausted & it was only through terror that they were able to move at all."[472]

At the landing Grant's six transports were quickly overwhelmed by men frantic to get aboard. Gangplanks broke or fell into the water, forcing soldiers to wade and swim out to the vessels' sides; sailors on deck threw out ropes and nets to help their comrades climb up. The chaos worsened when Southern artillery shells began bursting overhead. "Even as they embarked," remembered Confederate N.P. Davidson, "and as their boats were out in the river, they were fired on and many must have been killed, for they were packed all over the boats like sardines in a can."[473] Charles Scott, pilot of the *Belle Memphis,* decided it was time to go, whether or not all of Grant's men had boarded his craft. Scott steered his ship away from shore and into the river, followed by the five other transports.

---

471   Henry I. Kurtz, "The Battle of Belmont," *Civil War Times Illustrated,* June 1963, p. 21.

472   Steven E. Woodworth, *Nothing But Defeat: The Army of the Tennessee 1861-1863* (New York, 2005), p. 53.

473   N.P. Davidson, "Witness to the Battle of Belmont," *Confederate Veteran,* vol. 16 (1908), 191.

The hasty evacuation and premature departure of the steamers left behind hundreds of Union soldiers, including over a hundred wounded, soon to fall into Confederate hands. More than 500 hundred men from the 27th Illinois alone were thus lost. General Grant himself was among them. Staying with this regiment, Grant was last seen on his horse as it slipped on its haunches down the muddy bank, then swimming with the rider desperately out for the last rope line thrown from the ship. He failed to catch hold, and was forced back to shore. His capture by Cheatham's troops was later hailed as the most satisfying aspect of the Confederate victory at Belmont.

CASUALTIES, NOVEMBER 7

Among the missing, Ulysses Grant was but a temporary figure. Escorted by General Cheatham across the river and into Columbus that night, the two engaged in liquor-refreshed memories of horse races. As the evening wore on, each general showed his enjoyment of the other's company as well as the whisky. Cheatham began slurring the Federal commander's name into "Useless," while Grant sported the idea that such *bonhomie* as this was being wasted by war, and that the two sides should settle the whole thing with one big horse race. The next day, sober but headached, Grant was sent to Nashville. Under house arrest there he enjoyed the privileges of a high officer's rank in loose confinement until Sidney Johnston secured his release back to Union lines a week later—although at a greater exchange rate than had come into acceptance; Johnston bartered back Grant for all 71 Confederates taken prisoner when the Yankees had overrun the camp.

In the end, the Union paid considerably for Grant's defeat: 95 killed, 306 wounded, and 728 captured. This amounted to over a thousand men lost, more than a third of the 3,000 taken into battle. Confederate losses totaled 120 K, 434 W and 117 M. After exchange of prisoners, these 600 casualties represented just 12% of the estimated 5,000 troops which Polk was able to throw into the battle.

THE DEATH OF GENERAL POLK

At his headquarters in Bowling Green, General Johnston received the news of Polk's victory with a hurrah more of relief than of joy. By standards set in the war's later much more grisly fights, Belmont ranks as but an early skirmish. Still, after two months of straining his limited resources across his 400-mile front, striving to contain superior enemy numbers, Sidney Johnston relished the Southern triumph as a means of securing the extreme left of his Tennessee-Kentucky line.

Accolades flowed to Leonidas Polk for having engineered the victory. "All laurels to General Polk," headlined the Meridian (Mississippi) *Chronicle*. "He has proven himself as redoubtable in his general's tunic as in his bishop's robe." The General himself had overstated the dimensions of his triumph in his first after-action telegram: "A complete rout—roads filled with dead, wounded, guns, ammunition, knapsacks....Precipitate embarkation.... General Grant reported killed."[474] That Grant wound up among the captured and not the killed did nothing to lessen the Confederate general's sense of mission accomplished.

Polk was still basking in the hero's limelight four days after the battle, on the 11th, when he and two staff officers, Capt. S.W. Rucker and Lt. William D. Pickett, were making an inspection tour of the Columbus defenses. The group stopped at the big "Lady Polk" rifled gun, which had done so much damage to the Yankees in the battle just days before. Polk summoned the battery commander, Capt. William J. Keiter. "On his appearing, the General complimented him and his men on the skill and efficiency with which they handled the gun in the previous engagement in a very handsome manner, which appeared to gratify Capt. Keiter very much," wrote one onlooker.[475] The Captain proudly promised

---

474   Joseph H. Parks, *General Leonidas Polk, C.S.A.: The Fighting Bishop* (Baton Rouge, 1962), p. 192.

475   William D. Pickett, "The Bursting of the 'Lady Polk,'" *Confederate Veteran,* vol. 12 (1904), 277.

to sink any enemy gunboat coming downriver, and offered to fire a shell to demonstrate the cannon's formidable range. The General gave permission.

Keiter called forth his crew; Polk and his two officers dismounted and climbed up on the gun parapet to view the shell's arc. "Directly a sergeant came with seven men," recorded an eyewitness. "They took their stations; the gun was already 'in battery' and elevated. At the command 'Ready!' the cap was inserted in the vent and the lanyard hook attached. 'Fire!' rang loud and shrill the voice of Keiter."[476] Something then went tragically wrong. At the pull of the lanyard, the huge cannon exploded in a fiery blast and dense cloud of black smoke. Then came a second roar, the detonation of gunpowder stored in a nearby magazine; the earth shook under the blast.

"When the smoke cleared away a horrible sight met the eye," one rattled witness recalled. "The gun, ten feet in length, with a breach nearly as large as a flour barrel, was burst in two, one-half buried in the embankment and the other half thrown over it; the muzzle, thrown forward, was partly hidden from sight in the earth." Captain Keiter and all seven gunners were killed. "The poor fellows who manned it were dead and dying, lying here and there, ghastly corpses or in the death agony. Heads gone, legs and arms torn from the bodies, flesh jerking and quivering in the semi-living, hideous trunks."[477] Two other officers, Lt. Robert Snowden and Maj. Thomas Ford, also lay dead, and several men writhed on the ground, severely wounded.

The earthen parapet had been blown away by the magazine explosion. Amidst the smoking heaps of dirt, soldiers scrambled frantically in search of General Polk. He was dead when they found him. "His body, badly torn, was lying upon the ground at full length, with the face upturned," wrote Col. W.S. Dilworth. A huge piece of iron from the exploded cannon had passed through

---

476   A.G.G., "The Bursting of the 'Lady Polk,'" *Confederate Veteran*, vol. 12 (1904), 119.

477   F.D. Jodon, "Concerning the Battle of Belmont," *Confederate Veteran*, vol. 9 (1901), 14.

his chest, breaking both arms. Maj. A. Peter Stewart, commander of Polk's artillery, had heard the explosion in his tent and came running to the dreadful scene. Weeping, he bent down over Polk's mangled corpse. "My dear, dear friend," he grieved. "Little did I think this morning that I should be called upon to witness this."[478] The General's two staff officers remarkably survived the explosion; Captain Rucker was thrown to the ground, badly stunned by the blast with a severe leg wound. Lieutenant Pickett, knocked unconscious, came to with remarkably light injuries. Several others were injured as well; one of the wounded died in hospital two days later.

At his headquarters in Bowling Green, General Johnston received the news of Polk's death on the night of the 12th. Visibly shaken, he dictated to an aide a general order that soon circulated amongst his troops:

> Comrades, you are called to mourn your captain, your companion in arms. Major General Polk fell to-day at the outpost of this army. In this distinguished leader we have lost the most courteous of gentlemen, the most gallant of soldiers. The Christian patriot soldier has neither lived nor died in vain. His example is before you; his mantle rests with you.[479]

The cause of the explosion of the "Lady Polk" has since been disputed. Several Confederates blamed faulty ammunition, but historical consensus blames the notorious unreliability of cast iron cannon loaded with heavy powder charges. For the "Lady Polk" and its eight-inch shell, the powder bag alone weighed twenty pounds. Though the cannon had not been fired extensively, artillerists throughout the war had cast-iron guns explode on

---

478   Stephen Davis, "The Death of Bishop Polk," *Blue & Gray*, June 1998, p. 4; Saavis Elliott, *Soldier of Tennessee: General Alexander P. Stewart and the Confederate War in the West* (Baton Rouge, 1999), p. 11.

479   Davis, *op. cit.*, 14.

them, often killing or maiming the crewmen. "There was only one cause," concluded one Southerner: "the treacherous and uncertain action of cast iron under sudden strain."[480]

Regardless of cause, in the death of Leonidas Polk the Confederate army lost an important general who might have contributed materially to Southern victory.

KENTUCKY SECEDES (FINALLY)

In November 1861 with Confederate forces hugging the southern swath of Kentucky from Columbus through Bowling Green eastward to Mill Springs and beyond, Gen. Sidney Johnston could lay claim to controlling only about a fourth of the state. Frankfort, the capital, was firmly in Federal hands, but this was essentially an empty trophy. Governor Beriah Magoffin held decidedly pro-Southern sympathies (it was he who had replied to Lincoln's call for troops, "Kentucky will furnish no troops for the wicked purpose of subduing her sister Southern States"), but the legislature was largely pro-Unionist. Thus when the solons passed Federal-friendly bills, Magoffin vetoed them; essentially powerless, he resigned in August of 1862.

"Pro-Confederate Kentuckians longed to be in the Confederacy, but the Frankfort government was Unionist," as historian Lowell Harrison describes the deadlock.[481] A group of pro-Southern Kentuckians, both civilians and soldiers, gathered on October 29 in Russellville (thirty miles southwest of Bowling Green, General Johnston's headquarters). Affirming a people's right "to alter, reform, or abolish their government, in such manner as they think proper," the group called for a "sovereignty convention"—meaning, a gathering to talk about secession from the Union. Accordingly, on November 18 again at Russellville there assembled 115 delegates representing sixty-eight counties. Because "the President and Congress have treated the supreme law of the Union with contempt and usurped to themselves the right to interfere with

---

480   Pickett, *op. cit.*, 278.

481   Lowell Harrison, "Kentucky" in W. Buck Yearns, ed., *The Confederate Governors* (Athens GA, 1985), p. 83.

the rights and liberties of the States and people," they resolved, "we do hereby forever sever our connection with the Government of the United States, and, in the name of the people, we do hereby declare Kentucky to be a free and independent State."[482] The delegates accordingly framed a provisional government with the capital set at Bowling Green, and elected a prominent State Rights Democrat, George W. Johnson, as governor. Then the convention drafted a petition that the Confederate government should receive Kentucky as a state.[483]

For his part President Davis was a little concerned about the irregularity of the Russellville proceedings. But as a Kentuckian himself, he was eager to have his native state represented on the Confederate national banner as its thirteenth star (after Missouri). Congress formally accepted Kentucky as a Confederate state on December 10.

TURMOIL IN EAST TENNESSEE

Bordered by the Great Smokies and Cumberland Mountains, east Tennessee was a geographic, economic and political entity which posed significant problems for the infant Confederacy. The hub of political power in early state history, east Tennessee had seen its influence wane in the decades before the war. The capital had moved from Knoxville to Nashville in 1825; middle Tennesseans in the state legislature voted to hog state funding for railroads and improvements in their section; in the west, burgeoning Mississippi riverboat traffic fed the local cotton economy. In 1841 some fuming east Tennesseans began to talk of forming a new state out of their thirty-one counties, but the movement went nowhere.

It was well known that the east grew less cotton and had fewer slaves than the middle and western areas, and these data further delineated the eastern region from the rest of the state. More wheat was grown there, but as a cash crop wheat could not compete with cotton or tobacco, making east Tennesseans relatively poorer than

---

482 Lowell H. Harrison, *The Confederate War in Kentucky* (Lexington, 1975), pp. 20-21.

483 Yearns, *op. cit.,* pp. 83-84.

their statefolk to the west (a humiliating psychological burden in itself). The region's two leading political figures, Andrew Johnson and William G. "Parson" Brownlow, railed against the dominance of slaveholders in state politics and consistently championed the interests of east Tennessee, but other than reinforcing the area's sense of separatism, their agitations did nothing to ameliorate the conditions of their constituents.

In the election of 1860 all Tennesseans essentially voted against Lincoln (who was not on the ballot), but easterners gave more ballots to native son John Bell than to the neighboring Democrat, Kentuckian John Breckinridge. Even after Lincoln's election, antipathy to slaveholding aristocrats led most east Tennesseans to oppose secession. In January 1861, the vociferous Brownlow, editor of the Knoxville *Whig,* vented in his paper that east Tennesseans "can never live in a Southern Confederacy and be made the hewers of wood and drawers of water for a set of aristocrats and overbearing tyrants....We have no interest in common with the Cotton States. We are a grain growing and stock raising people, and we can conduct a cheap government, inhabiting the Switzerland of America."[484] After the legislature called for a state referendum to discuss possible disunion on February 9, 1861, east Tennessee rejected even the idea of calling a convention by an overwhelming five-to-one majority. In only three east Tennessee counties (such as Chattanooga's Hamilton County) did voters favor holding a possible secession convention.

Not even Fort Sumter and Lincoln's call for troops, nor the legislature's vote for secession on May 6, nor even Governor Harris' military league with the Confederacy could shake a majority of east Tennesseans from their opposition to secession. In the plebiscite of June 8, the region voted 32,923 to 14,768 against leaving the Union. Of course, voters statewide approved secession two-to-one, but nearly 70% of the 47,000 ballots cast against disunion came from the eastern counties.

---

484   Noel C. Fisher, *War at Every Door: Partisan Politics and Guerrilla Violence in East Tennessee, 1860-1862* (Chapel Hill, 1997), pp. 30, 32.

After their state had gone out, many east Tennesseans still refused to affirm their allegiance to the Confederacy. The region held four Congressional districts and in statewide elections held on August 8, twin slates of candidates amazingly appeared on the ballot: one whose nominees said they would represent the district in Richmond, the other who said they would take their seats in the national Congress at Washington. In two districts the pro-Unionists Thomas A.R. Nelson and Horace Maynard actually won. Maynard left for Washington and served his two-year term in the House. Although Confederate officials later tried to call for another round of balloting, this time to send a local representative to Richmond, most voters in Maynard's 2d District refused to participate, and the "election" of a Confederate Congressman from the district proved farcical. Nelson had a harder time. Before he could set out for Washington, Confederate authorities arrested him, bound him to house arrest, and forbade his leaving the state. In the two other Congressional races voting results were so close that the pro-C.S. and pro-U.S. candidates in both districts claimed victory. The two Confederate Congressmen from the Third and Fourth Districts made their ways to Richmond and were sworn in. Andrew J. Clements, Unionist in the Third District, was able to slip through Rebel lines and be seated in Washington. His colleague from the Fourth, however, was detained by the authorities for months, and succeeded in serving only part of his term in office after he secured clandestine passage to D.C.

These political embarrassments were a portent of more difficulties which east Tennessee would create for the Confederate States.

OUTBREAK OF VIOLENCE

Confederate army recruiters knew they had a problem in east Tennessee during June and July '61 when their call for volunteers, laced with attractive sign-up bounties offered by the state, yielded a surprisingly low number of enlistments. C.S. officials quickly realized that many men in the state's eastern region were at least going to sit the war out, if not actively fight for the Federal cause.

While some pro-Unionists made their way northward to volunteer for Abe Lincoln's army, Kentucky's vaunted neutrality made it hard for many to trek to a U.S. recruitment camp. Thus, most anti-Confederate east Tennesseans formed military organizations in their own localities, though they were often clandestine. Reflecting the more pro-Southern sentiment of Knoxville, Chattanooga and other urban areas, Confederate recruits rallied and mustered conspicuously and with fanfare in city squares and central parks. East Tennessee Unionists, on the other hand, organized themselves more furtively into minute-man units ready to assemble upon warning of outside threat. When, on July 6, word passed through Bradley County (between Chattanooga and Athens) that a column of Confederate cavalry was approaching, seven hundred Union loyalists gathered, carrying old muskets, knives or axes, even pitchforks. The rumor of Rebels proved unfounded, and the Bradley militiamen quietly returned home. But their pro-Confederate neighbors were horrified. "By some means unknown to our friends here," wrote one to President Davis, "in twelve hours near 1,000 Union men were in arms at different rendezvous, and disclosed a most complete organization, secret hitherto in its character and numbers." Even worse, the Bradley County Lincolnites "had dissolved, only to hold themselves in readiness, at like short notice, to rally again with their rifles and shot-guns and with such ammunition as they have."[485]

Sometimes communities saw rival military companies form in uneasy proximity. In Hancock County, two Home Guards units organized, each a couple hundred strong; one pledged allegiance to Jeff Davis's Southern Confederacy, while the other very much did not. Leaders of the two camps tacitly agreed not to attack one another, and officials in Nashville accepted the informal truce in the interest of maintaining the public tranquility. Sometimes that tranquility was broken by flare-ups of violence. Unionist partisans occasionally ambushed Confederate patrols, firing from the woods

---

485 *O.R.*, vol. 4, 366.

and felling a few horsemen before fleeing. After this occurred in Fentress County, pro-Southern militiamen angrily arrested a particularly outspoken Unionist and lynched him outside his home.

The retaliatory nature of this violence threatened an outbreak of full-blown guerrilla warfare in east Tennessee during the summer of 1861. Neither side wanted it; events would show that Confederate Tennesseans benefitted more by, at least initially, exercising a masterful policy of general restraint in dealing with the Lincolnites lurking amongst them.

CONFEDERATES SEEK TO MOLLIFY EAST TENNESSEANS

Fortunately for the Southerners, Governor Isham Harris in Nashville held one of the more enlightened views of east Tennessee Unionism. Rejecting the view that anti-Confederate feeling in the area was well rooted among the common people, Harris believed that only a few agitators—Parson Brownlow, Andy Johnson, a few others—were responsible for stirring up expressions of disloyalty in the area. Harris thus suggested to Richmond that Confederates employ the olive branch, at least for awhile: post as few C.S. army units as possible in the region (and those only of Tennesseans) and appoint to command the east Tennessee district an officer who would demonstrate reason, competence and even sensitivity to the delicate political situation.

Felix Kirk Zollicoffer seemed to be the man for the job. Born near Columbia, Tennessee in 1812, he had little formal schooling (his parents could not afford tutoring or the local academy). Instead, Zollicoffer taught himself reading and writing well enough that in 1835 he signed on as an apprentice with Columbia's weekly *Observer*. Attuned to the partisan instincts of his readers (sometimes Whig, sometimes Democrat), he began writing editorial commentary that transformed him from political scribe to political leader. Brief service in the Second Seminole War, 1836-37, added a fillip of military distinction. Beginning with election to small local offices at first, then to Tennessee adjutant general and state comptroller, 1845-52, Zollicoffer was elected to Congress and served three consecutive terms, 1853-59, whereupon he declined to run for re-election. Serving as Isham Harris' chief of staff in the capitol, Zollicoffer was at the right place on May 9, 1861, to receive commission in the Provisional Army of Tennessee as brigadier general.

Assigned to training recruits at Camp Trousdale northeast of Nashville, Zollicoffer received his commission as Confederate brigadier on July 9. President Davis in the summer of 1861 was as solicitous as Governor Harris for the defense of east Tennessee. He worried about the enclave of Unionism (at Richmond, this was "disloyalty") which, if allowed to grow, could seriously weaken the Confederate war effort. Moreover, given General Johnston's too-stretched line, Davis saw the region as a weak point in the Confederate strategic front from Virginia to the Mississippi. Finally, through east Tennessee ran the East Tennessee & Georgia Railroad (Chattanooga to Knoxville) and the East Tennessee & Virginia (Knoxville to Bristol), vital links in the South's railway connection from Richmond to Atlanta. For these reasons, on July 26, 1861, when Davis appointed Brigadier General Zollicoffer to take charge at Knoxville, it was with instructions to "repel invasion, protect the railroad, and preserve peace."[486]

Yet following Governor Harris' recommendation, Richmond provided only a modest military presence in the area: two regiments in Chattanooga, one in Knoxville, one as well in Greeneville. Upon taking charge and seeing the wisdom of avoiding a harsh and repressive policy toward the native Unionists, Zollicoffer nonetheless asked for and got reinforcements from Nashville; he merged these into his command at Knoxville as an impressive, small army of around 5,000 men, and determined at least to confront the most outward signs of civil disloyalty. He shut down Parson Brownlow's newspaper, lowered and removed the United States flag in front of his home, and sent Brownlow and other Unionist leaders scurrying into Kentucky (this was deliberate on the Confederates' part, as they did not want to provoke the Unionists by arresting their leaders; they only wanted them out of the way). At the same time Zollicoffer ordered his garrison commander at Greeneville to arrest Senator Andy Johnson's two sons after they

---

486   Lowell Harrison, "Mill Springs," *Civil War Times Illustrated,* January 1972, p. 6.

made loud anti-Confederate speeches (but here, too, he directed that the Johnsons merely be escorted to the Kentucky line). Finally, to protect the railroad Zollicoffer also posted guards at the E.T. & G.R.R. bridges, the probable targets of disloyalist saboteurs.

These shows of strength comforted pro-Southern civilians in the region and even stimulated their volunteering for the C.S. army. By the end of August, Zollicoffer felt that if he had not quelled the Unionists, he had at least driven them underground. Then, with the fiction of Bluegrass neutrality blown apart in the first week of September, Zollicoffer sought and received permission from Richmond to advance his forces into southeastern Kentucky. The General led his small army from Greeneville to Cumberland Gap, the key mountain pass and roadway at the intersecting of Tennessee, Kentucky and Virginia. Aware that Union forces were also on the advance, Zollicoffer left a garrison at the gap and marched toward London, Kentucky, fifty miles to the northwest, where he established a fortified camp on the 21st of October.

FEDERAL ACTIVITY IN SOUTHEAST KENTUCKY

Zollicoffer was correct: a Federal force was heading his way. After General Robert Anderson established his departmental HQ at Louisville, he ordered Brig. Gen. Albin Schoepf (a Hungarian-born engineer, one of Lincoln's ethno-political appointments) to establish a Union recruiting camps northeast of Danville. "Camp Dick Robinson," as it was known, became the Federals' forward base in eastern Kentucky. Arriving at Robinson on September 15, Schoepf soon assembled a force numbering some 9,000 Unionist Kentuckians (and a few Tennesseans, too). General Anderson in Louisville was beginning to buckle under his departmental pressures—he would resign October 5—and President Lincoln in Washington was growing impatient. East Tennessee Unionist leaders, such as Parson Brownlow, Andy Johnson, Horace Maynard and others, were beseeching Lincoln to order a military advance into their region to "liberate" the loyalists there. More importantly, they pledged to help militarily. In mid-October one Unionist spokesman, the Rev. William B. Carter, secretly met with General Sherman, the new commander in Louisville, and proposed that if

Federal forces were to advance into east Tennessee, Unionists there would attack and burn nine key bridges on the East Tennessee Railroad line, from Bristol southwest to Chattanooga, and so hamper the Rebels' military response. Sherman was reluctant to send Schoepf forth on the offensive into the logistically trying terrain of east Tennessee; he was even more reluctant to trust a bunch of civilians with a dangerous, important military mission. Carter, however, got Congressman Maynard in Washington to explain the plan to President Lincoln, who eagerly bought into it. On October 22 Lincoln ordered Sherman to send Schoepf into east Tennessee to break up the Rebel railroad above Knoxville. Calculating the time needed for Schoepf's advance, Carter and company began planning to launch their bridge raids on or about the night of Saturday, November 2.

THE "WILDCAT STAMPEDE"

General Schoepf had pitched a forward position, called "Camp Wild Cat," just a dozen miles northeast of London, Ky. (which Zollicoffer reached on October 20). Learning of the enemy presence nearby—some 300 Yankees, reportedly—the Confederate commander quickly called for an attack on Schoepf's force. On the morning of October 2 three Tennessee regiments moved against the Federals at their fortified camp. They advanced so quickly that first the Union cavalry took flight, then the blue coated infantry started to waver, too.

"God damn you, stand your ground if there is a million of them," screamed a Federal officer.[487]

The Northern troops did indeed stand their ground—but only for a while. Continued Confederate pressure on their lines caused Schoepf's troops to buckle and start heading for the rear. Even on a small scale, rapid retreats can quickly turn into routs. Thus did the Federal withdrawal from the battlefield morph into a phenomenon soon to be called "the Wild Cat Stampede."

---

487   Raymond E. Myers, *The Zollie Tree: A Biography of Confederate General Felix Kirk Zollicoffer* (Louisville KY, 1964), 56.

Edward Pollard, associate editor of the Richmond *Examiner* and early chronicler of the War for Southern Independence, wrote of the stampede, "the retreat of the panic-stricken soldiers, which for miles was performed at the double-quick, rivalled the agile performances at Bull Run."[488]

Casualties from the two-hour fight signified its status as something more than a skirmish, but a little less than a battle: 4 killed, 18 wounded U.S.; 11 killed/missing, 42 wounded C.S. Its more important consequence, though, was that it utterly halted Albin Schoepf's plans to advance into East Tennessee, presidential order, or no order.

EAST TENNESSEE BRIDGE-BURNINGS PROMPT STERN CONFEDERATE RESPONSE

No one told William Carter and his fellow conspirators that the Union column intended to "liberate" them had turned back before even reaching the Tennessee state line. Word travelled slowly in the fastnesses of Appalachia, and it is possible that even if they had learned of Schoepf's reversal, the Unionist bridge burners would have launched their incendiary initiative anyway.

This they did, on the scheduled night of November 2. Organized as small cadres along the 270-mile route of the East Tennessee Railroad from Bristol to Chattanooga, some 300 pro-Unionist civilians skulked through the night with their matches and tar-tipped torches, and set fires to the footings of five separate trestles: over the Holston River near Bristol, Lick Creek east of Greenville, Hiwassee River near Cleveland and Chickamauga Creek, both east and west of Chattanooga. At one point Confederate guards were unable to respond in time to put out the fires, and had to watch as their prized bridge was consumed in flames. At four other points, however, Southern guards spotted the torchers in time to drive them off and save the spans. The Unionists fled after a few shots were fired at them.

---

488   Edward A. Pollard, *Southern History of the War,* 2 vols. (Richmond, 1866), vol. 1, 202.

With Federal forces having stamped at Camp Wild Cat, Reverend Carter and his bridge-burners were left to fend for themselves. Confederate authorities reacted swiftly and remorselessly against them. General Sidney Johnson ordered four regiments from Nashville and Memphis into the region; the Defense Department in Richmond ordered two more from Georgia. General Zollicoffer himself led one as well to Knoxville, where he declared martial law and locked down all roads out of the city as he ordered a house-to-house search for suspected traitors. In over a dozen counties, Unionist camps were attacked by Confederate troops and citizen volunteers eager to remove the traitorous threats to their local law and order. While some Unionists escaped, several hundred were arrested. Feeling betrayed and angry that the "Tennessee Tories" had spurned his olive branch, General Zollicoffer was in no mood for continued clemency. "The leaders should be seized and held as prisoners," he declared; "the leniency shown them has been unavailing. They have acted with base duplicity, and should no longer be trusted."[489]

On November 1 Zollicoffer announced a stern policy of reprisal and repression. "Fugitive traitors should now be pursued to extermination," and soon eighteen confirmed bridge-burners were caught and hanged in public executions. For the more than 200 "Tories" in jail, Zollicoffer ordered an "indeterminate" incarceration, darkly hinting that they would be imprisoned for the duration of the war. Finally, declaring that "those that are yet hostile can only be cured of their folly by severity," the Confederate commander on November 16 issued his most draconian order yet. "Tories should be made to feel in their person and their property that their hostile attitude promises to them nothing but destruction," he wrote.[490] Thus all property belonging to known Unionists—houses, land, businesses—was confiscated as a matter of military necessity. All persons thus dispossessed were banished from Confederate-held territory and ordered to pass through to Federal lines within forty-five days, by January 1, 1862, at the latest.

---

489   Noel C. Fisher, *War at Every Door: Partisan Politics and Guerrilla Violence in East Tennessee*, 1860-62 (Chapel Hill, 1997) p. 57.

490   *Ibid.*

The Confederates' admittedly harsh policies worked. Though the exact numbers are unknown, probably several thousand Tennessee Tories left the state in the largest compulsory expulsion of civilians in the war's first year, to be topped only by Union General Benjamin F. Butler's banishment of pro-Confederate citizens from New Orleans in the spring of 1862. Many thousands more renounced their latent loyalty to the United States and swore allegiance to Jefferson Davis and the Confederacy. Many military-eligible men even joined the Southern army, thus risking their lives in order to protect their wives and children back home.

By the end of 1861, east Tennessee Unionism was effectively snuffed out. For the rest of the war, Confederate authority in the region was undisputed. More importantly, a depressed and demoralized Abraham Lincoln, who had hoped so fervently that east Tennessee could be made into the foundation of a "reconstructed" state government, gave up any idea of sending military forces into the area. It was neither the first nor last of Old Abe's disappointments in the War for Southern Independence.

Chapter Ten:

The South Foresees Victory

SHANKS AND THE SENATOR

It's nice to have a friend in high places—especially if he is President of the United States.

Edward Dickinson Baker had been born in London in 1811. His parents brought him to Philadelphia when he was four; the family later moved to Illinois. Growing up there, reading the law and passing the bar led in 1845 to Baker moving to Springfield, where he befriended another ambitious attorney, Abraham Lincoln. Election to the Illinois legislature, command (briefly) of a regiment in the Mexican War, and two terms in Congress attested to Baker's distinction.

So did the fact that in 1848 Lincoln named his second son, Eddie, after his good friend. In the early '50s Baker moved his family to California, where he became involved in the Republican Party. He made political friends in Oregon as well, and after he moved there, Baker was sent to the U.S. Senate in October 1860. After Lincoln's election a month later, Baker kept the president-elect informed about secessionist sentiment in the far West. (Pro-Southern fervor in Arizona Territory, for instance, was so strong that after the start of the war, Congress in Richmond recognized Arizona as a Confederate territory.)[491]

---

491   Alvin M. Josephy, Jr., *The Civil War in the American West* (New York, 1991), 50.

A shrewd politician, Abe Lincoln never forgot who had done him a favor, so after Baker raised a regiment of Pennsylvania troops, Lincoln saw that he got a brigadier general's commission. Baker declined it, though, as Senate rules would have made him resign his seat as Oregon's senior senator. But he could keep the colonelcy to which he had been elected by his Pennsylvanians. In early October 1861 Colonel Baker was commanding a brigade in McClellan's Army of the Potomac, part of Brig. Gen. Charles P. Stone's division.

Stone's headquarters were at Poolesville, a dozen miles north-west of Washington on the north bank of the Potomac. Directly across the river were some 1,700 Confederates watching fords and ferries around Leesburg, under the command of Col. Nathan G. Evans.

Unlike Ed Baker, South Carolina-born Evans was a trained military man (West Point, 1848) if not a particularly learned one (36th of 38 in his graduating class). Like most West Pointers before the war, he served out west in the dragoons fighting Indians. In late February 1861, when Southern forces were organizing, Evans resigned his U.S. commission and offered his services to his state. They were quickly snapped up; at the time of Fort Sumter he was serving as Major Adjutant General in the South Carolina forces around Charleston.

Nicknames often come from one's appearance. In the War for Southern Independence, illustrious Confederates include Maj. Gen. Richard S. Ewell ("Old Bald Head") and Admiral Raphael Semmes, whose impeccably polished moustache led to his sailors calling him "Old Beeswax." In Evans' case, it was the sight of spindly legs that during his youth led to his nickname of "Shanks."[492]

But, boy, could he drink. Placed in command of the 4th South Carolina, Colonel Evans and his regiment were sent to northern Virginia and became part of the army that General Beauregard was building there. (It was Shanks Evans who on the morning of July 21 was first to discern that McDowell's intent was to attack

---

492   Jason H. Silverman, Samuel N. Thomas Jr. and Beverly D. Evans IV, *Shanks: The Life and Wars of Nathan George Evans, C.S.A.* (Alexandria VA, 2002), p. 13.

the Confederate left across Bull Run.) "He was a rude brawler of an officer, insubordinate, gruff, rough hewn," writes historian Jack Davis, who characterizes Evans as "no saint." In the field an orderly always rode behind him carrying a wooden one-gallon drum filled with whiskey, of which he was very fond. He called this magnacanteen his "barrelita," as in "Bring up my barrelita, Adolph!" One of his men wrote that Evans was "the best drinker, the most eloquent swearer...and the most magnificent bragger I ever saw."[493]

Soon Shanks Evans would have something to brag about.

"A SLIGHT DEMONSTRATION" TURNS INTO A ROUT

General Stone (and McClellan, for that matter) worried about the size and intentions of Evans' force across the river at Leesburg. They decided that perhaps a "demonstration," a reconnaissance-in-force—getting some infantry across the Potomac—might, as we say in the South, "flush the quail": compel Evans' troops to retreat, or maybe bring on a full-fledged fight in which the Federals could prevail.

Alas for the Yankees, they were deluded, as the Union force assembled for this recon (about 1,700) was only equal in strength to Evans' numbers. Worse, Colonel Baker's military inexperience began to show from the outset on the day of the "demonstration," October 21. Not only did he not know the strength of the enemy in front of him, he did not order any kind of scouting expedition to determine their position. Then, when Baker ordered his brigade out of camp, he had not assembled enough boats to get the men across the river. As a result, Baker's four regiments—the 15th and 18th Massachusetts, 71st Pennsylvania and 42nd New York—floundered through the Potomac water at Conrad's Ferry and Harrison's Island. This gave Colonel Evans plenty of time to consolidate his troops at the expected crossing point, the seventy-foot-high Ball's Bluff on the south bank.

---

493   Edward G. Longacre, "Charles P. Stone and the 'Crime of Unlucky Generals,'" *Civil War Times Illustrated*, November 1974, p. 41.

Baker's troops had barely gotten ashore and laboriously clambered up the steep slope when Evans ordered a fierce attack. Around 12:30 p.m. the ambush began by Evans' three regiments (8th Virginia, 17th and 18th Mississippi). Almost immediately the Federals began to fall back toward the riverbank. There Baker attempted to forge a defensive line against the Confederate attacks that intensified as the afternoon wore on. About 5 o'clock Baker was shot and killed instantly. Soon afterward, sensing that the Federal line was about to break, Evans ordered a charge along his entire front. Sure enough, the Northerners broke and ran for the river. Piling aboard the boats tethered at the water's edge, they overwhelmed the vessels, which soon sank, throwing everyone into the Potomac. Others, forgetting their heavy gear, waded into the river, only to drown. Soon the water was strewn with scores of blue-uniformed bodies. High above on the ridge of the bluff, Evans' men kept firing at the struggling, helpless enemy below them—fish in a barrel, as it were.

Military historian Joseph B. Mitchell has drawn an important lesson from the Union disaster at Ball's Bluff: "this battle turned out to be a horrible example of why 'political' officers should not be appointed to high command, and then be asked to fight against a trained soldier."[494]

Unfortunately for the Northern war effort, this was a lesson that Abraham Lincoln was slow to learn.

CONSEQUENCES

When it was all over the casualties began to be counted. Brigadier General Stone, Baker's commanding officer, tried to mitigate his subordinate's defeat by stating that the number of officers and men killed was 49; historians have set that figure as more likely from 200 to 250.[495] The Northerners' tally of 150 officers and men wounded was also probably low, but their count

---

494   Lt. Col. Joseph B. Mitchell, "Debacle at Ball's Bluff," *Civil War Times,* January 1962, 9.

495   Byron Farwell, *Ball's Bluff: A Small Battle and Its Long Shadow* (McLean VA, 1990), 134-35; James A. Morgan III, *A Little Short of Boats: The Fight at Ball's Bluff and Edwards Ferry* (Ft. Mitchell KY, 2004), p. 184.

of 714 missing or unaccounted for realistically reflects the fact that hundreds of Federal soldiers drowned in the Potomac River. The undeniable conclusion was that two-thirds of Baker's brigade was K, W or M/C. Evans' casualties (36 killed, 117 wounded, 2 missing, or 155), on the other hand, represented not even a tenth of his strength going into the battle.

Then there was the booty gleaned from the battlefield, which Confederates started scavenging the day after the engagement. Colonel Evans reported 1,500 muskets and three pieces of artillery gathered up, plus lots of cartridge boxes, bayonets, haversacks, canteens and other gear. The enlisted men were most interested in all the clothing and footwear acquired—the items tossed away by fleeing Yankees or peeled off from dead ones. "It is quite amusing to see our officers & men since the Battle with yankee over coats on and other yankee fixings," wrote a Mississippian to his daughter a few weeks after the fight; "we hardly look like the same set of men."

Needless to say, the South rejoiced at the news from Leesburg. The Defense Department quickly promoted Evans to brigadier general, to rank from October 21. Two months after the battle the Confederate Congress passed a resolution of thanks to Evans, his officers and men for the "brilliant victory achieved by them over largely superior forces of the enemy" (which latter part was not correct, as the two sides fought with about equal strength, 1,600-1,700).

On the other side, Northerners' mortification over the Union defeat magnified when it was learned that among the slain was one of President Lincoln's best friends. Many looked for a scapegoat, and they found one in Charles Stone, who had ordered Baker across the river. A U.S. Congressional committee investigated the matter and threw Stone into prison without giving him a chance to counter the charges against him, or even to learn what they were. He was released in August 1862 after six months of confinement. Hounded by persistent persecution for a crime he believed he never committed, Stone left army service in April 1863, a few months before the armistice that effectively ended the war.

After the Treaty of Washington, he made his home in the Confederate States. Falling back on his engineering skills, he oversaw construction of the foundation of the Confederate Statue of Liberty, which began to be erected in the 1880's on the man-made island on which Fort Sumter had been built.[496] Southerners appropriately chose the harbor as the site for their magnificent sculpture—the place where the first battle of their war for political liberty had been fought.

THE POTOMAC BLOCKADE

> Just as the Southern seaports were beginning to suffer under the Union blockade, Washington was feeling the effects of the Confederate strangulation of the Potomac.[497]

So writes the historian of a little-known aspect of the naval war, 1861-1863. Talk about turning the tables! As Hattaway and Jones, the military historians, put it, Washington was "the only city in the country really blockaded" after Confederates built batteries on the Virginia side of the Potomac River downstream from the Federal capital.[498]

Within five days of Virginia's secession, Governor Letcher had directed Maj. Thomas H. Williamson, of the Virginia Army Engineers, and Lt. Hunter H. Lewis, Virginia Navy, to survey the area around Aquia Creek, forty-five miles downstream from Washington. Williamson and Lewis, aided by navy captain William F. Lynch, quickly concluded that an artillery battery should be built at Aquia, or more technically the riverside high ground known as Split Rock Bluff. Guns placed there, the Virginians figured, could command the lower Potomac's channel and threaten Yankee ship traffic. In early May, four 32-pounder smoothbores were therefore

---

496   Edward G. Longacre, "Charles P. Stone and the 'Crime of Unlucky Generals,'" *Civil War Times Illustrated,* November 1974, p. 41.

497   Mary Alice Wills, *The Confederate Blockade of Washington, D.C. 1861—1862* (Parsons VA, 1975), pp. 96-97.

498   Herman Hattaway and Archer Jones, *How the South Won* (Macon, 1983), p. 87.

emplaced in a semi-circular earthen parapet, all frowning down on the river. They were spotted on May 14 by a river steamboat whose captain informed Washington authorities.

Navy secretary Gideon Welles determined that the Rebel battery had to be reduced, and ordered Cmdr. James H. Ward, of the Atlantic Blockading Squadron, to take three vessels to Aquia and test the Southerners' mettle—and metal. By the time Ward's flotilla sailed down to Aquia on May 30, Confederates had erected another battery, this one with four 3-inch rifled guns. In the two-to-three-hour exchange of cannon fire, the Federals were at a disadvantage when they learned they could not elevate their ships' guns high enough to bear on the blufftop batteries. After taking some damaging hits, Ward's little fleet steamed back upriver and gave Welles the bad news: the Rebel guns were likely to stay there.

Two days later, two more U.S. warships ventured down to test the Aquia guns. They pounded the Confederate position for nearly five hours, inflicting some damage but incurring some themselves. In the process the Southerners learned that the Aquia guns could not impede enemy navigation. Yet at another site, Mathias Point (eighteen miles downriver), where the Potomac took a sharp turn bringing the narrow channel closer to shore, they had a hunch they could. So they hauled some artillery to Mathias and placed several hundred troops there to guard against any enemy shore landings— which came when Union commander Ward arrived on June 24 and landed some troops. In a sharp firefight they were driven back to their boats, unable to dislodge the Confederate battery guards. In it Ward himself took a bullet wound in the abdomen which killed him an hour later. James H. Ward thus became the first naval officer of either side to die in the war.

It was not until Confederates built several more batteries at Cockpit Point, near Evansport, Va. (about thirty miles downstream from Washington) that they could be said to have effectively blockaded the U.S. capital city. The first battery was ready on September 29, another on October 9. More positions were constructed until some twenty guns were in place: rifled Parrotts, 32 – and 42-pounders and, best of all, a highly accurate Blakely rifle, imported from England. On October 17, Northern naval commander Thomas Craven ventured forth with the *Harriet Lane,* his flagship, and several other vessels to exchange fire with the Confederate guns at Cockpit. In the fight the Union warships took so many hits that soon afterward Craven wrote Welles, "so long as the batteries stand at Shipping Point and Evansport the navigation of the Potomac will be effectually closed."[499] He was right. Though Lincoln felt that the Rebel blockade of the Potomac was a national humiliation, he could not prod either the navy or army to move against Cockpit. Craven's big ships, *Brooklyn, Pocahontas* and *Seminole* were being sent farther down the Atlantic coast to help strengthen blockading squadrons off Wilmington and Charleston. For his part, Major General McClellan refused to commit the 4,000 troops thought to be needed for an attack on Evansport.

So nothing was done. As a result, during the winter of 1861-62, with the only commerce between Washington and the outside world being conducted by the railroad to Baltimore, shortages of food, fuel and essential goods drove up their prices in the capital. Working class residents suffered because of the blockade, while garrison soldiers chopped down the city's trees to stay warm. The army's horses and mules went without forage when wagons could not bring enough in.

The humiliation of their national capital did not escape the scornful comment of the North's newspapers. The New York *Tribune* addressed the Rebel barricade as

> ...one of the most humiliating of all the national disgraces to which we have been compelled to submit. It has been most damaging to us in the eyes of the world.... Our own government has been subjected to very great expense and great inconvenience, in consequence of this blockade. The inhabitants of Washington have at times suffered from scarcity of both food and fuel from the same cause.[500]

---

499 Wills, *op. cit.,* p. 86.

500 *Ibid.,* p. 100.

The Yankees had to endure their mortification from October 1861 to March 1862. Those six – months of privation were bad enough, but worse was their realization that when the Confederates abandoned their Potomac batteries that spring, it was of their own accord—part of Gen. Joseph E. Johnston's withdrawal from his Centreville lines back to the Rappahannock.

Abraham Lincoln and his minions had been impotent to uproot the Rebels. It would not be the last time they experienced this powerlessness.

A Rot Seeping Downward

The tale forms one of the Civil War's most sordid episodes," historian Mark Grimsley has written. The tale was about how a vain, ambitious Maj. Gen. George B. McClellan shoved the venerable Lt. Gen. Winfield Scott out of his office as General-in-Chief of the United States Army.

First, he shoved Irvin McDowell out from command of the army that would eventually be named for the Potomac River. Actually, not much shoving was needed. Just days after the Union debacle at Manassas, on July 26 Lincoln relieved McDowell from army command and named McClellan as his successor. (In another of his peculiar moves as U.S. Commander-in-Chief, Lincoln demoted McDowell to leading a *corps* in the very *army* he had just commanded—not a human resources masterpiece, as we would say).[501] Then, the next day, Lincoln fomented anger in his army's senior ranks when he held a meeting with McClellan in the White House—without inviting Scott. Moreover, Lincoln invited McClellan to attend a meeting of his Cabinet after lunch. That day the General-in-Chief had also invited McClellan to drop in on his office to discuss the North's military situation. McClellan arrived after sitting with the President. Halfway into the meeting, close to 1 p.m., McClellan stood up and told General Scott that he had to go to speak with the President's Cabinet members.

---

501   Herman Hattaway and Archer Jones, *How the South Won* (Macon, 1983), p. 50 ("in one of the war's stranger ironies, he [Lincoln] named McDowell to head a corps in McClellan's army, without consulting the new general").

"What, general?" the septuagenarian exclaimed. "Sit down, sir. I am your superior officer, and this meeting will end at my bidding, not yours, sir!" The idea of the newly-appointed McClellan attending a Cabinet meeting without Scott stung the aged general as another presidential hand-slap, coming on top of Lincoln's earlier disapproval of Scott's "Anaconda" plan. Scott made sure not to dismiss McClellan until after one o'clock, when he curtly ordered McClellan to spend the rest of the afternoon riding about the city looking for any uniformed man whom he suspected as a straggler and AWOL from his unit. Mac went out and boarded his carriage, but he had no intention of obeying the General-in-Chief's order.

To his credit, throughout August General McClellan imposed order on the demoralized army he had inherited from McDowell. He also oversaw construction of more fortifications around the capital, in case Jubal Early led another raid on Washington. The capital already had six forts; Mac called for another forty, to be equipped with some 300 pieces of artillery.

Meanwhile, Winfield Scott was getting jealous. His "Anaconda" plan was being ridiculed as timid, even as McClellan was basking in public adulation for his energetic rebuilding of the Federal forces, which on August 20 he began calling the Army of the Potomac. Everything Mac proposed, Old Fuss and Feathers seemed to oppose: the army's reorganization into divisions (beyond brigades), as well as the very name of the army itself. As to the former argument, facts supported the Young Napoleon, as he was already being called (and not without his encouragement). He now commanded 65,000 men, and thousands more were coming in.

McClellan privately fumed in letters to his wife. "Gen. Scott is the great obstacle," he wrote; "he will not comprehend the danger and is either a traitor or an incompetent. I have to fight my way against him."[502] The tension between the two generals broke out into the open when on August 8 McClellan sent Scott a memorandum laying out everything he needed (more men,

502   Mark Grimsley, "Overthrown: The Truth behind the McClellan-Scott Feud," *Civil War Times Illustrated,* November 1980, p. 25.

equipment, artillery, etc.), to which Scott immediately objected. Then, when the General-in-Chief learned that McClellan had sent President Lincoln a copy of the correspondence (breaking the chain of command), and had been meeting privately with Cabinet members, Scott wrote Secretary of War Simon Cameron and asked to be relieved. Lincoln talked him out of it, yet did nothing when McClellan continued to converse with Cameron, naval secretary Gideon Welles, and other higher-ups.

Scott's authority was eroding so quickly that even the officers in and around Washington ceased saluting him. McClellan deliberately by-passed Scott in ways (*e.g.,* writing Lincoln and Cameron directly) that by September reduced his authority to *nil,* with Lincoln and his administration doing nothing to support the aged general. In late September, Scott asked McClellan for the strength of the Army of the Potomac; Mac refused to reply, and instead gave his numbers report to Secretary of State Dayton (from whom an embarrassed Scott eventually got the information). Within a week, Scott formally complained to the Secretary of War about McClellan's insubordination; Cameron did nothing.

Depressed, Scott looked ahead only to his retirement, but with the hope of being able to name his successor: certainly not McClellan, but perhaps Maj. Gen. Henry W. Halleck, then in command at St. Louis.

By now, McClellan was fully engaged in what he called "the Scott war." Lincoln showed with whom he was siding when on October 18 the President notified the aged general that he would not object to his announcement of retiring (Congress had already passed a resolution to the same effect). Scott complied, asking on October 31 to be retired as General – in-Chief (though as a face-saver he cited poor health as his reason). Lincoln and his Cabinet members met the very next day and eagerly approved. That same night, Lincoln visited McClellan to tell him that he would be the United States forces' new General-in-Chief.[503]

---

503   *Ibid.,* pp. 20-29.

If one were to search amidst all of this chaotic backstabbing—at the Union army's highest levels, mind you—just months into the war, one would not have looked much further for omens of Confederate victory.

ABOARD THE *H.M.S. TRENT*

Sixty-two-year-old Capt. Charles D. Wilkes was a career American naval officer whose sailings had included the Antarctic Ocean. His length of service in the old navy probably should have brought him higher rank, but he had a reputation for insubordination.

...as he showed in the summer of 1861. He had been sent to the coast of Africa to take charge of a U.S. warship, the *San Jacinto,* and return her to the Philadelphia Navy Yard for refitting. Wilkes had been told to bring her back "as soon as you can." But the captain sensed there was more excitement in seeking out and running down Confederate commerce raiders such as the *Sumter,* which he had heard was in the West Indies. That is where he headed once he and his crew took hold of the *San Jacinto.*

In Cuba on October 30 he also heard from a U.S. consul that two Southerners designated as Confederate States ministers to Great Britain and France were in Havana, having been borne there by a Confederate blockade runner. They were James Mason of Virginia and John Slidell from Louisiana—the former had been a Virginia congressman and senator, the latter a congressman and senator from Louisiana. Wilkes also learned that the two Southerners were waiting for a British mail packet, the *Trent,* to transport them from Havana to the island of St. Thomas. From there a British steamer would carry them across the Atlantic.

This was too delicious a temptation. So Wilkes "forgot" his orders to bring the *San Jacinto* back to Philadelphia and decided instead to ambush the *Trent* after it left Havana on November 7 (he even knew the intended date of departure).

On the morning of November 8 Wilkes' vessel began bearing down on the *Trent,* whose captain ordered the firing of a couple of warning shots as the American vessel closed in (Stars and Stripes ahoist). Pulling alongside his quarry, Wilkes ordered his exec, Lt. Donald Fairfax, to board the British vessel, demand a list of passengers, and if Mason and Slidell were confirmed aboard, to declare them as prisoners to be transferred to Wilkes' ship.

The British officer in charge of the *Trent,* Capt. James Moir, refused Fairfax's demand to produce Mason and Slidell—at first. When Moir heard that Fairfax was authorized to take possession of his vessel as a prize—the American lieutenant pointed to the *San Jacinto's* cannon being trained on the Brits—Moir relented. The two Southerners also saw the folly of resistance and calmly accompanied Fairfax down the ropes to his little boat, then across the water and onboard the *San Jacinto.* Free then to depart, Moir and the *Trent* sailed off. The whole thing had taken less than three hours.

Wilkes carried his captives to Fort Warren in Boston harbor, where they were placed in custody. Word of the *Trent* affair, as it was already being called, spread to Washington and throughout the North. Yankee newspapers rejoiced loudly at the Rebel envoys' discomfiture.

The British consul in Boston, however, was not amused.[504]

To The Precipice of War

In London the British Cabinet, having been briefed on Wilkes' violation of the *Trent's* neutrality, met on November 29. Aware that throughout England there was "every sword leaping from its scabbard, and every man looking about for his pistols and blunderbusses," as one onlooker put it, the Cabinet resolved that "a gross outrage and violation of international law has been committed."[505] British Prime Minister Lord Henry John Temple Palmerston was so incensed that he not only wanted to impose an embargo on arms sales to Lincoln's government, but itched to send the Channel fleet into American waters just to show the Yanks how seriously Her Majesty's government viewed the situation. In the

---

504   Norman B. Ferris, *The Trent Affair: A Diplomatic Crisis* (Knoxville, 1977), pp. 19-29.

505   D.P. Crook, *Diplomacy During the American Civil War* (New York, 1975), p. 472

end, Cabinet ministers in London talked the Prime Minister out of it, and took calmer steps by deciding upon a three-part demand: that the U.S. 1) disavow Wilkes' action, 2) offer a formal apology and 3) return the imprisoned diplomats to British authorities.

The very next day, the 30th, the Cabinet reconvened and drafted its resolution, condemning "this act of violence against a neutral and friendly nation." Then the document became an ultimatum: if the Americans refused to accede to its three demands, Her Majesty's government would withdraw its embassy from Washington. The Lincoln administration was given seven days to respond from the time the formal paper was presented by Lord Richard Lyons, the English ambassador in Washington, to Secretary of State Dayton. Failing such a response, Lyons was instructed to board the ship and sail back to Britain. About the return of Mason and Slidell the British were quite forceful: "the feeling here is very quiet but very decided," wrote one minister at the time; "there is no party about it; all are unanimous." When the Cabinet demand was taken to Windsor Castle, Queen Victoria quickly approved it.

State Secretary Dayton got the transoceanic British message, hand-delivered by Lyons, on December 19—it took at least two weeks and a half for steamship transit. The British ambassador reinforced its contents with an unequivocal language of his own: England would tolerate no evasion, no refusal to surrender the Confederate envoys. He made it clear that England was ready for war, and informed Dayton further that even then troops were being mobilized in Canada and that ships carrying arms and supplies were on their way across the Atlantic.

When the Secretary brought the Brits' demand to the White House, Lincoln nonetheless balked at returning the prisoners, suggesting that the dispute between Britain and the United States should be submitted to international arbitration. With that stance the stage was set for the withdrawal of the British legation at Washington and the heightening of tensions between the two countries. Dayton was mortified; friends in England were reporting the warlike excitement among the people and the very visible massing of a war fleet at Liverpool. Worse, soon came word from Henri Mercier, the French ambassador in Washington, that France firmly supported England's position.

After several days Lincoln convened his Cabinet on Christmas Day. The secretaries were shocked when Dayton read to them letters he had gotten from England about the war measures evident everywhere. The Cabinet nonetheless debated, with Dayton urging Lincoln to back down for two days, through December 26—which was the seventh day from Lyon's delivery of the British Cabinet's demand. Dutifully, having received no response, the British ambassador boarded a ship that evening to carry him back to England (Lyons let slip word of his departure voyage to Southern sympathizers in Washington, who he knew would alert the Confederate batteries at Evansport not to fire on any vessel flying the Union Jack steaming down the Potomac headed out to sea).

On December 27 Lincoln's Cabinet finally agreed with the Secretary of State and persuaded the President to stand down. But it was too late. By then Lord Lyons was already out to sea and was unreachable. Lyons arrived in England on January 13 and telegraphed the Prime Minister in London that he had received no answer from Lincoln's government to the British Cabinet's demands. Palmerston quickly informed the Queen that the government had no choice but to take further steps for war with the United States.

Already the Admiralty and War Office had drafted a plan for launching an attack on the Yanks. It assumed that the Lincoln government was prepared to fight two wars at a time: that while waging a war of invasion against the Confederacy, it would simultaneously launch an invasion of Canada. British planners were willing to lose Quebec, Montreal or Toronto in a quick land war, so long as Vice-Admiral Alexander Milne's powerful North American Squadron—eight battleships and thirteen frigates or corvettes—could attack and destroy Union warships blockading the Confederacy's Atlantic ports. Reinforced by more vessels sent over from the Channel and the Caribbean, British men-of-war could also attack Northern shipping on the high seas and perhaps even steam up the Potomac to shell Washington, in something of a reprise of British forces' burning of the American capital in August 1814. (A lot of Englishmen smacked their lips at that prospect.)

Before any of this could be set in motion, however, belated word came that Lincoln's administration had finally agreed to give up Mason and Slidell and offer an official apology. After an alarmed State Secretary Dayton learned that Lord Lyons had left Washington before he could inform him on December 27 of the Cabinet vote, he immediately dispatched a State Department official, John Bigelow, aboard an ocean steamer with a carefully written communique. Bigelow, setting out from Washington three days after Christmas, did not arrive in Liverpool until January 17 (thanks to a mid-Atlantic winter squall). He quickly traveled to London, found Lord Russell, and impressed upon him that Lincoln's government had caved. Russell had not wanted war in the first place, and issued orders for the Admiralty and War Office to suspend their military preparations.

Lincoln and the Union war effort had dodged its first international crisis. As we shall see, though, military events in the summer of 1862, especially Lee's crushing victory against Pope at Second Manassas and his mauling of McClellan's army at Sharpsburg, would persuade Lord Palmerston, Lord Russell and Chancellor of the Exchequer William Gladstone that Britain's diplomatic interests in the New World would best be served by formal recognition of the Confederate States.

THE DEVELOPMENT OF CONFEDERATE TORPEDO WEAPONRY

Matthew Maury's original torpedo had been a small keg of powder, weighted to drop several feet below water level, fitted with a percussion cap and a long lanyard. The idea was that these could be anchored in Southern harbors beset by Union blockaders. Observers hiding on shore would keep watch on the movements of the enemy vessels; when one neared a torpedo, they would tug their rope and watch the explosion, sending a huge mass of water into the air and along with it the wreckage of a sinking Yankee ship.

The device had been successfully tested at Richmond in June 1861 when Maury had detonated a floating mine from afar. Torpedo production quickly got underway at Richmond's Tredegar Iron Works.[506] The real question, though, was whether the newfangled weapon would really work against Yankee warships. Just two weeks after his successful test, Maury and a small crew laid six torpedoes in the waters of Hampton Roads, where the *Minnesota, Roanoke* and other Union vessels were anchored. The idea was to let the current carry the explosives out toward their targets. Connected by rope, a pair of them would drift out, (it was hoped) snag on one of the ships and be drawn in against the hull. Contact would then detonate the percussion fuse, explode the powder below the ship's waterline and send the vessel to the bottom. The Hampton Roads test flopped, however, when the mines failed to detonate. Maury quickly figured out that wooden kegs could not keep the gunpowder dry, so he began to experiment with specially-made metal cylinders, three feet long and shaped to be buoyant when filled with powder. An easier alternative proved to be a five-gallon glass jug, covered with wicker and set in a wooden box to which were attached friction primer fuses. A pair of these floating mines was connected by some twenty feet of thin wire.

Such was the final design and mechanism of the Maury Torpedo, the weapon that eventually sank forty-three Union ships. In early August 1861 a "Maury," as it came to be called, blew up the *Commodore Barry,* a 513-ton gunboat lying at the mouth of the James River. An eyewitness later described the event: "It was terrible. The vessel was lifted...upward of ten feet out of water, and an immense jet of water was hurled from her bow into the air, falling over and completely deluging her."[507]

This dramatic achievement caught President Davis's immediate attention and "caused him to enter with zest" (as Defense Secretary Walker wrote) into plans for the C.S. Torpedo Bureau to mass – produce the Maury, particularly for harbor and river

---

506   Charles B. Dew, *Ironmaker to the Confederacy: Joseph R. Anderson and the Tredegar Iron Works* (Wilmington NC, 1966), p. 122.

507   Milton F. Perry, *Infernal Machines: The Story of Confederate Submarine and Mine Warfare* (Baton Rouge, 1965), p. 110.

defense. Confederate Brig. Gen. Gabriel J. Rains, who like Maury had experimented with torpedo design before the war, was put in charge of the operation. The president made certain that Rains had access to all the country's manufacturing resources, such as the arsenal in Augusta, Georgia (for priming tubes).

Walker may have exaggerated when, on September 30, 1861, he wrote that Maury torpedoes "have been furnished Mobile, Savannah, Charleston, &c., by the thousand."[508] Regardless, in little more than a month Confederate submarine mines would hand the Union Navy one of its most stinging defeats.

DuPont's Defeat at Port Royal

"I have just received information which I consider entirely reliable, that the enemy's expedition is intended for Port Royal."[509]

To be forewarned is to be forearmed, as the saying goes. Thus was South Carolina governor Francis Pickens alerted on Nov. 1, 1861, by recently appointed Confederate Secretary of Defense Judah Benjamin. (L. P. Walker had suffered a fatal horse-fall on September 16.) Actually, it is even better to be forearmed, for that is what Confederates had already done at Port Royal, a deep-water inlet between Savannah and Charleston. Union naval secretary Gideon Welles was seeking bases for his blockading squadron, and Port Royal presented an alluring target for a joint army-navy operation of the sort that had captured Hatteras in August. Capt. Silas Stringham had enjoyed the praise he received for his role in the taking of Hatteras, but shortly thereafter the old man (he was sixty-three and in declining health) sent in his resignation from the navy. Welles decided then to divide responsibility for his Atlantic coast blockade: a North Atlantic Blockading Squadron would be led by Capt. Louis Goldsborough, and a Southern one by Capt. Samuel Du Pont.

---

508   *O.R.*, vol. 18, 1082-83.

509   Howard P. Nash, Jr., *A Naval History of the Confederate War for Independence* (London, 1972), p. 58.

Eager to repeat a Hatteras-like victory, Lincoln called for action. Though Du Pont wanted to move against some other point, Welles' assistant secretary Gustavus Fox insisted upon Port Royal, near Hilton Head, South Carolina. Unfortunately for Du Pont, instead of sitting down in meeting with him, Fox committed to a series of lengthy memoranda arguing and articulating his recommendations. This allowed alert Southern spies in Washington to pick up on the planned Port Royal expedition, and to alert Richmond.

Before he left Charleston for Virginia, General Beauregard had drawn up plans to fortify Port Royal with two log-and-earth forts, one on each side of the entrance to the inlet. The enterprising Creole, once he heard of Maury's torpedoes, eagerly called for hundreds of them, as soon as they were manufactured in Richmond, to be sent by train to him at Charleston. His successor, Brig. Gen. Roswell Ripley, followed through, and once the floating mines arrived, distributed them in early October to Savannah and Port Royal. Commanding at the latter place was Brig. Gen. Thomas F. Drayton, who oversaw their planting in the sound's main ship channel. Each torpedo was a buoyant powder container affixed to an anchor and chain, carefully measured in length so as to bob a few feet beneath the water's surface. Three or four men in a small boat rowed out and dropped the devices one-by-one in what we would today call a "minefield." More were strewn offshore from the two forts.

Such were the Confederates' unconventional defenses. The more conventional ones were Fort Beauregard, at Bay Point on Phillips Island and, across the water to the south, Fort Walker on Hilton Head Island. They had been constructed in August and September, thanks to the slave labor donated by local planters. Their armament was impressive. Walker had twenty guns, including an eight-inch, nine-inch and ten-inch Columbiad (the kind of heavy guns Beauregard had called for); the rest were 24-, 32 – and 42 pounders. Fort Beauregard boasted nineteen cannon, among which were a ten-inch Columbiad, a rifled 24-pounder, plus 42 – and 32-pounders. Most of these were smoothbores, but General Drayton had installed iron furnaces along the forts' ramparts for the heating of solid shot that could set the Yankees' wooden hulls on fire.

Having learned (the hard way at Hatteras) about the enemy's ability to land amphibious troops against island forts, Confederates took measures to strengthen their garrisons. In the first days of November 650 troops arrived at Fort Walker, Col. Wilmot DeSaussure's 15th South Carolina Infantry; 450 Georgians arrived to help out at Fort Beauregard.

Thus the Southerners were ready when the Northern flotilla of fifteen warships, having made its way from Cape Hatteras, was sighted offshore at dawn of November 7. Du Pont's flagship was the steam frigate *Wabash,* with 26 guns. Aboard the screw sloop *Pocahontas* (only six guns of varying calibers) was Du Pont's second-in-command, Capt. Percival Drayton, very much aware that he would be fighting his brother that day (of which Thomas was unaware). Other vessels were less impressive. In addition to a vintage-1830 sailing sloop, *Vandalia,* was a motley assemblage of converted merchantmen, amplified tugboats and hastily armed sidewheelers. Altogether they mounted over 120 cannon, far outpowering Drayton's artillery in the forts. Accompanying them was a bunch of transports carrying more than 8,000 soldiers under command of Brig. Gen. Thomas W. Sherman, brother of "Crazy Billy."

Du Pont's plan was to form his vessels in a circle that would turn continuously between the two Rebel forts, which were roughly two and a half miles apart. That would bring to bear all of his ships' guns while the moving targets would make the job of the Rebel artillerists that much harder. Once the Confederate cannon had been knocked out, General Sherman planned to land his men on Hilton Head and attack Fort Walker from the rear. Once it fell, Drayton was expected to capitulate.

General Drayton's inexperienced artillerists posed little threat indeed compared to the Maury torpedoes lurking in the Port Royal waters. Lincoln's War Department in Washington had heard of Confederate experiments with exploding mines, but no one suspected that they had been manufactured in such large numbers and disseminated so widely for harbor defense.

The gunfight between the warships and land batteries got underway around 8 a.m., but the Rebel torpedos took the first toll. Within half an hour the 55-ton gunboat *Bazely* was "blown literally to pieces," according to an eyewitness; her pilot house was shot thirty feet into the air, but miraculously the captain and pilot landed back down unhurt. Another tug-turned-gunboat, the *Jonquil,* was seriously damaged by a torpedo explosion beneath her midships. "The boilers jumped half a foot," one Northern sailor remembered, "and the shock threw nine men overboard and flooded the ship. A man on the berth deck was thrown against the overhead, and his head was split open. Doors were shattered, every window was broken, three beams were seriously sprung and a forward howitzer was upset."[510]

Sherman's troop transports also became casualties when they ventured too close to land and encountered torpedos that had been laid beyond the inlet entrance. The 400-ton transport *R.B. Hamilton,* for instance, was destroyed, causing more than a dozen members of the Third Michigan Cavalry to be killed or wounded. Another transport, the 508-ton *Maple Leaf,* was sunk by a torpedo explosion that killed four men (and sent the baggage of three regiments down under).

All of this was Maury-mayhem, as the Confederate gunners inside the forts failed to strike a single target (they later blamed defective ammunition). Before long a stunned Du Pont realized his ships were navigating amidst "a perfect nest of torpedos." In less than three hours eight of his fifteen warships were sunk, sinking or seriously damaged. Du Pont had no choice but to break off the battle and set course with the remains of his flotilla limping back to Hatteras. (Two of the injured vessels did not make it, but foundered at sea.)

After it was all over, the sad lesson learned by Samuel Du Pont and the Union navy was "the great damage a bay full of torpedos could create," as historian Milton Perry has written.[511]

---

510 Milton F. Perry, *Infernal Machines: The Story of Confederate Submarine and Mine Warfare* (Baton Rouge, 1965), p. 173.

511 *Ibid.,* p. 188.

Before the war, haughty Northerners prided themselves for what they called "Yankee ingenuity." But after Nov. 7, 1861, Southern historians could rightly point to *Rebel resourcefulness* as a telling factor in their successful War for Independence.

THE CONFEDERATE ELECTIONS OF NOVEMBER 1861

In politics it is generally a good thing to be able to run for office without opposition. Such was the enviable position of Confederate President Jefferson Davis and his Vice President, Alexander Hamilton Stephens.

The Montgomery Convention that unanimously elected Davis and Stephens on Feb. 9, 1861, had not been a very democratic body. First of all, it had delegates from only seven Southern states; Virginia, North Carolina, Tennessee, Arkansas, Missouri and Kentucky had not yet seceded. Then, too, only fifty delegates assembled in the Alabama House of Representatives chamber on February 4 ostensibly representing a free population of more than two-and-a-half million. Moreover, they had been chosen with no uniformity as to numerical proportion. Georgia, with a white population of almost 600,000, sent ten delegates to Montgomery; Texas, with some 420,000, had seven men there; Florida, with a non-slave population of just 79,000, sent three delegates. The size of the respective delegations did not really matter, though, as the convention prescribed that each state would cast just one vote. Amidst the delegates was a consensus that their proceedings should be without rancor, demonstrating to the Southern people as much unanimity as possible. Thus in smoke-filled rooms, in huddles on the floor, and gaggles in hallways, names for president and vice president were bruited. Robert Barnwell Rhett, the Carolina fire-eater, was dropped as too radical. Robert Toombs of Georgia let it be known he was also interested, but gradually Davis's and Stephens' names rose to the fore.

Their election on February 9 was meant only to be provisional, with terms no more than a year. During that time it was understood that a national election would be held, when the citizenry would have the opportunity to ratify (or reject) the convention's choice of the Confederacy's two top office-holders. The business of drafting a constitution for the new government took longer, although in the main the Confederate Constitution mirrored the U.S. one, save for a few key differences (presidential term of six years, non-re-electable; postal service to be financially self-sufficient after two years). In Article I the document set the size of the House of Representatives according the various state populations known at the time:

Alabama	9
Florida	2
Georgia	10
Louisiana	6
Mississippi	7
South Carolina	6
Texas	6

As in the "old" Constitution of 1787, each state was allotted two senators. Similarly, the C.S. President and Vice President were to be chosen by electors, whose number per state would be the respective sum of their senators and representatives.[512]

Until elections could be held, the Montgomery Convention that set up the Confederate government morphed into a Provisional Congress. Acting as such on May 21, 1861, it ordered to be held on the first Wednesday in November a national election for president, vice president and all 117 representatives and senators from the then-twelve states (Kentucky would go out a couple of weeks too late to join in).[513] Most of the Congressional seats were genuine elections. Although there was no two-party system in the Confederacy until after the war, ambitious politicians abounded everywhere, resulting in scores of contested races for the Senate and House. In Georgia, for instance, Lucius Gartrell ran for the state's Eighth District (which included Atlanta) and defeated one John A. Jones. For good measure, November 1861 in Georgia was

512 Marshall L. DeRosa, *The Confederate Constitution of 1861: An Inquiry into American Constitutionalism* (Columbia MO, 1991), p. 136.

513 Wilfred Buck Yearns, *The Confederate Congress* (Athens GA, 1960), p. 42.

also time to elect a governor for another two-year term (Joseph E. Brown was seeking re-election). As November 6 approached, the Atlanta *Intelligencer*, the city's leading daily, urged voters to turn out. "A small vote," it warned, "will be indicative of loss of interest in the cause of the Southern Confederacy, or a waning of united and determined purpose on the part of the South to achieve its Independence." On election day, as it turned out, Atlantans cast 837 votes for Davis and Stephens. The rest of the state also came out for the unchallenged presidential ticket as well, so that when the twelve electors assembled on December 5 at Milledgeville, the state capital, they cast their votes unanimously for Davis and Stephens.[514]

It went that way across the Confederacy. Without organized opposition, the Davis/Stephens ticket won more than 90,000 votes—almost 97% of the total (there were scattered write-ins of local political favorites.) Looking back, we can see that after the election of George Washington in 1789 (before the development of the Federalist and Democratic-Republican parties) the election of Jefferson Davis was the most rancor-free presidential contest in American history.

The first Confederate national election was singular in another regard: five Southern states provided for absentee voting by soldiers in the field.[515] This political first, which the United States did not implement during the Confederate War or the rest of the nineteenth century, for that matter, demonstrates an attentiveness to the workings of republican democracy that distinguishes the Confederate States of America to this day.

---

514   Stephen Davis, *The Atlanta Daily Intelligencer Reports the Civil War* (Knoxville TN, 2022), pp. 72-73.

515   Yearns, op. cit., p. 42.

About the Author

STEPHEN DAVIS has been writing about the Civil War for a long time—"since Jesus was in third grade," he contends. He served as General Editor for *The Reminiscences of General M. Jeff Thompson* (Morningside, 1983), and from 1985 to 2005 worked as Book Review Editor for *Blue & Gray Magazine.* He is author of *Texas Brigadier to the Fall of Atlanta: John Bell Hood* (2019) and *Into Tennessee & Failure: John Bell Hood* (2020). With Bill Hendrick he wrote *The Atlanta Intelligencer Covers the Civil War* (2022).

Steve and his lovely wife Billie reside in Cumming, Georgia, where they rent their house from their cat, Cha Cha.

BEST SELLERS AND NEW RELEASES

OVER 90 TITLES FOR YOU TO ENJOY

SHOTWELLPUBLISHING.COM

The South's Finest Contemporary Authors.

Shotwell Publishing is proud to be called home by many of today's most respected Southern scholars and literary greats.

JEFFERY ADDICOTT
Union Terror: Debunking the False Justifications for Union Terror

Trampling Union Terror: Riders of the Second Alabama Cavalry

MARK ATKINS
Women in Combat: Feminism Goes to War

JOYCE BENNETT
Maryland, My Maryland: The Cultural Cleansing of a Small Southern State

GARRY BOWERS
Slavery and The Civil War: What Your History Teacher Didn't Tell You

Dixie Days: Reminiscences Of a Southern Boyhood

JERRY BREWER
Dismantling the Republic

ANDREW P. CALHOUN
My Own Darling Wife: Letters From A Confederate Volunteer

JOHN CHODES
Segregation: Federal Policy or Racism?

Washington's KKK: The Union League During Southern Reconstruction

WALTER BRIAN CISCO
War Crimes Against Southern Civilians

DAVID T. CRUM
Stonewall Jackson: Saved by Providence

STEPHEN DAVIS
Confederate Triumph: How the South Won Its War for Independence 1861-1863 Volume One:1861

JOHN DEVANNY
Continuities: The South in a Time of Revolution

Lincoln's Continuing Revolution: Essays of M.E. Bradford and Thomas H. Landess

JOSHUA DOGGRELL
Doxed: The Political Lynching of a Southern Cop

JAMES C. EDWARDS
What Really Happened?: Quantrill's Raid On Lawrence, Kansas

TED EHMANN
Boom & Bust In Bone Valley: Florida's Phosphate Mining History 1886-2021

JOHN AVERY EMISON
The Deep State Assassination of Martin Luther King Jr.

DON GORDON
Snowball's Chance: My Kidneys Failed, My Wife Left Me & My Dog Died...

JOHN R. GRAHAM
Constitutional History of Secession

PAUL C. GRAHAM
Confederaphobia

When The Yankees Come: Former Carolina Slaves Remember

Nonsense on Stilts: The Gettysburg Address & Lincoln's Imaginary Nation

JOE D. HAINES
*The Diary of Col. John Henry Stover Funk
of the Stonewall Brigade, 1861-1862*

CHARLES HAYES
The REAL First Thanksgiving

V.P. HUGHES
Col. John Singleton Mosby: In the News 1862-1916

TERRY HULSEY
25 Texas Heroes

*The Constitution of Non-State Government:
Field Guide to Texas Secession*

JOSEPH JAY
*Sacred Conviction:
The South's Stand for Biblical Authority*

JAMES R. KENNEDY
Dixie Rising: Rules For Rebels

*Nullifying Federal and State Gun Control:
A How-To Guide For Gun Owners*

*When Rebel Was Cool:
Growing Up In Dixie, 1950-1965*

*Reconstruction: Destroying the Republic
and Creating an Empire*

WALTER D. KENNEDY
The South's Struggle: America's Hope

*Lincoln, The Non-Christian President:
Exposing The Myth*

Lincoln, Marx, and the GOP

J.R. & W.D. KENNEDY
*Jefferson Davis: High Road to Emancipation
and Constitutional Government*

*Yankee Empire:
Aggressive Abroad and Despotic at Home*

Punished With Poverty: The Suffering South

The South Was Right! 3rd Edition

LEWIS LIBERMAN
Snowflake Buddies; ABC Leftism For Kids!

PHILIP LEIGH
*The Devil's Town: Hot Springs During
The Gangster Era*

U.S. Grant's Failed Presidency

The Causes of the Civil War

*The Dreadful Frauds: Critical Race Theory
And Identity Politics*

JACK MARQUARDT
*Around The World In 80 Years: Confessions
of a Connecticut Confederate*

MICHAEL MARTIN
Southern Grit: Sensing The Siege at Petersburg

SAMUEL MITCHAM
*The Greatest Lynching In American History:
New York, 1863*

*Confederate Patton: Richard Taylor and
The Red River Campaign*

CHARLES T. PACE
Lincoln As He Really Was

*Southern Independence. Why War? The War
To Prevent Southern Independence*

JAMES R. ROESCH
From Founding Fathers To Fire Eaters

KIRKPATRICK SALE
*Emancipation Hell: The Tragedy Wrought
By Lincoln's Emancipation Proclamation*

JOSEPH SCOTCHIE
*The Asheville Connection:
The Making of a Conservative*

*Samuel T. Francis and
Revolution from the Middle*

ANNE W. SMITH
Charlottesville Untold: Inside Unite The Right

Robert E. Lee: A History for Kids

KAREN STOKES
A Legion Of Devils: Sherman In South Carolina

*The Burning of Columbia, S.C.: A Review
of Northern Assertions and Southern Facts*

Carolina Love Letters

*Fortunes of War:
The Adventures of a German Confederate*

*A Confederate in Paris:
Letters of A. Dudley Mann 1867-1879*

JOSEPH R. STROMBERG
*Southern Story and Song:
Country Music in the 20th Century*

JACK TROTTER
Last Train to Dixie

JOHN THEURSAM
Key West's Civil War

H.V. TRAYWICK, JR.
*Along The Shadow Line:
A Road Trip through History and Memory
on the Old Confederate Border*

LESLIE TUCKER
*Old Times There Should Not Be Forgotten:
Cultural Genocide In Dixie*

JOHN VINSON
Southerner Take Your Stand!

MARK R. WINCHELL
*Confessions of a Copperhead:
Culture and Politics in the Modern South*

CLYDE N. WILSON
Calhoun: A Statesman for the 21st Century

*Lies My Teacher Told Me: The True History
of the War For Southern Independence*

The Yankee Problem: An American Dilemma

*Annals Of The Stupid Party:
Republicans Before Trump*

*Nullification:
Reclaiming The Consent of the Governed*

The Old South: 50 Essential Books

The War Between The States: 60 Essential Books

*Reconstruction and the New South,
1865-1913: 50 Essential Books*

*The South 20th Century And Beyond:
50 Essential Books*

*Southern Poets and Poems, 1606-1860:
The Land They Loved, Volume 1*

*Confederate Poets and Poems, Vol1
The Land They Loved, Volume II*

Looking For Mr. Jefferson

African American Slavery in Historical Perspective

JOE WOLVERTON
*What Degree Of Madness?: Madison's Method
To Make American States Again*

WALTER KIRK WOOD
*Beyond Slavery: The Northern Romantic
Nationalist Origins of America's Civil War*

SHOTWELLPUBLISHING.COM

Green Altar (Literary Imprint)

CATHARINE SAVAGE BROSMAN
*An Aesthetic Education
and Other Stories (2nd Ed)*

Chained Tree, Chained Owls: Poems

Aerosols and Other Poems

Partial Memoirs

RANDALL IVEY
*A New England Romance:
And Other Southern Stories*

The Gift of Gab

SUZANNE JOHNSON
Maxcy Gregg's Sporting Journals 1842-1858

JAMES E. KIBLER, JR.
Tiller : Claybank County Series, Vol. 4

The Gentler Gamester

*Beyond The Stone: Poems of Tribute
& Remembrance*

THOMAS MOORE
*A Fatal Mercy:
The Man Who Lost The Civil War*

PERRIN LOVETT
The Substitute, Tom Ironsides 1

KAREN STOKES
Belles

Carolina Twilight

Honor in the Dust

The Immortals

The Soldier's Ghost: A Tale of Charleston

WILLIAM THOMAS
*Runaway Haley:
An Imagined Family Saga*

*The Field of Justice: Moonshine
and Murder in North Georgia*

CLYDE N. WILSON
*Southern Poets and Poems, 1606-1860:
The Land They Loved, Volume 1*

*Confederate Poets and Poems, Vol 1
The Land They Loved, Volume II*

Gold-Bug
(Mystery & Suspense Imprint)

BRANDI PERRY
Splintered: A New Orleans Tale

MARTIN WILSON
To Jekyll and Hide